LADY
OF
ISTOK

BOOK TWO OF THE QUEEN'S RED GUARD

ISABELLE OLMO

LITTLE
FOUNTAIN
PRESS

Cover Design by SeventhStar Art
Hard Cover naked back designed by Saintjupit3rGr4phic
Interior headers and dividers by Etheric Tales
Interior Art by Lunaris Falcon Studio
Maps and Family Trees by Abigail Hair

Editing by Faemance at www.fmbyfaemance.com
and Ashley Wessel at
https://sites.google.com/view/weasellywesselediting/home

Little Fountain Press, LLC.

To my readers who are my ever-supportive cheerleaders whenever I doubt my story.

HOUSE BALIK

CONTENT WARNING

This book contains elements of Ableism, abusive relationship, alcoholism, animal death, animal violence, blood (gore), bodies/corpses, body horror, bones (human), bullying, child abuse, sexual child abuse, childbirth, classism, death/dying, death penalty, decapitation, domestic abuse, drinking (recreational), drug use (mentioned), drug use (onscreen), drug use (prescription), forced captivity, graphic sex, homophobia, hospitalization, hostages, hunting, incest, kidnapping, medical procedures, murder, murder (attempted), pedophilia, poisoning, pregnancy, prostitution, PTSD, rape, rape (attempted), serious injury, sexism, sexual abuse, slurs, smoking, snakes, suicidal thoughts, swearing, terminal illness, torture, violence, vomit, warfare, weapons

PREVIOUSLY, IN
THE QUEEN'S RED GUARD…

For the sake of peace in her kingdom, Almira married King Alton, the man responsible for her husband's death. Calculating and methodical, Almira gathered around her a group of warrior women, amongst them her younger cousin, Hira Balik. Heir to the High Seat of Istok…

Before joining the Queen's Red Guard, Young Hira ran away from home. As a sign of defiance, she cut off her long, Balikian red hair, making a statement against the rules that constricted the women of her world. After pleading before Almira, and with the support of Captain Sanaa, Hira joined The Queen's Red Guard.

Hira was happy to remain in the shadows of Almira's unexpectedly happy union with her husband. But everything changes when Norr, the Northern Kingdom, rebels against Almira and Alton's rule. The peace that Almira fought so hard to achieve crumbles before her.

While Alton is at war, a desperate Almira seeks a witch to divine whether she's pregnant, because pregnancy would leave her vulnerable if Alton were to die in battle. She knows that the Norrians would kill her and the baby should they manage to take her. The witch confirms that Almira's pregnant, but also gives other important predictions. A Great Balikian War is coming, the witch predicts, and she calls Hira the Arm of New Verden. The witch also tells Almira she will suffer for four years. As the predictions end, Norrians attack the Queen and her guard.

Hurrying back to the castle, they discover that the king's soldiers have seized one of the Norrian attackers; Lord Ivar, heir of the Norrian High Seat. Almira locks Ivar in her dungeons, but soon realizes he could be useful. If he's the true heir, then he could bring peace between the countries.

Finally, there is a disruption to the weeks of waiting for news from the war front when another strange witch visits Almira. The witch shows her a vision of Alton desperate and dying on the battlefield, begging her to come. Almira and her Red Guard sprint to the war front only to find Alton in perfect health. Deceived at first, Almira finally connects a plot between General Hestian and Lord Arrigo to remove her from the castle to take it.

A battle ensues around her, with the Istokian Armada arriving with Commander Seaver at the helm. And Almira's uncle, Lord Thebo, descending on the castle with the Suidian Red Army. However, it's too late as Almira's father, Lord Beltran, dies protecting his daughter. Lord Arrigo escapes, her city lays in near ruin, but they save the throne.

Almira makes the tough decision to return Hira to Istok, as she is the heir to Lord Beltran's seat. Hira is now the Lady of Istok, even if she doesn't wish to be.

Unbeknownst to Almira or Hira, Lord Beltran instructed an unnamed, old drunk man to light the Corsikan torch upon his death. Across the world, the torches flared until hours later the light of the flames reached Istok...

PART I

Prologue

PANSY, CHILD OF ISTOK

Korkoran Fortress, City of Treveri, Kingdom of Istok

For the servants of Korkoran, the day began two hours before dawn.
Pansy considered herself quite the lucky person because she only
had to share a room with two other servants and neither of them
snored. As the youngest in the staff, they expected she wake before
all others. She slid her bony feet into her tight-fitting woolen shoes
and stoked the fire. It was a process not to be taken lightly, lest the
staff reprimand her when they awoke.

Quietly, she washed her face in the basin, and her fingers
reddened in the frigid water. She dressed in seconds and scuttled
down to the kitchens, hoping to arrive before Cook. She bounced
down the spiral staircase of the staff quarters and ran the blue path
of the parapet connecting to the main fortress. Under her breath,
she sang lullabies and skipped steps but the cheerful morning halted
as she saw a light flickering in the distance. Nestled between the
Mountains of Anaji, bright flames fought against the pre-dawn
darkness.

Pansy gasped and clutched the stone of the bridge. It was the
Dragon Torch! She'd heard of it, one of many legends of the past.

Whispers in hallways of times gone by when war plagued the land. The sun speckled its rays over the horizon and the small girl realized she'd lingered too long. With a cry of despair, she hurtled toward the kitchens.

Cook was already fuming, tossing pots and pans when Pansy entered. A basket of brown and blue eggs, fresh from the morning harvest, dangled from her arm.

"Where is the blasted girl, eh?" Cook asked the black cat, who despite not being allowed in the kitchen, was at least a sympathetic ear.

Pansy drifted to a halt and leaned forward on the cutting table, bouncing on her feet in excitement.

"The torch is lit! The large one atop the mountains!" Pansy shouted without taking a breath.

Cook whirled on the girl with a red, haggard face and white hair cropped so short it spiked every which end. She had a large mole on her nose that grew a single strand of black hair.

"That's your excuse, you *loitering* sack of bones?" Cook snarled.

The girl brightened. She'd always craved to be the ideal servant and show High Lord Beltran she was nothing but responsible.

"'Tis not an excuse, ma'am! See for yourself, the torch be lit!" Pansy pointed to the hall.

Cook scowled and waved around the spoon filled with sticky porridge. "What cares I for torches and things? Let Her Ladyship worry about the torch, you worry about delivering her the porridge!" Turning to the stove, Cook grumbled loudly under her breath about lazy girls from the North and when would the High Lord return to make sense of the happenings within Korkoran?

Defeated, Pansy launched into her routine of loading the Lady's tray, making sure she had plenty of black tea. She ensured the blue and gold tea pot was filled with piping hot water before loading the last of the drinkware.

The black cat pressed itself to the insides of her calf, purring and begging for food. Pansy peeked at Cook, who was continuing her tirade, then tossed the cat a slice of ham from the counter. The feline quickly snatched the meat and scurried out to enjoy his breakfast in peace.

"Girl, you keep giving that flea-infested beast of my good food and there'll be no fresh bread for you!" Cook slapped the porridge into the bowl and scowled at Pansy.

"But he's got to have breakfast like we all do," Pansy protested as she hefted the heavy tray onto the counter for Cook to add the porridge.

"Let it eat mice, so they'll stop making holes in my bags of rice. You keep the little beast fed, and it makes friends with the rats!" Cook slammed down the porridge. "Now get it to the missus before she rings—"

And the bell went off behind Cook, whose face soured even more.

"*Dependable*, that one!"

Pansy picked up the tray, breathing deeply as her thin arms tried to balance the heft. She prepared herself for the long journey up the five flights of stairs, as she did each morning. The first two flights were not too bad, but by the time the third arrived her knees ached and her arms trembled. She always paused against the large statue of a man, whose name she couldn't read.

"Bet you didn't have to carry trays and such," she said to the man's stony face. "You're important enough for a statue, so I reckon you were too important for trays."

She continued to climb the stairs when she caught her breath. It would've been a brief journey, but she heard the one door she dreaded most open. Pansy pressed herself to the shadows, the stone of the fortress burrowing into her back.

"Any word?" A woman's voice.

Pansy chilled and clenched the tray even tighter. It was the *Cruel One*. She prayed to all the gods that listened to servant girls like her for the Cruel One not to see her.

"Nay, m'lady, too soon, methinks," a man with a slippery voice said.

The Cruel One groaned with impatience. "I'll get dressed and see if that cunt has heard anything."

Pansy bit her lip and stayed as still as she could while the Cruel

One closed her door. The man walked down the hall, but she waited until his footsteps become smaller and smaller. She let out a breath of relief and hurried up the last flight into Her Ladyship's rooms.

Sweat drenched her forehead by the time she made it to the golden door. She readjusted the tray with one hand, then knocked with the other. She took a calming breath and prayed they did not leave her to wait long. Her elbows burned something awful.

"Who is it?" Her Ladyship's voice came from inside.

"Your breakfast, m'lady," Pansy said, like she always said.

It startled the girl that it was the royal Ley who opened the door. An ancient man, with wrinkled skin, spotted like soiled linen. He dressed in the customary black robes of Istokian Leys and stared at the girl with an interested expression.

"Come in, child," Lady Marai said from behind the Ley. "Place it on the table."

The Ley moved and Pansy shyly entered, ensuring not to meet any of their eyes. She wasn't important enough for stares. She would be quick in her task. Place the tray on the table and disappear. Servants were not to be seen. They were part of the castle and nothing else.

The dishes rattled in her unsteady hands as she set it down. She winced. She would have to be better. Truly great servants didn't rattle dishes. To Pansy's great surprise, the door to the rooms closed. She turned and stared at Lady Marai and Ley Wallace with wide eyes as her heart suddenly hammered. What had she done wrong? How could she explain she'd been as quick as she could, as steady as her thin body allowed?

Lady Marai, whose red-gray hair sat styled and braided, stood watching her with those eerie blue eyes. She crushed her cigar on her silver platter. It held many discarded butts despite being emptied twice a day by the servants.

"Come to me, don't be afraid," the gentle lady said.

Pansy, frightened for her life, took tentative steps towards the lady. The woman inspected her with an eagle's eye and Pansy nearly cried at the perusal, deathly worried they would dismiss her and get a girl who didn't rattle trays. Where would she go? Her parents were dead. She had no people. She only hoped to earn her keep well enough so one day she might become someone important within the household, such as a lady's maid.

"What is your name?" Lady Marai asked.

The girl looked back and forth between them and lowered her gaze. "They call me Pansy, m'lady. Because I'm from Lumbry where pansies grow."

Ley Coster stepped closer and met Lady Marai's eyes in an unspoken understanding. Pansy didn't know what the looks meant, but she didn't think them to be positive. Oh, she'd said too much! They didn't care where she was from!

"Lumbry? To the north?" The Ley asked.

"Aye, m'lord," Pansy whispered, a tremor in her voice. She hid her hands, embarrassed by the stains on her fingers, tainted by the dyeing of the winter wools.

After the strange morning, Pansy thought nothing would surprise her. Until Lady Marai took her chin to better survey the girl's face. Pansy trembled, clutching her tears between her lashes and keeping herself from begging for her post.

"Why do you serve this house, Pansy?" Lady Marai asked.

The girl blinked and quivered further. She didn't understand such a question. "To-to serve the High Seat, m'lady. There's no greater honor."

Lady Marai's red eyebrow curved as she studied Pansy's profile. "What is your age?"

She let go of Pansy's chin, and the girl sagged in relief. "Thirteen, m'lady."

Her nostrils flared, she smelled of ash, and Pansy held in the revulsion. "You're small for your age… and meek. People wouldn't pay you a second look."

"Indeed, they would not." Ley Coster nodded to the lady. "It might work."

Pansy was most embarrassed, and a tear dropped to her cheek. Her Ladyship took her hand and pulled the girl closer, though she hesitated and scrunched her nose at the fresh smell of cigars.

"I have a task of utmost importance. Do you know your way

home from here?" Lady Marai asked.

Pansy, to her credit, almost smiled. "To Lumbry? Aye, of course, m'lady. Everyone knows the way home."

Then Her Ladyship turned into her drawer and pulled out a letter. She touched it quickly, as if bidding it farewell. A most strange act.

"It's not to Lumbry that I send you, child of Istok," Lady Marai whispered. "It's to Easima."

Pansy's eyes widened, and she shifted back. Easima! That was a universe away and Pansy was just a girl!

She shook her head.

"I need you to deliver this letter to the hands of the queen. You must do so in all haste, and *they* must not catch you. Do you understand?" Lady Marai told her gravely.

Fear enveloped the girl as sweat drenched her back despite the winter chill. "Easima? The *queen*? Oh, m'lady, I'm no one, really! I'm a cook's helper!"

Lady Marai gripped her arm. "It is because you are no one that it *must* be you. A small, poor child from a tiny village can easily traverse New Verden undetected."

Pansy clutched her dye-stained hands to her face. "Please, m'lady—I've traveled nowhere other than by the cart that brought me here. I don't know the way to Easima!"

The lady glanced at the door and shushed her, and Pansy felt dismay bubble in her throat. Then Lady Marai choked on sudden wracking coughs that twisted her body. It horrified the girl when blood trickled at her lips, but Ley Coster quickly handed the lady a handkerchief. As the coughing episode ended, the lady seemed dizzy and placed her hands over the wood of her desk to catch her breath. Slowly, she looked at the girl, who stared aghast.

"Look at me. I'm *dying*. We have little time." Lady Marai's voice was hoarse. "You see that torch?"

And she pointed out her large balcony window, which faced the Mountains of Anaji. There was the Dragon Torch, still bright and beautiful. Pansy nodded.

"They *murdered* High Lord Beltran and our entire kingdom

hangs on a precipice," the lady croaked.

"*Murdered?*" Pansy asked.

"Aye, murdered by the bitch that walks my hallways," Lady Marai snapped.

Pansy's eyes went to the door. "The *Cruel One.*"

Lady Marai straightened and once more held out the letter. "If you fail in warning the queen of the impending danger… Istok will fall. Do you understand?"

Pansy stared at them both, looking at her with hope. At *Pansy.* As if she were important. As if she—of all people — could save the kingdom! It was like the stories Cook would sometimes tell her when she'd had wine and smoked her special weed. Of heroes, kings, and adventures. Pansy always wished to be like one of them, strong and brave and fearless. But she was nothing but a replaceable kitchen girl. It was something out of a dream, to be offered such an opportunity.

Fear still clung to her, but something else began to grow within the small girl. Hope that she *could* deliver such a letter, complete such a task and then perhaps the queen would reward her. Maybe she could indeed be one of her maids, which dressed her hair and straightened her gowns! No Cook to yell at her or stairs to climb or Cruel One to hide from! *And* she could save Istok, her beloved home.

Gathering that hope, she slowly nodded. "I'll try my hardest. For Istok."

Before she comprehended what she'd agreed to, they pulled her deeper into the chamber. The lady dressed her as a boy, then smudged ash on her face, neck, and hands. The girl trembled and protested when Lady Marai took her long thick braid and sliced a knife through the locks, effectively leaving her with chin-length hair. They provided no words of comfort when she clutched the ruined strands. As Ley Coster helped the girl into winter boots, the lady had another coughing fit where she lay on the chaise, barely able to stand.

"Tuck the letter in your pants," Lady Marai whispered.

The girl did as she was told, even as she sobbed over the loss of her hair. She chanced a glance at the lady's water mirror. She'd only looked at herself in a mirror once before. From this angle, she looked like a young boy.

"Speak to no one. If anyone stops you, you're traveling to Easima to get medicine for your sick mother," Ley Coster told the girl, who nodded as she rubbed her cheeks.

The Ley handed her a sack filled with food, water, a blanket, and a bag of *moja* coin.

"But m'lady, they'll see me leaving the castle!" Pansy moaned as she gripped the sack to her chest.

"You know how to sail?" Lady Marai slowly stood from the chaise and hobbled to the girl.

"Of course, m'lady. I'm Istokian," Pansy hiccupped.

The lady smiled. "Good girl."

The Ley moved aside the chaise and pulled back the rug over the floors. It revealed a small hatch opening, large enough for a person to fit. He grunted as he bent and opened it. Stairs went down into the belly of Korkoran.

Pansy reeled at the sight and stepped back with wide, fearful eyes. Lady Marai grabbed a lamp and turned to her.

"Remember your task, child. You must get to the queen at all costs. All of Istok depends on you. Take these stairs to the back of the dungeons. Follow the stone hallway to the gate—here is the key. Lock it after you pass and toss the key into the sea. You'll descend many steps, but keep going. You'll find a cave opening where a small boat awaits. Sail around Korkoran and land on the beach," Lady Marai said, and pushed her towards the stairs. "Buy a pony and ride hard north towards your home. When the Star Mountain comes into view—you know the one?"

The girl nodded; her eyes fixed on the bleak stairs. Fear and dread covered her. She'd always hated the dark.

"Good. Veer west once you see the mountain and travel the Ouestern road. You'll reach Easima in a few weeks," Lady Marai said.

The door to the chambers thundered with a harsh knock.

"She's here!" Ley Coster gasped.

Pansy shuddered as she stepped onto the blackened stairs. "I'm scared, m'lady!"

Lady Marai bent down and took her little hand, clutching it tightly with clammy fingers. "You're Istokian, born under a dragon banner. You *must* succeed or we will all die, including the queen."

Pansy paled, but a sudden resoluteness bloomed within her, and she nodded. "I'll succeed. I'll save Istok."

"Go, child," Marai said, and pushed her down.

As the latch closed, Pansy heard the Ley sigh. "We'll never know if she succeeds," his defeated voice filtered down to her. "Doesn't matter. The future is not for us."

And Pansy, small as she was, inconsequential as she was, afraid as she was, trembling as she was, was never more determined to succeed at something in her life.

Isabelle Olmo

Chapter One

ALMIRA

Seven months later, Mavros Castle, Easima

For the Queen of New Verden, pregnancy was a cruel thing. Almira's ability to rest remained limited because of the debilitating pain in her back, while Alton slumbered with ease. She couldn't even benefit from his warmth, as she needed cushions under her limbs to find some comfort. Alton asked if she was enacting a siege, a little game for them to play. Impossible man. She wished for details of the war, and he wanted to lap his tongue between her legs. He said she tasted different when pregnant.

The lack of sleep made her irritable along with the baby, who kicked with frequency. As she pressed a palm against her swollen belly, the child kicked again. The queen found she missed *Nanai*. Almira wished to ask questions of someone familiar with not only pregnancy, but herself.

She also desperately ached for her mother. Instead, she had midwives—who were knowledgeable—but it was not the same. *Nanai* would not return until next week when the Suidian entourage would arrive for the season.

It didn't help that as of late a darkness plagued her with a pressing sensation, like something was wrong in the world. A shadow outside of her political intuition. Naturally, she attributed it to a combination of pregnancy and Alton being at war. The feeling nearly overwhelmed her last night, and she'd clutched Alton tightly, crying against his chest. Her husband knew better than to jest about her tenderness towards him. The blackness ebbed, and she finally enjoyed his pleasures.

The child kicked, making her wince.

"Allow me respite," she murmured.

Alton stirred, his face against the pillow and his hair strewn and rumpled. "You've not slept."

Almira sighed. "Very little. Your child is attempting to kill me."

He lifted his head; sleep lines marred his face. His long golden arm reached for her, then he caressed her belly under the covers. The child kicked in excitement as if it could sense him nearby; as it always did whenever he was around.

The delighted look on his face spoke deeply to the care she held for him, and she sighed into his caress. She'd missed him desperately these months since he'd been at war.

"I never knew babies moved within the belly," he said, still in wonder over the entire experience.

While Alton had attended to battle, his letters to her contained a litany of questions about her and the child's well-being. However, Almira longed for news of the front, so she'd taken to writing General Vine for the information his letters lacked.

She groaned when a sharp pinch traveled up her spine. "You can carry the baby next time."

He smiled. "Gladly."

He tossed aside her pillow fort and slid in next to her to capture her in his arms, then nuzzled her neck.

"No, Alton, I can't. You've pleasured me enough," she said with little meaning.

"I've been away for weeks. That's days on end of not pleasuring you. I'm making up for the time," he said and chuckled, amusing himself.

His mouth descended on hers. His kisses were rich and

luxurious, and she arched into him. Alton's talent with his tongue properly distracted her from any discomfort. His hands caressed her back and ass, encasing her in his sleepy warmth. She grasped his hair and pulled him deeper into her; her legs opening of their own volition.

He pulled back and sported a pleased smile. He had a small scar on his cheek that he received in battle last week and a bruise covered his left eye. It didn't take away from his good looks and handsome smile. She carefully touched the scar and fear took over her senses. Last year she'd almost lost him to Arrigo and Hestian, and after the death of her father she didn't think she could handle any further losses.

"You must be careful, my love," she whispered.

"It was nothing. Some blighter got lucky," he said. "Dodging swords, arrows, and axes are some of my favorite pass times. Keeps me fit to come home and pleasure my wife."

It was the fact that he was out dodging swords, arrows, and axes that heightened her anxiety.

His fingers found her belly once more, and the baby redoubled its tirade of kicking her ribs to dust.

She groaned at the sharp pain that echoed up into her chest. "Stop encouraging it!"

He delighted in her scowl. "You'd have her be a simpering lady. My daughter will be a warrior, the Warrior Queen!"

"She may begin her training once she exits my belly, and not one moment before."

Alton didn't seem to care. He chuckled and refocused his attention on her neck, peppering her with kisses as his lips traced towards her earlobe. Behind him, a window fluttered and she could see the mountains beyond, capped with snow and feathery clouds that hid their peaks. No birds cut across the cold blue sky. It was too cold, and the only raptors that ventured the frigid tops were the rare silver owls. She often felt very much like a mountain in winter; distant and revered, but never accessible.

What if Alton didn't survive? The thought pierced her mind before she could stop it. Her fingers tightened into his hair. *Would Arrigo conquer him?*

Or was the worry because of Hira? Was she doing the right thing by sending her back to Istok? *Yes*, she reminded herself, she was. Hira *must* return to Treveri. The city was essentially leaderless. Compounding the issues at hand were growing rumors of a man called Kuimo. Was he, in fact, crumbling the Free Isle. Would she soon have a war on two fronts? Would her uncle Thebo be ready for such a calamity? Suid was closest to the island and could suffer significant attacks.

"I'm doing some of my best work here, and yet your mind is likely on some political machinations," Alton murmured against her skin.

But her mind was always focused on political machinations. They filled her head with points of contention, and the balancing act left her withered and exhausted.

"Will you meet Ivar again?" Almira asked.

"I knew it!" He pulled back with a sigh and turned her to face him.

She tried to pull away from him, but he hovered over her with a suggestive look. She scowled. "Alton, *please*, I'm worried... though I'm uncertain about what."

"I do believe you're worried about *everything?*" He twisted one strand of her loose curls around his finger, pressing it against his nose to inhale her scent.

"Perhaps," she sighed and settled into the pillow.

He sunk down next to her and stared at her with clear green eyes. The warmth of his cock pressed against her hip. "This is better. It doesn't make a husband feel too good when he's making love to his wife and she mentions another man. Especially one such as *that* man."

She almost laughed, a welcomed distraction. "*Please*, Ivar is a brute."

"I don't know. He's handsome. Tall," Alton teased her.

She rolled her eyes but smiled at his little tactics. "Likely has a larger cock, too."

Almira slipped out of the bed as he gaped at her, laughing at his comical face. He attempted to grab her, but she was out of his reach, taking the covers with her and leaving him bare on the bed.

"I can show you *exactly*—"

"No." She shook her head. "We have much to do."

Alton sighed dramatically. He laid back on the bed luxuriously, lounging with this cock half-hard against his leg. He watched as she covered herself in her robe and tied a large bow across the top of her enlarged stomach.

"Tell me to stay. Ask me to stay. I'll stay," he breathed.

"You know I can't. You know I won't."

He said this each time he left her. Her answer was always the same. He would write in his letters, *tell me to come home, ask me to come home, I'll come home*. She wished he'd stop asking. It made her feel like this was *her* war, that they fought on *her* whim. Arrigo was splitting the Norrian nobles in half. More and more ignorant men joined his side, fooled by his charismatic words.

She threw another log on the hearth. The people nearest to her once warned Almira of the harsh Easimian winters, and they hadn't lied. Entire days she'd spent sitting next to the fire, writing letters and sipping tea simply to keep the cold at bay.

"I fear Arrigo will set his sights on Istok," she said quietly as she watched the log catch fire.

"Your mood is dark," Alton sighed as he got up and robed himself, realizing she wouldn't return to enjoy their bed again.

They had precious little time to go over details before he rode out once more and she intended to discuss the pressing matters regardless of his enthusiastic cock.

"I still maintain the best course of action is Ivar. Dag is old and battle ridden. He's losing claim to the High Seat while Arrigo is gaining ground." She looked out the window once more. Somewhere out there, Arrigo was doing all he could to destabilize the land.

Alton came to stand behind her, embracing her. "Are you going to let loose the kraken in the tower? Your little *pet*?"

He reached for a grape from the table and fed it to her, kissing her jaw as she chewed and contemplated his question.

"He might be our only hope, but as we saw last night, he hates you." She glanced at him. "*You* don't help matters."

He smiled rakishly. "I'm hard to like. What that man needs is a good fuck. Must be hard being locked up in a tower. Where's breakfast? I'm famished."

She rolled her eyes as he reached for an apple and bit into it wildly.

"A fuck lasts a moment, and he would be back to hating us," she said.

He ambled to the door and effectively startled her guards and posted knights. While he demanded food, she sat to comb and braid her hair. As she interlocked her fingers into the strands, she stared at herself in the water mirror. It rippled and slowly stilled. Bruises covered her neck from last night's activities. The extra weight of pregnancy filled out her cheeks.

Her mind was a whirlwind of anxiety; the visit to Lord Ivar was her attempt to find a common ground and make him an ally. He'd been in a foul mood last night, made worse by Alton's presence. The two men had growled and hissed words at one another like two tomcats competing for dominance. *Fools.* Still, she wouldn't give up, she would try again. She just needed to find *something* he desired. If she could just find out what it was, then use it to her advantage, then Ivar could become an ally. With him at their side, they could squelch this minor rebellion once and for all. Then their focus would be on tracking down Arrigo and his troublesome nature.

The baby kicked her again as Alton returned, servants following behind him with large trays of sumptuous food. Nadim, her devoted Keeper, instructed them to place the items on the table. He was a stickler for household details, which pleased Almira as it took things off her mind and she could focus on important matters.

"Majesties, I apologize. I did not wish to interrupt," he said.

Alton, who sat down and grasped a piece of dried meat, shook it at her Keeper. "If it's food, interrupt. It won't stop us."

Nadim averted his eyes and flushed red. Almira attempted not to show amusement at Alton's jesting nature. He always woke in a good mood after a long night of lovemaking. It was certainly something to get used to. He'd had his dark days recently and there was little for her to do but to sit or lie next to him until they passed.

"Nadim, ensure Lady Hira comes to me before she departs," Almira said.

The Keeper nodded. "Yes, My Queen. As you know, because of the storm, the Istokian escort ships arrived late last night. Commander Seaver awaits her. Also, her attire is ready."

Almira brightened at the thought of the gift she'd planned for Hira. "Good. Did the commander bring a letter from my aunt, the Lady Marai?"

Nadim ushered the servants out to provide the crowns with privacy. "No, majesty."

Marai had been hard on Almira when she was a child. However, she and Marai had bonded during her preparations to marry Edgar. Her advice turned out invaluable.

Almira looked to Alton with worry, and he understood the concern in her gaze. "Thank you, Nadim."

Not needing dismissal, the Keeper was already at the door, closing it behind him as he left.

"I'm afraid my aunt's time is short," Almira admitted.

Alton's humor abated and he entered into the sphere of calculation with her. Not his favorite activity but she'd learned he was keen when he wished to be. "Can Hira truly handle such a responsibility? She can't be more than twenty."

Almira stood from the vanity and sat across from her husband. "She's *exactly* twenty. That matters little. The fact remains she is the High Lady of Istok, and she will *have* to be ready." She picked up a wedge of cheese and ate it with gusto.

He reached across the table, took her hand, and squeezed it tightly. "She's not you."

She pulled her hand away and gave him a withering glare. "And who shall I leave in the High Seat? Hira is loyal to the crown. It's more than we can ask at this point. She'll grow into her strength in time."

He exhaled and spread apricot jam on bread, then handed it to her. He knew she enjoyed it this way. She took the peace offering and bit into it with delight.

Wisely, he changed the subject. "When do Poelia and Lady Gita arrive?"

"Next week," she said and drank some water. "It will be nice to have the children here."

Alton nodded and pursed his lips. "They're no longer children."

No, they weren't. Teb was now a young man and one day he would rule Suid. The connections he would make with the children of other high-ranking nobles were crucial.

"It's vital they're exposed to court life," she said, ensuring her tone was light.

Alton was no fool, and his eyes narrowed. "You're planning their future before they realize they have one."

Almira looked up and controlled her annoyance at him, pointing out her dealings. "Young Thebo must marry a Norrian noblewoman. There's no way around it."

The conversation with Lady Gita would be a hard one. She'd be against it. She wanted Suidians to marry Suidians and, in times past, Almira would've agreed. But the world was changing, and alliances were frail.

Alton set down his cup. "I suppose you have one picked out."

His tone was keenly tense. He disliked her meddling with the future of Thebo's children.

"I have a few in mind," she said and focused on the meat on her plate.

They ate in silence, and it starkly reminded Almira of their first dinners. How they'd hated one another, how everything about the other annoyed them. Now that they loved one another, the intimacy turned into a different sort of vexation. One where she constantly had to think of the future of the kingdom while Alton wished for each person to make their own way in life.

"It's not fair, you know. They're children," Alton finally said.

She inhaled sharply and cut into the now-cold roasted potatoes. "I was seventeen myself when I married."

He leaned forward. "They're not *you*. Hira is not you. Thebo's children are not you. The child in your belly is not you." He pointed his fork at her. "You can't plot out everyone's future. We're going to be surrounded by unhappy and disgruntled family members. At this rate, you'll want to marry off Captain Sanaa."

She set her mouth. She didn't care for his wisecrack statement. "It is our duty."

Alton shook his head. "I love you. We're damn lucky we love one another because... wife, you're incorrigible."

She brightened and clutched her hands under her belly.

"Don't you think they deserve a chance at their own happiness? To choose who they wish? What if young Thebo prefers men? What then? What will you do?" He flushed. He hated arguing with her, and she hated it just as much. But she would not lose this claim.

She picked up her cup. "Then perhaps I can arrange something with a Norrian man. Lord Ivar is handsome—"

At this, he laughed, and his ill humor dissipated. "Oh, stop it!"

Almira smiled back at him and felt the tension ease. She was relieved because she didn't wish to disagree with him before he departed. Then she would regret it once he left and miss him even more. She studied the way he cut his meat, recalling how strongly her father heeded her against marrying him. Her father had been wrong.

"Father disagreed with our marriage; did I ever tell you?"

He looked up at her, suddenly interested in this revelation. Almira recalled the day of her unveiling, after a year of donning a mourning veil for her first husband, she was finally allowed to make choices. Her choice was to marry Alton for peace.

She nodded. "After I unveiled from Edgar's death, we had a terrible row. He even called me a whore."

The goblet to his lips paused. "Did he really?"

She looked away. She didn't like to dwell on dark memories of her father, days when he missed his dead wife so much he would lock himself in his study to speak to her portrait. Not even a young Almira could pull him from such moods.

"I don't want to have that sort of relationship with my daughter, but," she looked at him, "had I not had it, I wouldn't be here today."

He smiled slightly. "And we're glad you are."

Alton reached across the table, took her hand, and kissed it. She smiled at his attention and the softness of his eyes.

"You look beautiful. Full of life, pleasured by your talented husband, and happily plotting out other people's lives." He meant it to placate her.

She knew he didn't wish her to change, but he was within his rights to counter her ideas. That's what she wanted, wasn't it? A companion, not a servant. A partner, and partners may disagree from time to time.

"Make nice with Lord Ivar before you leave. Do it for me," she said and tightened the hold on his hand. "He really is our best hope. Peace in the North means you can stay here with our children and watch them grow."

There. She knew it was low of her, to use such a notion against him, but the situation was dire.

He groaned and leaned back. "Fine. But only because you've used my children as bait, you dragon."

Chapter Two

HIRA

Her hands trembled as she bathed, and she fisted them to hold in her rage. She knew plenty about holding in emotions. All her life, court politics required her to present an icy disposition. House Balik felt nothing. House Balik was *poised*. House Balik was an example for all. Her family discouraged emotions so thoroughly Hira felt she hardly knew herself. The first time Hira yelled in frustration, her mother dropped her knitting and clutched her throat.

This year, freedom was allotted to Hira. She could laugh freely and discover which mead she liked best. Now they would yank her back into the prison by the sea, like a caged bird deprived of the use of her wings. A prisoner who never knew freedom is happier than one who freely lived and was later incarcerated for the rest of their life.

As the servants packed her bags, Hira dressed and began to head straight to Almira before she was summoned against her will. It was pointless, though, because Keeper Nadim waited outside her chambers. The man informed her with an undue formality that the queen requested her presence.

Hira hoped by the time she arrived at her cousin's chambers, the king would be gone for his daily activities, whatever they were.

She didn't wish to have such a conversation while he watched on with levity.

Posted before the royal chamber were six Black Knights, along with M and Delara. Next to them were two new Red Guard recruits whose names Hira hadn't bothered to learn.

"I'm surprised you're awake," Delara said, and she exchanged an amused expression with M.

Delara acted like a *lady* despite her broad, muscular body. She didn't engage with random men and was never indiscreet. She was elegant and collected, yet deadly and serene.

"Leave her. She's young and enthusiastic." M smiled, "What did you do with your handsome soldier?"

From initiation, Hira quickly learned there was nothing more entertaining to a Red Guard than stories of war and sexual conquests. Lately, it seemed Hira grew quite a reputation, which filled her with pride. She wasn't a wallflower around the men, and she thrilled in luring them to her chambers and enjoying a pleasurable evening. She might as well do it now. The opportunities would be seldom when she returned to Korkoran under her mother's hawk-eye.

"I sent him away. Did the queen notice my coupling?" Hira glanced at the door. The faceless Black Knights passively watched them.

Delara raised a brow. "That one notices *everything*."

M made a noise of covert agreement.

"You can see her when the king leaves," Delara said. "I wouldn't venture in there while they're alone."

M chuckled, but Hira couldn't find the humor in the woman's statement. An awful burn coated her stomach at the thought of being away from Easima and the rest of the women she considered friends. No more happy evenings with ale, cigars, and stories. She saw her future as nothing more than a tomb.

"Are you packed and ready, my lady?" M asked.

The title jarred her ears, and she fought the urge to snap angrily at M. "Call me no such thing, "she said more gently than she wanted to. "I'm a Red Guard above all else."

M placed her finger over Hira's heart. "You are the High Lady of Istok and a Red Guard no more."

Hira flinched at her words, but she wouldn't spill her pain before them. When she first joined the guard, M took her under her wing, demonstrating her many skills. Tora would watch from the sidelines and add comments on her posture, giving advice on ways of improving her technique. Thinking about it now, all the women were open and willing to share their knowledge. Leaving them felt like imminent death.

For a sharp moment, Hira yearned to hug M and thank her properly, but was afraid the Suidian woman wouldn't be open to such a display in front of others.

After the king left, Hira braced herself to speak with Almira. She entered the quarters and closed the door behind her. When she turned to Almira, she found her smiling. The sort of smile of one deeply satisfied with their nighttime festivities.

Her cousin motioned for her to sit. "You seemed to enjoy your farewell celebrations."

Cunning. Always cunning and observant. The queen sat at her table, layered with breakfast, as her servants cleared the king's discarded dishes. Hira's stomach turned at the sight of the food. This felt like a slight chastising, the sort of delicate words her mother would use to point out a misstep.

"I didn't mean to embarrass you," Hira murmured.

Almira stopped cutting her plum and sighed. "I've permitted you these liberties before you leave because I think it's good for you."

Anger flickered on the edges of Hira's mind. "Yes, now I'll know what I'm missing."

The queen looked at her with deep sincerity, her eyes so wide and black it was hard to maintain her stare. Hira didn't wish to argue or plead with her again. She'd done plenty of that in the past months, delaying her departure as much as she could.

"I apologize, cousin. I'm ready to leave at noon for Treveri," Hira said.

A part of her, the part of her that was still a child, longed for

Almira to change her mind. But as Hira watched her sharp brows and calm demeanor, she knew she wouldn't. The queen was not rash; Almira had too much of her father in her. She calculated moves and plays as a Korkan player did. The pieces moved on a board delicately and with intention. If there was any part of her that was erratic, she suppressed it very well.

"You'll be well guarded. Commander Justan is quite capable," Almira said. "It's a shame he couldn't join us last night, but they caught a terrible storm off the Cliffs of Kempt."

Hira squished a rebellious grape on the table. "I can defend myself. I don't need that Garian to protect me."

Almira observed her with that same look. "I know you can. I know you're trained and brutal in battle, but you're no longer a Red Guard."

Hira's face reddened with both shame and resentment. Almira wisely dismissed her curious servant who dallied to listen to the conversation. Keeper Nadim entered and ushered the servant girls out, then discreetly lingered by the door.

Almira turned back to her. "Hira, you're the Lady of--"

"The Lady of Istok, I know!" She threw her hands up.

Their eyes met, and she saw how unyielding Almira's gaze was. Hira would garner no sympathy from her. She too had sacrificed much in this life, and each second around her reminded Hira how much of a petulant child she still was. A part of Hira felt that if she succumbed to her duties in Istok, she would soon turn into someone like Almira. Despite her great admiration for the queen, Hira saw her life as a litany of monotonous meetings with nobles and recurring dinners with her husband. Like they'd grown up, everything was orderly. No shouting, no burping, no laughs, just a silent castle pressed against the violence of the sea.

The issue was, Almira *loved* the order. Hira didn't. She wished she did, perhaps her life would be easier that way.

"I... please forgive me," Hira whispered.

Almira stood and moved next to Hira, then took her hands. Their knees pressed together, and they sat like when they were children, in confidence. Almira's fingers were incredibly delicate, and

24

she smelled of Ouestern roses and lily water. Comparatively, Hira washed with oat soaps and strength trained twice a day, creating calluses on her palms that made them rough to the touch.

"You don't know how much I wish there was another way," Almira said with great honesty. "I know how you strain against this. It's your greatest battle. But even when you swore yourself to me, we knew the outcome would be the same."

Ocean Fury, which Hira had strapped to her waist, warmed against her thigh. A stark reminder that she carried the legacy of House Balik. To be chosen, when one didn't wish for the task, was a lonely journey. She chewed on her words of protest, and digested them. Many would think her ungrateful had she not.

"I don't... I don't know how to be a lady," Hira admitted sheepishly.

Almira smiled a little. "I didn't know how to be a queen."

A ridiculous statement, for one so fully qualified. Almira didn't see how she spoke and how she operated, how she bore the weight of the crown with such ease and assuredness. Not even the king could compare to the manner her in the ways she faced her duties without fear.

"You were born to be a queen. Uncle Beltran, may the veils protect his soul, taught you from a young age," Hira said.

Almira looked down. She still deeply mourned her father, though she didn't express it often. He guided all her movements.

"Aye, he did." Almira looked back at her fiercely. "But you and I? We're the same. We're sea dragons, born from the same ocean pool. Father couldn't have lived forever and one day you had to take up this banner and lead. Bach's death cemented that. I know you've been prolonging your departure, but your mother ails, and our country is vulnerable." She tightened the hold on Hira's hands. "This is not about you, Hira. This is about our people; they need a leader. These sailors? They're *yours*."

Hira didn't feel like a leader. She felt very much like a fraud. It's not that she hated her people, on the contrary—she adored them! She treasured their oceanic way of life, the hills and mountains, and even the spring fiddles. She delighted in the summer celebrations and the onset of fishing season, when they hauled scalla out of the waters and prepared them with spicy peppers.

She studied Almira's brown hand, soft and cared for. She was beloved in Easima. Almira smiled a little and touched Hira's cheek, traveling her fingers over the scar that crossed her face. Hira flinched.

"Along with that, you marry *when* you wish and *who* you wish. I won't drive you to such miseries," Almira finally said.

Instant, tentative relief filled Hira, and she smiled brightly at her cousin. "Truly?"

"Truly." The queen laughed and kissed Hira's cheek. "Was this your fear? That I would saddle you with an octogenarian lord?"

Hira grinned. "I feared it."

Almira went back to her seat to finish her meal. "I hold no naivete about the realities of marriage. I've been fortunate in my unions, though I must admit I rather enjoy my second one better."

And she did. That was the truth. Almira blossomed since she and the king became intimate.

"Because you love him," Hira said.

"I'm afraid I do," Almira said as she ate a potato and gave her a knowing look. "Commander Justan is a pleasant and handsome man. He wears his colors well, and he's set to inherit Pinnacle Palace."

Hira fought the urge not to roll her eyes at her statement. "I hold little interest in marriage, especially for a *handsome* drunken sailor. He likely beds maids in each port."

Also, the Garian smelled of seawater and sweat. He had too much hair on his chest, and it distracted from his sharp jaw and corded arms.

Almira, however, quickly found a silver lining. "Then he'll not judge your indiscretions!"

Her words shocked Hira. Lately, the most inappropriate things amused the queen. In the past, she would've never made such a joke. Almira didn't seem to notice Hira's disturbance and looked back at her conspiratorially.

"I have something for you. A gift."

She turned to Nadim, who nodded and left them. The queen looked back at her with a pleased smile.

"I know you're a formidable warrior, but you'll have to learn balance. Many high lords have been both warriors and state leaders. There is no law that says a lady cannot battle *and* lead her people. I know, I've looked. In the entire kingdom, there is only one above you, the crown. Navigating the nobility is a treacherous path. Think about it like... a ship in a storm. The water under the ship is necessary to keep it afloat, but during a storm, only a capable captain can prevent a ship from sinking under the crushing waves."

This only erupted questions in Hira's mind, but Nadim interrupted her thoughts when he reentered with two men. They carried a wooden frame and on it was the most beautiful suit of armor Hira had ever seen. It was Istokian blue with a sea dragon embossed on the chest piece. It was a suit for a woman. She'd seen nothing like it, and she gasped at the sight, overwhelmed with the implications.

The queen rose and watched Hira's face with contentment.

"I had it made from my father's old battle armor and our grandfather's before. With a few alterations to suit you." Almira touched the armor with reverence. "This is yours by birthright and title. The armor of the High *Lady* of Istok."

Isabelle Olmo

Chapter Three

HIRA

Hira peered at the woman in the water mirror and scarcely recognized her. She recalled that moment of freedom, of unwrapping her bindings, the slicing of her hair, and escaping the fate she hadn't wished for herself. The pinnacle of her life.

Now it felt futile, like she'd only delayed the inevitable, and Master Elio's words haunted her mind, frayed her senses, and filled her with frustration. *"One day you will be the Great Dragon, like the High Seats before you. I just hope I live long enough to see it,"* he'd said as the old man helped her escape Korkoran.

Not long after Almira first married, Hira sat at the dinner table and decreed she didn't want fishbread, a staple of Istokian winter cuisine. Her mother's mouth soured, and her uncle's eyes sat heavily on Hira's face. She was to have fishbread. Balikians ate fishbread. They squashed any possibility of allotting room for her own desires. As always.

She picked at the neck of her armor. Well, she wouldn't have fishbread when she returned. They wished her to be the High Seat. Fine. She would make room for a Hira-shaped space within her duties.

Almira sent too many servants to fit her in the new armor. They flittered over her, as if she didn't know how to secure arm braces. Ocean Fury strapped to one side of her waist and Ruby Blade at the other. The only item left over from her time as a Red Guard; aside from her scar, which glinted silvery in the sunlight. She supposed she *looked* like a High Lady but she didn't feel like one. She felt as though she'd stolen armor from her uncle and played make-believe.

A throat cleared behind her and she found a smiling M lounging by the door with her arms crossed. "Look at you now."

Hira glanced down at her attire wistfully as M came to her. "I don't look like myself. I feel like an impostor."

M shrugged and helped her fix the Istokian cape. "At least you look good in blue. Suits you."

M smiled, and Hira felt an unforeseen need to hug her. She clutched M tightly and sighed in forlorn loss. At first, M startled, then slowly relaxed, holding her in return. She'd said once that Hira reminded her of her daughter, not that M ever knew her daughter. She'd left the baby in a home for girls in Norr, but she would've been Hira's age by now.

M pulled back, then gently pushed Hira's hair behind her ear. "Don't let them give you shit about your scar. You got it defending the queen."

As if she could forget. That night lived perpetually, vividly in her mind. The gasp that came from Tora's throat when the blade imbedded into her back. The surprise of death. Hira supposed all death was a surprise, even if one lived a long life. Like an expected friend's visit that arrived early and startled you when they knocked.

M tapped on Hira's leg. "Don't forget the Hytto step."

Hira quickly nodded. "Step back right, roll, and slide, pop up, blade at ear."

With her hand, M made a stabbing motion. "Stick a blade in a man's ear and he won't fuck with you much, will he?"

Hair fell across her face when Hira looked down. Her worries frothing behind her lips. "I've no problem with the men. It's the ladies at court, which will make it difficult."

M yanked at her belt and made Hira look up. "What did I say about courtly bitches?"

The sun caught M's gray braids and Hira was sure she would never see her friend again. Her throat tightened, and she held M's hand as words escaped her.

"You're the Lady of Istok," M said. "The *High Lady* at that. Don't you remember how your uncle entered a room? Like a king. You enter every room *exactly* like that. You command the largest armada in the entire world. Look at me, *don't* look down."

Despite the tightness in her chest, the vast chasm of inferiority, Hira obeyed.

"That's it. Chin up. Those bitches try to fuck with you? Show them who you are," M stared down at Hira with a dark gleam in her eye that spoke of her belief in the young woman. "You defied your uncle and mother, rode across a kingdom to find your freedom. You're no simpering maid. I know you're young and scared, but you won't always be young and one day you'll stop being scared."

"Not today." Hira grinned.

"Not today, my lady, but one day." M winked.

There was no use in dallying. Istokians ships always sailed at noon and the morning quickly escaped her. It was time for her to go. She wouldn't be embarrassed and have Almira come and escort her. She would go on her own and own the last taste of full autonomy.

"Take care of yourself and the queen," Hira whispered.

"I always do," M said.

Hira took her face in her hands. "Be well, Madhavi, the Suidian Warrior."

M grasped her hand tightly. "You too, young Hira of House Balik."

As Hira pulled away, she paused and looked back at M, standing like the perfect Red Guard. Her cape sharply pressed. Her armor bright in the morning light. She was everything Hira desperately wished to be.

"Is it worth it?" Hira asked. "All you've done?"

M pondered for a moment, then shrugged. "I'll tell you when I find out."

The streets of Easima were foreign and unwelcoming to Hira,

despite over a year of living there. Treveri always smelled of fisheries, but the scent was crisp, mixed with the tang of moving waters and salt. Easima, however, smelled rank. There was no freshness. The summers were intense and unbearable, then the rains muddled the rotting smell that rose from the streets with mustiness. Winter descended with a deluge of clouds and the sun refused to show its face for weeks at a time.

And it was bitterly cold. Hira felt it enter her bones despite the thick woolen cape she'd draped to cover her new armor. She didn't wish for recognition. Almira wanted her to take an escort, servants and ladies, for her journey, but Hira declined. Having an entourage of servants at her beck and call seemed tedious and bothersome. She wanted to show the crew she was merely one of them; she didn't need to be treated differently because she was the High Seat.

In her bags she carried sweet summer wine from M, who said she would need it for such a heinous journey and a sharpening rock from Delara. Stones of Kemp, the lady claimed, sharpened blades like no other.

Her dapple-gray mare, Jessa, snorted in mutual sadness. They'd once escorted a queen to her kingdom, but now trotted wistfully away from freedom. Jessa would be a lady's horse now. Gone was the delight of the adventure, the freshness of the wind. Jessa would be bored, just like Hira.

The road to the docks guided them through markets crammed with vendors perpetually hawking their goods. Men chopping heads off goat carcasses with a swing of their cleavers, wrapping the meat into brown parcels, and shoving them at displeased looking servants. Women with baskets laden with winter root vegetables for hearty stews, young children clutching their robes to find some warmth as their mothers finished the shopping for the day, and young lads attempting to purchase ale and share it amongst themselves in merriment.

As she meandered through the rows of magic crystals and vendors who assured her a black rock would provide emotional harmony, she discerned an intense stare. She paused, and Jessa snorted, alert as Hira. The horrible face made itself known in the crowd and she instinctively went for her blade. It was Nadim's witch. The same sorceress Almira went to see to confirm her pregnancy.

The sensation felt like a vision.

From that moment, she couldn't trust anything she saw, touched, or smelled. Hira was not afraid of incantations. After all, witches could falsify a sentiment but couldn't physically harm her. She needed to keep her wits about her.

"Marked one," the witch said with a smile.

Hira jutted out her chin. "You search me out, witch?"

Through the market she seemed to glide, as if the world ceased. Her presence canceled all noise. Had the world ended? Were they the only two people left? *No!* She couldn't believe anything. The world was still there. Commotion was present. Hira simply couldn't hear it.

"You leave for the East. Oh, what a journey it will be," the witch said.

Hira, knowing she must control the situation before it unraveled, rounded the witch with her horse. "I don't ask for my fortune."

The witched cackled, her white eye swirling from side to side. "Who says fortune swims your way? You will want what you don't want. You'll be willing to die for what you don't believe in. The girl before me will soon perish and be reborn a great one."

Every human had questions they wished answered. Hira was no different. The same question haunted her over and over in the night. She pulled it from her thoughts and allowed it to slither to her tongue.

"How will I die?"

She looked Hira over. "*Fools* ask how they will die. The wise ask how they will live."

Jessa stomped and neighed. The witch smiled her dark smile and Hira turned from her. She'd had enough of such shadow prophecies, she would not live by them. She rode her horse away, but from the slithers of her mind came the witch's words.

"Don't let them take the arm, my lady. Without it, you won't be able to save anyone."

Hira glanced back at her, but when she looked, the witch was gone. Noise filtered back into the world, a sharp cacophony pounded against her head. Her flesh prickled, and she shook herself of the lingering ilk. Enchanters and witches, liars, tricksters, and goons. Such magicians wouldn't spook her. *Shadow jumpers.*

With renewed purpose, she spurred Jessa to the port and gathered the hood of her cloak to protect against the wind and any other conversation.

The tang of the ocean air intensified as she reached the docks, The Sea Wife awaiting her arrival. It was her uncle's grandest ship. No, not her uncle's. *Hira's* ship now. This was *her* armada and *her* crewmen. *Her* Commander. The thought of facing them and ruling them twisted her stomach. She would have to pretend to know things she never wished to know.

The Sea Wife was impressive. It carried thirty-five fire throwers, with a hull longer than the blue whales of the Sea of Torkin. With emboldened assurance, it flew blue sails with embroidered golden dragons. The Sea Wife was the most spectacular ship in the world. Three other ships escorted the Sea Wife. One boasted black sails, which were uncommon in the armada. The sound of hundreds of men rushing across wooden decks sounded down the docks as they readied the ships for departure. Hira handed Jessa to the port-boy with instructions and a silver moja, then slipped into the Sea Wife undetected. Luckily, the men were busy carrying boxes and parcels filled with items needed for the voyage home.

Pulling her cape tighter around herself, she crossed the deck, hoping to find Commander Justan quickly. Aboard the ship were chickens housed in cages, angrily flapping their wings as black feathers danced into the air. A cat, always present on a ship, glared at her coolly from the top of a crate. Not even the cat respected her. Hira looked around, attempting to distinguish the commander from the rest of the men. She saw no suit of blue threads to signify the commander's rank.

She'd only encountered Commander Justan a few times. The last time they'd traded words was when she'd collided with him after fleeing an argument with her uncle. That was mere days before she ran away from Istok. Her boyish demeanor amused the commander. Hira was certain the commander, above everyone, was unhappy to have her as the High Lady.

This was the ship that carried them into Easima a year ago. She'd reveled in that journey, though the rest of the Red Guard had not. Perhaps she should've made acquaintance with the commander then. At the time, she'd thought it unnecessary. She'd freed herself from her duties to Istok, or so she'd thought. What a little fool she'd been.

As she studied a crate packed with spices, a commotion sounded from above.

"Get this *wench* off my ship!"

Chapter Four

JUSTAN

This Ouestern weather was a dreadful calamity. It'd been too damn close, and they were lucky they hadn't crashed into the Cliffs of Kemp. His shoulder smarted from the fall last night. How many times had he meandered through the wooden slates in the middle of a storm? Plenty! One swift northern wind and he'd fallen with a hard thump, smashing his shoulder blade against the mast.

The task at hand didn't help to soothe his ill humor over his fall and late landing. He felt his hands drench in sweat at the thought of Lady Hira coming aboard. He was plagued by visions of the same procession of madness that invaded his ship last summer when he escorted the queen. The woman brought eagles aboard, for gods' sake! They shit all over his floor and it took weeks to clean it up, especially because of the rumors their feces were flammable. But Lord Beltran said *nothing*, as if he wished the cavalcade to outshine any other Istokian arrival. And an arrival it had been.

Justan could only assume the new High Lady would subject him to the same manner of flippancy. The crew hardly slept last night as he tasked them with cleaning the deck until it shined under the Ouestern moon. But the frigid temperatures numbed the sailor's fingers. The water in the buckets filmed over with ice on the top, and the wind was merciless against any exposed skin.

He paused once more and looked into the high quarters. Everything was as it should be. He stepped around the bed, passed his hand over the duvet to straighten out the wrinkle left by his careless crew. As he did so, he felt the gaze of the queen's portrait inspect him. He studied the fine lines of her aristocratic face, the flat nose that spoke of her ancient lineage, and her full lips that made her seem more Sikorian than Balikian. Her eyes were pits of black sky, steady and unmoving. He would easily admit to being besotted with her when he first saw her on the day of her unveiling.

There was something in the manner she carried herself, an assuredness which he found most attractive in women. She scarcely glanced his way to welcome him before she turned and took her father's offered hand. Justan didn't blame the king one bit for falling in love with his bride. Justan could even understand why Lord Beltran had treasured her above all others, and the thought soured his belly.

He rubbed his hands over his face, his fingers shaking. The journey had not yet begun and his insides trembled. He had no stomach for such schemes.

His one hope was that the Lady Hira was demure and kind. It might be her only saving grace. A delicate flower could hardly be a threat. A lady easily loved by Istokians and the nobility, if not a little malleable. He opened the small closet, which held some dresses and elegant leather shoes, a woolen cape, and a fur-lined coat. Plenty for her to wear on her trip. He was sure she would scarcely leave this room, and he'd ensured there was a wealth of scrolls and a fine set of knitting tools to keep her occupied.

The last memory he had of her was before she'd run away. He'd captured a glance of her months ago, but she always wore a blasted helmet so he couldn't recall her face. From memory, he knew she had Balikian red hair and a pert nose. He'd recognized a wildness inside her, but who wasn't at that age? Likely she'd grown into her post and now held an air of patrician composure like the queen.

Gods help him. He must be calm. He must complete this task without a hitch. The door to the room opened and in strutted Mr.

Hyall. Blasted man, always with scrutinizing eyes.

"Commander," the man said with a slight mocking tint to his voice. "Deck all clean, floors all mopped, and spoons shined. It should make the lady happy."

"Have we spotted the lady's entourage?" Justan walked out of the quarters with Hyall close at his heels.

"No, Commander. I'm sure we'll see the fine gowns coming down the port," Mr. Hyall chuckled.

The crew was no happier than he was to transport the lady to Treveri. Some of them didn't believe women belonged at sea unless that woman was the beloved captain of the Night Serpent. They blamed the storm on the anger of gods. *Fools.*

"I want to be notified the moment she's seen. I want the entire crew lined up and ready to greet her, and I better not see one whisker on anyone's face," Justan said with a growl. He himself had to shave, but he'd not been able to do it with all the tasks at hand.

"Mustn't offend the lady with the show of prickly facial hair, can we?" Mr. Hyall stuffed a pipe into his withered mouth.

The commander paused and leveled the man with a look of distaste. Then, from the corner of his eye, he spotted a cloaked woman wandering onto the deck. A deep flush traveled up his neck at the sight of her stealthy steps as she surveyed the ship with wide, interested eyes. *Unbelievable.* An Ouestern urchin on the prowl for desperate Istokian men! He leaned over the railing.

"Get this *wench* off my ship!" He yelled.

The woman turned to him, but Commander Justan, Lord of Pinnacle Palace, was already snarling in anger. He hardly considered her startled expression before he pointed at her.

"I've a lady coming on board, and I don't need the likes of *you* on my watch!"

He jumped down the netting and landed in front of her with expert grace. His blue coat billowed behind him as he stalked closer. He took in her face as he stood before her and the blaze of blue eyes beholding him in narrowed anger surprised him. She was heavily scarred. There was a familiarity to her he couldn't place. He thought he knew her, but given she was only a pleasure-giver, it wouldn't surprise him if he did. Visiting pleasure houses was one of his favorite activities. Seeing her up close made him wish he didn't have an assignment; he could appreciate her loveliness despite the massive scar cutting across her face.

Her face brightened in indignation. "How *dare* you speak to me in this manner?"

Something in her tone as she spat her words stirred a shiver of desire. She was feisty. A good time indeed. He preferred his pleasure-givers to have a sharp mind and a lashing tongue.

He towered over her and narrowed his eyes. "You're on my ship, *red*."

A cloak covered her from head to toe. A pity. She wrinkled her nose in disgust and he couldn't help but approach her. That was a mistake, as she had, without him noticing, placed a knife against his throat. He almost laughed.

"Come closer, Commander, and it'll be more than a shave you'll receive from me." She pressed the blade deeper into his skin.

A warmth stirred in his belly. Perhaps she wasn't an urchin. Perhaps she looked for work and yearned to be part of the Istokian armada. Well, that wouldn't work out.

His lips twitched at the thought. "Have you any knowledge of your trinket, *red*?"

The steel bit at his neck, and he held in a wince at the sting. He didn't appreciate that. The last thing he needed was to greet the Lady Hira with a bleeding throat.

"More than *you*," she said in a low tone. She found no amusement in the predicament. "And from now on you'll address me as *my lady*."

He stared at her scar; the way it curved up her chin, pressed against her nose, missed her blue eye by a hair, and cut across her forehead. He sensed her disfigurement was something she hated— though he thought it took little away from her pretty face.

"*I'm* more a lady than you'll ever be," he goaded her.

Around them, his crew laughed uproariously. She pressed the knife to his throat with perfect precision and he flinched. Done with her game, and having limited time, he shoved her off and kicked her legs. Instead of collapsing or giving in, she twirled and pulled a sword from her waist and faced him. His own curved Garian blade was already in his hand. He'd never lost a fight with this sword and doubted the woman had sufficiently practiced dexterity to fight him.

The commander smiled to his crew, delighting in the manner her face flushed a deeper shade of crimson. "What say we, men? Twenty silver moja, I beat the marred red wench to port in five strikes!"

Chants of speculation rose from the sailors, now rounding and surrounding their little theater. They crammed themselves against the rails, leaned down, hanging from the nets, their mouths dampened with the prospect of a gamble.

"I'll take that wager!" one sailor said.

The commander smirked as he rounded and inspected her posture. She placed her feet correctly.

"You've got suitable form. You've studied a bit, but you're a little too confident. There's a tricky vibe to you, trying to stowaway in the Lady of Istok's ship," he said in near merriment.

He paused for a moment at the sight of her boots. Dusky brown leather, well-shaped, and well-cared for. He looked back at her face, which was transformed into livid ferocity.

"Is that what I'm doing, Commander?" Her tone changed to one of daunting fervor.

He side-stepped her, but she rounded and kicked back, aiming for his stomach. He jumped in the nick of time. The crew roared, and they exchanged bets. Justan smiled at the men, opening his hands in a great show of confidence. It was the wrong move to make. The clever girl found an opportunity and their swords clashed before he danced away, a laughter on his lips.

"You've trained. How'd you get that scar?" He asked.

He wished he hadn't.

"*Defending* the queen."

Justan's body froze when he turned to stare at none other than Captain Sanaa Cinege of the Queen's Red Guard. She stood in a near-casual manner, her golden eyes laid hotly on the commander.

Captain Sanaa was a well-known woman. She wore a fur-lined

cape and gold and red breast plate. The pelt danced in the chill air of the docks. Her long hair was in customary Suidian braids underneath her red and white feathered helmet. She exuded command and authority in a manner Justan had never seen before.

He looked from the captain back to the wench he'd begun to fight. At the realization of his behavior, he felt all the blood drain from his face. Instantly, Justan sheathed his sword. His apologies were scorching hot in his throat, and he swore he would be sick. He couldn't even meet the lady's eyes. What a fool he was! What a complete moron! He could've flung himself from the top of the castle tower, and that would yield more honor than this moment.

"My lady, I apologize," he said in a desperately sincere tone.

Of all the women he suspected her being, his own Ladyship was the last of his conjectures. *Of course.* Her eyes. Fucking Balikian eyes haunted him everywhere he went. Red hair. That was the last he recalled of her a year ago when he'd gotten a good look at Lady Hira. Hair so long it brushed her legs. Gone was her treasured hair. She was no longer a soft maiden who chattered amongst fellow noble ladies and was always at the side of Lady Marai. Before him was a woman with a sharp jaw and set mouth that looked to want to pummel him until he was a pile of weightless ash.

That same lady scoffed at his words. Her lips twisted, and her eyes narrowed. Not a tremble from a lash. Her anger was hematic, a sanguine thirst for respect. And he'd given her none of that. He'd mocked her.

"You best do good on your wager, Commander." Captain Sanaa took off her helmet and handed it to one of the Red Guards, who watched with interest.

The commander, crimson faced, floundered. He looked between the women. There was no salvation for the situation.

"I apologize, my lady and Captain Sanaa. I didn't recognize the lady—"

The captain, highly amused at his faux pas, walked to them. "You said you would beat the marred red wench to port in five strikes. Do good on your wager, Commander. Or have you no honor?"

A curtain of embarrassment fell over him. He was most ashamed, pride be damned. He looked at the Lady Hira, braving to meet her eyes. She beheld him with such little regard, he almost flinched.

"I'll not fight my lady and ruler," the commander said.

Hira remained unmoved, and pointing her blade at him, she called, "Your lady and ruler commands you to finish what you started. Unsheathe your sword."

His stomach once more stirred, and he cursed it. This was *not* what he needed at this moment, and he felt like an unpolished lad before her. Damn Balikian women. Were none of them normal? It was Beltran's fault; he'd raised them.

With a resigned grunt, he yanked out his saber. Then Lady Hira tugged at her cloak and revealed a blue armor crafted to perfection. He'd seen no one look fiercer in his life than at that moment, and his breath whooshed from his body. She tossed the ugly mantle to the side and turned back to him.

"Try not to kill him," Captain Sanaa said as she moved to the sidelines.

The commander's face reddened to the neck.

"Now that you've shown me how you fight, Commander, I'll know if you're going easy on me." Lady Hira provided him a smile. Her scar tugged her lip.

Because his breath came short, all he could do was nod at her words and pocket the fascination he'd suddenly developed over her features.

They rounded one another, a perfect synchronicity of steps. She was good, very good. He charged, and the swords clashed. Their breaths puffed against their faces; he could see the soft hairs on her brows. He had to pull away simply to escape the proximity. Hira ran after him, but he twisted and lunged at her. She stepped back just in time. Not before the cat scampered between her legs in an angry wail. She stumbled as he attacked her again. She twisted her ruby knife and blocked the hit. He raised a brow, almost smiling at the thrill of fighting her.

She was agile and calculating, her body muscled and sure. He swung repeatedly, and she met his blade. They pressed against each other, and his neck tingled. Despite his superior strength, she held tight. A crushing wave of the sea.

Their faces were close to one another until he could feel her breath against his cheeks. He almost lost his footing, and she smiled at him. *Minx!*

She craftily yanked back, unlocking the grip, and swung her sword down hard enough that his blade clattered loudly across the deck. He turned and stared at her, stunned, as she rose to her full height and stared him down.

The uproarious crew exchanged bets, some laughing and others arguing. He heard nothing, distinguished nothing, he only saw her. She looked like the heroes of old, High Lady Dominia reincarnated. A warrior of formidable strength encased in a deceptively sweet face. He would've never guessed the young girl he'd seen as a child would turn out like *this*. Gods of the sea, he was in trouble.

She brought her blade to his cheek, and he swore it was the touch of her skin. She panted as they beheld one another.

"Now, Commander… you'll bid me welcome to *my* ship."

There were many things he wished to say to her. Many more, he would never even allow his mind to ponder. Especially with the situation at hand and the complications this could cause. This was going to be a long trip.

"My lady, welcome to the Sea Wife," he said, promptly bowing his head.

She pulled back and sheathed her sword, which caught his attention. A dragon hilt on an ancient blade. He knew that sword. He'd held that sword on the day of her uncle's funeral. Shame flooded him once more. He'd sworn to protect her and instead he'd seeded hate and mistrust. The Favia harshly punished failed promises to the dead. He may not believe in much, but he believed in honor.

"I should have known," he mumbled.

"But you didn't, and that makes you a *fool*." She put away the ruby blade. "Get up and man my ship. You're lucky I don't dismiss you."

Without awaiting his response, she turned to Captain Sanaa, who sat on a crate.

His body felt hot and cold all at the same time. He did not know what to do or how to remedy the situation. He'd need to speak to her in private, but he didn't think she would take kindly to his words. Actually, from the pride of her stride he knew she would take kindly to nothing he told her.

He didn't blame her. He'd damned himself.

Chapter Five

HIRA

Hira's heart still beat erratically from the exhilarating fight with Commander Justan. She glanced back at him, finding his dark eyes lingering on her. She turned her head to ignore him, but also to hide the flush on her cheeks.

Sanaa regarded her with a knowing look. In her hand she held a large pouch of *moja* coins. She must've placed some bets while Hira was fighting for her life. Typical. Sanaa and M never missed an opportunity for a good wager.

The captain smiled, which was a rarity. "My lady, thank you for the riches."

"Use them wisely," Hira said and pushed her sweat matted hair from her face.

A few of the new Red Guards accompanied Sanaa, and they stared at Hira with something akin to reverence. She looked away from their appraising eyes. No one ever stared at Hira in awe, and her chest rose with pride.

The death of Tora and Keilly depleted the original Red Guard. The replacements were young and eager girls, easily trained. How Hira wished she could teach them what little skill she'd developed. It felt wonderful not to be the young one who lacked in training and instead be the wiser guard with tenure.

"How many new ones did you contract?" Hira asked.

Sanaa shrugged. "Twenty."

Twenty. Incredible that so many women continued to show up at Mavros wishing to join her majesty's personal protectors.

"A good number," Hira said.

"Should keep *cuzo* content for a while." Sanaa pocketed her winnings into her cape. "How you can choose to go home by ocean is beyond me."

The sea did not suit Suidians. They hated it, land is where they belonged. Hira recalled how badly most of the Red Guard reacted during their voyage to bring Almira to Easima. The captain spent the trip with a bucket between her legs, grasping walls to prevent from toppling over.

"I was born in this ocean. It's home." Hira wished she recalled the birthing pools; Almira always swore she had a memory of being pulled from the ocean and taking her first breath. An impossibility, to be sure.

"Will you be alright?" Sanaa asked, breaking through her thoughts.

Hira nodded and studied the deck that would be her home for the next few weeks. The men had gone back to their tasks but still laughed and recounted the entertainment.

"The Red Guard will miss you," Sanaa said.

Her words were a sharp end to a long line of hope within Hira. Perhaps a part of her was still that girl bowing before the captain begging for her post. Begging to be taken seriously. To be something other than an unqualified heir.

"I wanted to thank you. For taking a chance on me and standing up to the queen. I don't know what would've happened if you hadn't of shown me pity."

Sanaa seemed somber. "Her majesty took pity on me once. It was only right that I pass on the favor."

Hira sighed. "I'll miss wearing the red. I wore the red, and I was untouchable. Without saying a word, people respected me. When I entered a room, men minded me. No one gave a shit if my face was a mess. I'd earned it and it was valor."

The captain made a noise of understanding, as if she too hid behind her post and granted importance. "Let me tell you something about respect. It's *earned*. It's a gift. True, that women seldom receive it, but I believe you can. You're smart and stubborn enough to fight for it. You must go to your duty, you must lead your people and find love for them within yourself."

Hira beamed out at the sea. The sun was high, and she knew they must sail very soon. The waters were calm, and the birds wheeled through the harbor skies. Their calls were a comforting noise. She'd never thought of respect as earned. Many provided it to her without preamble and that was something she'd not dwelled on. For the first time in her life, she would need to earn it. She didn't even know how to commence. She looked at Sanaa, strong and sure of herself, earning respect just by her mere presence.

"What would you do if you were in my place?" Hira asked.

"I'm not you. I'm the daughter of an illegitimate lord and his commoner wife. They did not demand duty from me, but it became something I insisted on myself. You think your duty takes you away from your dreams? You equate the term 'lady' with a prison sentence, but how is the title of a lady different from that of a lord? Is a lord not allowed to lead his armies, sign treaties, discover lands, father children, sit in councils, hunt, drink, and whore? Then why shouldn't a lady do the same?"

Hira thought Sanaa had spent too long with Almira. Her liberal views on society were, admittedly, contagious. Few agreed with such statements. Especially her mother, the Lady Marai.

"You don't know my mother. Her idea of a lady is someone who dons gowns, marries the man she's told, and leaves the wars to her male relatives. I'll never be able to carry a sword, no matter the fine armor."

Sanaa seemed unperturbed. "Your mother is not High Lady of Istok, you are. The title went to *you*. What will she do? Clap you in your rooms? It'll be amusing for her to try."

Hira hadn't thought about that. Honestly, aside from hounding her, her mother's power depended on what her uncle had provided.

And he was dead. The Korkoran guards who protected the Istokian fortress now answered to Hira. They were loyal to the seat. *Not* her mother. She had it on good authority they didn't care for Lady Marai and her harsh, antiquated ways.

The captain nodded at one of the young Red Guards who stepped forward with a scroll.

"I brought you a gift," Sanaa said.

Hira took the old, leather-tied scroll. The pages were yellowed and weathered, many lives had come and gone since its conception. She wasn't much for reading. It bored her. She found it hard to concentrate if she stood still too long. Like she would wither like a fallen leaf.

"The Histories of the High Lady Dominia, the first of the royal House of Balik," Sanaa said as she stood. Her brilliant cape shined under the cool winter sun.

Hira turned the scroll in her hands, studying the deckled edges, frayed by time. "Where did you find this?"

Sanaa provided her with a conspiratorial look. "I stole it from the Royal Archives."

A lively vision of the captain sneaking into the archives, perusing the subjects, and then stealthily tucking the scroll into her cape came clearly to Hira's mind.

"*Stole* it, Captain?" Hira smiled.

Sanaa showed no shame as she took her helmet from the hand of the young Red Guard.

"It's good reading for such a long voyage. Lady Dominia began the Royal Line of Balik. She was one founder of the Council of Five, and she died in glorious battle at the ripe age of seventy," Sanaa said.

All of this, Hira knew. She'd listened to Ley Coster spout endlessly about the creation of the Balikian line. She'd discarded many of his lessons. Perhaps paying a little attention might lessen her apprehension at this moment. Still, people like Lady Dominia belonged in a category beyond Hira. Much like Almira, they were larger than life, and Hira was merely a girl with an ancient sword at her waist.

She looked down at the scrolls. "It won't be easy to be myself in a world that condemns individuality."

Sanaa laughed, her head thrown back in amusement. "You whine about this to *me*?"

She was right. Sanaa, with her large stature, solid face, and preference for women, was always true to herself. In the beginning, it must've been quite difficult. Hira smiled and nodded, admitting her erroneous statement. Privilege painted her words. She'd have to be mindful of careless statements. Almira always was.

"Well, I'll be off," Sanaa said.

Hira breathed deeply and nodded. "Thank you, Captain. I'll see again you for the birth of the baby."

Sanaa nodded and cast a dark look at Commander Justan, who watched them from the upper deck.

"A word of advice? Bury the hatchet with the Garian commander. It's bad luck to fight with the captain of the vessel that carries you." Then Sanaa slid her helmet over her head. "Just don't *fuck* him."

Enjoying the bawdy rebuke, Hira mocked a gasp, saying, "Ladies do not *fuck*."

"I thought you had no interest in being a *lady*," Sanaa called on a laugh as she left the ship. Hira's face reddened further.

The quarters of the High Seat were a vast improvement from the ones she inhabited when Almira came for her coronation. Her uncle had a beautiful painting of Almira hung by the desk and she was glad to have her watching. It was a spacious area with an inviting view of the sea and the accompanying ships. The gilded bed was enormous, with deep blue sheets signifying a true Istokian retreat.

They delivered her trunk, but no servant bothered unpacking. She supposed she was the only lady on board and that task would fall to her. No matter, she was used to taking care of herself. After all, she'd told Almira she had no need for servants. It was easier said than done. She had many things she'd collected and quickly became overwhelmed with all the tasks.

She removed her armor with some difficulty then changed to plain clothes appropriate for a sea voyage. It startled her when someone entered the quarters without knocking.

"Why didn't you tell me who you were?"

Hira turned and looked at Commander Justan. She tried to imagine how her uncle or Almira would address such an insolent question. Certainly, the commander would never storm into Lord Beltran's quarters and demand such things. Why did he believe he could do it to her? Perhaps it was time to set boundaries.

"Leave. Knock. *Then* enter again," she said, squaring her shoulders and holding herself up in her closest imitation of Almira. It felt unnatural, but she supposed life was all about discomfort in the things that would strengthen you.

His jaw twitched, and his eyes blazed. To his credit, he stepped back, closed the door. A few seconds passed. She thought he was gone for good and didn't dare move. Then a soft knock.

She swallowed and cleared her throat. "Come in."

He entered. He looked angrier than before. Good. She wouldn't stand with him barging in on her. She might not wish for the power of the High Seat, but he'd no right to behave as he'd done.

"Now. To answer your question. You assumed I was a wench trying to sneak into your ship under false pretense. You were wrong." She crossed her arms and gave him a withering glare. "You assumed I didn't know how to handle a blade, but the nick in your neck says otherwise. Wrong again. You thought me a hooligan with my scarred face when it's a stamp of my deeds. Thrice wrong. This is *my* armada, Commander. Seeing as you're wrong so often, why should I allow you to continue your post?"

She couldn't believe her words or how she managed to say them without a trembling tone. It didn't matter. This man annoyed her, and she had enough troubles to worry about ahead of his loyalty.

His face twisted. "My family has been commanding the ships of Istok for twelve generations."

She walked closer to him until she could see the sheen of the skin from the opening in his shirt. "Is that the extent of your qualifications? You were born into a house that, at one point, could read the night sky? I'm impressed."

She smiled when his neck reddened. Hira was an absolute no one around Almira. She didn't think she'd ever held anyone's interest for so long, and she found herself in a rather unsteady position. She could hardly believe in herself as a dragon when establishing her post felt so unnatural. Like forcing a leather trouser over wet legs. Still, the act electrified her senses, especially his reaction.

He stepped forward and pointed at his chest. "Me and my men defended this city when General Hestian tried to kill the king and queen! It was *I* who carried the high lord's body to the sea. I'll not have some redhead come and tell me I'm not fit for my post because she failed to identify herself and came disguised aboard a royal ship!"

She brightened and felt her skin burn. How she hated her paleness and how much it gave away without permission. "I am your High Lady, Commander. I will question you if I want. And if I wish to walk around naked for the rest of our trip, then I shall do it. If you want to have words with me in that regard, just let me know. I find your whiskers offensive and would gladly take a hand at shaving the other side."

Her entire body trembled, and she found it hard to breathe. She was floundering. He was getting to her; unmasking and unraveling her. She was holding on by a thread and thought she would faint. Sheer stubbornness kept her composed.

His teeth gnashed, but he kept a civil tone. "As my lady *commands.*"

They stared at one another for a beat. They were too close. The commander was an example of many years at sea, darkened by the sun, toned by the vigorous exercise. Well, he wasn't the only one filled with strength. She was a fucking Balik. A fucking dragon, and she'd not tolerate his berating tone. She straightened her shoulders and pointed to her unpacked things, realizing she might have made a mistake with the extra work she placed on herself.

"I shall require someone to attend to me. I'm certain you can spare a sailor. I'll be up to toast to the voyage in a few. You're dismissed, Commander. And don't enter my quarters again unless you're invited."

He needed to leave *now.* She was crumbling. The visage of the lady would reveal the softness of the girl.

Hira thought he would unsheathe his sword. She almost wished he did. His brown eyes were small but deep, they narrowed into slits. He towered over her, easily the height of Delara.

For a moment, she thought he would grab her. She would rather they grapple on the floor with fists and slaps. But he didn't place a finger on her. He turned on his heel and slammed the oak door behind him.

She sagged against the table, grasping the wood and feeling the need to vomit. How Almira maintained this composure was beyond her. She sunk into the chair and placed her face in her hands, feeling her strength drained, as if she'd battled physical enemies instead of a man who reported to her.

"You're a dragon," she whispered to herself without allotting it much meaning. Words were simply words and right now, words bled her.

Angrily, she yanked from her trunk a blue and gold fur-lined royal cape and tossed it over her shoulders. She felt Almira's eyes shine in approval. *Show them who leads, and they'll follow.* Hira would face the sailors once more and she *must* show command of position. She wouldn't have that commander make the men question her power. She would save her battles for her mother and not waste them on sea commanders.

When she returned to the deck, they met her with curious glances and slight bows. They made the last calls for the sail. The sun was high in the sky and the time had come to leave Easima. She attempted to focus on the good parts of the moment—which was hard to do amongst the clouds of her mind.

Hira recalled she *loved* sea voyages; the crispness of the clean wind, the splashing of rogue waves, and the mystery of the dark waters. It was enchanting and she would allow the happiness of it to strengthen her and provide her guidance.

The men pulled barrels of ale and out came the cups, passed to each man on board.

"My lady, your goblet," a sailor said.

She nodded in thanks but noticed her goblet was elegant compared to the cups used by the others. Someone had delicately filled it with a lady-like sip of ale. She sighed and looked for the distributor of the drink. It was none other than the commander. Fuck. She stared angrily at the goblet, curling her hand over the rail in annoyance. With a sharp breath, she confronted him once more. She was the Lady of Istok. She was the Lady of Istok. That was her mantra as she made her way to him.

He watched her approach with a tight face. "We've no wine on board," he said, and looked away nonchalantly.

She held out her goblet and cursed the trembling of her fingers. "Fill mine up to the brim, Commander. I'm no simpering maid."

He turned and bristled in her direction. Their eyes battled for a moment and she felt the hairs on the back of her neck rise. His face twitched, sharpening his jawline. The men watched them in near fascination, but she wouldn't back down. Especially when they had an audience.

Finally, the commander snatched the goblet and filled it so that it splashed down to her boots as the ship gently swayed. He smirked sardonically. She smiled back and refused to complain about his antagonism. Once everyone had a cup of ale, Commander Justan stood on the top deck and raised his cup.

"Gods of the sea! Dragons of the waters! Bless this here voyage, bless your Istokian children, and protect the High Lady of Istok on her journey home!"

"TO THE LADY OF ISTOK!"

Hira flushed as the men all chanted this. Commander Justan spared her a look, then drank deeply from his ale. The rest followed, then yelled, and threw the cups into the bay with gusto.

The dance of sailing began, and she pressed against the railing as the sailors rushed to their posts. They shouted orders and reported statuses. With a grunt, The Sea Wife pulled from port and away from Easima. Many city dwellers came to witness the spectacle. They threw flowers and waved as the small part of the armada left their city.

"Goodbye Easimian maidens!" one man shouted as he waved hanging from the rafts.

And an impromptu song started amongst the men. They spoke of Suidian beauties and the mercy of the waves when good sailors were lost at sea.

Hira felt a tightness in her chest; she was going back *home*. It was strange to think she was the same girl who'd cut her hair with a small blade, stolen a soldier's clothes, and begged her cousin for mercy. She was returning home with a ruined face and a questionable reputation. The nobles would scoff at her, and her insides twisted at the thought of having to wrangle them. If it was anything like wrangling the commander of her armada, she could look forward to many exhausted nights.

The commander shouted orders to his men. His agile body moved from place to place in a dance of motion. He knew the vessel, she could grant him that. His shirt billowed in the wind and his chest freckled with hair like a true Garian.

He caught her staring at him, and heat rose sharply to her cheeks. She looked away, angry at herself for lingering on his form. Even angrier at looking away. She'd let him win, and that burn scalded her stomach. His stare was poignant and bold, but she kept her eyes on the fading city. Still fuming at her reaction and with a curse under her breath, she serenely made her way to her quarters.

Her false calmness did not fool him. Behind her, he laughed raucously.

Chapter Six

SANAA

The captain of the Queen's Red Guard had certain liberties the rest of the guards did not. Without her consent, it had turned into a sort of diplomatic post where random nobles from houses she didn't recall would greet her and inquire after the queen's wellbeing. The first time it occurred, the moment left Sanaa feeling rather startled. She was used to being invisible in a world that liked her imperceptibility, her ability to mold to the background and take her rightful place as a bastard.

This was no longer the case. The queen was pregnant, and the kingdom acted as if no one had ever borne a child before. The questions they asked were rather ludicrous. Normally she wouldn't mind their plebeian speculations but they directed these inquiries at *her*. Sanaa fucking Cinege. Gods of the sea, they were ridiculous.

"And has the morning sickness ebbed, Captain? I recall mine was rather terrible! Not that we should admit such things in good company."

Sanaa, confounded, stared at the woman. She'd never been around pregnant people and she'd attributed her *cuzo's* sickness to indigestion.

These days, walking about Mavros became a sort of game of

hide-and-seek. She would take the servant's routes to avoid being questioned and greeted. How she abhorred greetings. Pointless things.

Swiftly, she made her way up to the tower and just managed to escape nearly all of the inquisitive eyes. Over ten Black Knights and a fretting Ley Wallace who worked the stone floor with his pacing guarded the door to the Norrian's cell. He paused when he saw her and let out a sigh of relief.

The captain didn't know why he should be relieved to see her. Had he misplaced the king? If he had, it was not her problem.

"Oh, Captain, thank goodness you're here! By the gods, you were sent!"

The gods had nothing to do with it. Her own worry over the queen's security brought her here and nothing else. The king was hard to catch when he wasn't sparring or fucking his wife into oblivion. You'd think pregnancy would slow them down. Almira had discovered pleasure and there was no mercy upon the castle and those residing within its walls.

"Is the king still speaking with the Norrian?" Sanaa glanced at the door behind him. It was a solid structure made of Duncan wood.

"Alone!" Ley Wallace cried, clutching his cheeks.

Sanaa raised a brow and glanced at the Black Knights that stood by helplessly around the hall.

"Her Majesty, the queen clearly instructed that he shouldn't be left alone with the prisoner," Sanaa said tightly.

"Yes, but he threw us out!"

The captain tried desperately not to sigh as the absurdity of all involved parties consumed her. She pushed past Ley Wallace and went to the door. Voices came from within and she peered back at the Ley, who was paler than usual. Ouesterners were the strangest shade of beigy-pink she'd ever seen.

Before Sanaa could push open the door, the king himself stormed out with a red face and a jaw clenched so tight with anger, Sanaa nearly laughed. She stared at the Norrian behind the king. The man winked and smiled rakishly, which only served for her to roll her eyes. Brute.

"Lock him," Alton said and strode past her. She kept up easily with his long strides. "You're not my guard, Captain, and you don't have to escort me. You can tell my wife I went and did as she asked."

"Yes, Your Majesty," Sanaa said, and he glanced at her as she did not leave his side.

And she wouldn't, not until he addressed her concerns.

"Now she has you guarding me?" He stopped and looked at her. Standing before one another, they were the same height, and she coolly met his eyes. Sanaa suspected he feared her more than he did the giant in the tower.

"No, Your Majesty."

The escort came to a halt when he squared up to her. "Then? Have you something to say to me?"

Oh, *plenty*.

The captain pointed her chin back towards the cell. "What says the Norrian beast?"

He bristled, nostrils flaring at his inability to make the Norrian see reason. Sanaa had zero confidence in anyone's faculty to convince the Norrian to aid in ceasing the war.

"Same as he always says. He said I could go fuck myself," he said.

A small smile quirked her lips. "I figured as much."

Alton rolled his eyes and kept walking. She maintained herself next to him, and he sighed. "Anything else, Captain?"

Sanaa stared at him coolly, amused by his demeanor. Tall, strong, and handsome as he was, he did not impress her. She admired his fighting skills and his ability to calm down Almira when she'd worked herself up to a frenzy. That was the extent of the admiration she held for him. Where Sanaa found Almira's determination somewhat annoying, the king found it endearing and, dare she think it—*alluring*.

There were times the king seemed to appreciate Sanaa's lack of respect towards him. Other times, he felt she should at least pretend. It made a man feel like no more than a decorative rug in a room already well-furnished.

"The queen cares deeply for you," Sanaa said slowly.

He let out a breathy laugh. "You're a bit late for the hurt her or I'll maim you conversation."

"I assumed that was succinctly implied," she said, holding in a smile of amusement.

He chuckled, enjoying the salty banter. "We've yet to spar, Captain. I still maintain you'd be quite a challenge."

Inside, she laughed heartily, though her face didn't twitch. She'd like to see him try.

"As His Majesty wishes," she replied in the same neutral tone.

They moved down to the main level of the castle. Servants flittered back and forth preparing for another evening dinner. A gardener chased a cat, and maids carried thick plush blankets freshly washed to the high quarters. The king paused, as if suddenly taking in the imperceptible changes to *his* residence. Despite the winter, all the fires roared, and flowers decorated tables and atriums. Mavros had slowly changed under the sure guidance of Almira. She'd brought the place to life and turned the mausoleum into a warm home. It was rather clear this was *her* castle.

He turned to Sanaa with a frustrated glare. "*What* is it?"

She looked him over and took a deep breath. Words were not her forte.

"The queen wishes to give birth in Istokian waters." Her jaw tightened. "It's most unwise to travel while she's so close to the birthing date."

"And you've voiced this opinion, and she's ignored it?" Alton asked.

How many times? She'd stopped trying. Almira had this mad notion that if the child was not born in Istokian birthing pools, both she and the child would die. Sanaa understood it was her clouded past speaking. The Lady Lamya birthed Almira in the ancient birthing pools, but she'd hated it. Sanaa herself thought it was most unnatural. Children were born in beds. And so, Lady Lamya birthed her second child in the Suidian manner. Ultimately, it led to her death and a sickly baby. Sanaa knew it had nothing to do with the water or place of birth, but who was she to convince her *cuzo* otherwise?

Sanaa nodded, and he turned to continue walking. "She's stubborn. She's always been, even before she married you."

"Oh good. I thought she did it to annoy me." He took the stairs and nodded to the passing nobles.

"No, I'm afraid it's part of her personality."

At that, Alton laughed. "Captain, I worried you had no sense of humor."

Sanaa raised a brow. "It's made available to me from time to time. I humbly ask that his majesty attempt to make her see reason. If she wants to birth the child in the sea, there's water here."

He shook his head. "Making her change her mind is as pointless as convincing Lord Ivar to join with the rest of New Verden." He entered the area of his chambers.

There were new tapestries along the wall and a table with a vase of flowers, dark purple. His humor turned dark. In those dark thoughts, he whirled on the captain, who remained stoic and impassive.

"What exactly holds your loyalty, Captain? It's obvious that you have little regard for me. You respect me based on the notion that I am husband to your queen. So, what is it, eh?"

Oh *fuck*. Naturally, he *would* inquire after her loyalty. Life-debts were not to be kept in secret. No matter who asked, she would have to share it. To encourage manifestation or some other ludicrous notion.

"Is the king familiar with life-debts? Suidian life-debts?"

"No, I am not." She knew he wouldn't be.

Sanaa scratched her neck and sighed. "It's a sort of oath that one makes to another who saved them or changed their life for the better. It's got to do with honor. My uncle, Lord Edgar's father, had a life-debt to my father, who saved him once from a wild boar. In turn, he took me under his wing, and raised me in the royal house, along with my cousins. *My* life-debt is to the queen." Sanaa swallowed, abhorring to recall the day she begged, cursing him for asking. "She saved me once, and allowed me to train and be the warrior I'd always wanted to be. I shall repay that debt one day on *my* terms and how I wish. Until then, you're right. You have my respect because you're her husband and we have the same goal in mind."

He nodded. "Do you love her?"

She raised her brow and smiled, always amused at people's inability to understand friendship.

"Not how *you* do, majesty."

"Good. I'm afraid I wouldn't stand a chance otherwise."

None.

"Try to convince her. She has no business traveling to Istok to give birth. It is folly." With that, she turned around and stalked toward Almira's quarters.

Chapter Seven

HIRA

She fell asleep in her lounge chair, wallowing in her loneliness. A knock startled her awake, and she hesitated. Hira didn't want to deal with the commander again, but she would hate even more to hide like a scared child. She gathered her wits and turned her face stony.

There was a young man, no older than thirteen, waiting when she opened the door. Confused, she stared at him, trying to discern his presence. His cheeks reddened, and he looked away and coughed into a cloth.

"My lady, Commander Justan, sent me."

His voice was squeaky like a small mouse. He was average height and skinny, of Garian ancestry, with short hair, which was badly cut and oversized clothing. His eyes were wide and light gray, sharp against the dark olive of his skin. He looked petrified.

"For what purpose?" She leaned against the door frame.

He blinked at her, stuttering and shifting on his feet. There was an innocence to his demeanor which made her pity the young thing.

"He-he said you asked for a servant, my lady."

"And he sent a boy?" She raised a brow.

She almost scoffed. *Of course*, the commander would mock her and send this poor child. Bristling with exasperation, she had no one to blame but herself. They'd just begun the journey, and nothing was going right. She had no one's respect and had no clue as how to earn it.

The boy looked around her with curious eyes. He twitched his fingers and stared at her with open sincerity.

"We've no ladies on board. Except for you, of course, my lady."

Unbelievable. This man purposely did things to annoy her. She sighed and opened the door wide for him to enter. He looked into the cabin and took a tentative step. She waited, but he lingered, as if he feared being beaten if he even sniffed inside her rooms.

She held in her exasperation. "Don't be shy, come in."

The boy entered, but stood unmoving in the center as he perused the quarters. His enormous eyes idled on her furnishings, the rugs, the warm light, the large window that opened to the afternoon sun, her weapons, her trunk, each piece he studied with precision.

"Blooming sea gods!" he said with a slight gasp.

That made her smile. She could only imagine that a boy such as he had seen little finery in life and for a moment, she felt she'd answered him too harshly. She'd not meant to make him cower; it was not like her to be brusque.

"My uncle had comfortable quarters, didn't he?" she asked pleasantly, an attempt to put him at ease.

The boy looked at her, still bathed in shyness, as if he couldn't believe she addressed him so openly. She smiled a little and his shoulders relaxed.

"I've never been allowed here before, my lady. I've only peeked in when the High Lord entered and left." He had a small lisp that made him sound younger than he was.

When she didn't respond, he sniffed and wiped his nose against his soiled sleeve.

"No one's used it since," the boy said.

She raised a brow and doubted his words, despite the sincerity of his tone. "The commander doesn't use these quarters when royals are not aboard?"

It was one reason she didn't care for napping on the bed. She assumed the Garian commander's body hairs covered the duvet. Not that she'd seen anything because she had indeed checked. The linens were fresh and straightened by someone.

The boy's eyes widened, and he coughed. "Never, my lady. The commander sleeps with all of us, down in the jumby jet."

She almost laughed at his adorable accent. "Jumby jet?"

He nodded vigorously and stepped slightly towards her. "Aye, we hang the hammocks from the rafters, and we jumble and jet about when the waves hit. You can feel everything down in the belly." He spoke animatedly, his hands showcasing the toss and turn of the sea.

She walked to her dining table and tried to hide her annoyance. She was certain the boy knew little. "Commander Justan is a lord. There's no reason for him to sleep in *hammocks*."

The boy's face reddened. "The commander is the best commander there ever was, my lady."

His voice was firm and slightly defensive, which startled her. She realized there was appreciation and loyalty there. Naturally, the commander would have the devotion of all those aboard, *including* this poor kitchen lad. Had the men openly offered the commander their respect, or had he earned it? The question perplexed her further.

"What's your name?" She crossed her arms and studied him.

He squared his shoulders. "Quent, my lady."

She idly wondered how such a young man came to be in her uncle's greatest ship. Seeing as the boy was Garian, perhaps he was a child of one of the commander's sailors. That seemed likely. Justan was smarter than she cared to admit; he knew such a move would gain even more admiration amongst the crew. So, he was cunning. Hira hadn't counted on some sailor being cunning and now she felt rather inadequate. She could only imagine what he thought of her in the confines of his mind. Shaking off her hostility, she smiled at the boy.

"I'm Hira. A pleasure to meet you."

He stared at her, aghast. "I can't call a lady by her name. I wouldn't dare."

She took a raspberry from the fruit bowl and sat down. Why couldn't people address her as who she was? It was vexing. She had to constantly reminding others that she was not a *lady*. A lady embroidered. She refused to embroider.

"I'm not a lady," she said forcefully.

He studied her trousers and boots. His eyes were keen, and she held herself back from shifting self-consciously.

"You might be dressed like a lad, but you're certainly a lady, my lady," Quent said as he pointed to her attire.

When at ease, he was a bold little thing.

She bristled. "Seems to be the consensus. What experience have you as a servant?"

Quent studied her quarters once more. "None, my lady."

"None?"

He looked worried and fiddled with his fingers. "Not a bit. I help Cook with the meals when I've messed up, like when I spilled the tar on the deck and took three weeks to clean the mess... I'm still doing penance for that, actually."

She pressed her lips together and clutched her hands, attempting not to take out her anger towards the commander on this innocent boy. "And Commander Justan, Lord of the Five Seas, thought you were best suited for the job?"

Quent brightened and looked down. His brown hair fell over his forehead. She realized, with a start, that she embarrassed him. She'd not meant to. Hira witnessed Almira and uncle Beltran embarrass plenty of people, but they were usually deserving of such a treatment. Gods, she had so much to learn. She was constantly mucking it all up!

"There's no one else, you see. We thought you would come with—"

She swallowed. "With ladies-in-waiting? Servants?"

He looked at her. "Aye."

She took a deep breath and glanced at Almira's portrait. Her cousin's brow seemed amused, as if it said, 'I told you so.' Almira would never enter a ship for a cross-world trip on her own. She'd have helpers, maids, keepers, guards, and counselors. The entourage alone would demand respect. Hira had fought with Almira just last month, refusing a retinue of people. The queen wasn't happy—actually, she had been rather angry. A few days later, she acquiesced to Hira's appeal simply to get her back home. Had she been here, she would've frosted Hira with one of her looks. Even the boy had more sense than she did.

Hira nodded. "Fine. You'll need to avert your eyes occasionally."

He looked startled, bewildered at the suggestion, as if it wasn't clear. "What for?"

She paused the perusal of the meaningless scrolls on her table and looked at him. "For when I *dress*."

"Oh!" He laughed, which morphed into a cough. "Right."

"Are you a cook's boy?" She asked, largely for lack of conversation. Not that she would admit boredom. With her luck, the rumor would reach the commander.

Quent gave her a lovely smile. "I mean, I help the cook, if that's the question." His eyes lingered on the fine items in her room. "But I'm mostly here, so my brother can keep me safe. He worries a lot."

At that, she paused and studied him once more. There was a slight familiarity to him, but she couldn't place it.

"Your brother?" Hira asked.

"Commander Justan, my lady."

The realization that Commander Justan had a ward was hard enough, but that it was *this* sweet lad was even more discomforting. She didn't care to paint the commander with any good attributes at the moment. This was certainly a respectable attribute, and she was unsure what to do with it. Imbalanced in all of her conjectures, she flooded with shame.

"I'm sorry, my lady. I thought he told you," Quent whispered.

Hira felt her heart soften towards him. It must be lonely with no one his age in a ship full of sailors. She actually understood such a position with acridity. Once Almira left for her marriage, there were absolutely no companions for Hira. She spent many an isolated afternoon wallowing in the gardens and idly studying the clouds. As if waiting for her life to begin. Youth was such an odd thing. You were too young to know much, but when you crossed the threshold into adulthood, they resented you for not knowing enough.

"He didn't. It's alright," she said.

Quent glanced at her, unsure, his eyes still wide. "You're certain? I'm not very good and Justan says I'm clumsy, which I am, but I want to one day be sure of myself and not trip over things or... accidentally set the kitchen on fire."

She almost laughed. "Please don't set my quarters on fire."

He brightened, and his smile made him look younger than he was. "You're an amazing fighter! I wish I could be like that! And Captain Sanaa! I heard of her from the stories of the other sailors and she's grander than anything! Strong and tall! I'll never be that strong and tall! Did she really battle twenty men at the same time?"

Sanaa would laugh at the tumble of words that escaped the young boy. Or maybe she'd mortified by them. Either way, it would be a delight to watch.

Hira settled into her chair as he spoke. "I don't think we were counting."

Undeterred, Quent continued, his hands wildly gesturing the tales. "I've heard *all* the stories! How the Queen's Red Guard took down the entire castle guard the day they killed the High Lord! And then the queen herself slit the throat of General Hestian with Ocean Fury! And my brother told me there was a man in the tower, a Norrian so big and strong that he slaughtered forty men with his bare hands!"

"It was more like a dozen."

"A dozen!" He looked star struck, then he coughed into his cloth. "Wow! When I grow strong, I'm going to be part of the Queen's Red Guard! Defend the crown, wield a sword, protect the kingdom!"

It wasn't until that moment that Hira realized exactly what they had accomplished simply by being the queen's protectors. Their legend was growing, and she was intrinsically part of it. Until now. She fought against a bitter taste settling in her stomach. A part of her knew she acted petulant, and she truly wished to stop. It was bringing her nothing but misery. Yet, reminders such as this baited her fragility, threaded with youth.

"How skilled are you at fighting?" she asked him.

He paused and looked down. "Not very good. My brother says I can't practice yet. Not strong enough."

Hira, seeing a fantastic opportunity to tell the commander what to do, leaned forward. "You must start! When I was your age, I would sneak out of my room at midnight to train and tone my arms so I could carry the weight of the swords."

But Quent seemed unsure. "My brother says when I stop being sick, I can fight, but I always watch him and the other sailors spar."

She suddenly realized how ill he looked. He couldn't be contagious. He slept with the rest of the crew, but his eyes seemed tired and his skin held a slightly sallow tone. His cough, she gathered, was constant. And he was thin, a mere wisp of a boy.

"You've been ill for a while?" She murmured.

He tugged at his badly fitted shirt. "Aye, but I'm not infectious, my lady!"

"I believe you." She nodded, and she gestured for him to sit on a chair.

He glanced at it and slowly sat, as if he was afraid he would dirty the satin covering. "Since I was little. These are nice. Remind me of home."

Questions erupted in her mind as to why the boy was here and not on Istok. A child of House Seaver grew up in Pinnacle Palace. She'd never seen the castle, but rumor held it was beautiful. Had the commander and she not been at odds, she would've ventured to ask him.

"How long have you been away from Pinnacle Palace?" she asked him.

Quent bounced on the chair, amused with the construction. "I've been a ward of my brother for five years."

"Well, when you get better, I can teach you some moves," Hira said. It would give her something to do on this long, boring voyage. Also, she could show off the skills she'd mastered.

He smiled brightly at the prospect. "Train me like a Red Guard?"

He was endearing, and Hira felt a sudden need to protect him and keep him safe. She returned the smile kindly. "Yes, with a Ruby Blade, lighter and easier on one not so strong."

Quent's eyes went to her waist where she held her blade, the constant reminder of what she no longer was.

"Can I hold it?" He asked.

Before she could offer him the weapon, a harsh knock at the door interrupted them.

"Quent, stop dallying!" It was the commander, interesting that he did not barge in.

The boy swiftly stood and did the worst bow she'd witnessed in her life.

"I've got to go. I'm on onion duty. Excuse me, my lady!" he cried and stumbled on his oversized boots.

She nodded. "We will speak later, my lord."

He paused and turned to her with wide eyes. "No one's ever called me a lord before."

Gods of the sea, she would eventually need to have a conversation with his brother. This boy was a lord. She didn't understand why he would dress in rags. As if the commander was hiding him.

"That's what you are, aren't you? The second son of House Seaver, born in Pinnacle Palace?" Hira stood and smiled down at him as kindly as she could.

"Third son." Quent raised up three fingers.

"You've another brother?"

This was certainly a surprise, but again, she knew very little of the lineage of other houses. One more thing against her. Perhaps she should take the voyage as a time for study, cram in all the information she should've known. No, that sounded dreadful.

"Aye, our oldest brother died when they were fifteen, I think. Justan was his twin. He was supposed to be the commander, but when he died, well, Justan had no choice but to take the position." He shrugged. "I don't remember him because I was a little baby. That's why Justan is overprotective. He won't lose another brother."

Hira swallowed uncomfortably. She was learning too much

about the commander. The information painted him more human than she cared to admit.

She placed a hand on his shoulder; it was thin under the cloth and the bone poked into her palm. "You're still a lord. Third son or not. If *I* have to endure the title of a lady, then you have to get along with the title of a lord."

He smiled slightly, then rushed out. He coughed into his handkerchief, stumbled outside, and Justan let out a distinctly annoyed grunt. Through the door, Hira heard the brothers speaking and smiled.

"What did you do in there?" Commander Justan asked.

"She called me a lord!"

"Lord of the Onions, get to your task."

Chapter Eight

JUSTAN

His sailors were jittery and when he entered the sup hall, he found two of them at the cusp of an altercation. It was the last thing he needed with the lady on board, especially after dealing with her that morning. He was himself tense. His neck felt stiff with unwarranted stress that she'd single-handedly caused. Her furious face painted the particles of his mind and he tittered between complete frustration and panic. Once he calmed the two men and separated them to the other side of the room, a few sailors remarked good-naturedly about his inability to best the lady in the morning's fight.

He was not ashamed of losing his fight with the Lady Hira, he would admit she was a brilliant fighter and she'd caught him off guard. So, he smiled and allowed the jokes on his behalf to continue.

"Didn't know the commander had a weak right turn," a sailor said as he shoved a piece of bread into his mouth.

"I always leave my right turn open should a lady wish to access it," Justan said with a rakish smile. An excellent example of posturing, but he'd been posturing for so long he scarcely knew exactly who he was.

Plus, the men enjoyed such quips, and they laughed, slapping his back and beckoning him to sit with them. He'd not intended to share his meal, his purpose in coming into the sup hall was to grab the lady's meal and deliver it himself to her quarters. He became distracted by an old sailor's tale of a scalla hunt that sunk a ship. A welcome diversion from the Lady Hira.

One man shared a crude joke which made Justan laugh. Her Ladyship chose that moment to enter on the arm of Mr. Hyall, no less. He felt his face heat at the sight of her, and the room was instantly quiet.

Her wide blue eyes took in the scene. There was an uneasiness in her stance, as if she also postured, but Justan had no wish to have anything in common with the lady. She shifted, likely caught in the uncertainty of sup hall etiquette. He fought the urge not to groan when Mr. Hyall smiled at her, then met Justan's eye with a wink. He left her alone and there she stood, the Lady of Istok, watching them all with her Balikian bearing.

Why couldn't she simply have waited until he brought her dinner to her quarters? Why must she insist on leaving her room and milling about on *his* ship? Lord Beltran never meandered around. He knew better than to interfere with Justan's authority while on board. It confused the men. But she knew little, and though Justan was aware, he'd have to have patience with her. He could feel his nerves fried and singed from their earlier encounters.

"Good evening," she said, her voice strong and sure despite the contradiction of her flushed cheeks.

The men turned to Justan as they awaited his response. He'd told them last week she wouldn't enter the sup hall and here she was. Damn the woman and her aristocratic pert nose. He stood, pushing back the Duncan wood bench, and stalked to her. He fought bravely to uphold neutral features. When he stopped before her, she lifted her chin in that proud manner of hers. His nostrils flared.

"Lady Hira, I will have your meal brought directly to your quarters," he said in a clipped tone. His neck burned, and he itched to yank the collar back.

The lady's face brightened, and the flush captured her chest, which he could see from the unlaced top of her blouse. Her mother, the Lady Marai, wouldn't tolerate such a display of female flesh. The lady was tyrannical in her beliefs, and he didn't blame Hira for her rebellion. Perhaps she'd been just as trapped as he'd been.

"There is no need, Commander. I'll eat here," Lady Hira said.

It took all his composure not to grab and drag her back to her rooms. He refrained from doing so mostly because he knew he would simply have to battle her, and suspected they also trained her in hand-to-hand combat.

He closed the distance. "No women allowed in the sup hall, my lady."

She looked over his face in a manner that told him she would welcome a fight with him. It would be an excellent way to end her eventful day. Did she have no reason in her stubborn mind?

"You need not worry about my honor, Commander. I can handle myself," she smiled with false pleasantries.

His eyes lingered—of their own volition—on her clavicle and the soft shape of her neck. She could handle herself alright. That was the problem. *Gods of the sea.* What a fucking complication. He wished he didn't hold tight to promises and honor or he'd take Quent and get as far from here as possible.

"I'm mindful of that, *my lady*," he said between clenched teeth.

Their eyes locked, and it took all of his training to maintain serenity on his face. The men skewered their eyes on them, and Justan was keenly aware their power struggle was the most interesting event the ship had experienced in quite some time. This was not good, but he floundered with how to handle it properly. None of his discipline covered this.

"Then I don't see a problem," she said.

He cocked his head, and his jaw twitched. "It's a distraction… for the men."

A distraction indeed. He couldn't recall a time in his life that his mind had become jumbled so. As commander, Beltran trained him to be composed and focused, but she… blurred things. He didn't like when things blurred. He had a task and gods knew what would happen if he failed.

Oh, couldn't she see he was trying to *help* her? The trip had the men tightly wound. He'd promised them a day in Easima but the storm mucked that up. With no merriment, they would have to wait until they arrived at Zuri before they visited the pleasure houses.

The lady, fully affronted by now, pulled back her lips in anger. "Each of the men in this hall has seen tits and cunts, *my lord.*"

His level of fury rose, and he thought they would grapple in an instant on the dirty floor. She would get herself killed; he was certain of that.

"The answer is *no*. And don't challenge me in front of my men." His tone was as hard as a polishing stone.

She bared her teeth, her anger radiating off her in waves. "Do you honestly expect me to be locked in my quarters for the rest of the journey? Doing *what?*"

He felt his body mirror her stance; he couldn't control it. *Blurred.* Everything blurred. The way she stared up at him, no one had ever stared at him like that, and he was desperate to find a corner to take calming breaths and gather his thoughts.

Naturally, he lashed in exasperation. Beneath him, but his frustration with her behavior corrugated his good sense.

"Play the harp or sharpen your sword. I don't care. I never asked the High Lord what he did, but he kept himself out of my way," he snapped.

One could hear a pin-drop in the room, as if all of them held their breath at the display. She crossed her arms and lifted her chin up to him. He had to swallow, or he would choke.

"I'm not my uncle and I'm out of state letters to write. This is *my* ship, and I am not your prisoner. I'll sup *here.*"

She stepped around him and ensured her boot smashed into his. He grunted deep in his throat as his body burned with unexpected intensity. He'd no choice but to take a moment to settle himself. His hands were trembling, but he didn't know why. What the hell was the matter with him?

The men parted for her as she went to the cook.

"Good evening," she said with a smile that was forced and direct.

Justan didn't think he'd ever seen the cook look more stricken. He was usually yelling at everyone. Now he stared down, cowered.

His eyes darted from Lady Hira to the commander.

"Give her the plate," Justan said for the sake of not escalating the situation and having to throw her over his shoulder.

She opened her mouth—likely to insult him—when the cook plopped food on a plate.

"M'lady." The man handed her the meal with a shaky hand.

She took it and smiled, then turned to Justan with a frosty brow. "Perhaps you can show me to my seat, my lord?"

Her little tone rattled him once more. So, to hide traitorous emotions, he pointed to an empty table.

"This way," he said.

On instinct, and because he'd grown accustomed to it, he gently reached for her elbow. He'd done it to many ladies in his life. It was polite. He should've known better than to attempt any manner of politeness around *her*. She instantly froze and gave him a death glare.

"Don't touch me!" she hissed between clenched teeth.

Unwilling to admit defeat—and with his men observing—he refused to obey. He pulled her to the table.

"I don't want you to lose your way, *my lady*."

The flush went to her ears, and her skin turned the color of her hair. It was absolutely worth it.

"If you do not unhand me this *instant*, I will slice your throat before all your men!"

Finally, he let go and smiled. He'd taunted her enough. "From ear to ear?"

She pushed around him and slammed down the plate. She sat, and the silence defused as the men in the sup hall went back to their other topics of interest. Justan hesitated, seeing her alone and indignant as she stared down at her food. With a grunt, he sat across from her, folded his hands, and regarded her coolly. Within himself, he faltered, but she wouldn't know that. The picture of a carefree, gallivanting man was a brilliant facade he'd perfected. It was a role he scarcely knew how to end. Because ending it would sacrifice too much.

"We need to establish some ground rules," he said.

She studied the meal of cured scalla, boiled potatoes, and onion tart. As she inspected the tart, she spared him a glance. "By saying *we*, I assume you mean *you*."

He nodded as she cut into the potatoes. She diced a small piece and ate it, all the while glowering at him. From his perspective, Lady Hira was manners and grace. Her back was straight, her shoulders squared. The elegance in which she held her utensils spoke of high breeding, the sort that Lord Beltran often displayed. She may not see it, but she resembled him. Justan felt clumsy. He'd long forgotten the way one should properly hold their goblet in good company.

"I'm not interested in your rules, Commander," she said after she swallowed.

Naturally. She liked to pretend she wasn't a lady of the highest standing. As if her head wasn't worth half the gold in the world. As if a war wouldn't erupt, should something happen to her while under his protection.

He smiled forcefully. "You might remove me from my post the moment we dock in Treveri. That's your right as our ruler. But, while we sail, while inside of *this* ship, the safety of each person is on my head. *Including* yours." He leaned back and considered her. "I know you're very young and bold, but it's my job and responsibility to account for the security and harmony of my crew. Had I known you'd waltz in here by yourself with no escort, I would've asked the queen for land transport."

The lady clutched the knife in her hand. She was almost amusing, so easily rattled. It was likely her age. With this in mind, he furthered his determination to ensure her safety.

"Now," he took a deep breath. "I'm sorry you're bored in your quarters, but I'm not here to entertain Her Ladyship. I've a ship to run, sailors to control, and the safety of a high-born lady on my hands. The men are offensive and crude, so I don't want you in the hall. Some nights, fights break out. It's the pressure of the high seas."

She banged down her fork and stared at him. Her fists clenched, her neck cherry red as she opened her mouth to snarl at him, but he held a hand up.

"You can hate me, that's allowed," he said passively, so self-assured that he surprised himself.

She shoved the plate away. "I'm *not* a delicate flower, Commander. I've seen the ugliness of soldiers and it neither offends nor frightens me. The only thing that frightens me are your manners."

That felt like a slap, but he held his face still. He supposed he deserved that.

He paused and beheld her carefully. "May I remind Her Ladyship that she's no longer a Red Guard?"

She flinched. His stomach turned at her reaction. She couldn't control her expressions. That soiled any hope he had of being honest with her. He'd flayed her raw, and it was visible. He felt himself drenched in regret, but she would never know. *No.* She could not know. He rather she'd hate him than place her in such dangers. Tears prickled her eyes. Justan wished to look away and apologize, but he didn't. He couldn't. He was trapped in this damned ship, in this damn mess with her, and there was no escaping it, no matter how much he wished it.

The tightness in his chest morphed into an animal, and he sighed, trying to fix things. "My lady, you're the queen's cousin and—"

"I am *very* well aware of who I am, sir!" she cut him off sharply.

Her voice raised, and he glanced at the room, then back at her. She was a second away from crying, and he felt mortified. She was a lady, and he'd insulted her. He didn't know what to do with his hands, so he clutched them tightly and attempted to swallow.

She pushed off the table; the stool scraped sharply across the floor. He sat frozen.

"I shall retire, Commander," her tone lost in a whisper. "If you'll excuse me."

He watched her storm off, her meal barely touched. He sat there for a long time, his eyes speared on her plate. His thoughts were a whirl of madness. Gods of the sea, he couldn't do this. His hands shook so violently he had to press them flat. The hurt expression on her face would haunt him.

He dimly recalled his mother and how she would hide her tears whenever his father insulted her intelligence or addressed her brusquely. How angry he'd been as a child to witness such a spectacle.

He shoved himself away, uncertain of where he was going when he ran into Mr. Hyall on the deck. The man stood in the shadows, smoking his pipe and watching him knowingly.

"The little lady was right upset about something, Commander," Mr. Hyall said in that tone of his. That slithery tone. "Perhaps some *appeasing* might be in order."

"Mind your tasks, Mr. Hyall. She's not your concern," Justan snapped, and walked away before he could retort.

Justan's feet led him to the high quarter. Her light was on, and he went to knock on the door. He would at least apologize and attempt to calm her. He wasn't sure how he would manage that, but he would attempt it—if he wished to sleep at all tonight.

As he raised his fist, he heard diffused sobs.

He paused and listened carefully. He'd made her cry. *Fantastic.* The commander didn't know what to do. He'd never made a woman lament before. He stood like an idiot and accepted the damning sounds of her pain. Why did he say the things he'd said? He'd not wished to have such animosity with her. On the contrary, he hoped she would at least trust him.

Oh gods, Beltran, how do I fix this? He felt very much like the boy at the window. Alone. Only this time, there was no happy young Hira singing songs. This time, it was sorrow. And he'd caused it.

He placed his hand against the wood and exhaled. He'd swore he would shield her as best he could, just as he promised. But he couldn't bring her into his confidence. Not without endangering her life. Quent's life. And his own.

Chapter Nine

HIRA

The resentment and embarrassment from the dinner fiasco tormented Hira for three nights. She lingered in her rooms, like a failure. Commander Justan's words affected her dreams and waking hours.

May I remind Her Ladyship that she's no longer a Red Guard?

Cad! Absolute brute! How Almira could ever consider this man as the one best suited to lead her armada was a joke. A well-placed jest at Hira's expense. She went over and over in her mind all the responses she should've thrown at him. Instead, she'd left. Like a child!

It all rankled her. The way he'd seen through her, through her inability to govern, through her childish notions and idealism. How he'd stripped them crudely with a mere string of words. Tears stung her eyes once more, and she angrily wiped them away.

Yes, Hira scarcely knew herself. Yes, she floundered constantly. She didn't even know which ale she preferred until a few months ago.

"Ladies, do not partake in the drinking of ale," her mother once told her.

Everyone was so eager to tell her who she was, what to do, who to be. It was maddening.   She felt the frustration flare up within her. She wished to scream and destroy each piece of furniture in her fancy room.

Wasn't that what life was about? A constant journey of self-discovery? So what if she still teetered at the edge of full confidence? So what if she attempted things she was not certain of? It was no reason for a man to discard her. No one had ever spoken to her in such a manner, and it made her realize how sheltered she was. They'd done this to her; Uncle Beltran and her mother. Kept like her a prisoner in the castle and expected musty scrolls would teach her to rule. They were at fault!

It still gave no reason for the commander to unearth her insecurities and realities. Hira violently hated his actions. She would remove him from his post the moment she arrived in Treveri. She would not work with a man who held such little regard for her. Damn earning it! She was his superior, her position in relation to his demanded respect!

In the evening of the third day, she heard the commander's laughter outside her door. She broke a vase by smashing it against a wall and growled in his general direction. That *she*, daughter of kings, should shelter in her quarters was *mortifying*. Her hate bounced from Almira to Commander Justan to her uncle, even General Hestian for killing uncle Beltran and making her a High Lady.

Hira's thoughts scattered. They were sporadic by the time she settled in bed that night. She stared sadly at the ceiling and felt tears once more drip from her eyes onto the pillow.

"I wish I was strong. And brave. And smart," she whispered to the air, to the gods who would listen. She wished for a miracle so she could wake already strong and brave and smart. If such a miracle would occur, she might be a wise ruler. She wouldn't fear what was coming. She could be a dragon.

She hadn't slept long when a large hand grabbed her face, preventing her from screaming. She fought wildly against the man who towered over her. He pressed her into the bedding and straddled her hips. She could hardly see his features. He seethed and

82

frothed at the mouth; his body was acrid with unwashed odor. She tried to grasp his neck, but he held her down tightly. Hira bucked under him with all of her strength, but he didn't waver.

"Got time for a poke before I kill ya," he said, drool dripping down to her nose.

Hira screamed, but his large hand smothered it. She twisted under him, and he backhanded her so hard the world rotated on its axis. Here was the Queen's Red Guard, held down by a common thief! The thought burst through her mind and her mouth opened in a wild, desperate yell.

He cursed and grabbed her face and pressed a sharp knife to her eye. It pushed into the soft skin of her eyelid. She stilled as the implications of this moment descended over her. He would rape and kill her. Despite her strength and training, he overpowered her.

"If I were you, little lady, I'd stay quiet and still," he whispered.

She trembled as he slid the blade slowly down her face. Tora flashed into her mind. How she'd died to save her and here she was, pinned on a bed. He kissed her neck as she cried. Instinct told her to push him off, but the knife was at her breast.

Then a rapping at her door! A voice she never thought she'd be relieved to hear.

"Lady Hira?" Commander Justan pounded on the door.

The man paused, and she took that moment to punch the filthy man as hard as she could in the face. She heard the snap of a broken nose. He rolled off the bed and fell with a thump on the floor. She scrambled up, but her legs twisted in the sheets.

"COMMANDER!"

The insistence at the door increased and Commander Justan shouted and thundered against the heavy wood. But the man had apparently locked the latch. He was already standing and rushed at her. She stumbled from the bed and made for her knife, but he grabbed her from behind and lifted her clear off her feet.

Her legs were stuck into her gown as she kicked the air. She thought the commander would pound the wood down as he continued his tirade.

"COMMANDER!" she screeched.

Then the dagger was back at her throat, but she grasped his hand and bit into him with all the strength she could. Blood gushed into her mouth and the man screamed, shoving her to the ground. She coughed, spitting his vile blood from her mouth as she fell hard on her knees, but pushed herself up and reached again for the table with the knife. Before she could grab the blade, he harshly kicked her away.

She lost her breath and landed on the carpet with her cheek pressed to the rug. As she struggled to push herself on her elbows, he yanked her back by her hair and brought the knife down. She felt the flash of it and saw her coming end. With a wild scream, she shoved herself up and into him, and he fell backwards. They scrambled on the floor, a fury of kicks and punches.

Her small size allowed her to slip from his grasp a few times, but he was stronger and knocked her down. The knife cut her arm, and she fell across the table. It tumbled her weapons to the carpet, and he kicked them away as she scurried for a blade.

But her fingers finally grasped the ruby knife, the hilt heated in her fist. They stared at one another, both bloody, both out of breath. She could see him clearly now, Istokian, with dark hateful eyes and a gaping mouth. His flash of hesitation was her salvation. She jumped and straddled him, then punched him as hard as she could with the fist that held the hilt of her ruby blade. He blinked stupidly and, with a ferocious yell, she imbedded the blade into his eye and buried deeply within his head.

Commander Justan chose that moment to crash through her window. He landed on his knees with his sword in hand. He looked up with a grave and enraged face and they stared at one another. The commander saw the man she'd killed and let out a deep sigh and a curse. He stood and pulled her to stand, then yanked the knife from the man's head and set it on her table.

Hira didn't realize she was shaking and covered in blood and bruises. She'd almost died. A man attacked her. She killed her attacker. That man attempted to assault her! Where was Almira? Where was her mother? Her uncle? She'd never felt more vulnerable in her life, even as she began to repeat shaky words.

"I'm fine." A bald-faced lie, but she repeated it to herself, to anyone that would hear them.

The commander made her sit and stared at her with such concern, she almost didn't know him.

"Gods of the sea, you're not fine," he murmured as he looked her over with wide, petrified eyes.

She couldn't reply. The words were a jumble of consonants in her tongue. Her mind raced and her skin burned. She'd been touched without permission. She'd had to battle for her life. *Alone*, in her nightgown, in nothing but a scrap of cloth.

"No, I'm fine," she repeated, but she was certain her pale face gave her away.

The commander kneeled before her and hovered his hands over her as if afraid of touching or startling her.

The men broke the door to her rooms and both she and the commander stood as a dozen sailors, swords at hand, tumbled in. They gaped at the grizzly sight. Without her realization, Hira had grabbed a vase and held it over her head.

The commander, noticing, gently took it from her and motioned for her to sit.

She did so because she didn't have the strength to argue with him. She could scarcely breathe.

Quent ran to her, faltering over his feet. "You killed him, my lady!"

Commander Justan turned to his brother and pointed out of her room. "Fetch her fresh water, clothes, my kit, and some brandy."

Quent charged to his task, and the commander looked at the crew with a red, angry face.

"Who the fuck is this man?"

His booming voice startled Hira, and she jumped and crossed her arms over her chest, still dazed at the entire evening.

Mr. Hyall came forward and studied the body. "Newcomer. Came to us from Rybar. We thought we could trust him, given the lady's father was Lord Rybar."

"Rybar? Rybar!" Hira noted the hysteria in her tone.

The men looked at the body, then back at her. They each

studied her as if she were for display, some in fear, others in disbelief, and others with a certain amount of calculated admiration. She'd done well for herself. *For a woman*, they must've thought.

"Take the body out of here! I'll deal with this later," Commander Justan said.

The men carried the corpse out, and they left her alone with Justan. Her thoughts froze in her mind. House Rybar was small but honorable. The line was nearly dead, and the family owned but few lands to the west of Istok.

Once more, the commander kneeled before her. He wore his night clothing, the shirt open to the belly with his sword still at hand. She dimly noticed he was shaking.

"Be he from Rybar or somewhere else, it's certain someone wanted you dead," he said.

Hira looked at him and she felt the panic and frustration bubble up within her.

"If they want the bloody seat, they can have it! I don't crave it! I've never wished for it. The queen ordered it, so I'm going home to rule a land that wants me dead! I swore when I cut my hair and rode in disguise to Suid that I would never return and now look! I'm stuck in a vessel with a man that despises me, that *might* also be trying to kill me!"

He looked at her incredulously. "You think *I'm* the one seeking to kill you?"

"I'm on *your* ship, Commander, and you've made it clear how you feel about me," she snarled the words.

He stood sharply and pointed to the billowing curtains. "I've jumped through a fucking window to save you!"

Hira rose to face him, her emotions erupting out of her, lacking all control and decorum. "I've been attacked in my quarters! The same quarters you insisted I stay in, so forgive me if I don't trust you very much right now."

He looked at her as if she'd lost her mind. Honestly, perhaps she had. She didn't know what was real. A sharp pain in her arm made her look down, and she noticed blood seeping down her forearm into the carpeted floor.

86

Commander Justan took a deep breath. His words were calm and measured. "I understand you're upset. You've every right to be. You were attacked, but I swear on my life—on Quent's life—that it's not me whom you have to fear. There may be others, there likely are… but as long as you're on my ship, I swear I'm trying to keep you safe."

His hand was at his chest, and his eyes were wide and sincere. She almost believed him. But her senses still stung at the words he'd said days earlier. She wasn't willing to believe in sincerity from him.

A red-faced Quent rushed in, arms laden with the instructed items. The commander broke eye contact with her—which soothed her. Each time it was the two of them in tense conversation, she felt she lacked all sense and serenity.

The commander snatched the waterskin and thrust it at Hira. Quent carefully took her ruby knife and cleaned it with a rag as he coughed into his elbow.

"Drink," the commander said. "Let me look at that wound."

Hira shook her head and pulled back. "It's only a scratch."

He sighed in complete frustration. "Are you really going to fight me on this?"

She glared at him, sat, and offered him her arm. She winced when he inspected the cut and drank the water to calm her nerves. Her insides were quaking. This never would've happened in the Red Guard quarters; it was one of the best guarded places in Mavros. How wrong Almira had been to think she would be safe.

Hira scanned the walls, nooks where an intruder could hide in the vulnerable angles. How long had the man waited in the shadows? Watched her undress? She shook once more.

"Brandy," Commander Justan snapped.

Quent filled a small cup with golden liquor and handed it to her. She took it gratefully with a nod.

"Thank you, my lord," she said, and Quent blushed a furious red.

Her statement made Commander Justan pause and look at her with obvious annoyance. "You'll have to be better guarded. I'll place four men at your door at all times."

Hira shook her head. "I don't—"

"I think you do," he interrupted her as he cleaned her wound. "Given what's happened. I can't parade in front of your room the entire night." It was as if he were murmuring to himself.

She watched him; his bent head. His hair was deep brown, almost black. It was thick and grew over the back of his neck. His hands were warm against her chilled skin and his movements were steady and careful, so as not to cause her discomfort.

"It's a good thing you're trained," he said as he wrapped the wound in fresh linen. "Did he say anything to you?"

Hira swallowed, hating to recall the man and his remarks. "He said he would rape me before he killed me."

The words were sluggish and nearly unreal in her mouth. As if it happened to someone else, long ago.

The commander paused, his eyes tightened, then he nodded. "That's all, Quent. Leave her clothes on the bed."

Quent seemed to want to protest, but a look from his brother silenced him and he slumped out of the room.

"You can't protect him forever." She didn't know why she said it. It was not her business. Perhaps it provided her with a welcome distraction from the evening's events.

The commander glanced up at her. His sharp jaw twitched and his thick brow furrowed. "I'm well aware of that."

The wrap felt tight and secure. He'd done a good job. The pain ebbed as she sipped the brandy. He stood and considered the room. The broken window allowed in the chilly sea air and her thin sleeping gown provided little warmth.

"You can't sleep here tonight," he said as he kicked some glass out of the way.

She took a shaky breath, running her hand over her hair. She became keenly aware she was in a sheer night cloth. Most indecent with a lord before her.

"I won't sleep anywhere tonight," she admitted.

He placed his hands on his slim hips and turned to her. "I'll clear up another room."

Hira nodded and stood slowly. Quent had laid out a clean

sleeping gown for her, but her stomach recoiled. She didn't want to wear it. She'd rather carry armor.

"How long till dawn?" she asked.

"A few hours." He rubbed his hand over his face. Whiskers covered his chin, the beginning of a beard.

"I'll dress and stay up," she said and went to her trunk.

She pulled out leather trousers and a jacket. She found the commander watching her. His eyes were intense. He seemed not to look at her in any other manner, and it unnerved her. Men didn't stare at ladies in such an open fashion. It did something funny to her stomach, and she straightened her shoulders. She gathered all of her strength and hooked him with a withering glare. She wouldn't allow him to continue his berating. He was a sea commander. She ruled a country. He would remember his place around her.

"You're dismissed," she snapped.

He clenched his fists, opened his mouth, but thought better than to retort. As he stormed out, he muttered, "difficult woman," then slammed the door close.

She couldn't explain her rudeness. Perhaps it was the shaking of her hands, or the jumble of her thoughts. She'd never felt more exposed, and she didn't need an audience for her chaotic behavior. The intruder's blood stained her carpet, and it spurred her to dress quickly.

Hira didn't want any part of her flesh visible or uncovered. She slid the ruby blade into her belt deciding she would go nowhere unarmed again.

Isabelle Olmo

Chapter Ten

HIRA

The night turned frigid as the clouds covered the stars and the wind blew them course-forward. A few men were still awake when Hira stepped onto the deck. They spoke in harsh whispers as they recounted the tale of the lady and the intruder. She lingered in the shadows as their words made her tremble.

"Right through the skull, I tell ya," came one man's voice.

"Mercy me!" another hoarsely whispered.

"Trained with Suidians and Free Islanders, I hear."

"Rather unconventional for a lady, if ye ask me."

They paused their murmurs when they saw her, and Hira tucked her cloak tighter around her shivering body. An attempt to make herself as invisible as possible.

Hira always knew she was an oddity. Hira never felt as poised as Almira, and she didn't command a room or know how to put a noble eloquently in their place. From birth, Hira seemed to be born to disappoint people. Or perhaps from birth, women disappointed people. Women's freedoms were conditional, distilled by unspoken commandments embedded into a society who suspected them based on their sex.

Some days, such as this pallid midnight, she hated being a

woman. Sometimes she'd thought of the freedom a cock between her legs would bring her. The temptation to imagine a world where she could do as she pleased, then laugh at the end of the night with ale and friends in a seedy tavern, was tempting enough. To grasp a man by the lapels of his coat, shove him into a closet, and press her body against his… no. That made her think of the man who attacked her. She shuddered.

What she wished for was a cleansing. A new body to touch her, one that was welcomed, one that smelled of must and sea air. She froze when she realized the face that she saw in her mind was the commander's, and the memory she experienced was of their battle. For the mercy of the Favia, she couldn't actually be allowing her thoughts to stray towards such heinous daydreams. She needed to compose herself. She was a wreck of a person. What was wrong with her? She'd need to light incense and provide a prayer. Surely, she was cursed.

Seeking to be alone with her raging thoughts, she went to the uppermost deck. Naturally, the commander was there. He smoked a pipe and glowered at the escorting ship, the Night Serpent.

When he saw her, he sighed darkly. "I'll let you be." He pushed himself off the rails.

Hira, unsure of how to handle this entire situation diplomatically, straightened and opted for maturity. "It's fine. I didn't know you would be here. I did not mean to intrude."

She turned to go back down because she had no wish to argue further. Her nerves and thoughts were already erratic and frayed. She was tired of fighting him and her mind was obviously in need of soothing.

"Stay, just *stay*. We don't have to speak. I'd actually like it if we *didn't* speak," he said it so tiredly, she hesitated.

When she glanced at him, he angrily smoked his pipe in the darkness so that all she could see was the ember when he inhaled. Tersely, she walked to the other side. She found a large box to sit on and stared out into the dark night. The three other ships trailed them, their lights flickered, and their sails glinted off the moon's glow.

In the midst of her tormented thoughts, she felt a sudden sense of pride at what her family had accomplished through the years. They built an *armada*. Now it was hers. *She* was the master of the seas. She didn't feel like the master of much. Not even of herself. Not even of her thoughts. She recalled watching Almira pick out her gown for a dinner with the king; she'd known exactly what she wanted. It had overwhelmed Hira on Almira's behalf with so many alternatives. What if she'd made the wrong choice? The feeling of honor soured. All her life, choices were not hers to make. Now they expected her to enact the appropriate ones. How so? What if she carried out a mistaken judgment? What then? Would people die? Or get hurt?

Angrily, she polished the ruby blade with the stone Delara gifted her. Not that the knife needed it, but the task kept her thoughts from wondering into choices. The commander had been so quiet she almost forgot he was there. She expected him to remain silent until his voice startled her.

"Why don't you want to be the Lady of Istok?"

She glanced at him. "I thought you had no wish to speak to me."

He shrugged and stepped closer. She could see the outline of his jaw and how his brown hair danced in the sea air. "You're sitting there looking like this entire voyage is a prison sentence."

Because it was. *He* wouldn't understand. He was a seasoned commander. He didn't think seven times about his decisions.

She went back to polishing. "We're not in each other's confidence."

He worked his pipe but kept his eyes on her. She felt him studying her scarred face. She knew her wound made her horrid; she didn't need this man to... *judge her*. Handsome men in Easima would politely glance away once they saw it. She was used to disappointments. Along with that, she'd never been lovely like Almira. Almira captured all the attention in the room with the way she spoke and walked. Hira was an afterthought. She was accustomed to that. It didn't bother her, but she was still keenly aware of it. Pale and pasty, flat-chested and clumsy, lacking all eloquence. Hira Balik was the boyish wonder born from Lady Marai, the example of ladyhood amongst their peers.

"You going to tell me how you got that scar?" he said, almost gently as he puffed on his pipe.

Her hair fell over her face as she continued sharpening her blade. She paused as she ran the stone over the knife and finally quietly told him of the night Tora died. Why she would share such a meaningful memory with him, of all people, was beyond her.

He was silent, and his nonjudgmental look was strange. He didn't seem to scorn her wounded face. When she met his eyes, she became short of breath. Under the light of a thousand stars, he was beautiful and wild, like a storm in the northern seas. And he entranced her, pinning her down without remorse. She swallowed thickly. She'd not acknowledged that she found him attractive until this very moment and she was at a loss as to what to do with such a realization. She didn't admire him so finding him attractive was a confusing sensation.

She quickly licked her parched lips. "After they sewed me up, I saw myself in a water mirror and… I was glad."

He came closer and looked down at her. "Glad?"

She set down the stone, frustrated with his interest and warm voice. "Because no one would force me to be a lady. Great joke, that was. Look at me now." Her hair fell over her face again, and she tossed it back, angry that it wished to hide her. "My mother doesn't know of my disfigurement."

He surprised her when he smiled as he exhaled smoke. "It's hardly a disfigurement."

Annoyed, she slid the blade into its sheath. "She'll be horrified. No lord will wish to wed a beast like me."

He didn't experience self-hate or people expecting things from him. He was young, rich, and healthy. Powerful in all Istok, with many ladies likely vying for his hand. Why should she open like a spring blossom and allow him entrance to her inner most thoughts?

She wished he'd left her alone. She wished she hadn't lingered on the color of his eyes. She wouldn't be one of his conquests, she was certain of that.

"You're exaggerating. *I'm* a lord," he said, as he opened his arms. He looked almost comfortable around her.

With the pipe in his fist and his disarming smile, she *could* describe him as charming. Oh yes, many ladies vied for his attentions. She would wager on that. A ridiculous part of her yearned to be an alluring coquette. Such a woman would know how to lure a man like the commander to her bed, and then have him waiting and willing at their feet. She supposed all women craved to be something they were not, even for a moment.

"You certainly don't behave like one." But her words were not corded tight, they were easy and conversational. A *tease*. She'd never teased a man before and it was... liberating. She felt her chest bloom with a sort of risqué thrill she'd never experienced before.

He may be a lothario, but as Almira loved to remind her, *she* was the Lady of Istok.

Sensing her change, he smirked. "And you don't behave like a lady. So, we're even."

A flush crept up her freckled cheeks, and she bit her lip. A statement such as that was downright flirtatious. Suddenly, she realized no man had ever flirted with her. She bedded men, lapped in liquor, but there was no art to it. It was a floundering of limbs. This was different. This was sex, but with words.

Having little knowledge of how to respond, she was silenced. There was no dexterity to her opinions, and she realized she still had much to learn on certain human exchanges.

When she didn't answer, he carefully stepped closer and inhaled his pipe once more. It smelled of mint and lavender. He cleared his throat, perhaps sensing her hesitation to continue the improper conversation. Or her lack of knowledge.

"I still don't understand your hesitation on taking up your post as our High Lady," he breathed.

That got her properly riled up. All propriety flew out of her mind. She scoffed and looked out at the great expanse of the ocean.

"*You* wouldn't. You're a man. You live on a ship and have the freedom to see what you will, do what you like, fuck who you want to fuck, drink to your heart's content, and not have the weight of responsibility of an heir for a while. Even then, a quick poke to a chosen young wife would fulfill your duty."

She froze when she realized what she'd intoned. Gods of the sea. Such conversations were acceptable amongst the women of her acquaintance, such as Sanaa and Almira, but *not* around Commander Justan. Instantly, her palms sweated, and she had to rub them against her pants.

But he surprised her when he laughed with vigor. He threw his head back and exposed his throat as he delighted in her sharp words.

"I think your scar and trousers should be the least of your mother's worries," he said, mirth still dancing in his tone.

She smiled without wanting to. The thought of such a tirade in the halls of Korkoran was rather amusing. Her mother, for one, would never allow such a thing. Lady Marai was all lineage and nobility. She knew her place and expected the same from Hira.

It was strange to speak so openly with a man of her standing and not have them grasping her hands in reverence and sticking to topics such as the roast and the pleasant weather.

"You'll have a hard time filling your uncle's shoes," the commander said. "Perhaps it's best to do things your way. That's what I've done. The first two years of my command were a constant litany of Commander Tikan did it in this manner. Commander Tikan would never."

The change in his demeanor surprised her. It was an easy, flowing conversation. The exchange allotted time for her eyes to linger on his lips and the way he shoved his hair back to keep it out of his face.

"And what changed? The men seem to respect you." She motioned with her chin to the crew below.

He smiled and winked. Her stomach tightened at his open flirtation. And then, as if he could finally manifest his true self, he moved about and enacted his story. He seemed different in that moment, like he was allowing her perusal at one of the pages he often kept closed.

"Our first sea battle." He pointed out to the ocean. "Seven pirate ships at dawn. Four days we chased them to the Isles of Hipata and there defeated them once and for all."

He was so lively in his words, lacking all pretense of being 'the commander' that she found herself relaxed and smiling, dreaming of such an adventure. She would love to chase pirates beyond the great seas, pounce on their ships and battle to victory.

"You must be a great warrior," she said with little thought. Then blushed and was grateful the night covered her flush.

Pulling back his shirt at the neck, he exposed an angry scar across his collarbone. "Nearly took my life, but worth it."

The wound must've been grave at one point. It began at the base of his throat, long and jagged, and disappeared into his tunic.

"Impressive scar," she said earnestly.

"Not as pretty as yours." He gave her a disarming smile.

She looked down and tucked her hair behind her ear. She wasn't certain if his words were a tease or mocking. While in Easima, she played a good game of pretense around the men she bedded. Hira posed as an experienced lady who knew the correct manner to twist her hips. But, to behave dexterously as a consummate lover, she relied on their thirst for liquor and cunny.

Justan smoked his pipe and studied the night sea with keen eyes. He let the silence linger, and she shifted. She didn't know how to respond to a compliment from a man such as him. Desperate to end the torture, she clutched her hands and glanced at him once more.

"How ill is Quent?" she asked.

The commander became lost in thought, then he looked down at his pipe. Shadows covered his face, and she noticed his fingers trembled slightly.

"Very."

His voice spoke deeply of loss and emptiness. He loved his brother dearly, and Hira was uncertain what to make of such a revelation. She'd mistook the commander as uncaring. She didn't know how to adjust her views on him. He seemed so very different when it was the two of them. As if he were being himself, where nothing seemed expected of him because she hated him already. What was strangest was that she felt the same.

"For that, I am sorry. He's a sweet boy," she whispered.

The smoke covered his face, and all humor left him. He studied her, and the potency of his gaze made her tug at her collar. Why must he stare at her so? What was he attempting to see? She had nothing to hide. She was who she was. There was little to it.

"Why don't you sleep in the commander's quarters when us royals are not onboard?" She asked.

"Because... having my little brother also sleep there would seem as preference amongst the men," he said with a slight shrug.

"You're protecting him," she realized.

"That's what I do." His jaw twitched, and he clutched his pipe tightly. "He was born when I was a grown lad and our mother died with his birth. Father is retired now, as you know, lives a good life with a new wife that says very little and has no opinions, just as my father likes it."

Hira swallowed as the implications descended upon her. "Why doesn't Quent live with him? What of his studies?"

He laughed, but it was a sardonic dark laughter. "My lord father is, like many men of his generation, cold and unfeeling. Quent showed up on my dock five years ago. He stole our mother's ring and sold it for clothes, food, and a horse. I knew what he ran away from. It's a lonely life to live in Pinnacle Palace with a man who pretends you don't exist. Quent's not said much, but I know my father. I know his sharp words and his demeaning tirades."

There was a slight burning in Hira's stomach at the thought of poor darling Quent being mistreated.

"I was transitioning to commander, and I could protect him. The High Lord allowed him a post, and he's been on this ship since." He met her eyes quickly, but peered away. "Soon after he got sick, medics explained the sickness." He paused, sadly considering the fate of his young brother. "He won't live long. He knows this. I've made peace with it. But I'll make sure that while he lives, he's happy and cared for and safe. Allot him the cheerful life I didn't have."

A thickness coated her throat, and she retracted from his sincere gaze. It made all her griping feel rather juvenile. Sure, her mother was strict, but deep inside Hira knew she'd been loved. Even uncle Beltran loved her in his own way. She'd grown up in a castle pampered, never lacking for attention—just freedom. She studied the manner in which Justan smoked his pipe and she saw the man who looked after his little brother despite his impending death. Despite the inevitable pain of the eventual loss.

"That is decent of you, Commander," she said.

He stared at her with a surprised smile. "That's the nicest thing you've said to me since you boarded this ship."

She turned to him and bristled. "You attacked me and called me a whore!"

He didn't bother denying it. "I was angry."

Hira could not help but feel affronted. As if fury could account for all actions. "And that justifies your words?"

His jaw tightened, and he looked away. "I'm not a man to give into anger. I've never been but you—" he pointed at her and let out a frustrated growl. "You have a hot temper."

Insulted, she stood to face him. "As do you, you fly off the handle as much as I do, you might as well admit it!"

The commander's mouth flopped open, and he shook his head. "Because you're *nothing* like what I thought you would be."

She flushed to the tips of her hair. "And neither are you! Each time I've met you before our trip, you've been glad to ignore me." She surprised herself at her words.

"Ignore you?" he asked, aghast. "*When?*"

Hira realized it was not that he'd ignored her. It was that she wasn't important enough to notice. In the presence of Almira, her uncle, and even her mother, why would he pay attention to the freckled Hira?

"Never you mind," she mumbled, mortified.

His jaw tightened, and he opened his arms wide. "Well, since we cannot come to an agreement, we are at an impasse, my *lady*."

She felt a keen loss at what she'd believed was tentative friendship. She rather enjoyed having friends and, despite Quent being a pleasant companion, naturally there were conversations she couldn't have with the lad. She'd also foolishly thought she could consult with the commander about some of her roles as High Lady. It was a momentary reflection, fleeting, but it was most appealing.

"It seems we are. It's a shame. Under other circumstances, I think we could be friends, Commander."

He looked at her doubtfully and she, having nothing more to say, turned and rushed to the lower deck. Hira paused when she realized she had nowhere to go. Annoyed at having to continue speaking to him when he blocked any offer of friendship, she groaned.

"What room have you for me?"

Following her down the stairs, he took her elbow to help her steps. Like a *lady*. She yanked her arm and stumbled. He grabbed and pulled her against him. Each part of his body molded against hers in the most improper manner. *Gods of the sea.*

"Unhand me!" In the torch-light, he would see the pink of her cheeks.

"Let me know when you stop believing that all of my actions are an effrontery, *red*," he barked.

He set her against the railing, and they stared at one another, breath sharp on each other's face. His fingers lingered on her waist, but he slowly extracted his hand. Her entire body felt suddenly alight at the thought of such a man interested in being intimate with her. His stare was so intense, she felt he would kiss her under the ashen moon, but he did not. She didn't know where she gathered such fantastical notions from. Obviously, it was all in her head. Perhaps it was loneliness. Perhaps the havoc of the night.

He swallowed thickly and held his hand against his chest, as if preventing it from touching her. He pushed past to the bottom of the stairs.

It took her a second to follow him, but she did, her knees still wobbly.

The commander walked her to the cabin and opened the door. He dramatically pointed to a small bed, a humble writing desk, and a slight port window. It was the room she occupied with the rest of the Red Guard when they escorted Almira to Easima. She wandered to the desk, inspected the room, and nodded in thanks.

Hira unlaced her cape and set it on the chair, then turned back to him with a raised brow. Why hadn't he left? The commander pulled a key from his pocket and held it out to her. She attempted to snatch it, but he didn't let go. They remained connected via the key. A petulant struggle ensued within her mind as he watched her. Then his other hand went up to her hair, touching the strand of red that fell over her eye. She stayed still, not sure what game he played.

Her skin prickled at his proximity. Then his fingers weaved their way to her cheek. She sucked in a breath as he touched her scar and lingered over the jagged flesh.

"Good night," he whispered as he let go of the key and departed.

He left her even more confused than before, her heart eating at the inside of her throat, her mind swirling in madness. Effectively, all she could think about was the complications caused by having any attraction to a man who disliked her. A man who reported to her. A man she knew very little about, and the little she understood was like two faces of a coin. The angry posturing commander and the endearing brother of a dying boy.

Life was certainly simpler in Easima. However, it was the first time her thoughts cemented themselves on one particular man. The litany of reasons such a complication would bring was another problem. It was in that thought that she realized she was pausing to think of the consequences and repercussions of such an involvement.

Chapter Eleven

SANAA

Sanaa looked over the training yards as the new recruits practiced mock battles. Below, a few of the castle soldiers watched them with interest. She disliked not having the training yards to herself because she knew the weight of critical eyes when one was young.

In her youth, when she was only twelve, she would wander into the yards and take lessons from whatever Mesedi was kind enough to volunteer. It seldom happened, and she quickly learned they did it for sport. They enjoyed her stumbles and lack of strength. She recalled the laughter and amusement each time she landed on the ground; her face painted red with the clay of the sparring ring.

Her uncle's voice came through her memories. It was long ago, before Edmee ever left. Sanaa was young and forced to partake in unpleasant dinners. Her uncle insisted she wear a dress like a lady should.

"Captain Utuan says you won't leave the training yards."

Sanaa chanced a look at her uncle's hard face. She displeased him constantly. Hated he owed Sanaa's father a life-debt, hated that to host the bastard child in his home with his poised children.

"Oh papa, little Sanaa wants to be a Mesedi," Edmee purred, a smile of pure malice on her beautiful face. "She confessed it to me."

And what a fool Sanaa was to trust such a secret to Edmee. She'd confused beauty with goodness and that was a lesson hard learned.

Her uncle set down his fork with a thud and leaned back in his chair. He belched as he beheld Sanaa. Her stomach iced and her knees trembled.

"Foolish girl," he growled as grasped his goblet of summer wine.

Sanaa's face heated and her neck flushed. When she was young, she would sit quietly through his tirades, but lately she'd grown bolder. She enjoyed searching for the edges of his temper.

"And why can't a girl be a Mesedi, uncle? I would serve you well, protect you at all costs," she said.

And she would, she would protect the bastard because a bastard he may be, but he was still their High Lord. Edmee laughed, and Edgar sighed. His large shoulders—even for his age—tensed at her antics.

"Let her be, Edmee. She's done nothing wrong," her twin said, and Edmee's eyes sharpened like an eagle. The golden hue darkening.

"Nothing wrong? She's our cousin, unfortunately. The Mesedi are servants, Edgar. Didn't you hear her? She would serve papa. How degrading." Edmee's elegant neck twisted to look at Sanaa, her full lips pursing in disgust.

Sanaa's inspection of her beautiful cousin was interrupted by her uncle who slammed the palm of his hand on the table. The fruit rattled. Breadcrumbs clung to his lips.

"Your sister is right, Edgar," he glowered at Sanaa.

Tears caught in her throat.

"No niece of mine will ever serve. You're young still, but old enough to know better, girl. You're not to go to the training yards or even look at the Mesedi —"

"But uncle!" Sanaa's tears betrayed her.

He stood, and with a powerful swing, he smacked her across the face.

"Father!" Edgar rose in shock, and Edmee laughed in delight.

Sanaa stared at her uncle as she clutched her face. His mouth frothed, his eyes narrowed into slits, and Sanaa swore he would kill her.

"You have the blood of high lords in your veins, no matter how watered down your lineage is. That little cunt of yours will one day bring me a trade alliance, you hear me?" he snarled.

Biting into her plum, Edmee relished in Sanaa's abuse. The juices coated her lips and ran down her chin. "What man will marry her with a face like that? It is a worthless pursuit."

Sanaa glanced at her. "I'm not worthless."

Edmee gave her a look of supreme doubt, staring down at her as one beheld an insect. How could Sanaa love such an evil person? Her chest heaved, and she sobbed.

"Don't you dare cry. Go to your rooms. I can't stand the sight of you." Her uncle sat down and grasped his goblet, the belted out, "Now!"

"They're getting better," Delara pulled her to the present. She lounged on a wooden chaise, casually sharpening her knife.

Delara's voice was unplagued by the acrid memories of a haunted past. Sanaa grunted, still shaken. It happened all too often; the past had a clutch on her life that she couldn't shake.

The captain looked back at the recruits as they practiced. She wasn't certain they were improving. There were a handful of good ones. Spotting a deficit in one recruit, she sighed.

"Zoya, this is not a dance, girl—swing like you mean it!" Sanaa barked.

The other girl disarmed her, and Zoya ended in the dirt. She missed the sword by an inch, and Delara hissed, "Don't kill one another!"

Sanaa cursed and turned to sit next to Delara. It took her months to find the perfect five women for her team, and now Almira breathed down her neck to train an entire battalion. It was impossible to manage control with so many.

Delara cracked her neck. "We have at least a solid ten. That's a good number."

"It won't be enough if this war continues," Sanaa said.

"It'll continue. The Norrian in the tower will refuse to broker peace with Norr. He's more stubborn than the queen and won't yield, I told her majesty as much." Delara tossed her long braid over her shoulders, her eyes glazed in contemplation, her lips set in worry.

Sanaa agreed with her. Almira went once more to meet with the Norrian and it ended in innuendos and another punch from Delara, which the Norrian enjoyed a little too much.

"You know the queen, she won't give up," Sanaa said as a servant girl came with a tray of steaming hot tea.

Sanaa knew the girl; though she didn't recall her name. A pale thing with unimpressive brown hair and soft eyes that followed the captain each time she saw her. With a timid smile, she set the tray on the table.

"Some fresh tea to warm you up, Captain." The girl carefully pulled back a cloth to reveal fresh cookies. The scent of butter, peanuts, and berries wafted up. Sanaa raised her brow and looked up at her.

The girl blushed prettily.

"How kind. Don't you think, Captain?" Delara asked, amusement clear in her tone as she reached for a biscuit and caught Sanaa's eyes with a knowing look.

"Agreed," Sanaa said as she reached over and slowly took a cup and sipped from it without taking her eyes off the girl. "I also enjoy tea before bed. Perhaps you can bring me some later."

The girl seemed to almost gasp at the prospect. "Of course, Captain! I will make sure I bring you... tea. Before bed."

Delara, enjoying the entire exchange a little too much, said in between bites of her biscuit, "Tea before bed. How enticing."

Sanaa nodded to the girl who left, bright in the face, and with a spring to her step.

Slowly, Sanaa looked at Delara, who innocently sipped her tea. "That's the third one this week. Leave some for the men, Captain."

Sanaa smiled and burrowed down into the seat, enjoying the warmth of the tea and the lingering scent of the girl. A moody M, wearing her casual robes interrupted them.

"You're off today," Sanaa said.

The older woman sighed and sat. "I know, but I'm bored. I'm alone wandering a city I'm not keen on, and you two having all the fun. It's not fair."

From the grounds, one girl yelled when a sword accidentally nicked her.

"Gods of the sea." Sanaa clutched her forehead. "Go down there."

Delara chuckled and stood to check on the girls. M poured herself some tea as they sat in silence and the bitter chill.

"What do you think the little lady is doing now?" M asked as she sloshed the warm liquid in her cup.

"Hira?" Sanaa asked. "Probably teaching those men who's in charge."

At least she hoped that was what she was doing. It would be a shame to have her fail a task she must succeed in. Sanaa agreed with Almira; Hira carried Balikian determination in her.

M smiled. "Good. She'll be a great High Lady."

"I sincerely hope so." Sanaa studied her cup. "Are you going to tell me why you're really here? What distraction do you seek?"

M winked knowingly. "You're sharp, I'll give you that. Those who are saddest are the most observant."

Sanaa found herself amused, as if she would provide confirmation. "You won't get stories from me, Madhavi. I'm a closed book and you're aware of that."

And she intended to stay that way. The last time she spoke of the past, it was to Almira on that awful mountain. The voice of Edmee haunted her for days, though none knew how she struggled.

M nodded, still with her pleasant ease. "You'll make soldiers out of those girls. I know you will."

Sanaa studied her profile as she focused on the yards. Shadows over a person's face meant pain, the sort not physically seen.

M lit a cigar and blew smoke into the cold air. "I won't be long with you."

"You must leave?" Sanaa sipped her tea as she mulled over the implications. This severely depleted her original Red Guard.

"Aye, but not like you think." M glanced at her. "Medics have found a growth in my breast. You know the type."

Sanaa swallowed her tea and set it down. Yes. She knew the type. There was no way to prevent it or treat it. It simply grew and grew until the pain became unbearable. Perhaps this was the ill news Almira fretted about lately. She'd complained nonstop of sensing something was wrong, though Sanaa thought war was bad enough.

"Are they certain?"

M nodded, but there was no hopelessness in her countenance. It was her same relaxed gait, as if she'd not shared life-changing news. "I ignored it for a while. The thing with ignoring this is that the more you ignore it, the more it invades your thoughts."

Sanaa didn't know what to say or do. She wasn't the comforting type, and she didn't think Madhavi would be receptive. To have lived so long and battled so many and to face such a death seemed unfair.

"You're turning your blade in?" Sanaa asked.

M had a far-away look. Her eyes lingered on the mock-battles below. "I want to die sword at hand, Captain. Not lingering in a bed in pain. If I can protect the queen in the process, that's enough for me."

Sanaa looked away and understood her very well. Perhaps she too would one day die for Almira and all that she stood for. Repay her life-debt. She'd welcome such a death with open arms.

"Don't feel sorry for me, girl. I know you carry your own pain clutched tight to your heart, but I can assure you, you're more than capable." M firmly gripped Sanaa's shoulder and squeezed it. "You've done well and don't need old Madhavi."

Sanaa smiled slightly and grasped her hand—it was as much comfort as she could provide. After all, she knew little of comfort.

"Don't leave me yet, old woman. Your smiles delight my sour moods, though I might not show it."

On her day off, Sanaa took to the city for a distraction. She'd kept M's secret. Perhaps she attempted to cusp it in her thoughts, mull over it before sharing it with Almira. A great sadness washed over her, and she couldn't shake it off. A sense that the Red Guard was dissipating permeated her senses. It was difficult to remain positive when she could only watch as what she'd worked so hard for unraveled. After a hearty dinner at her favorite pub, she meandered into the nighttime. The city was dark and held an enchanting aura in the frigid winter. The ground crunched under her boots from the snowfall that still lingered from last night. After an ale that lightened her spirits, she began the trek back to Mavros. She made her way through the labyrinth of Easima when she sensed a change.

Pausing, she placed her hand on her blade, eyes and ears alert. It didn't stop the intruder from landing a kick to her spine. She slid flat on her face.

The attacker wasted no time, and before Sanaa could grab her sword, they slit her hand. Sanaa dropped the ruby blade and screamed a curse. They stepped back, but not before they booted her ribs as she rolled up to counter the assault.

"Get up, Captain. I want to kill you armed!" the assailant growled.

It was a *woman*.

Sanaa jumped up and unsheathed her sword as she clutched her injured hand to her chest. *Now* the captain was indignant. She never thought it would affront her that someone dared to attack the queen's guard.

"If you know who I am, you know what a mistake this is."

The woman laughed; her body still bathed in shadows. "You exalt yourself, *mighty* Captain Sanaa."

Instantly, the woman sliced her blade down and Sanaa barely deflected. She rolled to the side and implemented her preferred steps, but to her surprise, the attacker was familiar with them. Sanaa couldn't catch an opening or gain the upper hand. She was on the defensive. The woman was better than she was. Quicker, smaller, and moved in the shadows like she belonged to them, like she was an enchantment sent to haunt Sanaa.

"You're a Free Islander," Sanaa grunted after she survived her last pounce.

While she panted, the masked woman seemed relaxed.

"I've dreamt of this moment. Look at you. Is that what you call a Jalibo step?" The woman sounded amused.

How dare she insult Sanaa's technique? Her steps were perfect. She could do them in her sleep! But the woman did the required brisk movement. She gracefully swashed her saber so dexterously and elegantly that Sanaa almost wished to admire her showmanship. But she had no time. If she didn't move as fast, the woman would gut her. Sanaa, admittedly, floundered.

"*That's* a Jalibo step," the woman said.

Sanaa's sword nearly flew off her hand, but experience and strength prevented that. She rounded on the woman and tried to catch her breath. Questions of the woman's identity erupted in her mind. Sanaa had no enemies on the Free Isle that she could think of. A few jilted lovers, but none so terrible that would seek revenge.

"Do you require a break to compose yourself?" came the woman's sarcastic question.

Sanaa brightened. She fisted her hand and pointed her saber at the woman. "You hide behind your mask like a coward! Face me like a warrior. Let me see my attacker!"

She moved to battle her, but the woman, executing a perfect Karten Corner, finally disarmed the captain. Her sword flew into the air and landed a few feet away. It was something that hadn't happened in years. She stared at her sword dumbly.

Sanaa turned back to the woman but a dagger was sharply pressed against her throat. Even a swallow would split her skin.

The woman leaned closer, and the moonlight illuminated her masked face. With an evil smile, she tugged off her mask.

Sanaa blinked at the sight of her.

Well. She'd not expected a beauty. The woman looked like she belonged on a dancing stage, not lying in wait down shadowy alleys, besting captains of the queen's guard. A true Free Islander with hooded dark eyes, pale skin, thick black hair and puckered pink lips.

"Do you recognize my face, Captain?" The woman sneered.

"I've never seen you before," Sanaa said quietly.

"Are you *sure?*" The woman's grin deepened.

"I'd remember your face," Sanaa admitted.

She'd certainly recall a face like hers. If she wasn't trying to kill her, Sanaa would've deeply desired her.

"I'm Kaia Lu Kait. Does that mean something to you, Captain? Was her death so inconsequential that it escapes your thoughts?"

The woman said slowly and pressed her blade closer.

Sanaa looked over her features, and her stomach dropped. *Yes,* she knew that face and that name.

"Tora's sister," Sanaa whispered.

A flash of Tora's wicked humor flashed before Sanaa, her deadly skills, and how she could out-drink them all. How small she felt in Sanaa's arms as life quickly left her broken body.

"Don't you speak her name!" Kaia's mouth twisted in rage.

Sanaa raised her hand. "I sent for you, and you never replied."

She'd worried about the sister, forlorn and defenseless. What a useless worry. Sanaa had delusions of a young child, a small girl that needed protection. She'd not expected the deadly hate before her.

"What a *fool* you are to think that you had to send for me." Kaia pressed the sword closer to her skin. She might've injured Sanaa. The blade was warm, and perhaps the captain now bled.

"You'd strike me down? Me, whom your sister defended?" Sanaa inched forward against her better judgement.

"A lot of good that did her. Her body laid on an Onyx stone! Polluted and desecrated! Her hair cut without her kin! Dying for a queen that would never, ever represent her! Bowing before a captain that steals our skills and passes it off as her own. Then rises to legend on art that was not hers to practice!"

The girl's angry words wounded Sanaa deeply, and she swallowed the unwelcomed shame.

"I -"

"Shut up! Or did you not pride yourself on your ability to execute our steps, which our masters crafted for a millennium? The only reason you're a fair fighter is because you took and gave nothing but death! Where were your stolen movements when my sister perished, huh? You were responsible for her and still—"

"She died in my arms!" Sanaa snarled and a visceral pain erupted in her heart.

This time, the blade cut through her. She felt its sharp bite. Sanaa had not allowed herself to think of Tora's last moments. She constantly hid it behind a curtain. It was the original loss of the women she'd gathered. A part of Sanaa thought to protect them too and keep them from harm. Yet they kept slipping from her fingers. First Tora, then Keilly… and now M.

"I chanted the prayer. I held her hand! It was my voice she heard as she passed to the light!" Sanaa's fury and frustration rose. "Damn you for dishonoring her in this manner! I swore to her I would protect you --"

Kaia's mouth twisted and, with a kick, she landed Sanaa on the floor. In the glistening winter landscape, Kaia looked like a goddess.

"Protect me from *who*?" Her voice dripped malice. Slowly, she pulled out the bow that was strapped on her back and dropped her saber on the wet ground. "This is my preferred weapon." She nocked an arrow into her bow and pointed it down at Sanaa. "I won't miss. I never miss."

Sanaa's heart thundered. She could fight, she could try, but she sensed she shouldn't. Something bid her to remain calm because this wouldn't be her terminal moment. She raised her bloodied hand up to show it to Kaia, then slowly lowered it to her belt satchel.

"No weapons, I swear it. It's a gift you should have before I die," Sanaa said quietly.

Kaia's eyes shifted, and they focused on her fingers, her mouth set with intent. "My arrow would fly before a blade can," she said.

"I'm aware of that." Sanaa pulled out the rolled hair, which she always kept with her. With a quick motion, she dangled it before Kaia.

Tora's thick braid hung between them, and the woman stared at Sanaa. Slowly, her shoulders relaxed, and her face transformed. Sanaa gathered her bravery and met Kaia's eyes.

"I know the customs and fighting techniques because they were granted to me. Given willingly by Master Otto, who was a great friend. He believed in me when I didn't believe in myself. He taught me the language and what to do when a warrior dies. I placed Tora on an Onyx stone because I couldn't find one made of Jasper. Jasper is scarce on the mainland. They don't understand it. They don't feel the vibrations. Take her honor, Kaia Kait. Keep it always and kill me."

Kaia looked younger and vulnerable. She lowered her bow, and the arrow clattered to the ground. With a trembling hand, she snatched the braid and pressed it against her nose. She closed her eyes and inhaled the scent that perhaps still lingered there. As if she could embrace her sister.

"I'm sorry I couldn't protect her. I want to protect everyone, but lives keep slipping through my fingers." Sanaa looked away. "I've never admitted that to anyone."

"I only needed you to protect *one*," Kaia whispered. "She was all I had. The Favia has taken *everyone*. What is a person without people? A ghost, that's what they are. I have followed you for twelve days and people fill your unworthy life. The queen, the guards, and the women you take to your bed. You never saw me, never sensed me. I was invisible. Not even today did you sense me."

And Sanaa hadn't. Not a sign of someone watching, or a foreign presence. It was admirable. Any warrior prized such a skill above many. She almost asked her to join the Red Guard, but knew Kaia would consider that an insult.

"You know I cannot take this. It has to be you who must return it to Agamora," Kaia said.

Sanaa slowly rose and realized how much taller she was than Kaia. She was a small petite thing, deadly but tiny. "The kingdom is at war, and I have a queen to protect. I cannot travel to the golden city."

"And what is Tora's need compared to a queen's?" Kaia spat.

Sanaa meant to protest, but Kaia let go of the braid and tossed it back to her. Sanaa deftly caught it. Kaia grabbed her weapons and strapped them on her body. Her movements were methodical, sharp and unwavering. She'd been in survival mode for a long time. Kaia's boots showed heavy wear and her trousers lacked mending. She was thin. Perhaps many days without meals.

Sanaa cleared her throat. "Return with me to Mavros. I have Tora's contract payment. It belongs to you."

The captain would triple the coin owed to Tora and provide her clothes and whatever else she required.

Kaia turned back to her with sharp eyes. "I don't want your coin."

"It's yours by right. Get better boots for this godsforsaken winter," Sanaa said with frustration.

"I'd rather starve than receive anything from you." Kaia's even tone showed she was resolute in her intentions.

Frustrated, Sanaa grabbed her weapon. "Are you staying in Easima?"

Sheathing her blade, Kaia spared her a glare. With that, she turned on her heel and disappeared into the night. Sanaa stared at the spot Kaia had occupied as her mind raced. She cursed and held her arm close to her chest. It would need stitching and she'd have to explain to her inquisitive, perceptive *cuzo* exactly who attacked her.

If she was honest, it shook her to her core. She grazed her fingers against her nose and hidden in between the digits was Kaia's scent. She would have to wash her hands.

Chapter Twelve

HIRA

Quent woke Hira the next morning, his thin arms laden with all of her things. The items fell down the moment he attempted to greet her. She rushed to help him as her items rolled on the ground and scattered to make a mess.

"I'm so clumsy," he apologized as he ran after one of her shoes, which slid under the bed. He was all limbs that lacked coordination, his excitement the driving factor to his mayhem.

"I could've gotten my things myself," she said in amusement as he struggled to grab the runaway shoe.

"Actually—" he grunted, coughed, and finally grasped the shoe, pulling back with a wide smile. "Justan said I should get your things."

At the mention of the commander's name, Hira looked away and pretended interest in the scattered scrolls on her desk. She'd had a rough sleep last night, her thoughts a volcanic wasteland. She attempted to decipher all the commander's words and actions, turning them over and over in her mind until everything was mush.

All the ways she should've responded, or acted, or looked played over and over in her mind. So what if he took her elbow? Was it truly so bad to allow a bit of softness? A part of her didn't think it would take away from her ferocity as a warrior. Another part of her doubted he did it because he didn't think she could descend the stairs on her own, but as a matter of courtesy.

She cleared her throat and chanced a glance at Quent as he attempted to get all the fallen items from the floor. "Is that all the commander said?"

Quent paused and thought about it. Hira's breath hitched, desperate for more. But Quent shrugged and shook his head. "Then he said I had to go to sleep."

Hira's shoulders deflated, but Quent didn't notice.

"Jacoby says he's never seen a stab like the one you did on that fella. Your window won't be repaired until we make port in Iguanta. Have you been to Iguanta? I'm not allowed to go on shore unless Justan is with me. Seeing as he goes to Iguanta to see Cevilla, I'm sure Justan won't allow it this time either, but maybe he'll allow me to accompany you and I can enjoy the town!"

The insinuation of the commander having wenches in various ports made a strange animal erupt in her stomach. She attempted to finagle the flush that her body produced with no control from her rational mind.

"Cevilla?" she asked as neutrally as she could muster.

Of course, the woman in question would carry a name like *Cevilla*. She was likely elegant, composed, self-assured, and laughed like the whispers of sparkling wine. Hira wondered how often Commander Justan took her elbow.

"Cevilla is of the old race and is *beautiful*. She owns a brothel on the south-side of Iguanta. I'm not allowed on the south-side. Too dangerous, Justan says."

Her cheeks brightened.

Yes, the commander was well versed in seducing ladies everywhere he went, wasn't he? She thought. *Well, I won't fall for it.*

Last night was simply her, in her youth, misunderstanding his affections. She'd been vulnerable after the horrible attack. She sought comfort in the wrong place and had wished for things that were most improper given her position. The arms of a philandering sailor were no place for the Lady of Istok.

"Does your brother allow you anywhere without him?" She sat

116

on the desk chair and pretended to study the parchments.

Quent sat across from her and shrugged. He seemed a little defeated. "He's very overprotective. He says it's dangerous because I'm so young. But I think I can stab a man if I'm attacked. I don't need to be swaddled."

Hira understood this with acridity. "Do you know how to stab?" she asked.

He looked downcast as he coughed into his elbow. "A little."

She perused her scrolls and thought how dreadful the afternoon would go if she did nothing but sit here with no activity.

"I can teach you if you like." She smiled.

His head swiveled so fast, he had to grasp the corner of her bed to keep from swaying. "You will?"

"Of course! Don't you want to be a Red Guard?" She laughed at his innocent charm.

His smile faded quickly, and his shoulders sagged once more. "Justan wouldn't like that."

Oh, screw the commander! The boy wished to learn, just because he was ill meant nothing, he was alive now! She felt her rebellious nature course through her at the thought that, for the first time, she could influence the life of another. She was the High Lady, and the commander answered to *her*. She just needed to ensure the boy didn't feel he disobeyed or displeased his adored older brother.

She raised a brow and attempted to look innocent. "What if I'm attacked again? Don't you want to be able to save me?"

He laughed, clearly not believing the angle. "I doubt you need saving. You're too good."

Hira's heart swelled at the thought of anyone believing her to be *that* good. She'd been so used to being surrounded by the Red Guard from Sanaa to Delara—the women were untouchable and far above her own abysmal skill.

"A few tricks won't exhaust you. Come here."

She showed Quent defensive moves—easy ones that didn't send him into coughing fits. His favorite was the slashing by the groin. He said it made him feel like a pirate. By the time she said enough, despite how tired he looked, he was ecstatic.

117

Later, when the door closed behind him, isolation descended upon her like a thick curtain. She heard the men laugh outside. Every once in a while, Commander Justan gave orders, and the men scurried to abide by their leader. She didn't know *why* she kept to herself. A part of her didn't wish to argue with the commander or grow confused by his presence. They brought meals to her, and she ate them alone, staring at the wooden beams under candlelight.

Hira didn't leave her room for days. Lapping waters didn't pause its rhythm for pouting girls.

Tick. Tock.

Lingering in bed, she didn't bother washing her face. What was the point? The life she loved so much was being slowly peeled from her future. No matter how she rounded her thoughts, she didn't see a silver lining, not for all the gold in her Balikian coffers.

One night, when the waves were harsh against the hull, she pulled a quill and paper and began a frenzied letter. She sobbed as she scribbled, pushing aside the knowledge that Almira would have no mercy but still remained teetering at the edge of hopelessness.

Queen Almira,

My cousin, you must allow me to return! Each day closer to home brings me closer to the end. I'm alone and desperate. You know me above all others. You know I'm not fit to rule! I am not you. I don't want this, please believe me I shan't survive. I shan't find happiness in this task! Give me anything else to do! Send me to war! Allow me to look after the king on the battlefield so that I might find glory in death and not death in life! I am on my knees imploring your mercy. I care not what happens to Istok! Istok is no longer my home. It is a prison, a punishment!

Then she stopped and scrapped the letter. She sounded desperate and Almira would pull it apart for what it was. The letter would serve one purpose; to confirm Hira was a child and nothing more. A child that couldn't handle responsibility and ruling—a failure to her family and her name.

She tossed it in the corner and threw herself dramatically on the bed; her frustrated sobs echoed against the walls.

Mr. Hyall stopped by to check on her the next morning with a hearty cup of ale. He paused when he saw the state of her room. Her things were strewn about and paper littered the floor. After handing her the cup, he quietly cleaned up the room, gathering the discarded papers from the floor. He put some of her things away as she drank the ale.

At the door, he paused. "Loneliness solves nothing, lass," he said and left.

The thing with loneliness is that when you're in it, it feels eternal and the malignant thoughts housed in one's head come out for a midnight dance, delighting in one's sorrow.

On the evening of the fourth day, she went to the deck. The fresh, salty sea air greeted her. It filled her lungs, and she let out a sigh of pleasure. She leaned on the railing and looked out across the arching waves. The sun was setting, and it was those magic minutes of glow when everything is picturesque. A surprising tug ignited her stomach. *The sea.* She was *of* the sea. She'd been born from its waters, pulled from her mother's womb, emerged from it, with its salt still clinging to her naked flesh. The feeling was so vivid her hands trembled and she shook her head to dispel such ridiculous thoughts.

When she turned back to the ship, she found Mr. Hyall watching her with a keen look. He sat mending netting and slowly offered her a kind smile. He was missing his right hand and in its stead was a hook.

"And she emerges." He smoked a pipe and his sparse hair danced in the breeze.

"Mr. Hyall, good evening." She came to stand by him and watched his diligent work.

He continued his task. "I got a sense you were hiding, my lady."

Hira looked away, her face aflame. She hated her sentiments were blatant for all to see. Even to a lowly sailor.

"I wasn't," she defended herself, despite the obviousness of her behavior.

Mr. Hyall twisted the netting with dexterity and chuckled. He pulled at his pipe and provided her a knowing look. She glanced at the quarterdeck, where Commander Justan spoke to some of his men. The sunset made his skin golden and his brown hair looked sun kissed from this angle. He turned to her, but she looked away before their eyes could meet.

"You know I saw her once?" Mr. Hyall interrupted her perusal.

Hira, desperate for a distraction from the commander, turned to him. "Saw who?"

Mr. Hyall's eyes twinkled. "The Lady of the Seas. The last of the sea dragons."

She laughed. "Mr. Hyall! I'm not Quent to fall for tales."

Rumors of sea dragons hiding in the endless oceans lived for centuries. Only the old sailors would ever claim to see them and everyone else laughed at their fantastical stories, mostly meant to amuse children and to share in port taverns after too much ale.

But Mr. Hyall bristled. "'Tis not a tale! We were lost by the Straits of Bula, the fog thick and heavy. It blocked the sun during the day and the stars at night. For five nights we sailed aimlessly, and the mood was as sour as the weather." He pointed to the top of the ship. "I was on topsail duty and that's when I saw her. The fog parted, and the moon shone down her light. And a dragon jumped right out of the water! Not five meters from the ship. Long thick body covered in golden scales that glimmered. She turned her great colossal head and looked right at me with sapphire eyes."

He paused and allowed Hira to ingest his words.

He leaned forward. "Believe in dragons, m'lady. They're the last bit of magic left in this world. You were born in Istokian waters. Pulled from the birthing pools you were. The dragons blessed us all."

Hira smiled at his words and patted his shoulder. He was dear, and she wouldn't scoff at his honest beliefs.

"Are you telling tales, old man?" Commander Justan stood before them.

Hira had been so enraptured by Hyall's story that she didn't notice Justan come down from the quarterdeck.

"Commander," she said quickly and tensed.

"My lady Hira." He bowed.

Mr. Hyall pushed himself and stood. "I'll stay my tales, Commander."

The commander glanced at him. "Sup is served, Mr. Hyall."

The old man nodded and hobbled away, and she was once more left alone with the commander. She didn't care for how he dismissed the sailor; he'd done nothing wrong other than provide her a little entertainment.

"He was only speaking," she said tersely.

He ignored her jab and walked closer. "You've come out of hiding."

Her face flushed, and she fisted her hands. "I wasn't hiding, Commander. I had letters to write and scrolls to go through."

He gave her a sideways glance. She could smell the scent of his sweat. It was not unpleasant and unbidden to her mind came the memories of their previous proximity.

His eyes softened as he studied at her. "I didn't behave like a gentleman the last time we were together."

Surprised at his words, she stared at him. He seemed frank and looked equally embarrassed. "Is this how you apologize?"

He smiled, amused. "I'm not apologizing."

They were silent, and his hands tightly gripped the rail. She caught a glance at the cords of his arms. The veins protruded from his skin, covered with soft brown hair. Despite his muscled arms, his skin seemed soft and welcoming. Straying to such thoughts was most inconvenient.

The commander turned to her. "How do men usually speak to you? They bring your little hands to their foreheads? Give you the utmost respect? Speak in pleasant, bland tones?"

She startled at his harsh tone and squared up to him. "They speak to me like a nobleman should."

He scoffed. "No wonder you want to be in armor and hide behind a scar."

She reddened as she stared at him incredulously. "Sir, I am a high-born lady."

He smirked. "I thought you wanted to be treated like a guard, sup with the crew, and trade insults with the commander."

At that, her entire face brightened to her ears, and she shoved her finger into his chest. "You are *hateful!*"

He looked down at it and then back at her with a raised brow. "Hateful?"

"Aye, hateful, my lord!" She felt all the frustration at his behavior bubble up within her. Also, frustration at her own inability to have a normal conversation with him. "You treat me horribly, but then you tell me of your noble deeds with your brother. You laugh with your crew, but you scowl at the mere sight of me!"

He openly *laughed* at her, unperturbed by her outburst. "What a load of jokesters you're used to. You know what your problem is? You haven't had a man meet you eye-to-eye and tell it to you the way it is. All these simpering fools treating you like a delicate porcelain doll. Who cares if you're in trousers or not? You've never been addressed like a real person, so you put this getup on because you're secretly hoping someone will respect you enough to speak to you like you desperately want to speak to others! Oh, don't shock yourself, my lady, I'm leaving!"

She blindly grabbed his arm and dug her fingers into his forearm. He was all muscle. His face was suddenly too close. "And you know what *your* problem is, my lord? You haven't been around a woman that you didn't have to pay for. You've no idea how to behave unless I'm a wench or a sailor. Well, I'm not one of your port whores, *Commander*. I won't straddle your lap for a silver moja!"

"You'll do it for free, then?" His words were quick and sharp.

She gasped so loudly it resounded from the entire deck and silence descended around them. The crew stopped and watched them with unwarranted interest. The fact that she'd been thinking of doing such a thing flooded her with shame, and she instantly let go of his arm. They stepped away from one another with both of their tempers still sizzling.

"I apologize, that was low," he whispered, but the fire in his eyes did not ebb.

She should've stabbed him. Instead, she had *gasped* like a simpering lady. She became irrationally angry with herself.

"My lady, I am—"

But she didn't let him finish. She turned to return to her rooms. He followed right along, shoulder to shoulder, as they thundered around the ship.

"You don't have to hide in your room," he said tightly. "I apolo—"

"I'm *not* hiding," she countered. Her lips were trembling.

His shoulder pressed against hers, and his face was sharp in the evening glow. She could scarcely breathe. They sidestepped a sailor who yelped to get out of their way.

"Look, I apologize, that's a genuine apology there," he was hissing.

Hira scoffed, desperately wishing to punch him, but it wouldn't be right, it wouldn't be proper. She hated the impropriety of his words, as well as the mottled sensation of lust said words arose in her.

"I'm so *thankful*, Commander, that you can apologize like a civilized individual," she spat and turned with him right next to her, as if he escorted her.

She speared him with a glare and quickened her steps, intent on locking herself in her room until she could control her body and her mind. And her temper. Quent watched them with wide eyes, but Justan snapped his fingers loudly and the boy scrambled away.

He growled, "Oh, why can't I think straight with you around?"

"I'll leave you to work out your own issues," she said, nearly reaching her door.

He stepped around her and opened it, staring down at her, breathing deeply. Their eyes latched onto one another. Her fury was so great, she felt it sting against her lashes. She would cry in anger and she'd never hated that more.

She moved into her room and before she could dismiss him, he moved back.

"Don't worry, I'm dismissing *myself* before you have the chance to do it. Sleep with a knife. Slice my throat if I'm stupid enough to march back in here," he said tightly.

All the rage in the ocean flooded her veins, and she felt if she had some magic, she would burn down the entire ship and let them all drown.

"If you march back in here, it won't be your throat I'll slice," she spat and cast her eyes between his legs.

He looked her over with an infuriating smirk and then bowed in the most ridiculous manner. "Most temping, red."

He slammed the door behind him, and she rushed to lock it. She swore she heard him laugh on the other side. A scoundrel! A heartless mercenary! How her uncle placed such a bastard as commander escaped her. Her first order of business was to banish him from her lands.

Chapter Thirteen

HIRA

One solitary evening, the reverberations of shouts and steps thundered on the deck, dissolving Hira's solace. The walls to her small room trembled, and she couldn't slide on her boots fast enough. Once she'd strapped her sword and blade to her waist, she opened the door to find organized chaos.

"SEA PIRATES, M'LADY!" a sailor shouted.

Her heart leapt at the thought. A fight! She couldn't have asked for a more opportune distraction from her wandering, morose thoughts. She itched to join the fray, Ocean Fury at hand.

Around her, soldiers pushed their bodies against the ledge to identify the attackers. She ran up the deck stairs to where Commander Justan stood with legs planted wide and a visionscope pressed against his eye. Any feelings of hatred towards him evaporated. She wanted to fight! She wanted action! The seas were dark, and heavy clouds draped the moon and stars with a foggy mist. How could he see? Visibility was not on their side.

When he felt her presence, he turned to her with a tight face and displeased brown eyes. "Get back to your quarters!" he snarled protectively.

Hira flushed at the expectation that *she* would follow *his* orders. Orders barked like one addressed a servant.

She squared up to him with a determined look. "Commander, tell me the situation."

He started at her tone, and she realized her words were a sort of haughty nasal sound that manifested when she was angry. She flushed as the mask of utter loathing filled his eyes.

"You're the Lady--"

"That's *right*. I am the Lady of fucking Istok and, as your sovereign and High Seat, I *command* you to answer my question. Speak!"

She surprised herself with the brusque way in which she answered him because, for a mad moment, she meant every word. She meant the strength of each one of her words. Ocean Fury heated as if it commended her for finally taking her place of authority.

Justan's jaw looked so compressed it seemed it would protrude from the skin of his face, but he sighed in defeat and pointed out into the night. "Four pirate vessels closing in fast. There *might* be more, but it's too dark to see."

Hira peered out into the ocean, distinguishing very little. "Our other ships?"

He went back to the visionscope, the skin between his brows creasing. "Ahead by twenty leagues. Captain Gunn is turning the Night Serpent, but the pirates are closing in fast."

Hira's heart was at her throat. She glanced around at the men on her ship. "How fast?"

The commander shook his head, his face grim. "We cannot outrun them."

A thrill filled her, something she hadn't felt in a long time. Perhaps since the Siege of Mavros. She was about to clash steel. Each nerve ending within her crowded with light and purpose and she yanked out Ocean Fury in one swift pull.

"Commander... ready my ship for battle," she said.

He watched her for a moment, their tempers combating one another in the manner of ships destroying each other at sea. His brown eyes became flecked with gold, as if his fury was so great it ignited from within him. Mustering as much confidence as she could, she lifted her chin. His nostrils flared and his body leaned into her. He bit back the nasty words he likely wished to hurl at her.

The commander broke their silent argument and turned to his first mate. "You heard the lady! Ready the ship for battle, Mr. Torrent."

He turned sharply to her. "I hope you know what you're doing."

"*Me?*"

"Yes, *you*."

Around them, the men rushed from one end of the deck to the other, pulling cannons, grasping weapons, placing boxes packed with firebombs by the cannons. The anticipation of the fight inebriated her senses and her body burned with excitement.

"I'm not even going to tell you to take care of yourself because from the looks of your getup, you're warring with the rest of us," Commander Justan grunted as he tucked his visionscope into his coat.

She smirked, delighting in his annoyance at having to follow her orders. "You should be relieved you have a Red Guard on board."

He scoffed. "*Ecstatic.* Stay close."

She gave him a sarcastic, sideways glace and said, "In case you need saving?"

"In case," he said, rolling his eyes as grasped a rope and swung down onto the main deck. She watched him as he landed neatly and turned to look at her. For a moment she felt bewitched by his stare, but she attributed it to the feeling of coming battle.

A few sailors viewed her doubtfully, but most of them had no time to think of why she was in the tussle. Hira unloaded boxes of ammunition and slid them next to flame throwers. She urged men to their positions and to arm themselves.

As the pirates came into view, she clutched the edge of the ship to get a better look. She'd never seen pirates before. She only knew what passed in rumors: they were non-conformist, they owed allegiance to no one, they attacked vessels and killed the crew, or stole the ships they didn't sink.

"That's Strauss alright," a sailor next to her said.

She glanced at the man, whose face was grim, then back at the vessel. "Strauss?"

"Aye, Captain Strauss, the most notorious pirate there is, m'lady. That there is the Red Dragon, a *beast* of a ship," he said in near awe.

The massive ship with red sails led another three. They moved as a though threaded by a cord, a perfect coordination for attack. Above, the moon shined down on the ships, and the silent approach through the dim lunar light sent a chill down her back. The Red Dragon was impressive. Almost as large as the Sea Wife. A ship that size would surely be a challenge.

"Has anyone ever defeated him?" she asked.

"Nay, m'lady. But the Night Serpent can outrun it."

The sailor pointed to their accompanying black-sailed-ship. She was plowing through the dark waters at full speed. Still, she would not make it in time to aid in their defense. The hairs on her neck stood on end as she realized all the vessels would clash in one spot. It would be mayhem.

Commander Justan came to her and took her arm. "I want you to not argue with me for a moment. I'm trying to save your life. Take Quent and board the Night Serpent."

She studied him with realization. "You don't think you can defeat him?"

He peered at the red sails of the pirate ship. "It'll be difficult."

She was stunned at his stance. "And you think shoving me off to another ship will do anything for the morale of the men? I don't think so, Commander. I'll not run away while my sailors and armada face its foes!"

To even her own surprise, she turned to the crew and cast her sword into the air. "Prepare for battle!"

This was her family's legacy, their *prized* ship. Her uncle would never have allowed a pirate to attack it and get away with it. She may not have known much about court politics or the correct way to hold her teacup, but she knew war. She knew swords. And she knew they must best these pirates.

The commander's eyes widened when the men cheered the

same and lifted their blades in consensus. The crew seemed to come alight, delighted in the prospect of battle, and she felt that energy pulse right to her heart. She pulled herself up on a crate and pointed with Ocean Fury to the cannon on the side of the ship.

"Load the flame throwers!" she shouted.

Commander Justan, seeming to shake himself of the notion that she'd taken over leadership, turned to his men.

"You heard Her Ladyship! Starboard side!" he cried. His voice was angry, but resigned.

She looked at him, rather stunned that he was going along with her plan. He'd fought her each step of the way and here he was, both falling into his place of authority and following her lead.

He met her eyes with a furious blaze. "You won't listen, so I might as well let you go down in glory!"

She was titillating with delight at not only getting him to agree with her but the fact that she was about to do actual battle! Now she understood why her uncle had sailed so much. Such an adventure!

Captain Strauss didn't wait for a curtesy warning shot. As the men loaded the canons, the nostrils of Strauss' boat opened, and four heavy artillery pipes emerged. Then fired.

BOOM! BOOM! BOOM! BOOM!

Her inner ear rang as one bomb hit the Sea Wife, and the wood crunched. Hira crouched and Commander Justan covered her with his body. He stared at her, still angry, but assuring himself she was uninjured. Before she could take offense, he jumped up and rushed towards the throwers.

"FIRE WHEN READY!" he yelled.

She went after him to the Cannon-lead. They loaded the cannons with ironbombs, rounded balls of iron crafted to provide the maximum damage when propelled through the Istokian shooters. Strauss was reloading, they had mere seconds. She covered her ears.

BOOM! BOOM! BOOM!

They could hear the crushing of wood from the Red Dragon when the ironbombs hit their marks. Then the Red Dragon shifted, as it turned to aim with the full onslaught of her throwers.

"FIRE!" Commander Justan urged them.

The men reloaded ironbombs into the compartments just as the Red Dragon completed their shift. The wooden body was of wide berth and ten chambers opened and out came the pirate's cannons.

"FIRE!" Commander Justan cried and once more she covered her ears.

BOOM! BOOM! BOOM!

Wood splintered on the Red Dragon. Then Strauss' canons were upon them. She saw the glint of red fire before she heard the noise. All ten of the far superior mortars thundered in sequence like piano keys.

A flash of silver came straight at them, and on instinct, she grabbed Commander Justan and yanked him down. They stumbled to the floor, their limbs tangling around one another until they lay pressed intimately together. Just where he'd been standing, an ironbomb landed and destroyed the beam.

He looked at her, surprised, but she was too shocked to claim her victory or linger in the impropriety of their position. Their men reloaded without pause as the Night Serpent came within range and fired at the other pirate ships.

"FIRE!" Commander Justan stood, helping Hira up by yanking her by the arm.

BOOM! BOOM! BOOM!

It didn't matter, the Red Dragon was upon them.

BOOM! BOOM! BOOM!

More shots and more damage to the Sea Wife. Chunks of wood fell around them. Quent, on cleanup duty, swept up the deck to remove hazards from the floor. The men rushed to reload cannons, and the rest armed themselves.

Despite the Night Serpent's attacks, the Red Dragon focused on them. They were out of time! Hira looked to the men, focusing on the cannons. They weren't ready for a close-hand attack. They needed blades!

"PREPARE TO BE BOARDED!" she shouted.

"Stay on the cannons, Mr. Ilk, fire at will—everyone else with us!" Commander Justan pulled out his sword. "Quent, downstairs, safe room!"

The lad disappeared into safety, and Hira turned to the commander. His shoulder pressed to hers, and she realized he hadn't left her side once. Without thinking, she pushed further into him, ensuring herself she was not alone. He glanced down at her, his chin tight and corded. His eyes flickered into something akin to genuine worry, but it was gone in a moment.

"You drop your--"

"My left shoulder, yes, I know," she peeked at him. "And you drop your right."

His nostrils flared. "What a pair we make."

His words sent a fuse of electricity through her. In the midst of the chaos, the splintered wood, and the smell of cannon smoke, she had a mad desire to kiss him. He looked like he would welcome that at this moment. They pulled their gazes from one another as hooks, followed by ropes, landed on the deck. They hacked at the cables, the blades splintering lines, but soon the pirates boarded. She found herself in full battle, the likes of which she'd not seen since the day her uncle died.

The pirates were sneaky, ignoring all the rules of engagement. Just when she would have the upper hand, they would slick a blade at her side or yank her hair. More than once she'd nearly lost her life, barely managing to deflect blows with her ruby knife.

One hairy pirate held her back by her hair while another ran at her with an ax. Had it not been for Hira twisting and kicking the one who held her, she would've been disemboweled. She turned to fight the ax-wielder, unarming him and slicing his throat with a yell.

Ocean Fury was in its element, delighting in pirate blood, as if it recognized its preferred liquid fare. Hira could only imagine how many pirates the blade killed through generations of Baliks.

Commander Justan found her, and they battled back-to-back, their swords slashed through a sea of riotous pirates. They cast orders to the crew and the cannon handlers. Despite the onslaught, their men held up, and the raiders abandoned the quest.

Another pirate kicked her but she managed to gut his belly. She almost toppled over, but Justan grabbed her and pulled her flush against his chest. Their eyes met for a moment before she turned him sideways and deflected the sword of a man headed for the commander. Justan nodded in appreciation, and they were once more back-to-back, his firm ass pressed against her back.

Then she saw Captain Strauss, his face twisted in rage as he had boarded the Sea Wife. His eyes were intent on the commander. The pirate rushed at him with his sword to skewer Justan from behind like a coward. Hira threw her ruby blade the way Sanaa taught her. It missed and imbedded itself in the wood by the captain's head. He turned to her with surprised wrath. She bared her teeth and pointed Ocean Fury at him.

"Face *me*, Captain," she sneered.

He paused for a moment, then jumped off the Sea Wife and back to the Red Dragon. She ran past the commander with her sword flailing wildly in the air.

"After Strauss!" She yanked her knife out of the wood, but Justan stopped her and grabbed her hand, pulling her in.

"Our men are wounded. Let him go. We'll fight him another day," he breathed.

She stared at him incredulously. "And allow him to escape?"

He came closer, an intimacy she'd not allowed him. "Look at the sailors!" he hissed quietly, and when his fingers lingered on her hand, the moment wasn't lost on her.

He was right. The men were relieved the battle was over. Many of them wounded, all of them exhausted. There was a small fire on deck and sailors moved with hurried gestures, attempting to put it out. Their faces were drawn, they leaned against beams and grinned haggardly in relief.

She paused, her breath came sporadically, and she conceded with a nod.

The Night Serpent had her own damage, but she fired a few more rounds of ironbombs as the pirates retreated.

The commander, to her surprise, stared at her with an unreadable expression. "Saved my life twice. Are you hurt?"

His clothing was dark and grimy in a mixture of sweat, dirt, and the residue of ironbomb powder. Hira likely looked the same. She wanted to mock his worry for her but didn't. She didn't think it was the time. Not when his face was so momentarily sincere, like she'd surprised the hell out of him.

She shook her head in definitive denial. Exhaustion set in as the rush of adrenaline abated, but she knew she held no injuries worth attention. She leaned against a wall, which was splintered and damaged to catch her breath.

"You?" she replied as she sheathed Ocean Fury.

He shook his head but still looked at her. There was an intensity in his gaze. Perhaps he also felt the thrill of the fight and how much it resembled the thrill of a fuck. He licked his lips and cleaned his mouth with his shoulder. He pushed his hair back and let his hand linger on his forehead as he held her stare. His eyes dilated and darkened.

But the sailors pulled his attention away when they asked for directions on what to do. He looked away from her and cast orders as she watched him. He was not terrible to behold when at ease.

They tended the wounded, and the commander ordered the cook to get meals started for the men. The commander inquired after the status of the ship and demanded to know how many ironbombs remained. Hira took a seat at the steps which led into the upper decks.

Quent clambered up to her with a mug of ale, which the men were enjoying post battle.

"I saw as much as I could from my window!" He said, nearly spilling the entire cup.

She took it from his hands before he could, chuckling and bidding him to sit with her. The ale was biting and refreshing post-battle.

"How many pirates did you kill?" Quent's overly excited voice spoke of his thirst to be in the fray himself.

"I can't recall, Quent," Hira admitted.

And he launched into an explanation of how he would fight if he were allowed to engage as such. His hands were everywhere, a thespian of imagined skills. As he spoke, Hira's eyes found the commander in the lower deck. She gazed at him over the rim of her mug.

The commander paused hauling the dead off the ship and rolled up the sleeves of his shirt. He revealed well-shaped forearms covered in veins and soft brown hairs. She drank more of her brew, delighting in the welcoming sight of his muscled body. He took the steps up to her, ruffling Quent's hair when he was before her.

"Did you get dinner?" The commander asked.

"Soon!" Quent sweetly looked up at his brother with admiration.

Justan smiled down at him and then glanced at Hira. "We will make port at Iguanta in a few hours. If we see no more pirate attacks, that is."

"Captain Strauss is a threat," she concluded.

But even as she spoke the enemy's name, her thoughts and feelings were wrapped up in the man before her. Quent spoke to the two of them but their eyes lingered on one another until Hira could scarcely recall much from the battle other than the commander never leaving her side.

Chapter Fourteen

JUSTAN

Late into the night, Justan still found it impossible to find sleep. In all the madness he'd lived through, this was the most dangerous game he'd ever played. He ran his hand over his face and groaned. Fuck.

Fuck!

What the hell was he doing?

Amid the mess, how could he desire his High Lady? His body was still alight with the closeness of Lady Hira, the roundness of her lips, and the tone in which she argued, the slant of her shoulders when she fought. Thirty-one years he'd wasted on this earth, not allowing himself to be interested in a woman in this manner. He couldn't be interested in anyone; it wouldn't bode well for anyone involved and would simply result in pain.

What he didn't comprehend about himself was why he antagonized her so? Why did she respond as she did? It was as though a magnet connected to his belly was yanking harshly in her direction. He'd wandered before her door for days as she martyred herself in there. Posted himself like a damn guard to ensure no one bothered her. Made sure no one tried to kill her.

It was the way she raised her chin—that recalcitrant Balikian air. A proud arch to their brow that spoke of power and lineage and not giving a shit about the process of things. He'd admired it for years, and now this lady sported the strongest of these traits he'd ever witnessed. A part of him always knew the young girl running around Korkoran was a little wild and untamed, but his interactions with her had been minimal. Mostly watching her from afar. He'd been only fifteen himself when he first laid eyes on her and even back then she was a storm.

The timing of this attraction was atrocious.

Hira would surely be dead from the attack a days before, had she not learned to defend herself so well in her training for the Red Guard. His panic was so great, his mind skewed in desperation that he'd barely slept since then. He could hardly stay still, thinking another sailor would be bold enough to assail her. Adding Strauss into the mix didn't help matters.

Justan had *one* task, and he was so close to failure he could taste it. A bitter aftertaste on his tongue.

"I'm asking of you something I wouldn't ask of anyone else," Beltran said, standing over his desk, the fire roaring behind him.

He didn't like when the High Lord asked things from him. He was never in a position to refuse.

"More than what you already have?" he asked, attempting to lighten the High Lord's darkened mood.

Beltran sighed and placed his pipe into his mouth, his eyes trained on the two small portraits on the desk. One was Queen Almira, and the other was a rendition of Hira when she was ten. His Lordship's face shadowed in deep thought.

"Hira must take the seat. When she does, I'll no longer be around," Beltran said with great grief. "My girls will be alone. All I can do is send them envoys. Helpers." He looked up and met the commander's eyes. "Be Hira's envoy. Help her make the right choices and wise decisions. She'll be young and rash. Promise you'll protect her. You above everyone know the danger she's in. You alone can help her, even if she hates you for it. She'll not like it, but she'll need all the protection available. Promise it, on your life. On your little brother's life."

He'd swallowed the discomfort then, glanced down at the portrait. He barely saw the Lady Hira nowadays, but sometimes he would catch a glimpse of her bright-red, long hair in the halls of Korkoran.

"I promise I'll do all I can to keep her alive. I swear it on the Favia."

Justan recalled feeling inept for the job Lord Beltran saddled him with. He wasn't a guard; he was a lord. Back then, the Lady Hira was a small thing that ran from place to place with hair loose, and a dirty nose. But she was no longer a child. She was very much a woman. A very *attractive* young woman, and a bold warrior. It awoke something in him he'd long lost hope of. But she was the last Balikian princess, and far above his station, especially given the reality of his *particular* situation. His task was to serve her. Not only as her secret protector, but as her commander.

He looked at his hands, callused and rough. The commander couldn't recall what it was like to be soft and open. He'd been a stone for so many years that the pit of his heart was a calcined organ long left to rot.

She belonged to the kingdom, though she may not know it yet. In the stillness, Quent coughed above him from his hammock. The commander was instantly on his feet.

"Justan?" Quent's voice was weak.

"I'm here, I've got you," he whispered and helped the lad sit up, rubbing his thin chest as the cough wracked his small body. "Breathe, relax, look at me."

Quent's eyes watered as he tightly grimaced. Justan placed a cloth against his mouth and patted his back until the phlegm dispelled from his cracked lips. The boy sighed in relief as Justan discarded the napkin to the waste bag, along with the others.

Justan comforted him as the coughs cleared. The sharp pain that always lashed his heart whenever he witnessed Quent like this coated his insides. Justan clasped his brother's small hands and rubbed them, ensuring he was warm, ensuring he hadn't missed any signs of the coming end.

He attempted a smile. "Better?"

The lad sniffled and nodded, rubbing his eyes sleepily. "My chest hurts."

The commander smoothed his palm over it, as he always did, alleviating him as best he could. Quent sighed and blinked up at Justan.

"Why do you argue so with the lady? She's very nice." The question was very innocent.

The commander fought the urge to chuckle. "I'm sure you think so."

He groaned and settled into his hammock. "I don't like you speaking to her the way you do. It's not proper, is it?"

At that, Justan grinned. "You lecture *me* on etiquette?"

A small cough caught in Quent's throat and Justan quickly helped him sit up, then laid him back down with a sigh once the fit was over. Shadows covered his frail face, which troubled Justan constantly.

"I just… I don't want you to make her cry." Quent flushed.

The burn in his stomach erupted. His jaw clenched, and he groaned and wiped his eyes. "Her Ladyship is more than capable of defending herself. Now, stop worrying over her," Justan sighed, now understanding Quent's obvious crush.

"*Me?* You're the one who's constantly visited her hallway since we departed. I've seen you at night, standing outside her door while she sleeps." Quent smiled that soft, childlike smile.

Justan almost faltered at being read so clearly.

"If you like her, you should be nice to her. She'd like you better," Quent said.

"I *am* nice to her." Justan didn't meet his eyes.

Quent shook his head, his brown hair falling over his cheeks, and he sniffed. "You're not yourself around her."

Heat flared in his cheeks, and he took a sharp breath. No. No one could see the real him. He'd allotted Quent that honor and he was too close to revealing it to Her Ladyship.

"Time to sleep," Justan said and smoothed his palm over Quent's face, but the boy caught his older brother's hand. He looked up at him with their mother's eyes.

"She's a proper lady, isn't she?" Quent asked, a little crestfallen.

"Aye," Justan nodded and tightened his hands in his.

He chewed on his lip. "I like her."

The commander raised a brow. "I'm aware of that."

The boy flushed a deep red. "I'm too young, ain't I?"

"Aren't I," Justan corrected him.

Quent gave him an exasperated look of disdain. Justan well knew Quent hated when he improved his vocabulary. Proper speech distinguished him from the rest of the men. He didn't like to be singled out. It was bad enough he was sick.

"She likely has to marry someone important," Quent said with a shrug.

"Most likely," Justan agreed in a whisper, though the words formed a sour settlement in his stomach. He couldn't digest those implications. "Now…" Justan smiled and set aside their conversation. "What do I always tell you?"

Quent swallowed, his lids dropping. "That you love me, you'll protect me, and no one will hurt me. Oh, and even if things are bad, we are family. We are Garians, the star-sons of the night sky. We're all we've got."

Justan's throat tightened, and he kissed his forehead, inhaling his scent. "I won't ever leave you; you are my treasured one. I promise that every day, don't I?"

"Yes," Quent said as he yawned.

When he settled Quent down, he noticed a small scrap of cloth in the boy's pocket. It was a lady's handkerchief. He pulled it out to study the elegantly etched letters.

H. B.

Taking it with him, he laid in his hammock, examining the delicate threads. He followed the pattern of the initials with his fingers. Then he dared to press it against his nose and the scent of Hira's perfume oils overtook his senses. He sighed as he lingered in memory.

"What happens if I fail?" the commander asked Beltran the final time he saw him. They were in the High Lord's rooms in Mavros before he would sail the armada back to Treveri last summer. "That woman suspects everything. I have not a moment's peace."

Beltran's blue eyes were cool and unwavering. "You think I give a damn about your peace? Your happiness? You remember what I did for you? I saved you, pulled you from death, gave you food, clothing, a roof over your destitute head when you had nowhere to go. Provided you with the means to care for your brother. Now I demand you save my heir. That was the deal. You do what you have to do, fuck who you have to fuck, lie if you have to lie. Kill if you must kill. You and I don't matter. If we fail, Istok will fall. My house is depleted, and Almira and Hira's life will be in danger. Along with the whole fucking world."

The commander closed his fist around the handkerchief, Hira's initials pressed against the callused palm of his hand. Her face came sharply to his mind. *He* didn't matter. Only *she* and Quent did, and he would do everything in his power to fulfill his promise. Because promises to the dead could not be broken.

Chapter Fifteen

ALMIRA

The queen led a small entourage of guards escorting Lord Ivar into the rooms she'd selected for this last hope at negotiations. Lady Delara held his arm in a vice grip while two black knights stood by. Ivar had not fought them, and still chained, he regarded his captor with a cool expression. Delara ignored him, though he'd verbally goaded her the entire journey from the tower.

He perused the room, inspecting it with less than subtle amusement. The fine bed, the desk and chair, a modest table to write, read, and eat at. All the minor comforts afforded to any other notable guest. Except for a balcony. The window was small and high, but still brought in a nice brightness into the space.

"This is a lovely bribe," he said as he turned back to Almira with a full smile.

She resisted the urge to showcase her emotions, something her husband was fond of pointing out.

"You're under a great belief that you hide your feelings well, my dragon, when in reality they're painted clearly on your face."

She opted to glance away from the Norrian and walked to the desk to ensure he had plenty of ink and parchment. "How many times have I reminded you we're not enemies?"

He chuckled, a deep rumbling that escaped his bear-like chest. His bound hands gingerly touched the offered bedding. "And yet, I am still a prisoner."

Almira didn't blink at the bait. "You'll have a servant, which will tend to your needs. Food, drink, baths, and you can write any letters you wish."

If Alton knew she was in a room with the Norrian lord, he wouldn't be happy. But her husband didn't need to know of her "schemes", as he called them. But she didn't do things lightly, and she'd executed her actions with precision.

He paused and raised his brow. "And I can have these letters delivered to whomever I wish?"

"After I inspect them, of course," Almira smiled with a sly grin.

Ivar looked her over appreciatively. "I wouldn't expect anything less from *you*, Majesty."

She lifted her chin and walked closer to him. Behind her, Delara tensed, but Almira waved her hand to calm her guard. She was certain the Norrian wouldn't harm them. A beast he might be, but he'd defended a Ley in the middle of the siege. There was honor there.

"You must promise me not to kill the servants or anyone else. I'll have to trust you on this." Almira met his stare intently.

He was a little amused as he glanced at Delara, who refused to acknowledge him. He clicked his tongue as his eyes lingered on her guard's form. "Despite what *certain* people's opinions of me are, I'm not a murderer."

Delara scoffed.

That offended the man, and he turned crimson. "*Arrigo* is the murderer, not I and you know it!" Then he looked at the queen. "And you've not found him despite the months. Now he gains strength and allies!"

The intimidatingly large lord wasn't wrong, and she didn't blame him for his anger. It was justified. Arrigo's ability to elude them at every turn frustrated her just as equally.

"Yes, he does." Almira closed the distance between them.

"Majesty," Delara warned.

Ivar cut Delara's rebuke with a glare. "I'd not hurt her."

"Like you didn't harm the guards in the throne room?" Her guard replied while rolling her eyes.

Almira physically placed herself between the two. "*Fools* will always follow deceitful vows without understanding repercussions. It's in human nature to fall for the luring siren's call of false promises. It delights the imagination of the weak minded because they lack the balls to do the work themselves. They seek saviors, and in doing so, damn themselves in the process. Arrigo is the perfect conduit for such fancies."

Ivar observed her with a twitching cheek. "I can see why the king is so taken with you. You speak your mind quite boldly."

Almira opened her hand to Delara. "The key."

The guard's nostrils flared, and she shook her head. "Majesty."

"The key, my lady. His Lordship is not a murderer, you heard him." Almira didn't break eye contact with Ivar.

Delara slowly unstrapped the key ring from her waist and handed it to Almira. The queen took it, and Ivar raised his shackled hands. She breathed deeply, attempting bravery. It was not only her life she needed to protect, but the child.

"I have your word?" She gave herself credit for the steadiness of her voice.

Bold decisions, that was all she had left. She would do what she could—trapped in this castle with a body that betrayed her daily—to save her husband and his men from war.

"On my honor and that of House Benici," he said slowly, meeting her steady gaze with his own.

"I do hope you are as honorable as you claim to be, my lord," she whispered.

She inserted the key into his lock. The chains rattled open, and the shackles dropped loudly to the stone floor. He continued to hold his wrists out, bruised and raw, scarred from months of the iron cutting into his skin. His eyes didn't leave hers as he slowly opened his arms in a wide stretch.

"I wonder what the king would say to this," Ivar said with a slight smile.

She handed the key back to Delara. "He would be most upset, but I don't answer to the king. I have my own mind and I make my own decisions."

Ivar rubbed his wrists, still observing her. "Why don't you just kill him and rule the damn world?"

His words startled her. "Because, my lord, like you, I'm *not* a murderer," she said as she walked past him. "*And* I love him."

Ivar laughed, and it cut to Almira's heart. Her lover was out there, likely dodging axes and swords, and she could do little to protect him.

Almira paused and stared at him. "I'll have fresh clothes and a bath brought to you. You need a haircut and a shave. Perhaps we can even enjoy a dinner."

Delara reached into her pocket and tossed him a vial. It was a healing ointment. He deftly caught it in the air and studied the bottle, then met the guard's eyes in confusion. The lady equitably beheld him as if she'd not just been slightly kind to him.

The Norrian lifted his chin. "We're still *not* allies."

Almira placed her hand on the door to leave. "As long as we're not enemies."

Delara gave him one last glare and tossed her braid over her shoulder.

"How about conjugal visits? It's been an arduous time and things that before were appalling begin to lure," Ivar said as he inspected Delara appreciatively.

Before Almira could urge Delara not to fall for his bait, her guard looked at the queen with a blank and serene expression, and said, "Majesty, it'll be a challenge to bring a horse up the stairs, but we can attempt it if the Norrian wishes."

Ivar let out a belly laugh as they closed the door behind them.

The next night, a letter from Alton confessed a crushing defeat in the fields of Mineau. A thousand soldiers were dead. It sharply felt like the lingering notes Edgar would send her. How many more dead before one day it would be General Vine who would arrive with news of Alton's death? *No.*

Her fingers lingered on her map, and she swore she heard the Favia laughing from the corner of her room. She *must* end this war. She faced the shadows with sharp eyes and a set mouth. Almira was the fucking queen and she wouldn't let this happen again. She was certain this defeat was the growing gloom in her mind, that plaguing thought that something was wrong. She'd been right. Something was terribly wrong.

Shoving herself from the table, she yelled Nadim's name to begin preparations. Almira took extra care to ensure the meal was authentically Norrian. Roasted hares in a plum mint sauce, and duck fat confit potatoes, fried and seasoned with black coal salt. A stew of mashed carrots and coriander. Finally, a pint of the darkest ale she'd ever seen accompanied all of it.

Ley Wallace paced nervously next to her, and she requested that he calm himself.

"It's much too risky," he said in that nasal tone of his. Not meaning to tell her what to do, but still showing great displeasure in her choice.

"I must concur with the royal Ley," Nadim said. He stood calmly with his hands clasped before him. Today, he carried a small, curved blade with a jewel-encrusted handle.

Unnecessary, she thought.

"I've no husband at home for any other man to advice me what to do," she said hotly as she glared at them. "Much less *two*."

Ley Wallace drew near, his face drawn and haggard. "But

Majesty, this man is a *brute*. We should at least stay with you for the duration of the meal."

"So he can kill you too?" she bristled as she adjusted her skirts.

"Aye, I rather he kill *me* than you," Ley Wallace said with great sincerity.

"That's very sweet of you, Ley Wallace." She smiled, "But I'm certain the Norrian will not hurt me. Norrians revere the pregnant woman. I've read of their multiple statues of Orta the Wild, pregnant seventeen times, and still led armies to war."

His face reddened, and she dismissed the Ley. However, Nadim stayed to aid her with serving the meal. She knew he remained to guard her, but she didn't mention it and allowed his fretting.

She waited, as serenely as she could, for the prisoner. Sitting here, in this same dining room without Alton and his green eyes made her miss him deeply. She placed her hand against her swollen stomach and the child gently moved. Because Alton was out there, in muddy trenches, constantly at the mercy of feral arrows, she did this. She risked everything to end the war.

Sanaa and four black knights escorted Lord Ivar to the dinner quarters. He entered the room unshackled and refreshed. Finally, he looked like a nobleman. Despite being plain, his clothes were clean and someone had trimmed and styled the giant Norrian's hair. He was frighteningly massive and could still assassinate her with ease over the confit potatoes. He paused when he beheld the feast and found her smiling.

"Are you planning to kill me tomorrow morning, Majesty?" he joked.

Sanaa, who was also against this entire arrangement, stared at the man in disgust. She placed her hand on her ruby blade. "Your death will come sooner if you dare touch her," Sanaa's words were ice.

He smiled as he said in return, "I'm delighted by your choice in guards, Majesty. I say your fine captain would make a fitting Norrian warrior."

Sanaa's lips twisted. "I'm Suidian, born and raised, and I *will* kill—"

"*Cuzo*. It's alright. Lord Ivar is a gentleman, and I aim for a pleasant dinner. I'm sure he would love some familiar cuisine after his long imprisonment."

Sanaa glared at Ivar one final time and stepped away to allow them some privacy. Ivar raised a brow, then turned back to Almira.

"Where's my usual lovely custodian?" Ivar walked to the table and calmly pulled back a chair for her.

The queen sat with difficulty. With her extended belly, it was impossible to find an enjoyable position. "If you're inquiring about Lady Delara, the lady in question is on a small leave visiting her family on the western coast."

Ivar paused. "The western coast, really?" Then he stepped around her and took his seat with surprising elegance. "It must be a delight to see one's family."

"It must be," Almira said with a pointed look. "I, too, miss mine."

They were arriving this week, but he didn't need to know this. The Suidian escort left Zuri a week ago and was currently making its way across the world carrying *Nanai*, Hester, Lady Gita, and the children. Thebo would follow once Hira had safely sailed past Suid.

He arranged a linen napkin over his lap and offered her a glass of ale. She scrunched her nose, which made him laugh. "You've made notable efforts to seduce me into a peace treaty."

"I don't seduce." Almira draped her napkin over her gown and motioned for Nadim to begin the meal.

Her Keeper set the plate before Ivar and stared at him until the Norrian met his eyes.

"A room full of people wishing to slit my throat if you so much as cough, Majesty. I've never felt safer," Ivar chuckled.

"Nadim," Almira said in warning.

"Apologies, My Queen." The Keeper's nostrils flared, and he set the ale before the lord.

The Norrian took the ale, his massive hands dwarfing the large cup. He watched her over the rim. The bright fireplace brightened his crimson hair.

"What made you do it?" Ivar sipped his ale.

She looked up at him. "Marry the king?"

He nodded and set down his drink with a delightful sigh. She picked up her spoon and braced herself for the soup. The overcooked carrots (preferred in Norr) floated in her bowl.

"Lord Ivar doesn't know me, but I am, above all, dedicated to my kingdom," she drawled. "Loving my husband has been a benefit, but I would've ruled, regardless."

She took a spoonful and was relieved it was not horrid. Ivar chuckled and dug into his soup. The pause in his movements made her guess he delighted in the familiar flair.

"He killed your husband. I hope you recognize this," Ivar said quietly.

A part of her liked to pretend Alton was nowhere in the fields where Edgar died. She'd never asked him directly if it was his blade that ended Edgar. She didn't want to know. A little ignorance in one's life allotted room for happiness.

She opted for a measured answer. "He defeated Lord Edgar, yes. I'm aware."

The Norrian stared at her with hard, unfazed eyes. "I would've slit his throat as he slept."

Almira paused and contemplated her next words, "He tempted me a few nights. I'll admit that he drove me to an anger I didn't expect."

She figured she'd have to reveal a little about herself to gain his trust. It was a tactic her father taught her, though he seldom gave anything of himself. He was a great pretender, posturing with dexterity.

Ivar finished his soup and cleaned the residue from his beard. "And why didn't you?"

Nadim took their bowls as she met the Norrian's eyes, opting for sincerity.

"It would've destabilized the kingdom. I've buried my parents, my brother, and a husband. I think I've worn enough veils; don't you?" She cocked her head, and he gave her a small smile.

"Did you know that in Norr, women don't veil themselves?" he asked.

"I do," Almira nodded. "It's an old, antiquated custom; I'll admit as much. I questioned it myself the first time they made me to do it. Why should women hide under a cloth while men didn't? But then I realized, a veil is a socially permissible way a woman can mourn and reflect on her emotions. Yet we do not encourage men to reflect on their own loss and turmoil. They rage against it, and so it feels foreign to have feelings of loss and emptiness. They react in a manner that might not be conducive to their mental wellbeing. My father never granted himself acceptance of the loss of my mother and it morphed him into a cold being. And others…" She met Ivar's eyes. "Others rage because they never mourned the loss of a sister."

He flinched. His wound seeped to the ground because he'd never allowed it to cauterize.

"We don't speak of the dead while we eat," he said in a sharp tongue. "The dead cannot eat and so we don't call forth their spirit to gloat over what we still enjoy."

It was a custom she didn't know. It surprised her to learn something about the Norrian way of life.

"I apologize," she said sincerely.

They placed the main course on the table, and the combination of mint with plum invaded her senses. Ivar immediately dug into the roasted hare.

She changed her tactic as she saw he enjoyed the fare. "It's a pleasant thing to enjoy a meal, especially with those we've often thought of as enemies."

He glanced at her. "You continue claiming Norr is not your enemy. Yet, as we sit before this fine, slightly bland dinner, your beloved kills my people. Your diplomatic angle is bold but could use some help."

Regardless of his critique, he ate heartily. Annoyed, she stood and startled the men. She took the salt, and Ivar paused as he watched her. She slowly walked to him with the dispenser in her hand.

"We encounter problems everywhere, my lord. Things that are not to our liking. It doesn't mean the situation is lost. It might simply mean that," she looked pointedly at him as she sprinkled salt over his hare, "it needs some tweaking. You wouldn't toss the hare just because it's bland. You would merely add salt."

He watched her as she sat down and leaned back in his chair. "You're very good," he stated, a bemused smile crossing his own face.

Almira took a bite of the hare and stopped. She wiped her mouth and smiled. "You're right. It's bland."

He watched as she salted her meal, his fingers drummed on the table. "Why won't you let the North be independent?"

She breathed deeply and set down her fork. "You're independent. Same as Suid and Istok."

His face became hard, his nails dug into the grains of the wooden table. From the corner of her eye, she saw Sanaa move behind him. "Suid and Istok have representation in *you*. Norr has no representation."

Almira raised her chin and leveled him with a look. "How many men would you like me to marry, my lord? I have just one cunt."

At that, he threw his head back and laughed. "Oh, I can certainly tell why he loves you. You're a *dragon*, my lady."

Almira flustered as she recalled Alton's first words to her, how he taunted her and teased her. How his name for her slowly changed to one of endearment. To hear it from another man was hurtful. She strengthened her resolve. She wanted Alton *back* and she wouldn't idly wait for news of his death. This bastard stood in the way when she wished him safe.

"I want friendship between our countries. A treaty that is mutually beneficial." She swallowed and looked for the bribe. The one that came to her when the word of Alton's defeat reached her. One she was afraid of saying out loud, but the more she thought on it, the more it seemed like the correct path. "Perhaps one day my child will marry yours."

Sanaa's head snapped up, and her eyes narrowed. She trusted her *cuzo* with many things, but this was something she felt Sanaa would *actually* tell the king to dissuade her. Ivar shook his head, still amused. Not realizing she was earnest.

"You bargain with your child? You haven't even *birthed* it."

When she didn't respond, he stopped smiling and gawked at her. "Are you serious?"

"*Cuzo!*" Sanaa hissed.

Almira, flushed in fury, looked at her and demanded, "Quiet."

Sanaa's face was of pure rage and Almira knew the argument later would be great. Ivar was still stunned, unperturbed by the power struggle. The queen turned back to him and nodded.

"I wouldn't jest about my child." Almira clasped her palms under her enormous belly. "I'm in earnest. I shall birth an heir to the throne. You shall father an heir to Norr. A union would be most beneficial."

He contemplated the offer as he studied her. "You don't even have the support of your captain, much less the king. He'll not agree."

Almira's hands shook. Had she made a mistake? She'd placed her child on a bargaining table. To consider something and to do something were two different things. One day she would have to orchestrate the child's marriage, but she hoped that day would be far in the future. She'd just set down the comfortably curled baby in her belly before the feet of Norr. She thought she would vomit.

"You leave the king to me," she said with a certainty she didn't possess.

"He would rather cut off his balls than have his child marry a child of mine." Ivar leaned forward and smiled. "But, I'd like to be there when you tell him."

She would delay that as much as she could.

"Will you agree? Join our houses? Is that a good enough *seat* for Norr?" She stared him down as her heartbeat erratically fluttered against her throat.

She idly wondered how much of herself she would have to give for the world to stop its madness. And what would happen when it was finally enough? Who would she become?

"Aye indeed it is. A most generous offer, majesty." He leaned his chin on his palm and perused her. "One problem. I've no heir and I'll not make plans for myself until Arrigo of House Markey is dead."

Almira slowly nodded. "Fair enough. Why don't we strike a deal—hear me out—I shall travel to Istok for the birth of my child. After the birth, Lady Delara herself will escort you home safely. Discuss the offer with your people."

Ivar raised a brow. He was hard to read as he considered her offer. "Really. You'll let me go with your little guard?"

"Captain Sanaa?" Almira glanced at her *cuzo*.

"Aye, Majesty, I heard you," Sanaa said in a snarled tone.

Almira ignored her and watched Ivar. "There. You have my word. I swear on the Favia."

She could attest she heard hissing laughter in the air.

He contemplated her as he stretched back. "What caused you to hate war as fiercely as you do? I wouldn't give up my child for anyone and yet you would give your own child for the sake of peace."

Almira's hands instinctively went for her belly. The past few months made her violently protective over the little one. She would burn the entire world down for their safety, but she always kept such thoughts to herself.

"We should *all* hate war. And I don't give my child away, my lord. They will be the crown that will rule this land when our time ends. Such title, such responsibility, comes at a substantial cost." She felt herself crumbling. Tears were pushing against her eyes. "Trifling things such as vengeance are not for the crown to feel. We must separate selfish sentiment for the good of the people. Right now, as you complain about your hare, there's a young man lying in a field somewhere. It doesn't matter if he's a Norrian or a Ouesterner." She took a deep breath. "The blood is the same color. He lies on the grass staring one last time at the night sky filled with stars. It's his final moment. *You* and *I* have killed him. He is one of many."

She stood up and stared down at him. She was finished with this meal.

"If I have to sacrifice my child's happiness to stop more deaths, know that I damn well *will*. I'll not sit here in this warm castle awaiting news anymore."

She left the dining hall and stormed back to her quarters. Sanaa was hard on her heels along with half a dozen Red Guards. She entered her rooms intending to slam the door behind her, but Sanaa shoved herself in and closed it with a harsh bang.

"I'm sorry!" Almira cried as she desperately clutched her belly.

Sanaa stared at her wildly. "Are you mad? Have you lost all sense?"

But Almira couldn't register her words. All she felt was the baby within her, innocent to her bargain.

"The king won't agree," Sanaa said harshly.

Almira sunk into her chair and pressed her face into her hands. "She'll wish she was born from another."

"Damn right she will." Sanaa stood over her, her anger bristling out of her in waves. "How *could* you? How could you damn this baby so?"

She grasped her stomach and sobbed into her sleeve. Alton would fight her on this, he wouldn't understand, no one would. Not even Sanaa. Almira wished she didn't care; she wished her father hadn't raised her as he did. She wished she could be as cold and unfeeling as he'd been. He'd married her off to Edgar without thought. It was a good match, that's all that mattered.

"Everything I do is for…" the expression died in her throat and her face crumbled. The words that once gave her a sense of purpose and comfort drowned her. "*Fuck* the kingdom."

Sanaa sighed and kneeled before her with a hard face. Almira looked at her best friend and took a sharp breath.

"Promise me something and swear it on your life."

Sanaa said nothing. She hardly moved.

"If I die. If Alton dies. You take the child, you protect it. Until the child is ready to take their rightful place on the throne. Swear it to me." Almira grasped Sanaa's shoulder. "Swear it."

Sanaa's face turned to pity, and a great sadness overtook her. "You don't realize what you've done, do you? You've placed this child on the bargaining table. You've named its fate. This child no longer belongs to you. It belongs to the Favia. And they seldom play fair."

Isabelle Olmo

Chapter Sixteen

HIRA

Iguanta was situated on the east coast of Suid, an oasis for nonconformists from all five territories. It was a seedling of debauchery and hooliganism. A shanty town that spread over the sand and uneven ground, a place where seedy merchants and pirates frequented. The homes were shacks with plaster and clay roofs, which needed frequent replacement given the assault of the salty sea air. Children played in the shore dunes, barefoot and underfed. Their voices carried the joviality of ones not yet affected by the underbelly of the lifestyles that surrounded them.

The port also called for repair. Docks of rotting planks speckled the coastline, covered in ropes that required oiling and mending. Cats scurried after mice and whatever scraps of fish the anglers discarded. Dogs seemed to have a task as they walked themselves from place to place, chasing their favorite generous vendor.

Despite the early morning hour, Hira could hear the rowdy sounds of drunkenness as she disembarked the Sea Wife. The crew was delighted with their arrival at the port city. The men jeered at a passing pleasure-giver. She had a shaved head—like all pleasurers. Bangles covered her arm to the elbow, an indication that she specialized in *everything*.

From the dock, Hira examined the commander as he contracted services to fix the ship, including the window to her quarters. He seemed relaxed and relieved to arrive in such a city. She also couldn't help but study the way his trousers fit nicely against his backside. After the battle last night, she'd lingered in her bed thinking of his shape and the way his eyes darkened when he regarded her. She now understood that some of her reactions to his words were born out of a confusion of feelings. She couldn't deny that found him very interesting, even desirable.

"Many people find it surprising to learn that, as a boy, he would read his brother's poems," a female voice said, startling Hira.

It surprised her to find, who she could only assume was, Captain Jutia Gunn of the Night Serpent. The woman was raven-haired, with pale skin and crystalline blue eyes. She wore an intricate hat with a single feather, and leather trousers that accentuated her sharp curves. Her body and face whispered allurement making her the most openly sexual person Hira ever beheld.

The captain took off her hat, twirled it in her hand, and bowed with a charming smile. "We've not been properly introduced, my lady. I'm Captain Jutia Gunn, second cousin to the commander."

"A pleasure, my lady," Hira returned with a smile. There was a certain delight in once more being in the company of fellow women.

They shook hands, and Hira found the woman's grip was strong and sure. Jutia set her hat back on her head to shield from the morning sun.

"It's Captain, if you will. I've bled for that title," Jutia said with a playful wink.

Military titles were to be respected, especially in Istok. Hira blushed. She should've known better. The captain must be a fine sailor if her uncle approved of her captainship. Afterall, he was hard to please. She must be ferocious indeed. Hira felt submersed in jealousy towards the captain for she herself would rather captain a ship, shout at the men, battle sea pirates, and live her life as she pleased.

"Of course, Captain. Apologies," Hira said.

Captain Jutia's eyes were cool and undeterred. She studied Hira with amusement and Hira could only image what she thought. That Hira was an inexperienced girl who was lucky enough to inherit the title of High Seat. Jutia brought a cigar to her lips and lit it, then offered Hira one from her case. Hira declined. The last thing she wished was to cough and make a fool of herself in front of such a woman. She turned back to the commander, who'd finished his bargaining.

"You've known the commander since childhood?" Hira asked.

Jutia leaned against a crate and crossed her booted legs, openly appraising the commander's taut form. "Aye, my lady. He's changed a bit, I can say that much. Filled out in all the *right* places."

She winked at Hira in conspiratorial amusement. Hira tried not to blush, but the captain had obviously seen Hira admiring the commander's physique.

"How has it been for you? Quite a change, I imagine. From Red Guard to High Lady," Jutia commented before she took another long drag from her cigar.

Tucking a wild strand of red hair behind her ear, Hira looked away. "I was born to be High Lady. I'm afraid there's no escaping it."

Jutia chuckled and pulled from her coat a small bottle of liquor and drank deeply from it. "I didn't mean to mock your plight," Jutia said as she tipped her bottle for another pull.

Hira found Commander Justan watching them with slight curiosity when she dared her next glance at him. Jutia noticed and let out a sigh. She straightened up and dusted her leather trousers. She looked down at Hira with a dimpled smile.

"I might as well enjoy Iguanta," the captain said.

Having insufficient knowledge of how to open up to someone she so immediately admired, Hira became nervous. "I didn't commend you, Captain. You fought bravely last night."

The captain shrugged as she perused the bustling streets. "It has little to do with bravery. Had the pirates succeeded, we would have perished at sea. That would've denied me the quality cock this city consistently provides."

Hira laughed nervously, confused by the sudden impropriety,

but also delighted by the sincerity of it. It was like being with the Red Guard once more. She wished to invite her to have ale, but she didn't want to ruin Jutia's plans of… quality cock.

"If you'll excuse me, *my lady*." The captain winked and strolled past Hira.

Jutia walked to Commander Justan, and their interaction transfixed Hira. The change in their body language was instantaneous. The commander looked down at her as the captain said soft words to him. He glanced at Hira, who reddened in embarrassment at being caught watching them. Then Jutia chuckled a throaty laugh and slid her hand over the commander's chest. It was a caress. Then something happened that Hira didn't foresee. He laughed *with* her and grasped her leather-clad derriere in an all-too familiar manner. Her gloved fingers went to his neck, and she stroked it, then she strode away as he watched her retreat.

The display flushed Hira scarlet and she had to look away. Her mind blanked as she tried to speculate. Obviously, the commander and the captain were involved, and Hira was the ignorant, stupid girl who lusted after him and could never ever be someone like Captain Jutia Gunn. She imagined they would laugh, naked and tangled in sheets, discussing Hira's subpar capabilities. She wished to die.

The commander came to Hira, and she met his eyes, hoping he didn't see how embarrassed she was. She was familiar with the flirtatious manners of flings, but she hadn't expected the commander to be involved with any sailor within the armada. Also, she'd just imagined him and his lover naked, that did no favors for her freckled flesh.

"Don't let her scare you. She likes to talk big," he said.

"I don't scare easily. However, your cousin is quite interesting." Hira shielded her face from the sun, but also from the embarrassing conversation at hand, and looked away.

He stood before her, effectively blocking the sun. "She's always been."

Hira nodded, still sensing her face was flushed. "Is she your lover?" She couldn't even meet his eyes.

He laughed a little. "She's my fiancé."

"You're *betrothed*?" Hira stared at him incredulously.

Justan, unaware of her shock, nodded and packed his pipe. "Ah, yes. Since childhood."

She felt hurt. Hurt for *what*? He'd not led her on or trespassed on her sexually. Still, a part of her thought she'd seen interest in him, that a part of him enjoyed her company. All the while, he frolicked with another. She gathered all her courage and sought not to be deeply disappointed. What a little fool she was. What a *child*.

Clearing her throat, she attempted nonchalance. "Why haven't you married?"

Down by the end of the docks, almost reaching the streets, Jutia laughed as she greeted men. She was so carefree and wild, so desirable... no wonder the commander loved her.

"Because I don't want to and neither does she." Commander Justan followed her line of sight.

A perplexed Hira shook her head. "But you're lovers."

He chuckled.

It was like she hardly understood the complexities of human relations. Naturally, she'd taken on lovers, but a betrothal was different. A betrothal meant a union. A public announcement.

He smiled. "At times, yes, my lady."

She tried not to continue the conversation that caused her such mortification, but her curiosity was all-consuming.

"I don't understand," she admitted, suddenly realizing that Justan had to be at least a decade older than herself. She knew her ears must be cherry red. He was a full-grown man with experiences and stories, while she knew was ignorant of plenty.

His tone changed, as if he were trying to explain something that was evident. "We're not in love with each other. It's as simple as that," he said with surprising sincerity. "It affords us liberties to continue the farce. She gets to live the life she wants, and I get to live the life I want. We respect one another and, when the occasion calls, we couple."

Hira had to look away. He didn't. He still watched her, and she resented the fact he could be so calm in such a scandalous declaration. Jutia was a lady of a house and he was a lord with titles.

Was the entire world allowed to do what they liked except for Hira?

"Respect is essential," Hira whispered, twisting her hands.

"Aye. She's earned her captainship fair and square. She's a brilliant swordswoman and strategist and holds the respect of her men."

Gathering her bravery, Hira acted worldly about this entire calamity. Though she wasn't certain why she looked at it as a calamity. She tossed her hair back, attempting very much to look unaffected.

"With such a woman, Commander, you're a fool to dally," she said and her voice came steady. She didn't allow him a moment to respond, and smiled brightly. It was a falsity. "Right. I'll see about this town then."

"I'll escort you," he said. "I'll escort you," he said.

Before she could open her mouth to deny him, he slid on his coat, snatched his pipe, and followed her.

Chapter Seventeen

JUSTAN

The walk down to the city was a familiar route for him. The temptation to glance back at the woman next to him was too strong. He couldn't help it. There was something about the way she stared ahead, attempting to mask her annoyance at being escorted, that absolutely delighted him.

Two men, drunk as they could be, staggered before them and fell in a heap of laughter on the ground. Hira startled, but straightened her shoulders and walked past them. The lady was determined to appear worldly, and nothing like the girl who'd lived most of her life trapped in Korkoran. It amused him greatly.

"It tends to get rowdy," he said before he pulled from his pipe.

Her lovely mouth tightened, and she kept her eyes on the road ahead. "I've survived *your* company. I think I'll be fine, Commander."

He laughed at that, which earned him a glare from the lady. Something he found he didn't mind. There was a subtle tact to her glares. An innocence within them, like a petulant child that hid behind the woman she loved to parade for the world. He suspected she was still learning things about herself. Digging into her likes and dislikes. There was a part of her that lived in perpetual wonderment, and because he'd long lost his wonder of the world, it was intoxicating to behold.

He led her down one of his favored streets, mostly because of the liveliness. It was a mistake. The road smelled like a mix of vomit and ale, but also cinnamon; the port's largest export. Shipping boxes filled with cinnamon and other exotic spices left the port daily, and the scent combined with the evening's *delights*.

They stepped gingerly over and around the puddles of questionable substances while peering into different shops. Some had chocolates and sweets, others had cheeses aged in cellars, and others sold silks and gold chains.

But it was her face which he enjoyed. How she peeked into the windows, studying the wheels of matured cheeses and giving kind smiles to the vendors who grouchily stared back at her from behind the glass. His suspicion was right. She'd lived her entire life trapped in Korkoran with little chance of seeing the world beyond.

He recalled how her family seldom allowed her outside the gates, and when she was finally granted leave, Korkoran Knights followed her every move. He supposed being a Red Guard took up most of her time in Easima. And despite her theoretical freedom, she still had the queen and Captain Sanaa watching over her with eagle eyes. Her freedom had only been an illusion, and he understood such emotions more keenly than most.

Justan looked into the window of the cheese monger and asked, "Would you like to taste the Suidian Blue? Smells like feet, tastes like heaven."

She seemed slightly disarmed by his words and glanced away from him, then back at the merchant. The man wordlessly sliced her a small piece, and she took it.

"Only if it can be dunked in honey," she said with assuredness.

He grimaced at the thought, but the cheese monger beamed at her in approval. "We have the best honey. Produced from the northern fields where the lavender grows. Gives it a nice floral taste."

The man plopped a pot of honeycomb before them both. The sticky sauce dripped over the edge and Hira slicked it up with her cheese, then brought it to her mouth, making a delighted sound. Justan was a little fascinated by her actions, so much so he nearly missed the vendor waving a small piece for Justan to take.

"Thank you," Justan said as he took the cheese. "No honey for me, though."

"Don't be a bore, Commander," Hira said as she leaned against the counter. Her eyes studied him with amused appreciation. She licked her fingers, all the while watching him. "I command you to try it."

Each time she responded with "I command this", or "I command that", a strange sort of flippancy danced through his stomach. He didn't like being told what to do—he damn well hated it—but there was something about the way she said it. As if she wasn't comfortable yet with her commands, but he knew she soon would be. Strangely, he wished to witness her growth, but knew there was little chance of that.

Slowly, he dabbed the cheese against the honey pot and brought it to his mouth, expecting nothing but madness to descend upon his senses. What he found was paradise. His eyes widened as the mixture of flavors resonated over his tongue. He stared back at Hira, who watched him, pleased with herself.

"I believe you've discovered something new about yourself," she said in that flippant tone of hers. He'd learned it meant she was ecstatic to win this round and delighted in slapping his face with the victory.

He would not give her the satisfaction. "It was fine. For a Suidian custom."

She handed the vendor a few coins for his samples and walked past Justan. The smirk on her lips said more than any words could.

They made their way to the market and lost themselves in the shouts of vendors, the scent of fish, and the pleasure-givers lounging by doorframes, smiling at them both and beckoning them to enter for morning delights.

"Are any of them in your acquaintance?" the lady asked with mock innocence.

Yes. But he wouldn't relish her with the truth.

"No."

The lady, a tiny minx with a deadly arm, clasped her hands before her. "So many that you forget them, Commander?"

Justan looked away and did not answer, especially when one girl called out, "Commander Justan, won't you join us once more? He fought the urge not to brighten under such a blatant reveal of his lie. He'd inadvertently took his frequented route and led himself into an embarrassment.

Hira didn't comment further, but when their fingers accidentally brushed against one another while walking, she quickly pulled her hand away. He'd startled at the intimacy of touching hands. Hand holdings were between lovers and those married, not for acquaintances who disliked each other.

She spotted a particular vendor, and her face lit with excitement. "Conjan!"

Before he could heed her caution, she rushed ahead, and left him to jog after her quick steps. Conjan was a firm fleshy fruit that was tart and seedless. The scent of the ripe fruit sharpened a memory he'd not allotted himself to peruse in many years.

"Boys! Come down from the tree!"

It was their mother.

Justan was no more than ten and seldom listened to his mother. The massive conjan tree that grew in their garden was perfect for climbing. The twisted limbs were thick and inviting and the boys spent many afternoons attempting to reach the ripest fruit the crows had not yet devoured. Justan was obsessed with mixing the juice of the crop with stolen liquor from their father's cellars.

"We best listen to her," he said.

"She worries too damn much," Justan said.

And the memory was gone. He felt a tightness in his chest. He didn't like to linger in memories of his brother. It was a useless pursuit.

"Commander," the Lady Hira watched his reticence with intrigue.

He took a sharp breath. "I don't like conjan. Too tart."

She raised a red brow. "Is there anything you *do* like?"

He didn't answer, but provided her with a small knife for her to cut into her fruit. She, the tease, pulled out her own Ruby Blade and brandished it to show she'd no need of his musty weapon.

"Almira and I used to eat them under the walnut tree when we were young," she said with a smile.

The relaxation in her words stirred something warm in him, like a swift memory of childhood that brings comfort. He'd witnessed the act she described, and the memory left him a little breathless. Truths carried within him flittered out of the tight fist of his mind.

The vendor, observing the lady, set eyes on her knife. The commander sensed a feeling of dread enter his body. Hira was too wide-eyed to notice.

"I know such a blade. Queen's Red Guard," he said with a brown twisted finger.

His eyes clouded with old age, but he stared at her knowingly. Justan's stomach dropped, and he came closer should he need to threaten the man. But Hira didn't seem to understand the dangers surrounding her.

She nodded. "Aye."

Blasted girl!

"You stole it?" The vendor looked delighted, showing a mouth of rotted teeth.

Hira pulled her cloak tighter. "Gifted by the Queen herself."

Her little tone, that chesty enunciation of pride that covered her sentences, was a sure giveaway. Did she believe the world would respect her based on the lineage in her blood? Was she truly so ignorant? One look at her face confirmed it.

"*Hira*," Justan snapped, but she ignored him.

He'd have to drag her through the streets if she insisted on waving a flag that said "*Kidnap me because I'm the Queen's cousin!*" throughout all of Iguanta.

The man eyed her carefully. "I didn't mean to insinuate anything, my lady."

"I'm *not* a lady," she said, flushed with frustration.

Oh, *gods of the sea*. He tossed a coin to the vendor and grasped her arm, then pulled her away. The lady struggled, as he knew she would. She glared up at him with snarled pink lips, and his groin tightened.

"How dare you!" she hissed.

Justan didn't let go and navigated her until they reached a small pocket where they could speak. He turned her to him, but before he could chastise her, she poked a finger into his chest. Sharply. He'd have a bruise in a few hours.

"Might I remind you, *Commander*, that—"

"At the rate you strut around with your paltry words, waving your royal blade about, you won't have to tell anyone who you are. They'll know, alright!"

Her cheeks turned scarlet with a mixture of anger and hurt. How she enjoyed pretending she was not the second most important woman in the kingdom.

"I can defend myself," she sneered.

"This is *not* Treveri, or Zuri, or even Easima. This is Iguanta. The only port on the continent where Agamorian ships from the Free Isle dock. You're a tasty morsel for any keen Free Islander who figures out who you are. You'll be taken straight to Agamora and used as a bargaining piece, causing further misery, adding to the war that the kingdom doesn't need," he said, out of breath as he shoved his hands into his hair in frustration. "What trouble you are."

She flinched, and he instantly felt sorry. He'd have to follow her to hell itself at this rate. He saw himself getting kidnapped for the sake of keeping her alive, since she had no survival skills. How he wished to tell her the truth, how she was in a nest of vipers and demons with their narrowed eyes placed firmly on her.

"No one knows who I am and all you've done is make it obvious," she said with a sharpened face.

Her hands were curled, and he was certain she daydreamed of scratching his cheeks bloody until they sported matching scars. He wouldn't mind that bit of foreplay.

"Ah yes. *I* did *all* of that." He couldn't help himself. She got under his skin until he felt the need to rip it off and lay raw before her. At least he could stop this madness.

"You'll not grab me again," she stated resolutely. "I can find my way around alone, thank you. And if *anyone* tries to set a finger on me, I'll split their belly in twain—*you* included."

Justan had to take sharp breaths to calm himself. He'd made a promise and couldn't endanger the plan so callously. It could imperil Quent and certainly her, despite her infuriating nature. When he opened his eyes, he found her staring at him, with the flush on her cheeks ebbing.

"Oh, why do we fight so?" she asked, tossing the half-eaten conjan on the ground for the ravens to peck.

Why indeed? Because she was a stubborn woman and a peevish child, all at the same time, and he was going mad with all the worries housed within his head. Thrown between what he must do, what he should do, and what he *wanted* to do.

"I don't do what I do to annoy you or question your authority," he said lowly with controlled rage. "See that man there?" He indicated the Norrian sporting furs casually staring at them.

She glanced, to her credit, imperceptibly. When she looked back at Justan, she nodded slightly.

"His eyes are pinned on you. Now, it just might be that you entice him, but maybe he suspects who you are." He sighed and scratched his beard. "Allowing someone to concern themselves with your wellbeing doesn't make you weak."

His statement startled her, as well as did himself. Perhaps he gave away too much, but he was clumsy with his words, as if they were foreign objects never felt by his tongue.

"And who takes care of you, Commander?" she asked, her eyes so bright blue he almost flinched.

There was a change to their tones and Justan's anger officially abated, sinking down to his feet, confounding his brain and body. His breathing hitched and his hand dropped to his side, slacking his shoulders. In this moment he felt strongly like his true self, it was too close to the edge, to showing her the plains of his mind. He pulled back, terrified of the implications of such a discussion. Petrified she would see him like no one had seen him for over fifteen years. He might be free to walk the markets of Iguanta, but he was still very much the boy in the tower.

"I didn't inherit a country. I'm simply the commander of

your armada. As you've made it clear, you can replace me if you wish and I would be nothing more than another noble in your court." He looked away from her because her eyes softened and the dangers of himself outweighed the dangers in Iguanta. "Take this street, stick to the walls, and look everywhere before you turn. Stay armed and aware. Anyone touches you… well, you know what to do. Afterwards, run back to the ship and I'll find you there. You, above everyone else in all of Istok, must live. That should be your constant priority."

He turned from her, unable to be near her for another moment. His hands shook violently and the shifting of his heart felt strange within a chest so long left dormant. He lingered in the market, ensuring she took the route he suggested. She did and from then on, her eyes were sharp and cautious. Good. Shoulders slumped, he walked past the merchants, past the beggars, and the whores. What once invigorated him and provided him a distraction now soured his mood.

Finding a small corner, he smoked five cigars and wearily watched all those that meandered the streets. Hira's scent painted his insides, and trapped him in delusions he had no business perusing. He downed an ale before he stumbled into his favorite establishment and into the distracting arms of Cevilla.

Chapter Eighteen

HIRA

Inexplicably confused, Hira stormed through Iguanta, rampaging thoughts within her mind. She bounced between violent dislike for Justan Seaver and confusion over his words. She felt he hid something deep within, and that bothered her more than anything. Just this morning she'd spied him speaking to Quent, bent down to stare at him eye to eye. There was a softness in how he doted on his little brother, and the way in which he worried about the safety of the crew. Then there was the part of him that was clearly a knave.

She couldn't comprehend his fretting over her wellbeing, as if someone tasked him to protect her. As if *her* life was in *his* hands. Perplexing man. He continued to catechize her every decision, chastising her when she'd done nothing wrong other than provide niceties to commoners. On many occasions, while living in Treveri, she visited the market with her mother and conversed with vendors. Nothing happened.

His insinuation that *she* was in danger. Ha! That someone would *dare* kidnap the Balikian heir was laughable. Almira would bring down the entire Verdian army along with the Istokian armada and blow the Free Isle out of the water.

Still, his words slightly frightened her. No one had ever

kidnapped her before. Or threatened to. So, she covered herself well and studied each inch of her path, each face that looked in her direction. The blasted commander made her feel unsafe, and she didn't like that. She didn't enjoy herself very much after their argument or his feeble attempt at an explanation.

A lively tavern caught her attention, and she noticed the crew of sailors within. Her Istokian sailors seemed to revel in it, so she entered to take in the ambiance. It was a large establishment with quality ale and affordable grub.

Loneliness covered her as she watched others laugh and cavort with one another. They shared stories she'd never partaken in. It was a good quarter hour before a barmaid noticed her and Hira quickly ordered an ale. The maid stared at her curiously with a raised brow. Justan's words sharply entered her mind, and she wondered if they could all see through her. See the fine shape of her nose and know her for what she was. Someone who didn't belong.

"Put her on my tab, Penny," Captain Jutia said as she took a seat across from Hira.

Hira brightened in relief. "That's not needed, Captain."

Penny ignored Hira and obeyed the captain, then went to get the order. Jutia planted her boots on top of the table. A mannerism that allowed her to fit in with the rest of the rambunctious crowd.

"My pleasure," Jutia said, waving her hand as she inhaled her cigar.

Hira's envy towards the woman morphed to new heights. There was something alluring about the captain, a sexual undercurrent to everything she did. No one would dare kidnap *her*, would they? *She* wouldn't be yelled at by egotistical commanders.

"How did you gain the men's respect?" Hira asked.

Jutia chuckled as the blue smoke covered her face. "Men seldom respect us despite our abilities. At times, they fear us, but respect is something they hand out only selectively to women. Unless we remind them of their mothers, daughters, or sisters, we're subhuman. Don't you agree, my lady?"

She sounded like Almira. It was like a rant the queen would have after a War Council.

"Please call me Hira. We're both ladies. I rather we capitalize with such familiarity." Hira leaned forward simply to be closer to her presence.

Jutia smiled and blew out smoke. "I must first apologize, *Hira*. I've not been around civilized society for many years. Drinking, smoking, cursing, and impropriety are a commonality of my life."

Again, jealousy. It burned in the pit of Hira's stomach. "But you're high born."

Penny brought the ale, and Hira sipped, enjoying the freshness of the barley.

Jutia tapped her cigar, and the ash fell on the floor. "I'm not *your* type of high born. I didn't inherit a country. I was born in a noble house in Ciraton, raised by Garians on my father's side."

"Ciraton," Hira said softly. "My cousin is the Lady of Ciraton. Lady Furia. I've not seen her since we were children."

Jutia slowly smiled. "Aye. The Lady of the White Tower. I believe that's what they call her."

Hira nodded and took another sip of her ale. "What house are you?"

Jutia glanced about the room, then back at Hira, inhaling her cigar once more. "Justan's father gave me the Seaver name. He was good friends with my family."

"Is that how you ended up... committed to the commander?" Hira said with a weak smile.

It was wiser to be honest if they were engaging in open conversation. Best wash the wound with soapy water and endure the discomfort. Though she didn't quite grasp why it should hurt her so when she was so confounded by the commander.

Jutia savored her ale, watching Hira from the top of her rim. Her blue eyes were bright and clear, despite the imbibements. "I see he spoke to you. Care to tell me *his* side of the story?"

A little confused, Hira explained what he'd shared. Jutia listened quietly. Every so often she smoked and drank, but her eyes remained preternaturally still.

"I appreciate your sincerity. I'm unaccustomed to it," Jutia said as she stubbed her cigar against the sole of her boot, watching the ash smear with the saddest face. Her countenance changed so drastically that Hira felt she'd gained access to a chapter of Jutia's book not meant for public consumption.

"Forgive me, but is it not the truth?" Hira asked in a low tone.

Jutia gave a bitter sort of smile before she continued, "Yes, it's the truth. It's Justan's truth and, at the end of the day, it's what matters."

Commander Justan chose that moment to enter the bar, and both women turned to watch him. He went straight for Penny. He pulled her into his arms, and she squealed in delight. A few other maids went to him, all accepting his kisses and greetings. Hira's stomach twisted. Torn between something she wouldn't dare name, which mingled with hurt over his lingering words. She regarded Jutia as this happened, but the captain remained relaxed and unconcerned.

"I don't understand," Hira said.

Jutia smiled and took a gulp of her ale. "That's because you've never been in love."

The captain pulled another rolled tobacco and lit it. She glanced imperceptibly at Commander Justan. Her eyes softly lingered on his form. As if she wished for him. As if she couldn't get to him, though he shared the same space.

"You *love* him?" Hira asked with a slight surprise.

Jutia made a noise of agreement. "The lies we tell to protect ourselves are the most important lies we ever tell."

Hira floundered, looking between the two. Justan unaware. Jutia deeply desiring him. Hira was in the middle, a child witnessing adult play. "But... he said you didn't love him."

Jutia took her time answering. Her fingers slightly shook as she brought the cigar to her lips before she said, "That's Justan's truth."

The lady attempted to wrap her thoughts around this contorted notion. Over this devastating theater. That someone would conceal their feelings for self-preservation was something she'd never considered.

"You told him you didn't love him," Hira said, and Jutia nodded. "But you *do* love him."

"*That's* Jutia's truth."

Hira watched uncomfortably when a beautiful Suidian woman came to Commander Justan. This must be Cevilla, whom Quent spoke of. She was indeed stunning, with a long neck, soft shoulders, and skin like the night sky. Justan embraced her with vigor, kissing her openly and with passion.

"What is the queen like? Her mother was a legendary beauty. Has she become as lovely as Cevilla?" Jutia's eyes were on the display.

Hira looked back at Jutia. "The queen is not her mother."

She was heavily relieved by the change of conversation. It was intrusive and not Hira's business. It was most improper and, despite her desire for impropriety, she realized even *she* had limits.

"I've seen the portrait of Lady Lamya. She was quite stunning, like all that come from the first people. They can't help it, can they?" Jutia smirked. Her dark mood seemed to abate.

"Have you not met the queen?" Hira sipped more of her ale, enjoying the last bits in the bottom and wishing for another, but Penny remained otherwise *occupied*.

"I've not had that pleasure. If she's not a beauty, then she's a tempest." Jutia bit her lip and glanced at Hira with a wink.

Hira smiled. "How do you know?"

Justan kissed Cevilla desperately in the background, as if he wished to escape into her mouth. Such an exhibit was impossible to ignore. Jutia, however, carefully protected herself and kept her eyes on Hira.

"I keep up with the times," Jutia said as she downed the last of her ale. "The moment her husband dies, she proposes marriage to the man responsible for killing him. She conquers Easima with a dress, wins the king's heart, and slices the throat of the man who plotted against her. She *must* be a tempest."

Hira looked away from Justan's shenanigans. "She's a tempest alright."

"Are you like her, my lady?" Jutia's tone was that of curiosity and amusement.

"I am *nothing* like Almira."

For starters, Almira would never allow herself to be in a place such as this. Much less having conversations with a woman like Captain Jutia or lusting after a commander under her service betrothed to another while he frolicked with many more. *Especially* after he dared speak to her in the manner he did.

Cevilla led Justan up to the private quarters. She tentatively looked at Jutia, but she watched Hira with a slight smile. Hira flushed at being caught staring at the commander and his recreational activities. She could only imagine what the captain felt.

"Why do you do this to yourself?" Hira asked.

The captain shrugged. "I suppose it's hard to comprehend. Especially given the woman I've made myself to be. Strong, independent, nonchalant, and unbothered. I carved her out of tears and pain. I don't recall the young lady I was," Jutia said with utmost sincerity. "My life has been… rotten. It's molded me and I can adjust and pretend quite easily. I've had to since I was little."

"You loved him since you were children?" Hira asked her.

Jutia nodded, though she flinched.

Hira looked away and desperately wished for more ale. "There's no happiness in such a life."

But the captain was unconcerned with the notion of unhappiness. As if she were well familiar with it. "There are days when I find happiness to be overrated. I find comfort in the small things. I built my life in small moments, and I always keep my eye on the goal. *That* brings me comfort."

"And what is the goal?" Hira couldn't imagine going on with scant hope of the situation changing.

She peered at Hira, as if realizing the truth she'd let slip in front of a stranger. "I've said much with little ale. It's been a long time since I've confided in someone." Jutia blew out the last of her smoke and put out the stub. She stared at Hira intensely before saying, "I'd like to be friends, if you'd allow that."

Hira smiled. "I've missed female camaraderie, or *any* companionship, in general."

Jutia raised a brow. "Is Justan not a gracious host?"

Gracious indeed! Hira brightened at the memory of their

argument. She intuitively felt he'd wished to grab her and shake her. Or kiss her. She wasn't certain.

"He's combative. Argumentative and rude. I can't see how you love him. He's a lord, but he acts like a sailor without title or class. And he *hates* me," Hira snapped.

It was harsher than she expected, but perhaps the ale loosened her tongue too.

"He doesn't even like conjan! What Istokian doesn't like conjan?"

The captain stilled slightly before saying, "Justan loves conjan."

Hira shrugged and waved her hand before blurting out, "Well, he doesn't anymore."

Jutia studied Hira's face in the way she wished people didn't. Breaking down her faults. The permanent mark of her unskilled failure that led to Tora's death tattooed on her skin.

"How did you get the scar?"

Hira hesitated before answering, "Protecting the queen. At the time I thought, stupidly, 'Now they'll never make me go back.'"

Jutia smiled widely. "Why did you think that?"

"Because I'm disfigured," Hira spat. It was impossible for Jutia to see. *She* was beautiful.

The captain leaned forward and reached out and pushed back a hair on Hira's forehead. It reminded Hira of a mannerism Almira had. It was a way of comforting the younger one. "You're not. Yes, you have a scar, but you're a few things most women will not be. You're a royal and no marring will ever change that. And you're a *lady* and I don't mean by title or dress."

Hira shifted even as Jutia's fingers lingered on her face. "I don't understand," she said nervously.

The captain pulled back and chuckled. "You're a *lady* and you can't help it. You were raised as such. Even in the way you enunciate your words." Jutia studied her. "There's also an innocence about you. It's really quite enchanting and I'm understanding something I didn't before."

Hira, confused by Jutia's words, shifted. "What?"

But Jutia smiled and stood, placing her hat back on. "Let me have my little secrets. Have another ale and then make your way to Portia's Landing. It's the nicest boarding house in town. You'll find comfortable bedding." She tipped the brim of her hat with a wink. "Until we sail tomorrow, my lady."

Hira nodded and watched her walk away. Jutia paused, grabbed a willing sailor, and left with him in tow.

Quent woke Hira the next morning with a harsh knock. He had many questions about her stay, and it surprised her he was alone. She suspected he'd snuck out of the Sea Wife to find her. Justan would likely blame her for the boy's actions.

In the morning, the port town changed to business. Men rolled carts over the broken cobblestones and children ran chasing one another as they played games. Women sat in circles, placing bets with a lizard on a leash, and tossing dices made of dried brown nuts.

Quent chatted incessantly as they meandered. The only time he stopped was when they passed by a sweets shop that boasted baskets of taffy and honey fudge, warm and fresh. She purchased some for him since he'd never enjoyed it. Hira was aware they were late, and the entire crew likely awaited them with one angry Commander Justan. She didn't really care. He had no choice but to wait. He was, after all, escorting *her*. They animatedly made their way to the docks to find the Sea Wife ready for sail as the noon sun crested the sky.

Jutia had already sailed the Night Serpent and Hira dreaded the argument, which would surely erupt when Justan explained that the other ships started without them.

She and Quent rushed up the ladder and landed on the deck to find it empty. Hira paused and looked around as Quent stumbled aboard with a cough. The hairs on the back of her neck prickled. Something was wrong. Where was Justan and his angry face? Where were her men?

Instantly, her sword was at hand. "Quent, get behind me."

"Yes, *boy*, get behind her."

She turned, but someone hit her head. She remembered landing on the floor and Quent's screams before the world went dark.

Chapter Nineteen

HIRA

A pounding headache woke Hira. It flittered through her thoughts and jarred her awake. Her throat was so dry she could scarcely swallow. She was bound against a pole. She heard men laughing and others groaning. Shifting, she tried to move her strained muscles.

"Good, you're not dead." It was Commander Justan.

She blinked and stared up at the sky. It was well past noon, and she panicked. She turned with a grimace to seek him out.

"You've been out for four hours or more. I thought you died," he was snarling.

Hira squinted but saw nothing. *Panic.*

"I can't see!" she struggled to say, but her words came out hoarse.

"You've been in the sunlight all day," he said.

She shifted and tried to move. Her face was hot and painful. Sun burned. Her vision slowly returned, and she found the commander watching her worriedly. He labored against his own bindings, along with the men and officers bound to her left. She took deep breaths, but all it served was to further dry her throat.

"Quent." It was all she could croak.

"I'm here, my lady," Quent said, and she felt relief. "Justan tried to move you, but they knocked him good."

The commander glowered. He had a badly bruised eye and a split lip. "I've had worse."

"Me too," she laughed humorlessly.

There was something comical about the way he stared at her. He looked thrown between anger and worry. She didn't know why he should be angry at *her*. They had bested her as much as him.

Slowly, she sat up and groaned as the pain in her head intensified. The world whirled, but there was a sharp breeze, and she realized they were at sea. They were all *kidnapped*, out in the open ocean with no chance of Suid learning of her predicament. No chance of Lord Thebo being notified. No chance of Almira knowing. She was alone. And these sailors, these men, were hers, *her* responsibility. She was their High Lady, and she was uselessly bound and dying of thirst.

She turned to the commander. "Water."

He shook his head. They didn't have any. She tried to swallow, but it came out like a cough. Commander Justan sat up and pulled against his restrains. "Strauss! We need water, you pirate!"

"No, Justan!" Quent's tied hands clutched at his brother. His voice was pure hysteria.

"She needs water, Strauss!" Commander Justan ignored him.

The name Strauss registered, and she realized the danger they were in. Captain Strauss. The Red Dragon. The pirates tracked them down. They followed them to Iguanta. And Justan had needlessly worried about Free Islanders.

Furthermore, this pirate threatened her crew! *Her* Istokians, these were her fucking people. She wouldn't stand for this. She would make them pay dearly.

Steps thundered towards them and the men next to the Commander begged him to shut up. They didn't want the attention, but he continued calling Strauss. For her.

She tried to push herself up, but they also wrapped her ankles in rope. She attempted to reach for her ruby knife, but it was gone.

"My blade!" she cried.

"They took it. Save your words," Justan said.

"My sword! Ocean Fury!"

"Shut up!"

She felt blinding anger erupt inside of her. How *dare* they steal her weapons? Those were heirlooms and gifts! Ocean Fury was birthed with House Balik and she wouldn't be the one to lose it.

From the top of the deck, a good dozen pirates walked to them, and she blinked up to see Captain Strauss limp closer. He was in late age, missing an eye that was replaced with a shiny gold orb. He wore a red cloak covered in diamonds and jewels cinched at the waist in an antiquarian style.

"Ah, the blade thrower wakes!" he delighted when he spotted Hira.

He carried Ocean Fury on his belt, and she instantly sat up. "That is *not* your sword! How dare you!"

"Hira!" Commander Justan snapped.

Captain Strauss laughed, and he slapped the handle of the weapon. He pulled Ocean Fury out and brandished it before her. This sent his men into a gaggle of laughter. Then the iron was on her face. He traced her scar with the tip as she held herself still.

Anger rose in her, the likes of which she'd never experienced. It felt like a tidal wave, taking over her veins as she met his eye. The sight of the sword in *his* fist reminded her of who she was. Not only was she House Balik, but she was the ruler of these men. Their lives were in her hands, and it was foolish of her to waste them in a tantrum.

"Leave the lady be!" Quent screamed, and Justan chastised him and bid him quiet.

She took a deep breath and held Strauss' gaze. "Water."

"*No*," the captain chuckled.

She bared her teeth. "Water or we do not discuss terms."

He let out a devilish belly laugh. "Discuss terms! Oh, the pride of the royalty! Just like your uncle. I've been waiting for you to wake, you cunt." He pressed the blade into her skin, and she winced. "Your ugly head will fish me a pretty price."

She licked her lips. "I'll *double* it."

"Have you the coin? Where? In your tits?" He chuckled, making his belly dance. "Can't be that much!"

The pirates laughed and slapped each other heartily. She glanced at Justan, who strained like a madman against the rope, then she looked at Strauss.

"Give her water." The captain waved his hand dismissively as he pulled back the sword. "If she keeps talking, I have an excuse to kill her!"

They threw Hira a water bag, and she clumsily opened it as best she could with bound hands. She drank greedily, making the water splash down her shirt. When she stopped, she corked the bag and flung it to Quent.

As she breathed deeply, she attempted to gather her thoughts. She had to be careful and find common ground. Like Almira would. She was, after all, a royal. She had plenty to offer them. With pirates, the only accepted currency was gold. That shouldn't be a problem.

"How much, Captain? How much for my ugly head?"

He paused and slowly turned to her. He twirled Ocean Fury with a wicked smile. "At least ten thousand golden moja. But seeing you now, I'll take no less than thirty."

Hira lifted her chin. Thirty was nothing compared to the riches in the vaults of Korkoran. "I can get you *sixty.*"

The blade was back, but this time at her clavicle. He exposed the skin of her chest, and she flinched at being displayed in such a fashion.

"Is it just your face that is scarred?" he asked with genuine curiosity.

She yanked herself away from the steel. The pirates and Strauss guffawed. Shame filled her at being discussed in such a crude manner. She was a lady of House Balik. These peons had never seen or imagined royal tits!

"I'll take that as a no, boys! Drag her to my quarters. I want her naked and bound!" Strauss said and waved *her* sword in the air. "Sixty! Ha!"

Pirate hands were on her, and her sailors shouted in horror.

Quent and Commander Justan sent curses to the men.

"You coward, you filthy coward!" she yelled, trying to catch his attention.

Captain Strauss turned and sneered at her. "How am I a coward? I'll fuck you in your own bed and then kill each sailor on this ship. After I've broken you, I'll hand you over for whatever price anyone wants to pay for a cut up, used up, redheaded bitch. I'm not a greedy man. I don't need sixty, but you and your rich lot of dancing bastards think you can buy anything by tossing the peasantry a few coins."

Hira thought quickly. She had little time. What would Almira do? She would negotiate. Use what strength she had, her cunning. But Hira was not cunning. She was good with one thing—her sword. Then she knew what she must do.

"I challenge you, Captain Strauss of the Red Dragon, to a duel. For my honor and for the life of my crew. Defeat me and you can do what you like." She swallowed, "I beat *you* and you and your men get the fuck off my ship and leave my Istokians unharmed."

He studied her with his eerie eye. The pirates shifted, unsure of what to do now that she'd challenged him. She knew little of nomadic life. However, she recalled Uncle Beltran instructing Almira that if pirates ever kidnapped her; she was to challenge them to a duel. Then have someone fight in her proxy. Hira would remove his head from his body all on her own.

He came closer and ran his finger down the scar on her face. She could smell his fowl breath. "There's an old Suidian proverb. It says, 'Never trust a redheaded woman,'" he whispered.

"There's an old Istokian one that says, 'Cursed is the man who refuses a challenge. May all his voyages be damned. May they know him as a coward,'" she spat and lifted her chin.

Justan hissed her name, but she kept her sight on Strauss. The captain's face twisted in anger. He'd not counted on her knowing their own rules. He'd not counted on anything from the moment he boarded this ship, and she would make him pay.

"Or perhaps you're afraid of fighting scarred up, used up, redheaded bitches, Captain? Maybe you can only handle us when we're tied naked on a bed for your tiny cock's pleasure," she hissed and smirked as his face shifted, as if she'd slapped him.

His men murmured as they looked at the captain, whose face was red with rage.

"What little you know of the blade is nothing compared to my knowledge. I'm the greatest swordsman that ever was," he sneered as he grasped her face tight.

She strained, but still smiled. She'd gotten to him. Men were proud of many things, but above all, they were proudest of their concocted virility. What was it M used to call them? Four-minute men. Never knowing how to provide pleasure but delighting in recounting tales of their manhood.

"Then it shouldn't be a problem with all of your... *talent*," she said as she glared at him, taking him in slowly.

"Hira!" Justan wrenched forward until he snapped his bonds, but the pirates grabbed him and howled as he stumbled to the floor.

"Look at that, Commander. A *woman* must save your crew," Strauss said with a chuckle as he turned back to Hira.

She lifted her bound hands to his eye level. "My sword, *Captain*."

The captain acquiesced to the shouts of excitement as the pirates decided this would be a show worth enjoying. They pulled Hira to the center of the deck and unbound her hands and feet. She rubbed her wrists as she regarded Captain Strauss. He was a seasoned swordsman, and he would be tricky to defeat. She must be quicker and wiser than she'd ever been.

Justan was also dragged out, and their eyes met. At least they had released him from the restraints, but two men tightly held him.

"Hira, listen to me! He'll cheat!"

Strauss marched to him and backhanded the commander. Justan landed on the floor, and the other pirates jovially kicked him. They threw him down next to Quent and the boy sobbed as they pummeled his brother.

"Stop it! Your quarrel is with me! Your quarrel is with the High Seat. Here I am." Hira opened her arms wide and pulled back his attention from Justan.

Strauss turned to her and spat in her general direction. "Your house delights in making nomads out of honest men. I've stories to tell you, little girl, of your dearest uncle. The *Great Dragon*."

She snatched Ocean Fury from the pirate as he handed it to her. She sneered at the captain. "I'm not my uncle and I hold no delusions of the man he was. He wasn't perfect and neither am I. Are we dueling or not? I don't have all day."

Strauss' evil smile sent the pirates into more fits of delight when he took out his own long, curved saber.

He brandished it before her. "I'm going to gut you, redhead."

Hira moved to stance, but he rushed at her, upper cut and *CLASH!* Their swords met, and she twisted away from him as she brought the sword up. She swung and jutted it in, then out. *CLASH!* His footwork was brilliant, sure, and decisive. She jumped defensively and attempted to stay ahead of his forceful strikes.

CLASH! CLASH! CLASH!

"You think Istokians want a brat like you as the High Seat?" Strauss shouted as his blade nearly gouged her shoulder before she rolled out of the way.

CLASH! SLICE!

His sword brushed her leg, and she felt a stabbing pain. It was a scratch, but he had outmaneuvered her. She looked back at him in shock as her mind erupted in outrage.

"You don't know what Istokians want, you pirate!" Hira turned quickly, coming close to slicing his belly. He moved out of the way just in time.

"I bet you've pouted this entire trip!" he growled before he hacked his sword down.

She had no defense for his words. She *had* been pouting like a spoiled child and demanding preferential treatment. Not listening to Justan as she frolicked around Iguanta. Well, when she bested this madman she would change, she swore it. It was high time she stopped her pity party. The world didn't offer flowers to those who'd not earned them. And so far, she'd done *nothing* to earn it.

CLASH! SWIPE!

She jumped as his sword nearly took the second half of her face.

She twisted, turned.

CLASH!

She pushed him back with all her strength, and he stumbled. Then suddenly, he rushed forward, then right, twist, turn, and *CLASH, CLASH!* She desperately tried to stay ahead of his movements. Panting as he chased her around the deck.

"Left counter, Hira!" Justan said.

She moved out of the way in the nick of time and elegantly danced through a set of steps Sanaa taught her. She brought the sword down on him. He almost lost his grip, but he recuperated.

"Those are Free Isle moves! Where have you studied, girl?" the captain asked as he panted.

"A bit here," she said as she snapped her weapon to his left and grazed his thigh. "A bit there!"

Another twist and she jumped through his turn. Her sword came down in a manner which Keilly once taught her.

"A little Norrian, a little Suidian, and a lot of Istok!"

Their swords battled in the sun as the men screamed and Justan shouted instructions at her.

She attempted to stay ahead of the dance when she felt a shift in the captain's actions. Master Elio always said the ability to keep up meant someone would tire. True to the master's teaching, fatigue claimed the old pirate. He might've been the greatest swordsman once, but he was a gray-haired man now, and she was young and light. He realized this and raged. His emotions made his movements clumsy. In a maneuver she learned from Tora, she twisted her wrist and Strauss' sword flew through the air.

She capitalized on the moment, and with a thrust, she backhanded him with the hilt. He fell on his knees, and she placed Ocean Fury at his throat. The pirates gasped as her crew cheered.

She rotated the blade against his artery. "Get off *my* ship."

"The Night Serpent!" a pirate shouted.

At that point, all chaos broke loose. The Night Serpent sailed at all haste, with Captain Jutia at the helm. Her face was fierce and deadly. Hira's chest exploded with happiness—they were saved!

That's when Commander Justan screamed her name and Hira

felt a stab in her arm. She looked down and there was her ruby blade, buried in her elbow. Captain Strauss held it with a wicked smile. He yanked the knife down and she gurgled in pain. Her legs collapsed as he split her arm wide open. She felt him pick her up and then he threw her overboard.

The water was frigidly cold, and she sunk fast and deep without a chance of saving herself. Her left arm hung limp, and she had no sensation in it other than excruciating agony. She screamed into the water. Her legs twisting to flee the blinding pain. It burned right into her head. Hira couldn't escape it. She couldn't even swim. Any attempt created more torture. She sobbed under the sea and fervently prayed to the sea gods for a quick death. To end her torment, allow her quickly into the darkness.

Then someone jumped into the ocean and grabbed her waist. It was the commander. He pulled her up, kicking furiously in the currents. As he jolted her, the agony intensified, and she fell unconscious.

She lost track of where she was. But when she came to, they were above the waves. The pain dulled after she coughed. She was dying; she was sure of it. Cannons fired, men shouted, and the universe was on fire.

"Stay awake, you stubborn idiot!" Justan said into her ear, then called Quent's name, who lagged as he swam after them.

"It's too late. Let me go," she whispered.

He paddled as best he could and pulled her like a rag doll. When she blinked, she saw the Sea Wife ahead, but they swam *away* from it.

"My legacy," she said as her head went under the water.

He didn't answer and continued the course away from what her family built. She cried. The *men*. She'd left the men behind. Hira had doomed them. She'd failed. She didn't expect it to hurt like this. Despite all her talk of not being ready, those men counted on her and here she was, dying. She'd left them at the mercy of a pirate.

More hands grabbed her. They hauled her out of the water and the jostling reawakened the agony in her arm. She screamed and thrashed before finally blacking out. The torment was too much. She felt weaker and weaker.

When they placed her, without ceremony, on the floor, she awoke. Captain Jutia hollered orders. Hira was aboard the Night Serpent. How did she get there? Her breathing was ragged as the suffering overwhelmed her. It was hard to even breathe.

"FIRE!" Jutia cried.

Cannons exploded, and Hira heard Quent cough. He wept into her ear as his little hands pushed back the wet hair from her face. She could barely take in his outline against the sky. Did he jump in the water? Was he safe? She couldn't see anything. She was sinking quickly into the void. Both brothers moved over her, she felt Justan tear open his shirt and wrap her upper arm in a tourniquet. But she was unfocused and gasping. Air was scarce.

"She's dead!" Quent sobbed.

"She's not dead. Move aside!" Justan said and yanked harder on the tourniquet. "Hira, look at me!"

"Her arm, Justan! Her arm!" Quent cried as he dug his fingers into her hair.

"Look at me, Red!"

And she did. Then he yanked out the knife and she gurgled in the back of her throat, her vision blackening. He pressed cloth to her wound, frantically yet methodically. Justan was saying more things but she couldn't understand him.

"Gods, she's going into shock," he murmured.

Hira blinked up at him, and she shook as the pain ebbed to allow a coldness to enter her body. Frigid cold. Her lips trembled, and she convulsed. She was in a frozen lake, lost. Lost and floating. Her heart slowed as if each beat was a massive task. In the haze she reached for his face, felt the stubbles of beard against her thumb. It grounded her.

"The witch said don't let them take the arm. Promise me, Justan. Don't let them take my arm."

And she sunk into the frozen waters of her mind.

PART II

Chapter Twenty

HIRA

For the next few days, all Hira registered was pain. It was a constant source of agony. She babbled incoherently and wished it gone. Wished *herself* gone. She would arch off the bed and beg. She begged endlessly. She didn't feel any other part of her body but her arm as if she were her arm. And yet, without the arm, she was nothing.

She was always aware of people. They dabbed her face and tried to give her medicine and drink. None of it worked. In terrible moments, strangers would touch her wound, then speak to the commander in harsh voices. She would scream during those times, beg, and cry for them to stop.

The pain was so intense it invaded her dreams. She dreamt of her uncle, a figure of disappointment at the destruction of his legacy. A golden Almira who would have faceless guards torture Hira, stripping the skin off her arm. Her mother would appear and soothe her and beckon her home, crying for her daughter, the lost heir of a once mighty house. But there Hira lay, a broken thing, shattered and agonizing each moment. In her delirium, she saw her abandoned crew being burned alive, pleading to be saved. But she couldn't save them. She was dying herself.

The one figure constantly present was Commander Justan. He

was the personification of desperation. He would make her drink water and wouldn't blink when she coughed it up on his clothes. When he would re-wrap her wound, he wouldn't flinch at her scratches.

For days, Hira flittered in and out of consciousness. A floating cloud that would descend to storms as lightning hit her arm and erupted with fire-hot pain.

Once, she woke to find Justan staring at her. His handsome face was haggard and worn. He'd not shaved. He gripped her shoulders and pulled her up, gathering her in his arms, as if she weighed nothing. Pushing her matted hair back, she found him broken.

"It's infected. Do you understand? I can't save it, you'll *die*. You'll die if we don't remove the arm." The words choked him.

She grasped his shirt and yanked him in. "Save it or let me die. That is an order."

"Hira, you're *dying*. You *can't* die. I promised him I'd look out for you," he whispered, as if his remarks were only for her.

As the restless sleep claimed her again, she swore she felt his lips against her clammy forehead.

The same people would haunt her over and over until she realized she was in Hell. Then, in the depths of the night, she saw them. Her skin chilled, and she backed into a corner. They slithered over the ground, their lower bodies gone, their bony hands dragging them towards her. Their faces were human but distorted, with wide mouths and gashing teeth, others with empty eye sockets.

The Favia.

She gasped and shook her head. They came to claim her. They came for her.

"*Vishap*," they hissed, their tongues forking out of their blackened lips.

"I'm not ready!"

They would grab her feet and drag her into a black hole.

There was finally a blissful numbness when she woke up. She panicked. She sat up and looked down and was relieved to discover her arm still attached. They'd wrapped it in linen gauze so she couldn't see the wound. Then bile rose in her throat and Jutia was there with a bucket. Hira vomited stomach acid. She'd not eaten in days.

She sagged on the bed, wet with her own sweat as her body shook. "I can't feel my arm."

The captain sat next to her and looked grave. "Rot has set in. It's beyond the skill of medics."

Jutia watched her with a truthful, grim expression. Her face held a heavy burden.

"Am I dying?" Hira asked.

"Yes," Jutia sighed. "We're almost to Calisto."

"Calisto?" The chill was in her bones. She shook violently despite the blankets over her.

"Two surgeons have seen you. Amputation is the only option. Justan refuses to go against your wishes," she breathed. There was an underlying snap to her voice. "There's talk of a woman, a witch, in Calisto. If you believe in such indigenous magic."

Hira licked her lips. She was so tired. "A witch told me not to let them take it. Perhaps a witch will save it." She closed her eyes as she dizzied. "My head hurts."

Jutia nodded. "You've had a fever for two days. It won't break."

Rot had set in. The skin was dying. The bones were dying. *She* was dying. It was taking her with it. Stabbed with her ruby blade, the same blade which gave her hope of a new life, now took everything from her.

"Can you pen a letter and send it when we arrive to Calisto?" Hira asked.

Jutia leaned closer. "A letter to the queen?"

Hira nodded and tried to keep her eyes open. Jutia moved about the room, pulled out paper and quill, then sat ready.

"Almira," Hira said, and Jutia wrote. "I've lost the Sea Wife and I'm dying. Please forgive me. My intention was to obey your command. Save the crew and trust Commander Justan and Captain Jutia, for they'll know the events which transpired. I leave Istok to you. You'll know what to do. I've had no greater honor than serving as your Red Guard. Your dearest cousin, High Lady Hira Balik."

Jutia finished the message, then brought the pen, inked and

ready. Hira signed it with a feverish shiver. She watched Jutia roll the letter and stamp it with red wax. Her lids felt heavy and sluggish.

"Have you ever seen anyone come back from such a wound?" Hira whispered.

Jutia chewed her lip and shook her head. "No," she said. "Rest, my lady."

Hira tried to smile but couldn't manage it. "I'm at death's door. I hear the Favia, Captain. They call my name. I have all eternity to rest."

Despite her words, she fell asleep without meaning to and didn't wake for a while. Not until someone lifted her. They neatly tucked her arm to her side, and she blinked up to see Justan carrying her down onto the shore. He was warm, and he smelled of soap and ocean air. His muscled chest was soft and inviting. She burrowed into him.

"Are we in Calisto?" she asked him.

Justan looked down at her. "Yes. If it doesn't work, it's too late, you understand? Not even an amputation can save you now."

His jaw was hard and resolute, and she recalled how he'd hardly left her side, tended to her in a caring manner.

"You're very handsome," she said sluggishly.

He raised a brow. "Now I know you're dying."

She smiled and slumbered against his shirt, curled into his embrace.

A shrill foreign voice woke her. "You're late! She should've been brought straight to me. Wasting time with surgeons! Come in, come in, set her down!"

They placed Hira on a bed, and she saw a tiny figure. The witch was no more than three feet off the ground, a small person. They were extremely rare, and she'd never seen one up close before. She was of the old race, with a hard face. Her eyes were a golden hue that gave her an unnatural look. She moved about so fast and determinedly that Hira couldn't keep up with her movements. She came closer to Hira, who recoiled.

"You're going to hate me before this is done," the witch said.

Hira took a sharp breath. "Can you save my arm?"

"Save it?" the witch chuckled. "Can I save *you* is the question, you stubborn girl! Damn Balikians, all stubborn!"

They pulled back the binding of Hira's arm. It smelled, and the stench rose in the small hut until she gagged, as did Jutia. The acridity of a rotting corpse. Like eggs left in the sun and covered in maggots. Quent retched.

"Take him outside!" Justan said to Jutia.

Hira decided if she was going to brave this process, she might as well look. She shouldn't have looked. She let out a cry at the sight of her mangled arm.

"Don't look at it," the witch said and turned her head, but it was too late.

The grizzly sight would haunt her the rest of her days, however long they were. The scent coupled with the vision of blackened fingers made her sob. She knew the blackness of the skin meant there was no hope for the fingers. She would never use them again. It was a lost cause. All the pain was for nothing. She wanted Almira. She desperately wished to be a child and curled in Almira's bed, safe and warm.

"Almira," she whispered as she cried. "Almira, help me."

"The queen can't help you now." The witch cursed and shook her head. She opened Hira's eyes and made her stick out her tongue. She pulled back with a grimace. "Blood is poisoned."

"Can you save her?" Justan glared down at her.

The woman's eyes moved about, as if she was calculating her abilities. "I *might*."

"Can you save the arm?" He came closer.

The witched chewed her lip. "She's young and strong, but it'll be hard. If she lives, it's because the gods want it. The Favia laps at this wound. We must hasten. It will be a long and horrible process, but if she lives… well, if she lives, she lives. If I save the arm, then I save it."

Then she shoved a piece of wood into Hira's mouth, who struggled but was too weak to do much.

"Bite down. There's no other way. It's going to hurt more than anything you've ever felt, you hear me?" The witch's voice was harsh.

and without pity.

"Save the arm—" Hira tried to gargle around the wood. It was the last bit of bravery she had left. She had nothing and had no one. Surrounded by strangers, decomposing despite being alive. She was so scared. Naked and alone, she trembled violently.

"Let's start with saving your life, child of Istok. The arm can't live without you, but you can live without an arm." The witch tsked, "Hold her down!"

Hira quaked. She couldn't do this. Justan should just slice her throat. End it now. Jutia reentered and grasped her legs. Hira sobbed in anticipation. Her tears drenched the bed.

"Give her something for the pain!" Justan cried.

"Not enough time. We've got minutes." The witch met Hira's eyes. "Scream if you have to scream, but I can't stop once I start. Today you'll find out what you're made of."

Her body convulsed, and she shook her head. Hira didn't wish to find out what she was made of. She wished it to end. She wanted no more. She wanted *nothing*.

But Justan held her shoulders and loomed over her. "Look at me."

She did. His eyes were lovely. He was worried and his concern anchored her to the earth. In that moment she realized she didn't hate him, in that moment she wanted to start over, to forgive him and stand as equals who shook hands.

The witch started a chant in the old language and threw herbs into the fire. Their fumes covered the rotting scent. Then she brought a smoking bottle. She continued chanting in a near-melodic sound.

Hira bit hard into the wood and stared at Justan. He nodded, encouraging her.

"Keep your eyes on me, I've got you," he breathed.

She could do this. She was a dragon. She was a *dragon*. She was—

When the witch poured the contents of the jar over the arm, she arched off the bed. It burned and ate her skin. Hira screamed, and at the same time, her teeth crushed the wood. Justan's face was all she could see.

"Stay with me," he begged, but she shook her head. She wanted to leave, she wanted to be gone!

"Again," the witch said, and Hira wailed preemptively.

STOP HER! STOP HER! But thoughts jumbled with words, and she couldn't speak. She was beyond speech.

"Look at me!" Justan urged.

Hira met his eyes, but it was brief because the witch poured the liquid repeatedly and Hira spasmed. Hell consumed her, and she knew no more.

Chapter Twenty-One

HIRA

When Hira woke, pain consumed her before breath did. She moaned in agony, kicked and thrashed. She breathed sharply and attempted to shake off the overwhelming awareness of the end. Why hadn't she died? Why was she still here?

The witch hovered over her once more, her toothless mouth widened into a smile. Hira almost hit her—if only she had the strength to do so.

The witch nodded. "Pain is good, means there's feeling, means there's hope."

She brought a cup to Hira's lips. She tried to turn her head, but the witch held her still with a small, but determined hand.

"It tastes like bastard's cum, but you need to drink it all," she hissed.

Jutia came and kneeled by her, holding Hira's head and aiding her to gulp back the liquid. Hira couldn't taste anything, but it smelled like her arm. A rotting sludge that almost made her vomit. She was trembling by the time she finished. Jutia watched her with pity as she dabbed Hira's tears

"I'm going to clean the arm again. We must do this once an hour and then I have to scrape off the dead skin. Do you understand me?" the witch asked in a sharp voice.

Jutia sighed, her mouth souring, "Can't you give her something for the pain? She'll weaken if you continue this."

"Yes, please!" Hira cried at the prospect of more torturous *healing*. Why did healing have to hurt so? The wound was bearable, the healing felt impossible to survive.

"The draught will help." The witch prodded the wound, making Hira gasp and pull away.

Hira shook once more, thinking of the boiling liquid. She couldn't endure this. She wasn't strong enough. She was naked in a dark room. Alone. No kin to comfort her.

"Jutia, kill me, *please*. Slice my throat, make it quick. Make it end. I beg you."

Jutia's face hardened as she held Hira's shoulders. "I cannot do that, Hira. I truly am sorry. You *need* to live."

Hira wailed, her good arm grasping her, digging her fingers into the captain's shoulder.

"I can't, it's too much!"

But Jutia placed the wooden stick back in Hira's mouth. The captain met her eyes and nodded. "Justan is resting. He hasn't slept in days, so try not to buck me off."

Hira took a sharp breath to steady herself. She prayed fervently that she would die. That it would kill her. When the witch poured the liquid again, she blacked out in yowls and screams.

It wasn't worth it.

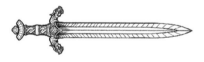

In the night, she heard their voices. It sounded like blades against metal. They called her name, but *they* had no name. The Favia were in the wind and in the water, rippling the ceiling and floating through the fire. They were the air she breathed and the ground she walked on. They'd always been there, only now she entered their realm and could sense them.

The Favia had come for her. Relief flooded her. She was dying. She opened her arms, welcoming them to take her.

"Don't listen to them, *vishap*," the witch whispered in her ear. "You're not theirs *yet*. Do you hear me?"

The torture of cleaning and scraping the arm went on for hours until finally, when she woke, the pain had ebbed. Her body was limp and numb. As if they had sucked life from the very marrow of her bones. She slowly turned her head to find Justan asleep next to her. His long arm lay draped over her leg. He looked terrible. Shadows marred his face, and he'd not shaved in days. She thought he'd held her through the night, but she couldn't be sure. She wasn't certain if she imagined it to provide herself a little comfort.

"Water," she whispered.

He instantly sat up and looked at her with hopeful eyes. She watched as he moved around the room and brought a cup to her lips. She drank, then coughed, spewing liquid everywhere. Gently, he dabbed her face as he watched her with a careful gaze. This was not a bad way to die, she supposed. He felt warm and inviting. Like she could fall asleep, and he'd watch her, ensure no harm came to her. In a sweet gesture he sighed, ran the cloth over her lips. She swallowed. She couldn't imagine how she must appear after her odyssey.

"How is it?" she asked.

He nodded. "Better. I think."

She felt relief flood her and, without meaning to, she cried. The sobs shook her, and she trembled in a mixture of liberation and finally hope. She'd never lived through such horrors, and she'd come out on the other side with vitriolic memories of the happenings. As if the girl before died and a battered woman was born.

Justan instantly came closer, and he softly pushed her hair back, his eyes crinkling in sympathy. He was so close she could smell the salt on his skin.

Hira shook her head. "I wanted death. Why hasn't it come for me?"

He pulled up her chin and brushed her tears away. His

tenderness made her cry even more. She'd not deserved it.

"You are... rather magnificent. Hira, you've *survived*. You've battled fiercer than anyone I've ever seen," he said in such a soft voice it erupted further sobs from her.

"I lost the ship, Justan," she wailed. "I've *failed*. I know I said I didn't want to rule, but I never stopped and thought what it would mean for everyone else. I'm such a little fool. Now the sailors are *dead*."

He swabbed at her face and ran his fingers over her cheek. "They're not dead. We'll get them back."

She closed her eyes and tried to find solace in his caress. A caress that didn't belong to her. But it didn't matter at this moment. Cocooned as they were, he belonged to her now and it was wonderful to have someone belong to her. Someone to hold on to after so much darkness. His fingers created patterns on her face, and she sighed into his embrace.

"I'm so tired. I can't feel anything. Justan, I don't want to do it anymore," she hiccuped and then sniffled.

"It's almost over," he said, his tone filled with lies. He pulled her closer. "You don't know what I've seen you endure. You've battled each moment, grasping to this life with all your strength."

She wished to deny his lovely words. She'd rather not melt into his touch and sweet intonations. Even if she was well, he was betrothed and was not for the having. She didn't recognize when she'd started to yearn for him, but somewhere along the line, with his constant presence and mollifying expressions, her heart leaned to him.

"I've cried like a child," she reminded him.

"You've cried like a *human*." He dabbed her face again, his deep voice soothing her.

They were quiet, and she realized he'd pulled her closer so that her cheek rested against his chest.

She swallowed and calmed herself. Slowly, she relaxed as his presence stilled her. Glancing down at her covered arm, she braced herself. Bravery was something she would learn from now.

"I want to see it."

He seemed to hesitate, but he obeyed her request. Justan helped her sit up, attentive, and gentle as he propped her up against pillows. She had no strength; she was a rag of a thing. With careful fingers, he pulled back the linen from the wound.

She gasped at the state of her arm. In her mind, she thought if she endured all the pain, the arm would be unscathed. That the violent fight would give her back her flesh, but that was not the case.

The skin had rotted, and it was a terrible, grizzly sight. She could see the bone of her elbow and the surrounding skin, angry, swollen, and pink as the infection battled for territory. The jagged edges along the elongated wound underneath were a twisted feat that left half of the skin missing. Even if she lived, the arm could never wield a sword. She was maimed. They'd wrapped her fingers in gauze, but she saw the blackness prevailed. She would lose them. They were gone. How she resented her arm, as if it was at fault for her perils.

"It's a sight better than before," he whispered.

Hira cried in despair, "I should've allowed you to take it. I'll never be able to use it. My fingers…"

He looked at her, his warm eyes saddened. "We can't save them, Hira. I'll be honest with you. But the witch said you *will* heal. In time…"

She shook her head as her lips trembled. "Time enough to save the men? To save the ship? To save Istok?"

Gods, she hated herself. She hated what she'd been. How heedlessly she'd behaved. What would happen without her? Who would rule? She had damned people with her own egotistical behavior.

"If you live, it'll probably take years before you're able to use the arm." He didn't mince words. She appreciated this. It didn't stop the words from burning a hole in her mind. The stark reality of the situation brought on by her own conduct.

She looked away. "Cover it. I don't want to see it."

Apparently, bravery took time.

He carefully re-wrapped the wound in fresh cloth. "Listen, you're going to need to heal. Jutia and I will go after the Sea Wife, then we'll come back for you."

The mere thought of being left behind like a useless lump of flesh captured her attention away from the helplessness of the change in her life. "You'll *not*. I'm coming with you."

"You're at death's door," he said, shaking his head, watching her incredulously. "I can't wait for you to recuperate. Think of the men."

She leaned back and closed her eyes. "Don't you see if I cannot save my own men, then I cannot rule? I know I can't be there in each battle, but this is my first. This was a test and I failed. I was arrogant. Pride filled me when I fought him, pride filled me when *you* tried to help. I was a prideful child and here I am, the consequences of my *pride*. I *must* make amends."

He sat, and she felt his palm slide over the bed. He clasped her good hand, and she gripped him.

"I thought you didn't want to rule," he whispered.

She hadn't. But losing it all had done something, or perhaps it was the odyssey of the past few days. Perhaps the voices that attempted to claim her, or perhaps her dreams. She woke determined to win this, to beat the odds. Live and rise to be the leader her uncle wished her to be. To save her crew from this pirate, to arrive home and start making changes that would positively affect her country.

If she lived. And she wanted to live. She *desperately* wanted to survive.

Hira spent so long thinking that being like Almira was the only course for growth that she'd not allowed room to pave her own way.

She pictured herself clearly with sudden determination. Wearing her blue Istokian armor, leading her army and being the Lady of Istok. There was a warmness in her belly at imagining her future. *She* was the Lady of fucking Istok. She answered to no one.

"It's what I was born to do," she said, and her voice became strong as she tightened her fingers in his. When she opened her eyes, she found him watching her with a surprised look.

"Then, my lady... I'll make sure you get to Treveri," he nodded.

Justan came closer and before she could comprehend it, he held her, pulling her against him, encircling her in his kindness. Perhaps it was inappropriate, but she didn't care. She'd been desperate for someone to hold her for days, and here he was.

Her body filled with warmth. She wished they could start over. That she'd boarded the ship as she should've and they would be friends and confidants instead of existing in false spaces. Stolen spaces created for her swift death.

"I'm sorry, Hira," he breathed.

She curled her fingers into his arm.

"I wish I hadn't spoken to you in the manner I did so often," he confessed. "You're going to rise from this. I'll be proud to have you as High Lady. See you sitting in the Dragon Throne."

She blinked up at him as his remarks filled her with something she couldn't even describe. That she should have to endure such pain to hear such pleasure. His eyes brimmed warm and Hira felt she saw him for the first time. She wondered if this was how he cared for Quent when he was ill. The soft intonation of whispers that showcased the real man behind the posturing. She wondered *why* he hid this man. He was absolutely enchanting.

"I forgive you," she said. "I shouldn't have responded in kind."

Then he did something that took her breath away and made her forget all about her arm. He seized her small hand and held it, intertwining their fingers.

"Thank you, Commander. For everything."

She watched him visibly swallow. He smiled slightly. The dreaded exhaustion drenched her, which he noticed. He helped her lie back down. She was out of breath as he tucked her in. Hira did something that she might pay for later, but felt that she must tell him. Mostly because she recognized the guilt over her own feelings. Over the tenderness filling her heart. She'd never held tenderness for anyone before. Above, wishing him *with* her, she wished him happiness. Which was a strange desire indeed. She had to think of others before herself, even if it hurt. She'd learned pain could be managed. Pain could be endured. And there was someone who had loved him and appreciated him before Hira ever did.

"Captain Jutia loves you, Commander," she murmured.

He stopped and considered her, confused.

"She's an excellent woman and I command you to make good on your promise to her."

He stepped back and looked down at her. "Hira, there are things you don't—"

"*Lady* Hira, Commander. I'm still alive, and I'm your liege." She closed her eyes and drew a deep breath. He grasped her unharmed hand once more.

"Let's talk when you're better, *Lady* Hira," he said, but she saw a mask of sadness cover him. It was as if she were dying, but also healing. She felt better.

"Don't leave without me. That's an order."

Sleep knocked steadily at her door. He agreed, but she swore she saw sorrow in his eyes.

Then his tender, deep words recanted ancient tales as she rested. "In the beginning, Garians traveled the seas from land mass to land mass. They were the star-sons of the night-sky. The sky would speak to them and they, in-turn could paint messages in the stars…"

She sighed, falling into slumber at the tone of his voice.

Hours later, she died.

Chapter Twenty-Two

JUSTAN

He stared down uncomprehendingly at Hira's body. He'd not left her side, though falling asleep had been out of his control. *She* looked asleep. But she wasn't. She was dead. The idea didn't cut through the fog of his brain. Trapped in this room filled with smoke and fumes from the herbs, he couldn't think straight. He'd held her. She'd been warm in his arms. How could she be gone?

Dimly, he heard Quent crying and Jutia cursing. His brother draped himself over the lady and pressed his face against her as he sobbed. The act was so final, so accepting of her death that Justan raged.

"No!" Justan pushed Quent away.

He grabbed Hira's shoulders and lifted her up. Her head rolled back and her mouth fell open. She was limp in his arms. Her skin was eerily pale. After days spent lingering at death's door, her body lay decimated. And she'd fought—fought harder than anyone he'd ever seen. But the Favia clutched her soul and dragged her down to the abyss.

She'd lost her battle. He had to watch her fall.

No!

"Hira! Wake up, Hira!" He shook her. She didn't challenge him.

She didn't yell to remind him of his place. "Wake up, you stubborn woman!"

And he slapped her.

"You fought all this time, fight now! Fight me! Wake up!"

Nothing. She was gone. A strange wail erupted from his mouth as he clutched her to him.

"Justan!" It was the captain. Her face was red with frustration and anger, her blue eyes blazing. "It's done!"

He pushed her off, making her stumble back, which served to infuriate her more. Let her be angry. Let her rage. He understood rage at this moment. He'd done everything he was supposed to and still he lost Hira. The girl in the window was gone. Gone was the warmth of the world.

"Get off! It's not over, she'll make it, she'll live!"

He was drowning in her agony, how much he made her suffer by attempting to save her. Justan knew he should've slit her throat the moment he rescued her from the waters. He shouldn't have allowed her to linger if this was the eventual result. It was *his* fault. He'd done nothing but harm her and cause her pain. He recalled her eating the cheese with the honey in the market and smiling at him. Oh, why didn't he say something to her? Why did he act the way he did? Damn his soul, damn it to hell!

"*Justan*," Jutia said with a near hiss, an unbelieving hurt that etched her face in two. She slowly shook her head, watching him cradle the body.

He had to look away, pressing his nose into Hira's hair and closing his eyes. He breathed out a shaky sob, feeling the sense of overwhelming failure. *Doomed.* That's what they were. Doomed. He was trapped. He'd never get out. He too would linger and suffer and die. Quent would be taken. He couldn't protect Quent. Sons of an ancient lineage and all he had was his ability to act like the Justan everyone knew.

He turned to his brother, whose little face was broken in pain.

"She's... she's not really dead, is she?" Quent asked him. "She's just tired, right?"

Justan wished to assure him, to tell lies and make him believe in fantasies, but he didn't have the heart to do so. The exhaustion of the past five years descended on him like torrential rain. Hira's screams as they tried to heal her echoed in his mind. The zenith of his charade.

Quent reached for Hira and cried. "She was getting better. You said she was getting better!"

His heart broke for his brother. He was soft and open because Justan had shielded him. Protected him from the harshness of life as best he could. Now life, and the maladies it contained, raked its fingers over them all. The Favia laughed and danced. *A feast*, they sang.

"Life works that way," the witch, who'd remained out of the scene, said in a cryptic tone.

He turned to her with unjustly placed anger. "Bring her back! Do your magic, pull her from the abyss!"

The witch slowly smiled then laughed sadly. "Not even incantations can drag souls from Hell. The Favia clutched her good. She's gone, Commander."

He was suddenly a lad and listening to his father coldly tell him his mother had died.

"At least the baby is healthy, that's what matters," Commander Tikan said to his son, with his hands behind his back as he stared out into the port. "Three sons. The name Seaver will live in the three of you for many generations to come."

His father took a deep breath.

"I didn't care for being married. Women constantly need things. Attention. Love. Promises. It's tedious."

"But father..." he'd whispered with the sorrow thick in his throat. "I didn't get to say goodbye."

Commander Tikan turned to his son with sharp eyes. "Goodbye for what? To provide her with more assurances? That you would look after your brothers? That you would remember her?" he scoffed. "What a weakling she birthed."

He'd ran off to cry in a corner because he knew his father wouldn't stand his tears. Alone with his grief, he assured his mother's spirit all the promises his father forbade.

And now he'd failed another. Another goodbye never intoned.

Justan let go of Hira, placing her body down and attempting to remember her face. Her smile. That child-like wonderment she held. That stubbornness that cut right through him and made him desire someone in a way he'd not desired in a long time. Her bravery and words as she cried in his arms and wished to lead their people. For a moment, he'd seen the real Hira. That dragon she didn't yet know how to wrangle. That Balikian heroism that never ceased to amaze him. She was there, she'd arrived. He'd seen nothing as beautiful.

He'd failed so completely and utterly. He'd not been able to save her. Protect her. Watch her from the Dragon Throne and stand by her side as she ruled. Hope was lost.

"Let her go," Jutia snarled as she stood next to him. "We have work to do. The Sea Wife, we need to get her back. We've wasted enough time."

He rose and grasped the captain's arm and studied her beautiful face. "How is saving someone's life a waste of time?"

Her wide blue eyes took him in. He knew he disappointed her. He didn't care. Let her bathe in disappointment. They were all used to it by now.

"There are days I don't believe I know you at all," she drawled.

There were days he didn't know himself. He shoved her off. "I'm going to wrap her and bury her. She deserves that. She at least deserves that."

Her nostrils flared. "I sail at noon. We need to think of those who are still alive. Those we *can* save."

He let her leave. He didn't want to look at her. He didn't wish to think about her. All he wanted was to entomb his head in the sand and have a few moments' peace. He shoved his hands into his hair and watched as Quent pitifully cried against Hira's shoulder.

"Commander," the small witch said next to him. In her hands was a white linen cloth. "We must wrap her. You can leave her with me until you find the Sea Wife and then come get her body. No one will harm her. I swear it on the Favia. She'll be safe."

He shook his head, hardly believing it was falling to *him* to organize the details of the High Seat's death. "I can't leave her here."

"What are you going to do? Drag her back to the ship? Think

of what's honorable and right. She deserves an Istokian burial. You can come get her when the time is suitable," the witch said, and leaned closer.

She had sense, but at this moment Justan had no sense left. Leaving Hira alone in the middle of nowhere felt wrong. But he had no time to mourn or process his feelings. He had to think rationally. There was no time to contact the queen. Time was his potent enemy. The kingdom was about to be split in half with no Hira to save it.

"Critical thought separates man from animals," Beltran said when he was only seventeen and sat listening to the High Lord's speech. "The moment we lose reason, we might as well be animals. The good of the kingdom, the good of Istok, is what matters at the end of the day. You understand, boy? Not even I matter that much."

He'd understood then, and he understood it now. He had to think of Istok. He had to think of the men at the mercy of a pirate. Hira would want that. She'd not want him to despair on the beach because of her loss. She would rise, dust herself off, and leave him behind too. Hira would do what she had to do. She was brave like that. He had to be brave, too. He had to make the choices that broke hearts. Even if that heart was his.

With great care, he wrapped his Ladyship's body. He braided her short hair, committing to memory the feel of the strands. He allowed his fingers to linger over her soft skin, and let himself imagine what he would say to her if she'd lived. If he'd shared with her all the things he'd kept housed in his head. She'd likely hate him for a while, which he understood. But he dreamt of her understanding his story and perhaps accepting him for who he was.

Recalling his mother's words, he took sand and mixed it with sea water to make a paste. Carefully, he coated her face and urged Quent to find the two best shells he could. The brothers placed the shells over her eyes. In this light, she almost looked Garian.

As he finished, he pushed back her hair and stared at her one last time. At the curved scar, that to him made her even more interesting. He traced it with his finger.

Slowly, he closed the door to his heart. He'd allowed it an opening for a few days and all it'd done was hurt him more. For as long as he lived, he would never forget her last night. Though it was brief, for a moment, she'd belonged to him. For a moment, he'd held Hira Balik until her name sounded like music on his tongue.

The stars dulled their light, for he'd seen her face in their sweet brightness. And that's where Hira Balik would live. In the night sky so that each time he'd stare up into the emptiness, a sliver of her memory would warm his heart.

"*Elas stelas la viv,*" he whispered.

In the stars she lives. The final Garian goodbye.

"I'm sorry, Beltran. I'm sorry, Hira," he said. "You'll be avenged. I swear it."

And he grabbed a crying Quent and left her in the hands of the witch.

Chapter Twenty-Three

ALMIRA

The arrival of the Suidian escort was the perfect distraction for Alton's delayed letters and the haunting of her dreams. The sense that *something* was wrong continued to plague the queen, but she couldn't see *what* it was. Her nerves were a tight fist that had her pacing rooms the past week, and last night she'd woken with someone calling her name. The perception that the Favia laughed from the corner of her bed had her covering her belly protectively for hours. Sleep was a luxury at this point.

Nanai's presence was certain to help.

Almira stood at the top of the stairs with her guards and Ley Wallace to her side as they aided *Nanai* out of the carriage, along with Hester. Almira felt a brightness take over at the sight of her grandmother. Especially when the elder looked up and smiled. The women embraced, and *Nanai* cooed over Almira's stomach, pressing her hand over it in delight.

"You're glowing," *Nanai* said.

"Only because you're here," Almira said as they walked back within the caverns of Mavros. The relief of her company was instantaneous.

"Pregnant women always glow," Hester said, and Almira noted

happiness in her seamstress.

She clutched Hester's hand, which surprised the old woman. But there was a steadiness to Hester, which Almira felt she needed. A stable stone to stand on.

"My dresses need your eye, dear Hester," Almira said good-naturedly. "The girls you left behind, though talented, splay the feathers."

Hester glanced critically at the queen's gown. "I can see."

Almira laughed and urged the party into the dining hall, where a grand luncheon spread out over a long table. Nadim awaited them and warmly welcomed the ladies, indicating he'd ensured their favorite foods—if not bland were served.

As the group settled in a comfortable delight of reacquainting themselves with all they'd missed, Almira finally relaxed. This was what she needed. She needed her family. She studied her cousins, Thebo's children seemed to have grown in the past few months. Teb, a strapping lad, was tall and muscular, with a sharp jaw and a handsome face. He was mostly quiet, annoyed at the female chatter which surrounded him. His sister, Lianna, looked equally bored. Almira remembered she had a gift for the girl. She motioned for Nadim, and he understood what she wished. Her Keeper brought two bound scrolls, which Almira discovered in the old section of the royal archives.

Lianna's eyes instantly lit up.

"I found these and thought you would enjoy perusing them," Almira said with a smile when the girl clutched the scrolls to her chest as if they'd given her the most wondrous gift.

She was indeed a beauty and would be coveted come her time. Her skin was a smooth, beautiful Sikorian black, her cheekbones were elegant, and she boasted warm golden-brown eyes that took up half her face.

"Oh majesty!" Lianna cried even as her mother, the Lady Gita, looked on worriedly.

"She really needs no more scrolls. She has plenty," Gita said in disappointment.

"Too many," Teb grumbled.

Almira ignored them. If Lianna wished to read and learn, then it should be allowed. "They are ancient, very hard to decipher. I've no knowledge of their contents, but perhaps you can translate them, cousin."

This excited Lianna even more. "Oh, I will! Mother, may I be excused? I wish to start on them right away!"

Gita's mouth soured, but she glanced at Almira, who watched the scene passively. Naturally, she wouldn't interfere with Gita's parenting, but to discourage the girl when she thirsted for knowledge was not to the queen's liking.

"Very well," Gita said and turned back to her honey cake with a shove of her fork. Lianna wasted no time and scampered off to her selected rooms, clutching the scrolls in her small arms.

Teb leaned forward and addressed the queen with interest. "Majesty, is it true that you've captured a Norrian giant?"

Almira attempted a neutral face. She didn't care to think of Lord Ivar lately, especially after their dinner. "He's hardly a giant."

"The man's a giant," Hester said, pointing her fork at the lad. "As large as two men! With a wild beard and arms the size of logs!"

Teb's eyes lit in excitement. "May I see him?"

"Absolutely not," *Nanai* said with a displeased look thrown at Hester.

Almira deduced Hester fed the boy stories, and now he hungered to see the tangible proof.

"Cousin, Lord Ivar is a prisoner, not a spectacle," Almira said to appease the situation. *Nanai* and Gita visibly relaxed.

"I've seen prisoners. We have plenty ourselves. But not a *giant.* I'd very much like to see him." Teb's brows furrowed.

"No, Teb," Gita said with a shake of her head. "The man is clearly a barbarian and dangerous."

Almira ran her fingers over her belly. "He's not wild and untamed, Lady Gita. He's a lord and the heir to Norr."

Unperturbed, Teb grinned delightedly. "*How* was he captured?"

"Took twenty men to bring him down," Hester said and smiled, enjoying adding fuel to the young man's speculations.

Next to the queen, Lady Delara stared at the boy and placed her hand calmly on her ruby blade. "The man lacks manners and breeding. He's hardly worth idolizing."

Almira looked around the room and recognized Sanaa was not there. She turned to Delara. "Has the captain returned from her morning ride?"

Nanai too searched for the captain, but it was clear she was missing. "Oh, I knew we were missing someone. Where *is* Captain Sanaa? I very much long to greet her."

Delara's posture stiffened, as if she realized the captain was overdue and would've certainly been here for the party's arrival. Almira stood, as if this confirmed her premonitions. Something was wrong. It's not that she didn't think Sanaa could take care of herself, but with their enemies growing, *everyone* was in danger. When had she last seen Sanaa? Yesterday, during lunch. Oh gods.

"Nadim, send out a search party," Almira said quickly and walked to the balcony, where she could see the long road that led to the castle. Aside from a handful of passing pedestrians and soldiers, there was no sign of Sanaa's iconic red armor. Her stomach soured.

"Do we think something happened to the captain?" *Nanai* stood next to her.

Almira shook her head. She really had nothing to prove why her senses remained so frayed. "*Cuzo* is very capable, but there's still a witch out there and gods know what else slinks in the shadows."

Nanai fretted at her words, glancing at Hester, whose face darkened. "I'm sure the Black Knights will find the captain. She likely stopped for some ale. Tell me about our dearest Hira." *Nanai* grasped Almira's hand and pulled her into the room.

"Yes!" Gita brightened at the change in topic. "She must be arriving to Treveri soon. Thebo said he would come join us the moment he heard she'd arrived safely. The Lady Marai must be excited to have her daughter back after such... circumstances. I know *I* would."

Almira forced a smile at Gita's idle chatter, but her mind turned sharply to Sanaa and her whereabouts.

"Oh, the girl's miserable alright," Hester said plainly. "She would've liked nothing more than to stay here for her entire life."

Almira sighed and rubbed at her stomach because the baby pinched her ribs. Where the hell was Sanaa? She should be here. It was unlike her. She glanced at Delara, whose face was also tight with concern.

"Majesty, would you like me—"

"Yes," Almira said.

But as Lady Delara opened the door to the dining quarters, Sanaa herself burst into the chamber without preamble, a small person in her arms.

"*Cuzo!*" the captain placed the person on a chaise.

Almira was instantly on her feet, staring in wonder at her *cuzo*. Sweat and grime covered Sanaa. The pudding forgotten, the room erupted with shouts of concern as the women rushed to the captain and her small companion.

"Where were you? Who is she?" Almira fired questions faster than the captain could answer.

Hester was sharp with her fingers as she inspected the small young girl who laid unmoving. A pale thing with matted brown hair, she was nothing but skin and bones dressed in rags and bloodied bare feet.

"Istokian," Hester murmured. "She looks at death's door."

"Oh, poor child!" Gita kneeled and waved to her son. "Teb, water!"

The lad scrambled to get a cup as the queen turned to Sanaa.

"Found her on the side of the road, beaten and starved... nearly dead." Sanaa's breaths were still coming in brief spurts.

She pulled a mangled letter from her cloak. Almira quickly took the note and paused, her throat constricting. The queen felt the blood drain from her face.

"This is my father's seal," Almira said slowly and met Sanaa's stare.

The room quieted as the women looked at the letter in Almira's shaking hands. How many times she'd wished to receive such a message these past few months? Now that a letter arrived, all it did was cover her in dread.

"The girl claims your aunt sent her. Marai said you're to be warned of impending danger or… or Istok will fall. There was truth in her eyes. She wasn't lying," Sanaa confided.

Nanai and Gita audibly gasped, but Almira's skin prickled as she clutched the sealed letter. A warning. *Hira!* Her breaths came sharply as she tore the seal and scanned the contents. She was so nervous she couldn't comprehend the writing.

"Sit." Nadim was next to the queen as he placed a chair for her. She was incredibly grateful as her legs shook and her hands trembled.

"It's my father's handwriting," Almira said darkly. "This is an old letter… what if he tried to warm me of his capture?" She felt dizzy.

Had there been a chance to save her father? Was this his meaning as he lay dying in her arms? There were so many questions, but also so many ears and eyes. She looked around the room as they all watched her. Whatever was in this letter would have consequences. She needed only her family and trusted guards.

"Servants and guards out!" Almira shouted.

Nadim quickly turned to comply as he ushered the curious servants and the young Red Guards out of the chamber. Surrounded by only her family and Sanaa, M, Nadim, and Delara, Almira shook her head and closed her eyes, then shoved the letter at Sanaa.

"Read it out loud," the queen said.

Sanaa sighed and, breathing deeply, she opened the letter. "My dearest daughter, it pains me you have to receive this letter. Five years ago, I uncovered a plot to overthrow Istok. Before you were born and before I met your mother, I had an affair with Lady Ignatia, whom you know as your aunt," Sanaa paused and they stared at one another as she processed his words.

Goose pimples erupted in the back of Almira's neck at the implications of his letter. A confessed affair such as this meant an *heir*. A secret heir.

"Gods of the sea," Gita breathed.

Almira reddened in embarrassment. A sibling. She clutched the arms of the chair. "Keep reading!"

Sanaa stumbled with the paper and continued. "This affair

resulted in the birth of a child and that child is Furia. *Fuck!*"

It left the women speechless. Teb stood with wide eyes, the cup of water fell from his hands.

"I knew it!" Almira covered her mouth with her hands. A girl. She had a sister. Oh, where was Alton? She needed him! "Keep reading."

"Majesty—" Delara stepped forward, concerned when Almira's chest heaved.

"I said keep reading!"

Sanaa cleared her throat. "You know Lady Furia. As you believe, she's your distant cousin and inheritor of Ciraton. Knowing your mind, I understand you're angry with me. I've robbed you of a sister."

"Robbed me of peace!" Almira burst. How could he? How could he leave her with this mess? The nobility could contest the High Seat and declare Hira a usurper! Hira was out there, bold and ignorant of the realities. Having little dexterity on how to handle such a calamity.

"Knowing your mind," Sanaa continued. "I know you're calculating the consequences of my actions."

"Gods absolve me, but what has he done?" Almira finally stood and paced. "Oh, you foolish old man! Keep going, what are his other sins?"

Sanaa grasped the letter tighter. "Your sister's heart is filled with bitterness. I admit she has the right, but it's combined with her mother's ambition and hate. You must forgive this old man."

"I shan't. I cannot. I will not!" Almira raged.

How *dare* he ask for forgiveness from the great-beyond where she couldn't deny it? How dare he believe she would discard his actions with his soft words? He'd kept from her a grandmother *and* a sister, heedlessly holding Almira tight while keeping her away from others.

"*Cuzo,*" Sanaa looked at her fearfully. She respected the Favia and would never insult them. The dead were not to be cursed.

"Let them hear! I've sent Hira to the mouth of the wolf! I've doomed her! I foolishly thought her safe because I trusted all would be well, but it's not. She may have needed me and where am I? Eating pudding!" Almira clutched her chest.

"The dead are dead and gone. He's gone and his deeds are done." *Nanai* suddenly stood and turned sharply to Gita. "This is *not* gossip, and this information doesn't leave this room. Am I understood?"

Almira tried to wrap her mind around the revealed facts, but she struggled to maintain calm. How could he? A sister! An heir! She took a deep breath and attempted to contain her screams. M kneeled next to her and pressed a cup of water into her hand.

"We can get to Hira if we ride with all haste," M said with assuredness, and Delara nodded.

"We don't even know where she is," Almira hissed. "They might've captured her already—she might be dead." and the words sputtered out her anger. Oh gods. Her darling girl. She let out a cry and pressed her palm to her face. All she could recall was the smell of her hair when they were little, and how Hira would curl herself against Almira and beg her to tell her stories.

"You're conjecturing wildly," Hester hissed. "Drink your water."

Almira drank as everyone stood with their heavy thoughts at hand. Her fingers trembled as she lowered the cup. "That awful feeling I've had for weeks. I thought it was because Alton was leaving for war, but it wasn't *that*. Hira won't see it coming, she won't see it."

"Let me finish the letter." Sanaa held up the damning item.

"I don't wish to hear it," Almira spat angrily.

"Will you be blind then, to this sister you've discovered?" Hester asked sharply.

Almira looked away from her and stared at the young woman who'd traversed the world to bring her this calamitous news.

"Go on then," she whispered.

Sanaa sighed and read. "You must forgive this old man. I never had the heart to kill my child. She has my eyes and some nights they haunt me, reminding me of the weakness I hide from others."

Almira shook her head. "What have you done, father? I don't

know this sister and if she hates me, she'll turn my country against the crown. Istok will break all alliances."

Nanai rubbed her face and gratefully took the seat Nadim brought her. She sat next to Almira and held her hand. "Read on, Captain."

The queen felt primed for battle, as if she could wield a sword. As if she could hunt the dead and demand answers.

"If you've received this letter, Furia has attempted the unthinkable. Istok has fallen. I know not the fate of Lady Marai or Hira, but you must take back Istok immediately or I fear for the outcome of our people," the captain finished somberly.

Almira and Sanaa stared at one another; the implications of the letter drowning them. Istok had collapsed. Her aunt could be dead. Hira could be dead. It was an act of war. Another war on another front. *Nanai's* hand tightened in hers but Almira could scarcely breathe.

"I was too late then?" a small voice said from the chaise and they all turned to the forgotten child who watched them with hallow eyes. She'd woken and now sat out of place amongst the fineries of the upper houses.

Almira swiftly stood and walked to the girl who stared at the queen in wonder. She studied the girl's bony cheeks, her dirty matted hair, and chapped lips.

"Majesty, I'm sorry. I tried my hardest—" The girl wailed.

"What's your name, girl?" Almira interrupted her.

The girl cried and clutched the cloak tightly around her. "Cook calls me Pansy because I'm from Lumbry, where pansies grow."

Almira felt her heart soften towards the pitiful thing. Like her, there were others. Istokians of her own blood who innocently tended fields, pulled nets from the sea, and heartily enjoyed ale. All blissfully unaware that her father had destroyed the possibility of peace because of his eager cock. His sins were not hers. Yet, she would be the one to pay the penance.

"Have you no proper name?" Almira asked.

Pansy looked on at all that watched her, such fine eyes watching such a wretched girl. "I'm just a servant, Majesty. I worked in the kitchens in Korkoran. I used to bring the High Lord his supper each night. I've not eaten for days, and my coin was stolen. I—I can't read, so I didn't know what the letter said. Robbers beat me. But I had to find you. Lady Marai said that if I didn't warn you of the danger, Istok will fall. Please don't let it fall. It's my home. I've got nowhere else to go."

And the child dissolved into sobs. The queen thought of the odyssey this poor ignorant girl went through. How she traversed the world for months just to bring her Queen this dire warning. In her was the strength of Istok, the resilience of its people. Conquerors of the oceans, fearless even in the face of impossible odds.

Almira gently grasped the girl's chin as she studied her Istokian bone structure. She looked to have Garian in her and the queen saw how her aunt couldn't have picked a better person to save their country.

"You've not failed in your task. You've warned me and I know what I must do. You have given us a *chance* to save Istok, and because you've done so, your name will be Pristok. The Pride of Istok."

The girl gasped and took Almira's hand and pressed it to her forehead. "Majesty, I don't deserve that."

Almira sat next to her and pushed back her oiled hair. "Listen to me, Pristok, you must tell me everything, absolutely *everything,* you can about Lady Furia."

Pristok's face paled, and she looked down, her lip trembling. "Oh, majesty, you don't understand. There is no one in this world as cruel as she. She's *evil.*"

Later, Gita closed the door to the small room and turned to Almira, who waited with her hands clasped over her belly. Sanaa stood next to the queen and signaled for a Black Knight to be posted.

"I would say the poor girl hadn't had a decent meal in months."

Gita's lips pursed, and her face pulled tight, wrought with concern.

"Nothing but skin and bones," Sanaa said in agreement.

Today was supposed to be a joyous occasion, and it had morphed into a nightmare. Almira needed to write to Alton the moment she retired to her rooms. She had to operate under her darkest fears. Istok was splitting with the top half, joining Norr. Her lover had to know what waited in the wings.

The women joined *Nanai* and Hester in the sitting quarters, where the fire roared warmly. Ley Wallace sat before *Nanai* and listened as she carefully relayed the details of the letter. The Ley's face looked taut, and he seemed as worried as Almira felt. He looked up at her as she entered.

"I need you to be honest with me. Based on the laws, what can we expect?" Almira sat across from him.

He sighed as he rubbed his forehead, "It depends."

"On *what?*" Almira snapped and *Nanai* inhaled sharply.

"*Proof,* evidence," he said, and scratched his bald head.

Almira's mind raced. The letter claimed Furia had their father's eyes, but that could hardly be used as concrete evidence. Everyone knew documents could be disputed and falsified.

"If you're lucky, this letter," he pointed to the letter in Nanai's hands, "is the only proof. May I see it?"

Almira nodded at her grandmother, and the elder handed the Ley the letter. They watched as he read it over again. He sighed and scrunched his eyes, then read it once more. Almira felt her patience thin. Just as she opened her mouth to convey urgency, he paused and held it up to the light.

"Fire, I need fire. Heat." He stood.

"Are you burning it?" Almira gathered and followed him with a grimace at the sharp discomfort her belly caused.

"Captain," he said, glancing up at Sanaa, who grabbed a candle and brought it to him. "Hold it so it heats the paper, do not burn it."

Almira stood behind him to see what he revealed. All she could see were those damming words inscribed by her own father.

"There," he pointed at the bottom of the paper.

Faintly, Almira could discern lines but she couldn't make it out. Like faint scratch marks of another letter, written on top and the indentations seeped into the paper below. Nothing more.

"Is it a message?" she said in a near whisper, hovering as Sanaa concentrated on not burning the frail paper.

"Yes," Ley Wallace said almost proudly. "Haliondi ink, very impressive, my lord."

They watched as the note turned darker and, as if by magic, letters appeared. It was her father's handwriting with two lines.

"The key to his jail cell is in the hidden drawer of my desk. Trust Ryker, he is true," Almira said the words out loud.

As if her father spoke to her from the great beyond, her mind buzzed, and she stepped back from the implications. She had to sit. Gita noticed, took her hand, and walked her back to a chair.

"Who is Ryker?" *Nanai* asked. "Who is this man?"

Almira shook her head. "I don't know. But I know the jail cell he means. Under the Korkoran fortress is a hidden labyrinth. Seldom used. Father only mentioned it a few times, as if he wished me to recall. It's a system of caves on the cliff. There's one jail cell there. Impossible to escape from. He said it was empty, and perhaps it was at the time he spoke of it."

The queen looked up as they all watched her. Her hands shook, her mind imagining who exactly her father left there to rot. And more importantly, if they were still alive so many months after his death. Or did her aunt know about this prisoner?

"Could it be Furia?" Sanaa had the look of someone ready to ride with all haste to Istok and slit the throat of whoever was there.

"He says *his* jail cell," Almira said, and licked her lips. "It's a man."

Nanai shook her head and pressed it against her hand. "Oh Beltran, you old fool!"

"What does a man matter in all this?" Hester snapped.

But Almira saw the path her father took, like a map laid out. It was one of his puzzles. A political puzzle he'd created to test her. A younger Almira would've spent days deciphering them, reveling in finding the clues and messages. Queen Almira, however, was not awed. She saw the direct trail. Whoever was in that cell was very important. Her father wouldn't have thrown just any prisoner in there for no reason. Whoever was in there knew of Furia. Whoever was in that cell was to give Almira an upper hand.

"That man matters because he means something to Furia. He means *a lot* to Furia." Almira looked at the fire, her mind resolute in what she must do. "If Furia has captured Hira... that man is my bargaining chip. Because she would care enough about him to trade. Whoever this Ryker is will aid us. We must wait until he reveals himself, for it may be unsafe for him to leak his true identity. This Ryker will tell *no one* who he is. He's my spy. He's likely been a spy for years, living under a false identity. No matter what, he won't act until I arrive. My father would've instructed him as much. Ryker is our only ally in a sea of vipers."

Isabelle Olmo

Chapter Twenty-Four

HIRA

Death. Mourning.

Hira watched it all from above, like a floating specter.

She saw poor little Quent crying. He clutched her body and pressed his cheeks to her shoulder. Justan turned to Jutia, grasped her arm, and yelled something furiously. Jutia shoved him off and stormed out of the hut. Justan buried his hands in his hair. His mouth twisted in defeat. Then he wrapped her in a white gown of death. Composing a Garian burial mask, he covered her face as his fingers lingered and he seemed to ask forgiveness. She didn't think he needed to be forgiven. He'd done his best.

Within her sphere, she didn't feel the need to reassure them. She felt so warm and content. So free of the suffering she'd endured that she preferred to linger and simply float, watching time happen below her, freed from its sorrows.

Then she watched them leave.

Hours passed, and the ceiling caught her, trapped amongst the herbs that dangled from the rafters.

Into the sphere came the witch's voice. It was so sharp and urgent that it startled her. As if the claws of life latched themselves to her soul, it yanked her. She struggled at first because she didn't wish to go back! She was a happy floating speck of air!

But life and its determination won, and the drop was swift. Her mind dove sharply back into her body, rushing in with the madness of the world. Hira scrambled, her hands going for her face. She found it packed with sand, and seashells that pressed into her eyes. She tossed them off and frantically looked around. She was no longer a specter. The noise was too sharp, the colors too bright. She gasped and screamed, trembling as she became accustomed to her old body. It felt too tight, like it didn't fit right. As her breathing calmed and she settled, a shadow moved over her.

She was in her *dead* body. She was alive. How could this be? What witchcraft was this?

The witch laughed, as if the vision Hira'd experienced these past hours was false.

"I wondered when you'd wake. I didn't know what you were before, but I know *now*." The witch snapped her small fingers in front of her face. "You were buried deep. Very smart of you, *vishap*. You were always clever, my old friend."

Hira shook, not because of the pain. She had no pain, but because of the vision of her death.

"I died!" she cried, then touched the gown she wore. "I floated. I was nothing in the air."

She'd *seen* it, she'd *felt* it. She'd *lived* it!

The witch watched her with calm eyes. "It *seemed* like it, didn't it? It was certainly very convincing to those who needed to be convinced."

No. This couldn't be. This was… magic. *Dark* magic.

"How did you do it? *Why* did you do it?" Hira recoiled from her.

The change within her left her petrified, as if she didn't know who Hira Balik was and had to recommence her journey of discovery.

The witch shook her head. Hira disappointed her. "You're asking all the wrong questions."

Hira looked around the hut and found it empty. Only the two of them. It was a cramped thing with hangings of skulls and bones in various stages of decay. Perhaps she too decayed. She too slowly died. Cursed to live in visions. Where was Justan? Where was Quent? Why was she alone?

"Did they leave?" Hira asked.

"Soon they will, and *we* have little time."

The fire roared, roasting the air within the hut. The witch threw herbs into the hearth, encasing them in bitter fumes. Hira coughed and asked her to stop. Her lungs contracted against the acridity of the dense smoke.

"The moment has come, *vishap*," the witch whispered through the flames. Her eyes turned an eerie white.

Fear grasped Hira. Its claws wrapped around her throat. It was too much. She trembled violently. Her skin itched, and she wished to strip it off.

"Time for what?"

The witch moved closer, her eyes wide in a sort of manic delight. "What do you recall of the histories, *vishap*? Come now, you used to know them well!"

Hira rubbed her eyelids against the onslaught of smoke. It stung and made her disoriented. She didn't understand these question; it was pure nonsense. "No more herbs!"

The witch's face peered at her from the fog. "The first people had never seen sea serpents, so they made them gods."

She threw greenery into the fire, more smoke wafted and floated within the space.

"Stop, please—" Hira coughed. Shaking her head because she wished for peace, for a moment to think. She wished to be a specter again.

"Listen, *vishap*!"

"Stop calling me that!" Hira roared, and anger erupted within her. She almost felt her mangled arm move. A fiery pit burned in her belly as if flames would overtake her mouth. A flash of a vision smacked against her mind, and she was suddenly a general. She was a queen. She was a warrior in fur, hacking down enemies with a ferocious yell.

A blink and it was gone. Hira was gasping, a torrent of questions floating from her tongue.

The witch noticed, and she cackled in delight, throwing her hands victoriously up in the air.

"You slumber, *vishap!* The time has come for you to wake! The cost? Your arm. Everything hangs in the balance and if you don't rise, war will plague this land for a thousand years. Only a Balik can kill a Balik, as it's been foretold!"

Hira shook her head at such a crazed prophecy. There was only one other Balik. Almira. It made no sense. She wouldn't kill Almira. Ever. She adored Almira, even in her darkest moments when she was angry at her.

"The birds fly south, the fish swim from the shore, the bears of the North hide in their caves. The world feels it. It feels the coming war. It's in the water. In the air. It's waiting for you, *vishap*. It's waiting for you to *wake*," the witch hissed. "Like you were *before*. For who will save the queen, if not you? Remember how you led the southern armies? Fifty thousand men followed you to battle, and you were at the helm. Suidians, Istokians, Garians, all manner of people!"

"Stop!" Hira closed her eyes. "Stop the madness, I can't!"

"You *can* and you *will!* You hold yourself back! Stop being afraid!" Her rotten teeth darkened. "Fear is a ravenous beast. If we allow it, it'll devour us. The only thing you have to defeat is fear. When you stop fearing death, that's when you'll wake!"

She snapped her small fingers in front of Hira's face, making her jump. She felt that snap deep within her heart, within her soul. Hira clutched her chest. She couldn't breathe. There was a slithering under her bones, a dormant power she didn't recognize.

The witch glanced at the door, as if something enticed her. She looked back at Hira with a smile. "There's someone calling you," she crooned in a sing-song voice.

The witch turned and fled the hut. The leather door flap clapped behind her. She left Hira alone, ensconced in fumes. Hira stumbled forward. She felt a sudden, desperate need to follow her. To discover what was calling out to her in the night.

"Wait!"

"Come, *vishap*," she heard the witch's ghostly voice.

Hira wondered if it was a vision, like another witch once made Almira see. Or perhaps the herbs had hallucinogenic properties, and this was all an intricate, elaborate dream. But her feet moved, and she slowly stood.

Hira staggered and held on to the chair next to the bed. Her left arm hung limply at her side, making her off-balance. She wore the death robe, so she hadn't dreamed of that. She *had* died, and they had mourned her. Mourning sand still clung to her face. She panicked at being left alone in limbo yet again, so she went after the witch.

Right outside the hut was the sea. The waves crashed against the grainy land. The moon hung low and bright, commandeering the entire earth to her attention. Hira stepped through the growth, over narrow stones, broken seashells, and dried seaweed. The waves creating an orchestra, a concerto for the willing.

Hira spotted the witch, who waited for her. She looked like a myth, dressed in a tunic as she opened her arms wide, beckoning Hira further.

"Where are you taking me?" Hira asked her. "What's out here?"

"I've been waiting for you for a long time, *vishap*. I read it in the stars, the Favia whispered it to me. They wanted you, but I said '*no!*'" the witch growled. "*They* want the war, they want to devour the dead. They know *who* you are and *what* you are."

"Did I die?" Hira swayed.

The witch shook her head and beckoned Hira forward with a small hand. "Your lifeline is long and steady, *vishap*. But only if you wake!"

The small witch looked like a painting, like a creature from olden tales.

"You call me *vishap*... what does it mean?" Hira asked.

"Old language." The witch smiled, then crooned one word, "*Dragon*."

Cold settled in Hira's stomach and she clutched a tree as she swayed against the wind. She looked at the moon, then back at the witch. It couldn't be, but... that anger, that fire which bloomed each time she raged. Did Almira feel this too?

"We are the dragons," Hira breathed.

The witch laughed. "It came to us long ago. The whispers of the night. It told us of four Balikian women birthed in sacred Istokian waters. One was born to rule the world. One was born to destroy it. One was born to save it. And the fourth... well, she has not yet been born."

"Almira's baby," Hira whispered as she clearly saw the vision of Almira with her full belly.

"Yes, *vishap*. It'll be a girl and she *might* be a queen like her mother, but the end is never written. Only the beginning." The witch nodded, as if all her madness made sense.

Then she turned from Hira and walked towards the sea. Hira followed, grasping branches along the way. They came upon a hidden clearing and the witch began to sing in the old language, swaying her slight frame. The waves crashed and thrashed against the rocks. Louder and louder the witch sang, and the waves crashed, as if a storm settled itself upon the small cove.

Hira felt a sudden stabbing strain in her dead arm. She cried out and doubled over, holding on to her useless limb. As if the wound was fresh. As if it were being scraped anew.

"She comes, *vishap*, she comes!" the witch screeched.

Hira gasped as the burning pain intensified. She screamed and fell to her knees. Her teeth gnashed against her lips.

Then an eerie silence descended, and Hira knew they weren't alone. She looked up and what she saw paused the rotation of the earth. The moon cleared her way and shone down, illuminating the lagoon.

The waves, which a moment before battered the rocks, now were calm like a water mirror. No birds, no fish, a complete silence. As if the sounds of nature muted. Then, as if the veil between what was real and what was myth lifted, Hira saw *her*.

Out of the ocean came a giant head. Then a neck. A thick neck, as wide as a tree trunk. It glistened with golden scales.

A *dragon*.

The creature's gaze met Hira's and speared her to the ground.

The witch delighted with laughter and fell backwards. Ancient words stumbled out of her mouth, but all Hira could think was, *dragon*.

The dragon's eyes were needles into her mind. She opened Hira's thoughts like a roses' petals, pushing past the resistance of time and space. Until she was *in* her. Hira gasped and shook. She cried tears at the sight of this wonder. Surely, she'd died, for here she saw the gods.

"Come to me, child of Istok," the dragon whispered against her mind.

Hira rocked back and forth. Her mouth was agape, her thoughts bared to the dragon. A desolate desert. Void of any life. A small infant standing before a legend.

"My blood has cleansed yours so that now we are one," the dragon said.

Hira shook her head, denying her words or that a creature could speak to begin with. It was impossible. Animals didn't speak. But this was not an animal. This was a god. A god of the seas. Creators of all. The golden scales glinted, and the sapphire blue eyes twinkled, as if it smiled.

"Be not afraid, human."

Slowly, Hira's bare feet stepped forward as her toes dug into the sand. The cold water touched her skin and still she walked, as if pulled, as if she had no choice. The dragon's long body circled her; it circled the world.

"I am the last," the dragon said in her mind.

Hira felt the scales of the serpentine body brush against her bare calves. Like a soft whisper, a caress. A kiss. The water reached her waist and still Hira walked into the ocean. As if it were only a pool. The water around the creature warmed. Like a bath filled for a child. A cleansing.

"Are you real, or are you in my mind?"

Hira pressed her palm against the creature's nose. It breathed, its nostrils flaring, and Hira laughed. She was warm, like her horse, but massive. The dragon's head was three times the size of a horse's head. The scales felt like porcelain plates, curving and molding its body.

"You're real," Hira whispered.

"Give me your arm, child," the dragon said.

Without meaning to, Hira extended her arm. The water bubbled, as if boiling, and heat seared her. It boiled her. Hira gasped as she strained against the agony. Her joy was gone, replaced by torturous suffering.

"You'll find them in the Isles of Hipata. With this arm, you will end the war," the dragon said. "The queen will need you. Remind her of who she is, remind her of her kindness. Remind her of the love you shared as children under the walnut trees."

Pain took Hira under until the water covered her. The dragon sunk with her, and Hira truly saw her. All of her. She regarded Hira with eerie stillness. She was long like a ship, body thick like a pine tree. It curved around her, her golden scales reflecting off the moonlight. Her head came before Hira and locked her in a hypnotizing gaze.

Hira realized she didn't drown. She breathed the water as easily as if she had gills.

"You're the rightful ruler of Istok, blessed by the last of the sea serpents. You are a dragon," it said.

"I am a dragon," Hira whispered in her mind.

"Rise and lead your people."

Her words reverberated into her thoughts until Hira's entire frame shook. She felt the creature's body coil around her. It squeezed her, and with one final compression, Hira welcomed the darkness.

Chapter Twenty-Five

HIRA

It was near noon when Hira woke face-first on the shore. She pushed herself off, noticing she was naked, sand wedged between her buttocks. Beyond the beach, the waves of the ocean industriously washed the coast as they'd done for millennia. Seagulls squawked, battling one another for the transparent crabs that sidled the rocky formation of the southern lands.

No dragon.

No moonlit lagoon.

No witch.

Had she dreamed it all? Was it a hallucination? She breathed deeply as the events of the previous night overwhelmed her and a sensation of rebirth flooded her mind. An ocean breeze ruffled her hair, the salt was thick in the wind, and the sun freckled her skin.

As she spat the strands and sand out of her mouth, she paused. She'd used her left arm. She could move it. The fingers were no longer blackened and rotted. They were *heavily* scarred; her entire arm was. As if it had burned a long time ago. It boasted the trauma of the past days or weeks. Time had lost some of its meaning in the darkness.

Hardly believing such an event, she gasped as she stared at her flesh and touched the new thickened skin. She flexed her fingers and fisted her hand. Nothing. No pain. It was a ghastly sight but *healed*. She had movement and *strength*. She'd endured and found she was made of more than just flesh and bone. Though she carried the mark of her trauma, she *lived*.

She stood with shaky legs, still staring at her arm. A miracle. Or a dragon. Looking around, she spotted her ruby blade discarded on the sand. She grasped the hilt with her left hand. Fingers of iron creating a vice grip.

She glanced at a palm tree, its body curved down into the ground. She aimed the blade and launched it. Flying swiftly, it imbedded itself into the trunk.

Slowly, she looked down at her hand, then back at the knife.

Not even Sanaa could imbed a blade like that. She went to the tree and grasped the hilt with her healthy arm. It was unmovable. A moment of hesitation passed quickly, then she switched hands. The fingers of her mangled arm closed around the base, and she yanked. It slipped out with little effort. So swiftly, she stumbled back.

Hira studied her left hand, holding the blade with its inhuman agility.

"With this arm you will end the war," she whispered the words the dragon said.

She looked back at the water, and the waves innocently splashed against the terrain. Hira Balik was born from the ocean and re-birthed within it last night. Hira had the strength of the powerful sea in her veins, and she felt a sudden hope and thrill run through her.

She *was* a warrior. She *was* a lady. Hira would like to hear anyone voice their displeasure at her dual nature. Today she felt an untamable fire rising within her. Out of the countless cells in the universe, life chose the ones which formulated Hira and stitched them together to create her mind, body, and soul. Forged from millennia of star-residue, here she stood. Yes, her body held unfathomable scars, but her body also chronicled her endurance.

"I'm the Lady of Istok," she said to the waters. "And I will lead my people."

Then she recalled the Sea Wife. The Isles of Hipata. *Her* crew.

Noon was almost upon her, and she hoped Justan had not left. She ran up the beach and found the hut abandoned. Her clothing, boots, and cape left neatly folded over a chair. Gone was the fire, the bones, the herbs, and any trace a witch ever lived there.

"Thank you," she said to the emptiness. It felt right to thank the sorceress for saving her life and her arm. For recognizing a strength, Hira didn't know she possessed.

She was a Balik. She was a dragon. *Vishap.*

Dressing quickly, Hira tucked her blade into her trousers. She wandered outside and hoped to find a road that could lead her to the docks. Before she could set foot on the sand hill to find a road, she stumbled into Quent.

His face was red and blotchy, eyes swollen as if he'd been crying. He fell backwards and landed on the gravel.

"My lady! Y-you're alive!" he sputtered.

She almost laughed. *Yes!* She was alive! She had life, and she'd stared death in the face and come back. Yanking him up with her mangled arm, it as if he weighed no more than a rice sack.

"But you died!" Quent's eyes were still wild in disbelief.

"Did you sneak out of the ship again?" Dumbly, he nodded, and she laughed, lifting him up into the air and swirling him as he floundered. "Keep disobeying, Quent! Have they left?"

He stuttered, then clasped her. "No-no, but soon they will. I only snuck out to stay with your body until they returned…"

She kissed his forehead in relief. Bless the boy and his incorrigible ways! Just seeing him filled her with happiness. They were going home!

"We need to catch them! Run, Quent! To the docks, hurry!"

Startled, he did as he was told. The moment her boots landed on the road, she felt strength and energy course through her like it never had before. Her feet were light and sure. It was a near dance over the dirt pathway. She sped past farmers and mills, braying mules, and alarmed gardeners. Dogs barked, unsure of the need to run but becoming excited none the less.

They ran until they came upon a hill where she saw the other side of what looked like a peninsula and a small town at the tip. The coast was winding, settlements clutched against the terrain, peppered with trees and palms that swayed in the cool breeze.

Calisto.

In the distance, by the port, she recognized the Night Serpent. Her sails were up. They were readying to leave. They'd better not.

"Run Quent!"

But he couldn't keep up. He was coughing and wheezing and bright red in the face. Hira grasped him and hefted him onto her back. He yelped and protested, but to her, he was no trouble.

Without pause, she ran down the hill at full speed with strength she didn't recognize. Her heart pounded in desperation. She jumped over fences like a racing mare and landed in perfect synchronization on steady feet. No matter what, she needed to be on that ship.

"Slow down!" Quent screeched, clutching her neck and shoulders, but she paid him no mind as she thundered down the road.

When she reached the town, she sped through streets, pushing vendors, soldiers, and anyone in her way. People shrieked curses at her, but she didn't pause. The noon sun was high in the sky and Istokian ships were never late. When she saw the bay, she shouted.

"STOP THAT SHIP!"

Quent slid down her back and rushed next to her. She ran through the docks at a thundering speed as anglers screamed, sea birds startled and quacked. Men dropped their catch as she careened through fisheries with Quent barely keeping up with her dash.

"COMMANDER!!"

"Lady Hira!" Quent panted. "It's too late!"

"CAPTAIN JUTIA! STOP THE SHIP! STOP THAT SHIP!"

Folks, noticing the commotion, shouted at the Night Serpent to stop and soon chaos surrounded her as the people of Calisto joined the fray.

"COMMANDER!" she yelled.

When the sails dropped, she screamed in joy. She rushed the last few docks and jumped on crate boxes. She waved her arms chaotically.

"COMMANDER!"

Justan ran to the back of the ship, and he stared at her with an open mouth. His face paled and his eyes seemed on the verge of panic. Captain Jutia was instantly at his side and watched Hira in equal astonishment. Hira cupped her hands over her lips.

"You said you wouldn't leave!" Hira shouted.

His expressions were nearly comical. Then his face changed to something like relief, the sort that weighed him down the past few hours. "Hira Balik?"

"That's *Lady* Hira Balik to you, Commander! Now turn my ship around!" And she laughed.

Justan was still too shocked to comprehend. "You fucking died last night!" he said, pointing to her accusatorially.

She threw her head back, feeling the sea air in her hair. It filled her lungs, and she suddenly needed to feel water. Submerse herself in the ocean's freshness. She was born in this ocean. She'd died in this ocean. And she'd return to this same sea.

"Well, I'm alive *now*," she screamed. "And I'm coming with you!"

Then she dove into the bay and swam with a capacity she never possessed. She stroked through the water like a fish, never tiring and gliding over it as if the strength of a dragon was in her veins. They threw the ladder down and with ease she reached the Night Serpent and climbed up the ship with Quent lagging.

Commander Justan grasped her hand and hauled her in. She shook the water from her hair as she landed on the deck with a bright smile.

Justan touched her face and pulled her to him. He gaped at her with wide brown eyes. Awed. She awed him. She'd awed no one before. He pushed back her wet bangs and, for once, she didn't care that her scar was in full view. Her scars were battles she'd survived. She was a beast in all the best possible ways.

He was so confused—seeming to round between fear and relief. As if the gods answered his prayers for the first time after a lifetime of disappointment.

She felt her heart go to him and she reassured him with a smile. On her deathbed, tenderness for Justan Seaver filled her. He'd held her and comforted her. He'd been real and open. Seeing him now, the tenderness didn't ebb. On the contrary, it was morphing into something else. A warmth she wasn't brave enough to name because to give it a name was to provide it meaning.

He shook his head, and his shoulders sagged. Hira did not lose sight of the softness in his brown eyes as they settled on her, taking her fully in.

"You *died* last night," he whispered.

She *had*. She was glad it had been in his arms, but at this moment, she wouldn't confide that. Not when she had a task, and a pirate to kill.

Gods help the one who messed with a woman reborn. She was a Balik for a reason. Ocean fury ruled her veins.

"I know where the Sea Wife is, Commander!" she said, then turning to Jutia, who watched her with trepidation, "Set course to the Isles of Hipata, Captain. Let's go get *my* crew."

The sailors of the Night Serpent differed from the Sea Wife. The men remained devoted to Captain Jutia, and eyed Hira with suspicion. Jutia assured her they were superstitious. People didn't come back from wounds such as the one Hira had.

Once Hira changed to clean, dry clothing, she felt more like herself. Jutia provided her with a long leather ribbon and the lady listened as the captain and commander updated her on the other two ships, which had originally escorted them. They had instructed the other ships to go straight to Treveri to give details and information on Hira's dire condition.

Because of the men's prying eyes, Hira found a corner to hide in. A stack of crate boxes served as her temporary shelter so she could digest the occurrences of the night. She sat and faced the afternoon sun as she carefully wrapped the leather around her arm. The fingers looked like burned scar tissue and the deformity covered her to the elbow. She didn't care. It gave her strength and resolve. Still, it was a frightening sight, and she didn't care for constant explanations and judgmental looks.

"It's impossible for that wound to have healed so quickly," came a gruff voice from behind her.

Justan watched her wearily. He must've searched for her, slipping between the tight spaces of the ship. His white shirt was open, and the breeze revealed his muscled chest peppered with dark hairs. She looked away and focused on the binding. There was much she needed to ponder, such as his dedication to keeping her alive. How he'd mourned her.

"You took me to a witch. What did you think would happen?"

He shook his head and ran his fingers through his dancing locks. "I thought... she would save you, but still have to amputate."

She expected the same thing herself. After the happenings of the night, she feared she now walked a path between what was human and what was not. Something she wasn't willing to explore just yet.

Instead, she smiled, attempting to ease his worry, but it didn't work.

"You were dead. I saw you *die*. No breath," he said with wild, intense eyes. "I... I wrapped you in funeral cloth. *Hours* passed."

She recalled glimpses of him doing so. Watching him from the ceiling like a specter. "I remember little."

His jaw tightened. "Because you were *dead*."

She didn't know what to divulge. He'd think her mad if she told him what she experienced. Even Almira herself wouldn't understand and dismiss it as a dream. But it was so tangible. She'd felt the scales of the dragon against her legs and palms. She smelled its sea-scented body. It was the most vivid memory she carried.

Justan carefully came closer, and Hira slid sideways so that they sat shoulder to shoulder, staring out into the ocean on top of a small box.

"What happened after we left you?" he asked.

Hira peeked at him, enjoying the momentary glimpse of his profile, of his nose painting a perfect silhouette. She realized how close they were. She could study the grain of his skin, the pores where his beard grew.

"You won't believe me."

"Give me the benefit of the doubt. I washed your body for burial," he breathed.

Her heart leaned to him, but she reeled it in. He was not for the having and she had a country to rule. She could not lose focus of the promises she'd made. Instead, she stared at her wrapped hand, the fingers still visible to allow for the dexterity of a blade.

"I was dead... From the ceiling, I saw you wrapping me. But I couldn't speak. I couldn't even feel anything other than recognition. Then... you and Quent left, and someone yanked me back into my body. At first..." she sighed and shook her head. "It felt all wrong and tight. The lights were too bright and sound too loud."

She looked at him and found him transfixed in her comments, lapping them up and believing her.

"The witch was there, and she took me to... a dragon." She cast the words out of her mind because saying them made them real.

"A *dragon?*" he laughed incredulously. When she didn't share his humor, he stopped and studied her, his mouth slacking. "You're serious?"

She blushed, sensing that each time she recounted the occurrences, they would promptly label her a babbler of tales. One that crafted lies for a bit of attention. Or simply one that hallucinated. None of that was good. Especially if she wished to be trusted with leading her people and representing them before the crown.

Still, a silly part of her wished she could confide in *someone*. Someone like the commander. Not that she *should* confide in the commander. He was to be the husband of another. The last thing she wanted was for Jutia to believe Hira had ulterior motives in their friendship.

"I know it sounds like a fanciful tale, but it happened. You don't have to believe it." She didn't wish to force intimacy between them when he'd only allowed it as she lay dying.

He looked out into the sea. "Tell me."

Softly, she told him what occurred, with all the detail she could muster. He said nothing, nor did he provide any indications of his thoughts, but listened with respectful silence. When she finished, he sat quietly, mulling over her words. She flushed, feeling like she must explain herself and assure him she was of the right mind. Hira didn't quite understand why his good opinion should matter so.

"Perhaps it was a dream, Commander. Perhaps I *did* die, walked in the beyond, and met the gods of old. Either way, I live *now*." She fisted her bandaged arm and flexed it. "I was told the location of the Sea Wife. If we find the ship in the Isles of Hipata, then we'll know. If the child is born a girl, we'll know."

To her astonishment, he reached out and gently took her battered arm. His fingers lightly ghosting over her mangled ones. A part of her wished to recoil. She didn't wish him to feel the roughness of her new skin. But his touch lingered as he contemplated her story and her wound.

"I cannot deny that this healing is a miracle." He looked at her. "And I cannot deny that you being alive is also a wonder. There are old Garian tales, ancient. Before Istok invaded us, when Garians were free people."

"You *are* free," Hira said, almost offended.

There was an archaic anger flittering in the brown expanse of his irises. "For fuck's sake, Hira. We were independent and you should know that. My father's castle was once the capital of our small kingdom. It wasn't much, but it was ours."

His remarks were awful to hear, not that she didn't know them. Everyone knew the Garians were *different*. Long ago Istokians forced them to integrate with Istok in exchange for protection against Norr. Given that her family ruled Istok for centuries, somewhere along the line, a Balikian ruler, had perpetuated these crimes.

It felt strange to suffer guilt over something not of her making, but still part of her heritage. It caused her great discomfort, but she had to bear it. She had to bear the discomfort. Ruling was uncomfortable, and all she could hope was to be cognizant of it and do better.

"What I'm trying to say is that I understand legend and whispers of magic. My people believed—*believe*—in the wizardry of this old earth more than the skeptical Istokians." He flushed. Perhaps not sure how to showcase this part of his beliefs. "We have a word. It's called *vishap*."

She felt the blood drain from her face as her skin prickled.

"*What* did you say?"

"*Vishap*. It means -"

"Dragon."

"Actually," he smiled, self-consciously, and had she not been shocked, she would've thought him lovely. "It's not cut and dry. *Vi* means return and *shap* stands for—and this is a loose translation—life. Together, their meaning changes. Together they mean returned by a dragon."

She stared at him, acutely aware of the swaying of the ship. That's how she felt herself, lost in the ocean, having little comprehension of the complexities surrounding her journey. How much she'd changed since she stepped foot on the Sea Wife.

"Returned by a dragon," Hira whispered.

He shrugged and pushed back his hair from his face. "In the old tales, they said that those who were *vishap* were... a sort of reincarnation of one who was once powerful. One that Zeita deemed needed."

Hira's stomach lurched. "Who is Zeita?"

Justan looked at her almost as if she should know, but Hira didn't know. She'd never heard these fables. Her uncle had little time for indigenous beliefs, so it did not surprise her she was unfamiliar with them. If hard fact and science couldn't prove it, he often dismissed it. Legends were children's tales. The earth didn't speak, to him, the earth was dead.

"Zeita. Our goddess. The Great Dragon." He pointed to the sails of the Night Serpent. Though they were black, they had the outline of the Istokian dragon on them. "Istokians took her and made her their symbol without understanding what she was."

Hira stared at the emblem she'd seen all her life. The Istokian High Seat was always called the Great Dragon, and all this time, they'd stolen it from the Garians. She grimaced at the shame that filled her.

"If she came to you, if she saved you, it was for a reason," Justan said.

"But what does it *mean*?" Hira asked. "Am I still me? Who am I, or *what* am I?"

Justan's smile lit his handsome face. "You're Hira. Heir of Lord Beltran."

There was a soft cadence to his voice when he said her name.

She shoved his shoulder in frustration. "You said reincarnation. Not even the Suidian and Norrians believe in such concepts. To live again? To be a vessel? It's ridiculous."

The entire conversation veered into madness.

Justan nodded. "Yes, it is. It's an ancient tale. The Garians believe Zeita gave birth to all living things on this earth. She shed all her scales and as they washed up to shore, they became the different people of Old Verden."

"From the sea our bodies came…" Hira whispered in realization.

"To the sea our bodies go." Justan shrugged, then looked to the sky. The sun was almost gone, and the small sparkle of stars peppered the horizon. "And in the stars are those who are lost to us. Like my mother."

It startled her how much she enjoyed his company. That deep tone of his voice, and his words filled with wonder and history. She was never one to learn things written in scrolls, but when he spoke, she sat enraptured. She suckled the meaning and painted her heart with it. She realized there was much more to Justan than she'd thought. It was as if she'd not wanted to see him.

"And your brother," she reminded him.

He sucked in a breath and nodded, then agreed, "And him."

The intimacy was breathtaking. She realized she enjoyed his words and the tone of his voice.   "What if it was Zeita who I met? Maybe it's not magic or mystical belief. Perhaps it's simply healing we don't understand because of our limited knowledge. Maybe there are properties that certain animals exhibit that are beneficial to humans. Ancient people had no explanation for it, so they called them gods, but I am real. My arm is real."

They were quiet as they took in the waves.

Then the commander sighed and glanced at her. "You confided in me before you died."

She remembered. She told him Jutia loved him. Words

carelessly spoken because she believed she wouldn't make it, despite her desire to live. She'd wanted to do something nice for Jutia, for her help during her illness. A part of her wished Jutia didn't love him. Or perhaps a part of her clearly understood *why* Jutia loved him.

"I've ended the engagement," he said.

Her head snapped up to stare at him in horror. "But—"

"There's so much you don't know. Things I'm… ashamed of," his voice broke, and he looked away.

Hira could imagine the acts played out in ports and pleasure houses where they frequented while Jutia watched a man she loved couple with others.

He glanced at her, face still red and jaw locked. "I am a bit of a romantic at heart. I sleep with random women because… I suppose I don't have to give anything of myself. My life has been chaotic for a long time. Quent takes precedence, so I've pocketed desires I had as a youth to please my father and *others*. But there're days when I wonder how life would've turned out had I stood my ground. Been stronger."

Hira couldn't believe his words. Aside from the women she'd left behind in Easima, Justan seemed to her one of the strongest people of her acquaintance. He constantly worried about his brother, he fretted about Hira herself, and nobly broke his engagement to Jutia when he realized he was hurting her.

"You *are* strong," Hira insisted.

He shook his head. "Most days, I don't feel powerful. I'm like a small ship in a great storm, teetering between survival and capsizing. I spend each moment worrying about Quent, the men, this voyage, Istok…" He cast his eyes away as he exposed himself. "*You*."

She flushed and severed contact with his intense gaze. She wished he didn't look at her in that fashion. "Well, you no longer have to worry about me." She raised her mangled arm. "I've been blessed by the gods."

He smiled, and she was bold enough to hold his stare. It was strange to sit with a man—a *lord*—in this manner. Lords were such foreign, intimidating people. As if they saw her as a walking cunt, a possibility for either a pleasurable evening or a title to be gained. To be regarded as a regular person and spoken to like one would to a peer was exhilarating.

She tucked a wild red strand behind her ear. "You've been very kind to me, despite our tumultuous beginning. I'd like to be friends, if you would permit."

At this, his face hardened, and tension entered his shoulder. "I don't deserve your friendship, my lady."

She had a hard time swallowing. It was the most intimate conversation she'd ever partaken in. Despite the clothing she wore, she felt naked. "I bestow my friendship to whom I wish. So, it's yours. Friendship would be a refreshing change, don't you think? It would certainly take less energy than hating one another for no reason."

Justan stared at her in wonder, then slowly nodded. He stood sharply and dusted his trousers. He patted himself down, searching for his pipe. When he didn't find it, he seemed at a loss for what to do with his hands. With himself.

"Well, I'm going to go over the maps again. Make certain we're on course. Excuse me, my lady." He bowed, turned, and left.

He exhibited excellent navigational skills. They wouldn't have veered off course, but she understood the discomfort. He was a lord, and she was a lady. For them to speak in confidence was improper enough as it was. Almira would disapprove of such a familiarity or even such a friendship unless they tied it to a marriage. Unless Hira would take him as a husband, everyone would discourage such intimacy. He was her commander. He answered to her. She governed his actions.

Hira watched as he walked away. He'd wrapped her in funeral cloth, had *mourned* her. At that moment, she couldn't think of any other man who deserved her more.

Isabelle Olmo

Chapter Twenty-Six

SANAA

Sanaa stood next to M on the queen's balcony. The preparations for the trip to Istok—or, more realistically, the invasion—were at hand. The queen had no time for rest. The implications of the past few days were a raw wound that made Almira pace from room to room.

Sanaa's nerves frayed in the quake of the queen's wanderings. It if felt as if the walls of the castle closed in and drowned them. Somewhere out there was Hira. Impulsive and stubborn, easily swayed with a complimentary word, accepting smiles and allowing them to pass as friendship.

"I fear for our young friend." M's tone was dim as her thoughts meandered in the same direction as Sanaa's.

Not that Sanaa disagreed with her, but she didn't speak life into the dark thoughts of her mind. She glanced away and held her own judgment deep within her, as she always did.

"We can hope she is the dragon Almira believes her to be," Sanaa said.

M, having no qualms about voicing her own worry and allowing it to flow freely, looked at the captain with something akin to frustration.

"And what happens if they've killed her? What happens if the heir is gone?" M asked.

Sanaa stubbed out her cigar with a grimace. As if she, a bastard child of a disgraced house, had the answers. "Then Lady Furia claims the seat. Could she be a good ruler? We don't know. What we know is her hate for the queen might supersede her reasoning. And so, to unseat her would be a legitimate act of war. Many of Istok's bannermen would side with her."

M inhaled sharply and cursed, tossing her cigar on the ground and mashing her booted foot on it. "Hira is a skilled warrior and won't be easily killed. We've taught her much and must have faith in her."

Despite wishing to place her doubts in permanent suspension, Sanaa's mood was sour. She simply grunted as a response, not yearning to fall into colloquies about Hira's abilities.

The Balikian women held a fanciful notion that because they were from a noble house, that they were untouchable. *Dragons*, Sanaa scoffed inwardly. Legends couldn't protect the human body and death came for them all. The Favia were constantly waiting for the demise of warriors; it was a battle none could win.

"Nothing?" Almira snapped loudly from inside of her rooms.

The poor royal Ley had tirelessly scoured law texts with Almira as his violent task master. Her pregnancy did little to discourage the queen from her uncontrollable frets.

"If he finds nothing, then there's nothing to concern ourselves with," M said quietly, for Sanaa's ears only.

But Sanaa was uncertain. Laws, though mostly enacted in good conscience, could easily work to the detriment of others. Their carefully worded clauses allowed leniency for a beguiling noble to have the law serve their purposes and schemes. Sanaa had an awful feeling that Furia was no Arrigo. She was a shadow, a specter, painted in plain sight as she syphoned the information she needed for her ultimate act. She was a child of Beltran, and in many ways, she was Almira's equal. That alone tightened Sanaa's stomach. Almira succeeded because no one was like Almira, but the world where she was unique in temperament was quickly diminishing.

Sanaa stepped back into the room.

"No sign of Delara?" the queen asked.

"No." Sanaa stood passively next to her and looked down at her oldest friend. "You should be prepared for Furia to take the seat by force."

"She won't," Almira said, shaking her head. "She can't."

"She *will* if her plan fails," Sanaa warned.

Almira took a deep breath and met her eyes. "My father wouldn't have gone to such lengths to warn me of a blood-thirsty person. Disappearing ink? A spy? A secret prisoner? No. He understood Furia very well. She's been planning this for a long time, her moves are calculated, and I'm already behind in the game."

"Agreed. But if you thwart her plans, if she's cornered, she'll resort to fire and iron," Sanaa said, tossing a scroll the Ley had on the table, making him jump.

"And we'll be ready for her," Almira said as her face reddened.

Sanaa looked at Lady Poelia and Hester, who sat before the hearth. Both seemed exhausted. The lady had her head on the seamstresses' shoulder while Hester carefully sewed feathers to one of the queen's gowns.

"Politically, what is the *worst* she can do?" Lady Gita paced and wrung her hands.

"Split Istok," Hester said without looking up from her task.

Gita took a sharp breath. She had a right to anguish. As the closest neighbor, even half of an armada could decimate Suid's capital, and they would have little ability to defend themselves against such a coastal attack. The pride of Istok was about to become the threat of the world.

"We must hope for the best. We must hope our Hira can maintain her seat," Poelia said tiredly. She pressed her mouth to Hester's shoulder, and the latter intertwined their fingers. It was a sweet display in a sea of pestilence.

The Ley chucked the scroll and rubbed his scalp. The captain almost felt sorry for the poor man at the mercy of the queen's desperation.

"I apologize, majesty." Ley Wallace hardly dared to look at the queen, who bristled with frustration.

Almira groaned down what was most likely a yell and resumed her pacing, her eyes dark as she clutched her belly. "She knows something I don't."

Ah, that was the problem, Sanaa thought. Almira was used to out-thinking and planning. The captain was certain that not even a vocal love-session with her husband could improve the queen's mood.

"How about Antilay?"

The room turned to the inconspicuous tiny figure by the door. It was the young Lady Lianna who sported a self-satisfied smile as she clutched scrolls. The girl was in her sleeping gown, barefooted, with hair wrapped in a lovely lilac scarf.

Sanaa raised a brow as Almira looked at her, torn between confusion and intrigue. The Lady Gita did not, however, seem bewildered. As if she were used to the child appearing with strange stories of laws and legends. She flushed and walked to her daughter with a frustrated expression.

"Why are you out of bed?" Gita demanded.

"What is Antilay?" Almira ignored her aunt and came closer to Lianna.

The girl, not impressed with her mother's demands, considered the queen. Her chin lifted, and it took Sanaa aback by how much she looked like young Almira. The same set mouth and straight brows. Like mirror etches of one another set in separate decades.

"Antilay is a sort of… ritual. A trial per se. The Fillimians—the nomadic sailors who ruled over Istok before Lady Dominia founded House Balik—had a process in place when they wished to replace a ruler. When a High Seat is found to be unfit they can be removed by bringing proof of their corrupt, disingenuous, or erratically based actions. It ensures a relatively peaceful transfer of power. Granted, new edicts would have to be enacted with the new regime as a proceeding such as Antilay would sever all established alliances. But I'm certain you know that, Majesty. A rather clever plan, if you ask me," Lady Lianna finished with a proud smile, without realizing her words were a sword embedded in the rest of them.

"Where did you read such nonsense?" Gita growled.

Lianna looked at her mother with wide, golden eyes. "Last year, Lord Beltran gifted me the Historical Laws of the Coastal Lands."

"My father..." Almira walked to the child and stood before her anxiously. "Exactly *when* did he provide you with these scrolls?"

Lianna shrugged. "He caught me in the royal library. I snuck in there because I was bored with your wedding festivities. He asked what I was reading, and I told him about some fictional account from the Free Isle. I mentioned I wished to be a Ley, and he was greatly amused. He said my father would '*love that*'. Then he gifted me a scroll from his personal collection. He mentioned that he would quiz me when he saw me again," and at that, she looked a little crestfallen.

Sanaa could imagine the scene and how much the child would've reminded Beltran of his own daughter before she snatched her independence from his influence.

"Do you think he planned it?" Sanaa asked Almira.

The queen slowly shook her head. She walked around, twisting her fingers together. "No... for once, fortune has benefited me. Out of all the scrolls father traveled with, he presented *that* one to our dear Lianna."

"But majesty, ancient Fillimian laws are hardly something to concern ourselves with," Ley Wallace said, a little red in the face. Sanaa could only imagine his embarrassment at not knowing a vital law, which the small child provided.

"That's where you're wrong, Ley Wallace," the queen snapped. "In Istok, they didn't eradicate Fillimian Laws. Are they rare and seldom used? Absolutely. But once in a while, a Fillimian law is followed. My father himself had a penchant for them."

Poelia stood and walked to Almira to grasp her hands. An attempt to calm her. "But you are forgetting, Furia would have to bring proof of Hira's corrupt, disingenuous, or erratically based actions."

Sanaa sighed and rubbed at her eyes. "The girl sliced off her Balikian hair and escaped wearing a stolen soldier's uniform to cross the world, denounce her inheritance, and become a *guard*," Sanaa said with a harsh tone, fully understanding that many noble houses would see such behavior as erratic. Damn them all!

Almira had to sit down. Her face was flushed red as she closed her eyes and breathed through her frustrations. The shadows of the fire danced over her features, and it reminded Sanaa of the Favia—lapping at her for all her actions.

"That's it. That's what she'll use. Furia needs Hira *alive* to proceed with Antilay. She'll bring her before the Istokian court, present her shackled to the nobles, then read her sins. The nobility is fickle, easily swayed. At least we know Furia will try all in her power to ensure Hira lives until that moment because you can't unseat a corpse," Almira said darkly.

"Bless us…" Poelia pressed her hand against her mouth. "Poor child."

M strode into the room from the balcony, her face bright, her eyes wide. "It's Delara! She's arrived!"

"Oh, thank the gods!" Gita cried.

"Yes, the *gods*," Hester murmured. "Nothing to do with the girl's ability to ride without rest."

"Off to bed!" Gita didn't hear Hester as she pushed a protesting Lianna out.

A few moments later, Lady Delara rushed into the quarters, flushed and panting. Her armor was muddy and her frame shivering against a chill the last of winter brought. M quickly gave her water and Nadim provided her a chair by the fire.

Delara wiped her mouth against her hand and pushed back her hair.

"Lord Thebo says… Suid will ride with Ouest into Istok," Delara said grimly.

Gita gasped, as did Lady Poelia. The women huddled together joined in their worry for the High Lord.

Almira, however, showed only signs of increasing agitation. "Then we must go. Alton can catch up to us. The Red Army will be enough. Any word on Hira?"

Delara nodded and looked hesitant in her next words. "The Sea Wife arrived in Iguanta a week ago. Sources say they saw Hira in perfect health, along with the rest of the crew. They docked for the night and left the following morning."

"Fucking Iguanta," M murmured darkly. "A cesspool of thieves. A good place for Furia to hide."

The room seemed to sigh in relief. Poelia murmured a quick prayer and sat by the queen.

"Well, that's good news," Ley Wallace said, but Delara shook her head.

She took the food offered to her by Nadim and stuffed a roll into her mouth. In between bites she said, "Lord Thebo just received word that a Captain Strauss of The Red Dragon attacked The Sea Wife. They fought the pirates off and the next morning, they docked in Iguanta."

"Captain Strauss, you say?" Nadim carefully stepped forward.

They turned to stare at the Keeper, whose brown eyes were solemn. He never interrupted Almira's talks and to have him do so, made them all shift with uncertainty.

"Yes," Delara nodded.

"I apologize, Majesty." Nadim's cheeks tinted pink. "But Strauss is an old sea-pirate, vicious and cunning. I had some dealings with him many years ago. He mostly sticks to the Free Isle these days. But above all, he has a golden eye."

Almira's face paled.

"The underbelly of the world knows of Furia's plans." M's lips were curled in distaste. "If they can capture Hira before Furia has her, they will sell her to Furia for a pretty price."

She voiced what Sanaa thought. She could almost see hands attempting to grasp Hira ahead of landing in Treveri, while the girl happily wandered the markets and engaged with vendors. No one to protect her or make her safety their priority.

"She's being hunted, and she doesn't know it," Sanaa said.

Almira stood suddenly, her marbled black eyes pointed at the fire. Sanaa walked behind her. She realized what the queen saw. A man with a golden eye attempting to capture Hira because he'd learned of the sinister plans of Furia, and wished to make extra coin meant that...

"Furia is in league with Arrigo," Almira whispered and shook her head. "He'd told me he had allies that would turn my blood cold. They've been planning this for years. He knew I had a sister. During his captivity, Arrigo probably tormented my father with that knowledge. *That's* what father tried to warn me about before he died."

The room silenced as the knowledge now drenched them with the implications.

Almira's breathing was harsh. "It means Arrigo and Furia spoke openly of the plan in front of Strauss. The pirate, seeing an opportunity for a little more coin, attempted to capture Hira and sell her to Furia or Arrigo."

"That's not all, Majesty," Delara said.

Almira tensed.

"They instructed two of the escorting ships to sail ahead," Delara looked to the queen.

Almira turned sharply to her, her eyes wide and her face pale. "What do you mean? The escort has *left* her?"

Delara nodded. "They sailed to Treveri without her. Informants spotted them off the southern coast, past Calisto. And… only one ship remained in Calisto and it was *not* the Sea Wife."

Sanaa glanced at Almira, knowing full well where her thoughts led. "We don't know anything yet."

"What else would you like to know, Captain?" Almira snarled. "How she's trapped? Chained? Tortured? Held hostage so she can be dragged before Furia and pay for my father's deeds before they decapitate her?"

The queen rounded on Delara, who could scarcely meet her eyes.

"Where is the Sea Wife?" Almira asked.

"They don't know," Delara said quickly.

"Damn them all to hell!" Almira roared. "If Hira is captured, which there is a high likelihood of that being so, it's *done*. I'll have *no* choice than to march the Suidian and Ouestern armies to Istok and kill *my* people to remove my sister from the High Seat!"

Almira took a sharp, shaking breath and pulled away when Lady Poelia tried to comfort her. She was having none of their pity. She was a raging fire. They quieted around her as she paced, her mind likely working all scenarios to prevent a war of this magnitude.

"I want us out of this castle in two days, Sanaa. Two days. I'll send word to Alton. I require at least half of our army. The Norrians have been playing hide and seek with Alton for months. I won't let my soldiers linger in uselessness while I need them. I shall not lose my house and country to this. I shan't lose Hira. We march to Istok *now*."

"Will you call a war council meeting?" Ley Wallace said, watching her with wide eyes.

"By the time the fine lords finish delighting in their decorous speeches, Hira will be *dead*," Almira growled, and Ley Wallace blanched.

As she yelled, Almira pressed her hand to her stomach and grimaced. The happenings constantly excited the child. The queen was also dangerously close to her birthing day. Any attempt to convince her to change her mind failed. Not even the king, with his head between her legs, managed to do much of anything.

"*Cuzo*, you'll excite yourself into a premature birth," Sanaa muttered.

Usually if they were alone, her words would be more forceful, but she had no intention of poking a dragon before all to witness. Gods knew who would have to pay the price.

Almira ignored her and turned towards her side room, which was completed a month before. Sanaa thought it would've been the nursery, but no, her majesty wanted a *war room*. They'd set a large table with the map of New Verden laid over it. Almira used it more and more the longer the Northern Conflict dragged.

She stood before the map with her belly advancing over the country's rendition, as if the child already joined in matters of state. They followed her in and waited for her machinations. She stretched her hands over the table, her eyes studying and calculating the moving plays.

"Where will Thebo find us?" Almira glanced at Delara.

Her guard cleared her throat and pointed to the map. "The High Lord plans to march the Red Army to the Pas of Gul, past the

Mountains of Anahij."

"And how will the king be able to cross into Istok and meet us there without being seen? He'd have to cut straight through Ciraton—isn't that Furia's castle?" Sanaa asked as she leaned forward and followed the path indicated with her finger. "Furthermore, you're leaving the Norrian border vulnerable."

Almira's eyes shifted back and forth, her thoughts racing. She paused at the drawing of a dark black forest that ran along the edge of Istok and Suid. It was a thickly wooded area, spanning for miles.

"The Black Forrest cocoons Ciraton on the westside so Alton will have to go through the forest." Almira pressed her finger into the rendition of the zone. "And with the Norrians preoccupied with their own internal battles, I can only hope they don't notice half our army missing."

A weak plan indeed, Sanaa fumed and fought the urge to yell. The pounding in her temples was unbearable.

M scoffed and shook her head. "Half an army through a forest? They'll be seen. It's an impossibility."

But Almira's face was tight with concentration, her brows a straight line and her shoulders hunched in anger and worry. "Alton will do it. He's a skilled leader. People don't wander into that forest. Ciratonians are afraid of it, they believe it's haunted. On the other side of the woods is Suid. Once they're in Suidian land, it won't matter."

The queen grabbed one of her metal pieces she used for strategizing and placed it in the forest. The crown on top of the piece signifying the king.

"They march down the border of Suid and Istok and can meet us at the Pas of Gul. I'll write to Alton. Nadim, I need the fastest rider we have. Right now, our enemy is time."

Chapter Twenty-Seven

HIRA

When they entered the Southern Seas, large scalla appeared against the hull. They jumped into the air, then crashed down in enormous splashes that drenched the crew. The white scaled bodies of the scalla hid the favored sea fare of Istokian people. Their giant, triangle shaped tails forced their large bodies to the surface and up into the air as the ship cut through the waters.

Captain Jutia was at the helm, and she laughed a beautiful, crystalline laugh when she spotted them. "Fresh fish tonight!"

Justan stood at the bow with a huge harpoon in his hands, the wind blowing his hair about. Hira watched him, transfixed. His face was a mask of concentration as he aimed the weapon, and in an expert move, he threw the harpoon and speared a massive scalla right through its eye.

The men shouted in excitement as they hauled in the beast and Hira helped with the nets. Upon landing on the deck, the crew and Hira roared in delight. She'd never had scalla this fresh before. With her newfound strength, Hira slid the net across the planks with ease.

Jutia bent down and sliced the side of the animal. She dug her fingers into the raw meat, popping a sinewy chunk into her mouth.

"Pepper them well, Friar! I want it *spicy*." Jutia laughed as she wiped the bloody knife against her trousers.

The sailors spoke excitedly in anticipation of the feast. Hira herself was ready for a true roast and it made her miss being in Korkoran, enjoying her uncle's famed suppers. Her gaze wandered to Justan, who yanked out the harpoon from the animal. Their eyes briefly met, but he was called by one of the men.

"My lady," Jutia said with a smirk. "We've entered the Sea of Jacobin. Did you know that this is the only place where scalla grow this large?" Jutia asked as she came to stand next to Hira. With a devious grin she continued as she looked on at Justan, "He didn't learn how to use a harpoon like that until five years ago. He has great aim, now. I'll give him that."

Hira blushed a deep red at being caught lingering her gaze on the commander. The captain stepped back to the netting and began rolling it in precise, practiced movements. Hira bent down to aid her in the task, and together, they made quick work of it before placing it into its crate.

Since the Night Serpent was a smaller ship, Hira had to share quarters with Jutia But the two women had barely spoken a word in the days they'd spent at sea. Hira felt she needed to clear the air of what felt like a prolonged awkwardness.

"I'd forgotten how much I love fishing," Hira said with a smile.

Jutia leaned back on the rails, her long dark hair dancing in the wind, her slim legs encased in black leather that looked to be made for her. She lit a cigar with a smirk and puffed out smoke.

"Fishing is in our blood. Our people have always lived off the ocean and its bounty," Jutia said.

They stood in silence and Hira pondered on what to say to the captain.

"I haven't thanked you, Captain," Hira finally said.

She'd noted a change in Jutia's behavior towards her. Granted, they'd not spent much time together but Hira wandered if the chilliness was caused because of Justan's decision to end their engagement. Perhaps the captain simply attempted self-preservation.

"No need," Jutia said rather casually, with a smile.

Hira's stomach burned. It was such a throwaway, false statement. "I think there is."

To her surprise, Jutia abruptly pushed herself off the rail and placed her hand on Hira's chest. She was taller, and it felt combative. The lady froze, tittering between matching Jutia's energy or being a much-needed pacifist.

"I didn't do it for *you*," Jutia said harshly. The captain realized her move and quickly pulled back, turning to face the sea.

Oh, no, she thought.

Hira chewed on her lip as shame flooded her for hurting a person who'd tried her best to keep her alive. Held her down as she was healed. Brought water to her lips. Wrote letters to Almira while Hira agonized on her deathbed.

Words were so difficult when the meaning was shadowed. She felt she'd meddled with things not of her business. It sharply felt like something someone worthy of the High Seat shouldn't do. Almira certainly avoided meddling with other people's personal affairs.

Hira took a tentative step towards her. "I betrayed your trust. It was not intentional. I thought I was—"

"Dying. You were. You *did*. You're a little bit of a miracle." Jutia glanced at Hira. "That's always a novelty."

Hira was unsure of how to respond. The implications of Jutia's cutting words only left her with more questions. A novelty for *who*? *Justan*? What a mess, what an uncomfortable mess. She'd never desired so badly for a pirate attack. A respite from such a confrontation.

"I wish you would've died with that secret," Jutia admitted softly, her face crestfallen. She was beautiful in her despair.

Hira's heart broke for her, for what she'd caused in her delirium. Even good intentions could have disastrous consequences. "I shouldn't have said anything. I'm sorry. Now I'm afraid I've ruined your opportunities for being with the one you love."

Jutia smiled a little, her attention still on the ocean. They were the color of water. "That opportunity has long been gone. Long before you stepped foot on the Sea Wife. So, don't take all the credit,

Isabelle Olmo

or martyr yourself for that throne."

The scalla continued to dance and jump, twisting in the air with cold black eyes as if they delighted in Hira's discomfort. Hira caressed the grain of the wooden rails under her hands. She was drenched in guilt. Jutia loved Justan and, in her ignorance, Hira thought her death-confession might allow them happiness after she passed. But she'd not stayed dead and she couldn't ignore her own attraction to Justan. She couldn't deny that all she'd done since this journey commenced was ruin everything. She swore she would never interfere with another's relationship again.

"I was angry at you," Jutia said solemnly after a while. "I'd noticed Justan's reaction to your injury."

Hira's stomach twisted, and she swallowed thickly against the keen feeling of bile.

"I wanted to wish you agony, but I saw how death slowly claimed you in such a painful and horrific manner... my anger quickly dissipated. What you did and what you endured... I'd never. I'd slice my throat first." Jutia glanced at her. With shaking fingers, she brought the cigar to her lips. "I almost admire you. Jealousy is not a pretty thing."

That Jutia should be jealous of *her* was comical.

Hira shook her head. "I wanted to die, truly, I did. I'm not brave. Reckless is a bit more like it."

Jutia threw her tobacco bud into the sea and the wind blew her hair about. Then she fiercely looked at Hira. "I've never wanted sainthood. To be one of those ladies who knit and gossiped. Bore babies all their lives and never felt the thunder of an ocean storm hang their fate in the balance. They have denied me *many* things in my life. I'm afraid I hold grudges rather thickly. I won't sit around and pine for Justan, so don't you worry, I'll be just fine."

The captain studied the waves and Hira allowed her to settle her words. As the sun painted its last masterpiece of the day, the world turned a golden amber. The heart was such complicated chaos. Hira wished she didn't delight in Justan's attention. She wished she didn't recall the scent of his skin.

After the scar destroyed her face, she made sure whomever she

260

bedded was beneath her social position. Someone with no possibility of forming any legal attachment. In the morning, when she would toss them from her chambers, they would point out her ugliness. Then she would remind them who she was, remind them of *their* station.

It was a game. A stupid game. A part of her wanted to show them that despite her deformity, she was still *royal*. She talked big about not wanting the High Seat, yet she cowered under it. Hadn't she thrown it in Justan's face upon meeting him? Yes. She had much to learn.

Here she was. No armada, no High Seat, and she'd likely doomed a ship full of sailors to their death.

Jutia pushed her hair out of her eyes. "When you were in delirium, you kept asking about the ship and the sailors. *Begged* us to go after the Sea Wife to save the men. Even as your fingers rotted, and the stench became unbearable, you worried for them. Must be the Balikian in you. That stubbornness."

Indeed, it was. Hira wished she were more aware of her stubbornness. She didn't think it was a particularly outstanding trait to have. She'd often viewed her uncle's stubbornness with contempt and now she herself inherited it.

Stubbornness could be detrimental and might cloud the truth otherwise readily visible.

"I think enough dark words have been spoken." Jutia suddenly smiled, and her ill humor seemed to evaporate. "We should have dancing tonight. To celebrate the scalla. What is peppered scalla without some music?"

She turned to her men, and they stared at her with awe and respect. She'd *earned* that. Hira looked at her mangled arm and saw how foolish she'd been. Pompously fighting Captain Strauss despite Justan's warning, then recklessly losing so much.

She couldn't wait to get home, to see her mother and show her what she'd become. Even if Lady Marai didn't approve, she was still her child and she would love her, nonetheless. She was sure of it. Hira would aim to heal their relationship and perhaps confide in one another. Her mother was loyal to House Balik and, by extension, would be loyal to Hira. Lady Marai wouldn't agree with her decisions but she'd not agreed with all of Uncle Beltran's either. It mattered little. They would be a family once more and protect each other. Hira would work towards that.

There would be no greater honor than serving her country and carrying on the Balikian name. Regardless of what became of Justan and Jutia.

The scent of peppered scalla filled the entire ship and, despite the direness of their journey, the men were in excellent spirits. They joked and Hira joined them in partaking of ale and wisecracks.

Each time she would laugh, head thrown back, Justan noticed a slight dimple on her left cheek. He found himself wandering how it felt to touch it. To dip his finger into the divot of her flesh. Usually, he had pristine control of his mind. He'd had no choice these many years. Yet lately—specifically since the lady arrived on his ship—he was a storm with no beginning and no end. The promise to the dead should've been easy but selfish desire slithered under his door of resolution.

He helped Hira move the long tables made of Duncan Wood to the center of the deck. Since the Night Serpent had no dining quarters, this would make do. At one point, their fingers brushed against each other, and she straightened and stared at him. He felt his neck run cold and hot at once. It was the second time their hands had accidentally touched. The other times had been intentional, and the feel of her skin remained tattooed to the memory of his palms.

She hastened away with an awkward smile. He had to take a sharp breath to steady himself. He'd not felt this silly since he was a lad. When he looked up, he found Jutia watching him with darkened eyes.

He cursed internally when she sashayed her way to him, cigar in mouth, and a smirk firmly in place.

"It's sweet, really," she purred.

Justan glanced away, clenching his jaw against what he truly wished to say. He busied himself with helping the men move the benches and refused to discuss the situation with her. He should've known she wouldn't let it go so easily.

They served large pots of peppered scalla along with freshly made bread, still warm and pliable, perfect for sopping the red sauce. Though Justan attempted not to stare, his eyes wandered on their own as Hira moaned in delight when she ate the delicious fare. When she licked her fingers clean, his groin tightened, and he forced himself to focus on Quent, who was sharing a most exaggerated story.

After the meal, ale was served, and the mood turned lax and inviting. When he looked up, he found Hira watching him between the candles of their evening feast. The soft glow of candlelight brightened her face and when she smiled softly at him, he felt his heart drop from his chest.

In a bold move, which he welcomed, she raised her glass and drank to him. He bowed his head in thanks as they silently communicated through the crowd of sailors. The gaze was so intense he had to glance away, lest they become obvious. That's the last thing he needed.

A few Garian sailors pulled out their Jujupi, a fretted instrument about five feet long with seven strings. A man sang in old Garian, something about lost love, and death coming too soon. Hira delighted as the two men began a sort of musical duel, both trying to outdo one another in their talent. Once more, he felt besotted with her smile. At ease and allowed the space to be herself, she was magnificent. How bright she was, a bright shining light in a world filled with darkness. Despite the years, she was still much the same as he recalled. The warmth she exuded with her joy was enchanting and he envied whoever was lucky enough to receive her smiles.

Quent stood next to him, his eyes wide on the lady, equally charmed. The commander nudged his brother and Quent flushed red at being caught staring.

"Why don't you ask her to dance?" Justan murmured.

The boy shook his head. "I wouldn't dare. She's much taller."

He bent down and stared at his brother. "What did I teach you?"

"To dance like mother taught you," Quent said and chewed his lip in self-doubt.

Justan raised his brows and whispered. "We're the star sons of the night sky. We've no fear. Now, go. Show the lady a good time."

His brother nodded and took a deep breath. "We're the star sons," the boy said to himself. And gathering his courage, Quent went to her and extended his hand to Hira.

She happily took the offer as the guitars began their rhythmic battle. They twisted and turned, their feet stomping at the right moment. His short stature made it awkward for turns. They laughed, and she had to take the lead and twist him.

STOMP! STOMP!

It was a chaotic but amusing display, and his brother recalled all the steps he'd shown him. Hira turned, and Quent caught her. He stretched to provide her a twirl as she bent. They giggled and again—STOMP! STOMP!

When they hopelessly tangled, Justan set down his drink and walked to them. He couldn't have the Garian dance maligned so. Grasping her hand, he pulled her out of the web they'd accidentally created.

"Allow me to finish, Quent," Justan said.

Quent bounced away, dancing on his own around and around.

The commander took the lady into his arms, her small body fitting neatly in his. Her breast pressed intimately against his chest. He momentarily floundered, and he felt the tightness in his neck. He'd never danced with someone like her before, and he almost trembled. Recalling the moves, he expertly turned her round. She looked up at him with wide eyes, allowing him to lead her into the dance.

"How does a sailor learn these steps so well?" Hira asked with a small, flirtatious smile.

There was only one person in Pinnacle Palace that cared for the

Garian customs and that was his mother. Her long hair was always intricately braided, and she only wore the color blue. She had soft brown hands that wove tapestries which detailed the olden stories passed down from generations.

He twirled Hira in a perfect circle, stomped and caught her. "My mother."

She raised a brow. "Tell me about her."

He pulled her around the floor as the guitar dictated the rhythm. Then he placed his hands on her hips, as was customary, and despite the leather, he felt her warmth through the cloth. She met his eyes as she set her palms over his. Her cheeks colored as they stared at one another.

In her arms, he allowed himself to recall his mother. Though she was a woman filled with much sadness, she'd loved her children and wished them happiness. Whenever he was sad, she would lift his chin and say with a smile, *"You're entitled to happiness, darling."* And how sour those words felt now.

"She would take me to her quarters and teach me all the Garian dances," he said with a slightly bashful glance.

"She was proud to be Garian," Hira surmised.

"Aye." He studied the way her brow curved over her bone structure. Her scar, a perfect pathway for kisses, to discover the planes of her face. He dared himself to believe that his mother would've liked the Lady Hira, she might have admired her fearlessness and confided in her son that perhaps she had a little Garian in her.

"You loved her dearly," she whispered.

The statement was so simple, but it split him in two. Love was such a luxury, the price so high he'd only allowed himself to love Quent.

"I did, and she loved me." It was a whisper of a truth which had belonged only to him for all of his life.

She softened within his embrace, her eyes wilting in sympathy. "What was her greatest wish for you?"

Her question caught him off guard. He could scarcely draw breath, having her so close. In his arms, she was momentarily his.

She wasn't vital to the survival of their country. She wasn't anyone but Hira, and his heart softly leaned into her. He dared imagine a different life. A life where she knew everything, each secret he kept, and accepted him, though he was heavy with faults.

"Happiness. She wished I would find happiness," he breathed.

Her hand shook slightly, but she tightened her grip on him.

"And *are* you happy?"

No.

All he could see, feel, and taste was Hira Balik. His hand on her back, molding to the arch of her spine. Imagining what her skin felt like without the cloth that protected it. Imagining her nails scraping over his chest, painting him as hers. Her hand tightened around his arms. An invitation. And how he desperately wished to accept it. To sneak into her bed and make her his. But she wasn't his. She belonged to the kingdom, and he was no one. A ghost. He was acutely aware that she was the most prized possession of the crown, and he could never compare to her worth.

When the music stopped, they still touched. Her mouth was open, and her eyes were so dark he swore they were a pit at the end of the world. In that moment he nearly shouted the truth, but if he did, she would surely die. Seeing and smelling her now, he couldn't place into words what he felt, but he felt *something*. That something superseded any promises and so he made a new one. He would ensure she lived and found happiness, even at his own peril. Under the starry night, the promise glowed and bound him to it.

The clapping shook them. They looked around and their hands dropped away. The loss was sharp, like the splitting of a soul. Hira was red in the face as she realized their audience, the obviousness of their entanglement. Justan was flushed but he disguised it by making a big show of bowing. Then he extended his hand out to her. She followed his lead and curtsied with a mock smile.

A shadow from the corner of his eye caught his attention. Jutia moved away from the main deck and into her quarters, but not before casting him an expression of offence.

Fuck. Fuck it all. Damn Beltran.

He quickly excused himself and went to find her. The hallway leading to her door was dark. There she stood, smoking her cigar. She'd drank too much. Her frame swayed slightly.

"You used to look at me that way," she whispered. Her voice was thick with hurt. She took another swig of the wine bottle in her hand.

He turned away and clenched his jaw tight, holding in his words.

"A woman doesn't forget looks like the ones you used to give me." She came closer and his skin prickled. "I was your *entire world*."

She slid her palm down his arm and he tensed. She pressed her lips against his shoulder. A kiss. He couldn't look at her because he knew what he would see. Pain. It wasn't a show; it wasn't an act. He hurt her each day, and he hated that it was up to him to placate her.

"The only thing that was ever good in my life was *you*." She inhaled a tearful breath. Her voice was a precipice. "After everything I've gone through, you were the one who was supposed to understand. You're the love of my life. My *one* constant and now I lose you, too."

He closed his eyes and rubbed his hand against his face. He would break. He swore he would.

"I'm still here," he said in a hushed tone.

But when he didn't turn to her, she scoffed and drank more.

"No, you're not. You *smell* of her," she spat. "We're not like *them*, Justan."

No. They certainly weren't. With one last scratch of her nails down his arm, she slithered away, stumbling into her cabin, and closing the door behind.

He groaned as he pressed his forehead to the wall, fisting his hands. He didn't know how much longer he could do this. How much more he could stand.

Isabelle Olmo

Chapter Twenty-Eight

SANAA

Their party comprised of twenty-nine people, plus a very pregnant queen. Sanaa still didn't think it would be enough. They were too susceptible to a Norrian or nomadic ambush, and it made it difficult for travel orchestration. Her majesty was adamant. The child *must* be born in Istokian waters. Never mind battling a newly discovered sister and saving Hira. It took all of Sanaa's willpower not to lock her in her chambers and refuse her demands.

Almira was loaded to her carriage along with servants and a midwife. They were all enacting the plan of a madwoman, and Sanaa had little patience for it. Almira sharply looked at her from inside of the carriage. She wished to leave and not a word needed to come from her bullying mouth for Sanaa to register her wishes.

"Mount your horses, Red Guard! The queen is ready!" Sanaa yelled to the girls, who scrambled onto their beasts.

Black knights also accompanied them as extra protection, but mostly to lead the way. The matter of safety logistics was up to Sanaa. Her head hurt and they hadn't even begun the journey.

From the corner of her eye, she spotted the girl, Pristok, who watched the chaos with fascination and rosy cheeks. The days of good sleep and meals gave life back to her.

Sanaa moved her horse to her and smiled down at the young woman. Pristok startled, so intent she was in watching the loading of the queen and the servants, she hadn't noticed Sanaa.

She looked up at the captain with a bright smile. "Captain, I never got to thank you."

"You are welcome, girl. You look a fair share better than before." Sanaa leaned forward in her saddle, satisfied she was not beyond saving.

The girl straightened her servant's skirt and nodded. "I've got a post in the kitchens. Like I did in Korkoran. The queen's much nicer than Lady Furia."

Sanaa's horse stomped, ready for the voyage. "That's a relief."

Pristok's wide eyes went back to the rest of the Red Guard. "Impressive, aren't they? A battalion of warrior women just for the queen. You must be very proud to lead them, Captain Sanaa."

Sanaa glanced at the girls. One of them couldn't mount her stubborn horse, and the others chuckled at the display. She sighed.

"Yes," Sanaa said sardonically. She looked at Pristok and noted how neat her clothing was, ironed and well snatched. "Do you like the kitchens, girl?"

Pristok startled in confusion. Servants did not get the luxury of being satisfied with their posts in life.

"It's a fine job, Captain. A girl like me can't ask for much more, can she? To serve the queen is an honor," she said with a tone of innocent sincerity.

Sanaa forged a plan as she studied the girl. She'd grown strong after the care she received in the castle. She showed a remarkable deal of determination and perseverance during her task of delivering the letter.

"How about protecting the queen?" Sanaa asked.

One of the younger Red Guards, Zoya, came closer. "Captain, we're ready."

"In a minute," Sanaa dismissed her and turned back to Pristok, who observed her. "How about it?"

Pristok's face was one of shock, as if she feared it was a game intent on hurting her. Poor chit had seen nothing but dismissal and abuse. Sanaa knew that position well.

"You're saying *me*? Protect the queen? Be a Red Guard?" Pristok asked in a hushed whisper.

Sanaa almost smiled. "You are still too young. We've got a page in the training yards. He's a fine boy, but lazy and forgetful. Seeing as you traveled half the world to deliver a note— even if it killed you—I think I won't have trouble with you forgetting to polish swords."

She'd long realized that if the Red Guards were to be a permanent fixture in Mavros, the girls needed to be scouted from an early age. For generations, the Suidian Mesedi also recruited and trained in the same manner.

Pristok's mouth dropped open. "I'd never forget such a thing, Captain!"

Sanaa pulled at her horse's rein as the beast brayed. "Good. If you work hard and earn your place, then perhaps, when you're of age, you can train."

The girl's face paled even as she slowly smiled. "Train to be a Red Guard?"

"Aye, girl. Would you like that?" Sanaa turned her horse.

"Oh, Captain!" Pristok stepped forward. "I would love nothing else in the entire world! But… I'm absolutely *no one*. I don't come from a fine family or have any skills."

"Everyone is someone," Sanaa said sincerely. "And skill is simply practiced action."

Pristok took a sharp breath, her eyes watering with hope. As if her horrible journey suddenly made sense.

"Nadim!" Sanaa yelled and waited until the Keeper reached them, his hands folded neatly before him with a serene expression. He'd taken to staying armed with his jeweled knife. Sanaa didn't blame him.

"Captain, we're ready. The queen is impatient to leave," he said.

Of course she was. Almira had dallied, ensuring she took the correct gown to enter the Istokian capital, and *now* she was in a hurry.

"Take young Pristok here to the training yards. I'm making her our new page for the Red Guard. Show her what needs to be done.

The boy can work in the kitchens and keep a post in the castle."
Sanaa turned back to Pristok with a hard look to ensure she
understood she wouldn't go easy on her. "Until we meet again, girl.
I want all the armor in that weapons room shining like the Sea of
Jacobin."

Pristok clutched her hands together. "Thank you, Captain! I
shall do my duty and more. I shan't disappoint you!"

"Good. And Nadim? Make sure they teach young Pristok to
read and write," Sanaa said.

Nadim raised his brows. "I will see to it *myself*, Captain."

Sanaa gave the girl one last look and galloped to the front of the
envoy. She pulled her horse next to the queen's carriage as M
watched her with a knowing smile.

"Keep your words to yourself, Madhavi," Sanaa grunted.

M lit her cigar. "This is the second girl I've seen you rescue to
be a soldier."

Sanaa ignored her as she went to Almira, who bid her last
goodbyes to Lady Poelia, Hester, and Lady Gita. The women
clustered against the queen's carriage.

"We're ready, *cuzo*," Sanaa said.

"Alright," Almira said, and held Poelia's hands tightly as the
elder cried.

"I should go with you. It's not right that you'll be alone," Poelia
said.

"She's got the girls and the king will meet her there. Though
I'm not sure what good he'll do. Men are seldom levelheaded during
childbirth," Hester said.

Almira forced a smile. Sanaa could clearly tell she was trying to
appease them, to keep them from distressing, even if she'd bathed
herself in worry.

"You'll be safer here, far away from the dangers. I'll be back
soon with our darling little baby for you to fret over," Almira said.

"We will pray for your wellbeing each night. She'll be alright,
cen-nai," Gita said.

Cen-nai, mother-in-law.

"Oh, but I wish I'd been there when you were born. And now

I'll miss this one too," Poelia bemoaned.

Almira leaned in and kissed her cheek. "Perhaps the next one, when we're not on the precipice of yet another war."

Hester pulled at Poelia. "Yes, time your childbirths better."

Sanaa chuckled and moved her horse forward. "We move out. Come now, ladies."

But there was something about that moment. She nearly stopped the entire procession. A feeling haunted her. *Haunt.* A ghost. Instantly her eyes scanned the area, the corners where those who wished to remain unknown hid. Someone watched her. Someone who didn't want to be seen. There was only one person who would do such a thing: Kaia Lu Kait.

Fuck. Sanaa wasn't afraid Kaia would try to kill her again. It was that she wondered about the woman's new motives now that she'd finished licking her wounds.

Let Kaia reveal herself in due time.

It was going to be a *long* journey.

A week later they finally reached the outskirts of Suid. Almira's discomfort was obvious, despite her attempts to hide it behind her veil. Sanaa was certain the jostling in the carriage didn't help and the captain was afraid they'd have to birth the baby in the fields of the Valley of Ucello. Sanaa finally decided the queen had enough travel for the day. The lady protested, but Sanaa ignored her, and they camped at the foot of the stone mountains.

That night in her tent, Almira spread her legs for the midwife. The woman inserted her hand into her, which cemented Sanaa's desire to never have a child. The midwife wiggled her hand inside and the queen was close to yelling when the woman pushed against her internal walls.

This is absolutely ridiculous, Sanaa fumed. In her late term, she should rest comfortably. At least it's what Sanaa would do if she were the one swollen and lethargic.

When the midwife paused and furrowed her brows, Sanaa's entire body tensed, as did Almira.

"What is it? What's wrong?" Almira held herself up by her elbows.

The woman dragged her hand out and took the linen cloth Sanaa offered her. Her mouth was down-turned.

"The child has dropped. It readies itself," the midwife said.

Oh, for the fucking sake of the gods! Sanaa had a violent desire to drag the tiny queen straight to Suid and lock her in Thebo's palace until she birthed and save them all the headache.

Almira cursed. Her obsession with birthing in Istokian waters would get them all killed.

"How long?" Almira asked her.

The midwife had the decency to meet the queen's eyes. "Not long at all. Two weeks, maybe a little more. Depends. If you settle and stopped this travel, it could delay the child. This constant movement brings the child faster."

Sanaa looked at her *cuzo* with bristling anger, but she held her tongue.

"Your counsel is noted." Almira sat up with a grunt and closed her legs.

The woman's face soured. "Majesty—"

"That's enough. Thank you." Almira nodded to Sanaa.

The captain, suffering from the worst headache she'd ever had, aided the midwife to stand. Almira waited until the woman left and finally looked at Sanaa, M, and Delara.

"I know what you will all say, but I *must* get to Istok." Almira winced and leaned back against the pillows.

Delara, who usually held in words and spoke with her eyes and the shifting of her body, sighed loudly and ran a hand over her face. Sanaa seldom saw her angry, but there was a severe displeasure in her countenance. Good. Sanaa wasn't alone in thinking this plan was idiocy.

"Any manner of things can happen, but I will do my best to get

274

you to safety if they attack us," Delara said with an infuriating level tone.

She was the queen's runner. Her savior, should they suffer an ambush and need to flee. She would ignore the royal protests—at Sanaa's command—and ride without pause through the valleys and hills of Suid right into Zuri and lock her there. There would be little Almira could physically do.

Before Almira could plead her case once more, Sanaa roared, "It's a *foolish* venture! You risk *everything* each day you continue this irresponsible pursuit!" Sanaa's mouth wound tightly, her lips pulled back, and her shoulders bristled. Almira's eyes widened at her outburst, but on the gods, she could hold it no longer. This was *enough!*

Delara and M looked hesitantly at the exchange. Sanaa never questioned the queen's authority in front of them, it was always in private where their tempers would crash in a tug and pull. Almira's neck flushed and her breath hitched.

"That's *your* opinion, Captain," she said coldly. "But this child *will* be born in Istokian waters. I *will* find Hira. I *will* defend Istok from usurpers. I'm the queen of this land—of this entire world. If not I, *who* then? Shall the lord of Suid invade its neighbor in my name? How well do you think that will fare? Shall Alton? No, *cuzo*. It cannot be them. If I—a child of Istok—is not at the helm, then it is an act of war against the people of Istok, not against one polluted person."

Sanaa thought she would surely shake the queen to death. She had to pace the floor to prevent herself from doing just that and spending her life in the dungeons of Mavros.

"What if the king cannot make it? What if he's too late? What if *we* are too late? What if Hira is dead? Consider *that*. What if Furia has named herself High Seat? If that is so, then we are invaders into her land, and she has a *claim*."

Almira, having no desire to heed her good council, looked away. The queen was drenched in Balikian stubbornness—not a bit of Sikorian sense left in her at this moment.

"She'll have no proof but what stories her mother told her. For all we know, we are the only ones that know of this family secret, and I intend to keep it that way. I hope to make her see reason," her *cuzo* said.

M sat and watched them quietly, her hand pressed against her chest, her mouth set in a grimace. She too ailed, but she wouldn't say it out loud. "She plotted to kill her own father, majesty. What reason do you think such a person will see?"

Ah, exactly, Sanaa snapped internally.

Almira swallowed and fisted the cloth of her dress. "I cannot lose hope, Madhavi. And we stay the course. We can be in Treveri in two weeks with - at the very least - the Suidian army and my uncle. Enough time—"

Sanaa madly needed to laugh at the entire plan. "For you to jump quickly in the waters, birth a child, then take back a country? In between those actions, rescue Hira, just in time for evening tea?" Sanaa placed her hands on her hips.

Almira took a deep breath and sunk into her bed. She was clearly in pain and wouldn't admit it. "I shan't abandon Hira. I shan't abandon Istok. This child *will* be born in Istokian waters, or you might as well kill me as I sleep."

Sanaa stormed out of the tent in a cloud of anger, the likes she'd not experienced in a long time.

"Guard her," Sanaa ordered, but M and Delara hardly needed to be told.

She had no concept of direction as she stalked through the camp. The new Red Guards jumped out of her way, and the Black Knights apologized, even if they were not in her path. She cared not, her annoyance and worry too great. She had little time to placate those that knew nothing of the reality of their predicament.

Damn Almira! Stumbling around Suid, marching towards certain death. Goddamn her ridiculous ventures! Sanaa seethed with such wildness that she found herself at the outskirts of the camp, alone at last. Just as she liked it. With sharp moves, she rolled her tobacco, lit it, and inhaled the blue smoke to calm her shaking hands.

"You're careless when your mind is clouded," a voice said in the shadows.

Instantly, she dropped her cigar and pulled out her ruby blade when she turned to find Kaia. The woman casually leaned against a tent pole, still cast in darkness. Her eyes were painted black, and she languidly scratched her chin as she eyed Sanaa with amusement.

"Seems like a waste of good cigar, Captain." Kaia glanced at the ember on the grass.

Sanaa took a breath to calm herself, uncertain if the woman would attempt something as stupid as attacking her in the queen's own camp.

"What are you doing here?" Sanaa snatched back her bud from the ground. "You're going to get yourself killed. My guard will attack anyone they don't know."

Kaia tossed her braided hair over her shoulders. "Good obedient little girls, aren't they?"

The way she said it sent a minor shiver through Sanaa's stomach, but she ignored it. Instead, the captain glared and sheathed her blade. Was the entire world conspiring for the single worst day of her life?

"They protect the queen. They're more deadly than obedient," Sanaa snapped.

Kaia chuckled and bit her lip. "You've ensured that, haven't you? Hand-picked them yourself? Do they worship the ground you walk on? I would wager you enjoy having so many women… on their knees."

Sanaa's nostrils flared, intent on disguising the effect the little tone Kaia's voice had on her. She opted to take a long drag of her cigar and leaned across from her so that they both regarded one another in the same manner. Both pretending at boredom, yet both intrigued by the other.

"Why are you following us?" Sanaa asked.

Kaia shrugged. "Because I can."

Sanaa inhaled once more, and Kaia's gaze flickered to her lips. This was a different sort of game than she'd ever played, but at least it distracted her from her ire at Almira.

"I sensed you as we left," Sanaa said.

Kaia glanced at the camp, then back at her. "I allowed you to sense me. I wanted you to feel *hunted*."

It had been a long time since the captain truly felt fear. Fear reminded her of her past and she was in no mood to linger in bygone anguishes. Kaia, believing Sanaa would cower, was comical.

"If you wished me dead, you would've let your arrow fly."

That changed the chit's attitude. Kaia's eyes narrowed, her mouth soured, and her small body tensed. "A fact you knew. Which is why you dangled my sister's honor before me."

Damn right she'd done that. She wouldn't die at the hand of Kaia. Not then, not now. Not when she'd sworn to a dying woman to protect her. Promises to the dead could not be broken.

"Survival instincts?" Sanaa couldn't help but smirk, especially when she felt it would anger her. She was tired of the cloak and dagger game the woman wished to play.

This rightly angered the girl. Her cheeks flushed and her lips thinned. "You're very good at that, aren't you?"

"I'm good at many things," Sanaa drawled. "But when you grow up as I did, you quickly learn to survive."

She didn't know *why* she divulged such details to someone who'd tried to kill her, but it seemed like she had to explain herself, or provide justifications when she felt so wrongly judged. Kaia knew nothing of Sanaa. She'd spied her through windows lacking all context for Sanaa's behavior and made her own deductions.

"Oh, spare me the sad story of Sanaa Cinege." Kaia rolled her eyes and looked away. "You were raised in the house of the High Lord. You never had to scrounge for food, never had to mend the holes of your robes in the hopes the cold didn't freeze your malnourished body. Never had to work as a child to help place bread on the table." Kaia kicked a small rock with her foot. "You're to be commended for surviving such a life, Captain."

Her words burned a hole in Sanaa's stomach. She studied Kaia's slight frame and dimly wondered if it was genetics or a scarce childhood that made her diminutive.

"Physical ailments are not the only sort of struggles."

Kaia turned back to her with narrowed eyes. "Need someone to talk to, Captain? A shoulder to lean on?"

Sarcasm dripped from her tone. It held a sting of mockery, which infuriated Sanaa. She no longer enjoyed looking at her, no matter how attractive she was. She was a shelved vial of vinegar, and the captain didn't like embittered people.

"I've no intention of discovering what haunts your thoughts. No interest in what makes you hate me so. I've *actual* problems at hand, and you have nothing to do." Sanaa turned away. "Get out of this camp. I won't save you if the Red Guard attacks you. You've brought it on yourself."

As Sanaa moved to leave, Kaia stepped forward with a smirk. "I'm surprised, Captain."

Sanaa paused but remained quiet. Let the woman drip whatever poison she had to extract.

Kaia slid closer to her. The slight woman almost touched her arm but didn't. "Surprised you haven't asked me to join your squadron, given you recognize my skills."

Sanaa glanced over her shoulder and took her in. Kaia was small and perpetually walked as if she marched into battle. No. She wouldn't have such a warrior on her guard if she was the last person alive.

A realization formed in Sanaa's mind. She knew why Kaia haunted them. She knew the woman's plan for her so-called revenge.

"And I won't. Above skill is trust, and I don't *trust* you. You're volatile. For all I know, you've now placed your blame for Tora's death on the queen," Sanaa said with a tone of warning. "Her death would pain me in the way Tora's pained you. But you won't kill her with child, you're not heartless. That's your little plan, isn't it? That's the best way you can think of hurting me."

Kaia's face tightened, as if slapped. "You're right. I would never harm an innocent child. But the queen is not innocent."

Sanaa loomed over her as she stretched to her full height. She met Kaia's eyes with intense fury. It was time to put an end to this chaos.

"You attack what you don't understand. You can think only of your pain, *your* suffering. Fuck the world, right? The queen tries to keep the kingdom at peace, and yet you rage because you lost someone. Let me tell you something." Sanaa held a finger before Kaia's face and the woman reeled back. "We've *all* lost someone. You're not the first to drink of its waters. Your life is pointless because you don't have a cause. Tora was more a warrior than you are. She was selfless and saw the good, even in the darkest days. She smiled despite having the same upbringing as you and she didn't hesitate to save another. What a *child* you are."

Sanaa enjoyed the look of shock in Kaia's eyes. Let her linger with Sanaa's words, let the message fester. With a grunt, Sanaa turned on her heels and left the petulant woman in the dark.

Chapter Twenty-Nine

HIRA

Time on the ship was strangely normal. Hira and the commander continued their awkward dance, filled with hesitant moments or strangled words which all sounded wrong in her head. They were friends, but friends didn't dance in the manner they'd danced, or flush at the feel of one another's skin.

Quent was the lovely balm that soothed all burning. Hira had taken to finding him better fitting clothes, cutting his hair, and showing him how to pull back his shoulders when he walked. It distracted her from her scattered thoughts, which bounced from Istok, Almira, the Sea Wife, Captain Jutia, and—most fretfully—Justan.

After she'd polished the young lord, she'd invited him to live in Korkoran with her. Despite his initial excitement, he quickly turned her down. He'd told her he wished to be with his brother. Hira wanted to protest, but she understood the difficulties. None knew how long the boy had and what if his health declined? Would Justan, out at sea, make it back to him? There was too much uncertainty.

When they closed in on the Isles of Hipata, the weather changed. The skies darkened as murky clouds blanketed the area, encasing them in torrential showers. This area of the sea had no mercy for passing vessels that dared traverse its coarse waters.

"After the Dragon's Teeth, it should be one more day," Jutia said to Hira as they stood at the helm watching the spectacle of crew members attempting to keep the rigging where it belonged despite the strong winds and bruising rain.

It was called Dragon's Teeth because the protruding rocks that jutted out from the ocean destroyed many ships. It was a place that only the most skilled of captains would ever venture. Hira trembled at the sight of the mammoth boulders. There was little they could do if a wave tossed their ship against the stones. They would perish in chaotic agony.

Jutia morphed into a serene stance the moment the storm developed. "Have you been in many sea storms?" she asked as she flicked the butt end of her rolled tobacco and turned to Hira.

Hira's blue eyes intensely focused on the swirling black cloud that seemed to chase them as she replied, "Once, when I was a child, but it was close to the Treverian coast."

The captain took off her enormous hat and tucked it under her arm. "Treverian storms are not the same as these Southern ones, my lady. My crew and I will maneuver through the teeth, but it'll be some of the worst moments you'll ever live through."

Hira hated uncertainty. She sent up a prayer to the gods who played with the fate of their ship.

Preparations began in organized mayhem as the sailors tied things down and moved what they could into the bowels of the vessel. Whatever Captain Jutia thought to be unnecessary, they cast overboard. Including the sup tables, they were too heavy and were a dispensable luxury.

Hira attempted to stay out of their way and went in search of Quent to ensure he had a good place to ride out the storm. She found the brothers arguing in Jutia's quarters. Justan towered over his younger brother, his face flushed, and his eyes narrowed.

"You stay *below*. That is my final word on it!" The commander jabbed Quent's chest with his finger.

Quent's hands fisted as he stood his ground. He was red to his ears. "I'm a sailor as much as the other men! *And* I'm a lord, I'm ashamed of hiding down here!"

Justan gritted his teeth and yanked at his locks, which were wet with the rain. He took a calming breath and enumerated reasons for his decision.

"You're thin and light. One strong rock of the ship and you'd end up in the dragon's mouth! You stay down here—"

Quent stomped his foot, making him look younger than his age. "Lady Hira won't be down here! She'll be up there braving the storm and making sure the men make it!"

Hira, fearing the two were at a precipice of damaging words, cleared her throat. They both turned to her. "My lords, I apologize for the interruption."

Before she could distract them, Quent rushed to her with a pleading face. "Lady Hira, please! I want to be upstairs! I can help with *anything*, even if it's bringing water to the tired sailors."

He looked so hopeful that she knew it would break his heart to hear her words. But Justan was right. They wouldn't concentrate on maneuvering the ship if they had to worry about Quent and his whereabouts.

She gave him a sad smile and took his hands. "Lord Seaver, the commander worries about the coming storm. You must understand his side."

The boy's face showed genuine hurt, and he recoiled. His face twisted as he attempted to keep his frustrated tears at bay, then he glared at Justan. They looked alike in this moment, both furious and both believing the other to be at fault.

"You play a nice role at pretending to support me and telling me encouraging words about being a star-son, but you still treat me like I'm a child! I'm *not* a child. I'm a lord and a sailor on this ship!" Quent coughed violently and looked defeated at his inability to argue without proving how sick he was. He jerked his hand over his nose to wipe his snot. Tears of frustration filled his words as he said, "I may be ill, but I *matter*! I've got a life to lead, but you won't let me lead it! When we get to Treveri, I'm getting off this boat and I'm moving to Korkoran! What's the good of being on a ship if you don't allow me to be a sailor? I *hate* you!"

Hira flinched as he stormed past her and slammed the door. He left Hira and Justan in the penetrating silence, with nothing but the echoes of Quent's young words. The lady could scarcely breathe. This was an intimacy she'd not counted on.

Slowly, Hira looked at Justan, who'd not moved. His shoulders were tense. He was glaring at her, his eyes narrowed into slits, and his nostrils flared. She met his stare and waited for his inevitable vitriol.

"You blame me for this," she said.

He nodded, cheeks bright with fury. "I do. *Fully.*"

His words were so tight she thought he would break.

"Justan—"

"Oh, don't *Justan* me! You've filled his head with nonsense! Before you came, he was happy to look, behave, and be who he was. You come aboard and he's obsessed with being a Red Guard, which you and I know will *never* happen! He's repeating statements you've made word for word. He *escaped* a ship to be with your dead body! You dress him like some little doll of yours—"

"Stop!" she cried and threw her hands up, scarcely believing the accusations he lashed her with. Justan didn't deter.

He paced, snarling in her direction as he did. "*Now* he believes he's *invisible* and untouchable! As if he's grown, but he's not!" He pointed out the door, yelling at the top of his lungs. "He's still a child and you've got him following your every thought! The latest being that he's moving with you to Korkoran. Do you really think I'd allow that?"

Hira scoffed as she squared up to him. "He'd be safe in Korkoran, I'd ensure it!"

He laughed, the sort of laughter one has when in utter disbelief. "You can't even keep *yourself* safe!" he said, pointing at her arm.

She winced, and he backed away, aware that he'd insulted her beyond reason. They stood quietly, facing each other. She felt rather exposed at his statement. Yes, she'd been young and irrational not a few weeks before, but so much happened since. A part of her wished—hoped—that he thought better of her by now. Noticed her change, recognized the shift in her mind. That he still viewed her as careless and wild damaged her ego in more ways than she'd expected.

"Commander, I never intended to get anything in his head about the Red Guard—"

"You've been training him with your Ruby Blade. Don't think he doesn't talk, that's all he does is *talk*." He threw his hands up in the air. "He's *ill*, Hira. Do you understand that? He's going to die—" but he choked on his words. Fear bathed him.

He'd claimed to her facts he himself did not dwell on, as if they belonged to another brother and not *his* brother. Not *his* Quent. Not his little one. Not the boy he looked after and likely comforted at night. He grasped his mouth and looked away from her, eyes wide as he blinked.

Hira's heart went to him, to what he must go through, knowing that one day, nothing he could do would save Quent. Loving a dying person was a shattering pain that slowly ate at a fragmented heart. She took a tentative step towards him and placed a hand on his forearm. They were silent as she stroked her finger over his forearm. He didn't move, but the muscles in his arm gradually disentangled.

"Every night he wakes up coughing with pain in his chest and I… I tell him the same thing. Over and over. That I love him, that I'll protect him, and no one will hurt him. That he's my family. My *only* family. But not even love can save him, can it? He's all I've got. Do you understand?" he asked, and she nodded. "Lately, it's slipping right through my fingers."

His words broke Hira's heart as she envisioned Justan holding Quent each night and assuring him that his older brother would protect him and love him. The slow bloom of tenderness within her opened its petals a little more, and she hated the pain that would cover him when the time came. With all the vigor in her arm, she couldn't save him from such sorrows, and so she understood at that moment that strength was more than bone cast with muscle.

Hira came closer to him, and she placed her other hand on his chest. "He's still with you. He loves you more than he loves *anyone*. I might be a novelty, but even when we spoke about Korkoran, he was determined to stay with you. He's well aware he's dying. And he wants to be with you when it happens. No one else."

Justan's jaw tightened, and he nodded. He took a deep breath and finally looked at her. "I actually think he looked good. Fit as you dressed him. Never seen him happier or prouder."

She squeezed his arm. "He's a growing boy. He needs stability. A home. Privacy for his, you know... young man *needs*."

At that, the commander looked confused. "Needs of *what?*"

Hira blinked at him, incredulously. Almira was right. Men were absolute imbeciles sometimes.

"Oh, sea gods! This is a most inappropriate conversation." She rubbed her eyes. "Commander... Quent is growing up. Don't you recall when you were his age? You discover your desires and the... well, the sexual needs and such."

Justan's face turned a deep shade of red at her words. "*Oh.*"

She marveled at how they went to being permeated with future sorrow to amusing themselves at the realities of the human body.

"Yes. He may be ill, but he's still... you know, alive. It'll be good for him to be amongst other young nobles of his age. Develop social skills."

She smiled a little as he watched her dumbfounded and his flush crept down to his neck as he took a sharp breath.

"He's never told me he needed privacy," his voice sounded so confounded it was endearing.

"He'll say nothing. He's likely mortified. Have you even spoken to him about intimacy? You need to. He likely understands little about himself. When we get to Treveri, he needs proper tailored clothing. He also needs his own sleeping quarters, where he has privacy. And he needs to know *some* means of defending himself. You won't always be there to save him. It's a dangerous world we live in."

She honestly didn't comprehend why she laid out so much for him. The brothers were not her concern, but somehow it felt the two were afloat without knowing how to manage their affairs. Justan was busy with being a commander, and Quent was running around like a peasant.

He regarded her with an open expression, and his tension slowly lifted. His gaze shifted to something intimate. It was in the softness of his eyes and the slacking of his mouth. She cast him a glance and turned to leave, but he grabbed her scarred arm. She tensed. Without the leather covering, he could easily feel the jagged texture. To her surprise, he brought her hand to his mouth and kissed the back of it. He didn't flinch at the skin or the way the wound folds formed around his lips.

His eyes met hers. "You have my gratitude, my lady."

It was the most intimate gesture. One performed between a committed couple. Far beyond the friendship bounds. She wondered what else of his did she have? At that moment, she wanted it all. It was a crushing realization. She cared for Commander Justan Seaver. She desired him more than any other before.

Commander Justan was a far greater person than she was, even though she had royal blood. He watched over his brother in a nearly overprotective manner. He took his post as commander without complaint or pouts. When he realized he was hurting Jutia, he ended the engagement.

Hira was impulsive and arrogant, self-serving, and drowned in her own mistakes. He'd sacrificed going after his own crew to save her fucking arm. An arm! Half the men were likely dead.

She nodded and pulled her hand away. "You're welcome, my lord."

Then left the room, her skin a burning inferno that traveled right into her heart.

Isabelle Olmo

Chapter Thirty

HIRA

Dark clouds packed with wind, and rain moved swiftly over the Night Serpent. The storm pried open the ocean's mouth, and the ship danced in the bitter carnage of the sea. The harsh, cold pellets slammed into them, and heavy waves lifted the hull as if it weighed no more than a child's toy adrift in a puddle.

Jutia and Justan stood like twins at the helm.

Hira grasped the ratline with a vise grip as she took in the violent spectacle. Through the raging waters protruded the Dragon's Teeth. Jutting black rocks as ancient as the world made it seem as though they entered the very edge of Hell itself.

"Brace yourselves, lads!" Jutia shouted, her voice carrying over the intense winds and pelting rain.

The ship rocked each direction and Hira fought to stay on her feet as wave after wave tossed them without mercy. Justan maneuvered the vessel between the teeth as the wind unleashed its fury. The waves, a coiled menace of deadly savagery, grew in size until they were titans of some ancient world, tossing their boat like orbs in a field.

"Secure yourselves!" Jutia cried.

Men ran for cover as the deck flooded. Hira worked with the

sailors to throw back the water, returning it to the gods, an insulting act of ungratefulness. In retaliation, the sea fed them a merciless attack of more and more waves.

The ship tumbled and tipped ever so to the left. Justan's face remained set in concentration as Jutia helped pull the wheel. Together, they battled the gods themselves.

Hira's feet slipped, and she grasped the base of the mainsail. A deluge crashed into her, but still she held on, clutching it like salvation from death.

"Give me your hand, my lady!" Quent stood behind her with his arm outstretched.

"Go back inside, Quent!" she shouted over the gale.

"I can help you!"

That's when she saw it. A wave so tall it seemed as if it were an entire building. The water rushed like a stampede of wild horses. A veil of death. All she could do was gasp as the milliseconds ticked. It would be too late. She reached for his hand, but he turned from her to look behind him and she couldn't grasp his fingers.

The wave came down and Hira swallowed half the ocean. All she knew was that her mangled arm held on to the mainsail. And when she looked up, Quent was gone.

"QUENT!"

She could distantly hear Justan also screaming his brother's name. But it was as if the earth snatched him and dragged him down its esophagus. She was left with empty hands.

"MAN OVERBOARD!" Jutia took over the wheel.

Justan dashed down the stairs, but another wave crashed over him, and he slipped on the wood, landing with a thud on his back.

Hira didn't hesitate. She shed her coat and jumped off the ship into the turbulent ocean.

It's a strange thing how below the briny depth, the world is at peace. The currents felt like caresses to her, versus the onslaught that raged above. She swam with a voracity she never had, erupting to the surface as another wave descended over her. It turned her over and over in its chaos. She battled with the water and emerged to gasp for air, her lungs protesting the assault.

She looked frantically around the mountains of waves, desperate to spot Quent's head. Hira almost drowned a few times until she finally saw him. He'd made it to one of the protruding rocks, sobbing as he held onto his life by mere fingertips.

"QUENT! I'm coming!" she gurgled as she went under yet again.

She dove lower into the peace of the depths and swam, renewing her efforts to reach him. One wave threw her against a rock and scratched her knees, but she grasped the boulder and pulled herself up. She tried to find Quent, but the storm was ferocious.

"HIRA!" she heard him distantly.

The stone was slippery under her feet and she dug into the seaweeds that lived in a perpetual tumult adhered to barbed rock. When she reached the top, she saw Quent crying, cocooned in the small alcove of another boulder.

"I'm coming!"

"I can't hold on!" he despaired.

"Don't you let go!"

The distance between them was only a few meters, but the ocean was tyrannical in its attack. It seemed like a pot of boiling water, ready to consume crustaceans for a feast. She took a deep breath and jumped as close to him as she could. The waves awaited her with open arms, dragging her under. She swam and swam, kicked her legs with such ferocity she lost her boots. It didn't stop her. She *must* get to him. She couldn't let him die in this manner, she'd never recuperate.

Then, by luck or by the calculating hand of the gods, a wave pushed her against Quent's rock. She held it with all of her might. His fingers stretched out to her, and she clutched and pulled him as he sobbed against her.

"I got you! I got you!" she whispered as she attempted to gather her breaths.

"We're going to die!"

She looked at the Night Serpent. Despite her selfish desperation, she saw they couldn't come to save them. They would lose the ship, torn to shreds on the rocks. Hira knew Justan was beside himself, probably being held back from jumping into the tumultuous storm.

"We need to swim to them, Quent," she said against his hair.

He shook his head and coughed violently. "I can't! I can't do it!"

She pulled his chin up. "You can and you *will*. You hear me, sailor? If we don't, we'll *die* here!"

He hiccupped and stared at the ship. "It's too far!"

It was a frightening distance in this ocean as the waves pirouetted the uncoordinated dance of coming death. If they made it, it would be a miracle. But it would be sure demise if they stayed here. Already she felt her grip slip each time a wave landed.

"I can't hold on much longer. We have to jump and swim," she shouted.

He shook his head, his mouth agape as he spat out more water. "I'm not strong enough! Leave me to die, save yourself!"

"Look at me!" she demanded. "I wasn't pulled from the ocean pools of Istok to die in them! This water birthed me. We're amongst the sea gods now!"

She almost believed it herself. A part of her expected the sea wouldn't snuff out a life it once created. It simply wished to play, and she was ready to win that game.

Let it *try* to take her down.

She grabbed his face as they slipped. "*We* are the dragons!"

His eyes were wide, and his lower lip trembled as he repeated her words, "We are the dragons."

"JUMP!"

Instantly, the storm pummeled them. They flailed and swam, using their strength against the onslaught of the waves. Quent tired and she held his head over the water even as she went under to ensure he didn't drown. She urged him to keep going. The closer they got to the ship, the stronger the currents became, as if the water was angered that they were slipping from its claws. Just when she thought she would lose the game, a rope landed on her face.

"Grab it!" Justan screamed.

Hira placed Quent's hands on it. "Hold tight!"

Instantly, they pulled him. She grasped the bottom of the rope, and somehow, they were lifted up. As she dangled, another wave hit her, making her grip slide loose. She slid all the way down, falling back into the ocean.

It swept her deep into the bowels of the earth. A circular, twisting motion, an underwater tornado. She scrambled for air, but she was too far down. It seemed life would snatch her back into the womb it once produced her from. She tangled into a bramble of seaweed that clawed her limbs. She tried to peel herself away from them as the pain in her lungs launched her to desperation. Then an eerie stillness surrounded her.

Her lungs were no longer constricted. She stopped struggling and blinked as she took in the dark ocean. She must have sunk hundreds of meters. Surely death was seconds away, but strangely, she felt no fear or panic. There was an acceptance blooming within her consciousness. She'd saved Quent. She'd directed Justan to the Sea Wife and knew he would find them.

Hira wondered if death had already come, and she'd not seen it passing. But the ocean shifted in the softest of manners, like a curtain parting. In the darkness, she saw a golden glint. A twirling ribbon in the night. Undulating, it moved through the sea as if it had created the waters.

Zeita!

She *was* real, and Hira was seeing her again! Her tired body renewed with energy as she watched Zeita dance under the ocean. The dragon circled around Hira and the scales brushed against her skin. They were solid like armor, but smooth as polished obsidian. Hira realized she breathed as easily as if she had gills again.

"You're real!" Hira said in her mind.

"I am the last, my Lady of Istok." The dragon's voice was soft, angelic, but with an underlying strength no human could emulate, not even a queen.

Hira placed her hand over the scaled body. It rippled against her palm. "Have I died again?"

"You've never died, child." The dragon sounded amused, as if humans delighted it.

The majestic head pressed against her as she nuzzled Hira's face. She cupped the creature to her as it filled her with completion and love. It was an indescribable feeling. A connection so deep she felt she'd experienced it before. Long ago, before she was born. As if it belonged to another life, which Hira no longer recalled.

"Many lives are at stake, child."

She didn't care. Here she was safe, here no one could harm her. The gods would protect her. In the dragon's belly, she was untouchable, and the world ceased to exist.

"House Balik is in grave danger," the dragon said.

Hira couldn't comprehend if she was in earnest. If this was all an illusion crafted from her watery grave. Through her mind flashed a vision of her mother, weakly pale on her bed, chapped lips as she took laborious breaths. It was as if Hira was in her room in Korkoran, feeling the waning warmth of her decaying body.

"Mother! She's dying, she needs me!" Hira gasped as the picture faded.

"She doesn't have much time left," Zeita whispered. "She used to believe in me once. Child, she wants you to be aware. She calls for you to know the dangers within Istok," the dragon circled her, creating soft ripples cocooning Hira.

"What danger?" Fear clutched her chest. No one would hurt her in Korkoran. It was *home*. One could always go home.

"Furia is at your throat," Zeita whispered. "If you are not wise and brave, she *will* win. War will plague the land and hope will be lost."

Hira shook her head. "My cousin Furia Pesce? In Ciraton?"

Furia was years older than Almira and Hira. She was their second cousin. Hira met her twice when they were children. Once, she had made Almira cry, a difficult feat. Hira recalled her as a bully and an angry child.

"She wants the High Seat. Each morning she tastes it. She *yearns* for it. I can feel her malice deep in the dark waters. The fish whisper her name," Zeita said. "Be brave, Hira. Do not fear death. Death should be afraid of *you*."

Hira studied the giant head that caressed her cheek.

"I have missed you, my friend. It's been many eons." The dragon seemed to smile. "It's time for you to return, *vishap*."

Before Hira could argue and demand she stay under the calm waters, warm in her embrace and floating for all of eternity, Zeita thrust her up with her great tail. Hira sped through the waters, breaking the surface and rising into the air as if she could fly.

When she landed back on the top, it was soft, just as though dipped. She took deep breaths, as if she'd merely held her head under for a few seconds. The ocean had calmed, and she gently floated next to the Night Serpent.

"There she is!" Jutia cried from above.

They threw a rope down, and it smacked Hira's forehead. She grabbed on and, as they pulled her, she stared down at the sea. There was no sign or trace of the Great Dragon.

When they dragged her on the deck, Hira glanced at the sailors. "How long was I gone?"

Jutia kneeled before her and shook her drenched head. "Just now. The ocean suddenly stilled. Are you hurt?"

"You got her!" Behind Jutia, Justan grasped Quent tightly as the boy coughed.

It was as if mere seconds ago she'd lost her grip on the rope. As if the lengthy minutes under the water hadn't occurred. She looked around the deck uncomprehendingly. Had it happened? Yes, it had. She was with Zeita, she spoke to her, she'd swam with the gods.

"But..." Hira murmured. "I was underwater."

Jutia wrapped a thick wool blanket over Hira's shoulders even though she was not cold. The captain rubbed her hands up and down Hira's arms.

"For a second, but I got you," Jutia said with a smile. "Come, let us get dry clothing. I can't believe you survived that. I begin to feel you have seven lives."

Hira followed her, but as they made their way to her quarters, the sun burst through the dark clouds, causing them all to look up. As if the storm never happened. Hira glanced at the sailors, but they were busy cleaning up and arranging loose items that'd came undone. The ship was in complete disarray and much work needed to be done before it resembled normalcy.

Furia. Her heart tightened at the thought. Zeita had warned her. Furia was out there, waiting for her. Waiting for her to arrive and take her seat.

"Do you think I'm cursed, Captain?" Hira asked Jutia, as they entered her cabin.

Jutia glanced at her as she opened her trunk. "I don't believe in curses. I believe in what I can touch, what I can kill, and what I can influence. Things outside of that are dreams, and dreams have helped no one to achieve anything."

Hira nodded and dried her face with the blanket. "We Istokians are cynics."

Jutia smirked at her, then tossed her a clean shirt and pants. Hira took them and undressed as the captain did the same.

"We were not always cynical," Jutia said as she peeled her soaked coat off her body. "There was a time when Istok hosted the largest gatherings of earth-witches. The coven ruled and protected the women, but the men didn't care for that. They didn't like that they couldn't threaten their women, and so declared the witches evil. Heathens against the gods. Their destruction was sanctioned by the Council of Five."

Hira glanced away as Jutia removed her shirt and her breasts spilled out. Now Hira wanted to be alone. Her thoughts raged as she attempted to digest her experience while Jutia wished to speak on the histories.

"The Council of Five was a mess," Hira said, attempting to undress without showing skin.

Jutia pulled her blouse over her head. "It was. Representative government is not always the best solution. Still, the queen can try her best to maintain peace, but how long before the Norrians unleash their wrath? How long before Suid is no longer loyal? How long before the Free Isle decides it wants a stake in our world? And you think Istok is stable? Be sure you're on the right side of things, Hira Balik. Rumors of war plague this land. You can't be blind to it."

Furia. The air whispered the woman's name.

She turned away slightly as she pulled her own shirt off and quickly slipped the dry one over her head. "Almira will know what to do."

"Does she always know what to do?" Jutia asked.

She always appeared to know. Even when she didn't.

Hira's brain kept shouting *Furia*, as if the woman was imbedded in her thoughts.

She sighed and sat down, desperately wishing she had Almira's political cunning. The queen could pick apart this situation and find an angle. The entire thing made Hira's head hurt. It exhausted her further, after the happenings of the day. She had no mind to deal with the complications of a chaotic cousin who might wish to overtake her seat.

Justan chose that moment to enter. He paused, his face brightening to red as he noticed he'd caught them in the privacy of the female space. This was most improper, but the captain didn't seem fazed—she laced her trousers and neatly tied the leather binding.

"How is Quent?" Hira asked him as she quickly closed her shirt.

"Completely worn out," he said as he stared at her. A slow smile, dripping with awe, formed on his lips. "How the hell did you do that?"

Hira shrugged. "I wasn't going to let him drown, was I?"

To think of Quent perishing while they watched helplessly from the ship was ridiculous. She did it without thinking. But had she not, she wouldn't have seen Zeita again and wouldn't have received her warning.

"I've seen no one swim like that," he said to Hira before glancing to Jutia. He studied her posture and raised a brow. "Is she filling you with political talk?"

Jutia glared at him with a red face. It made her look even more beautiful with her dark tresses wet on her cheeks and her lips a sour-cherry color, as she said, "You used to delight in political conversations."

Her tone was tight, and there was a shadow of deep disappointment. Hira felt she shouldn't be a witness to such an ex-lover's quarrel.

"It bores me," he snapped, and shoved his hair back.

Hira cleared her throat, an attempt to diffuse the situation. "Captain, did you send the queen my letter?"

"I did." Jutia nodded.

"What letter?" Justan's head swirled to stare at Jutia.

"I asked her to pen a letter to Almira," Hira said as a way of explanation to what seemed like a miscommunication.

Justan crossed his arms and glared down at her. "And *when* were you planning on telling me this?"

Jutia's face morphed into anger. "You were busy holding the lady's hand as she laid convalescing."

Hira blushed to the roots of her red hair and looked away. Justan flinched and sucked in a breath. Gods, what an odd place to be. This was most unnavigable. She would rather swim back into the storm.

"Regardless, I sent it, my lady," Jutia said and turned to Hira. "I also sent her one of my own and told her your prognosis was grim. I'm sorry if I overstepped my boundaries."

At her words, Hira realized something she'd been blind to. Something that made her stomach clench. If Almira had received her letter, then she was on her way to Istok. At all haste. She could march into a trap. A Furia-shaped trap.

"Excuse me," Hira whispered and walked out. She went to the rail to look out at the calm sea.

Her breath came quick as realization fell into place like pieces of a puzzle. Perhaps it was the many hours around Almira, or maybe she'd always been capable of analytical thought, but just lacked the discipline to hone the craft.

What was it Captain Strauss said? There was a prize on Hira's head. She was being *hunted*. Goose pimples erupted in her arms. A sense of the mystery penetrated her thoughts, and once it formed in her mind, she knew it to be the truth. As if Zeita spoke to her from the waters.

Furia *orchestrated* uncle Beltran's death.

Why? Why would she do this? Think, Hira! *Think!*

She looked down at her hands and gasped when she stared at them.

With Lord Beltran dead, the seat would be in Hira's hands.

She was young and inexperienced. A *weakling*.

Manipulatable, easily killed, or removed.

If this was true, which she strongly felt it was, it meant that Furia was in league with Arrigo. Furia must've provided Arrigo the details to kidnap her uncle. Perhaps she bedded a sailor for information? Perhaps spies lingered in the armada's ships. This was planned. They'd fallen into a trap. Hira, a lamb to the slaughter.

Her hands trembled, and she gripped the rail. Her mother was *dying*. Once she died, Korkoran was without a Balikian until Hira arrived.

She *must* get to Treveri. No matter what. For her mother, for Almira, and most importantly, for her people. And once there, she couldn't break. No matter how rabid Furia's wrath was.

Hira was a Balik. She was the Great Dragon. And dragons didn't cower.

Chapter Thirty-One

HIRA

After Hira's ordeal, exhaustion overcame her, and she slept well past noon. A commotion on deck woke her, and she hastily dressed then emerged to find Captain Jutia shouting at the men.

"Lower the anchor, Mr. Tithe!"

Surrounding the ship was an outcropping of rocks. The sunset quickly approached, and the waters were calm as they lapped against the wooden hull. In the distance, seals noisily nursed their pups atop flat boulders. A few seagulls mewed, their droppings landing on the rails in liquid spurts.

Commander Justan walked past Hira with a narrow face. He wore a heavy coat and carried his visionscope.

"Are we there? Are these the isles?" Hira asked.

He paused, then pointed to the formation arising from the sea. "This is the farthest we can go before the ship is seen."

There was hesitancy born of fear in her. If Zeita was right about the location of the Sea Wife… she was also right about Furia.

Hira followed him as he aided the men, unlocking a longboat. "How will we know if they're here?"

The commander threw a rope over the side of the ship and glanced at her. "I'll take this boat and spy on them. I have to wait for nightfall for cover."

They floated next to a large rock formation that concealed the Night Serpent from being seen by any other vessel. Hira helped pull the heavy wooden boat. The sailors tied lines attached to a pulley.

"I'm going with you," she decided.

Justan's jaw twitched. He looked at her with a raised brow. "*I'm* going. I'm taking a couple of men and we'll be back in a few hours. It'll be dangerous. Stay put."

Infuriated with him for his stubborn bossiness, she slammed her hand over the boat's rail and paused the descent. "Commander, this is *my* mission."

He turned his body so that he hovered over her, his face closing in. "Those are my men."

Heated from both his dismissal and the closeness of his chest, Hira angered. She wasn't certain she wished for such a display before the sailors but she wouldn't be left behind.

"May I remind the commander that it's not his place to tell *me* what to do?" she hissed.

Her voice was steady, much to her credit. However, she was barely composed. The whetted words and his proximity awoke something in her, something akin to desire, and she didn't know if it was shown on her face.

Jutia strode to them, her hat on her head, and a cigar in her hand. She looked from Justan to Hira with raised brows. "Why don't you *both* go and stop fighting about it in front of my crew?"

Hira was rightfully ashamed when she saw the men watching them wearily. This wasn't the etiquette of a High Lady. She left to grab her weapons and when she came back, Justan was climbing on the boat. He yanked a bag from Jutia, and the two looked like they'd had an unpleasant conversation.

Perhaps Hira shouldn't go. Perhaps it wouldn't be proper for a lady and a gentleman to be alone in a small ship, away from prying eyes. In Treveri, a lady could lose her reputation participating in such acts. A silly notion. As if one could misplace one's reputation as they did buttons.

Before Hira could back away from her insistence to go, Jutia turned to her with a neutral look and an encouraging smile. "Ready, my lady?"

Hira tentatively nodded. Was she ready? Alone with the commander encased in darkness? She would have to be.

"You'll have to hurry. The sun is almost gone, otherwise we'll have to wait another day. I gave Justan some food since it'll be a few hours." She helped Hira up onto the barge.

Jutia slammed her palm twice on the siding. The sailors lowered them, and they rocked back and forth as Hira held on to both sides until they landed on the water. Without sparing her a look, the commander grasped the oars and handed her one. They rowed in the direction he indicated. Left, right, left, right. He easily maneuvered, even with the spiked sea.

As the last rays of light disappeared, he stopped and pointed to a flat rock they could disembark on. Silently, they crept up to the stone. The boulder was small, and they had to jump to a larger one. He spied around the base, then turned to her. His face was lit by moonlight.

"Look," he whispered.

Hira pressed herself around him and, as steadily as she could, peered past the formation. There, in the lagoon, was the Sea Wife along with the Red Dragon.

"I *knew* it!" she hissed, and Justan shushed her.

She pulled out the visionscope. Lanterns were lit and men moved about. She couldn't see Strauss, but the pirates seemed jovial and the high quarters she'd inherited from her uncle glowed with golden light.

A rocky outcropping anchored the ships. They'd chained the Istokian sailors against a large gibber outside of the vessel. It looked like a fair amount of them were alive. She sighed in relief and turned back to Justan. She'd not failed *yet*. She still had time to make up for the wrongs her idiocy caused.

Justan placed his hand over her shoulder and squeezed. Their eyes briefly met, and in the proximity, she felt the world pause. Then laughter and merriment sounded from the ship, pulling them from their trance.

They made it halfway back to the Night Serpent when they slammed into a jutting rock. Justan stopped the boat until the waters calmed and some light came into the horizon. That would be hours from now and the temperature was dropping. She tightened her coat and huddled in the corner.

They were quiet until she noticed he silently watched her.

"The night you were attacked in your rooms…" his voice was hollow. "When I showed you to your new quarters. Did you wish to kiss me?"

The question was so ridiculous she laughed and looked away. He didn't laugh. He stared at her with unwavering eyes. She studied the motions of the water and fiercely wished they could go back to the Night Serpent. She didn't want to have this discussion. She feared exploring her sentiment would mean disappointment and heartache.

But yes, she'd wanted to kiss him. *Desperately.* And when he'd not, she felt foolish and hurt. Misled by his lingering eyes after their intimate conversation that night.

"Does the answer matter?" she lingered, running her thumb against the wood grain of the rail.

"It does," he whispered.

She glanced up at him, but he remained unmoved, as if he were afraid.

"*Why?*"

"Because," and he swallowed, his shoulders hunching together. "I didn't wish to be alone in my delusion."

Her throat felt dry. "May I remind the commander that, at the time, he was betrothed?"

His face tightened and the muscles of his jaw twitched. From this angle, he looked haunted. Perpetually oppressed by something he wouldn't discuss.

"I don't wish to speak of Jutia," he said in a rather metallic tone.

She flinched at his harshness. The water lapped against the boat and it was as if anything she could say at this moment might come out wrong or lead to misinterpretation. Especially when she refused to study her own feelings. Slowly, the tension dissipated.

He studied her with a calmer expression. "Why did you run away and join the Red Guard?"

Why indeed? It seemed like something which occurred in a past decade, so long ago she scarcely had memory of it.

She shrugged. "I wanted a different life. I was eighteen and suffocating."

He leaned back on his elbows and stretched out his legs. "That wasn't long ago."

"Feels like lifetimes ago." She fisted her scarred hand.

"There had to be a catalyst. What was it? Did the Lady Marai saddle you with an overgrown pompous lord for a husband?" There was a twist of humor in his voice.

She glared at him, and he laughed as she scowled. She didn't wish to discuss the event that had transpired before she sliced off her hair. The angry words she'd spat to her mother. Her defiance of all that made her a Balik. A part of her was a little ashamed. Another part of her had no regrets.

"What's his name?" He asked.

"I can't recall, my lord." She sniffed. She knew the lord well enough and never let her thoughts stray to him, his little head, and his little bow. She disliked everything about the man.

Justan leaned back and admired the stars. She drank in his profile, the upturn of his nose and his fine throat. She warmed despite the chill in the air.

"You know his name. It haunts you some nights. The thought that, had you not escaped, you would be his little *wife*." He looked up to find her staring at him. "Come, tell me."

She focused on the moonlight reflecting on the waters. "Tell you *what?*"

"His *name*, my lady," he said with a chuckle.

She took a sharp breath and prepared herself for the mockery that was sure to happen. Out of all the men her mother could've chosen, she chose the absolute worst, and everyone knew it. Before Hira could deny the man, her uncle had announced her engagement. It was done. There was no turning back from such a spectacle as the announcement of a union. It would've doomed Hira. She had no choice but to run away.

"Carrian," she admitted.

The laugh was more of a howl. He pressed his hand to his mouth to muffle the noise, but still he delighted. She glared at him wishing to shove him into the waters.

"*Barnabus* Carrian?" Justan asked, his delirious laughter finally dying down.

"Well, I didn't marry him, did I?" She grew frustrated with the entire conversation.

She did not appreciate his teasing or the fact that he felt comfortable teasing her. It tasted much like a friendship, like something M or a brother would do, and her affections were clearly more than of the sisterly kind.

"Lord Barnabus Carrian, that self-important loaf of bread? He comes with suitable lands. I can see the reasoning, but he's in his fourth decade!" Justan's smile was more than she could bear. She felt her entire neck flush.

When she didn't respond, he pulled out some dried meat and fruit from the knapsack.

He glanced at her. "He could never have handled you. Not even on a good day."

Hira stared at him, aghast at the implication. "What is that supposed to mean?"

He bit into an apple, still delighting in teasing her. "You're a handful, that's all I'm saying. You never would've been happy with gentile words. Doing nothing but ensuring his scalla was properly smoked. You'd die of boredom."

"Lord Carrian is an excellent prospect." She sat up, making the boat rock.

She didn't even know why she was defending Barnabus Carrian, his mere existence had been torture. But something about the way Justan implied she was unmanageable was insulting. It insinuated that she was a wild horse to be tamed.

He raised his brows. "What I mean to say is that you wouldn't marry a man you didn't love."

She looked away. Mostly because he was staring at her so

intensely and they were alone. He was a lord, and she was unmarried. And too attracted to his dark eyes and olive skin. How good he was. And how he behaved in moments like this, as if he showcased the real Justan Seaver that he allowed no one else to see.

Hira shouldn't have come. This was an improper conversation.

"I've embarrassed you, I apologize," he mumbled.

"I'm a lady. You seem to forget that when you're around me," she said.

He pointed his finger at her. "*You* seem to forget that when you're around *me*."

She leaned forward. "You continuously provoke me! Since the moment I met you, you've been combative! I don't know if you're a friend, an ally, or *what*."

Justan looked genuinely hurt as he flinched. "I've sailed half the southern seas to save your life. Every day I think of new ways of keeping you safe, scouring words to protect you. At least consider me an ally," he breathed.

He was right. He'd done her bidding, but *why*? Why did he wish to save her so badly? What was she to him? If she'd died, they would've appointed another High Seat. He wouldn't have lost his post. On the contrary, Almira would have rewarded him for attempting to save Hira's life. A noble act.

"*Why* did you? You could've left me to die. You could've ignored my words and had my arm amputated. Why didn't you?" Hira asked the questions which plagued her, the questions she'd painted into the air as she laid pursuing sleep these many nights. Questions she didn't dare voice.

"I respected your uncle," he admitted and glanced away. "He was… one of my only friends. I couldn't abandon his niece and heir, even when everyone urged me to."

A strange statement. She'd not expected him to think highly of Lord Beltran.

"So, because of my uncle? That's the only reason? Out of respect for a dead man?"

He looked at her with those stormy brown eyes. Here, sitting so close to him, her mind drowned in the notion of how handsome he was and how disfigured she'd become. Now that he had no attachment, he was quite the catch. Despite her own insecurities, which she knew she would have to work through, he didn't seem to dislike her scars.

"Also, because you asked me to. I may be many things, but I'll not deny my lady's bidding," Justan said. The tone in which he said "my lady," lead her to somehow feel as though she, Hira Balik, belonged to him in some way.

"But you've not trespassed on our friendship. I know I'm not beautiful like Jutia, but I thought…"

Hira couldn't even form the words or meet his gaze. Perhaps she should've been the one to be forward and state her interest. Still, she hesitated. She could battle an army but had little notion for the softness of feelings.

Days at sea and the commander, despite watching her with warm eyes, hadn't asked her about attachments or conversed about the future. For them both.

She realized that she'd been lapping an angry wound in her heart. Hira had been sure that he didn't want her from the very moment he attacked her on the boat. Didn't think her attractive enough to cherish. Called her a 'marred wench'. He'd been a friend, yes. And she valued his friendship, but he'd done nothing more. Not even after their dance. The longer time went on, the more she was certain that he simply respected her as a ruler and would never consider her as a partner.

But he stared at her in disbelief. "You think I didn't kiss you because of your scar? Or spoken to you of attachments because of it? Oh, *Red*. There are moments when I believe you see nothing of the truth," he said, then he smiled sadly. "There's a lovely, idyllic innocence to you. Like you think there's still good left in this life. Gods… it's been over a decade since I've seen some brightness outside of Quent. I don't know how… how to be around you."

Her cheeks flushed bright red. She would understand someone like Almira intimidating a man, but never Hira. She said all the wrong things and angered too quickly. She was flat-haired, flat-chested, clumsy, and impulsive. She'd grown up never being allowed to explore the world for herself.

She was a painting where only the edges were drawn and all the wild, vibrant colors were yet to bring the image to life.

"And what is the truth, Commander?" she asked in a hush.

His mouth slacked opened, and he seemed to wish to speak, but he stopped himself. He looked down and played with the sack in his hand. "The truth is complicated. But there's one thing I know. You intrigue me. Things seldom intrigue me anymore. I've seen too much. You've been a puzzle since the moment I fought you. Each time I think I have the last piece, you reveal something else, and I understand *nothing*. But you're important, where I am dispensable. The world can manage without Commander Seaver, but not without Hira Balik."

She studied her hands in the moonlight as he tossed the apple into the ocean.

He took a deep breath. "When I was a young man, I never knew what I wanted. I was the eldest, so naturally I would become the commander. My brother... always knew what he wanted and *who* he wanted. He never questioned it. He was bold and rash, and I tried to keep him out of trouble. By the time we grew into teens, I knew nothing about myself, but he knew *all* there was to know about himself."

Hira listened in silence, wishing to ask more questions about his brother. That secret that he carried and wouldn't allow anyone to look upon.

"Why don't you speak about him?" she asked.

He laughed without humor. "Because all it causes is pain."

Shadows traveled across his face. They painted such morose pictures he became easy to pity.

"And once Quent dies... I'll be alone," he said and looked up at her. His hand slowly trembled. "I'm rather used to loneliness."

He didn't have to be. That's what she wished to say. For a mad moment, she wished to open herself to him. To tell him about her fears and her thoughts. To not be so alone in the desolation of life. Instead, she crunched the words between her molars. This was a different sort of bravery, and she had very little training for this manner of war.

"Loneliness is a silent killer, isn't it?" she sighed as she looked out into the sea.

His head turned to the expanse under the moon and stared at the stars. "The night before we left to join my father on our maiden voyage that would take us from home for a year, my mother took me to the window. She pointed to the sky."

The melodic sound of his voice covered Hira like a warm winter blanket as he said, "She said that Garians would paint the name of their loved ones into the sky, to be close to them. That each night I would be away from her, she would paint my name into the stars and watch over me."

Hira felt emotions thicken in her throat. "But she died," she whispered.

He nodded, pulling deep into himself. "The day I found out, I hid from my father. He wouldn't permit anyone to mourn her loss. From the back of the ship, I stared at the night sky, and, for the first time, I could read the tales of the past. Thousands upon thousands of names etched in their glow. I searched and searched until I saw my name. The light damp, confirming she'd died. As the years passed, the light ebbed more and more until one day I gazed up and it was gone. Like the pain that dulls after years of grief, so the light shined until she knew I would be well."

Hira was breathless, encased in his story and the rawness of his beliefs, which she desperately wished to adopt for herself. To paint loss across a canvas of night and allow it to act as a reminder of death, love, and loneliness.

After a while, he sighed and looked at her once more. "I thought Lord Beltran would leave Istok in the hands of someone—"

"More capable," she whispered sadly, keenly aware of the truth.

He met her eyes. "In the hands of someone who wanted the seat. Who *wanted* to rule Istok."

She swallowed as her emotions rose to her throat. "Things have changed since then."

He smiled. Truly smiled. And under the stars, he was beautiful and haunted. "Yes. For the better, I think. You've... grown. I've seen you selflessly risk yourself in heroic ways. You're becoming a fine woman, Lady Hira. *Admirable.*"

She felt her stomach freeze as they stared at one another. As she allowed his words to drench her. "Are you saying you admire me, Commander?"

He popped a piece of dried meat into his mouth and chewed it carefully as their eyes remained locked. "Very much so," he said.

His eyes were so intense she could scarcely move.

"I admire you too," she said.

"Don't." He shook his head. "Let me earn it first."

The boat rocked and all she could do was hold on to both sides.

She was afraid she would fall over. Or perhaps she'd already fallen.

Isabelle Olmo

Chapter Thirty-Two

ALMIRA

It was the evening of the seventh day when they saw the Pas of Gul. The light faded from the world, casting golden Suidian warmth over the small traveling party. The Pas was no more than two massive mountains split in half, which allowed Suid to connect to Istok. In ages past, the area was more heavily guarded, but since her grandfather's time, the countries had been allies and there was little need for security.

Sanaa wanted to make camp, but Almira refused in light of her desperation to find her uncle. Another hour of fast pace and they would be at the mouth of the pas. Small rumblings of labor pains begun the night before but Almira said nothing. Her discomfort grew with each passing day, and she cursed herself for not leaving sooner. The soreness in her lower back was nearly unbearable when she jostled against the carriage. There was a change in her belly, as if it shifted.

She veiled herself. She was, after all, still in mourning. Underneath her veil, she grimaced, hoping her Red Guard wouldn't notice. She prayed fervently to the sea gods and the spirits of her dead parents to guard her. The child must delay. It *must*.

The thought of not bearing the baby as she floated in Istokian waters sent a panic over her spine. The vivid memory of her mother perishing in bed as she refused to birth her second child in the sacred pools admittedly haunted her. Balikians must be born in water or tragedy would follow in their wake.

"Please little one, await a week, my love," she would murmur when alone.

Sanaa halted the party the moment they reached the base of the mountains. Evening was a hair's breath away and there was meager light to secure the campsite and unload.

The captain was so angry that she didn't look at or converse with Almira. This suited the queen, as she had no intention of pretending in front of Sanaa's eagle eyes.

There was no Red Army in sight, and Almira pondered reasons for her uncle being late. She would wait for him for two days, no more. Any longer and they risked the child being born or losing Istok. She daydreamed of her Red Guard storming Korkoran on their own despite it being an impossible feat. Korkoran was an impenetrable fortress, as her father often boasted. It had one way in and one way out; through the front gates. Her guard would die speared to the dragon stones.

That night, she slept deep and didn't rouse until noon. Perhaps she underestimated how tired the travel made her. When she woke, M brought her food.

"I tried to wake you two hours ago, but you wouldn't stir," M said as she set the tea over the queen's legs.

Almira sipped on the hot drink and thanked her for the meal.

The older woman sat slowly and grimaced as she clutched her chest. She'd declined quicker than Almira expected. Sanaa had confessed M's illness and her determination to stay by the queen until she no longer could. At first Almira protested, but Sanaa said—in a tone that left no room for questions—that the choice of guards was always Sanaa's and not the queen.

"Why did you come, Madhavi?" Almira studied the woman, the way her fingers encased her breast.

M spared her a glance and slowly lowered her hand, as if she'd not realized she openly revealed her illness.

"And lay writhing in a bed in Mavros? No, Majesty. That's not for me. The journey distracts me from the reality, and I almost want an envoy to attack us so that I might meet the death I seek."

Almira nearly gasped. To think that someone would wish to place their flesh before her so that she may live… it reminded her too much of her father. "Don't seek death."

"I never sought it." M smiled her mischievous smile. "It's sought *me*. I've no intention of running from it, but I'll defeat it by naming my terms. I began the game with the Favia at an early age and in that game I shall perish."

Almira set down her cup, the taste of her tea soured at the thought. The queen herself was in the middle of a game, one she scarcely knew the rules to. Her hand strayed to her stomach, the place that ensconced her baby, the baby she'd placed before a bargaining table.

"I know you don't believe in the old gods," M said quietly, slithering words into Almira's dark thoughts.

To distract herself, Almira buttered the bread. "I was raised in Istok. We have little time for gods."

"Well, be that as it may, they came to me in dreams last night." M shrugged.

For a Suidian to admit such an occurrence was bold indeed. Suidians didn't dare dream. Almira never mentioned dreams to Sanaa or her *cuzo* would curse and offer prayers to the gods so that the queen might be forgiven.

"In them, I saw Lady Hira." M leaned forward on her elbows. "I know in my heart she's alive and she will outlive this old woman."

M's face was sincere and filled with assuredness. How Almira wished to hold Hira, to assure herself that her cousin was safe and unharmed. She still clearly recalled the scent of her hair when she was a child. She would curl against Almira, seeking comfort and warmth, like a young kitten.

"What did she look like?" Almira asked in a whisper.

"I saw her dressed in the garbs of a High Lady. She was older and carried your family's sword. She looked magnificent and grown, like a true warrior. Like a *dragon*. Like you always knew she would

315

be."

The women smiled at one another, and the vision filled Almira with reassurance. She'd known Hira was a dragon, but wondered how long it would take for her young cousin to see it.

Almira rubbed her stomach. The sharp pains had subsided, and she felt much better than she had the past few days.

M slowly stood. "They're called false labor pains."

The queen paused and stared at her.

"You think you hide things well?" M said in a tone of amusement. "The girls don't know because they are not mothers. But it happens, sometimes a few times. We'll get you to the waters of Istok in time, Majesty. I swear it."

Her words infused Almira with a sudden appreciation towards the woman. "I am glad you ended up in my rooms that night and defied me with your interruption."

M walked to the tent entrance. "Not more than I, Majesty."

Almira's thoughts strayed to Alton, his whereabouts, and his opinions of her decisions and task. He likely hated them. He wouldn't hate it as much as her offer of their child to the Norr. It felt as if all her choices, since the moment she banished her father, had become cursed and questionable. She wondered if ousting her maker would unravel her.

Because the thought of Alton mixed her with longing and apprehension, she focused on the matter at hand. Furia. A *sister*. She didn't feel like she had a sister. It wasn't a warm sensation that filled her heart. It was so nebulous and unfathomable that no tenderness captured her feelings. She recalled Furia as a child, she whom she called *cousin*—how Furia hated her.

The desperation to get to Treveri sent her to quick breaths and shaking hands, which she had to calm alone in her bed. She reminded herself of Alton when the darkness overcame him, and the memories of his own brother crushed his smiles and good humor.

It was in the dimming of the evening light when a noise like a powerful thunderstorm reached the camp. Almira quickly exited her tent. She'd tried to rest, but the sound was deafening. The wind had chilled, and she wrapped her golden robe over her body, attempting to shake the shivers.

"Rain? This time of year?" She asked Delara, who stood outside, her green eyes on the horizon.

"That's not rain." Her guard pointed to the distance.

Almira turned and gasped.

The Red Army.

It was the most beautiful sight she'd ever beheld. Like a river of rushing blood came the men of Suid decked in red, with eagle banners, and her beloved uncle at the head of the cavalry. His great red eagle, Ushga, swept down on the small envoy and screeched as she announced the High Lord. She landed on top of the flagpole in the center of the encampment. Opening her wings, she proudly showed off her girth. Her wingspan was over three meters and her massive claws sported talons as long as Almira's fingers. She watched them all as if she herself brought the entire army to save them.

Their camp cheered when Thebo raised his hand and waved at Almira. She could almost see his smile. Her heart leaped, and she inexplicably cried.

The moment Thebo reached her, he dismounted his horse. He took three steps to Almira and embraced her. She clutched his armor and trembled as she filled with gratitude. She had an army. He had come, as he always did.

He studied her, his own face etched with concern. "You push yourself, Majesty. You're nearly due. Gods help us. Let me take it from here. Go to Suid and we'll march into Istok."

But Almira shook her head and pulled him to her tent. "No, my dearest uncle. *I* shall enter Istok, swollen feet and all."

"Then we better get you a horse." He smiled slightly, wrinkling the corners of his eyes.

The Red Army settled camp. They scattered over the pass, covering each inch of grass with tents. Fires roared to life as they roasted wild game. The scent of it wafted into her tent, where they set up a small reunion feast for them to speak over their plan. They loaded the tables with fruits and cheeses, which were hard to acquire in Easima. They seasoned the fowl with black pepper and lemons until the crispy skin cracked, displaying the juicy meat beneath.

Almira's appetite was suddenly open like a gaping dam, and she ate with a ferocity she'd not allowed herself before. Her uncle watched her as he smoked his pipe and exchanged glances with Sanaa.

"Each time Gita was pregnant, I had to produce a hog, for she could consume one all by herself," he smiled.

Almira paused and cleaned her lips with a napkin. "We've traveled light. We haven't had a decent dinner in days."

Sanaa made a noise of agreement as she lit her cigar and joined Thebo in a good smoke after a pleasant meal. Delara opened a bottle of fermented golden berry liquor and poured them all a small serving.

"Any word on the king's whereabouts?" Thebo asked as he took his drink and sipped it to savor the taste.

Sanaa tossed her liquor back, setting the cup down to indicate for another. "None. He's crossing through the Black Forrest to avoid detection."

The high lord raised a brow. "The entire army?"

"Half of it," M said.

Thebo shook his head. "He won't make it. Not in time."

At this point, it mattered very little. The queen took a deep breath. "I can't wait for him."

"No, you can't. I have a confession." He looked around at the ones who partook in the meal. "I take these women are in your confidence, seeing as they're your *ladies-in-waiting?*"

The queen raised a brow, but her eyes twinkled at his joke. "Confess then."

He placed his elbows on the table. "I have a spy in Korkoran. Actually, I have two."

Almira's appetite officially subsided. It was something *she* should've considered. At that moment, she felt rather silly. To trust people would welcome Hira with open arms was fanciful. Her father likely had spies everywhere, secret plots he concocted. She'd not thought ahead, and she was already behind.

Her uncle could see her tight face and he provided her with a small smile. "With Beltran dead, Marai ill, and Hira hiding in Easima… I had to learn the happenings within Istok."

"Did you know about my sister?" Almira asked what haunted her.

How many knew and how many kept it from her? It made her feel not only betrayed but also separated from her family. Like a child not allowed to partake in the conversation of adults. Cast aside, not able to handle the harsh reality.

"No," Thebo said quickly and with sincerity. "Did I know of Lady Furia? Yes. Did I know her as anything other than your cousin? No."

Almira braced herself. "Speak, sir. I need to learn everything."

He smoked his pipe and took a moment to compose his thoughts, like he often did. "Furia arrived at Korkoran the day after your father left to escort you to your wedding. She appeared at court and your aunt allowed her. Beltran was aware of it. He received word the night before The Cutting. They assumed she would simply be in Treveri for a season. She was entitled to do so as a relative to the High Lord."

"Only she didn't leave," Almira said darkly. "She's *still* there."

"She's not." Thebo's lips thinned. "That's why I was late. I obtained a delayed message from my spies. Furia has left Korkoran… and no one knows her whereabouts."

Almira's stomach froze as she processed the implications. "What do you mean, *left?*"

"Gone. An argument with Lady Marai and she went in the night." Thebo gestured with his hand.

Almira's mind was wild with thoughts. "She could be *anywhere!*"

"She could," Thebo admitted and smoked his pipe. "Along with that, Marai's health has considerably declined. She won't last long. My spies tell me she's hardly able to leave her bed."

Almira sighed and pressed her face to her hands. How she wished to see her aunt before she passed. To hold her hand and assure her all would be well. The agony of not knowing what would happen to House Balik likely haunted her these many nights.

"Marai's time is short and with Furia out of the way, Hira can easily ascend to the High Seat," Thebo continued. "However, there can still be dangers within Korkoran."

"You don't believe Hira can handle it?" Almira set her water down.

Thebo sipped more liquor. "I think Hira is young."

She wouldn't argue with him about that notion. "Indeed, she is, Uncle. But if not Hira, then *who*? My presence there will be vital. I'll rouse the nobles to be as loyal to Hira as they were to my father. We'll root out Furia's influence."

"And what of Furia?" Sanaa leaned forward. "She's your *sister*."

Almira looked down to her hands and admitted the thought of destroying one of her own blood made her feel ill. In other circumstances, she would have welcomed an unknown sister. It felt like a curse cast from the mouth of a dark abyss. A plague upon their world.

"I wish to speak to her, but I doubt she'll wish to. She likely blames me for the sins of our father," Almira said.

"Most certainly, but you mustn't blame *yourself*. This was not your doing." Thebo blew out smoke from his pipe.

"I absolutely do not blame myself, but I would blame myself if I sent Hira to her death by forcing her return only to face such dangers." Almira looked at him. "Even if I wasn't aware of them."

Chapter Thirty-Three

HIRA

Jutia spread the map of the southeastern seas over the table. Hira wasn't skillful at map reading, but she'd learned Jutia and Justan were. It was a nautical map that showed sea depth and important markers. The captain imbedded a knife down over the Isles of Hipata, exactly at the position of the Sea Wife.

"How do we do this?" Hira asked.

"The pirates have chained our men and we don't know if they've been fed or tortured. We can't count on them." Justan placed a stone where the Istokian sailors were located. "Them being tied up *outside* of the ship works for our advantage."

Hira leaned forward. "Someone needs to unshackle them without being seen."

"I'll do it!" Quent said.

The three of them turned to Quent, who stood as tall as he could, his hands on his waist, sporting a bright and stubborn face. Justan tensed and she understood why. The boy, being weakened by his illness, wouldn't fare well in such a task.

"I'm small. I can crawl through the rocks and get to them," Quent continued, undeterred by their obvious doubt and concern.

Justan stepped closer to him, shaking his head and putting his hands up. "It's too dangerous."

"Horseshit, Justan! You told me you would treat me different! You were killing pirates at my age!" He squared off with his older brother. His little face reddened, likely embarrassed at being denied once again.

The only thing this could lead to would be another argument. They didn't have time for this and with all of them in such peril, she didn't want the last words spoken between the brothers to be cold and biting.

Hira placed her hand gently on his shoulder. "You could cough and give your position away. It'll risk you *and* the men."

But Quent met her eyes with an offended look, as if he'd not thought about it. "I'll dunk myself under the water and cough there. No one will see me! You need all sailors on deck for this plan to succeed. I survived a bloody storm. I can survive this!"

Justan shook his head. But Jutia, to Hira's surprise, was the one who spoke, "Very well. You'll silently swim through the *cold* ocean and release the men. Hopefully, some of them are in a condition to help us fight."

Justan's head swiveled to her. His glare was intense. Jutia, long done with pleasing him, shrugged.

"Like the boy said, he lived through the storm. He'll live through this," the captain answered.

Hira had to agree. The frightening episode he'd endured and recuperated from proved that. Justan found himself outnumbered. Annoyed, he slammed a stone next to the one representing the captured sailors.

"Quent's position will be here. He'll release the men so they can join the fight. *And* he'll try to stay alive," the commander said in a harsh tone.

At first, Hira felt surprised by Justan's acquiescence to his brother being placed in such dangers, but there was a part of her that was proud of him. For unclenching his hand and allotting him the responsibility he craved.

"He will," Quent nodded eagerly, bursting with pride.

Jutia turned to the map. "Alright, what else?" She ran her long fingers over the remaining stones and looked at the commander.

"They have more men than we do," Justan said, and the captain agreed, but she did not look deterred.

Hira studied the plan and the pieces present. Somewhere, in the back of her mind, a lesson flittered through her memories. It was Ley Coster, her old Ley, who attempted his best to school her. A wealth of knowledge, having served House Balik for two generations, he often droned on about battles. Hira would've rather experience the battles than hear about them secondhand, but she recalled a story… about Lady Dominia.

Dominia was most revered amongst Balikians. She united Istok in a time when the Corsikan empire ruled the world. She joined forces with Suidians, Norrians, a rebellious Corsikan princess, and brought forth the Council of Five. In a decisive battle, she waited until dawn and attacked the Corsikan ships with the rising of the sun. The Corsikans couldn't load the cannons fast enough with the glare. She decimated their fleet and won her first sea victory.

"What if we attack from the east? If we maneuver the Night Serpent around." Hira took a stone to represent their vessel.

"That'll take hours." Justan shook his head.

"I can do it. We'd have to leave soon, in the next hour." Jutia looked at Hira with a smile. "The glare will be in their faces."

She'd never been more thankful for Ley Coster and the moment she saw him she would tell him of the success his droll lessons had on her. The ancient stories could very well save their modern-day ship.

"It might work to our advantage. At least canon-wise. It'll be hard to make ready cannons if one cannot see," Hira said.

Jutia brought the large stone and set it in the east. "The Night Serpent will attack at sunrise."

Hira pointed to the plan. "Commander, you'll have half of our forces in long boats. Circle around the northern rocks and wait for the right moment."

She took stones from the pile and laid them at the bottom of the map, where their weak spot was. Whatever happened, she couldn't allot Strauss to gain the upper hand.

"You come in from the south," Hira said.

"Wade quietly in the early morning cover, then storm the Sea Wife." Justan nodded. "Jutia can focus on the Red Dragon."

"Where will you be?" Jutia looked at Hira.

"Cutting off the head." Hira pointed her ruby knife at the Sea Wife. "That's where I'll find Strauss. I'll go in first, sneak into the ship."

Justan's warm brown gaze met hers, and she felt the same flutter in her stomach. She had to look away, so she focused on the map.

"How do you know he'll be there?" Justan asked.

Hira thought of the fine tunics Strauss wore, the polished gold of his eye, and his false modesty over coin. He might've stated that he was not a greedy man, but he painted himself with greed. And his greed would be his undoing.

"Because he will be delighting in the comforts of the High Quarters. I'll go for Strauss. I'll be aware of his tricks this time. You take care of the men. Jutia handles the Red Dragon and with no captain to issue orders, it'll be chaos." Hira looked proudly at the two of them.

She scarcely believed she'd come up with a solid plan. She desperately wished her uncle could see her from the great beyond. As she explained the idea, she glowed with warmth. As if her soul filled out the cracks long left gaping from her resistance to her destiny. She was their leader. Their High Lady, and today, she would take back her ship and rescue her men.

Justan slowly nodded. "It might work. Many will die."

Hira pounded the map with her fist. "Many have *already* died. We need to do this swiftly. I must get to Istok."

"Never thought I'd hear those words out of your mouth." Justan smiled at her, and she blushed to her ears.

Despite the hours between their conversation, his kind words continued to coat her insides and provided her strength. He recognized her change for the better, and there was pride in his tone. She'd made someone proud, and that was worth more than all the gold in Istok.

Jutia leaned back and crossed her arms. "I'm impressed, my

lady. It is a good plan. Don't let Strauss distract you. Finish him quickly, or he'll feed you lies."

Hira agreed and nodded. "Let's do this."

Once they issued orders, the ship went into quick motion. They assigned half the men under Justan, and the other half were to stay with Jutia. Justan's men made quick work of rounding up as many long boats as they could. Hira helped sort weapons and tally up the ironbombs that were left. They had forty rounds, enough to cause serious damage if done in proximity. There was no doubt in Hira's mind that it would be a bloody battle.

Hira planned to swim up to the Sea Wife, climb up the side ladder and slip into the high quarters. Her wounded arm itched to meet Captain Strauss and bring him the death he'd nearly caused her. This was revenge, and she knew it. The Favia might claim payment later, but right now she was willing to play their game.

When Hira finished outfitting herself for a cold swim, Justan knocked on her door as she slid on her gloves.

"Sixty men in long boats, my lady," he said.

Sixty! Her mind wanted to calculate how many would make it, but she had to push that aside. Istokian sailors knew the risks they took when they signed up to serve in the armada.

She nodded. "Quent?"

"He's never been happier," Justan admitted.

She walked to him and smiled. There was a tender feeling within her that was mixed with gratitude at his loyalty. He was her commander and answered only to her. He was her righthand man. After their conversation a few hours ago, she felt torn between desiring him deeply and restraining her feelings. Somehow, it always seemed the wrong moment to act upon her impulses.

"Let's go save our men, Commander."

His eyes softened, and he nodded.

They threw the longboats over the side and the sailors slowly climbed down, packing the boats to the brim. Luck was on their side, for the waters were calm because of the frigidity of the night.

Jutia stared down at Hira with a smile. "You're a fine strategist, Lady Hira."

Hira looked at the captain and her shadowed face. There was no trace of sarcasm to her tone and the lady admired Jutia for seeing the closeness between her and Justan and not allowing it to impede solid reasoning. The matureness of her actions cemented her determination to ensure they remained friends. She was a valuable member of Hira's armada, and she wouldn't forget all Jutia had done for her during this tumultuous voyage.

The women shook hands. "Captain, good luck."

"You too," Jutia replied.

The captain gave Justan one last look, then slapped the boat before her men lowered them into the ocean. They slowly rowed in complete darkness, as the danger of the jutting rocks was ever present. Hira's stomach knotted, but she never let it show. This was her moment, and she wouldn't falter.

It took hours, in the mists of their journey, she found Quent shivering under his coat. "Are you sure you can do this?" she whispered.

He gave her an incredibly hard look. "I can and I *will*. I've got to prove myself somehow."

Hira tightened her hand over his arm. "You don't have to prove yourself to *anyone*."

But Quent's eyes narrowed. She could see his determination by the light of the moon. "Yes, I do. We all do, even *you*."

Such insightful words were not for the tossing and Hira backed down. She prayed that whatever god guarded the Istokian children would watch over him and wrap him in protective arms.

About an hour before sunrise, they arrived at the rock outcropping where Justan anchored, then stepped off the boat. He pulled Quent with him as she jumped after them. The commander kneeled in front of Quent. He looked so worried, and she had no words to appease him.

Quent placed his hand on his older brother's shoulder. "I'll make it, Justan. You've got to believe in me. We are the star-sons, remember?"

"I believe in you," Justan whispered in a hoarse tone, as if his little brother had matured before he'd had the time to digest it. "Just be careful. First sign of trouble, you duck in the water and swim back here. I'll come get you."

Quent nodded. "I promise I will."

Then Justan grasped him and pressed a loving kiss into the boy's brown locks. "Garians always survive."

"Garians always survive," Quent repeated the motto.

Hira waited until the brothers' tender moment finished and Justan turned to her. The chill cut through them both, and Hira shivered. He stepped forward and rubbed her arms up and down, pulling her to him. She almost gasped at the intimacy, her heart at her throat.

He visibly swallowed. "Don't die again."

She smiled, warmed by his concern. "Humans can only die once."

"And you've already used up your chance." He looked grim.

On impulse, she hugged him. Instantly, he pulled her closer and buried his face in her hair. She felt his lips press a soft kiss on her temple and she sighed into him. His warmth enveloped her, and Hira clutched him as tightly as she could, delighting in the feel of his body against hers. The gods better not touch him, or she would swim to Hell to get him back.

"Go kill the bastard," he whispered in her ear.

There was something about the way he said it. Like he knew she could do it, like he would stand by in case she needed help, but fully comprehended the weight of revenge. He had confidence in her ability, and she'd never been more deeply attracted to him than she was at that moment. Hira caressed his face, and he leaned into her touch. She felt the stubbles of his whiskers, those same whiskers she'd found offensive when she met him. She delighted in them, delighted in their coarseness. Hira realized she'd grown to care for him, for his deep voice, and the fine lines that decorated his eyes when he smiled.

Quent, ever studious, cleared his throat.

Flushing, they pulled apart and Justan's hand lingered slightly against her marred arm. Then he turned away.

Hira took Quent's hand, and they silently jumped through the slippery rocks to the spot closest to the target. When they looked back, Justan was already in the craft with the men as they navigated to their task.

They waited alone, but Hira's eyes were on the commander's boat.

"He cares for you, my lady. He probably doesn't even understand it, given that he's been with Jutia for so long. Justan has a funny way of showing he cares, but he does, and I see it." Quent's voice was sincere.

"I greatly admire Commander Seaver," she admitted.

Quent huddled under his coat and after a while he spoke once more, words she wasn't ready to digest. "I know you'll probably have to wed a Norrian High Lord or someone equally important."

Almira might ask such a thing and Hira was not certain how she could defend her attachment to the Commander. There was so much more to think and consider now. Especially if the conflict in the North continued and spilled into Istokian land. Marriage with a Norrian lord would calm it and save her people from war. She felt a bitter pang enter her stomach.

"Let's not speak about that. We have a task ahead, my little friend."

She crawled over the rocks and peeked into the bay. It was much the same as it was before, only quieter and less rowdy. She glanced at the sky. They didn't have long. The sun would rise in the next half hour. She rubbed her hands together as she tried to warm them. The water that lapped against them was freezing.

"I'm going. Don't stop swimming or moving. The moment you do, the body gets too cold," she warned him.

He nodded.

"You have your knife?" she asked.

He pulled his small blade from the inside of his coat and showed her.

She grasped his little face. "Good luck, my lord," she said and kissed him.

His eyes were wide in wonder, and Hira smiled.

She turned and slipped into the water as silently as she could. The cold overcame her for a moment, but she pushed through. The waters lapped at her cheeks, and when she went under, she felt the chill to the crown of her head, small spikes of pain as her body adjusted. She swam the thirty meters as stealthily as she could and found the ladder.

The ghost of the early rays of light were coming. She didn't have long before a pirate would spot her in the water. Hira grasped the bar and hefted herself up. Quietly, she climbed up to the deck and pulled out her ruby knife. The first man she spotted was easy. She grabbed him from behind and slit his throat. Then dragged his heavy body into the shadows. She had minutes before they would discover the corpse. Then the alert would sound for the rest of the crew that someone was aboard.

As she rushed to the high quarters, she encountered two more men and dispatched them the same way until their blood drenched her hands. Then she was before her door, where she knew Captain Strauss would be. When she reached to open the latch, a blade pressed against her back.

"Looking for me?" a voice asked.

Isabelle Olmo

Chapter Thirty-Four

HIRA

Hira slowly turned to find Captain Strauss flanked by four of his men. In his hand, Strauss held Ocean Fury. It seemed to glint at her in greeting, as if it were the maiden that needed rescuing all this time. It was sacrilegious that her family's sword was used by a common vagrant.

"That sword belongs to me," she said.

He couldn't see her face because of the shadows that bathed her. He grabbed a lamp from one of his men and moved it forward. The light slowly crept up, confirming her identity. Hira brought the ruby blade before her with a wicked smile, her body alight with the coming fight.

It was as if he'd seen a spirit of the dark night. "You died," he whispered.

The surrounding pirates shifted, and she recalled how superstitious pirates were. They believed in ghosts and goblins and shadow walkers. She would use that to her advantage. He'd had the upper hand before. That wouldn't happen today. She laughed wickedly.

As she stepped forward, they inched back. "I *did* die, Captain. A *witch* brought me back. Chanted prayers over my corpse. Scraped the dead flesh from my fingers. And when I rose from the dead, she led me to an enchanted cove. And in a midnight pool, a dragon came to me."

She moved to reveal the gory sight of her mangled arm. Twirling her fingers to ensure they saw each scar, highlighted against the luminosity. Strauss, pale and petrified, stared at her wound, then back at her.

"Do you know what the dragon said to me?" Hira stepped closer, offering him her limb.

Strauss visibly swallowed.

"She told me where to find you," Hira said.

He shook himself off his stupor, then yelled and moved to attack her. But, as he brought down Ocean Fury, the sword seemed to shift on its own. It was enough for her to sidestep and pull out her weapon. The swords clashed. He stared at her in utter horror.

"How did you do that?" he hissed in her face, and the stench of his rotting mouth assaulted her.

"You better hope that steel kills ghosts," she grunted and shoved him off.

His men struck at her from the sides. She deflected the blows with a twist of her blade. Before they could retaliate, a cannon exploded. Wood shattered in loud cracks.

They all turned and stared at the Night Serpent, coming fast as she attacked the Red Dragon. Captain Jutia was at the helm, a malevolent smile on her face and a cigar on her lips.

"WE'RE UNDER ATTACK!" the men yelled as they woke and wavered about the ship.

Chaos surrounded her, but she concentrated on Strauss. She turned and kicked open the door to her room. To her delight, Strauss followed. She twisted and their swords clashed. She pulled back and threw a chair at him. He stumbled against a wall, and she hacked her blade at him, narrowly missing him.

She twisted from his onslaught, and he stabbed the sofa, sending goose feathers into the air. It was a madness of steel and kicks.

"One doesn't return from that wound!" he cried.

Hira punched him, and he faltered. She slashed with her sword, and he met her blow.

"I know your master, you sack of old bones! After I kill you, I'm going after Furia. One by one I'll take you down!" Hira perfectly executed steps beyond his knowledge, and he went on the defensive.

She wouldn't be foolish like before and allow him to distract her.

"The blade that moves is not the dangerous one," Tora had said.

Hira spun her sword and kept her ruby blade steady. It worked. As he concentrated on her sword, she turned and buried the knife in his elbow. He screamed, and she sliced it out. Now she wounded him in the same manner he'd wounded her.

"You bitch! You know nothing!" Saliva sprayed from his lips.

With a limp arm, he brought his sword back down, but she easily deflected it. More blasts from the cannons, then two more pirates, entered the room and joined Strauss. She battled them, quick and methodically.

She reached Strauss, slammed her blade against his, making him drop Ocean Fury. It rolled on the floor and came to her, as if it traveled a path. A desperate little thing, salivating to be back in Balikian hands. She picked it up, and the hilt heated in her hand, as if it missed her.

She brought it to her forehead and smiled. Strauss took one look at her and ran out of the room.

"You coward!" she yelled.

The other Pirates descended on her, and she sliced her rightful sword through the air. She dispatched them quickly, gutting the two and leaving their bodies in her room.

The main deck of the Sea Wife was in turmoil.

Justan and his men had made it on the ship and the sailors Quent released were climbing in. Everywhere there was the sounds and sights of clashing steel. Men held bloody stumps in their hands, screaming in torment. Blood splattered the floor, and she almost slipped. She rushed through the sailors, desperately looking for Strauss, and finally spotted him trying to escape on a long boat with two of his pirates.

She ran to him, hacked men down until blood painted her and Ocean Fury. Her face covered in the spray of pirate gore, her hair matted with sweat.

She reached Strauss before he could leave. She dispatched the first man next to the captain. The sword slid into him swift and sure, and his body dropped to the water. The other turned to her and their blades met before she brought the ruby knife from the side and imbedded it in his ear—just like M taught her. She felt the crunch of bones as it traveled through his skull. He gasped, let out a gurgling wail, then fell into the sea.

Captain Strauss was alone and unarmed. He observed her as she pointed Ocean Fury at him. The tip of the blade dripped blood; her hands were crimson. Today, she'd not only played the Favia-game, but she'd also led it.

"Your men killed Tora. She was my friend and a great warrior. Know her name!" Hira snarled.

"I've killed many people, girl. The Favia and I are good friends."

Good friends or not, he'd met his end and she would ensure herself of that. She wouldn't have vermin like him wandering her coastline and targeting any other Istokian.

"Do you know how it feels to have your skin scrapped from your rotting arm?" Hira took a small step toward him, her blade still steady.

His jaw tightened, but he kept his one eye on her as she pressed Ocean Fury to his face.

"If you don't, I can show you. I'll hold you down as I slice your skin off, inch by inch. Allow you to fester and when your fingers blacken, I'll scrape it off. You can scream all you want but I can assure you, the pain doesn't stop," she spat.

His men died around him as he clutched his wounded arm tighter. She pressed the blade into his upper cheek next to his remaining eye.

He smiled slowly. "I serve the *true* Lady of Istok. You… are a fool. You'll know it before this is over. I delight in that, you cunt."

The temptation to stab out his eye was great, but before she could, the Night Serpent attacked with a strong cannon shot. It rocked her back, and she fell on her ass. Strauss pulled a knife from behind him, but she brought Ocean Fury up and in one swift move, she sliced his belly. Gutted.

He staggered and looked down at himself, then at her. His hands went to the protruding organs which hung down to his legs. Outside of her rotting arm, she'd seen nothing as awful.

Blinking, he let out half a chuckle, then he fell forward and landed dead.

Hira lay listening to the battle and pressed Ocean Fury against her forehead and sighed.

"Uncle... I did it," she whispered.

Someone grabbed and lifted her. It was Justan. He hugged her tightly, then pulled back to stare at her. He shoved the hair out of her eyes. His face was sweaty and covered in dirt and blood.

"I saw when he took out the knife. I thought I would be too late," he murmured.

She smiled and clutched him tighter, the exhilaration of the success singing in her veins. "I told you to trust me."

Around them scuffles ended as it was clear, they were successful. She could scarcely believe it. It worked. She stole back the Sea Wife; she was in the arms of a good man, and she was going *home*. The excitement that filled her to the brim was indescribable.

"CAPTAIN STRAUSS IS DEAD!" she shouted.

Their sailors cheered in victory, and the remaining pirates threw their swords on the deck. Hira let out a sigh of relief as she leaned against the pole of the mast. Justan and she stared at one another, wordless in their happiness.

Quent ran to them with a wide smile. Soaked to his core, he shook with the cold and his teeth chattered, but his delight was palpable.

"I killed two pirates, my lady!" He jumped up and down and showed off his bloodied knife.

Justan laughed and drew him in, and she hugged both brothers, assuring herself they were both well.

"Oh, Quent! You brave lad!" Hira said.

Quent, too excited to be suffocated by embraces, pulled back and wildly recounted his adventure. "I snuck onto the rock where they had the men and I cut five of them loose, then they all helped, and then the Night Serpent attacked, and then pirates came with swords. And then I stabbed one and the rest of the sailors took him down! Then I climbed onto the Sea Wife and I was going to get slashed by another pirate that saw me coming, but I pushed my knife into his knee, and he screamed and fell on the deck and then I jabbed his chest twice!"

"I told you to stay on the rock!" Justan clutched his shirt and looked him over to ensure he wasn't hurt.

"You needed help, and I helped! Lord Seaver will never again cower!" Quent raised up his small knife.

Justan sighed, grabbed his head, and kissed his forehead. "You did great, Quent. You make me proud."

Quent beamed so brightly, she'd never seen him happier. Watching Justan with his brother, her admiration for Commander Justan morphed into such warmth that she turned away to focus on the sailors. Afraid of what her face would show without her permission.

Wrangling the leftover pirates, her men tied them up and pushed them to their knees. Some grappled with their captors, but her crew indisputably outnumbered them. Victory was theirs and the sense of success had them all drunk.

"What should we do with them, m'lady?" It was Mr. Hyall. He looked healthy and unharmed as he shoved a pirate face first on the deck.

"Mr. Hyall, I'm sorry it took so long." Hira helped him tie the man's hands behind his back.

Hyall's eyes lingered on her exposed arm. "We thought you were done for."

Pausing, she stared at him and recalled the awfulness of the weeks after her injury. "I thought I was too, but the Favia didn't call my name."

She and Justan lined up the captured men as Jutia did the same in the Red Dragon. Hira turned back to the released sailors, who sported wide, relieved grins.

"Does any Istokian sailor have any quarrel with any man here?" She pointed to the tied pirates with Ocean Fury.

"I do." Mr. Hyall stepped forward and his eyes zoomed on a small man, who stared at him with pure hate. His lips twisted against his broken teeth.

She walked to Mr. Hyall. "Do with him as you will, Mr. Hyall. Be honest about your justice before the Favia."

Mr. Hyall looked at her and nodded.

"You bastard!" The pirate screamed.

Mr. Hyall sliced his hooked hand across his throat and the man landed on the deck with a gurgle. He walked back to Hira with a firm nod and he wiped his metal appendage.

"Anyone else?" She asked, and no other came forward. "Very well. Raid the Red Dragon. Empty its belly and set it adrift. Take the prisoners and place them on the rock with two days' food rations. If they live, they live, but I'll not kill any man who has surrendered his sword."

Later, she entered her quarters. Much of the furniture lay overturned and broken. She found a music box behind a chair; the small twirling lady's head was gone. She opened the lid and wound the crank. The soft Istokian melody sharply reminded her of her mother.

She recalled her mother sitting on her bed the night her cousin Bach died. Her back straight, her eyes shadowed.

"Why can't Almira play today?" little Hira asked.

"Because... little Bach has passed, girl."

Hira recalled the servants and nurses flittering in and out of his room for days.

"She's sad," Hira surmised.

"Yes. Very," her mother said and sighed.

Then she did something she'd not done in a long time. Reaching over the covers, she took Hira's small hands and caressed them tenderly.

"You're very special, Hira. Do you know that, my girl?" her mother whispered.

Hira didn't think she was special. She wasn't pretty like Almira, and she tripped when she ran. Her uncle cared very little for her wellbeing. Her mother mostly ignored her.

"*One day, you'll be High Lady of this land,*" *her mother confided.* "*All of Istok will bow before you and you, in turn, will protect them.*"

Hira had an indescribable need to cry. She held the box to her chest. "I'm sorry, Mother. I didn't understand. Soon, I'll be home, and I'll *never* leave my people again."

She stood and looked about the room. To think that weeks ago she sensed this was her uncle's rooms, and she was merely a spectator in his world.

Hira found the scrolls Sanaa gifted her, the histories of Lady Dominia, and clutched them tightly. She must get to Istok. She had to warn Almira, and not allow her to walk into a trap. Her people needed her. And she, surprisingly, needed her people, too.

Justan entered with a small knock and watched as she yanked the bed linens and threw them on the floor.

"His smell is all over my room," she said over her shoulder.

He shrugged. "Sleep somewhere else."

"These are my quarters. I sleep here." She tossed the pillows. "How soon can we set sail?"

He glanced outside the windows of her cabin. "We need to tend the wounded and evaluate the damage to the ships."

Hira knew all of this was required. Even so, she was eager to get going. She didn't know how long her mother had and she wished to... What? Tell her she was sorry?

She wasn't sorry for leaving. The only thing she regretted was not having a better relationship with her mother. Almira's painting caught Hira's attention. She studied her older cousin. Her sharp brow and knowing look. The queen needed them and here they lingered.

She looked away from her cousin's stare. "How far are we from Treveri?"

"Less than a week, with favorable winds. I'll have some men help tidy this room," he said. His voice was soft, and she appreciated his calming presence.

Who would've thought? In these same quarters, they had their first quarrel and now she looked forward to him soothing her nerves.

It felt a hundred years had transpired between that day and today.

Wearily, Hira sat down. She was so tired, as if the madness of the past few weeks had descended on her and incinerated her.

"I want food reports. Do we have enough to get to Treveri? I want the amount of wounded and dead men. How gravely are they hurt? Will they make it until we arrive?"

When she looked up, it surprised her that Justan watched her with such softness.

He came closer and smiled a little. "You did it."

A compliment so small, yet it filled her heart with warmth, and she shifted, unsure if she truly deserved it. Or at least merited it from *his* lips. "*We* did it. I'd be dead in the bottom of the South Seas if it weren't for all of you."

He nodded, then winced when he touched his stomach. She'd been so focused on everything else that she'd never asked if he was well, even when he'd always checked on her.

"You're hurt." She stood and went to him.

"It's nothing," he blurted.

She shook her head and pulled up his shirt as he protested. He stood shirtless before her, and she concentrated on spotting the wound. They cut him on his side, a slice with a clean blade that wouldn't need sewing. His torso was taut with soft black hairs that covered the brown skin. His muscles rippled under her touch. She glanced at him and found his eyes darkened at her proximity. She felt a flush creep into her cheeks.

"It's nothing," he repeated, but she turned to find clean linen and a bottle of disinfectant.

Reminding her of the night when an attacker entered her quarters, she almost smiled at his protest.

"Are you really going to fight me on this?" She signaled to her desk chair with a smirk.

He didn't miss the irony as he glanced at her with a knowing look. He sat down and she kneeled between his legs, then pushed him back. A strange position indeed.

"There are men with worse wounds," he said, perhaps because the closeness made it impossible to think of anything else.

"They'll be taken care of." She leaned over him and tenderly cleaned the cut.

His eyes watched her intently, and she felt herself redden, so she focused on disinfecting the skin. He helped her wrap the linen around his torso. When she was done, their faces were mere inches away. He was so close a push would have them in an embrace.

Taking her scarred hand, he slowly brought it to his lips and kissed it. She gasped at the feel of his mouth, at the intimacy of such an action. Actions of such were between lovers, between those wed, a stunning act that left her lacking sense.

He let go of her hand and she instantly felt the loss. She madly desired to have his lips permanently pressed against her flesh.

Trembling, she peered at him. "I remember you once told me to slice your throat if you were ever stupid enough to march into my room."

He smiled a little, and it took her aback by how handsome he was. Smooth skin that desperately required a shave, thick brown hair that fell over his forehead, and warm eyes encased in curled lashes. A few freckles of gray hairs danced in his temple. It was the small reminder that he was her senior by over a decade. A truly good man. A patient man.

"Now that you've got your old room back, I'll have a difficult time attempting to steal into your bedroom." His lips quirked in amusement.

That properly reddened her face, and she decided to tease him, a petty revenge for all the teasing he'd done to her.

"Perhaps you should wait until you're invited," she said.

But there was no mirth in his actions. He reached out and touched her chin, caressing her skin. Surprised, she leaned into his touch without meaning to.

"I'm at my lady's beck and call," he whispered.

Her heart began to beat erratically, and in an act of pure boldness, brought his hand to her lips and kissed it. He didn't move, and she didn't dare glance up. Such a return in gesture in ancient Garian culture would imply a betrothment and they both knew it. His fingers softly touched her hair, and his thumb caressed the scar on her cheek.

She flinched and pulled away.

"Look at me, Hira," he said.

He was no common soldier that she could kick out of her room and brandish her title over him in mockery. She had no path to follow or guidance for the affection of a lord that respected and desired her despite her shortcomings, which she found to be plenty.

"Sometimes I think you're an enchantress." He pressed his lips to her temple. "How have you done this to me? After so many years..."

"Justan—"

He gazed at her intently, and the words choked in her throat. What could she say to him? What did she feel? Did she love him? Was she simply grateful? She realized she enjoyed his smiles and a funny feeling settled in her belly when he argued with her. She knew she stared at his chest and wandered at the denseness of the soft hairs there. Then she recalled his face, when he told her the stories of dragons and the Garians. She supposed she would admit that she cared for him. That each time he had a private word with Jutia, her stomach burned; that was something she didn't like. She didn't care for her jealousy. It was a detrimental trait which she would have to work on improving.

When she said nothing, he bowed his head, the thick hairs covering his forehead, then he stood. And walked out.

She stayed on the carpeted floor, staring at the chair he had occupied. His warmth still lingered in the cloth. Why hadn't she said anything? Lord Justan Seaver was quite a catch, but above all, he was a *great* man. But she'd lost his greatest ship, gotten herself mutilated, and didn't know what conditions she would find in the capital.

Too much depended on her. She couldn't allow herself to fall in love. If there was a battle, she had to focus on the end prize, not on her lover's wellbeing. She had no time for pleasure. Still, she pressed her palm on the seat cushion and enjoyed the lingering warmth he left behind.

Isabelle Olmo

Chapter Thirty-Five

ALMIRA

After the Pas of Gul, the land turned arid and barren. Small rocks littered the road and made it difficult for the army to maneuver. It was a landscape of sharp winds and harsh sun that beat down on the party, slowing their pace. A thing no one prepared her for was the constant sound of metal, horses, and wagons that came from an army marching for hours. Almira's head hurt so much she thought she would demand they all stop and provide her a few moments of rest.

"It doesn't last long," Thebo assured the queen as she looked out of the chariot at the seemingly endless horizon. "By the end of the day, we should enter the valleys of the west. I used to take this route each time I went to see you and Lamya."

And what excitement he would bring whenever her dear uncle would appear in Korkoran for a visit. Her mother would have the fortress in an uproar with music, feasts, and dancing to celebrate his arrival. Thebo would place Almira on his lap and tell her grand stories of his adventures.

"I remember how joyful mother was to see you," Almira said.

He remained silent as he marched his horse forward and the queen knew how much the death of his sister pained him. Pained them all. Out of all the happy guests in those cozy sitting rooms, only the two of them were left.

"No sign of Alton." Almira hoped he was safe. Hoped he'd not encountered Furia or war parties or anything that would harm him. But she wouldn't voice her fears. She'd rather bite them tightly in her tongue and allow them to fester her insides.

Thebo, however, seemed to recognize her troubles and smiled good-naturedly. "None. I'm sure he's fine. He was king for a long time before you came along to fret over him."

Almira irritably sat back and yanked the curtain closed. She did not *fret*. She knew Alton could take care of himself. Unless she had to go rescue him when he got captured by Arrigo with half his men killed or tortured. Aside from that, he was excellent at keeping himself out of harm's way.

"Would you like to rest, Majesty?" Delara watched Almira with cool, wise eyes.

"No. We need to get to Treveri with all haste."

And so, they didn't stop. Not even when Almira nearly screamed with the pain in her head. Each minute was agony and grated on her nerves. It was at dusk, as they set up camp, that she finally found peace. With an aching back and a headache, she eventually relaxed on the cot they placed in her tent.

After an hour of resting, she woke and paced. Her worry for Alton, Hira, and for Istok maddening her senses. Robing herself, she stepped out into the cool night. Sanaa was sitting down on a small folding chair and looked up at her with a raised brow. She made to toss her cigar, but Almira shook her head.

"Any sign?" Almira asked.

Her *cuzo* sighed. "You've barely rested."

"The same can be said of you," Almira said. "I know you're irate with me and I don't blame you. I'm aware I drive everyone to their brink with my determination."

Sanaa inhaled her cigar and met her eyes. "I knew you were determined the moment I met you, that's not changed. Pregnancy and this madness we live through do not help."

"They don't," Almira admitted. Her eyes lingered on the camp, the men settled down, joking, and enjoying a smoke and an ale. "I wonder what my life would be like if Edgar hadn't died."

"Boring," Sanaa said and the two met each other's eyes, smiling.

Just as she was about to voice her worry over Alton, movement was heard beyond the camp boundaries. Almira's heart leaped and Sanaa was instantly at her feet, whistling to five other young Red Guards who surrounded the queen.

From the clearing, seven cloaked men emerged as Thebo and the Mesedi moved forward. They pointed all arrows at the men as they immerged from the shadows of the night. Almira felt Sanaa move closer to her, her own blade already in her hand.

"Hold or face death!" Thebo cried.

"Forgive this wandering fool, me'lord. I've heard rumors of the queen's beauty and wish to behold her me'self," the cloaked traveler said in a heavy colloquial accent.

Sanaa pulled Almira back before the queen could ask that they allow the peasant pass.

"Who says we travel with the queen?" Thebo's voice remained unmoved, and the men's tension rose even further.

"Oh, I can smell her perfume oils from here."

The man in the middle shoved back his hood and there stood Alton, looking exhausted but providing Thebo a delighted smile. The high lord laughed at the jest as Almira let out a cry of relief. She pulled up her skirts, rushing to the men who greeted each other with hearty handshakes.

Thebo nodded. "She'll be most relieved; she's fretted all day, though she won't admit it. Stubborn, that one."

Almira would've yelled at him had she not been so comforted to see her husband. Alton chuckled for a moment, then turned to his wife and embraced her, burying his face into her braids.

"What took you so long?" she nearly cried, attempting to control the wail from her voice but failing.

Alton pulled her back and kissed her soundly, and she forgot all about her anger at Thebo. The High Lord laughed and ushered them into the camp.

"How did you find us?" Thebo asked as they walked to Almira's tent.

The king brought out from his pocket a tattered red feather. Thebo took it and raised a brow. All Suidian war lords tamed Red Eagles, and the beasts traveled with them into battle, actively using their claws to attack opposing soldiers. Their long feathers were majestic, red and spotted with white and black. When they last camped some of the eagles must've shed feathers and Alton keenly discovered them.

"The feathers!" Almira smiled, and Alton held her closer to his side, rubbing her back. The relief of feeling him eased her headache, and she sighed into his embrace.

"Good thing it wasn't eagle waste," the high lord said with amusement.

"Why?" Alton asked, confused.

"It's explosive." Thebo chuckled and left them to their caresses and greetings.

Alton looked down at her and kissed her temple. "I rode as fast as I could. Marching half an army through your Istokian forest is no easy feat, my dragon."

Almira didn't care, she had him *now* and all would be well! Sanaa met them outside of the tent and the king and she nodded at one another.

"*Finally*," Sanaa said with a sour mouth.

Alton, unperturbed by Sanaa's ill humor, smiled rakishly. "I'll take the night watch, Captain. Find yourself some delights," he joked, then pulled Almira into her tent.

The moment they were alone, Alton led her to the cot. She clutched him as he sat next to her. He held her tightly and rocked her back and forth. Almira buried her face into his neck, kissing his skin and inhaling his scent, no matter how grime-ridden it was. Her husband was safe, and it was one less person to worry about.

"I've been so concerned!" she sighed.

"I figured," he chuckled. "I rode ahead because I was afraid that you'd attempt to storm Korkoran with just your guards."

She wouldn't admit that she had this same thought not a week before. He pulled back and stared at her face, as if he assured himself that she was well and unharmed. When he felt satisfied with his perusal, he kissed her, and she moaned. Grappling against his armor and shivering when his fingers dug into her braids. He took her hands and fervently caressed them with his lips, then touched her belly, greeting their child.

His face looked bruised, and a cut healed on his bottom lip.

"They attacked you." She stoked his mouth.

"Aye, nothing we couldn't handle," he sounded unconcerned while she was frightened for his wellbeing. Massaging her stomach, he sighed. "You're too far along, my love."

She shook her head. "Don't come to dissuade me. You know I've not traveled half the world to stay behind. My body may be weakened, but I'm more determined than ever."

Almira could handle the criticism from many, but not from him. Not when she needed him to be with her and stand by her in her decisions, regardless of how outlandish they sounded to others. He said nothing else. He could be perceptive when he wished it. Instead, he took her in his arms and held her close, kissing the hair at her temple.

"I've missed you. I've missed your tongue, and your eyes, and your nipples." He grasped her thighs and squeezed them tightly. "I'm hungry for my wife. I want to eat you."

Almira delighted in his words. They were *exactly* what she needed. A little distraction. His musky aroma mixed with the hardness of his muscled body. It aroused her beyond anything she considered possible. The desire for him had built these months and her sex contracted at the thought of him within her.

He laid her back, and she bent her knees and opened her legs as he watched her. His eyes darkened with lust as he slid his hands over her skin and spread her wide. The cool air of the tent fanned her cunt, and she gasped, just imagining what his eager mouth could do.

"Look at you, I can see you glistening," he muttered, and kneeled as his kisses peppered the inside of her thighs. "You smell like heaven." He brushed his nose against her, lingering licks on her skin. "All thick and tender."

And he nibbled on the fleshy part of her inner thigh, making her moan, delighting in her weight gain, and having more of her to worship. She writhed as he traced her outer folds, so close to their destiny, yet so far away. Her heatedness mounted, and she thrust her hips up to meet his face, desperately in need of his tongue.

He latched on to her and she let out a strangled cry. She hated that she could no longer reach his head to grasp him, to demand more. Steadily he suckled and lapped, then he pulled back to stare at her. His lips wet with her desire. She knew he loved watching her in these moments, her gasps. How she panted and shook in the beautiful moment before the edge came.

Satisfied with her reactions, he quickly undressed. She watched him stroke himself, pull lightly at his cock, his eyes shuttered. His muscled chest sported a bruised rib, and he looked like a marbled god of the ancient world, a warrior to warm the bed of his demanding queen. Her sex quivered, so close to the edge but needing him in her.

"We should abandon all wars and fuck until we die of exhaustion," he said hoarsely.

"Why do you think I married you?"

"For my kingdom?" he teased as he grabbed her legs until her ass sat on the precipice of the cot. He kneeled and aligned himself against her.

"Alton, I'll fall!" she hissed.

He looked up at her, his blond hair fell over his forehead, and he seemed younger, as if war didn't dominate most of his life. "I'll catch you. I'll always take care of you, even when you don't want me to."

Her heart warmed to him, and he leaned forward and allowed her to caress his face.

"And our child?" she asked.

He nuzzled her hand. "Much more. At least you can make all those around you quake in fear."

He positioned himself once more, the tip of his cock pressed against her, and she gasped. She was so close. Gods, she was so close!

348

"Just watching you tongue lash generals and men—"

His words suddenly stopped. He bit his lip and groaned as he entered her, stretched her, and made her grasp the bedding. His words filled her with lust and joy. She never had to hold back with him because he adored her, even at her very worst.

"*Fuck*... I fucking—" his voice strangled in his throat as he pushed all the way in. "Why are you so enticing? I'd give my life to watch you rule and thunder..." He slowly plunged into her.

"Faster! Fuck me into this bed, by the gods of the sea, hard!" She couldn't believe her words. Let the entire army camp know that in this tent she fucked the king.

"I cannot help but crave to please you, wife—" he thrust with meditated speed, and their bodies covered with sweat. "I rode half the world to enter this cunt."

She was mad with want. She swore like a barmaid and arched into him like a common whore. Her lust magnified with his statements and the familiarity of his body. He delighted in the entire display, his frame rock solid from the sight of her in such a common position.

"Faster!"

"As my queen commands." He changed his angle so that his thrusts penetrated her so deeply that his sack slapped between her cheeks. The feel of their softness made her shudder.

Her edge was close when he began to buck like a horse, deeper and deeper until she had a mad thought that he would hurt the child. But his hands caressed her belly as he chanted nonsensical words to her and the baby. Her breasts flapped every way, thick with the coming milk.

"Promise me," she panted. "Promise me you'll keep the baby safe."

"I swear it," he ground out. "On my life."

"No matter what," she gasped, at the edge of a cliff.

His eyes were tightly closed, and the chords of his neck strained. His shoulders bulged. She'd never desired him more. This beast of a man, who towered over her, would sell his soul to the Favia to keep her safe.

"Gods help those who hurt my family. Come with me, Almira."

And she did.

He let go of her legs and she slid down into his arms until they were on the floor. He held her tightly against him as he shuddered through his pleasure. His head buried into her neck and there he panted.

She caressed his hair and allowed his heat to surround her, to hold her, and—for the first time in a long time—she permitted someone to carry her.

"You are my beloved," she whispered.

Chapter Thirty-Six

HIRA

They scrubbed and cleaned her room in an attempt to strip the evidence of the past few weeks. The stench of Strauss tainted the area. Never in its history were the Sea Wife's quarters polluted, and it happened under her rule.

She felt dirty, sticky between her legs. She smelled and longed to cleanse herself. A bath would do her good to keep her mind steady and focused. They brought a large basin to her rooms. She stripped and sunk directly, without ceremony, into the warm water. She'd not bathed properly since before her injury. She lingered in the bath, having no strength to do much more. Almira's portrait watched her, and Hira sighed.

"I did my best, cousin." Hira closed her eyes.

In that moment, she longed for a cigar and perhaps a glass of summer whiskey with a twist of lime to brighten the senses. Yes, she was changing at an alarming rate.

A few days later, when her nerves were soothed, she sat down on her desk, pulling parchment and a quill. In her shaky handwriting, she documented the happenings that led to this moment. The last lines read;

we sail in all haste to Treveri. I do not know the conditions that await me or if Lady Furia has killed my mother and taken my city by force. But I will do all in my power to ensure the safety of my people and the queen.

She paused before ending the journal entry. Then, with resolve, she signed

High Lady Hira, House Balik.

It felt like her first genuine act as the High Chair.

There was no turning back. This document had officially gained historical importance and Istokians would speak about Hira for generations to come. Perhaps a girl, her descendant, would peruse the letter and wonder at the history of Lady Hira, The Maimed.

Quent came by later and recounted once more the tale of his adventures, which she listened to with a sympathetic ear, but eventually her mind wandered to his brother.

She'd not told Justan the dangers she suspected awaiting them all. Perhaps it was wrong of her not to confide in him, but the time never felt right; just in case she was mistaken. She didn't want him to judge her for jumping to false, ignorant conclusions.

While she went over the documents she'd ignored before, Quent fell asleep amongst the polishing rags, since he volunteered to ready her armor for her entrance into Treveri. She didn't wish to wake him, so she made her way to the deck careful to make as little noise as possible.

When she stepped onto the deck, the sailors murmured, but there was an overall joviality at the prospect of going home. As she walked around the ship, the men greeted her with smiles and slight bows. This time, she did not feel awkward. She embraced the fact that something set her apart from them, but that was not a bad thing.

She was their High Lady and ruler, and she couldn't blend into the invisibility of the crowd. Yes, she'd been a Red Guard, and yes, she'd enjoyed it. But her people needed her, *these* men needed her. They needed a High Seat far more than they needed a Red Guard.

She found Mr. Hyall, whom she greeted with a smile.

"M'lady," he said with a nod as he puffed his pipe.

"Mr. Hyall," she said then looked out into the sea with her arms crossed.

He studied her face. "You seem different."

She cast him a look, then kept her eyes on the Night Serpent. Jutia maintained the ship close by, escorting them to safety. "I feel different," she murmured.

She and the crew enjoyed the serenity of the evening. The dancing breezes and the dolphins that occasionally jumped from the water and happily splashed down as they playfully rode in the wake of the ships.

"Do you know why I became a sailor, m'lady?" he asked as he studied the ocean.

It seemed to her that he'd lived one hundred lives. Pockets of lifetimes hidden in the markings of his weathered face, in the sadness of his eyes, and the frayed hairs of his ancient head.

"I was a Keeper once. A respected man, serving House Seaver. I loved my job. I loved the Seaver children that ran down the corridors and stole summer apples from the kitchen to eat them by the walls of the palace. Sometimes I would sneak out a pie and hand it to them. Oh, and how they would delight, pocketing their treasures and sharing it amongst themselves..." His voice began to roughen as his eyes glazed with sadness. "Then my wife died. She was carrying our baby. Wild Marchers attacked our caravan as we traveled with the family that year. There were a lot of attacks during that time." He glanced at her with a somber face. "Someone from House Seaver saved me, and all I carry now is her memory."

He fell silent.

"I saw her killed. Happened quickly. She didn't suffer. I always pray to the sea gods that the baby didn't either." He puffed his pipe.

Hira looked away, the memory vivid, drenched in loss, love, and remembrance. "Did you never marry again?" she asked hesitantly.

He glanced at her. "No point after Dresdie. We'd been together since childhood. Life became something else after her."

She nodded. "May the sea gods keep her and the baby."

"May the sea gods keep her." His eyes were hardened pebbles that studied the horizon.

She left him to his dark thoughts as a deep sadness sank in her. He was one of many who'd come to know deep loss. This was what Almira meant when she'd told Hira that the lives of their people were in the hands of royals. This was her meaning when she emphasized there was no room for selfishness. An innocent decree against a band of Marchers could cause an attack on a caravan, and a man could lose everything.

With that morose reminiscence, she found her way to the sup hall again. It surprised her when Justan glanced up and smiled. He looked clean and well fitted in a white shirt. Too handsome for her to ignore, and her desire for him mounted. Some sailors greeted her with cordiality and this time she took her sup without causing a ruckus.

When she went to sit, Justan offered her a seat at his table and the men surrounding him allotted them privacy and left. She attempted to keep her face neutral. The dinner was simple, a hearty fish stew with dried herbs and some old bread which needed to be soaked in the broth to make it palatable.

"You look well," Justan said.

She could smell the fresh scent of his skin, the soapiness, and could only imagine the softness of his arms and chest. It was a dangled temptation that she wasn't certain she could pass over.

"I was tired, and the rest was beneficial." She took a spoonful of soup.

They ate in silence, and she watched from the corner of her eye as he slowly dunked his bread into the stew and brought it to his mouth. His eyes didn't leave her form. The food overheated her.

"I assume Quent is huddled up in your rooms, concocting whatever scheme you two are planning." He set his chin on his palm and studied her.

"Yes," she said in a teasing manner. It amused her he felt the need to inquire.

He cocked his head and smiled slightly. "There's a coyness in your tone. I'm not familiar with it."

They stared at one another, her palms flat on the wooden table. "There are many things you don't know about me, Commander."

"Justan," he said.

She didn't reply because she couldn't. She looked down at the swirls in the wood of the table and traced the pattern with her scarred fingers. The words and the implications of his request were the loudest sound in the room, and she wasn't certain she could acquiesce.

He sighed, then questioned her, "Or was that only appropriate when we were in high seas and now that we inch closer to the capital, it's not proper?"

There was an underlying tone of hurt in his voice. She swallowed before she responded, "It was never proper and you know it."

"I know no such thing," he said sharply.

She met his eyes and felt a stab in her ribs. He asked things of her she couldn't give. Not right now. Not tonight. Not when so much was at stake. When so much depended on her. When she'd yet to share with him her suspicions of Lady Furia and the chaos awaiting her in Treveri.

"I think I should explain the complexities of my situation," she whispered.

He chuckled darkly. "I'm not a simpleton, *my lady*. I am aware of the *complexities* of your situation. The queen likely has machinations in mind for your marriage, an advantageous one. Perhaps to a high ranking Norrian that would stimulate peace and alliances."

She looked down. The stew was suddenly quite unappetizing.

"If needed. I'm the second highest lady in the entire kingdom. My hand could stop the war with Norr. It would save thousands of people. People like the men on this ship. I didn't understand that before, but I do now," she said as steadily as she could.

And even as she voiced the words, she hated them. But they were true. As true as the pain that lived in her wounded arm. The memory of it, always present, a carnivorous ghostly shadow that flickered its torment when it chose. The girl who ran away from home would hate the woman who now denied herself freedom.

"With your newly developed consciousness, this is something you must consider," he spat.

She was hurting him. A pain no skin could showcase. He cared for her. She stared at her bowl of cooling soup.

"Look at me," he whispered.

She bravely met his eyes. Sanaa once told her that if one had the balls to gut a man, one should have the balls to meet their eye. And so, she did. When she didn't budge, he slowly shook his head. The strong, stoic commander who issued orders to his men and yelled at her was gone. Slipped into nothingness. He was open, soft, and vulnerable. She was his harsh tormentor.

"Every moment since this journey began, I've been battling, waging war with myself to not care for you. I've lost that war. I'm not sure what the consequences will be," he said in a tone so low that the words belonged only to her. Not even the night could claim them.

Her neck felt chill and hot at once as his eyes bore into her.

"You feel the same for me." His voice was steady. "Or do you deny it?"

She clutched her spoon so tightly it molded into her skin. He'd pulled a truth right from her heart that she'd desired to keep dormant. Perhaps her love came suddenly. Perhaps it came slowly. Either way, he was the best man she knew. He was brave, loyal, charismatic, responsible, caring, and he *loved* her. And she loved him. Gods help her, she did. In another world, a world that belonged to other people and other lovers, she could've easily melted into his arms and allowed him to swaddle her with his desire. But she marched at all haste to a crumbling country and to precarious times.

She swallowed. She'd loved no man. Despite their differences, she loved Almira and her mother. She loved her fellow Red Guards. But never a man. She'd not permitted it; she'd denied any of them the mere chance. But what was love in a time of war? Or could war even exist without love? Without deep heartbreak?

"I care for you very much. Not just for how you saved me, but for how you tend to others." She studied the perfect rise of his cheekbones. "Your dedication, level-headedness, and your ability to put yourself aside for the good of all."

"I'm not a saint." he snapped, but his face was open with desperation. "I fear what you will think of me when you truly know me."

She shook her head. "I care for you, regardless. Despite being determined never to cherish anyone in such a manner. But..." she gulped and took a deep breath. "But... I've come to realize that I love my country more."

The realization that she'd led quite a selfish life shamed her. She'd not denied herself anything. Lovers, adventure, defiance, boldness... she'd had everything she could want. All she could need. A rawness entered her throat, and she had to look away from his soft brown eyes.

"Hira—"

"And if my queen asks me to marry to stop a war, to save Istokian lives... I'll *not* deny her," she said, hardly believing how true her words were.

It wouldn't be like before. She wouldn't be the one *saddled* with a man. This time, she knew who she was and recognized her power. A marriage would simply mean an alliance, not a lord to rule over her.

He leaned forward and his hands stretched to her, but she held herself still.

"You *are* entitled to happiness," he whispered.

His words were puncture wounds to her heart. His mother had wished him happiness and now he aspired for her to gain the same because he cared for her. It was too much to allot herself some selfishness for her wants after living vicariously in them and nearly abandoning her people. Abruptly, she stood and looked about the room. Too many sailors around that could mishear a word. She stormed out and desperately sought fresh air. The night descended, and the wind was chilled.

She meant to go to her quarters, but Justan came behind her and grasped her elbow. He pulled her to the shadows of the ship and pressed her back against the wall. He towered over her with dark eyes, clutching her shoulders.

"*You* are entitled to happiness," he repeated, but this time his tone was harsh and desperate. "*I* am entitled to happiness. I've not known happiness. Do you understand that? *Never*. It's always been a battle. A task."

He looked so desperately shaken that she had to place her hands on either side of his face. She finally touched him the way she'd longed to touch him for far longer than she could admit. In the shadows, she could. In the shadows, none of this was real.

"Please don't make me beg." He closed his eyes and leaned into her hand.

His skin felt feverish. Hira's fingers found the back of his neck and she pulled him until they pressed their bodies against one another. He was hard and solid.

"I want you, Commander," she hissed against his mouth.

He shook his head. "I'll not be a quick fuck for you."

"Will it truly be quick?" she attempted a smile but failed.

He looked away, and she realized she could do this for a lifetime. Tease him and banter with him. Feeling him against her in a way that sent a thrill into the very pit of her belly. A conversation with him, of unfolding him like a rose's petals, was the highlight of her day.

She held his head, and he leaned into her, melting into her touch until Hira felt she cupped his entire soul between her fingers. She kissed his temple, that small patch where tiny gray hairs spurted.

"I cannot promise you my life. But I can promise you tonight, my love. Won't you love me tonight?" she whispered.

No sooner were the words out of her mouth that his lips descended on hers.

Chapter Thirty-Seven

HIRA

They stumbled into the spare room, and Justan slammed the door. He grasped her face, and she desperately kissed him. His teeth bit at her lips and he trailed his tongue down her neck, making her shudder. She felt everything and nothing all at the same moment— a light-headedness at finally having him.

It was a race against time. Each minute became one less they could enjoy.

She grasped his arms when his mouth suckled her collarbone. He couldn't get enough and began tracing patterns under her ear, leaving a burn with his whiskers as he trailed along. She tugged his hair, and he groaned deep in his throat. He took her hips in his hands, lifting her feet from the floor as she wrapped her legs tightly around him. Against her sex, she felt the delightful bulge of his cock and rotated her hips to gain some pressure.

She would admit to herself that she'd yearned for this, to couple with him and whisper secrets in the night as only unclothed lovers could.

"Bed!" She tightened her thighs.

He complied, like an eager young lover. She fell onto the mattress, and spread out on the sheets. She stared up at him as his chest heavily rose and fell with his excitement. He threw his jacket off and she sat up to help him untie his trousers, but her hands shook violently.

"Wait," he murmured gently as grabbed her fingers.

Hira angrily growled. She was not about to be denied this. She longed for it too much! To feel him over her, to ride him until he gurgled with pleasure. She wished to study the chords of his neck when he spurted into her.

"No, please—I need it *now.*"

But he stopped her. His callused hands cupped her face, and he looked at her delicately in the moonlight. He brushed back her hair and smiled. He studied her, as if taking care to commit to memory this exact moment. Her heart beat against her ribs with excitement for him, and melted at his sweetness. She was witnessing a new side to him. The tender man who cared for those he loved.

"Hira," he whispered. "Hira Balik."

He said it with such reverence she wasn't certain of his meaning. As if he was in awe of even being allowed into her bed.

"Justan—"

"Shh," he hissed, and placed a finger against her lips.

He closed his eyes, and she watched as his chest rose and fell. He looked tormented, not a look she preferred to see on her lover. There was an ache she couldn't understand or grasp, and she wished to pull it out of him and allow him relief. Gods help the ones who hurt him. She would hunt them down and ensure they paid.

"What is it?" She caressed his cheeks, and he leaned into her touch. The softness of his beard danced between her fingers, and she combed it back, flattening it against his face.

Why did he dally? Her cunt was soaked and ready. Each inch of her needed him and still he lingered. As if he held secrets that he couldn't tell her. She recognized all there was to know about him. She knew the manner in which he tied rope and how he blushed when he argued with her. The way his body angled when he threw a harpoon.

"I..." he whispered. "I'm not..." he swallowed thickly.

He searched her face, as if words were a massive difficulty. The brown of his eyes was the beginning of the earth. The pits and hallows of mountains were painted in his irises.

"You're not what?" she asked, afraid of hearing the answer, afraid of the consequences of his response.

What if he actually cared for Jutia? What if there was another woman that she was unaware of? Impatiently, she scratched her nails down his arms, urging him to continue. But his face shifted, and he sighed as he shook his head. For a moment, she swore she saw defeat in his gaze.

"I just want to savor this, is all," he admitted. "This... this is different. For me."

It was different for her too, and perhaps he was the wiser man who urged her to pause and relish the feeling of their coupling.

Slowly, she nodded and brought his face closer and kissed him with exquisite patience. A tasting of courses, she suckled his tongue with deliberate calmness. He sighed into her mouth, then held her tightly, her chest compressed against his. She swore she felt his soul dancing out to her, their spirits twin flames that fed off one another and delighted in their mingling.

His hands curved around her body, palms soothing the heat searing her skin. He'd pause and massage her muscles, warming her even more. The fire increased, and the kisses became frantic. Hira demanded all from him. She wished for flesh against flesh, and she didn't want to wait.

"Such a desperate mistress," he mused.

She bit his ear and arched against him. "Is that what I am?"

"Yes..."

With one motion, he yanked his shirt off. She stared breathlessly at his chest. The small gauze she'd placed there unraveled, and she marveled at his sculpted body. He was all man, not boy, a perfect rendition of muscle and meat, ripe for biting. She raked her nails over his taut stomach, and he let out a rewarding gurgle of pleasure. The tempting trail of dark hairs dipping into his pants.

He untied his trousers, but she avidly yanked them down with a harsh tug. His cock bounced up between his legs, eager at her sight.

She warmed in anticipation. The bulbous head was pink and protruding from its sack. She desperately wished to feel the rigid shaft and its terse column. She reached for it, but he stopped her, his teeth clenched.

"Not yet," he said in a harsh statement. "You've too many clothes——"

Before he could finish his sentence, she pulled her shirt off and sat back to let him look. Her arm may look mangled, her face scarred, but her breasts were still pert, young, and lovely. She breathed deeply, watching his eyes narrow and his mouth dampen.

"Gods of the sea."

Justan's hands traced the muscles of her stomach, lingering on the freckles that covered her torso.

"Like the stars of the sky," he whispered, and she laughed lightly.

He hooked his arm around her and joined her in bed. Hira latched on to his lips and their chests pressed together. She loved the feel of his soft hair against her nipples. He tugged at her trousers and let out a curse of frustration which inexplicably made her laugh more, and he met her eyes and smiled.

"You couldn't wear a skirt today?" He grumbled.

"I thought you wished to savor the moment," she teased.

He kissed her again as his palm found her breast. She arched back in ecstasy and whimpered. His thumb flicked and pinched her nipples until her nails bit into his scalp. His lips assaulted her neck, lapping over the curve that led to her ear. The action erupted goose pimples over her entire body. She hissed and bucked.

"I need you *now!*" she demanded.

She kicked off her boots and slithered out of her pants, then angrily tossed them away. He looked between her legs with a sly smile. It made her flush as he openly admired her cunt... it was most improper. Not that there was anything proper about being stretched out on the bed of a sailor about to be fucked into oblivion.

"What?" she asked when he wagged his eyebrows.

He grasped her knees and spread her more. "You *are* a real redhead."

She laughed until he scooted down and pressed his nose against her red curls. She grasped his hair, those wonderful, dark locks she'd wanted to feel between her fingers for so long. His tongue licked at her cunt with slow, deliberate strokes, and she kicked fruitlessly at the sudden rise of pleasure. Her toes curled as she gasped.

Before she could succumb, he stopped and slid up her body. He grasped a nipple with teeth along the way. Then he kissed her, and she savored the taste of herself on his mouth. The syrupy salty tang of her own cunt. She wrapped her legs around him once more and his cock bounced against her center.

"Now, do it *now*." She tossed back her head.

"Wait, wait," he hissed.

He rested his elbows on either side of her head and looked at her. His thumb caressed her scar. She ran her hands over his muscled shoulders and arms, familiarizing herself with the dips of his body. He was rock solid muscle, and she wanted nothing more.

"I won't confess this outside of this chamber..." he whispered against her face. "But I thought about doing this from the moment I saw you slink onto my ship."

Desire flooded her cunt. She realized that she, too, craved it back then. She simply confused it with offence and anger. It'd been lust. She'd lusted after his brawny body and the preview he'd provided her with his opened shirts. Lust at how he spoke to her, and the flush on his face when she yelled at him. Like she would make him lose control. And she desperately loved it when he lost control.

"Fuck me, Commander. That's an order."

Her trailing hands found his ass. She cupped it with the firm grip of her mangled arm. In an act of boldness, she slapped his cheek so hard it resounded in the room. Gods, she hoped it left a mark.

Justan went wild with lust, needing to grasp his cock as the beast bounced against his stomach. He captured her mouth as he entered her with a slow, willful thrust. He stretched her fully, as if she would split open in a final injury that would end her life. They stared at one another as he touched her in the most tender ways. Caressing her hands and her face.

"We're all falling to pieces," he murmured as shadows danced over his face.

Sex with him was a most desperate struggle.

A battle of wills.

A tournament of extremities; from the gentle to the rapid, from the sweet to the pain, from the pleasure to the desperation.

Hira gripped his muscled ass and curved her leg, contorting it around his back. The angle made the penetration deeper. She could feel his thick cock raging deep within her, staking a claim over her for all those that would dare to come after him. She was so close, at the edge of the very precipice. His hand slid between them, and as he entered her again, he toyed with her clit. She screamed out in pleasure and grasped his shoulders. He produced incoherent noises, nonsensical words, until he released, and she followed suit.

She shattered. Surrounded by him, while she felt herself swallow him. She swore she saw the universe and a sharp vision invaded her mind. It was a flash that lasted a second. A woman, a redhead, and a man, a Garian. It happened long ago, centuries before. Ancient times.

"Find me in another life," the man said.

"I always will," the woman responded, and they kissed passionately.

And Hira woke. Startled from sleep. She turned her head to discover Justan next to her, still panting. As if she'd only closed her eyes and reopened them. She shook and Justan pulled her in. She cast the vision out and concentrated on him, on the feel of his arms and the rhythm of his breathing. He was so warm, like the center of the world, and she'd never felt safer. The realization that this would likely be it—their one chance to be with one another—brought her to tears.

She cried.

Anguished sobs wracked the very veins within her body. He didn't say a word. Perhaps he, too, had his chasm to survive. Perhaps he too lived through hell.

Not all those who hold back tears are happy. Sometimes sadness is so dire and deep that tears are inadequate.

Outside their small room lay a world filled with realities that neither wished to face. Would he have to see her marry another? Perhaps. He would know her heart belonged to him, but duty superseded all desires. She wished she was still the selfish girl who boarded this ship. That girl would've selfishly left with him to the ends of the realm. Somewhere Almira could never find her. They'd take Quent and sail and sail until the seas ended. Safe and happy. She would bear his children and raise them as nomads did, jumping from port to port.

But it was a dream, a fantasy.

When all her tears emptied, he rolled over and pulled her to him. He tucked her under his chin and allowed her to sleep enveloped in his arms.

They coupled various times that night and, in the blackness, she pretended they were married. Eventually, their mating left them in an embrace where she didn't know which body parts were hers and which were his. His cock happily sated against her inner thigh.

In the room's darkness, she exhaled.

"I saw Zeita again," Hira whispered.

He stirred and blinked at her, his hand coming to caress the arm she had against his chest.

"When?"

"When I rescued Quent from the storm. Remember that I went down into the water?" She still recalled the chill of that night.

"Yes," he said.

"I sunk many meters. It felt like I'd fallen into the belly of the sea. Where the gods live," she admitted, and their fingers intertwined. "And Zeita came to me. To warn me."

He tensed slightly. "About what?"

She turned her head and looked at him. "About my cousin Furia."

His face darkened, and he pulled from her, scooting back on the bed. She instantly felt the loss of him, and she studied his frightened visage. She'd never seen him like this.

"What do you know about her?" Hira quavered.

He scoffed and shook his head, running his fingers over his locks. "That she's awful. Evil. *Determined.*"

"And she wants the High Seat," Hira said, her lips set grim. "Why didn't you tell me about her?"

He exhaled. "Because... she has spies *everywhere*. And I mean everywhere. Even in this ship. That man, who tried to kill you? Remember?"

All too well.

Justan shook his head. "She means to hurt you."

"And Almira." Hira nodded. "I figured that out on my own."

"She doesn't play the games you play. She doesn't have *any* light in her like you do. Her smiles are smirks, her laughs are a warning of treachery."

He seemed so shaken that Hira bounced between confusion and wishing to comfort him, to have him once more, warm and safe in her arms.

"Look at me," Hira said with a strength she didn't think she possessed. "The girl that boarded this ship weeks ago would've let her have the seat. She would've done so gladly. That's not who I am now. I'm *not* afraid of her."

But he looked away. "Why did you say her name in this bed?"

Hira's brows knitted, and she wished to ask many questions of him but couldn't even form them. Then he slid closer to her and cupped her face with his hands.

"I promised I would keep you safe. I *promised*, and I do not break promises," he said harshly. "Now that I love you, now that you're mine, I'll do whatever I have to do to keep you as safe as I can. Not just for you or for myself. But for Istok. For the world. Do you understand me?"

Hira curled her hands over his and felt the tremors coursing through his body. "You're scaring me. Do you honestly think she'll start a war?"

His eyes darkened, and he looked at her with a sort of helplessness she'd never seen before. "Oh yes. That's her aim. She'll try to take the seat by blade and fire. And she has a witch. A powerful one. She makes people see things that are not real."

Hira froze as she recalled the witch that appeared to Almira and got her and the Red Guard out of the castle. "I've met her. Tall, pale skin, gray hair, beautiful with violet eyes?"

Justan paled.

"She came to the queen last year. It's how we lost Mavros. So, it confirms everything." Hira looked away as her brain raged furiously to decipher the plan. "Furia is in league with Arrigo. Captain Strauss worked for them. He recruited the men who infiltrated Mavros and killed Tora. Furia orchestrated my uncle's capture and eventual death, didn't she?"

"Yes. She did." Justan's jaw twitched.

She stared at him and felt herself resent his words. His silence.

"Why wouldn't you tell me this? Why would you let me go into the city defenseless and ignorant?" Hira pulled away from him, hurt dripping within her bones.

"Don't you see I've been attempting to protect—"

"That is not your place!" she snarled and stood from the bed, searching the ground for her clothing. "I don't give a shit what you promised my uncle. He's *dead*. You answer to me now. I'm your High Lady. I'm your ruler." She scoffed, "You're behaving just like everyone else. You hold things back from me because you think you're protecting me. What you're really doing is severing my power. And I'll not have my power amputated by anyone ever again."

His face brightened at her words, and he stood. His body coiled in anger. He grabbed her shoulders and shook her. "You stormed onto this ship as a brat! You said it yourself; you would've gladly handed Furia the seat if she wished for it!"

She yanked herself out of his arms and shoved him back with her mangled hand. He stumbled and almost fell.

"This cunt you just fucked," and she grasped her womanhood. "Belongs to a woman, not a girl. You hold anything else from me again, Sir, and it'll be the last conversation you and I will ever have." She took a deep breath. "Do *you* understand me?"

He stared at her with that same expression of trepidation, as if she continued surprising him. She was shaking, and she felt her shoulders deflate once she calmed. She collected her things, refusing to look at him as she swiftly dressed.

"Hira," he called her name as she reached for the door latch.

She paused. Damn, she wished she didn't pause. She yearned to be stronger and not lured by the tone of his voice. Then his arms were around her. At first, she stiffened, then slowly she relaxed into his embrace when he pressed his head against her neck and sighed.

"The night is not over, and I love you," he whispered. "Stay. Even if you're angry. Even if all you do is yell. But *stay*. Spend a night under the stars with me."

She bit her lip and gradually intertwined her fingers in his, holding him to her. She realized she'd been a little unfair to him. When she'd boarded this ship, he couldn't have trust her with something like this. What hurt her was that he didn't believe she could handle it now. That he should keep it as a secret to protect her. That hurt the most.

"I'll do all in my power to ensure you take the High Seat," he kissed her neck. "I swear it."

And in that moment, she believed him. She grasped his head and brought his lips to hers. Almira and Alton made it seem so effortless. Like love walked an uncomplicated path without disagreement and hotly contested discord. Perhaps they too had such arguments behind closed doors. Perhaps they too struggled. Perhaps everyone did.

Chapter Thirty-Eight

ALMIRA

Almira knew the reason they slowed their pace was because of her. She was certain Alton was the one to make that call, and Sanaa willingly agreed. The queen's mood was dark and combative, even against her husband, uncle, *and* guard.

As if none of them understood the vitality of getting to Treveri as soon as possible. For all they knew, Furia could've already taken over the city. Hira could be dead, and the hope she represented dead alongside her.

She sat in her carriage and glared at Delara, who seemed unperturbed. Her muscled body was relaxed against the seat cushions. She looked out the window as the forest scenery passed them by. The night before, the Ouestern army joined their journey, and the land became checkered with red and black soldiers traveling like spring snails over the bark of a tree.

"The king has set this pace. Don't dare deny it," Almira said.

Delara took her time and, finally, looked at her. "A full army is hard to traverse through thick woods, your majesty. Danger may hide behind any seedling, but the scouts are doing the best they can."

Almira almost growled and rubbed at her belly. It felt it would explode at any moment. The child was restless, as if it knew the impending doom and demanded to be part of the action.

"We should've gone the other way, south of the woods," Almira said with a grunt.

Delara raised a brow and Almira knew well she hid a look of amusement behind her solid face. "Her Majesty, the queen said herself that we needed to remain unseen for as long as possible. The woodlands are the best place to hide."

Damn this woman for her perpetual calm and steady nature. When in the past she found it admirable, now she found it insufferable. All elegance and consideration hiding under the body of a warrior. *She* didn't have to suffer with a lumpy, swollen and aching frame, rotund as she was. Annoyed as she was.

Her guard watched her carefully, not suspiciously, but more like to one who observes and arrives to conclusions after perusing factual information.

"You worry. I understand. We worry too. We also worry about you," Delara said.

"You can all stop this mollycoddling!" Almira fisted her hands. "I can withstand the pace needed to arrive on time."

As she worked herself up to a fury, Delara instantly drew her dagger and pushed her back. Almira startled, her mind crazed at her actions. But Delara's green eyes were intent outside, at the shift in the men. They'd halted and the Red Guard surrounded her carriage along with the Mesedi, Alton, and Thebo, who shouted orders. M jumped from her horse and placed herself against the window. She exchanged looks with Delara, a wordless conversation.

"Are we being attacked?" Almira asked breathlessly.

"Keep her down," M ordered.

The tension mounted, and Almira pressed up against the walls. An attempt to hear *something*. How she abhorred being kept like a prisoner because she could physically do little in her condition.

Delara's smooth face seemed to listen with each particle of her skin. "We're not alone."

Almira's stomach froze, and she clutched the blanket draped over her lap. It was a soft pink swaddle which Hester and *Nanai* sewed, each tendril of thread a ribbon of love. It made her feel safe.

"Alton."

"He's fine," Delara whispered.

Not daring to move, Almira's mind raced with a flurry of possibilities. They'd surely been found. Furia's men surrounded them. She was about to see a true battle the likes she'd never witnessed.

"State your name or face death!" Alton's booming voice echoed into the woods.

Almira pressed her ear to the wall of the carriage. The only thing she could hear was her erratic heartbeat.

"Don't come closer. This is your final warning. The Mesedi *will* shoot!" Thebo yelled.

A rustle, some murmurs. *Damn it all*—she needed to see what was happening.

"Apologies, apologies!" a high-toned male voice shouted from the distance.

Delara's gaze narrowed, and she glanced at Almira. "Strange. Four men, one of them a lord. Short of stature."

"I didn't mean to startle you, my lords!" the alleged lord said.

Alton said, "State your name and purpose, Istokian!"

Istokians! They had found them! Almira clutched the blanket tighter. *Gods protect him, protect our soldiers*, the queen fervently prayed.

"Oh, Majesty! I'm delighted to make your acquaintance!" the man yelled back, a laughter sounding in his tone.

Almira looked at Delara questioningly. Her guard simply raised a brow. That didn't tell her much. Gods *of the sea*, surely, she had the right to see a little of what was going on outside her carriage.

"It'll be a brief acquaintance if you don't identify yourself," Alton's voice was tight. She hoped he wouldn't do anything rash.

"I'm Lord Barnabus, a friend and an ally and an ardent support of her Majesty Queen Almira, child of Istok. I apologize for startling your party!" He let out an awkward laugh.

She sat up, but Delara's hard gaze and tight hold didn't abate. Her mouth set, her blade still drawn, and looking nearly inhuman. The woman didn't even bother to blink.

"It could be a trap," Delara said.

"He's a *supporter*," Almira hissed.

"The words men say, and the actions they do, are two different things," her guard muttered.

Almira scowled, but Delara ignored her.

"You claim you're an ally to my wife, yet you and your men surprise us. What business have you in these woods?" Alton's tone remained unchanged.

The man, she could only assume was Lord Barnabus, laughed a hearty laugh. Her party didn't share his humor. On the contrary, Delara's body hardened, the muscles on her exposed arm rippled. Almira tried to recall where she knew the name Barnabus. It seemed most familiar.

"Pardon me, your Majesty, but these are my woods. Why shouldn't I be in them? But if we're being honest, which I should, given the amount of arrows pointed at my person, someone warned me beforehand of your arrival," Lord Barnabus said.

M and Delara shared a look.

"Warned by *who*?" Thebo asked sharply.

More shuffle of horses, more metal grinding. Almira's frustration almost led her to push aside her guard, though she knew she wouldn't get far.

"Ley Coster, to be precise. He said, trust Lord Thebo, he'll know what to do," Barnabus said. "I assume that you, with your impressive plumage and even more imposing Mesedi, are indeed the mighty High Lord Thebo, brother of Istok and of our beloved Lady Lamya—may the veils protect her."

The men remained silent, Almira could almost see her husband and uncle exchanging wordless looks.

"How can I know it's not a trap? That you don't hold Ley Coster in your dungeons or that he's even alive?" Thebo asked.

"Well, I don't have a dungeon, never had much use for one. They're rather drafty, don't you think? Along with that, the honorable Ley Coster said to tell you, the torch is lit, the kingdom trembles, and oh—what was the other thing—long live House Balik, I believe. I'm paraphrasing. He said you would know what it meant. Also, you can't leave the woods. Furia's soldiers patrol the outer bank, and she has a system in place that will let her know if the entire black and red army marches on Istok. So... I bid you welcome, welcome to Carrian land! I'd be pleased to hide you and host the crown!"

Delara's hold relaxed, and she pulled back, then nodded at Almira. The queen sighed in sudden relief. That's when she realized exactly who Lord Barnabus was. She was almost sick.

"Get me out of here."

The armies were at a stand-still, spread out over the lush Istokian forest. Men rested, as far as the eye could see; tired and hungry. Many of them were fresh from war, having traversed across the world to come to her bidding. They parted and made a path for Almira as she strode—or more like waddled—to where Thebo and Alton stood with Lord Barnabus. The man became flustered at the sight of her.

"Your royal Majesty! Oh, what a delight, what an honor! I'm so pleased to find you well!"

His fleshy pink cheeks flushed as he bowed as best as his stocky body allowed him. He was bald but for a few wisps of hair with a fuzzy yellow beard and round spectacles, which hid his golden eyes. He leaned good-naturedly on a cane, which Almira suspected was more for the flair than the physical requirement.

"Lord Barnabus, it's I who is pleased," Almira said with a benevolent smile. "Please forgive our caution. These are dangerous times."

"No need for apologies, my revered queen!"

She extended her hands. He promptly took them and brought them to his forehead. His palms were clammy, and he shifted as if he didn't know how best to stand before her. Seeing him now, Almira could see why her youthful cousin ran away from her duty as she had.

This was not the prospect to bring to a young girl as an option for marriage. Still, she would need to appease Lord Barnabus to ensure he bore no ill will, though he seemed unconcerned as he beamed at them all. She thought best not to mention the broken engagement unless he did.

"The army can stay hidden in the woods, but I welcome your Majesties and Lord Thebo to join me in the manor. It's not a castle, but I have set up comfortable rooms for you and I always keep a stock of splendid summer Suidian wine!"

They found Carrian Manor at the edge of the woods. The large estate encompassed four adjacent buildings, including an outhouse, long stables, servant quarters, and a jousting ring that had seen better days. The grounds were lovely and the scent of wild freesias permeated the area. Goats languidly ate off the early spring grasses, their bells tolled softly as they moved from patch to patch.

Peppered around the manor's lands were dozens of distant farmhouses. It seemed like a peaceful, idyllic land which experienced prosperity in the quiet breezes that danced between the oak trees. She would admit Hira would've grown bored living here. She wouldn't have appreciated the gardens or gentle strolls of country life. Still, it was secluded from major cities, and would be a good place to hide while they prepared their plans to invade Treveri.

The inside of the home was vast, but badly kept. Lord Barnabus seemed to verge on an obsession with his tinkering. His inventions and prototypes were strewn about the halls. He owned scrolls upon scrolls, along with something he called a book. A bound scroll he'd sewn with burlap that allowed him easy access to scientific theories. They quickly learned not to ask him about them, or he'd begin explaining intricate details that none could understand. Still, he was a jovial, good-natured fellow, even if he was a little odd.

Almira tried to remain stoic and interested as Barnabus explained some explosive devices.

Finally, it was Captain Sanaa who stepped forward and loomed over a petrified Barnabus and insisted the queen needed rest. That they were weary. When Almira and Alton entered their room, she let out an audible sigh of relief. A bed! A proper bed! She almost tumbled sideways, but Alton pulled her to him and made her sit.

"I want you to lay down," Alton said, his face etched with worry. He tossed his cloak on a trunk and turned to her. "*I'll* meet with Barnabus—"

"Don't be ridiculous." She rubbed her lower back. As if she would permit him to ostracize her from such important conversations.

"You have me anxious, my love. Who knows how this will end?" He kneeled before her, and she placed her hand on his armored shoulder.

Yes, that's all she seemed to accomplish. Make everyone worry. Everyone fretted. Everyone eyed her as if she were about to have the child slip between her legs, land on the floor, just to stun them all.

"It'll end when we find Hira and ensure Istok is stable." She tired of repeating herself.

Her husband shook his head. He looked weary himself, but he was used to months on the road while she crumbled under her determination with a baby wedged under her ribs.

"Fine, I won't argue with you," he said dejectedly. "I'll have dinner with Thebo and Barnabus, and we'll wait for you before we speak on the matter. In the meantime, you need rest."

She grasped his chin and held his gaze steadily. "You wait for me. *I* know Istok. Not you or even Thebo know my country. Have Sanaa come get me when you're done with your *fine* wine."

And she dozed soundly, as if she'd not slept since the letter arrived from her father. The bed was comfortable. The room was warm. And when the knock came, she startled from a deep slumber with a cry. Which of course made Sanaa storm in, sword at the ready, and M close behind. She scanned the room, but Almira raised her hand to calm her.

"It's nothing. Gods… you alarmed me, that's all." She pushed her hair back, the curls wild and unruly. "Are they done with dinner?"

Sanaa's shoulders relaxed, and she sheathed her blade. "Aye."

Almira looked around the large room, the thick carpets of generations past, the warm fire, and a tray with fresh water, juice, and biscuits for snacking.

"I was tired," Almira huffed as she shoved off the covers.

Sanaa eyed her. "Stubborn as you are, I'm surprised you've admitted it. The manor is secure. Come, let me show you to the dining hall."

Downstairs, the men were speaking, and her uncle chuckled at something Alton said.

"I wonder if her Majesty will come," she heard Thebo say.

"I'm here," Almira said as she entered, with Sanaa and M on either side.

"Majesty!" Barnabus startled, and as he jumped his wine landed over Thebo's armor.

Thebo eyed him with a small snarl as he dabbed away the liquid.

Almira strode around them without preamble and perused the room. It was a nicely sized dining hall with a long dark table and chairs; both of which had seen better days. Two empty bottles of wine were in the center and, judging by Alton's glazed eyes, they had thoroughly enjoyed them. They'd covered the dinner table with various scrolls and a few opened maps. She held her annoyance in check and studied them, her finger tracing the path from the Carrian Manor to Treveri.

"We've not discussed them." Alton came to stand by her.

He placed his hand on her back. She hated that he knew her so well and controlled a snide remark. She'd assumed they'd made their plans over brandy, wine, and cigars.

She looked up at Alton and slid from his arm, perusing the rest of the scrolls.

"A four-day ride into Treveri, I assume?" she asked, glancing at Lord Barnabus, who seemed stunned she was asking him for details.

When he didn't answer, she raised a brow. His lordship stuttered and reddened. Almira classified it under liquor sluggishness.

"Oh! Yes, Majesty!" And he badly curtsied.

Almira made a pensive noise and spotted drawings of an

intricate manor that caught her attention. "Tell me about Lady Furia," Almira said as she perused the designs.

"Ah..." Barnabus came closer to her but set down his wineglass to the relief of the rest in the room. "I'm afraid I know very little."

"What does she look like?" Almira met his eyes. "What is she like?"

Barnabus opened his mouth, then glanced at the king and Thebo, which only infuriated her.

"It is *I* who asks you, my lord," Almira leaned against the table. "Not them."

Alton, delighting in the scene, sat with wine at hand and a smile on his face. He would have no coupling tonight.

"Well, you see, the thing is," Barnabus tugged at his collar. "I've not seen her, Majesty. I was in Treveri this past week, which is when I spoke with Ley Coster. She'd left by then, and the entire castle seemed reassured. Everything I've heard is secondhand."

Almira finally sat and spread out the drawings before her. "Tell me your second hand stories. They may help."

"We know she has men patrolling certain areas and a system of communication. We know she hates your aunt, the honorable and most gentile Lady Marai. Unfortunately, I could not see the lady. Ley Coster conveyed she is gravely ill and the situation with Lady Furia didn't ease matters."

Almira sighed and leaned her head against her hand. Her dear aunt had single-handedly warned her of the impending doom and bravely fought Furia as best she could—with a political tactic that would have little effect on someone as allegedly violent as her sister.

"Ley Coster described Lady Furia as a... terrible beauty," Barnabus said.

Almira flinched. *Naturally*, her sister would be the beauty.

She looked down at the drawings. "Tell me about these. What are they?"

Barnabus beamed. "Oh! My pyrotechnic invention! I sketched it based on some scrolls I acquired from the Free Isle. Brilliant people!"

It was a simple enough looking cart with logs attached

377

underneath and a string that trailed to a drawing of a man with a candle in his hand. The next depiction was the man lighting the string on fire. The flame traveled up the line into the logs. The final rendition had the cart exploding and the man at a safe distance.

"What are these logs?" Almira placed her finger on them.

Barnabus slid his spectacles further down and nodded. "It's a hollow cylinder filled with fire powder, works much in the manner flame throwers do, only no projectile launches. The fire powder explodes and creates great commotion!"

Thebo stepped around Almira and studied the drawing. "And a distraction."

"Yes," Almira said slowly. She peered across the table to Alton, who considered Barnabus with something between dismissal and interest.

"I suppose yes." Barnabus nodded vigorously. "In theory, of course!"

"What do you mean, in *theory*?" Alton asked him, crossing his arms.

"Well…" Barnabus looked between the three of them, his forehead wrinkling and his cheeks flushing. "It's just an idea. I'm afraid I'm not very good at executing. I'm a brilliant theorist!"

Almira sighed and laid her hand against the parchment. "So, this contraption, this pyro…"

"Pyrotechnic!" Barnabus smiled.

"That," Almira waved dismissively. "Is not real? Or you simply don't have one?"

Barnabus seemed to lose his words, placed in the spotlight as he was, he faltered.

"Well, which is it, man?" Thebo grunted and took a swing of his wine. Likely to not murder the lord.

Almira understood everyone's tension, and it seemed as if his lordship didn't comprehend the urgency of their predicament. She glanced at her uncle, bidding him to calm his annoyance, to allow the man a chance to form an explanation that would benefit them all.

"I have… a few. I'm afraid I've not been able to get them to work," Barnabus admitted, and Alton groaned.

She knew her husband thought they'd wasted time. The man was a dreamer, and dreams had no place in war. Thebo sighed in great disappointment, which made Barnabus blanch.

"You see, Istokian fire dust is simply not flammable enough. I light the chord, I wait, it fizzles and then nothing. Very disappointing. I've attempted to purchase a few kegs of powder from the Free Isle, but I'm afraid I've only lost my coin."

His lordship looked truly devastated, and Almira felt it keenly. A contraption such as this could create various distractions throughout the city if properly placed. Enough time to allow them to gain the upper hand on whatever Furia planned.

Thebo walked around Almira and went to what she realized was his sleeping eagle. The magnificent beast sat perched on a beam, likely enjoying the rest after many hours of flying over the marching army. Her uncle leaned down and took—to Almira's horror— droppings from the floor.

"Uncle," Almira grimaced. "Perhaps Ushga should sleep outside and not ruin his lordship's fine floors."

It was a lie. The floors badly needed polishing. But her uncle ignored her. He went to the roaring fire and flicked the droppings into the flames.

What happened next was not what Almira expected. The hearth exploded in a great noise that had Sanaa, M, and Alton instantly surrounding Almira with their weapons drawn and the enormous eagle flying around the room. They couldn't see Lord Barnabus because he'd fallen under the table, glasses lost and hair singed, but with a manically delighted look on his face.

Thebo, though slightly smoking, stared at Barnabus. "Suidian Red Eagles... masters of the skies, but also producers of very flammable feces."

"Gods of the fucking sea." Sanaa glared at Thebo as he opened his arm for the eagle to land on. It squawked in admonishment to its master.

Almira slowly stood and watched the fire, which still roared, making the room uncomfortably hot. She and Alton looked at one another and they understood Thebo's implication. Spreading explosives full of dung throughout the city, and detonating them, would create chaos.

"Incredible!" Barnabus beamed as he sat up. "Nature, nature is truly the most fascinating thing!"

He laughed and rushed to collect more of the droppings from his floors, carefully pocketing them into a satchel.

Chapter Thirty-Nine

HIRA

The next morning, she focused on avoiding anxious thoughts. She'd done a fantastic job of not speaking with Justan, mostly by keeping to her quarters.

There was little to be said. She had promised him *one* night. When the dawn cast its light on the earth, she was the High Lady. She had a duty. Perhaps one day the conversation of marriage would arise with Almira. If she and the commander felt the same once she settled her country, she would name him as her chosen spouse.

But right now, as they sailed with all speed to Treveri, neither a lover nor a husband was her priority. Furia was. Istok was. She had to be cunning and wise. Furia or any of her enemies could use her feelings for Justan against her. She couldn't let that happened, not when she already held enough marks on her record to make her seem like the worst choice for the High Seat.

No. Her selfish desires would have to wait.

The perfect distraction for her jumbled mind was the histories of High Lady Dominia. She'd so easily discarded them before, when Captain Sanaa provided them, and today she delighted in their narrative as Quent quietly helped her prepare for tomorrow.

"Interesting," she murmured.

"What is?" Quent looked up from where he polished her armor. He sat sprawled on the floor with all of his cleaning items laid out in an orderly fashion.

"In Lady Dominia's—which are now my mother's chambers—she had a secret passage built that led directly into the dungeons. She imprisoned one of her lovers and she would bring him up to her rooms, where she made him 'work off' his sins."

She laughed, but when she looked up, she found Quent red-faced. She quickly rolled up the scrolls and tucked them into her trunk, which was filled to the brim.

"I'm sorry. This is not a proper subject of conversation. You're still very young." She should know better. He likely had no experience.

Quent, despite his flush, shrugged nonchalantly. "I know what couplings are."

She tried not to smile. "I'm sure you do, my lord."

He was quiet for a moment, polishing the armor in sharp strokes. "I'll probably never be able to couple, but I realize what it is."

She stared at his bent head. He looked so much like Justan in this light, a little skinny thing, but with his life ahead of him. She'd noticed his health was improving lately. Hira dared to hope there was a chance for him. A true chance.

Quent looked older than when she'd first met him. He seemed to have spurted in height and musculature. She desperately wished he could live to be a grown man, to wield a sword with the strength of a knight, and to find happiness with someone he loved.

"I never thanked you," he said after a while.

She sat next to him and pushed at his shoulder with her own. "Thanked me for what?"

His hair fell over his face. "For the kiss. I'll never forget it. I'll probably never get a kiss again, so it was very nice."

She laughed a little. "Of course you'll be kissed again, and *plenty*."

He looked down. "I doubt a girl would want a sickly person like me."

She didn't know how to help this situation. It felt as if she were out of her league. "One day, a girl will love you just as you are. I'm certain of it." She took his hand and squeezed it tightly.

He tentatively looked at her. "You think so?"

She leaned into him and pushed his hair back, kissing his cheek. "Positive. You're kind, sweet, loyal, and brave. And *very* handsome, let's not forget. These are excellent qualities."

Slowly, he returned her smile and his chest puffed up.

It was mid-day when Justan finally broke into her solitude. She and Quent were finishing the last polishing of the armor and all of its complicated, interconnected pieces. Justan looked defeated, sagged like a lowering mast.

"Quent, give us a moment," he said.

The boy's mouth set in a determined line. He seemed taller, proud to stand between Justan and Hira. Grown from the clumsy child she'd met. She supposed she wasn't the only one who'd changed on this voyage. It would be selfish to think herself unique in that regard.

"Quent," his brother said in a warning growl.

"Fine! I'll get some oats, because I'm *starved*." Quent stomped out, and in a last-minute act of protest, he shoved Justan with his shoulder on his way through the door. Justan watched him with a raised brow, then turned back to Hira.

"I think you've enchanted both of the Seaver brothers," Justan said.

She paused and almost laughed at his insinuation. "He's a *child*."

He placed his hands on his hips. "He just turned fifteen. I know he acts and looks younger. Perhaps I'm to blame for that."

She shifted at the implication of his words. She'd not thought about that. Quent seemed so much younger.

"You've been avoiding me," he said in a hushed mutter. His face clouded as if he'd held himself as naturally as he could, but collapsed under his own demands.

Hira attempted to cast away the thought of his meaty thighs entangled in hers. How much she'd enjoyed their night and how she desperately wished to do it again. For the first time, she recognized her stubbornness and acknowledged it. They would be in Treveri by sunrise, and her lingering thoughts on the commander wouldn't help her.

"I was clear. One night," she said without shakiness.

He walked closer to her, and her breath hitched. Her skeleton seemed to recognize his scent, as if it knew the intricate patterns of cells in her lover's body. It turned to him in the way sunflowers gyrate with the sun.

"So now what? You see me in darkened rooms? Away from the queen's prying eyes? Your dark little secret?" His own voice wavered, the meaning lashing him raw.

Hira stood and crossed her arms, trying to hold back the wish of throwing herself into her feelings. The desire to allow him access to her body and soul. She recalled all his parts and the soft hairs that covered them. That lovely fold under his sack that made him jolt when she ran a finger under it.

"Our night together..." he whispered and shook his head. "It meant more to me than any other. I shall carry it in my mind until you allot me a space in your life once more."

She found it difficult to swallow, to breathe, or to live. It was the manner his eyes softened when she entered the room, or how he kissed and held her. As if for the first time in his life he'd opened a door he was determined to keep closed. And because he loved her and because she couldn't give him what he wished, she wouldn't drag him—or herself—through such a bed of burning coals. Loving Commander Justan shouldn't be her priority. Her people needed her, they required a leader. She sailed with all haste to face Furia. She had to focus.

"I know..." she swallowed. "I know you think that because I stand before you unshaken and determined that I don't care for you in the manner that you care for me. You ask things from me which I cannot yet give you."

"*Yet*," he came closer, his palms sliding over her arm.

"Yet," she repeated.

He touched her face, then tangled his fingers into her hair. It took all the dragon's strength within her not to react, to not become that woman who'd secretly made love to him.

As he observed her holding her emotions tightly, he smiled.

"I forgot how determined you are. When I watched you lay in complete agony as your arm rotted, you became resolved, hard, and unrelenting. A wall of water. You'd destroy everything in your path to get your goal. Even yourself." His finger caressed her lip, and his eyes followed his touch. "Maybe that's why I love you."

She shivered and tried to pull away. She didn't want him touching her. In his hands, her wall of water crashed against his coast.

"Come with me," he whispered against her skin. He pressed his nose to her cheek. "I've a ship of my own. We'll take Quent and settle on the Free Isle, distant from everything. No one can hurt us there. Let the world eat itself to pieces while we find our own peace. Our happiness."

She met his gaze and felt the water that dominated her will rush to her eyes, but not a drop fell. Her throat tightened. In that minute, she'd never hated her House more.

"I'm the High Lady of Istok. I've a duty," she said, cupping tears in her throat.

"The only thing between this point and war are the hours that constantly tick," he whispered.

"Justan—"

"Please don't speak my name," he begged, then rubbed his face. "Listen to me. You don't understand what awaits you. Furia is..."

"I'm not afraid of her," she said with strong conviction.

"You say that because you don't know her," he breathed.

She nodded. Her mind resolute. "Look at me," and he did. "I am not afraid of her."

Pulling back, a chasm opened between them, and he placed his hands on his hips as he studied her room. He said nothing for a while, as if composing his thoughts and she didn't dare add things that would only cause them pain.

"Have you packed everything?" He finally asked.

"I have."

He stepped away and the implications that soon she would not rise each morning to see him or converse with him gnawed her stomach. She wasn't certain at what exact moment seeing his face and observing his scowls became something she looked forward to. But she did. She couldn't deny that any longer.

"I'll let you be then," he whispered.

They stared at one another. Then he turned away and her heart lurched after him.

"Commander Seaver."

His name flew out of her lips of their own volition, a desperate rope in an untamed sea. A lifeline. She'd lied. She'd lied to herself, to him, to everyone. She wasn't ready to no longer have him. Not that she had him now, but she could... if she wished it. If she allowed herself the selfish allotment of one more night.

He paused and stared at her with a raised brow. His face was sharp, smoothly shaved, and his thick hair oiled and combed.

"I don't know how tomorrow will go or what will happen, but... thank you," she said earnestly.

He swallowed, she watched his throat work and his hands fist. "Don't thank me yet. The journey is not over."

She wrung her palms together because if she hadn't, she would grab him. She would pull him against her body and press her tits against him. "Thank you for many things. For saving me, for allowing me to meet Quent, and for bringing me to Treveri alive."

He looked away, and darkness overtook his handsome features. "I can't believe how stupid I was when this all began. I expected a lady in dresses with a flocking bunch of ladies-in-waiting, terrorizing my ship for weeks."

She smiled. "Instead, you got me."

"Instead, I got you," he breathed.

He took a step towards her, but she bridged the gap. She was in his arms in seconds. His mouth captured hers as his hand cupped the back of her neck. It felt so powerfully right to be like this with him. A stirring in her belly reminded her of what a wonderful lover he was and how she wished to wake next to him each day.

She had a maddening desire to lose herself in him when she'd just discovered her own strength. Hira didn't know how to extricate her autonomy from his kisses. Being in his arms felt like a precipice. One she might live on the edge of for the rest of her life.

He pulled back, ran his fingers over her locks, and kissed her scar and nose.

"I won't let anyone hurt you. I swear it," he said in a harsh tone. "Even at my own peril."

She was breathless. "I don't need a bodyguard."

"Stay armed, promise me," he said with a sudden urgency.

She touched his face to soothe him.

He took a sharp breath and shook his head. "Don't leave your rooms without me tomorrow. You and Quent remain here. I'll personally escort you."

Hira sighed into him and ran her fingers over his back, caressing him. "You don't need to escort me. Korkoran Guards will do that. They have received word of my arrival. My mother will send them—"

He shook his head. "Please listen to me, I—"

"How would it look if I entered my city clutching your hand?" She pushed his hair backward.

He took a deep breath and nodded. "I can take not having you in daylight. I can even handle you hating me. I can deal with you marrying another. But I cannot bear you getting hurt again." Then he said through gritted teeth, "Stay armed."

She smiled and kissed his lips lightly. "I will. No one can wrestle my blades from me."

He nodded and pressed his forehead against hers, then sighed. "Alright. I'll let you be."

Slowly, he pulled himself away and turned to leave.

"Would you care to spend the night? Here in my quarters. With me," she blurted, and he looked at her with a questioning brow.

Her chest tightened because she was afraid he would deny her. A part of her wished he *would*. Save her from the ill choices she would make. Save himself from the future realities of loving a High Lady that may not be his for many years. She shouldn't have to see him in dark corners, away from judging eyes, for the rest of their life. But what if she had no choice but to marry another man?

He looked her over, then a small smile swam into his face. "Lady Hira, I would be honored."

Justan moved across the room, quickly placed a chair under the handle, and turned to her with a smirk.

"In case the little nugget wants to make an appearance," he laughed.

"Poor Quent—"

But his mouth descended on hers before she could finish. She grasped his shoulders as he lifted her off her feet and she clutched him with her legs. Somehow, she landed on top of the bed. Clothes flew off in various directions while they attempted to keep their mouths glued to one another.

When they were naked, she rolled him over and straddled his lap. He panted as he looked up at her, his cock quickly hardening before her. She grasped it with the tight fist of her scarred hand and he arched, the chords of his neck straining, his hands grabbing on to her thighs.

"Look at me," she demanded.

He did, his eyes glazed over in lust, lips pulled back. His chest heaved, muscled and bristled with hair. She could dive into him and lose herself in the forest of his body.

"Tell me something true about you," she said and dragged his cock until the bulbous head fit between her thumb and finger. She caressed the mushroom-shaped tip.

"Hira," he gasped and tightened his hold on her thighs, bruising her.

"Tell it to me now or I won't allow you in me," she smiled wickedly, delighting in having him at her mercy. She rubbed the head of his member once more, her cunt tightening as he growled.

"I... I've written you poems," he said, and his eyes met hers. "Not on paper, but in my mind. In my heart."

Oh. She'd not expected sweet words from him while she held him in her fist. "You wrote me poetry?"

He flushed red, even as he bit his lip against the onslaught of her grip. "I did."

The bloom of a smile formed on her lips at hearing his

confession and having him in this manner. His cock, now fully erect, trembled in her hand and she let go of it and ran her nail up the underside following the vein there. He buckled and cried out hoarsely. She did it again, and he was cursing and snarling against the sheets.

Then she did something she'd not allowed herself to do, for this was not an act *ladies* did. Yet it was a thing she'd craved. Bracing herself, she bent over and tentatively took his cock into her mouth. His hands were instantly on her braid, but she pulled back, the member slipping from her jaw.

"Hands to yourself, Commander," she said, licking her lips, which held the taste of his skin.

His eyes darkened, and he grasped the headboard, the chords of his arms bulging as he watched her, lust ridden.

Satisfied with his ability to follow orders, she sank her head once more and took him into her mouth, until the tumid end pressed against her throat. And then she began to suck, inhaling sharply through her nose, acclimatizing herself with the rhythm of his hips and delighting in the purling sounds that emanated from his mouth.

"Hira!"

The desperation in his tone captivated her. Her fingers dug into his hip bones, designing half-moon shapes with her nails.

And his cock grew in her mouth until it stretched her lips, his thrusts becoming more frantic. She pulled back, and her tongue was slick with his pre-cum. Languorously, she licked her lips, ensuring he watched her. Her sex was slicked with her own desire at the act she'd dared attempt.

She moved up his body until she faced him, and his cock bounced against her cunt. She gasped, holding on to his shoulders. He stared up at her in almost awe.

"Fuck me, Commander. Finish inside me."

And he did. He slid into her, and she arched in pleasure. He fondled her breasts while he rocked his hips up to meet her desperate speed. Ecstasy hit her suddenly, and she screamed out, even as he placed his hand over her mouth to prevent the entire ship from knowing what they did.

She collapsed on top of him but continued to circle her hips and gyrate. He still raged hard inside of her, and he reached between her legs to prolong her pleasure. The pressure built again. Stunned, she rocked harder as they panted against each other's mouths. His eyes closed, head thrown back, and she pressed her nose into his throat. He spurted into her and she climaxed once more. She fell limp, and he held her close, kissed her shoulders and neck.

It was a few moments before she could catch her breath, and she blinked up at him. His face was haggard despite his obvious pleasure mere minutes ago. She caressed him and he pulled her closer.

Hira lay wrapped in him. The hairs of his body touched all of her, even the most intimate parts. There in the dark, she loved him. She wouldn't utter the words, she couldn't.

As his fingers trailed the nubbly bones of her spine, he sighed into her hair.

"Tell me your poem," she whispered.

"Not tonight," he kissed her temple. "Tonight, I just wish to hold you. I wish to pretend we're together."

Her fingers curled into his hair as they stared at one another. She wouldn't give him up. Not for Almira. Not for Istok. Not for anyone. Even if she had to hide him, even if all they had was poetry between rumpled sheets.

Chapter Forty

HIRA

Morning light woke her, and she found Quent asleep on the floor next to her bed. He kept a small knife at hand. She'd dressed after Justan left and Quent must've moved in quietly in the night. Hira stepped carefully around him so as not to wake him, but it was useless as someone knocked on her door.

Hira grabbed her robe and slipped it over her nightclothes. "Who is it?"

"Captain Jutia, my lady."

They'd arrived, they were at port. Hira pushed back the curtains and took in the blue city of Treveri. A vast difference from Easima and its gloomy skies.

Treveri was a land of sun and vast horizons. In the distance, one could see the faint outline of the Mountains of Anaji. In the legendary port city, every home stacked upon one another so that each Treverian could have a view of the Bay of Pasimin. They painted many of the homes in various shades of blue with large balconies to have access to the balmy outdoors and enjoy the sights of the sea. An azure stone wall surrounded the entire city, and yellow flowers hung from the sides where they grew wild in between the cracks. In the center, facing the ocean like a giant protector, was

Korkoran. The polished cobalt stones reflected the colors of the water, proudly daring any enemy attackers that would dare challenge the power of its armada.

She sighed in relief and turned to Quent. "We're home!"

Her excitement was contagious, and he quickly rubbed the sleep from his eyes. She opened the door to find Captain Jutia smiling.

"Late morning?" She leaned on the doorway and neatly cleaned her nails with a small pocketknife. On her head was her large, feathered hat. She looked spectacular, as she always did, with fitted leather trousers and a finely embroidered black coat. She'd missed the woman and her sarcastic, even temper.

"Captain, good to see you," Hira said earnestly. "I'll get dressed. Have the Korkoran guards arrived?"

Jutia glanced back into the city and shook her head. "No, Justan went to find them. He said not to leave your side, no matter what. He seemed nervous. What's going on?"

The captain studied Hira. She was afraid the various couplings Justan, and she enjoyed while Jutia was on her own ship, would be evident on her face. Hira flushed and glanced away. How to describe Justan's paranoia without making clear their attachment? She treaded unknown waters.

"He's become obsessed with my security. Thinks someone is trying to hurt me. Thinks I'm not safe." Hira shrugged, having little to explain since he'd been so cagey himself.

The city looked like it usually looked, full of life, vigor, and happiness. No chaos caused by the seat being violently taken. She'd seen this port a thousand times and nothing was out of place. Wherever Furia waited, she was not here yet.

"I noticed, he wouldn't explain much, just said to make sure not to leave you alone. Perhaps it's simply port-jitters. It happens." Jutia shrugged. "But don't worry, I'll do good with my promise. My men and I will wait with you until Justan returns with the guards. I'd like them to try getting past us." Jutia winked with a nod and thrust out her hip so that her fine sword glinted in the light.

Her reassuring words made Hira's guilt heighten, and she looked away. She would have to confide in Jutia. It would only be fair. She wouldn't blame the captain if she withdrew her friendship. The last thing she wanted was for Jutia to place herself in harm's way to secure Hira's wellbeing without being aware of the truth. But that moment was not now. Perhaps tomorrow, she'd invite her over for lunch and then they could speak. Best not delay.

"Thank you, Captain. Hopefully, the guards will be here soon," Hira said, and closed the door. She spoke to Quent, who washed his face with a wet rag. "Help me dress."

Quent helped as much as he could, but mostly she had to force herself into her armor without the aid of servants. She braided her own hair, then slid her Ruby Blade and Ocean Fury into their sheaths. When she finished, she turned to Quent, finding his face filled with admiration.

"You look incredible."

Slightly shaken, she wondered if there was something she'd missed. "I look like a High Lady?"

She didn't have a moment to give into her nerves, because before Quent could respond, Jutia knocked with sudden urgency on the door. The captain's eyes were wide and concerned under the shadow of her massive hat. She pointed to the docks, a little out of breath.

"Korkoran guards coming in fast," she said.

Sure enough, two dozen Knights stomped through the city at a full gallop. Not a procession, as she expected. Their armor was azure blue, and they carried the dragon flag high in the sky. In the pit of her stomach, Hira knew something was wrong. Had Furia made her move? She itched to clasp the hilt of her blade.

The sailors had saddled Jessa, her mare. They also readied horses for Jutia and Quent and some of her men as the Korkoran Knights came to a halt before the Sea Wife. One man with a large blue plumage jumped off his horse and strode to Hira.

He bowed low. He was older, with a lined face and bright eyes. She recalled him from her youth and knew him to be loyal to her house.

"High Lady Hira, I'm Lord Augustus, Captain of the Korkoran Knights. We've been awaiting your arrival. I come with terrible news."

"Captain, what is this?" Hira stepped forward, her nerves now singed to a crisp, her mind searching for a woman in white, with eyes filled with malice. Where was Furia?

He swallowed, shadowed and pained. "My lady... your mother. She's *dead*. The Lady Marai was ill, and just this morning she died."

Hira felt all the wild blood within her freeze and dry. Her breath hitched, and she steadied herself against her mare. *No!* She thought she had time! She thought she had time to at least make amends and say her goodbyes. This is not how it was supposed to be. Her mother... her mother was strong. Fierce and protective. The matriarch of House Balik.

She shook but fought against the thick bile that built in her throat. Even after Uncle Beltran died, Almira stood and continued to be the queen. She'd rose from the bloodied floors, and Hira knew she must do the same. There would be no transition, no celebrations for Hira's return. The country was about to plunge into mourning.

Where was Justan? Where was Almira? She desperately needed them. She felt so alone. A child with no parents to embrace and delight in her arrival home.

Jessa stomped her foot angrily at being made to stand by, and Hira pulled herself up to the mare. Captain Augustus mirrored her, and the Korkoran Knights fell in line.

"Quent, come!" Hira shouted. "Captain Jutia, stay close to me. I can't wait for Justan."

Jutia nodded and helped Quent scramble to the smaller horse. Hira dug her boot into Jessa, who reared up, then thundered down the road. Gone were all her dreams of entering the city, waving at her people, taking her time accepting flowers and gifts. Jessa galloped through the road that Hira knew well. Up the hill, into the winding streets. Anger, violent anger controlled her now. A full Balikian roar the likes she'd never experienced. Her mother dead, Furia crouching in the dark like a malevolent spider, Almira rushing at all haste and into peril.

As she galloped through the path, people peered out of their homes to watch as she rode straight to Korkoran.

All she could think of was her mother.

Hira had run away from her, rebelled against what she wanted, made her own rules, and abandoned her mother in a nest of vipers. One person was to blame, one person she saw in the back of her mind. *Furia*. Her sword itched to find her and make her pay for her crimes.

As they rode onto the White Path, the stones turned alabaster. The spires of her ancestral home rose high into the sky, built with the blood of her people. The guards posted down the passageway held shell-shaped shields, and when they beheld her, they pounded their bucklers in a chorus that signaled the arrival of the High Seat. The Great Dragon.

The golden doors of the fortress opened, and out rushed the last person she thought she would be happy to see. Ley Coster. Her old Ley, her teacher, that impatient task master she loved to question and ignore. He was an elderly man when she escaped, but he looked haggard now. He dressed in the same black robes of Istokian Leys. He greeted her with wide arms and a trembling smile formed on his withered face.

It filled her with a sudden need to hug him and listen to his advice. He was loyal to House Balik; he'd raised her and Almira. She quickly jumped from her horse and ran to him.

"Oh, my lady!" he cried when she reached him. He brought her hands to his forehead with shivering fingers.

"Is she truly dead? Am I too late?" Her voice was steady, but she drowned in unshed tears.

He looked up at her eyes clouded over with the sight of the old, and he nodded. "She'd been ill, but this was sudden."

Hira rocked on her heels as she clutched him, breathing deeply. His lips trembled, and he seemed to have lost the fight, that fight he often displayed whenever Hira or Almira would test his patience. Broken. They'd broken him.

The Ley shook his head. "It's been *terrible*. Ever since the High Lord left for Easima, our kingdom has been teetering."

His words filled her with even more brilliant determination. This was her home. This was *her* fortress. She was a warrior, and no one would harm her people.

"It'll teeter no more," Hira said sharply. "I'm here now."

Ley Coster looked at her with such sudden pride she could've hugged him, as if the gods had allotted him to behold the woman he always knew she could become. Inwardly, she shamed herself for her behavior as a child, how she'd discarded his words. Words he'd urged on her because he recognized this day would come.

"I want to see my mother. Take me to her," Hira said and turned toward the fortress.

He followed, lifting his robes as he went. Quent fell instep at her side, and she took his hand. The Korkoran Knights surrounded Hira as she made her way into her old home.

The castle bustled, and servants and guards stopped, bowing as she stormed in. Black veils were being hung from the windows to signify the death of the lady of House Balik. It was too real, the sharp reality of what she'd arrived at.

Captain Augustus led her to a small antechamber. Hira paused when they entered, for there, on a dragon stone, was her mother.

They laid her in her evening gown with a black veil over her head. She looked the same as ever, with soft, pale skin, and red hair. She'd been the personification of Istokian elegance.

"Mother..." Hira whispered and closed her eyes against the last memory she had of her. Of that awful argument that sent her running away from the castle and from her duty.

Hira gently took the veil from her face. Marai's mouth was wide open in culminating agony and her tongue laid out of her the cavity. She gasped and almost stumbled. Her mother's body was so frail and thin, as if she'd held on as long as she could and finally felt able to let go the minute Hira returned. As if the wind whispered her daughter's arrival on the morning breeze.

"She suffered greatly." Hira choked on her sobs. "She waited for me, didn't she?"

She could envision it, Marai clutching her covers, her blue eyes glazed with constant pain, and when she sensed Hira's scent in the air, she gasped her last breath.

"Yes, my lady," Ley Coster said sadly. "She knew you would

return, never lost hope of that."

Hira kissed her mother's cheek and at the feel of her cold, stiff skin, she cried in despair. Her heart shattered. She'd never been able to make peace with her mother. Marai always believed in the duty of their house. She carried it with aplomb. The matriarch was gone, along with Uncle Beltran. The old guard was dead, and all that remained was Hira and Almira.

Hira was cold, empty, and alone. She needed Almira. She'd know what to do, what to say, how to take over. Hira cried bitter tears of loss and regret, and in the silence she made a vow—she would carry on House Balik, just as her mother wished. She wouldn't let their house crumble. They would rise once more and be brighter than ever before.

Slowly, she pushed herself off the body and re-veiled it. She turned to Ley Coster, who dabbed at his own tears. His face folded in despair.

"Where is Justan?" Hira asked.

The Ley, confused at her words, blinked through his grief, his face paling. "Who?"

Hira sighed and rubbed her forehead. "Commander Justan Seaver. He came here ahead of me."

But the Ley seemed even more perplexed. He shook his head as he studied her. "Oh! Commander Seaver was last seen leaving to escort you, my lady."

Hira's stomach dropped as she sensed something was wrong. She turned suddenly to Captain Augustus. "Bring me Lady Furia *immediately*. Make sure she's well-guarded."

Ley Coster gently touched her arm, but there was a bite to his tone. "Lady Furia left Korkoran, weeks ago, my lady. She's not been seen since."

Hira glanced back at her mother's body. That *horrible* sight. "Who else could have tormented my mother in her last months? Who else could've orchestrated my uncle's death?"

"The rightful heir." Jutia took off her hat.

Hira realized Jutia had tucked her hair neatly into it so that it fell around her shoulders and cascaded down her back. She wore a brilliant, beautiful smile as she studied Hira with steady blue eyes.

Ley Coster gasped and pointed at her with a shaking finger. "*You!*"

"I, indeed." Jutia smirked at him.

The guard who stood behind Captain Augustus stepped forward and sliced his throat. Blood sprayed across the room as the captain fell to his knees. He clutched his neck and gurgled to his death. Quent screamed and Hira pulled out her sword, but half the Korkoran Knights killed the other half in a perfectly coordinated attack. Hira yanked Quent behind her, but they locked the door, trapping them in the small antechamber.

As they massacred the knights, Jutia walked to the middle of the room and regarded Hira with cool eyes.

Hira measured her breaths at the realization of the deceit. "*You are Furia.*"

The woman smiled wider and mocked a bow. Her hat danced in the air as she did the complicated curtsey. It took Hira a moment to register the truth, how all Jutia's confident smiles were indeed mocking smirks. How all of her words were double-meanings.

"Lady Furia the second, House Balik... *cousin,*" Furia said and laughed.

"You deceiver!" Ley Coster screamed.

Hira realized that in the grief of her mother's fresh death, Ley Coster hadn't even glanced at her companions.

Furia's sharp eyes flickered to the Ley in annoyance. "If you want your Ley to live, my lady... I'd have him be quiet. I have little patience for liars." She smiled, that enchanting, beautiful smile. A terrible beauty.

Hira wouldn't be afraid of her. She was still the High Seat, no matter what. "Do you deny it? Murdering my uncle? Deceiving me? Accosting my mother?"

Furia bit her lip as she slid her gaze up and down Hira's body. "Don't look at me like that Hira, we're *friends,* remember?"

"That's High Lady Hira to you, *cousin,*" Hira intoned.

Furia sobered at the statement. Her sharp eyes narrowed into slits, and her lips pulled into a mock pout. "You still think it's about you, you *stupid* girl? Spoiled *brat* that you are."

Furia raised a hand in a mock faint and whined, "Oh, I don't want my duty. Let me cut my hair and escape as if that will change anything!" She spat, "You didn't have to *work* for it. You didn't have to *kill* and *manipulate* and *fuck* your way in. They handed you the title without preamble, placing a most unqualified individual to rule this country. You stand there demanding *my* respect? Grow up, *child*. Time has come for you to truly know me. For the world to know me. I've worked very hard for this moment."

Hira tightened her grip on Ocean Fury. "What are you going to do? Kill me? You think the people will accept you as the High Seat? There's *four* heirs in line before you!"

Furia licked her lips, slow and languorously, before she spitefully continued, "I thought you would suspect by now. You believe this is because of a *seat*? Fuck. The. Seat. This is about my birthright! There is no one before me. No one."

"Lies!" Ley Coster shouted as he moved to stand before Furia, red in the face.

She released her sword and pointed it with frightening accuracy at Ley Coster. The blade inched under his nose. Hira recalled Furia's skill and dared not move, afraid she'd watch her royal Ley killed before her.

"Stop it," Hira cried. "You want me, I'm here!"

Furia paused and arched a brow. She glanced at Hira from the corner of her eye. "You've never been my goal," she all but purred. "Why do you think I needed you to live so badly? I needed you alive. Blasted Strauss nearly ruined that with his greed. I needed you so I could enter this castle. And I needed you as *bait*. That's right, you're nothing more than bait for the bigger fish."

Hira stared at her cool blue eyes. Her stomach turned. "It's the queen you want," she whispered.

"*Yes*," Furia hissed in delight. "My darling, sweet, cunning *little sister*."

It was too much. Hira shook her head, denying what she already saw as the truth. "You're a liar."

Furia shrugged, the blade pinned tighter against Ley Wallace, and he whimpered as she pulled it back. "I was born of a liar, so I'm not surprised I took some of his qualities, not just his eyes. You know these eyes, don't you, Hira?"

Ley Coster looked livid as he shook his head. "How *dare* you defile the name of our dead High Lord! He was a good man!"

A knight stepped forward without warning and punched the old Ley. The old man slumped to the floor making his body collapse like a tossed rag. Hira felt her world tilting on its axis, as if Furia had suddenly strewn the contents of her life across the ground and tread upon them.

"Stop it! I'm here, I'm listening!" Hira strode forward, but Quent was violently clutching her arm.

"Jutia, stop this!" Quent sobbed. "Why are you lying?"

Furia studied her blade and sneered at Quent. "I like you, Quenty, but if you call me Jutia again, I'll gut you. Let the lady hold your intestines in her hands."

Hira pulled Quent back protectively. "Furia, listen to me. The queen is coming with her guards. If there's even a chance that I'm dead, you stand no chance of surviving. The Red Guard will take you down."

Furia smirked, amused. The door opened and in stepped some of her sailors, along with Mr. Hyall. The men took in the room and laughed, congratulating one another. These were the same men she'd fished and dined with.

"Mr. Hyall!" Quent cried, but the man looked around, unperturbed. He met Hira's eyes in a chilling manner that went right into her.

How many had deceived her? On whom had she placed her trust?

An icy fear drenched Hira. "Where's Justan? What have you done with him?"

Furia glanced at Hira as she took some parchment from Mr. Hyall. "I've done nothing to Justan. He's safe, isn't he, Mr. Hyall?" Furia said, almost amused.

The old sailor chuckled and stuffed his pipe into his withered mouth. "As safe as can be. A bit angry, but safe."

Hira beheld the man uncomprehendingly. How many words had she captured as gospel from his mouth? "How could you? I trusted you!"

He stared at her with a face she'd never seen. One of utter contempt. "That's *your* mistake. My loyalties have always been to Lady Furia, since she saved me from the Marchers' attack. She even tried to save my wife and child."

Hira swallowed against the bile that coated her throat. Her hands shook. She looked around at the knights, dressed like normal Korkoran Knights, the ones she'd depended on for safety in her childhood. The feeling of desperation overtook her, realizing how isolated she was in this moment.

"Is there no one here loyal to the Lady of Istok?" Hira asked. "Have you all forgotten your vows?"

Furia laughed, her head thrown back. "Oh, darling Hira! Don't you understand? As first born to High Lord Beltran, *I* am the true Lady of Istok. Not you. You're nothing but a spare. I'm about to give you your greatest wish. *Freedom.* No High Seat, no need to rule. Only... after I kill my little sister, there will be no Red Guard, either."

"No!" Quent shouted.

He rushed at Furia with his small knife, but Furia backhanded him. He crashed to the floor, a coughing fit seizing him as he began to cry. Hira trembled as she calculated her odds against the knights in the room but realized she'd never make it.

Furia's blue eyes locked on Hira with a fox smile. "I like you, cousin. I truly do. I enjoyed our adventures together, didn't you? You're a *decent* warrior—smart, brave, a little reckless—but I like you still." The lady stepped forward. She touched Hira's face and traced her scar with her gloved finger. "Join me. Pledge your loyalty to me and together, we can rule this world. And though it would cause me pain—because believe me, when I say it would—you can be with Justan. I wouldn't stand in the way. That's what you do when you love someone. You give them their leave. Unlike the queen, I wouldn't care who you married. I would make you *General* of my armies. Imagine it, Hira. You could do what you wished. Be with the one you love. Strut around with your armor all day long. I think that's what you want, isn't it?"

Hira met her eyes and slowly shook her head. "And watch you kill Almira?"

Furia's mouth tightened, a flicker of hate. "What has that bitch ever done for you?"

Such malice was hard to comprehend. She couldn't even wrap her mind around the suggestion.

"She saved me, and she has my allegiance. I love her. She's my sister." She met Furia's eyes defiantly. "And I will fight you the whole way."

Furia sighed and caressed Hira's lips with a pout. "Pity, Hira. Quite a pity." She addressed her men. "I think we should clap them all in the dungeons. Mr. Hyall?"

"Aye, m'lady!" He said, and the knights pulled Quent and Ley Coster from the floor.

"Oh yes, I'd almost forgotten." Furia held out her hand to Hira. "My birthright?"

Hira grasped Ocean Fury tighter. "You've no proof. You have *nothing*."

Furia smiled once more, a grin from ear to ear. "But I do. Just you wait. I won't give you a crumb of proof without an audience. Too many truths have been spoken in whispers during my life. The problems I created by being born. It's time I shouted them for all to hear. So, I ask again: my sword? Or do I have to kill dearest Justan to get you to cooperate?"

Hira took a sharp breath, and Furia snatched the sword from her hand.

"Take the blade from her," she said, pointing to the ruby knife. "Toss it off the cliff."

"No!" Hira cried.

Furia swiveled Ocean Fury with a quick flick of her expert wrist and poised it with eerie precision under Quent's throat. Hira's stomach dropped at the icy look Furia cast on her. It was void of feeling, enraptured by hate and revenge.

"Have you no mercy?" Hira whispered as the knight yanked her knife from her waist before handing it over to Furia.

Furia took the blade and studied it. She caressed the steel, then turned to Hira with a frightening glare.

"Mercy? Where was *my* mercy? Where was *my* love? Where was *my* devotion? A fatherly caress? It was nowhere to be found because I came out of the wrong cunt! But Balikian blood runs through my veins and all he could do at the sight of me was curl his lips. Even in the end, he died for her when he wouldn't suffer a stomachache for *me*." Her tone was pure vitriol, a caged agony that festered into hate. "It ends now. I am first born, I am the true Lady of Istok, I should've been the Lady of Suid, *I* should have been the Queen! Instead, he pats my head, gives me a ship, and expects me to be grateful. I will take my birthright by blood and fire! Get her out of here."

The knights grabbed Hira as she struggled against their grip. The men yanked at her armor in furious tugs, bruising her until they left her in nothing but her underclothes, shivering before them. Furia delighted in the disgraced heir before her.

Unrelenting, Hira launched at Furia with a yell, but the men grasped her, wrangling her as she battled them. Her cousin laughed, watching her from above.

Still, Hira screamed. "The nobles will rebel. If you kill the queen, the king and the Ouest will come for your head! Lord Thebo and Suid will come for your head! They will burn Treveri to the ground! You're starting a world war! This is not justice!"

Someone slammed Hira into a wall and punched her in the stomach, leaving her without air. She coughed as they tied her hands behind her and dragged her over the stone.

"Furia, listen to me, please!" Hira cried from the dusty floor. "You don't understand how the king loves her. He'll be an unstoppable force! She's pregnant! He'll kill every Istokian man, woman, *and* child! Thebo will join forces with him, the Red Army will plow this city! You don't stand a chance! You are condemning our people to death!"

Furia straddled Hira's back and yanked on her hair. Then, with Hira's own Ruby Blade, hacked off Hira's hair, the strands landing around her as she faced the ground. It felt like an assault. When once she'd done it to herself, it had empowered her. Now, it having it done to her, felt like an attack. She gasped, feeling her chest constrict, feeling the blade scrape up against her scalp. Distantly, she could hear Quent crying and Ley Wallace begging for her to stop. When she was done, she leaned down to Hira, nuzzling her face.

"You are *nothing*. Do you understand? I will *break* you," and Furia licked her face as tears filled Hira's eyes.

The last thing she felt was a bold strike to the back of her skull.

PART III

Isabelle Olmo

Chapter Forty-One

HIRA

Hira woke to the sound of crying and someone saying a comforting prayer. She groaned as a sharp pain thrummed through her head. At the same time, a chill swaddled her neck. At least she was no longer bound. Slowly, she pushed herself up to see Quent curled on the floor with Ley Coster holding him.

"Are you hurt?" she asked.

Ley Coster trembled, but said, "No. The boy is fine, too."

Grunting, she leaned against the wall. She didn't have to look around to know they were in the dungeons. Hira recognized the musty stone smell. She wished to scream. To throw herself against the bars until her body shredded on the metal. She'd never experienced anger like this before. Like something within her was wide awake, something she couldn't name or describe. A slumbering beast. Curling her fingers, she touched her scalp and found a thick lump behind her ear with patches of her hair missing.

Vishap! Wake up, Vishap!

She looked around the cell, her eyes wide. The voice was clear, sharp, and deep. Like it belonged to another time and space.

"Did you hear that?" she asked in alarm.

The old Ley sniffled into his robes. "No, Lady Hira."

Sighing, Hira rested against the wall. She was losing her mind. Her sanity held by a string which had no master, a path without stones. Closing her eyes, all she could see was Furia. And hear her words, her taunting words. Words that crumbled her life. Words that could crumble a kingdom.

"Is there any truth in her allegations?" Hira asked.

The elder hid his face. There was candor in the downward turn of his mouth and the reality of the lies descended on her. Her uncle's hard face came into her thoughts, and she'd never hated the dead more.

"You mustn't judge your uncle too harshly, my lady. He was a good man and even good men make mistakes," the Ley whispered.

The blue stones of the prison were slippery and full of deceit. She was born into a house of lies and that would be their undoing. Her bones grew cold, her underclothes providing little protection against the chill.

"He fathered her then," Hira said into the darkness. She could envision their long Balikian tree, the roots that went deep into the earth corroded until only Hira remained. The final wisp of a once mighty house.

"He never wanted it brought to light, but he couldn't bring himself to destroy her. It's in the eyes, you see. She has his eyes," the Ley said.

Her face burned at the confession, and she pressed her hands over the patches of hair left on her head. "*How?* How did this stay a secret? How could he have left Almira and Istok so vulnerable?"

The Ley thought on his words, trained for years for the diplomatic solution. Today she had little patience for diplomacy. What she wished for was a blade and a belly to slice.

"He was young. Lady Ignatia was a woman of incredible beauty. She desperately wanted to be the Lady of Istok and truly believed Lord Beltran would accept the offer. Everyone wanted it. Lady Ethinea—your grandmother—was the coordinator of the union. But his lordship refused. He didn't want marriage. He didn't even want the High Seat. Your mother and Beltran had grown up with Ignatia — they were first cousins, they played as children. In this same castle! Ignatia would've been the natural choice for the Balikian line. When your grandfather died, Beltran became the High Lord. He refused to marry but... Ignatia was conniving, and she showed up to his rooms naked. He bedded her over and over for a week."

Ley Coster rubbed a shaky hand over his face. Hira ingested his poisonous words, her insides twisting at the truth so many kept hidden. She'd been surrounded by liars and from this moment on, she swore she would not fall for another. From this moment, she would mistrust each and every person she came across. A bitterness coated her heart and the voice that whispered *Vishap* shivered in delight.

"When he was done with her, he jumped on a ship and sailed to Suid. It threw the court into chaos. Lady Ethinea had to step in, but he refused to come home. He whored his way through Zuri until Lady Ethinea had an idea. Rumors of a Sikorian girl's beauty had permeated courts, so she wrote a letter to House Sikora."

Hira took a sharp breath. "That's when he met Aunt Lamya."

"All the while, shame descended upon Ignatia, for she was with child. She told your grandmother, but before a letter could reach him, your uncle married Lady Lamya under a Suidian Ley. It was too late. The child was a bastard." Ley Coster nodded with a grim expression.

Hira wished to speak to her uncle. No, not speak. Yell. The day of Tora's burial, he'd chastised her on duty all the while *he* was the tainted one. *He* was the one who destroyed them all.

"He just left her with a child! Furia *is* the Lady of Istok!" Hira yelled.

"I'm afraid that *patrilineally* she is, my lady. But your uncle *legally* left Istok to *you*, not to her. He named you his heir. He'd always tried to help her. Ignatia was even married in a rush into House Pesce. Her husband died when Furia was a baby and all the while that bitterness Ignatia carried passed into her daughter."

What was it with these men? They made their mistakes and explained it away with carefully crafted words that polished their image so that all who questioned them became the aggressors. The violent truth seekers that *ruined* things instead of their own decisions.

"She was his child! You know how he doted on Almira, but what about Furia?" Hira pounded her fists on the stone. "Furia is right. My uncle loved Almira without reason. He was mad with it, dedicated each day to her. You recall! Furia *saw* it! We met her as children! Furia understood, even then, that she was the unrecognized child. She was awful to Almira and would burn her hair!" Frustration overwhelmed Hira's senses, and she clutched her own ruined head.

"The girl was sent away—"

"She's his firstborn!" Hira yelled. The elderly man recoiled. Good, let him cower. Right now, she felt as though she could fight an army on her own. "Did my mother know?"

"Yes," Ley Coster whispered. "Lady Marai attempted to remove her various times. But Furia replaced some servants with those loyal to her. It happened slowly, covertly. I assume she's been planning the hostile takeover for quite some time."

"If she kills the queen..." Hira groaned and yanked at the bars with all her strength. But no one could breach the cells of Korkoran, not even by the strongest men, not even those blessed by dragons. She leaned her forehead against the metal, allowing the coolness to soothe her. "You *men*. You men and your *secrets*. You've condemned us all to death. Do you understand the war that is now upon us? Norr will join Istok against Ouest and Suid. Our land will *burn*."

Quent whimpered and Hira could hear the squeals of rats happily feasting on the food left discarded by the prisoners.

"I'm afraid that's not all," the Ley confessed.

Turning to him with narrowed eyes, she snarled. "What else?"

The Ley shifted, his face bright red despite the pallor of his eyelids. "Lord Beltran might not have been able to kill his daughter, but Lady Ethinea had no such qualms. When Furia was five, Lady Ethinea contracted Marchers to attack the caravan escorting her to Commander Seaver's home, where she would spend a few years."

Hira cursed. "That's when Mr. Hyall's family was killed. She saved him. That's how she met Commander Justan."

"I didn't know, my lady," Quent said. "I only met Jutia when I came aboard the Sea Wife and by then Justan told me they were engaged. Are you going to have me killed too? Will you kill Justan?" Quent asked.

"Quent, I know you're innocent." Hira pressed her hands against her face. "We have to warn the queen and the Red Guard."

How she expected to do that, she wasn't certain. Trapped and shamed as she was, she was of little use to anyone. She trusted no one and everyone outside of this cell was her enemy.

"I've sent word to her. Hopefully, information will intercept her ahead. But I cannot guarantee she'll have any knowledge of this. Last year, Marai and I sent a girl to bring her a letter from your uncle. Her Ladyship was afraid of sending any further letters in case Furia discovered it."

It was a dream indeed to believe Almira would perceive the happenings here. Otherwise, she would arrive to Korkoran with her escort and midwives, thinking she'd only come to birth her child instead of a slaughtering.

"Furia can kill me any day and set up a pretty ambush for Almira *and* the king." She sighed, angry at her current helplessness. "Take out the monarchy and allow Arrigo to rule Easima while Furia rules Istok."

The doors to the dungeons opened, and Ley Coster stood with the help of Quent. Hira braced herself for whatever was coming. What she didn't expect was Justan walking first, his steps long and sure as he stared at them.

"Why is he in here?" he demanded from Furia, who walked with a calm smile.

Furia wore beautifully crafted armor with a blue dragon pounded onto the chest plate. The turncoat Korkoran Knights surrounded her. Hira watched Justan, confused. Quent was his sole focus. Anger bristled off him.

"He's in perfect health, as I promised," Furia said.

Quent's face still had caked blood, and he sniffled pitifully.

"Get him out, he's sick and you know it!" Justan seethed.

Furia glanced at Mr. Hyall, who looked amused. They shared a covert understanding. "I have a suspicion our brave Quent will improve in health shortly," she purred.

"Plus, we're all out of Vindri oil." Mr. Hyall chuckled.

Hira realized the implications and her stomach plummeted.

"Vindri oil?" Hira glanced at Quent. "Vindri oil!"

Justan stared at Furia in horror, then he launched at her, but Furia's men grabbed him before he could choke her. He strained against them; his face enraged.

"You've been *poisoning* him!"

Furia blinked, providing him with a most innocent look as she walked closer to him. She ran a hand over his chest as he resisted restraint.

"You were hard to convince, my love," Furia said.

Justan studied Quent with a tormented expression, then back to Furia. "You! You stood by while all those tests and medical procedures.... you *found* the medics. You stood by while he screamed!"

The slow realization of Quent's mysterious illness coiled Hira's stomach. Furia smiled and leaned into Justan.

"You've always known what I'm capable of, and yet you still loved me." And her hand traveled to his face as he relaxed and the men let him go. "But your minor obsession with him was pathetic. It changed you. You are *nothing* like you were." Her lip curled back in disgust as she continued, "Do you recall how you were? Ever my partner, ever my equal. Until your little brother shows up."

The words were too harsh, they stripped the flesh from Hira and she was once more on a bed, dying, having skin carved out of her arm.

"Now, I say jump," Furia said in a tone of disgust, "you ask how high."

Justan's face broke into pain, shaking his head as he stared at Furia.

"I admit," Furia drawled. "You made me very angry at first when you refused to romance the Lady Hira, but you finally saw my reasoning." Furia cast Hira a delighted smile. "Look at her now. See how she watches you, lover? And I thought *I* was going to be the one to break her. I'll let you have this victory."

Hira stared at Justan as all the breath left her body. But he locked his gaze on Furia and Hira heard her heartbeat in her ears. She dizzied. All the fight left her, plummeting like an empty sack. She watched in horror as Furia dragged her long pale fingers down Justan's chest. He inhaled sharply.

"Did you think of me while your cock was in her? Was it my name you chanted in your mind?" Furia peered at Hira and smirked. "I *did* lie about Justan's truth, cousin."

Hira watched Justan's face, and he met her eyes. The self-hate there was overwhelming.

"Deny it," Hira whispered.

He blinked and swallowed, but to his credit, his eyes did not move.

"He can't." Furia smiled and slid her fingers over his arm. "It's always been Furia and Justan, hasn't it, lover?"

Justan shrugged her off. "Quent was off limits. Get him out of there *now!*"

"No." Furia turned to leave. "He's my little insurance. I can't trust you anymore, Justan. Not when you tried to save her because you think you have *feelings* for her. What a disappointment you've turned out to be. You don't even fuck me like you used to." She paused and seemed genuinely hurt as her eyes lingered on his defeated form. "I won't lose hope for us. I still love the man you were. How your eyes would brighten when I'd kill or torture someone? Do you remember? We planned to burn down the world *together.*"

Breath left Hira's body.

"Take it!" She slammed the bars. "Take Istok! I give it freely and renounce my post! I'll leave to the Free Isle with Quent and never be seen again."

Behind her, Ley Coster gasped. "No, my lady!"

But Hira was done listening to all the liars dressed as prophets. "That's what you want, isn't it?"

With a toss of her shining black hair, Furia turned to her.

Hira bared her teeth against the cell opening. "No one else needs to die for it. Have pity for my people. I'm standing in your way. I'll go. Be a wise ruler to them. It's your birthright."

Furia walked slowly to Hira, watching her with a cold appraisal. "You cannot give what was not yours to begin with, but I appreciate the character growth. I gave you a chance. You refused. Your trial starts tomorrow."

She speared Hira with such malice that the lady nearly flinched. There was only frigid blood in her veins, as if warmth seeped out of her. With one last glance at her prisoner, she left with the Korkoran Knights and Mr. Hyall.

Lingering, Justan looked at Quent, then spoke to Hira. "I told you. You don't know what I've done. Keep him safe. *Please.*"

Hira gathered all the hate within her. "You don't *deserve* him. You deserve nothing but death and damnation. I'll see you have it before my end. You'll have nothing, not pride, not Quent, not me."

The flinch that split his face brought her pleasure.

"Justan!" Furia called angrily.

Then he glanced one last time at Quent and followed his owner.

Bile erupted in her, and she fought to keep it in, clutching the bars. She lost that fight and she vomited on the stone. It spurted out of her and trickled down her chin onto the floor. She cried, sobbed, and yelled in pitiful anger.

Never again. Never again would she love. Never again would she care. She hated them all. She hated Justan Seaver with all the strength left in her. Why didn't he let her die? Why did he save her? To bring her here and break her? To think she thought him the best man of her acquaintance! To think how she fell asleep in his arms! She placed this man's cock in her mouth.

Damn him.

May the Favia hear her plea and grant her justice.

May he never find the happiness his mother wished for him. May he live for a hundred years and never grasp it. May someone always take it from him in the same manner autumn takes the warmth of summer.

"Does this mean I'm not sick?" Quent breathed.

"Vindri Oil is a poison," Ley Coster said. "A few drops in your food once a day would significantly weaken anyone and simulate symptoms of an illness that can never be identified or cured."

"So, I'm not sick?" Quent asked.

"No, Quent. Furia used Mr. Hyall to poison you daily." She turned to him.

He gripped his chest. "I'm not going to die?"

Anyone wishing to harm him was unthinkable, but so was everything else on this godsforsaken day. They lived and breathed the ashes of Hell.

"We might all die in this madness, but you won't die of a mysterious illness. It was a farce. She was poisoning you." Her voice was toneless, belonging to someone else. Someone new and freshly birthed.

Gradually, Quent laughed. Big, uproarious crackles of laugher came out of his small body. Hira actually worried for him as he coughed a few times and then he laughed after his coughs.

"The poison is likely working its way out of your system. It'll take a few more weeks." Ley Coster seemed equally concerned.

If Hyall had been the one doing the poisoning, it was likely that Quent hadn't received any poison in a while, since before her arm. Which explained why Quent's health had improved.

She thought of all the awful medical exams they had done to him. The scars she saw when she helped him dress; peppered across his thin back. A part of her almost pitied Justan, but then she sharply recalled how he'd willingly and purposively made her have feelings for him. To what end? To distract her? It had worked. It had all worked. She'd fallen like a willing child into this trap. Her uncle and mother dead, Almira's life on the line, her own life on the line, and the country in the middle.

Her heart was a pit of ashes where only the dead lived.

"What trial does she speak of?" Hira asked Ley Coster.

The Ley cleared his throat. "She's likely to invoke Antilay. It's an obscure, ancient ritual. Hasn't been performed for hundreds of years but the law still has it laid out. When a High Seat is thought to be unfit, they can be unseated by bringing proof of their corrupt, disingenuous, or erratically based actions."

Hira's stomach soured at the thought of the coming day and the tribulations she still must live through. "Before who? The nobility?"

"Yes. A sort of tribunal," he said in a grave tone.

She could do this. She wouldn't quake with fear. She was a Balik. A *vishap*. "It's smart. If she kills me without provocation, it's a hostile takeover. Presenting me before the nobles and stripping me of my titles allows her to walk away with their support of her claim. Istok will be hers."

It's why Furia fought so hard to keep her alive, held her down. What was it she said as the witch healed her arm?

"I cannot do that, Hira. I truly am sorry. You need to live."

To live only to die. Like all other humans, which came before the lady, they all lived only to die. Hira fisted her hand until the bone seemed to crush under her wrath.

"When the queen arrives unwelcomed, they can kill her for trespassing as they've made no allegiance between the new High Seat and the crown," Ley Coster said grimly. "The nobles would support a war and Lord Thebo would have a hard time justifying marching the Red Army."

But Hira knew Suidians and their fervent devotion to Almira and her grand shows of power. She'd seen the love for her in their eyes. The queen was their goddess and their religious fanaticism for their deity would be the ruination of all if Almira died. This would only be the beginning. Chaos would reign, just as the Favia wished. The Great Balikian War.

"It won't change anything. The Red Army *will* march on Istok. I must save the queen. At all costs. That's *why* Zeita brought me back. The baby must be born, the queen will live."

The three of them were quiet as they contemplated the calamity they found themselves in. Hira shivered as she discerned rats scrambling through the halls of the prison, their small feet pattering the corners as their whiskers sniffed the air for more food.

After a while, Hira looked at Quent. "If we live through this, you'll be able to be a Red Guard."

He seemed elated for a second, then his face fell. "But what about Justan?"

She took a deep breath. "Commander Justan is officially a traitor to the crown, and it is my duty to kill him on sight."

It was a frightful night, and as much as Hira wished to find sleep, it never came. The floor was hard, and the wet frigidity of the ocean entered the walls.

The bitterness of life entered her mouth and settled in her bones. Rage consumed her. Rage at herself, at Justan, at Uncle Beltran, at *everyone*. In her corner, she cried acerbic tears for her mother and for the possibility of Almira being killed. Would they extract the child in cold blood from her arching body? The coldness in Furia's eyes told her she would.

The reality of war was now a roaring fire.

She began to hate the love she still held for Justan. That fact mutilated her soul. How could she still love someone who betrayed her? She'd seen Jutia as a friend when her smiles were all smirks filled with disdain. Hira thought Justan loved her against his will because of her position when truly he struggled with false tenderness.

"Romance the Lady Hira…"

To think he had never loved her. What a child she'd been! A naïve girl. But never again. They viciously stripped innocence from her, and, like the brutality that made her, so too would she be ruthless. She would harden her heart like a rock and carry it like armor. They could mangle her body, but never her heart. It would be untouchable. If she slithered out of this mess, she would be an ice-queen for her people and only think about them. House Balik would end with her. She would be the last.

The world held no wonder. The world held no happiness. The world was dark and unfeeling. The stars had no warmth. The stars were dead.

"You're torturing yourself, my lady," Ley Coster said softly. He huddled in a corner with Quent curled into his Ley robes.

"I worry about our people," Hira said bitterly.

"You worry about Commander Justan's behavior," he said and shifted with a groan. "I too have been young and in love and spurned by the one I loved."

"Justan has betrayed the crown."

"He has betrayed *you*."

She clutched the metal bars. "He's betrayed *everyone*. My people

419

will die because of his actions and no fervent entreaty can ever allow me to grant him leniency. In leniency, the wicked thrive."

"The wound is still too fresh. It bleeds," he said.

"I've healed from the most painful of wounds, Ley Coster. Wounds of the heart, much like my arm, leave a permanent mark. Only the heart cannot be scraped or disinfected. No dragon will save me now. I'll have to save *myself*."

Chapter Forty-Two

ALMIRA

It was late in the night when a rider tore through the fields of tomatoes, corn, and grain. As a bell rang, the manor went to immediate alert. The tolling of the bell woke Almira and Alton from deep slumber, tangled in each other's limbs. It was Lord Barnabus who rang the bell as he frantically ran through the manor while wearing his long nightshirt, slippers, a cap, and a coat which made him trip, causing a commotion outside of the crown's chambers. As Delara and Sanaa wrangled him to the ground and pressed a knife to his throat, Lord Barnabus continued ringing the bell. That is, until Sanaa snatched it from him, leaving the man petrified on the cold floor and Alton opening their door, blade at hand.

"A messenger from Korkoran, Majesties!" the lord squealed while still on his back.

Alton closed the bedroom door, finding the entire situation incredibly amusing. He specifically reveled in the way Captain Sanaa's brows stitched together in a sour expression as she held the bell in her hand. He doubled over laughing while Almira admonished him and hoped his lordship didn't come to harm. But he was in good health despite the loss of his dignity.

The party rushed down the hall and into the study where Thebo awaited the crowns with a trembling Barnabus. Candles were lit, and a decently sized stone fireplace warmed the space. Almira's eyes went to her uncle, who held a letter in his hands.

The queen marched straight to him and snatched it as Alton brought her a candle so she could read it. There was no seal on the wax. Almira looked at her husband, who nodded in encouragement.

She opened it quickly and perused the message before handing it to Alton. She needed to sit. She needed to sit, or she would faint.

Alton, letter at hand, read.

Your honored aunt is dead. They have taken lady Hira prisoner on the order of the Lady Furia, which I hope by now you understand her to be your sister. By the time you receive this letter, you won't be able to stop Antilay. The lady will be found guilty of treason and sentenced to death. She wants the lady's head to land on your lap. I'll attempt all within my power to stall the beheading until the moment you arrive, even at my own peril. On the fifth day of the week, when the clock strikes midnight, I shall sneak to the dungeons and open the gate. A small group can infiltrate the castle and aid in breaking the defense. If no one is there, the lady will die. Istok will fall.

Your loyal ally,
Ryker.

The room fell silent as they absorbed the news. Except for Lord Barnabus.

"You have a sister?" he asked.

Almira drank from the water provided by M, who stood next to her like a protective shadow. It was as she'd imagined; they'd taken Hira prisoner. They were at a precipice so sharp that she couldn't contemplate its depth. Even if she wished it, nothing could repair the broken pieces already on the ground. There would be no way to control the nobles after this. No manner of placative annunciation could wrangle the allegiances her father moored for decades. Her aunt… she couldn't even process the madness. *Dead.* As if she knew help was close by, she held on until her girls were in Istok.

"To kill Hira, in such a manor, would surely make Istok descend into chaos," Thebo said quietly.

Almira nodded. She watched Alton. Gone was his humor. He slowly looked at her and recognized the smell of war in the air. No one knew war better than her husband. She could see from shadows cast across his face that he wouldn't like her decision.

"Yes, that's exactly what she wants." Almira licked her lips. "A country in chaos seeks stability and blames the rulers who oversaw it during the chaos. Naturally, they will turn to a savior. Someone that promises them a return of their former glory. Someone beautiful, someone eloquent, someone filled with lies that paint pretty pictures and promises."

"*Furia*," Sanaa said in a harsh tone.

"Yes. My dear sister with a Balikian mind made toxic by bitterness and pain," Almira nodded, and she stared at Sanaa. "*Cuzo?*"

Sanaa nodded and crossed her arm. "I'll do it."

"Do *what*? What's the plan? Can we explain it to the rest here?" Thebo stood by the fireplace, his long gray braids tossed over his shoulder, and despite his sleep clothes, he looked very much a high lord.

Sanaa glanced at him. "Me and a few others can infiltrate the castle, meet this Ryker, and try to take down Furia's guard as she focuses on Almira."

Alton and Thebo's head snapped to the queen, who sat calmly, her hands on the armrests. She met Alton's gaze and took a deep breath.

"Take the Red Guard. You have to find the hidden staircases that lead to my aunt's rooms after you're in the dungeons. It might take hours to find."

"The Passage of Dominia." Sanaa nodded and Almira startled at her words, looking at her questioningly. Sanaa shrugged. "I read it in scrolls. They lead to the west tower."

"Yes, that's right. My aunt's rooms. There is a hatch under her chair. We weren't allowed to play there, so Furia won't know about it."

Alton sharply realized that Almira was defenseless if she didn't have a Red Guard. And she would be. That's exactly how it must be, but her husband wouldn't understand. She didn't think anyone in the room would.

"A few of us could easily take down the flat-cocked bastards," M said next to Almira.

As an idea came to her, the queen raised her hand. Something that may appease her husband. "Not you, M."

It hurt her guard beyond her capacity to express, but Almira placed her palm on her forearm.

"You stay with me. We are going to ride alone into Treveri. To the steps of Korkoran."

"Alone? Alone? What are you talking about alone?" Alton's face colored. She felt his ire crackle off his skin as he shadowed her. Almira had not seen him angry since she first married him.

Almira's gaze remained steady. "Furia expects me. She knows my Red Guard is coming. Furia doesn't know that the Suidian and Ouestern armies have already arrived. She anticipates them *later*, after she kills Hira and myself. By then, she'll have access to Istokian and Norrian banner men. Surprising her is the only way to take her down and reduce the number of casualties. If Furia believes she has me, you and Thebo can enter the city with our forces. If not, we risk her killing Hira or even setting the city on fire."

Alton's mouth flew open, and he paced before her. Her uncle shook his head and Sanaa stepped forward, ready to fight her. The queen was so focused on the risks that she lost her patience.

"Listen to me. She needs to *believe* she has me. Do you understand? I need to divert her attentions from Hira—

"By placing yourself as a sacrificial lamb?" Alton thundered; spit frothed his mouth. "While carrying our child?"

Almira glared at him as her cheeks heated. "I am no lamb, my *love*."

The king didn't have any humor as he pressed his hand to his forehead. Almira looked away from him and turned to Sanaa, who was angry and ready to agree with him. In her captain's mind, it would be better for Almira to wander through dungeons, infiltrating the castle than for her to be placed before Furia.

"*Cuzo*," Sanaa hissed. "M alone cannot hold back Furia's forces."

Almira stood with curled lips and her muscles quivered. "The armies enter with all of our forces when Hira is secure. The pebbles of manure will explode in the city to create confusion. Chaos. We might find victory in the chaos. In the chaos, we may save Istok."

"*May*," Thebo said, still darkened by doubt. "If she can, she will kill you."

Almira thought about the plan and turned it over in her mind. "We should be reasonable about this. Killing me is easy. I'm a defenseless pregnant woman. This is a lot of theater for a simple death. Though she hates me, though she rather I die, I'm too valuable. She will trade me if she is able to capture me."

Alton leaned forward with a trembling chin as he set his hands on a chair. "What would the cost be, Almira? The world? My throne? Istok? How much are you willing to gamble now that you're fully in this game? Now that you've decided, you *must* out-think her to prove *what?* That you're smarter than she? This confidence you have in her is great indeed." His lips soured. "Mark my words. She will try to slit your throat regardless of how much she promises to Arrigo."

Almira flinched at his words, but her eyes fell on M's ruby blade. Slowly, she opened her palm and indicated for her guard to hand it over.

"You're right," Almira whispered as M handed her the knife.

"I'm *right*," he huffed as he pushed himself off the seat, he believed in her acquiescence.

"If she captures me, if she tries to kill me, we must make sure the blade most accessible to her—the blade that would provide her the greatest sense of satisfaction, is the one blade that would be most useless to her."

And with that, she pressed the ruby blade against her throat—the cool steel bit her skin but, with a harsh tug, she sliced it across her neck.

She wanted to startle them, not create chaos. M, Delara and Thebo screamed, and Alton had her in his arms with wild eyes and gasping mouth. Sanaa yanked the blade from her with a snarl.

"I'm well!" Almira pushed against everyone.

They were speechless as they stared at the blade. Alton looked at her and lifted her neck. He shook her shoulders angrily when he saw she wasn't hurt.

"Why would you do this? Are you trying to kill me?" Alton was speaking so fast she could hardly understand his questions. Thebo hovered behind him with fear in his eyes. Perhaps her uncle thought she'd lost her mind and there was a moment when Almira thought she might've.

"It cannot harm me!" She placed her palms on his cheeks to calm her husband. "It cannot."

This time, everyone looked at the blade in Sanaa's hands as she turned it over to inspect it. She pulled back after it nicked her finger.

She looked at the queen with disbelief. "What have you *conjured?*"

"Conjured?" Thebo echoed.

Almira lifted her chin. "Blades that protect a Queen cannot harm her."

"It's magic," Delara whispered.

"Magic?" Alton asked as he studied Almira once more, his brows furrowed, still holding on to his anger.

"Witchcraft!" Thebo shook his head.

"Likely science!" Lord Barnabus piped up, sidling to Sanaa to inspect the blade, which the captain pulled back from him.

Almira sighed and ran her hands over Alton. He remained wound tight as he continued to hold onto her as though she would fly away. A laughter broke into the room before she could say anything.

"You have a flair for the dramatic. I like that."

Every armed person quickly drew their sword, and Alton pulled Almira behind him. A woman emerged from the shadows of the study. A Free Islander. She had a bow slung over her back and various knives strapped to her waist. There was nothing but amusement in her countenance.

"I really thought you'd do it," the woman said.

Before Almira could demand she identify herself, Sanaa

surprised her by sighing in that manner of hers. The manner that signified deep annoyance.

"*What* are you doing here?" The captain asked, pointing a finger at the woman.

The woman gave a small smile to Sanaa. "Such charms, Captain. No wonder the ladies fall like daisy petals on your bed."

Almira raised a brow and looked at Sanaa. Her *cuzo's* face was a mix of resignation and embarrassment. Had her captain's libertine reputation finally caught up with her? Would Almira have jilted lovers arriving at all of her war meetings? That could be inconvenient.

"You know this woman?" Almira asked.

Sanaa nodded as her jaw tightened. "Not how you think. This is Kaia Lu Kait. She's been following us."

"Following us?" Alton echoed, staring at the captain with as much confusion as Almira felt. "And she's *alive*? I'm frankly astonished."

"As am I." Delara quipped.

Kaia chuckled. She leaned against the wall as they debated her life.

Sanaa rubbed her forehead and cast the intruder a sideway glance. "I *can't* kill her."

Almira thought nothing else could surprise her. "Well, why the hell not?"

"Because!" Sanaa threw her hands up. Almira had never seen her so frustrated and rather… flushed. "She's Tora Kait's sister."

Almira's eyes snapped to the woman. Yes. The resemblance was there. It did little to ease the questions of why she was following them and, more importantly, why Sanaa kept her presence from Almira and the rest of the group.

"Is she really?" M smiled as she stepped forward.

"Who is Tora?" an exasperated Alton asked as he looked to Sanaa for answers.

"Not certain," Thebo answered, though the question was not for him.

Lord Barnabus smiled as he looked at the blade that was set

down. "I find this night to be full of revelations."

Kaia Lu Kait, small as she was, seemed deadlier than Almira's entire guard. She walked closer to Almira, and Sanaa instantly moved closer to the queen as Alton also placed himself before Almira.

"Everyone, stop!"

Almira pushed away from Alton and Sanaa and strode to stand before Kaia, who watched her with levity. The queen ignored the curses and angry words from Alton and Sanaa.

"Did you come to kill me, Kaia Lu Kait?"

Kaia studied the queen. The woman was able to control each section of her face. "*No.*"

It was difficult to read the truth in her. As if she'd been hurting for so long, her emotions didn't belong for the perusal of others.

Almira nodded. "Swear it on your heart."

The woman flinched; her face pulled back. She remained silent. Almira inspected the weapons that were strapped to her small body. She would make a good Red Guard, but she had a feeling Kaia blamed Sanaa for Tora's death. That would explain the captain's silence.

"Your father... he was a great man."

"My father was a fisherman who happened upon an education," Kaia snapped.

"You think being a fisherman can discard someone from being great? He was great nonetheless. He was an honest man," Almira said slowly, and Kaia watched her, startled with a wide mouth. "Unfortunately, most honest men are idealist. Didn't he beseech the Agamorian council to join New Verden during the famine?"

Kaia looked suddenly smaller. Her hands fisted, and she stepped towards the queen.

"How do you know this? How do you know about my father?" Her words were bitter, like she'd carried them latched in her throat for decades. Many people in this room had the same thing in common. Pain so old it merged with their personalities.

"Because..." Almira stopped and stared at her kindly. "Tora told me. One night, under a heavy moon, as she escorted me across the castle. Now..." Almira placed her hands over her belly. "I don't know what your intentions are coming here in this manner, but if you wish to end me, you'll have to get in line. I have an heir to rescue, a country to save, and a child to birth."

The demeanor in the woman changed, and Kaia chuckled as she crossed her arms. "I listened to your plan. It's an admirable plan. But it's got a flaw. One that will end with you dead or badly hurt, whether you have a magic knife next to you or not."

Almira waited for her to continue.

"I took the Raoul Road on my way here and, as life and the gods would have it, I overheard a marksman speaking in a tavern. He was on his way to Korkoran, where he scored a lucrative contract to hide in the fourth tower... and bring down a queen," Kaia said with great satisfaction. "Avoid the stomach, he said."

As the words left Kaia's mouth, Almira felt cold, and the room fell breathless. She was only able to stare at Kaia, who had a neutral, unbothered look. This would ruin her plan. The thought of dying on the stairs of her ancestral home as Furia carved her child out of her belly was too much for her to envision.

Kaia smiled. "You don't need to worry, Majesty. What you need... is an archer."

And Almira saw her plan. She perused her. "And are you one?"

The confidence in her gait was evident. "The best there has ever been."

Almira understood her presence and leaned forward. "One problem."

"Amongst many," Alton snipped.

She ignored him. "There is no other building taller than the fourth tower. The closest would be the College of the Leys, but it's been sealed since the time of my grandfather."

The woman smiled and bit her lip. "I'm an excellent climber."

But Sanaa, with her ill humor, stalked to Kaia. "Since you're so confident in your skills, care to explain exactly how good your aim is that we would trust you to protect the queen?"

Catching the captain's attention seemed to be Kaia's aim, and she smirked. "Seeing as you don't have any more archers lying about, you're going to have to trust me... *Captain.*"

"Why? Why are you doing this?" A hiss of anger flittered through Sanaa's lips.

Almira peered at her. She did not think antagonizing the girl would help.

Kaia pointed at Sanaa's chest, smashing her index finger into her vest. "I don't do it for *you*, I do it for Tora. You can't return to the Free Isle and bring my sister's honor home if you're protecting your little kingdom."

"What honor?" Almira looked between the two. "What is she talking about?"

"So, it's selfish motivations," Alton said when Sanaa didn't speak. His hand slid on Almira's back as he stood by them.

Kaia smiled but kept her eyes on Sanaa, delighted in the simmering anger she found there. "Yes, mighty king. If you wish to call it that. I don't expect Verdians to understand our customs."

"I trust selfish actions," Alton nodded and glanced at Almira with a raised brow. "They're always predictable."

But Sanaa didn't look convinced. She grabbed Kaia by her upper arm and pulled her in. Kaia had the decency to flinch at the iron grip. Almira wasn't certain if her *cuzo* would listen to her at this moment. She had never seen Sanaa so worked up.

"If your little arrow misses and somehow slips and lands on the queen, I'll hunt you down, skin you, and make sure I toss both Tora's and your honor to the bottom of the Sea of Jacobin. You understand?" Her words came out as a hiss.

Alton, brow raised, stared at the two.

Kaia lifted her chin and smirked. "I understand Verdian very well." Then she glanced back at Almira with a placid smile.

The queen remained hesitant to place her life in the hands of such a woman. Yet she had little choice. Now it was time to shift to other matters in the sea of the many laid before her.

"Very well. Barnabus!" Almira turned and looked at his lordship, who probably didn't understand why he was dragged into this. He had to be her inside man, despite her concerns. She didn't have anyone else. He was a noble. "You need to get to Treveri. Tonight. I need your eyes and ears during Antilay."

"He'll never make it to Korkoran on time," Thebo said as he pointed to the man.

Lord Barnabus, who looked like he had only been in carriages his entire life, gaped at them all. To think he could handle a hard ride to the coast was comical.

"Unless he rides a Dundai horse." Kaia sported the same delighted foxy smile.

"And exactly *where* do you suppose we find a Dundai? There hasn't been one on the mainland in decades!" Sanaa said, seemingly at her wits' end.

Thebo rubbed his face after he sighed and sunk further into his seat. "This is madness."

"There's one outside, right where I left it," Kaia said with wide, innocent eyes.

Almira stared at her, aghast. It was unthinkable that someone could sneak such a horse into her kingdom. Those animals were so coveted, any manner of nefarious people would've killed her for it.

"How the hell did you get a Dundai into the mainland?" M asked. She sat with her hand against her breast and her lips set to a grimace.

Kaia looked at the crowns with childish pride. "I stole it from a man named Kuimo. Heard of him?"

The room was quiet as they processed the implications. From all they knew, Kuimo was a gambler and a criminal whose jurisdiction was mostly on the Free Isle. But his men infiltrated larger cities, such as Easima and Iguanta. Almira had enough issues to worry about without *that* headache. Maybe another day, but not right now.

"Are you mad?" Sanaa asked, aghast.

He'd hunt her down for certain. People did not steal Dundai horses from men like Kuimo. Despite all of that, a Dundai horse might be exactly what they needed.

"Never mind how she got it. She's got it now." The queen flinched when she felt a burn in her stomach.

She took a shaky breath as she pressed her hand to her belly. Allowing no one to inquire about her wellbeing, she squared her shoulders. Before this odyssey was over, she would have to bear a lot.

"What do you want in return for the use of your horse and arrows?" Almira was aware that the offers came at a price. She felt defeated at this moment. She continued to trade for the good of the kingdom and it flayed her raw.

Kaia pointed at Sanaa. "I want the captain to leave for the Free Isle and bring my sister's honor home," Kaia said in a clear voice.

As she pondered, Almira's dark eyes flickered from Kaia to Sanaa. Before she could open her mouth, Alton slammed his hand on the table.

Barnabus jumped in his chair and Thebo sighed as the eccentric lord accidentally scattered scrolls. They rolled about on the study floor, and he quickly went for them.

"Done!" the king announced. "Get up, Barnabus. You're going to Treveri tonight and pray to the gods you make it in time."

"I—I don't know how to ride a Dundai horse," Barnabus said from the floor as he searched for his spectacles.

Thebo shook his head. "Just hold on and hope you don't die."

Chapter Forty-Three

HIRA

When the doors to the dungeon opened the next morning, Quent clutched Hira's arm. He had been tossing and turning all night. She did not fare any better and neither did the Ley. There was no point in sleeping when death would arrive at dawn.

"I won't let them hurt you," Quent said desperately.

But she grasped his shoulders and stared at him, so he understood the reality of his expendability. Having them torture Quent to hurt her would be unbearable. No matter what, he was now hers to protect.

"I can take it if they hurt me. Do you hear me?" Hira asked firmly.

Quent's face morphed into an anger she'd never seen. He had dirt and tears on his cheeks, but he was defiant as he stepped back to Ley Coster. She didn't mind his anger, but defiance had to be carefully doled out when one was a prisoner at the mercy of the merciless.

The false Korkoran Knights entered the dungeon antechamber, dressed as though they were true honorable knights of Istok. She knew their armor well, as she would hide from them as a child. The Korkoran Knights wore golden armor, with blue sea dragons, and the design continued down their shoulders. Protectors of the Great Dragon. What a laugh they were now. She recalled how her mother would send them to find the young lady, and nothing would give Hira more pleasure than escaping and outsmarting them.

One man looked at Hira between the bars and sneered. "Hands where I can see them, bitch."

One last time, Hira looked at Quent. If only for his sake, she must survive today. And for Almira's sake and the child she carried.

"It's alright," she told him, then turned to the guard, coolly placing her hands before her. They unlocked the door, and one of the knights chained her up.

"You're not worthy of that armor," she said as she studied the dragon on the chest plate.

He looked up with disgust. "What happened to your arm, ugly?"

Hira chuckled. "It was sliced in half, then a dragon healed me. And my face? I defended the queen. What did *you* do for honor, *Sir*?"

He grabbed her shirt and pulled her to him, her breasts squashed against his steel plate. "Is it an honor to fuck a lady?"

His unshaved chin, and his red eyes spoke of long hours of drink. The real Knights were likely dead or imprisoned in these cells, and these were common mercenaries.

"You're no Korkoran Knight," she hissed accusatorially.

"Oh, because I expect coin and I don't come from a fancy family like you? Lady Furia pays well, and that's all that matters."

The scent of his decayed mouth drowned her senses. He held her buttocks as he moved his hands down the length of her body. She stifled a gasp.

"Unhand her, Sir! She's a *lady*!" Quent yelled as Ley Coster urged him quiet.

That distracted the man as he looked at Quent. It was a sadistic look, and it turned Hira's stomach. She twisted and kicked him after sliding from his arms. He landed on the floor, and she slammed her booted foot into his face with all of her strength. She stomped on him twice before the other guards hauled her off. They punched her in the stomach, and someone kicked her head.

She was sure they would kill her. But they didn't. They made her stand after hauling her up. When she looked at the man, she saw his nose was concave inside of his head. She'd disfigured him. His right foot twitched slightly, and then it stopped.

"You killed him," the knight who held her said.

She spat blood on the floor and cracked her neck. "I want to make sure I at least attempt to be as evil as I'm about to be painted."

"Get going!" the other guard yelled.

They dragged her out of the dungeon as Ley Coster shouted prayers she didn't recognize. Hira focused on breathing. The kick to her head made her woozy, but she still walked, chin high, as the Lady of Istok.

The castle was nearly deserted. She could imagine what she looked like when a few servants stared at her. In her youth, she walked these halls like a lady with long hair and a fair face. Today she was a shadow of her former self, but she never felt stronger or more ready to accept what would come. Surely, Furia would kill her after she found Hira guilty of whatever crime she concocted.

They took her to the throne room, a place she knew well, for it was where her uncle sat, and listened to people's complaints and met with his nobles. Here she first saw Almira sitting in her father's chair to practice being a High Lady.

There were giant murals of sea dragons encircling the walls of the entire room. The eyes were giant encrusted sapphires, the treasures of House Balik. A massive statue of Uncle Beltran stood by the throne. It was a tradition to keep the statue in the throne room for a year after the High Seat passed. Afterwards, it would be relocated to the stone garden amongst the rest of the rulers of the past. It resembled him so much that Hira flinched as he oversaw her fall from grace.

They shackled Hira to a witness box before the entire Istokian court, with Furia on the High Chair, a gilded throne decorated with sapphires. Sea Dragons made the crest and their bodies converted to the arms and legs of the seat. The cushions were the deep blue of the Istokian ocean.

Seeing Furia there made the chair look polluted, and Hira fought against the anger threatening to consume her. Especially because Justan stood next to her with his hand on the back of the chair.

She had blood in her mouth from the attack in the dungeons, so she spit it out and smiled at Furia.

"Cousin," Hira said.

Furia smirked. She wore a white gossamer gown, her hair braided down her back, and royal jewels on her head and neck. She looked like a terrible goddess to be worshiped.

"Have the accused state her name, Ley Olan," Furia said.

Hira was unfamiliar with the Ley who stepped forward with a sacred law scroll at hand. He was Suidian but wore the traditional black robes of the Istokian Leys. He was younger than Ley Coster and had a smooth face and bright eyes.

"State your name," he said to Hira in a deep voice.

"Don't you know your lady, Ley?" Hira said in a snipe voice.

She swore she saw the smallest of smiles in the corners of his eyes when he blinked. She had no time to think about it as Furia slapped her hand against the armrest.

"State your name!" She snarled.

Hira beheld her with contempt. "I am High Lady Hira, House Balik! My mother was Lady Marai, tormented by the woman before me! My uncle was High Lord Beltran, whose murder this woman before me plotted! I am the heir to the seat in which you sit and *defile!*" She looked at Ley Olan. "Do you know me *now*, Ley?"

Her voice reverberated against the walls of the hall. The nobles murmured amongst themselves. She turned to them. To their sniveling faces, their tiny hands clutched before them, decorated in jewels and pearls. Robes carefully threaded by master craft workers. Her house made them rich and here they stood, frothing spectators.

"Have you no honor?" she yelled. "Had you no loyalty to the High Lord? Did your pockets not grow fat because of his trade agreements? Did you not feast and drink in this very hall while pledging fealty to him? *This* is how you repay him? By bringing down his house?"

Some nobles looked away in distress or shame and refused to behold her. Others were happy with her fall from grace. Mangled, bloodied, bald, and torn as she was. The fall of House Balik would allow other houses to rise in ranks. They did it for themselves, not for the good of Istok. To line their purses at the expense of the people who toiled the land and manned the ships of the armada, which kept them safe.

"And *you*," she turned to Furia. "What charges do you bring against me? What could I possibly have done to strip me of my rightful place?"

Furia held that smirk in place, calm and unperturbed. Justan looked at the floor. Hira wanted him to look at her. Look her in the eye as he stabbed her and watch as Furia destroyed her. What a coward she'd loved. What a coward she'd fucked. Lingered in his arms like a fool.

Furia extended her hand to Mr. Hyall, who appeared to be the new Keeper of Korkoran. He gave her a scroll and scratched his face with his hooked hand.

"I will present to the Istokian nobility two letters. If you want, I will allow for your inspection to ensure validity. But first, bring forth the second accused," Furia said in a loud invocation.

Hira braced herself for whoever Furia would present to this crowd of vipers. To her horror, it was Ley Coster. They had beaten him, and Hira panicked at the thought of what happened to Quent. He would be defenseless. They dragged the old man to the feet of Furia. He slumped to the floor with a pitiful gasp, then coughed raggedly. Furia looked down at him, with the prettiest smile on her face.

"Are you Gray Coster?" Furia asked. Her tone was one of innocence, as if she did not know the man who lay helpless on the floor before her.

The Ley coughed again, and blood dribbled from his mouth. He moved himself up to a kneeling position. His spine shook as Hira held back her tears seeing her family's Ley in such a position. He'd been here from the moment she entered the fortress; in the same manner as the murals of the hall were.

"I am Ley Coster, Ley to the High Seat of Istok, my lady," he said in a hoarse voice.

Furia looked almost apologetic. A falsity. "You're no longer a Ley, I strip you of your title."

He shook his head as he swallowed. "Istokian law states that only the High Seat can do that."

Hira wanted to scream for him to shut up. She would kill him! She'd beat him for all to see! Furia paused and calmly stared down at him. Her blue eyes were almost white in the sun that flittered through the stained windows. She turned to the letter and read it.

Lady Ignatia,

High Lord Beltran has received your request to bring the young Lady Furia II to the Korkoran Court. The High Lord cares for his daughter and wishes for the best, but he won't be receiving her at the Summer Solstice. The Lady Lamya carries a second child, and the High Lord doesn't believe now would be a good time for such hard conversations. The High Lord will gift the Lady Furia a commission of her own ship on her eighteenth birthday. He would be proud of her to serve the Istokian Armada.

Yours truly,
Ley Coster
Ley to the High Seat of Istok"

Furia's gaze turned to Ley Coster and she let slip the letter down to him. It floated down so that it landed before his knees. The old man looked down at it. Hira swallowed and clutched her hands together. Oh gods!

Deny it! Deny it, old man, Hira chanted in her head. No one would come for him. No one would avenge him. What was a Ley compared to her own life? A pointless heartbeat that wouldn't matter to anyone. They would launch no wars for him. Not a single soldier would march in his name. He would be an unfortunate tale shared over a weekday roast.

"Is that your handwriting?" Furia asked in mock-innocence.

Ley Coster blinked, and a tear dropped on the old letter. Hira looked to Justan to beg him to intervene, but his gaze had not moved. It remained locked on the floor.

"It is, my lady," Ley Coster whispered in a hoarse voice.

Furia was like the fury of the sea.

"You admit to conspiring with my father to keep me from my rightful place. Is that true?" Furia asked, setting her chin on her open palm.

The nobles murmured. Hira looked around, a futile attempt to find amongst them a friendly face, someone as shocked as she was at the treatment of the Royal Ley. *Nothing.* The depravity transfixed them and frothed their usurious mouths.

"I have always done the bidding of the High Seat," Ley Coster said softly. His lips quivered as he breathed in a rough inhale.

Furia let out a humorless laugh. "I hereby strip you of your Leyship -"

Two Korkoran Knights stepped forward and tore and yanked at his black robes as Ley Coster cried for them to stop. His frail arms were no match for the strength of the mercenaries, and they easily disrobed him.

Hira yanked at her bindings. "STOP IT! LEAVE HIM BE!"

As the nobles chanted for his debarment, she was no more than a voice in the crowd. Delight overcame Furia's face when Ley Coster was finally naked before her. As he cried into his chest, he shivered and held himself as best he could. His translucent body hunched, folded upon itself, liver-spotted, and quickly rushing to its end. The creases of his skin prickled in the cold air of the throne room.

This was all too ugly to consider. Too acidic to digest.

Hira shook her head and cried for him as she pulled against her bindings. She sobbed for his shame and exposure. That he should lead such a prideful life only to have it skinned at the closing of the day.

The Ley slowly met Hira's gaze. His eyes filled with regret and kindness, despite his humiliation.

"You don't pay attention. That is why you don't know the answer." Ley Coster's *mouth soured as his spectacles slid to the tip of his nose.*

"It's boring! I don't care about the laws that govern treaties!" Young Hira

kicked under the table. It was the year she ran away. It was one of his last lessons.

He shook his glasses at her. "I won't always be there to advice you. The mind has no mercy on our needs and one day you will wish you remembered all my words."

"One day I'll get a new Ley that won't make these lessons so boring!" she snapped as she crossed her arms.

"Be that as it may, but today I'm still your Ley and you'll listen to the lesson!"

She'd rolled her eyes at his words and ignored him for the rest of the afternoon. Now he stared at her. Hira cried with him as his life pivoted on its last page.

"I'm sorry, my lady. I have failed you," Ley Coster whispered.

She shook her head and denied it. He'd done no such thing! He'd cared for her when she'd resisted him.

The voice of Furia broke through her thoughts. "Grey Coster for charges of plotting against the true Balikian heir. I hereby charge you with treason against the Lady of Istok. Death will be your end."

"NO!" Hira pulled so hard against the wood that it cracked and Furia's head snapped to her. Their eyes met.

Furia kept her eyes on Hira as she brought her hand down.

The Korkoran Knight next to Ley Coster yanked his head back and sliced his throat. The blade tore through sinew and bone, a crushing, macabre display of brutality. All the while the elderly Ley weakly struggled, his fingers grasping the last of life, his mouth shouting without sound. Blood painted the Balikian stones.

There was no breath left in Hira's body. She was only able to gasp at the act. Silence descended over the nobles as they realized the future they would share with such a woman in power.

Ley Coster's body twitched, and he fell backwards on the ground as his blood pooled around him. His wide eyes watching the last of the Hall of Balikian Kings. They were the ones he had served. They were the ones who'd failed him.

440

Chapter Forty-Four

HIRA

Her uncle's Ley was sprawled, naked, and desecrated. Butchered in front of the noble court.

"I'm so sorry," Hira whispered, not knowing to who she actually spoke anymore.

To the man they just murdered? To Almira? To her uncle and mother? To the gods? The same thing would happen to her. With her life, she would make sure the queen lived. She swore it.

Furia looked down at the court. In Hira's eyes, she was the epitome of evil. Arrigo did not compare with his show of removing Almira's undergarments. The true villain stood before the Istokian court, a thing of beauty and wickedness.

"The High Lord deceived each one of you and this man aided in his charade. I forgive you. Let it be known that traitors end this way. Naked. In their own blood. *Unveiled.*"

The nobility shifted. There wasn't a murmur. The silence was louder than words. They were afraid. She had dominated them with her strength in one swift kill. They were nobles, not warriors, they were rich merchants who ate at clothed tables and drank wine from goblets. The stench of fear overpowered the smell of blood. It was unbearable.

"Killing someone who disagrees with you is not ruling. It's madness. It's terror. *That's* what you've brought to Istok," Hira shouted as she met Furia's eyes.

The lady's nostrils flared. "*Cousin*, I'd almost forgotten you."

"Cover his body!"

Furia sat back down and fluffed her dress. Ensuring that despite her cruelty, she looked like a High Lady.

"I have a letter for you too," Furia said.

Hira remained unmoved, even though her stomach tightened. She wasn't going to give Furia the satisfaction. No matter what the paper said.

"Don't you think she's had enough, lover?" Justan said, curling his hand over hers.

She snatched it away, and he inhaled sharply. The tone of his voice was intimate, as if he'd often whispered it in the night, entangled in sheets.

"Did you just address me without title, *Garian*?" Furia hissed with her eyes still focused on the parchment in her hand.

Justan flinched. "Lady Furia," he ground out.

Furia grunted and straightened the piece of paper. "Lord Pyos, escort Commander Justan out if he interrupts proceedings once more. Perhaps he can join his brother in the dungeons."

Lord Pyos, the knight who'd killed Ley Coster, came to stand by Justan. The commander's eyes focused back on the floor and all that Hira could think was "*coward!*" He disgusted her. To think she'd admired his hands and the shape of his nails. He stood there, soaked in cowardice, and she'd been blind to it all along, focused on his fine chest and charming smiles.

"Lady Hira, did you run away from Korkoran two years ago to serve the High Lady Almira?" Furia glanced up at her. "Did you abandon your home, your title, your betrothed to serve as a *guard* to the High Lady of Suid?"

Hira said nothing. She'd yanked so hard on her bindings that the chains had cut her skin, and blood seeped down to the floor of her witness stand. She wished to strip all the meat from her hands and reach Furia with the bones so she could choke her to death right on the seat.

"Nothing to say? Commander, you said it was Barnabus Carrian, which they promised her to, didn't you?" Furia spoke to Justan but stared at Hira.

Hira's chest heaved. She'd given Justan all the tools to destroy her family. *Willingly,* she had done so. He'd lapped it up and fed it to Furia for a pat on the head. Like a dog.

Furia smiled. "Yes. I believe it *was.* Lord Barnabus! Is Lord Barnabus amongst us?"

A short man stepped forward as the nobles moved aside. He was a little disheveled, but still calm and self-assured.

"My lady," his voice was stronger than she expected.

Then he looked at Hira. Truly looked at her, and then back at Furia. Hira's breath hitched. She had cast this man aside.

"Did the Lady Hira spurn your agreement weeks before your union?" Furia burrowed into the seat with a mocking smile.

As he considered the question, Lord Barnabus cleared his throat and clutched his hands behind him. He looked like he'd truly pondered it. Hira wasn't certain what to think, as she'd only met him briefly.

"Well, my lady, one could hardly blame her. She was no more than a girl and I'm a bald old man," he said with a chuckle.

A few nobles laughed as Hira stared at Lord Barnabus, stunned. Warmth crept into her chest, and she was ashamed of how she had treated him. She turned to Furia, who looked positively enraged, and Hira felt a sudden fear that Lord Barnabus would end up naked and dead before the hour was done.

"But to answer your question, she did. I've since found happiness with bird watching. It's a lovely task, wouldn't you say? We have wonderful woods behind Carrian Manor and I find it a perfect place for the sighting of persils, alstrals, and the occasional eagles. There's a slew of them this season. Her Ladyship really should visit," Barnabus said as he finished with a delightful smile.

Hira held her breath as he leisurely completed his statement; poised and assured. She knew that Furia would kill him. Justan looked at him and then back to Hira with fear in his eyes.

Silence coated the hall. Furia stared at Lord Barnabus, but he calmly surveyed her with a pleasant composition. As if before them all was not a dead man, naked and humiliated.

At this moment, Hira admired no one more. She remembered how she wallowed in self-pity after her mother presented him as a prospect. All along, he'd been a brave man, and she'd discarded him in her shallowness.

Furia had wide, manic eyes. She went back to her letter.

Lord Barnabus melted back into the crowd, but Hira could have sworn he looked at her and gave a nod. She had an ally. It filled her with gratitude that at least one person remained loyal to her, that Furia had failed to manipulate. At least someone would have pity on her dead body after Furia killed her.

Furia cleared her throat.

Queen Almira,

My cousin, you must allow me to return! Each day closer to home brings me closer to the end. I'm alone and desperate. You know me above all others; you know I'm not fit to rule! I am not you. I don't want this, please believe me I shan't survive. I shan't find happiness in this task! Give me anything else to do! Send me to war! Allow me to look after the king on the battlefield so that I might find glory in death and not death in life! I am on my knees imploring your mercy. I care not what happens to Istok! Istok is no longer my home. It is a prison, a punishment!

Hira felt faint as she stared at the crumpled paper Furia held. She looked at Mr. Hyall, who had a smug expression, and she recalled how she crushed the letter and threw it on the floor. How he'd innocently cleaned up and offered her comfort.

Fool!

Furia let the silence sit, fat and happy. The nobles stared at Hira, but she couldn't look at anyone. She was overwhelmed with utter shame at the weak girl who had desperately penned that letter in the bowels of a ship.

"This seems to be your writing, my lady," Furia purred. "Do

you deny it?"

Hira clutched her bloodied hands and stood as straight as she could, even if she wanted to buckle. To beg for understanding. But she wouldn't. She must accept what she had been. Face it. She hadn't returned from death's door to humble herself further.

Today, she would have to be brave. Braver than she'd ever been. Even if one's deeds were mortifying. In that moment, she realized that bravery had nothing to do with swords and killing. Bravery was knowing who you were at all times. Even if your worst enemy held you prisoner; shackled, naked, and beaten. As long as you knew who you were and what you'd done, you were the bravest person in the room.

And she was Hira Balik, a descendant of royals. The last Balikian princess. Heir to a prosperous land.

"Might you want to see it closer? Commander Justan, take it to her. Perhaps she forgets her words," Furia said in a pleasant tone.

Hira looked at the empty wall of the hall. She wished her ancestors didn't witness the shame she brought upon their country.

Justan stood before her with the letter. His eyes were blank and neutral. They didn't judge her. Furia had sucked out everything that made Justan the man Hira thought to love. He was a shell. She stared at him and not at the paper.

"I do not deny it," Hira said with a steady voice. And perhaps she was not denying loving him, even now, when he crushed her with his indifference.

"Speak up darling, we can't hear you," Furia said with a laugh caught in her throat.

Hira swallowed as Justan turned back to stand next to Furia. It didn't matter that she'd been tricked and fooled and betrayed. She focused on the sapphire eyes of the dragons in the murals. Their cold stares were an unshakable strength that she allowed to arm her.

She was Hira Balik. She was a dragon. She was… *vishap*. She'd been that since she was born. She'd been that before she loved, and she would continue to be that through her hate and shame.

"I do not deny writing this in a moment of desperation," Hira said loudly.

Furia laughed, head thrown back. Had it not been for her malice, she would have been the most beautiful woman alive.

"Glory in death and not death in life! By your own hand, my lady."

The nobility appraised Hira. She was as calm as she could be. Then a bold one stepped forward and spat at her. When the spit landed on her face, she jumped back. Then another spat at her. And another. She held her hands up to shield herself from the attacks, but they quickly covered her hands with drool.

"There you have it!" Furia chuckled. Slowly she stood and walked over the Ley's dead body. She got so close Hira could attack her, but it would be folly.

"As you have named Istok, your prison and your punishment... I will deliver you. Lady Hira, House Balik, first of your name, I have accused you of treason and found you guilty. You are hereby sentenced to death by beheading on the morning the queen rides through the gates. By order of the Lady of Istok." She leaned forward so that Hira could smell her scent, the oils on her skin, the soap in her hair. "I want your head to land on her lap," she hissed quietly.

Hira realized something when she met her eyes. She didn't fear death. Not anymore, and Furia couldn't take that away from her. No one could. Perhaps her arm and her trials were to give her the dignity she needed for this moment.

"I have danced with the ghouls of the night, and I am not afraid of you." Hira smiled. "You do not know your sister. Almira will avenge me. She will carve my name into your skin, and you will beg for death before the end."

Furia reached out and gently, almost lovingly, touched Hira's scarred face. "Almira won't leave this castle alive."

Chapter Forty-Five

JUSTAN

It was not until they pulled Hira out of the hall that Furia turned her attention to the nobles. He was no longer in the spotlight. He made a grand show of heaving the Ley's body by his foot out of the hallway and, when he found a secluded corner, he slumped as he stared at the old man's body. He pressed his back against the stone, breathing deeply as he felt the contraction in his chest. He panicked and couldn't breathe. He had to put his hand in his mouth to stop the screams.

Oh gods. They wouldn't make it. He'd have to watch Quent and Hira killed in the same manner. He should have wrangled them out of the ship and tried to escape. Even if Hira fought him the entire way.

I cannot do this.

He thought of the scowl on the High Lord's face whenever Justan was overcome with his feelings. He felt tears in his eyes and pressed his fingers against them.

Breathe. He needed to breathe. He couldn't break down now, not when they were so close, not when help was only days away.

"Critical thought separates man from animals."

Beltran's voice was sharp in his memories. Critical thought. He needed to determine the angles, to find a solution, a way of appeasing them all, and attempt to save Hira from further torture. He was suddenly nineteen and listening to the High Lord as he paced before him and gave lesson after lesson.

Think of their objectives, he would say.

What did Furia want? She wanted Hira to suffer. She wanted to punish Quent for Justan's change. Alright. How can she continue torturing Hira? She wanted to break her. How could she break her? His skin was cold as he exhaled. She would allow her men to rape Hira as Quent watched.

No. Gods. How to deflect this?

"Appeal to their corrupt nature, make them believe you think like them," Beltran would've said.

Think like them. Be barbaric like them. He hadn't bedded Furia in months. She'd resented his lack of enthusiasm, serving only to fortify her beliefs that he wasn't behaving like himself. He needed to rectify that quickly. He had to calm her and soothe her. Convince her that he was with her. Distract her. How? When? It would be a lot of work. She thickly held onto anger. Like molasses in a jar, she wouldn't disentangle her ire with simple caresses. She would make him work to earn his forgiveness. He needed to be brutal, like her. Barbaric, like her. He had mere hours before she would concoct the idea of having Hira abused.

Then, in his mind, the dead body shifted. He stared at it in horror. The eyes opened, pure white. The mouth moved, encased in blood.

"Compose yourself. I don't matter. My time was long called," and the voice was a whisper of death. "We are not born for a good life. We are born for a reason. We serve this country. The dead are dead and gone and you, young man, are still alive."

And the vision left, and the body was unmoved and desecrated. Justan had a violent need to vomit.

Managing his shivers, he straightened out and dusted his pants. He swallowed and forced his feet to move. One foot before the other, focused on the end goal. Help would soon come, and then it would *all* finally be over. He could do this. He *must* do this. For Quent and Hira. For the queen and Istok. For Beltran and his schemes.

He found servants and instructed them to wrap the body and take it to the burial chamber. With one last lingering look at Ley Coster's corpse, he turned to continue the charade.

"I am a star-son of the night sky," he whispered and stepped into the hall.

Furia had dismissed the nobles. Furia lingered in the high seat, speaking with Mr. Hyall and her goons, who provided her updates and congratulations on her performance.

"There'll be not a tremble from the lot. You guaranteed that." Hyall stuffed his pipe and laughed.

Seizing a sharp breath, he strode with the perfect Justan stroll he'd perfected. His eyes locked on Furia as she lazily stared at him.

"Except for Barnabus Carrian," Justan sneered. "It would have been the ultimate lesson if I had speared him. Even better, dragged him to the dungeons to see if he would spot any astrals from there."

A slow smile captured Furia's face, but it was not a friendly one. He knew all her smiles. "Are you certain you don't hate him because he was once going to marry the fine lady?"

Justan snatched a cigar from a sailor who protested. He slapped the man with a turn of his hand. It was a harsh hit that resounded in the hall. The sailor looked uncertain if he should retaliate. The man backed down after Justan gave him a glare of disgust.

He slowly brought the cigar to his lips as he turned back to Furia. "Did you not *see* her, lover? A few weeks ago, she was something worth looking at. Now..." he snarled his lip. "I may be hard up, but I'd not give her the pleasure."

Furia's face brightened, and she looked at Hyall. "Maybe that is what the lady needs. A good fucking. I don't know why I didn't think of it before. I'm such a terrible host."

"Aye," Hyall said with a smile. "Many people would benefit from a good fuck."

His stomach erupted in such pain that it took all his strength not to scream No. He fisted the hand in his coat and stepped closer to Furia, ensuring his voice remained stoic.

"Pointless, if you ask me. Did I tell you she was desperate for it?" He glanced at Furia with a conspiratorial look. "The rougher the better. She couldn't come until I hurt her. Once I had to make her bleed."

Furia's chin lifted in contemplation. "No woman enjoys rape, lover."

Justan smiled rakishly. "This one *might*. I think there is no point given her days are ending quickly. Would be a shame to provide her pleasure when all we wish is to torture her. Listen to this bit. The last night, she demanded I tie her up and beat her. I was so damn tired at that point that I falsified a pain in my shoulder," he said with a chuckle, staring at the cigar, keenly aware that Furia watched him to detect his lies. "The stupid girl believed me." And he cackled, "She provided me a shoulder rub."

Furia smiled, an authentic smile of delight. "Was she truly terrible?"

"Aye," he nodded. "It's easy for a woman to fake it, but a man? The thoughts I had to conjure, lover."

She pondered on this, tapping the dragon heads with her nails. He was so desperate for the lies to be accepted that he almost screamed. He moved closer to her when she lingered in her thoughts. With expert hands, he slid them down her arm, caressing her along the way. She stiffened at first but didn't pull away. He called that a win.

He moaned like a desperate lover as he moved his lips closer to her hair.

"Maybe I could do it and you watch. What do you think? That might be a nice little game," he whispered.

At that, she yanked her hand back and waved it around. "No. I don't want you near her, and this entire plan bores me. There must be another way of making her suffer and entertaining ourselves in the meantime."

Relief covered his entire body, and his knees almost buckled. But he needed to look dismayed. Furia would regard his disappointment as part of his punishment. The malice he had to postulate would slowly suck out all the good within his soul. Had it not been for Hira these past few weeks, he would be nothing more than a crab shell who'd long lost its master.

He dimly heard them all speak about beating her bloody and, despite wishing to come up with another lie, another tantalizing reason for them not to hurt her anymore, he knew Furia's boundaries. She would recognize the farce if he protested again. He had to allow Hira to be hurt. She was stronger than anyone he knew. She could take it. They wouldn't break her because... *he* had broken her already.

When the time called, he chimed in, landing the perfect Justan statement for their malice and evil plans. Furia warmed to him as he joined in on their fervor. She put her hand upon his thigh after she allowed him to sit on the armrest. He disgusted himself, but he must do this. He kept Quent and Hira's face in mind the entire time. The hours would slog from here on out until the queen's arrival.

Furia took to her drink, as she loved to do, and he encouraged her. Bringing more bottles from Beltran's prized cellars, suggesting more vintages to sample, commenting on how angry her father would be at her so carelessly drinking his wine.

She was so drunk by the time night settled that her caresses and kisses became sloppy, just as he intended. He lifted her up and rushed her to Lady Marai's rooms, kicking the door open in the manner he knew would delight her.

He tossed her on the bed and watched her eyes become lethargic.

"Call me by my title, Garian," her voice was husky.

Perhaps he should've given her more drink. He might not get away with it now because he avoided bedding her for so long. He wasn't sure how he would manage. Nothing about her enticed him, everything about her disgusted him.

"My Lady of Istok," he whispered as he hovered over her.

Her smile was sleepy, but she grabbed his hair and kissed him. He put on a good show, digging his hands into her hair and hearing her moan into his mouth.

"This was a very good try," she purred. "But you're not fucking me. I'm still angry at you."

If he was a singer, he would sing the highest note he could reach and let it lift into the mountains in praise. But Justan would be angry, upset, and hurt. He sharpened his brow and frowned.

"It's been *months*. All I have is the redhead cunt's taste in my mouth," he attempted a complaint.

This delighted her, as he knew it would. She laughed and looked up at him flirtatiously, caressing his face.

"My poor darling," she murmured. "I'll allow you in my bed. Lay down and hold me. That's all you get today. Perhaps when I kill the queen, we can fuck drenched in her blood. A celebration. Right here on this bed so that Marai's spirit can watch me defile her room."

Her words were so outlandish and demonic that it left him breathless. His expression seemed to be appropriate because she read it as lust and laughed.

"We're going to burn the world down," she blinked, and sleep overtook her.

"And then… you'll be queen and I'll worship at your feet," he whispered.

And like the end of a terrible day, she slept. His shoulders slumped, and he blinked, taking in the room. Desperate to see something other than Furia. Something to center him and remind himself of who he was and why he did what he did.

He found it on Lady Marai's dresser. A paper folded with such care yet at the same time opened many times. It was a letter written in Marai's hands, edited many times as if sentiments came and changed as time came and went. The months spent composing it changed the woman's handwriting. The letters, once smooth and elegant, morphed to jagged jutted points, a symphony that spoke of her declining health.

~~Hira~~ *Daughter,*

~~I demand you return to your ancestral home.~~ I miss you. ~~You've no concept of what you've left behind, what you've caused in your departure.~~ When you were four and we rode the long carriage journey to come here, you fell asleep on my lap.

~~You've a duty to your country and people.~~ *I foolishly thought at that time that like me, you could stay in the shadows of these political games.* ~~Your behavior has shown me that you're still a child, rebelling so callously against your responsibility.~~ *But the gods had other plans and when that happened, I was keenly aware that I was no longer your mother but your guide.* ~~My ire for you knows no bounds.~~ *I knew I had to ensure you would be strong enough to withstand the tide that attacks with no respite.* ~~How dare you dishonor this house and opt for such a profession as a guard?~~ *It's not an easy life to lead a country. There is no praise allotted for the sleepless nights and the difficult decisions.* ~~I wasted years attempting to make you see reason.~~ *And I wish I could gather you in my arms and protect you from it all, but I cannot.* ~~That you should think your feelings more important that any one else's.~~ *I don't wish to leave you. I wish to hold you and care for you and shield you with my own weakened body.* ~~I am ashamed of you.~~ *I only had you for a few years, and I still recall the scent of your hair.* ~~Upon receiving this letter, pack your things and return.~~ *I love you more than anything in this world and I beg the gods, if they would listen, that you will live.* ~~You'll study harder and more fervently than ever in the hopes that one day you'll understand your duty.~~ *I pray they send you protectors and helpers so they may watch over you when I no longer can.* ~~I will not go easy on you for you do not deserve it.~~ *You are strong, Hira.* ~~And you'll pay your penance as you should.~~ *Don't let anyone ever make you believe otherwise.*

~~*Lady Marai, House Balik.*~~
May the gods protect you, my girl.

The letter broke his heart. Lady Marai played a fantastic role of not caring, much like he did. But inside, she held nothing but love for her daughter. Much like he did. He'd spent much of his time in this castle disliking the woman, and now they shared the same goal. Protectors. Helpers. Though Marai had vastly disliked him, little did she know that the man she held in contempt would answer her prayers. Afraid that Furia might find this letter and destroy it, he folded it as small as he could and tucked it in his pocket. He hoped to one day give it to Hira, as Marai intended.

Determined, he crept to the door as quietly as possible.

He could sneak into the dungeons if they'd posted no guards.

Luck was not on his side. The door opened and there sat Hyall, spearing him with a glare. The man had never trusted him. When Furia wasn't around, he saw too much of the real him.

Before the man could chastise him for attempting to leave his precious lady, Justan sneered at him.

"We require more wine. Send one of your little boys to do it and make it quick," Justan said, and closed the door.

Chapter Forty-Six

HIRA

They dragged her by the small patches of hair left on her head, then they threw her back into the cell. Quent instantly rushed to her.

Her knees slammed against the stone as she landed on the floor. She couldn't say anything. She was afraid that if she opened her mouth, a wail would escape. She could handle death; she didn't fear a painful end. But she was afraid of the world she left behind, jumbled, bleeding, and desecrated. Like Ley Coster's body.

He helped her sit and leaned her against the wall, then fretted. She hardly registered his movements. All she could think on was the hell she'd lived and the hell she still must see before the end. She envied those that died quickly.

"You're bleeding." His fingers touched her wrists.

Hira's mouth was thick with tears she'd clutched to herself. "Of my own doing."

Quent furrowed his brows. He already seemed older. Worry stole away that lovely childish energy he carried. Life was cruel that way. It sought out purity and pulled it by its root, exposed it to the harshness of the world and enjoyed how it dried out hope.

"Where's Ley Coster?" he asked softly. Innocence.

Hira closed her eyes. The memory of his death was raw, the

wound of his loss seeped pus. "They found him guilty of treason. Furia killed him."

There was no need to hide anything from the boy now. He would have to become a man faster than Justan ever intended. She would be the one to pull his roots. She rather he know, be *aware*, so he had time to dry. He needed to be wilted if he was going to survive. It was the only gift she could give him.

"No, sh-she wouldn't." His face was pale, and he shook his head.

"She did. She had him stripped naked before the nobility and had his throat slit. I assume his body is still there for all to see," she whispered.

He stumbled back, his hair falling over his face. "And you? Will she kill you as well?"

She leaned her head against the dragon stones. "When the queen arrives, I'm to be beheaded, in such a way that my head lands on her lap."

It left Quent without words. He looked around the cell, as if searching for ideas, for clues, for options.

He said the most innocent thing. "Justan won't let that happen."

Hira wrapped her hands around his tender soul, then wrapped her fist around it. Then, with of her might, she *yanked*. To save him, she harshly yanked on his idealism.

"He watched as they murdered Ley Coster, and did nothing. He will allow me the same curtesy."

A tiny sob escaped him, and he covered his mouth with his hands, shaking his head vigorously. Hira knew that pain well. It was a pain that could not be seen. She understood why Suidians pounded their chest when in pain. Because words were useless. Words are nothing but humanity's attempt to express what can never be expressed. An attempt to capture a moment, an emotion, a loss. But words were nothing. Words were vapor in the air. Words didn't provide life. Words didn't save.

"But he loved you. I saw it!" Quent cried.

"That was not love, darling," Hira said softly. "It was a role well-played and you and I the willing audience. He's a talented performer."

She sighed and looked at her hands. She'd scraped the skin from her wrists. It didn't even hurt; she felt no pain or discomfort. She could imagine her hands on Furia's throat. Watching the light expire from her eyes. But it wouldn't be her who would kill Furia. She'd not earned it. She'd tossed her country aside in the naivete of her selfish youth. No matter how much she wished it, Furia's death would not be hers. Death would come to her via someone else long after Hira's beheading.

To think all she'd lived through and survived, to die in such a manner without avenging herself, felt rather pointless. The pain of her wounds, that entire odyssey. The only thing she could hold on to—the one hope—was that Zeita brought her back for a reason. She wouldn't have saved her simply for her to face decapitation. She just needed to provide Almira and Sanaa with enough warning to save the kingdom and her people. Her life would be worth that. That would be her legacy.

"I'll save you, my lady, I promise!" Quent insisted.

"You'll *not*," Hira said. "Look at me. You'll survive on your own after I die. She'll hurt you. Justan won't be there to protect you. She'll hurt you to punish him. You submit to survive. You understand me?"

His jaw tightened as he swallowed. "I can take pain as well."

"She's evil. Do you understand? *Evil*. She told Justan she would throw him in these dungeons if he interrupted the proceedings again." She needed him to understand the danger he was in. His worth depended on what he meant to Justan.

Quent shifted away, coiled, as if burned. "But... but we're the star sons of the night sky," he cried with deep hurt as his chest heaved.

Hira grasped his hand and pulled him in. He sobbed as she took his face.

"You need to know what you're facing. You should *fear* her. Fear doesn't make us weak. Fear makes us courageous. Weakness gives us strength. We have to be weak before we can be strong."

His little face tightened as he nodded. "Show me how to fight because I *will* avenge you, my lady. I'll become the greatest swordsman in the world and defeat her. I swear it."

From that moment on, she showed him the battle moves that she'd learned from the Red Guard. These were rigorous movements and even when he coughed, she reminded him he wasn't sick. That thought made him push past his exhaustion. She would tap his face when he wanted to give up.

"Remember what she did to you," Hira would hiss.

His eyes would darken, and he would force himself further.

"Each time you feel you're too weak, remember how she tortured you for years and you endured it, and you are here now! You're alive and you made it. You survived!"

She reminded herself of her old Master Elio. She realized she had not seen him. Where was he? Her stomach turned cold. Furia couldn't have hurt him. He was skilled and smart. He would be hiding if he wasn't in the castle. He was waiting. Biding his time. Perhaps warning Almira. That *was* something he would do. Maybe he'd warned her already. Maybe *he* would save the kingdom. There was no one more loyal than Master Elio.

For days she trained Quent. It was harsh training, and they both succumbed to exhaustion at certain times.

Each day, when the afternoon was almost done, four soldiers would enter the cell, hold Quent back and beat her bloody. Hira never begged them to stop. She took it. She survived. She had to survive. For Quent, for Almira, for her people. Once the wooziness and sharp pain ebbed, she would sit up and hold Quent as he cried on her shoulder. Then she would shake him, and they would begin training again. Each day he cried less, and each day, despite the wounds she carried and her bruised face, she felt more resolute. She was the Lady of Istok. She would rather they beat her than hurt her people.

She woke up one night to find him practicing on his own. The more he practiced, the stronger of mind he became, and she thought he might survive. She hoped he would.

It was near the midnight hour on the fifth day when movement in the darkness woke her. Quent was snoring with his mouth open, so she knew it wasn't him. Hira didn't move and pretended to be asleep, keeping herself absolutely still. It might only be a rat, but she didn't want to take chances.

It was a rat.

"Hira," Justan whispered in the darkness.

He'd cloaked himself in black until all she could see was his beard in the shadows. He looked worse than ever, with pale lips and haggard skin. His eyes looked over her with a mixture of anger and sadness.

"Gods," he whispered as he took in her face.

"Came to gloat?" she said with a raised a brow.

He scanned the area, then looked at her. "I have little time. Is he harmed?"

A disgusted Hira stared at him. "He's in a dungeon watching me get bloodied night after night. What do you think?"

His hands slid around the bars of the cell and he stared at her in the way he used to. With wide brown eyes. "I've been doing everything I can to keep you alive. I need you to hold on."

Naturally, he would paint himself as her savior. She chuckled and looked away.

"Pathetic. How did I fall in love with such a pathetic man?"

A part of her delighted in trashing him with cunning words. She reminded herself of Almira and, though a part of her recoiled from such behavior, a greater part of her relished in them. There was such anger in her that she couldn't control her actions.

He was silent for a while before taking a deep breath. "I... I am playing a part."

"Yes, I know all about your thespian talent," she mused then leaned back. There was such freedom to be found when one wasn't affected by words.

He heard a noise from the door and looked around. "She'll realize I'm missing."

"From her bed?" She smiled at him in a dark, insidious manner.

He looked rightfully ashamed. "Yes. She's taken your mother's quarters."

She looked away from him and watched Quent, the gentle rise and fall of his chest. Justan said nothing. He pressed his head against the bars in the cell.

"The lies you must tell yourself. I almost pity you," she said.

A part of her was pitying him. He had the potential to be a great man, but people are not their potential, they are their actions.

"You can hate me. I don't blame you for that. One day I hope to tell you what I've had to do," he said, his voice drenched in regret. "What I've had to witness. How I've had to live. But everything you've seen from the moment we entered Treveri has been a part I've played."

"Played the part for who exactly?" Hira asked in a deceptive neutral tone.

He pressed his face against the bars of the cell as he grasped them. His eyes were dark and his knuckles pale. "I love my country, but I never—ever—intended to love you. But I did. Somehow, I did, and it complicated everything. But I don't regret it. My time with you meant more to me…" He sighed, "I knew what awaited—"

Despite his tortured tone, she couldn't forgive him. She couldn't understand him. His secrets could destroy a kingdom. When hundreds of thousands would die because he couldn't dispense with the truth.

She shook her head. "And yet you did nothing. You still do nothing."

He swallowed and nodded. "Beltran trained me for this moment. Do you understand? I made him a promise and I'll succeed in that, even if you hate me. Even if it kills me. As long as you and Quent are safe, I will succeed."

"Safe?" she scoffed and faced him so he could truly see her. She hoped he saw it all. The bruises, the cuts, her missing tooth, the butchered hair. All of it. "Look at me. Your lies did this. Try saying you love me now that I look like this."

He swallowed thickly and his eyes watered. "I love you, Hira. I—"

"Don't call me by my name. I am a lady, sir. I may not wear silks, but I am not your equal. You're a betrayer to the crown. A condemned man and I will die for the pleasure of the madwoman you fuck," she snarled.

His face shifted, as if she'd slapped him, and she desperately wished she could slap him. He'd deserved as much.

"I am your ally. I swear it on everything I am." His fingers curled tighter over the metal bars.

"Well, you're a liar, so that cancels it out." She looked away from him. "And I've no interest in your lies. I've fallen asleep to the tune of them, and I'll sleep no more."

His knuckles began to turn white as his grip on the bars hardened. "Can you even comprehend my self-loathing for what I've had to do? How many times have I placed a blade at my throat to end it all? Do you know what stopped me?" He pointed to Quent's sleeping form. "That one there. He's the only thing I have ever had. He is sacred to me!"

His words formed an opportunity in her mind. She very much doubted the love he claimed to have for her, but she didn't doubt his love for his brother. It was genuine. She'd seen it many times. At the very least, she would ensure Quent's survival. She moved closer to him.

"You understand that to hurt you and control you, she'll harm Quent."

Justan shook his head in denial, but she nodded.

"She will. She'll make you watch as they rape him. Do you understand that?" Hira sneaked closer to him. "And still you come to me warm from her bed to tell me Quent is sacred?"

The tears she'd not meant to spill sprinkled against her eyes. He was her greatest disappointment. The marionette to Furia's plans.

"No one will harm Quent. They'll have to kill me first," he said adamantly.

She formed the most malignant smile she could manage. She would slice him open in the same manner his deceit had gutted her. "Commander, she's already harmed Quent. What did they do to him for a 'cure'?" Hira paused and allowed her words to fester in his thoughts. "Where did they probe him?" She came closer until they nearly touched. His face twisted in agony. "Aren't you tired of your impotency?"

His eyes met hers and she swore that for a moment she saw the same fire and strength he had portrayed on the ship. There was a small flicker of that flame. He was in there, crushed and buried, but he was in there. She had to hope. She had nothing else.

"When the queen arrives, you're going to have to decide once and for all the man you're going to be. Not for me, not even for yourself, because you don't deserve it, but for Quent," Hira hissed. "If you wish to keep your brother safe, you're going to have to turn against her. And if you die doing so." She paused and studied his face once more, recalling his softness. "Then you die."

Chapter Forty-Seven

SANAA

In the evening of the fifth day of the week, Sanaa and Delara prepared to separate from the royal party. Woolen capes cloaked the Red Guard to hide their armor and weapons.

Outside of Treveri was a vast land filled with rolling hills. King Alton and Thebo hid their armies at the base of a mound half-a-mile ride to the gates of the city. They would have to march them at full speed in the morning to arrive on time to sack the city. It would be a bloodbath.

In the middle of this was Almira, pretending she wasn't in labor. As they crossed the Istokian countryside, the pains began. The midwife checked her, sprawled out over the grass with the Red Guard surrounding her and the king kneeling next to her, his face pale and gravely concerned.

The midwife pulled her hand back and smiled. "Good news. We have time. She's tightly closed. It'll be hours before the baby breaches."

Almira grunted and her head went back as she grimaced. The king held her up and demanded she stop this madness. But Almira's eyes were set into a determined line. The king cursed and raged, but

Almira wouldn't have it. With the help of Sanaa and M, she rose from the ground.

"You heard her. I have hours. I need my dress on now," she insisted.

And so, in the dark fields of Istok, they dressed the queen in her armored gown. She looked like a spot of red blood amongst a sea of metal.

As Sanaa made ready to detach from the group, she noticed Kaia take charge of the envoy. They would ride ahead and hide in the city. They'd disguised themselves, dressed in peasant clothing, ragged and full of holes. It also helped that they smelled. They'd been collecting the droppings of the eagles and carried them in their pockets.

"*Pidda*," Sanaa called to her.

Pidda, stupid girl in Freenian.

Kaia raised a brow and slowly turned to her. She placed a hand on her hip and smirked. "Don't give me nicknames, Captain. I'd think you like me."

Sanaa's nostrils flared, and she pointed her finger at her. "Get the best vantage point and try nothing heroic."

Kaia laughed and mounted her horse in one quick jump. She pulled the reins and smiled. "You don't need to worry. I'm not a hero. I leave that to you."

And with that, she turned her horse and led the envoy. Delara, ever watchful, stood next to Sanaa and studied her.

"Well, Captain," Delara said in silent amusement. "That's the first woman I've seen that doesn't melt into your arms."

Sanaa stalked away from her to where the Red Guard awaited. M held on to Sanaa's horse and softly petted its nose. Madhavi glanced at her and sensed her dark humor, but Sanaa had no intention of discussing anything.

"Say nothing," she said, and took the reins from M.

She paused and looked at M for a moment. They stared at one another, her Suidian companion. Her complete opposite in every way. From their likes and preferences to their temperament. Yet she'd grown used to the woman's presence and friendship.

On impulse, Sanaa extended out a hand and M looked at it, then back at her. She grasped her fingers and shook tightly.

Sanaa wished to say something like, "take care," or, "mind the queen," but all words seemed child-like, statements of a youthful mind. M noticed and she smiled.

"Say nothing." M tightened her grip.

A jagged pebble landed in Sanaa's throat, and she felt a sudden sense of emptiness. As they beheld one another in the dimming light, it was as if Sanaa were alone. As if she held a ghost.

The captain nodded tersely and jumped on her horse. She looked down at M as the Red Guard mounted around her. Despite desiring to express her gratitude for the woman, she'd never had the talent for such things. Words needed careful consideration, lest they be used against you. Sanaa looked at her one last time and rounded her beast, the rest of the Red Guard close at her heels.

They rode until the night was dark and foreboding and the ocean waves crashed against the coast.

As planned, they followed the side trail from the Cliffs of Lamya down into the pits that led to the forgotten beaches. The locals called the area forgotten because, once moored here, they did not find the men again. A barren rock inhospitable for horses. This was the path young Pristok used when Lady Marai and Ley Coster sent her on her journey. Sanaa committed to memory the steps the girl shared with her and now retraced them.

They tied their beasts in a crop of trees and descended onto the beach through a steep staircase seldom used. A few of the girls slipped, but Delara and Sanaa kept them going. It was cold against the wind and, at times, Sanaa swore she heard the singing of women deep in the ocean.

She shivered. Mystical land full of witches and enchantresses. Most unnatural.

By the light of the merciful moon, she finally set her feet on the sand. Most of the girls were shaking, their fingers cut from clutching the rock to prevent themselves from toppling forward. Sanaa allowed them a repose, but they didn't have long. Midnight was upon them.

They walked around the beach and Sanaa hoped to spot the small boat Pristok said she'd used. They meandered the sand for an hour, their feet wet with the waves, their hands chapped from grasping the stone. If they caught the high tide, death would quickly claim them.

Sanaa led, while Delara brought up the back. The girls seldom complained, and Sanaa gave them credit for their valor and endurance. This would be their hardest test yet.

Just as she thought the ravenous sea had eaten the boat, she saw a faint outline of a partially sunken rower tied tightly against a rail. As best they could, they pulled the rower from the belly of the sea. The small thing floated as if awaiting command. Sanaa gave Pristok credit for tying the knot so well, along with the oar.

Good girl, she thought.

Only seven could fit, which meant they needed to do three trips and time was not on their side. Sanaa took the first girls and with great difficulty she rowed them around the massive rock. Lord Beltran was not exaggerating when he boasted that Korkoran was impenetrable. Such a trip would be a massive disaster for a large crew.

One girl spotted the mouth of the cave as they rounded the cliff and Sanaa was relieved the trip took no more than ten minutes. Still, she had to be quick, for they still needed to get to the gate.

Once she offloaded the girls into the grotto, they clung to the walls and shook, their bodies unused to the sea waves. Sanaa herself felt faint, but she couldn't collapse, not now. She turned the boat around and went back for the next set and she did it once more until she had Delara. The lady took over the rowing and Sanaa sank in exhaustion against the gunwale.

"How much time do we have?" Sanaa asked once they all huddled against the cave entrance.

Shivering, Delara looked at her with drenched hair and pale lips. "Not long. We must make haste."

And so they did. One by one, they made a line as they began their ascent into Korkoran, the most protected fortress in the world. One way in, one way out. It was at least ten flights of stairs, only there was no landing portion. Just a steady spiral where the walls closed in on them until their shoulder plates scraped against the stone and it felt they were slithering to their deaths.

The atmosphere was damp and stuffy. Under their armor, they became desperate for breath. Some of the girls panicked, the sense of being trapped overwhelming them. Delara took off her gloves, grasped their temples, and chanted ancient Pistian hymns deep in her chest until they felt the vibrations, and calmed. It was a hellish time. Sanaa could do little if they were found. It would be a butchering, and their bodies would rot where they fell, encased in the Istokian tomb.

At long last, Sanaa felt the change in the atmosphere. A shy breeze flirted against her cheek. She rushed the last few steps and came upon the gate.

"It's here!" she hissed quietly. "Make no noise!"

The girls, ecstatic to reach their end, pressed forward, desperate for a particle of fresh air. Compacted as they were, they settled for resting on the steps, leaning on one another as they awaited their host.

"It must be midnight," some whispered.

"What if they captured the traitor? What if we're stuck?"

Sanaa paid them no mind, her eyes were in the dungeons. Distantly, the bells of Treveri rang as the hour struck midnight. They were on time and relief flooded her. She bid them all to quiet, her ears straining to capture any sound. The seconds seemed like minutes; the minutes dragged to weeks.

And finally, in the dark depth, she could discern steps. The lightest steps she'd ever heard. A skilled spy.

The enormous shadow formed into a body. Then, before her, was a person. They nodded at her as she rocked back in shock, staring at them. The blood in her chilled as she put the puzzle pieces together.

"Welcome to Korkoran, Captain Sanaa," they whispered with a wink.

Isabelle Olmo

Chapter Forty-Eight

HIRA

Death came at dawn for Lady Hira Balik. She'd carved her initials into the stone of the cell so that future generations could speculate on her final hours. Fear was a distant sensation she scarcely recognized. Her heart was still a toppled and broken vase, with pieces strewn about the floor. It didn't matter. She liked that it was broken. Had she undergone this while caring for Justan, it would've hurt far worse because they would've killed him to make her suffer.

She wished she could speak to Almira one final time and embrace her. To tell her all she'd learned. But that wouldn't happen. If she were to see her cousin again, it would be far too late.

Hira knew Almira had arrived in Treveri when more soldiers than usual entered the dungeon. Quent pressed himself against her as he gripped her arm. In part she wished to comfort him, but to provide him with reassurances would counter the work she'd done for him the past few days. His survival depended on the strength of his heart and mind.

Hira took his chin and met his eyes. "Remember all I've taught you. Even if you leave me behind, you must get away from here."

His lips slacked, but he bravely nodded. At this moment, he

looked like a grown young man. There was anger in him that wasn't there before, and she keenly missed the sweet boy who'd once stumbled into her quarters.

"My lady, it has been an honor," he said with teary eyes.

The hinges on the heavy iron door creaked as the men waited for her outside. Slowly, she untangled Quent from her arms and took a deep breath for bravery. *Know who you are.*

"Hands where I can see them, bitch," the fake Korkoran Knight said.

Hira slowly turned to him. There was no point in niceties if death was only moments away. "I'm the Lady of Istok, you mercenary scum. You'll address me as such."

He leaned forward, and she could tell he chewed takata leaves. They left his teeth yellowed and his tongue ashen to a dark gray. She flinched as the stench of rotten-anise reached her.

"You gonna bash my nose in too?" he sneered.

Hira smiled and held her hands before her. "If I can."

Drool seeped from his mouth as his eyes lingered on her body, the sheerness of the underclothes likely providing him an unwelcomed view to her skin. "I'm going to fuck your headless body."

He was alone and close enough for her to grab. So she did. She grasped his head, yanked his hair back, and pounded his nose against a metal bar. She heard the dull crunch of the smashed cartilage as his blood spurted over her face.

Swords were instantly at her throat. The man screamed on the floor as he clutched his contorted nose and he whined pitifully. She held up her hands, her fingers dripping blood.

"Step back!" one soldier screamed at Hira. "You try that again and we'll put an arrow through the boy."

"You mass of incompetent fools!" Mr. Hyall sneered at the man on the floor. "I said she's dangerous and still you see a little lady!"

Mr. Hyall, now dressed in finery, his hook polished silver and his boots made of smooth leather, turned to her. His eyes lacked all the warmth she thought she'd witnessed. He, too, had mocked her emotions and aided Furia in bringing down their kingdom. She longed to kill him with her own hands. She asked the Favia to give her that honor.

"Good morning, Mr. Hyall," Hira said in a pleasant tone.

He looked her over with a sadistic gaze. "Lady Hira, will you take on the entire Korkoran guard on your own?"

She shrugged and smiled before saying, "The opportunity keeps presenting itself and I have little self-control."

His keen eyes studied her. "You've right changed since the sneering girl you were when you boarded the ship."

Hira was bound at the hands, but she kept her gaze on him. "I'm smarter now, Mr. Hyall. This is true. But I could *always* kill with one hand."

He scoffed and leaned forward, his eyes delighting in her predicament. "I've always known that. You and Lady Furia are not very different. You should've taken her offer when you had the chance."

Hira lost her smile and raked him over with disdain. "I'll die a loyal Istokian High Born. You'll die a *traitor*. I wonder what your wife would think of the man you've become."

His hook connected with her face with a speed she hadn't anticipated. It was a harsh hit, and she collapsed the ground. They hauled her back up, and she spat blood. He'd hit her with his hook, tearing her mouth and reopening the beatings she'd received over the past few days. All she could taste was metal.

As she opened her mouth to yell at him, someone grabbed him from behind. She expected to see a lot of people, but not Captain Sanaa. She snarled and pressed her mouth to his ear.

"Hook this," Sanaa said, and imbedded her sword into his back, skewering him in one swift move.

The Red Guard invaded the prison and killed the Korkoran guards. Blood splattered, men that were once standing now laid out, decapitated and maimed. It happened so quickly that Hira had to push Quent behind her to ensure he wasn't accidentally hurt.

When they finished, Hira let out a cry of relief as Sanaa looked up at her. The captain was in front of her when Delara sliced Hira's bindings off. Hira cried out in desperation as he hugged Sanaa and

Delara. Sobs wracked her as she dug her fingers into their backs.

"You're alright, girl, you're alright." Despite her comforting words, Delara looked at her with concern.

Hira shook her head and stared at the two of them, scarcely believing her saviors were real. She'd lost all hope. *All* of it. They beamed at her as if she had never left them. It felt like years had passed. She almost forgot her purpose because she was so overcome with relief.

Hira grasped Sanaa's arm. "Almira, she's walking into a trap!"

The captain shook her head. "We know everything. Almira is prepared. The king and Thebo hide the armies over the small hill. We are going to take down the fortress. Are you free to join us or are you too hurt?"

Hira laughed, hugging her again. Hurt? She didn't feel any pain or exhaustion. She was ready to kill each and every one of the horsefuckers herself. She was prepared to take back her castle and slice Furia's throat. They'd created a monster, and her claws itched for blood.

They heard a moan from the floor. It was Mr. Hyall. He still lived, dragging his body as best he could through the stones. She held out her hand to Sanaa, who wordlessly gave her the Ruby Blade.

Hira walked to Hyall, flipped him over, and straddled him, watching him with disdain. He gasped as he looked at her. She took his hooked hand and held it up.

"I need this," she said.

With a harsh grunt, she slashed the blade, slicing through the bone of his arm, then yanked the last bit of skin until his hook was in her hand, along with dangling sinew. She didn't stop until done, even though he screamed and thrashed. Then she leaned forward, delighting in his gaping mouth of horror.

"I hereby sentence you to death, *traitor*." And she pounded the tip of the hook into his forehead. Hooked.

He died between her legs. She silently thanked the Favia, for they had given her a wish. Now she was thirsty for Furia, and her yearning was great indeed.

When she stood up, she found Delara and Sanaa watching her

in apprehension.

"Gods of the sea, lady, you've been through *something*," Delara breathed.

"Yes," Hira swayed, glanced down at herself now drenched in blood. A random bit of sinew was stuck to her chest. "And I got a souvenir," she said as she maliciously smiled and held up the hooked arm.

The girl she'd been when they last saw her wouldn't recognize her now. There was a level of emotionlessness that permeated her being. Like nothing mattered. She had lost it all locked in that cell and she'd been reborn as a machine with lead in the cavities of her soul.

Sanaa looked back into the cell, then back at Hira. "What do we do with the boy?"

Quent pressed himself against the wall, his gaze fearful, especially when he saw what she held in her hand.

"Come, Quent," she said.

He slowly pushed himself off, his eyes on Sanaa—widening in awe.

"This is Lord Seaver. He's under my protection. Furia killed many of the real Korkoran guards, but some must be in these cells. We have to get them out. Furia has hundreds of swords at her disposal, so we need as many as we can get. By the time the armies come over the hill, the queen could already be dead."

She was talking so fast that she had no time to dwell on her plans. Without overthinking them or second guessing herself. Like she was meant for this.

"All attention will be on *cuzo*, and then we can make ourselves known," Sanaa said.

Hira shook her head. "That's risky."

"Just as her majesty wants it."

Naturally, Almira wished to make an entrance. Hira could only imagine how Sanaa and the king took the plans once Almira delivered them. She was sorry she'd missed it. There was an endless row of cells in the hall. Her men were in here.

"Let's find the keys," Hira said.

Sanaa agreed, and they searched the dungeons. The captain posted two Red Guards by the entrance to take out any soldier that came down to check what was taking so long.

"We have little time, but I need to make it to the armory," Hira told Delara, who raised a brow in question. "I need my armor."

Chapter Forty-Nine

ALMIRA

It felt very much like the year before. A shaky plan, someone she loved on the line, and nothing but her wits and her Red Guard's blades to succeed. Only this time it coupled the stress with the pain that split her body in twain, taking her breath away so that the mere act of conversing was a struggle. Before, when respite would come between the labor agony, she could speak. Now, words were a monumental task. She'd assured Alton she could manage. After all, what did he know of the reality of childbirth? Nothing. He wouldn't have left her side if she'd not lied. The lies felt sticky on her tongue.

As the pain lessened, she opened her eyes and her horse neighed. She had little time.

"Majesty?" M asked.

Almira looked at her guard. "I'm ready."

She slacked her hands on the reins. Pressing her hand over her stomach, she prayed. *Hold on little one, please hold on.*

She felt dizzy as the chaos of the past few weeks rained down on her senses. She'd piled so much on her back that it felt like stones bogged her down. She left her country a young woman, hesitant to marry a High Lord. Now she returned home, a Queen and a

Conqueror, dressed in golden armor.

She urged the horse forward. Each movement became a struggle of willpower. M rode steadily next to her, keeping close with her hand at her sword, eyes moving from side to side.

They were before the city gates in a few steps. When the guards spotted the queen, commotion erupted as they scrambled to open the golden doors. She looked at them and realized they were not loyal soldiers of the Istokian forces. Their faces were unshaved and their attire sloppy. She wondered what Furia had done to the Istokian military. Had Furia butchered them or hauled them into the dungeons of Korkoran?

The false soldiers sneered and laughed as she made her way into the city with her lone guard. Unconsciously, she placed her hand on the ruby blade, which was secured at her side. The way she was feeling, she would slice any man who dared touch her.

Regardless of what the duplicitous soldier's thoughts were, the moment she walked her horse through the streets, the real Istokians saw her. They dropped their goods and parcels. They abandoned their laundry and their bartering. They gasped and called her name and, in a mounting chorus, they cheered. Women held their babies up for Almira to see and, through her blinding pain, she smiled at the children's extended hands. Elders prayed, clutching statues of her mother, Lamya, who'd come to represent childbirth. The likeness in the rustic renditions brought her hope.

"Bless you, majesty!"

"Welcome home, m'lady!"

"It's the queen, child! Look at the queen!"

Her heart warmed to them as they recognized their sovereign. As they poured into the streets, their fingers reached out to touch her. So many, it created a procession of Istokians surrounding her as she took the well-known path to the fortress of Korkoran.

The road changed to the white stones, the same one young Almira witnessed her father ride through whenever he would return from his morning tasks. His red hair would be crimson in the sun, his armor polished and glinting like the noon sea.

She was *home.*

Almira prayed Sanaa made it inside. She prayed she'd been able to find Hira. She hadn't gone through so much to witness her little cousin's decapitation. Even as her body protested, she prayed the entire way up to the fortress. To be so close to the sea and not reach it would be her greatest failure.

As she turned the last corner of the white road, the castle opened before her and there was Korkoran. The most beautiful castle in the world. It shone like a beacon of hope, blue and polished, rounded edges that marked the pristine craftsmanship of her people. The windows were scalloped and curved with wide balconies for ladies to enjoy the ocean views.

They'd built a platform at the entrance of the fortress. It was open and welcoming for all to see. They'd hauled the golden throne out and on it sat a woman with the most stunning blue eyes the queen had ever seen. She was the incarnation of beauty.

Furia.

Her dear sister.

She wore golden armor, much like the mail the Korkoran guards wore. She looked like a goddess, with her hair flowing down over her shoulders.

A lot of Istokians came to see the spectacle, along with the crowd Almira brought. The nobles stood to the side, impotent as ever. Next to Furia was none other than Commander Justan Seaver. Almira held her breath as she saw the level of deception around her. Was this why her father insisted against a union between Hira and the commander? If he suspected the commander of double-play, why would he allow him to stay in his post? It made no sense.

The commander didn't dare meet the queen's eyes. *Bastard.* She'd handed Hira right to the hands of the wolf.

She searched the stage for Hira but didn't see her. An executioner held Ocean Fury and her anger erupted to such heights that it overshadowed the pain of her labor. She seethed until she felt it against her teeth, until she sensed the wings of a dragon protrude from her spine.

Furia embodied her name. She clutched the dragons on the seat and her face twisted as the people continued their cheers. The crowd was silenced when Almira halted her horse.

She met her sister's eyes. "I come in peace," Almira said loudly, so that it carried to the crowd. "*Sister.*"

As they looked at Furia, a murmur went through the crowd. When Furia flinched, a small thrill of delight flowed through Almira. She was the *queen*, and this woman was a usurper.

"You're well informed, *Almira*. But this is not Ouest and you're not welcomed in these lands." Furia's voice was a deep, silken twist.

Almira glanced around at the nobles who watched her with fear. At the Ley of Suidian heritage that stood where Ley Coster should stand. The only friend amongst them was Lord Barnabus, who beamed with pride. The fool would give himself away.

"Is this not all for me, sister? The stage? The royal execution? The nobles holding their cocks because not one of them knows how to use it or what it's for?" Almira asked in her most pleasant tone.

A few people in the crowd laughed. Furia's eyes deepened like a coming storm, her full lips pulled back to a snarl mixed with a malevolent smile.

"In another life, I think I might've liked you," Furia clipped.

And how Almira wished they had. How she wished her father had come clean. She wasn't certain her mother would've forgiven him, but she would've at least attempted to understand. She would have not cast the child out. But his fear—his massive fear that he would lose Lamya— sewed his mouth shut. He'd lost her regardless, and now Almira might lose Istok.

"Where is the Lady of Istok?" Almira asked. "Show her to me or we shall have no negotiations."

Furia laughed, a serpentine slither. "What negotiations do you bring? You're down to one guard and a lovely gown."

Almira dismounted with the help of M. She curled her fingers into M's shoulder as another sharp pain overtook her.

"You can do this," M whispered between them.

Almira nodded and pressed her lips together to face her opponent. She felt herself being split in half, as if she must walk with her legs parted or she would squish the baby's head between her thighs. She took a tentative step towards Furia. M held her hand, allowing her to squeeze it as the pain flowed through her. *Oh gods*, she would birth the child here and now, she swore it.

"My cousin. Or we're done speaking," Almira said between clenched molars.

Furia raised her hand and smiled. "Bring the bitch forth."

The dozens of guards around Furia tensed as Almira moved forward. "Surely your men are not afraid of *two* women. Allow me to get closer, so her head can land on my lap."

At her words, Furia stood and faced the commander, enraged. She grasped the lapels of his shirt.

"I've not left your side! You know you have my utter devotion!" The commander tried to grasp her neck in a tender caress.

A teen boy rushed out of the castle and placed himself before the commander, facing Furia with a brave look. Before anything could happen, Furia grabbed the boy instead and slid her knife against his cheek.

The commander's face transformed as he lunged for the boy, but Furia's grip was steady. Justan Seaver pleaded for Furia to let the boy go, that she'd promised not to hurt him. His face split into panic as he begged. Almira, sensing the situation escalating before Sanaa could arrive, stepped closer.

"Furia," Almira said calmly. "Let the boy go. Will you truly let your opportunity to kill me slip past your fingers?"

Her sister's eyes were wide and manic. "My *opportunity*? Oh, little sister, you're already *dead*."

Almira could see the shadow of the marksman meant to bring her down as her gaze flickered to the fourth tower. M's body coiled, ready to grab the queen at a moment's notice.

She looked back at Furia. "Let me guess? Marksman on the fourth tower? It has the best viewpoint of this courtyard. That's what I would do." She walked closer.

Furia's face was pure rage. She tossed the boy to the side, and he landed with a thump on the ground. "I'll not let you die that easily."

Almira fisted her hands against the pain coursing through her. Sanaa needed to attack. A momentary panic quivered through her, a thought that they'd somehow captured Sanaa, and she was alone with one guard. She wouldn't let her fears spread across her face. M was next to her as she almost reached the top of the stairs.

"Arrow to my thigh? Cripple me so you can carve out my baby as I gurgle in pain? Or will you torture me for days? To work out your issues with our father on me?" Almira laced her words with honey.

Furia turned to her guards. "Did no one hear me? I said bring the bitch out!"

"The bitch is here."

Everyone turned to the castle entrance where Hira stood surrounded by a well-armed Red Guard along with soldiers who'd seen better days. Only Hira didn't look like Hira. Instead, the actual High Lady of Istok stood before them in her imperial armor, which Almira had made for her. Her face was a stone mask of hate as she pinned her blue eyes on the usurper. She was nearly unrecognizable. She looked like the Great Dragon.

At the sight of Hira, Furia faltered to near disbelief.

Before anyone could react or draw a sword, Hira tossed before Furia's feet a gory stump of a hooked arm. The strings of torn ligaments still attached. Furia stared at it for a beat, then wailed while Almira recoiled at the sight.

She pointed at Hira with a shaking finger. "Kill her. Kill them *all*."

A zooming noise flew past Almira, who gasped as M grabbed her. Her guard's face twitched; her lips pressed together. More zooms and M's body convulsed against her. The queen began to scream and still M held on, staring at her with unblinking eyes as the arrows rained down.

"No!" Almira cried, clutching her.

M slid down as Almira tried to pull her up, even as the chaos of a battle resounded around her. A sharp birth pain invaded Almira's senses, and she swore at that moment they'd wounded her, but it wasn't that. A gush of water splattered between her legs.

"No, no, no–" She stumbled to the ground, her shoes tangling into her gown, M dying at her feet.

A fury of arrows cascaded over them. Where was the archer? Where was the—

Someone grabbed her hair and yanked it back. A face was before Almira as she twisted against the pain in her head. It was Furia. She thrashed her with the brutal strength of one who'd trained for a lifetime. She held a knife to Almira's face and the queen couldn't breathe. Between the terror of being in Furia's grasps and the pain in her body, she couldn't speak.

"You're a payment for a debt long owed," Furia cut the knife across Almira's cheek. A harsh tug to split her face in two.

Almira gurgled, anticipating the pain as she clutched her face, but the pain wasn't coming from there. She pulled her hand back and found it without blood. Furia looked at the knife in her hand and then back at Almira with slow realization. She'd grabbed the Ruby Blade, just like she knew Furia would.

"Try again, you bitch," Almira snarled in agony.

"Istok is *mine*! My birthright, you brat from a brown cunt!" Furia screamed and smacked the queen across the face, tumbling her crown to the ground.

The harsh blow was shocking. No one had never hit Almira before. Pain exploded against the bones of her skull, and she tasted blood on her tongue. She lost her sense of place and time.

Distantly, she heard Furia screaming and issuing orders, but Almira couldn't react. Her brain had molded to her cranium. It was not until explosions began all over Treveri and the sounds of people screaming in terror that she realized Furia dragged her. Dragging her *away* from her guard, away from Korkoran, away from help.

Her legs were gelatinous, caving under her as her body collapsed in pain. She felt herself lifted, and then pressed against a chest. Commander Justan had her, and he was stony with determination.

She screamed, her mouth wide to the sky.

Isabelle Olmo

Chapter Fifty

HIRA

Explosions erupted across the courtyard. Nobles and commoners alike frantically attempted to save themselves. Arrows rained down. Around her, young Red Guards staggered, either hurt or killed.

Hira hacked her way through a sea of Furia's henchmen. She jumped over the bench where she would've laid her head for decapitation, and snatched Ocean Fury from the executioner in two strikes. The blade rejoiced at being back in her hands.

She ran to Almira, who was already in the grasps of Furia. The sisters were facing one another when Furia snatched the ruby blade Almira had in her holster, and slashed it across her face.

Hira screamed at the wound that would've split the queen's face in half, but more soldiers descended on her, and she couldn't reach the queen.

A long horn sounded in the distance. Hira knew that horn. The Horn of Parko, the last Suidian High Lord to sit in the Council of Five. Each time the Red Army was about to attack, they sounded the giant horn. There was a momentary pause as they stared at the Gates of Treveri.

The horn sounded again, and there was the king on his black

stallion and next to him was High Lord Thebo, dressed in his full battle armor, a prince in red. Over the hill came the red and black calvary which merged to create a sea of checkered soldiers. The king raised his arm, charging forward and into the pit of Treveri.

"CLOSE THE GATES!" Furia screamed. She had a limp Almira in her arms. "DEPLOY ALL SOLDIERS! WE'RE BEING INVADED!"

The false Korkoran Knights rushed out from the castle and the chaos escalated. Hira ran to Furia, but she placed an unresponsive Almira as a shield before her. Another giant explosion and planks of wood flew into the sky as they all attempted to dodge them.

Then, to Hira's horror, Justan took Almira from Furia's arms, lifting her against him. Almira woke and screamed when she saw he had her.

Ferocious anger broke inside Hira as Justan and Furia escaped, covered by her loyal sailors from the Night Serpent. Justan cast one last look at Hira, and she could've sworn he urged her to follow. Then they rushed down the path towards the docks.

"Furia!" Hira screamed. "Come back and face me, you coward!"

But more soldiers joined in the attack. A sword aimed for her belly nearly skewered Hira in half, but she countered and cut off the man's arm. It landed with a sick thump on the stone. Sanaa sliced her massive sword down on a man, and Delara gutted two men at once with her knife and saber. The younger Red Guards viciously attacked the soldiers. Their blades moving fast and sure in a manner that spoke of Sanaa's tutelage.

Hira turned to M, who lay on the ground with multiple arrows in her body.

"Sanaa! The queen!" Hira pointed to where Furia and Justan had dragged the queen away from the fight.

The captain plowed her way through the men in her path, swashing her massive Suidian blade, killing all those in her way.

Hira slid next to M and helplessly took in her destroyed body. She had over ten arrows in her. She bled from her mouth as she wheezed her final breaths. Hira grasped her arm, and she squeezed back, though it felt like she was slipping, slipping fast into a place she couldn't follow.

"The queen?" M gurgled.

"We'll save her, I swear it." Hira held her tighter. She felt tears choke her throat. "Madhavi, I'm sorry!"

M blinked up. "Don't you be sorry for a warrior's death. It comes to us all."

Hira screamed with a sob and shook her head, desperately clinging to her. It didn't seem fair that this would be her end. She should be fighting with them, not agonizing in death.

"I will carve your name in the Istokian war stones. All will know the great Madhavi died protecting her queen on the steps of Korkoran," Hira swore even as she cried.

M smiled, and a tear dribbled from her eye. "I go with honor. Let the Favia feast on me."

With one final grunt and a sharp breath, she died. Hira cried in anguish as another arrow was imbedded into M's dead body. Enraged, Hira rose and looked at the tower.

Just in time as another arrow flew from across the city and landed between the eyes of the marksman. He fell down and splattered contorted on the stone. Hira sought the savior and there, perched on the topmost spire of the gates, was a Free Islander with a rabid face. She met Hira's eyes and nodded. Then began to shoot arrows quickly to take down the knights that descended upon the Red Guard.

Hira ran across the courtyard and the archer made a path for her, shooting down whatever man attacked her. Soldiers screamed with arrows imbedded in their eyes and mouths. Swerving past them, Hira jumped on the horse left by Almira and galloped past the scuffles and to the gates. Just then, the Red and Black army descended on the city as more people screamed, attempting to flee the battle. Some of their bodies became crushed in the stampede. The King and Thebo's forces destroyed all those who opposed them, hacking down Furia's soldiers in a brutal fashion. The Mesedi arrived, dressed in their eagle-helmets with dual swords, annihilating Furia's forces. The great warriors hacking limbs and heads faster than Hira could process.

Knowing they would secure the castle, she cut through the market to get to the port. Parts of the city were on fire as the explosions lit homes and market stalls. As she rounded a turn, Furia's mercenaries attacked Hira, and she fought her way through them. Commoners joined in bashing their heads with pots and sticks. It was a free-for-all as they all worked to take back their city. Hira saved a woman who was pinned down and beaten by a henchman. She sliced Ocean Fury across his back, splitting his spine in twain as she galloped past them.

She spurred the beast and ran into Sanaa, who'd also managed to get a horse.

"Lovely day for a ride!" Hira yelled as she led Sanaa down to the port.

Their horses leaped through the wooden planks. In the distance was the Night Serpent, its black sails rising. They halted their horses, watching in horror the happenings.

"There! They're sailing away!" Hira cried, pointing at the ship.

They urged their horses forward past startled fishmongers and children who rushed to get out of the way. Sanaa was on her heels, thundering to the port. When they came to the Night Serpent, it was already over six meters away from the dock. From the ship, Almira screamed.

"No!" Hira dismounted her horse.

Sanaa landed next to her. "It's too late, we need a ship!"

But there was little time and the Night Serpent could outrun any ship. Hira wouldn't have it. She ran with all of her speed, jumped, twisted, and fell on the deck of the Night Serpent. Ocean Fury, ready in her hand.

All the sailors turned to Hira and Justan gently placed Almira against the crate as she pushed against him.

Furia looked down at Hira with annoyance. "You're very determined."

"Hira!" Almira flailed towards her and almost fell, but Justan held her up.

Hira pointed her sword at Furia. "Lady Furia House Balik, I charge you with attempted regicide, inciting a war, staging a coup,

and the murder of High Lord Beltran as well as that of Ley Coster."
She slowly stood and brought her sword to eye-level. "How do you
plead?"

Furia slowly unsheathed her sword. "Oh, I'm very guilty,
cousin. But my biggest sin was being born from the wrong womb."

"Stop it, it's over!" Justan, to Hira's surprise, attempted to take
Furia's blade, but the woman snarled and unsheathed a knife faster
than he could deflect it. She imbedded it in his shoulder, and he fell
backwards with a grunt.

Hira, momentarily shocked, circled Furia. The men on the ship
moved closer, but Furia held her hand up.

"The girl thinks she can take me, boys," Furia said.

They laughed, and Almira screamed again. She clutched her
stomach as she stumbled against the crates.

Hira clashed Furia's sword once, twice. They separated, and
Furia smiled at her. Hira sensed that she'd not seen her true skill, like
she'd measured it until the time was right. She momentarily doubted
herself.

"You see, I *also* trained with the best." Furia twirled her sword
and brought it down sideways. Hira deflected it and stepped back.

Furia was far superior to her. Her skill was elegant, technical,
and mixed with natural talent. The footwork was a perfect execution
of control. Hira attempted a Karten Corner, but Furia easily
outmaneuvered her with a laugh on her lips.

"After your grandmother tries to have you killed as a child, you
learn a few things," Furia said.

"Almira is not at fault for that, and neither is Istok!" Hira
twisted and brought her sword down. She slashed through the air
and cut Furia's cheek.

Furia grabbed her face in surprise, and her mouth split in rage.
"Now we're even?"

"Not even close—"

Hira moved her sword in quick, rapid succession, but Furia was
too good. Hira didn't know how long she could battle her; she was
already on the defensive.

Furia slashed her blade down, and Hira stumbled. "I've been

practicing all of my life to take down House Balik."

Their weapons clashed as Hira turned. They ran at each other around the ship. Hira attempted to find a weakness in her form, but it was impossible. Her cousin's footwork was impressive, almost like a dance. She fell against a box and Furia landed her sword next to her face, missing her by an inch.

Almira despaired as Hira scrambled and brought Ocean Fury up just in time before Furia could stab her arm.

Furia outfoxed her at every turn. Hira barely managed to avoid a death-dealing blow when Sanaa joined the fray. She landed on the deck, wet and angry, and began attacking the sailors with vicious precision. The distraction allowed Hira to slash Furia. Nicking her shoulder, the woman reeled back.

"It doesn't have to be this way, sister!" Almira leaned against one of the boxes. Her face was drawn, and the queen sweated as she clutched her stomach.

Enraged, Furia brought her sword down. Hira deflected it.

"And how would it be?" Furia snarled and attacked as Hira ducked. "What will you give me? You've given Istok to this *deformity*. Will you marry me to a Norrian lord and hope it'll satisfy me?"

Hira climbed up the stairs to escape Furia's blows as they licked her feet. Furia slashed with her sword, barely missing Hira's knee.

"Or make me a Red Guard? You'd think I'd like protecting your little life for the rest of mine?" Furia mocked. "People are always scrambling to figure out what to do with me, where to place me. Where will I be less bothersome!"

Hira turned, and their swords met again. Furia slid her blade forward and shoved Hira back, pressing her against the railing. The wood pinned her spine and Hira cried out. Furia frothed at the mouth, her eyes manic and determined.

"We're sisters! I'm not your enemy! Will you burn the entire world for revenge against a *dead* man?" Almira stepped forward, her face grim and pale.

Grasping Furia with her mangled arm, Hira clutched Furia's chin and tightened her grip, making the woman scream and fall back. Hira punched her, plowing her fist into her face, hearing the crunch of bones as Furia's nose broke. She punched her again and again. Furia fell and Hira jumped on her. Finally, Hira snatched Furia's neck, choking her as she gurgled. She felt the accumulated hate she'd built for Furia rise within.

"Who's broken now?" Hira mocked.

Furia yelled and hit Hira's head with the hilt of her blade. Hira rolled off, scrambling to her sword. As she grasped it, Hira turned and pointed Ocean Fury at her.

Furia stumbled up, coughing as her face twisted in rage. With a maniacal scream, she raged forward and attacked Hira as Almira attempted to reason with her. From the force of her hits, Hira knew it would be futile. She kept up, but Furia was extremely skilled. Hira's breathing was harsh, while Furia seemed not to need air.

"I met him *twice!*" Her voice shook, and Hira realized it pained her. It pained her to recall her own father. The only truly broken person here was Furia Balik. "Do you know what he said to me the last time?"

The anger in Furia's blow was so hard that Hira stumbled, then fell down the stairs. She landed harshly on her coccyx, making Hira scream as pain shot up her back.

Almira pleaded for Furia to stop. Hira had lost Ocean Fury and tried to rise but was out of breath. Furia looked down at them, her eyes focused on Almira. She placed her fist on her chest and pounded on her armor.

"'Stay away from *my* daughter.' That's what he said!" her lips were thin shreds of vengeful rage. "'The only reason you're still alive is because you have *my* eyes,' he said! As if I'd stolen them. As if I asked to be born!" And then Furia cried, angrily shoving away her tears. "What father doesn't love their child?"

Almira clutched the banister and bravely faced her. "Furia, I'm not him. Allow us to find common ground, *please*. You are my sister _"

The queen gasped and clutched at her stomach, and that's when Hira realized she was in labor. She'd *been* in labor.

But Furia shook her head. "The world will know my pain; the world will know my vengeance. I won't let you take that away from me, too."

And she rushed at Hira as Almira screamed, but Hira grabbed Ocean Fury in time. The hilt heated to intensity, and with all the strength in her mangled arm, she swung the sword.

It connected with Furia's blade and broke it in half.

The broken sword flew into the ocean and disappeared beneath the cool water. Furia looked down at her hilt and then back at Hira as she stood, Ocean Fury still at hand.

"At your command, Majesty." Hira leveled her sword.

"*Please* sister," Almira cried. "Please, don't make me!"

Furia slowly shook her head, but her face twisted in pain so deep she looked to break. Her beautiful mouth contorted. Her eyes watered with angry tears.

"You have *no* idea what my life has been." She clutched her chest. "When I was twelve, I ran away. I rode my horse to meet you. He didn't even come out himself. Ley Coster put me in a carriage and sent me away. As I cried all the way home, I knew he'd never love me. While the two of you are blessed by love, I've had to scrape and pull myself by my wits using whatever means needed! Fuck who I had to fuck. Kill who I had to kill. Lie when I had to lie. All the while knowing my blood was as royal as *yours*."

"Now you'll know pain—"

And she twisted her hand behind her waist, yanking out a knife, her sharp eyes on Hira as she swung her arm back to launch a blade, she wouldn't be able to deflect.

Furia's tirade ended as a harpoon flew, imbedding itself into her shoulder.

Chapter Fifty-One

ALMIRA

The sound of a harpoon hitting Furia's shoulder startled Almira. Next to the queen, stood Commander Justan, his body bent at an angle, his hand outstretched where he'd just released the fishing spear.

Furia slowly looked from the injury to the commander. She cried, flooded with hurt, as her eyes softened.

"Justan…" she clutched at her shoulder. "Why?"

The commander straightened. "Because I'm not Justan."

Furia's face went through a variety of emotions, eyes broadening in realization, then transforming as her mouth opened and she twisted in rage.

"You *bastard*, you *fucking bastard!* What have you done to him?" she howled, a mixture of fury and pain, then tried to pull out the harpoon. Her feet became entangled in the rope behind her, and she tumbled, falling onto a lit lantern. Within mere seconds, Furia's hair and clothes became engulfed with flames. She battled the flames fiercely, but she was no match for fire.

"Furia!" Almira reached for her as the awfulness bubbled the skin of her face, but the commander pulled her back and held her steady.

"Leave her!" he urged her. "Let her burn. You cannot redeem her!"

Hira rushed to help but before she could reach her, Furia fell backwards, howling into the sea. Her hand still extended. Hira ran to the ledge, crying out her name.

Almira sank down to the ground as the commander helped her back, her tears of pain and sadness overwhelming her. The child was coming. She felt it. The head had breached. It was all for naught. No chance of reconciling with a sister she never knew, and now her child wouldn't be born in water. Her own death would soon come. The child wouldn't live long. She would bleed out in Alton's arms, and he would be bitter until the end of his days.

Hira shoved the commander, making him land on his back. Then she slid before Almira, her eyes wide and concerned.

"Take this off me!" Almira yanked at the breastplate that pinned her and didn't allow her to breathe.

She arched as Hira worked the buckles. The child demanded to come even as she clenched her cunt close, even as she begged it to stay.

"The baby comes, she comes and I'm not in the Ocean pools!" Almira sobbed.

Through her agony, Almira registered another vessel had gained upon them. She wept again and grasped Hira's hand and threw her head back. The earth coming down on her body with such force that she had little control over anything. She desperately fought the battle of her life to keep the child within her. But that life didn't answer to her and would come when it would come.

"You must hold!" Hira urged.

Almira twisted as she panicked. She would die here on this ship. "She must be born in the ocean pools! Or we'll *both* die!"

Then Hira left her, and Almira could scarcely register the surrounding mayhem. She stuck her hand between her legs, opening them wide and feeling between her folds. Then she felt it—a small lump with hair.

She shrieked and grabbed at whatever she could find. "No,

please—please! Gods of the sea, keep her in!"

Sanaa was before her and looked between her legs. Her face was sweaty and covered in blood. "You won't make it to the pools. The child is here. Stop fighting it!"

Almira grabbed the front of her armor and pulled her close. "If you do not get me into ocean water, I'm going to die! Do you understand?"

"Arrest that man!" Hira shouted as the Mesedi pinned down Commander Justan to the ground. "Search the seas! Cast the prong anchors, bring me Furia's body! Don't stop until you find her! We need more boats!"

Then Alton fell between her knees, his face pale and drawn, his eyes wide as he took her in. He pressed his lips to her forehead as he grasped her face.

"Your ideas will be the death of me!" he growled even as he kissed her.

Almira slumped against the boxes. She sweated and panted with a grimace. At being in his embrace, she bawled. Uncontrollable sobs wrecked her body, the pressure of the past month overwhelming her. He pulled her to him as she weakly clutched him. She felt she was losing herself already.

"It's all for naught!" She shook her head against his neck.

He held her tighter, as if his embrace could keep her there, as if her own mother didn't slip from her father's fingers into the depths of darkness and the Favia's waiting arms. She felt the child inching further and her body pushing without her asking it to. It had turned against her, and she grasped Alton tighter as she screamed in rage. It was a betrayal. She'd saved Hira and Istok and damned herself.

Then Alton wrenched himself away and when she looked up, Hira and Alton were arguing.

Alton stared at Hira in shock. "In the *middle* of the bay?"

Hira nodded. "I'll keep her safe, I promise. Tie us well!" Thebo and Sanaa wrapped her in rope. She was so changed, but Almira couldn't contemplate the change in the midst of the blinding pain and the coming death.

As her body squeezed the child, Almira screamed and Alton

cursed. Then he was lifting her in his arms and Almira clutched her belly. They tied ropes around her back. She begged for them to hurry, for them to make haste.

Hira climbed to the other side of the rail and Alton hefted Almira up with a grunt. He set her on her feet, the tips of her toes hardly holding on as she panted. She met his eyes when he grabbed her face. The green of his eyes were dark and ethereal.

"Don't you dare leave me," he gasped. And he didn't mean now. He meant forever. As if she'd passed her own family trauma to him.

She nodded. He pressed his lips to her forehead, and she curled her fingers into his hair as they separated.

Then Almira let go of the banister, and Hira pulled her against her firm body. The queen squealed as she almost lost her footing, but Hira pinned her tightly.

"I've got you. Put your hands over my neck."

She clutched Hira tightly.

Her uncle and husband slowly descended them into the ocean. Almira looked up and for a moment she saw Alton and Sanaa watching her with worried faces. She wondered if this would be her last time with them. She'd not properly said goodbye.

"Keep your eyes on me," Hira said.

Almira looked at her cousin as another wave of agony strangled her, and her folds parted.

"She's coming! She's coming in fast. Desperate. Ready for this world." She closed her eyes and then she writhed as another pain came.

And then they sunk into the waters of the bay. Hira lifted her legs and placed them around her waist, Almira floated backwards, her face to the sky. Birds flew overhead as she stared up at the clouds. She realized the pain was easing.

She sputtered water and looked at Hira. The sea warmed as if the gods were jubilant about the birth, curling around them like a blanket of comfort. Then it turned golden, light shining between their bodies. As if she floated once more within the belly of her mother. Warm and comfortable, secure knowing that all would be well.

"Let go of the child," she swore she heard her mother's voice. Felt her hands caress her face.

"Mother?" Almira closed her eyes, desperate to see her, frantic for one last look. As if her spirit was floating with them, there was no Lamya, only a feeling of her.

"Give her to the world. It is time, my darling," Lamya's voice said.

"I'm afraid, *nai*," Almira sobbed.

And her mother cooed and caressed her hair and face. Almira gasped, her fingers curling into her thighs, petrified of letting the baby go, of losing it. But she did. She unclenched her body, and her stomach rippled, her legs broadened, and her body opened itself wide. She felt the baby slide down, pushing past the birthing canal, breaching the folds and emerging into the Istokian sea.

Hira's hands were there, reaching between Almira's legs, caressing the baby's head as it emerged. Almira watched her eyes, wishing to witness the spectacle herself. Hira cried in happiness; she beamed as Almira's body expelled the child.

"Gods, Almira…" Hira whispered.

As the child left her body, Almira sobbed in a mixture of relief and overwhelming happiness. She'd done it! She'd held on and made it to the Istokian sea! All the weeks and months planning and contorting herself for this moment. She'd managed it. She never knew she had such physical strength.

"You are so brave, my girl, so brave," her mother whispered.

Almira finally cried all the tears she hadn't cried when her mother died, tears she'd held back because she wished to be strong for her father. She had been the brave one and never mourned her. Never allowed her memories to plague her or to recall the shape of her fingers. The curl of her lashes.

"*Nai*, don't leave," Almira begged.

"I never have."

But her voice was already faint, the water cooling. The moment the baby broke through the surface of the sea, she wailed. Taking her first gulps of air. Her small, shaky brown limbs battled the air.

The wonder of life in Hira's hands made her laugh.

Almira couldn't speak. Her eyes were on her child, on the soft tuff of light brown hair, slicked wet with salt water, her tiny hands flailing. She longed to hold her, so she pulled herself up by the rope that still held her. She stared at the baby. Its tiny body half covered in sea water.

"Oh, darling," Almira whispered, and her tears of loss became tears of joy.

She cupped the small head and pressed her lips against her daughter. She was so small, so angry at the indignation of her entrance that Almira chuckled. She'd made this. Her body had formed and molded this small thing, giving it a head and a mind. It took parts, not only of herself and Alton, but of the long line of ancestors that provided bits of themselves to gift the child. Almira gazed upon her daughter's small hands and the kicking of her feet, how they splashed the water, and she laughed and cried as she pulled the girl against her chest.

She met Hira's eyes, the bright Balikian blue. The cousins sobbed, their heads pressed together, and the child cupped between them.

"Today a queen is born in Istokian waters," Hira whispered. "We are the dragons."

"We are the dragons." And Almira, finally, after the long weeks, sighed."

Chapter Fifty-Two

HIRA

Her city was destroyed.

As they surveyed the damage, Lord Thebo rode next to her. They'd quenched the fires, but many lost their homes and businesses in the name of creating a distraction. People added hay to the collapsed roofs and boarded up broken windows. Ashen faces stared up at Hira and she realized the amount of work they would have ahead.

When people saw her, they stopped and gave her the royal greeting of Istok. All fingertips clutched in the shape of the Istokian tulip pressed against their forehead. She responded the same to show respect to the folk who trusted her with power. She didn't feel worthy of it. After she'd shunned them. After Furia used her words against her before the nobles. It felt as if the road to become worthy of the High Seat was immeasurable. As if she would fight her entire life to clasp a portion of what it took.

"We need to ensure people are fed," she muttered.

Lord Thebo pointed to an open area. "I'll have my men set up a tent by the training grounds. We'll take care of it."

They passed by a building burned to the ground. Children's shy faces followed her path with wide eyes. Their robes soiled and small bare feet spoke of the many tasks she still had to undertake.

"How came you by these explosions?" Hira asked.

Thebo peered at her with slight amusement. "Lord Barnabus. He hid the entire Suidian and Ouestern cavalry in his woods. Fed us, sheltered us, and showed us his predilection for pyrotechnics. He's a gifted inventor. Explosives all over the city. Red Eagle droppings ignited the fire logs. He's a little odd, but admittedly, his inventions worked."

Hira looked at the high lord. His face was grave and lined. She recalled the words his lordship said during Antilay and realized that he'd been attempting to communicate with her. "You were the eagles in his woods."

He smiled slightly, and small wrinkles pulled at the sides of his eyes. "Yes."

Despite all that occurred, the silver lining always hid in plain sight. "Lord Barnabus is a good man. A good ally," she said.

He wisely nodded and said no more.

They turned into the fortress. Puddles of blood and debris littered the path.

"Did you know about Lady Furia?" she asked.

He cleared his throat as they came into view of the fateful courtyard before the Korkoran gates. They had removed M's body, but other corpses remained. The servants had the awful task of distinguishing those who belonged to the usurper and those who fought and died for the High Seat.

"I knew Beltran lived a full life before he married my sister. He was handsome, young, and powerful. A most dangerous combination. But I never suspected a secret heir, and Beltran never spoke of it. What you know about your uncle is little. I watched him be a fool in love, a merciless warrior, and a devoted father to Almira. Little did I know that while he doted on the queen, he spurned his first born. He was both a good and a terrible father." He made a signal with his finger to signify two, a Suidian mannerism often used by the upper classes.

As they reached the platform, servants came and took their

horses when they dismounted. From the front doors emerged Lord Barnabus and Ley Olan. Aghast, Hira stared at the Ley. How dare they not incarcerate this traitor who oversaw Antilay?

But Thebo, seeing her visceral reaction and Ley Olan reeling back, grasped her shoulder.

"Ley Olan is to be trusted, my lady. He's been my spy for a long time," Thebo said. "He's a friend of both Istok and Suid."

Ley Olan pressed a linen cloth to a wound on his head. She'd not even seen him in the fray. He bowed in utmost reverence. "My lady, I'm ashamed we had to meet under such circumstances."

She observed him, still distrustful, still angry at the occurrences. "Was there anything you could've done for Ley Coster?"

The Ley shook his head. "Ley Coster, may the veils protect his soul, knew of the delicacy of my position. He insisted that above all, my allegiances had to be kept secret until aid arrived so I could continue providing information to Lord Thebo."

Hira's stomach turned, and she looked away. It seemed many understood the dangers she sailed to last month, and yet no warning or precautions came her way. Had she remained here and never ran away, she was certain Furia would've killed her while she slept.

"Ley Coster was in constant contact with me after the High Lord's death. It's why I sent my trusted Ley to serve House Balik," Thebo said. "In case anything happened to Ley Coster."

Hira nodded tiredly as exhaustion reached her. There was so much to process and take in, it felt as though this day lasted a month.

"If you trust him, Lord Thebo, then I too will trust him and pray to the sea gods that it's not a mistake. Forgive me, Ley Olan, if I'm skeptical of words such as loyalty and truth. I've been deceived too many times these past few days and my mind believes very little of what it hears," she said, and the Ley nodded in understanding. "In the meantime, you're my official Ley. We need restoration to the city as soon as possible. Our Suidian friends will begin feeding those displaced. I want to know how many are without homes and businesses. I want the number of casualties and wounded."

The Ley nodded. "Of course, your Ladyship."

Hira looked around, spotted discarded silken robes where the nobles once stood, prepared to ogle at her decapitation. The bastards. "Along with that, I want the names of all the nobles who attended Antilay and I would like to consult with you on which are now lost to me. Which should I be prepared to turn against my rule? I'll not be blind again."

When she looked at Thebo, she found him with a proud look and a secret smile.

"Come, let us feed people." Thebo walked away as Ley Olan followed him.

Hira turned to Lord Barnabus, who witnessed her exchange, and she realized she was alone with the man who would've been her husband. The man she'd spurned, the only man who stood up for her while her world crumbled. He didn't watch her in the manner many men did, as if seeking something from her. He beheld her neutrally, with little revealed in his placid, pale face.

"Lord Barnabus, I believe I owe you an apology." She took a deep breath.

The man blushed scarlet, and he chuckled. "*Please* do not apologize, I cannot bear apologies. They're disastrously awkward things." He graciously extended his hand for her to take and helped her up the stairs.

She allowed him to aid her because she was so tired that she could hardly walk.

"I must confess I'm not much of a marrying man myself. I'd much rather be locked in my laboratory exploding things than catering to a wife and children," he said with a slight laugh.

She glanced at him and couldn't help but smile. "I was young."

He waved her concern off and pulled her inside. "My lady, you need rest. Besides, the past is the past."

Servants tended to the wounded and covered the dead with blue cloth. In the center of the hall, she saw her uncle's post-mortem statue destroyed. As if someone took a drunken hammer to it and chiseled it piece by piece. She could imagine Furia doing it one night while Hira lay beaten bloody in the dungeons.

She met Barnabus' eyes because she couldn't convey her gratitude any other way. "You aided us in this fight, my lord. You stood up to Lady Furia when others wouldn't."

He smiled and shrugged. "I must admit, I find a slight pleasure in defying those who believe we cannot defy them. It's the Norrian in me. My mother was Norrian, so we can blame her for that, and for my pale and pasty complexion."

She grasped his arm tighter. Despite the complete lack of attraction, Lord Barnabus was enchanting and funny. She appreciated humor.

"You were quite admirable too, you know. Your mother would've been proud. You knew death was coming, and you faced it without hesitation," Barnabus said.

She shrugged, not wishing to take any credit for the occurrences of that awful time. She knew a piece of her had forever broken on that day, though she wasn't willing to admit it.

"Facing death is easy, isn't it?"

He smiled. "Is it?"

She supposed not.

"Well, if I can assist the High Seat in any way, please do not hesitate to ask," he said jovially.

Hira paused and studied his face, the willingness to help, and his marked bravery despite his appearances. "I believe you *can*. The explosions you caused were very advanced. Your work, how developed is it?"

His entire face brightened. "Oh, I'd get much more done if I had a team, but I'm afraid I scare the local peasantry. The poor are very superstitious and believe I'm conjuring up the Favia. It's a malady we inflict upon the poor, isn't it? Keep them ignorant so they clasp to religiosity with fervent fingers while we voraciously hold back truth to control them."

He spoke so fast Hira could scarcely comprehend his meaning. But what he said made sense. "Yes. I suppose we do. We're not very good people, are we?"

He chuckled and his belly seemed to laugh with him. "Oh, no, not at all. We're the very *worst* kind."

Hira's mind was rounding option after option as she beheld him. "I'd like to fund your work. What I saw today made me think of a weapon. Today, the queen was out of reach. We couldn't get to her. If we had a sort of weapon, that can be... I don't know, held by one individual. One that uses fire but doesn't burn the one who handles it. And kills in the sort of manner that the ironbomb does."

He looked pensive for a moment, then nodded. "An ironbomb handled by hand that doesn't burn the user but kills the opponent." He worked the words as if she'd provided him with a riddle. "I've heard of an innovative weapon developed on the Free Isle, which I've been wanting to get my hands on. It's called a Baller, a type of ballista, but with more precision."

Her stomach tightened in excitement. "My lord, are you open to travel?" she asked with suddenness.

"I..." he searched for the words and then grimaced. She heard of his adventures on the Dundai horse and hoped it wouldn't deter him.

"I'd like to give you a special task." She plowed on, not allowing him the opportunity to decline. "Not a minor task, but a large one. Such a weapon would be vital. I know I've no right to ask—"

"You've every right to ask. You're our High Lady," he interrupted her.

She nodded, still trying to comprehend that a word from her meant a command. In the manner that Almira spoke. The difference was that now she was not afraid. "Then I ask as your High Lady."

He bowed. "Then, as one of your nobles, I'm open to travel."

Hira delighted in his acquiescence, and she realized she'd just politically maneuvered a situation. She couldn't believe it. She'd stated her intention, and a noble agreed. She almost laughed.

Without her realizing, they'd made it to the infirmary. They stood before a door guarded by six Black Knights.

"Why are we here?" Hira asked tersely, her good humor instantly dissipating.

"The young boy, Quent, I believe. He sought you out. A charming fellow, I must say." He pointed to the door. "He's in there with his brother... Commander Justan. I've heard the king has called for his head."

Hira instantly wished to vomit.

Lord Barnabus provided her with a knowing look over his spectacles. "I find it is often good manners to allow people to explain themselves. An apology doesn't always have to be accepted, but it does one good to hear it, none the less."

She stared at him with understanding. "You're very perceptive, my lord."

He smiled widely. "You know, people seldom say that about me. I'm glad you noticed. Thank you!"

Hira nodded and bid him good day as she slowly made her way to the sickroom, which seemed a lot more like a jail cell. It would suit one condemned. The Black Knights posted immediately stood to attention, and she stepped in, bracing herself for whatever lies might dance on Justan's lips.

As she entered, both Quent and Justan turned to her. Quent ran, and she embraced him tightly. She pressed her nose into his hair and sighed.

"*Why* did you run from me?" she chastised.

Hira and the Red Guard had hidden behind the doors of Korkoran as Almira arrived. But Furia had attacked Justan and Quent had torn through her fingers to save his brother. He'd nearly given them away. Had Sanaa not held Hira back, she would've rushed ahead before the right time.

"I was scared. Please don't be angry at me!" Quent looked up at her with wide eyes.

"You could've been hurt," she said, pushing back the hair from his face. "Furia would've killed you."

"But she didn't, and you saved the day!" Quent said with a wide smile.

"She didn't do it alone," a voice stepped in behind Hira.

Captain Sanaa and Lady Delara stood there. They closed the door behind them and stared at the boy.

"Captain Sanaa!" Quent instantly let go of Hira and quickly forgot her as he stared at Sanaa with open admiration. "You were amazing! I've seen no one fight that way."

Sanaa looked greatly embarrassed as Delara watched her with open amusement. Sanaa opted to ignore such praise and glanced at the commander, who'd said nothing the entire time, as he sat on the sick cot with his shoulder bandaged.

"Commander, we're in your debt," Sanaa said with a nod.

Hira's head swiveled as she gawked at the two.

"The commander let us into the dungeons last night, my lady," Lady Delara lounged by the door as her perceptive eyes studied Hira. "We have taken the queen and princess to your mother's quarters. She insisted the High Chambers belonged to you."

To think that she would now sleep where her uncle slept, touch the furniture he touched and write state letters from his desk.

"She requests your presence," Sanaa said. "Afterwards, we'll pay our respects to M."

Hira swallowed and nodded. "I'll be right up." Hira looked at Quent and forced a smile. "Get cleaned up, then you can come back and sit with your brother."

Sanaa glanced at Hira with a raised brow, then stepped out of the room with Delara at her heels. Quent could not help but follow them in a trance-like manner.

She was alone with Justan. She didn't wish to be, but Hira had too many questions. Half of the questions she didn't wish for answers to. Her hate for him, for his betrayal slithered through her veins instead of blood. His actions with the harpoon erupted into even more uncertainty within her. She cast him a side look.

"She's not dead. My aim was off." He pointed at the wound where Furia had stabbed him.

"No. She's not. Heavily wounded but alive," she said tersely. Despite the dozens of ships that now patrolled the bay, no fisherman's hook brought up a body. The only thing found was Justan's harpoon. Without a corpse.

He stared at the sheet over his legs, his fingers curling into the cloth. "I suppose I owe you an explanation."

She scoffed. As if explanatory words would suffice his actions. Pain parted her soul, splitting her like a summer melon and flaunting her raw and pink insides.

He nodded and met her eyes with great difficulty. It took effort to allow his brown eyes to linger on her without feeling the need to end the course Furia's blade began across his body.

"Did you let the Red Guard into the dungeons before or after we spoke?" she asked harshly.

He cleared his throat and winced as he moved his arm. "After."

"*Why?*" she snapped.

He sighed and sat up, his hands clenching. "Because I had a mission, and I couldn't jeopardize it. No matter *what*. I swore it on my honor and it's the only thing I have left. It would've risked Quent's life. The queen's life. *Your* life."

Listening to his words, she laughed without humor. "A *mission*. What are you, a *spy*? For *who*?"

That he would hope she would fall for such lies was a hilarity indeed.

He flinched but kept his eyes on her. "For *you*."

She rolled her eyes and turned to leave, done with his falsities. She had no need to speak to him any longer. Her initial assessment was correct.

"My lady, you've no reason to trust me, but I urge you to read your uncle's secret scrolls in which he documents the happenings of sixteen years ago." he said, pleas filled his voice.

It made her pause, and slowly, she turned and glared at him. "No. You tell me what happened, and I will confirm your deceitful words when I read his scrolls. Not the other way around."

He swallowed, his face ashen as he drew a sharp breath and began to speak.

Chapter Fifty-Three

RYKER

About sixteen years ago

He fell on his knees before the gate, his hands weakly reaching out to the legs of the Korkoran Knights. He'd not eaten in days, but he barely noticed anymore. All he could feel was the pus-filled wound on his chest, the pain radiating out, filling the veins around his skin. He knew it was infected, but he had no means to fix it. How to heal himself. Not when he wore rags and had nowhere to go. He'd never felt less like a star-son of the night sky, like his mother always told him he was.

"Off the door, scum!"

The Korkoran Knight kicked him, and Ryker fell backwards. He landed on his cheek and coughed into the polished stone. A terrible feeling of failure and helplessness nearly overtook him. To give up and simply find a corner to die in, like his brother wished he would.

"Please sir, I need to see the High Lord," he whispered. He felt his strength waning.

"His lordship doesn't have time for the likes of you," the

Knight said, and he chuckled with the other one posted. "Off the steps before you soil the stone."

He wished to cry. He wished for his mother, but his mother was long dead. Wishing for his father was useless, after the conversation he'd just heard in the tavern, he knew to return home would mean certain death. Justan's haughty look didn't abandon his thoughts. How he'd sat delighting in Ryker's death when Ryker himself would've been distraught if anything ever were to happen to Justan.

Then the gates of Korkoran opened, and he distantly heard a horse walking out. He weakly lifted his head, and that's when he first laid eyes on the High Lord. The Great Dragon. A massive man with red hair dressed in azure armor on top of a white stallion.

"Apologies, my lord, we tried to get him to leave," the Korkoran Knight said, bright in the face.

High Lord Beltran studied the boy with a raised brow. His face was so cold that Ryker recoiled. Perhaps he would take Ryker back to his father and sign the death-order.

"What ails you, boy?" the High Lord asked.

Slowly, Ryker pushed himself up, crying out as the wound reminded him of its infection. "My lord, I need help. My father… my father is Commander Tikan."

This halted the High Lord as he studied his features, features Ryker knew were clear on his face. Both twins strongly resembled their father, the sharpness of the jaw, the Garian coloring, the rise of their cheeks.

He hesitated for a moment and dismounted, leaning over Ryker. And the boy was ashamed of how he must look. Bedraggled and ill, nothing like the young Lord he'd once been. Lord Beltran pulled back the cloth that covered the wound on his chest. Ryker gasped and doubled over.

His lordship leaned back and contemplated him. "That wound is angry, boy."

And Ryker finally cried. He was most ashamed. His father didn't permit crying, but Ryker sobbed. His desperation and the awfulness of the past few weeks descended on him like a deluge. He dimly heard the High Lord instruct his knights to take him to the infirmary.

The first few nights were painful. The wound had to be cleaned and disinfected. He developed a fever that split his head in half. He shivered violently and tossed and turned even as the medics diligently worked. Ryker recalled little of that time other than wishing for his mother and calling for her.

On the fourth day, he could sit up and take in his surroundings. He was naked, his chest bandaged, and a thin sheet covered his legs. They had laid him out in the Korkoran infirmary. A clean, cool space that had only one patient. Him. He was thin and scraggly. The weeks spent at sea did little for his frame, and he could see his ribs through his skin.

The door to the infirmary opened and in peeked a set of blue eyes. He stiffened when he saw a young girl staring at him. She had shocking red hair, her cheeks were flushed pink, and she openly beheld him with plenty of curiosity and marked bravery. Another girl, with wild brown hair and Suidian coloring, ran up next to her.

"Got you, Hira!" the other said with a laugh.

Then both girls turned to him.

"He's naked!" The girl named Hira cried, and they erupted into giggles. Ryker brightened when he realized these were the Balikian heirs. In vain, he attempted to cover himself. Their giggles turned into loud laughs.

"Daughter!" The barked reprimand made Ryker flinch, as if he'd been the one to do something wrong.

The girls gasped and scuttled out, running down the hallway. Within moments, Lord Beltran entered with a set face. He slammed the door and stared at Ryker. The youth shrank back. Ryker lay there, mortified at his predicament now that he could truly process the situation.

"My lord—"

"You're better. Good." The cold eyes held no pity, just facts. "Can you walk?"

Ryker wasn't certain. He'd barely just sat up, wobbly in his movements, but the tone of the High Lord's voice didn't allot room for disappointment. "I'll try, my lord."

Lord Beltran nodded and tossed him some clothes. "Get dressed, let's go."

And Ryker did. With trembling fingers, he dressed, even as his breath came short. The clothes were ill-fitting, swallowing him up, and the shoes slipped off. Even then, he followed the High Lord through the halls of Korkoran with tentative steps. He'd never been inside of the castle. It was a delight for the eyes. But he had little time to take it in. The High Lord walked with sure, quick steps that made Ryker rush to keep up with his strides.

"There are certain rules I will have you follow. For starters, my family is not to know of your existence. You're not to speak to my daughter or niece," Lord Beltran snapped.

Ryker wished to explain that the young ladies barged into *his* room, but he didn't think his lordship would be pleased with that answer. "Aye, my lord."

"The girls are young and curious, and my sister is most inquisitive. You're to be invisible." He paused and swirled on Ryker, who stumbled back. "Do you understand, boy?"

He wished to ask *why* he must be invisible. As if he didn't exist. As if he wasn't the heir to Pinnacle Palace. But he didn't dare open his mouth. He simply nodded.

"Good lad." He turned and walked down onto a dimly lit staircase that rose before them. Lord Beltran took the stairs, and Ryker desperately attempted to keep up with the lord's steps. They climbed what seemed like years. The youth clinging to the stone walls to keep from faltering.

Then his lordship led him to a small door and opened it. Inside was a room, with little furnishings, a pitiful window, a sagging bed. It was a servant's quarter. Lord Beltran turned sharply to Ryker and set his hands on his waist.

"I went to see your father," he said, and Ryker's stomach plummeted. "I provided him with ample condolences for the loss of his oldest son."

Ryker's mouth dropped open before he said, "But... but I'm alive, sir."

"No, you're not." There was a hint of amusement in Beltran's face. "You're dead, boy. Ryker Seaver is *dead*. Lost at sea. A tragedy, really."

He didn't understand. He'd simply come for aid, in desperation, when he overheard his father and brother speaking about his death at sea. How their father mocked Ryker's death and congratulated Justan on not having to kill his older brother to inherit the post of commander in the Istokian Armada.

"But, sir," Ryker whispered.

"You're a ghost, Ryker. A dead man with no title, no inheritance, no prospects. You show up at my home and ask for help. I'll gladly help you. I'll provide room and board, education, training with weapons, sailing, and politics. I offer you all of this." Lord Beltran opened his arms wide as if he showed off an elegant room, not a pitiful space.

"In exchange for what, my lord?" Ryker shook his head. "I've nothing. You've said it yourself."

His lordship slowly smiled. "Oh, you have plenty. Most importantly, you have the face of the man who will one day be my commander."

"Justan," Ryker whispered in realization.

"Aye, Justan. Met the little bastard. I wouldn't trust him with my back turned to him." He went to the window and beckoned Ryker forward.

Below were the gardens of Korkoran. Between the trees, children played, their cheerful voices echoed up. It was the two girls who'd barged into the infirmary and a nurse held a baby in her arms.

"You see them? My children? My niece?" Lord Beltran said. "They're the only thing that matters to me."

Hira, the little redhead girl, sang songs to the baby boy who squealed with delight.

"One day my son will be High Lord. My daughter will be wed to a High Seat. House Balik will rule half the world." He turned to Ryker.

The sharp blue of his lordship's eyes took him back. He knew those eyes. They were the same as Furia's. At the thought of the girl, he recoiled.

"I should confess, my lord. I know your daughter, and I don't mean the young lady below." Ryker said as he pointed with his chin out the window.

His lordship's face transformed to solid stone. A curled twisted his lip. If there was one thing Ryker knew, it was how much Furia hated her father and, by extension, so did Justan.

"She's... she's promised to my brother Justan," Ryker confessed in a whisper. As if the walls could hear them.

This didn't have the effect he thought it would have. Lord Beltran changed to contemplation. "Does she love him?"

Did she *love* him? Did Justan *love* Furia? To obsession. Ryker and Justan might've been womb-twins, but he'd lost his brother the moment Furia arrived at their home. From that moment on, Justan was loyal to one: Furia. And her to him. A passionate sort of madness that understood no reason, answered to no throne, and would die, kill, and destroy for the other.

"More than life," Ryker breathed.

His lordship slowly nodded and left Ryker to continue his journey to recovery. Not for long though, because Lord Beltran began a sort of rigorous training. History, politics, nautical laws, etiquette, even dancing. The youth's health became a priority for the High Lord. The meals were rich in fish and meat, and soon his bony legs filled out and formed muscles. At night, he'd take Ryker out and practice horsemanship and sailing. When he was available, he trained under Master Elio, his lordship's own swordman. Master Elio and Ley Coster were the only two who knew of the youth's existence, but both mostly ignored him, just as his lordship commanded.

At night, when the sky would fill with stars, Ryker would stare at them for hours. Counting them and naming them, crafting messages to the sky. But he had no one to provide messages to. He had no friends or family. The stars became his friends, and they would amuse him with their sparkling light.

The only brightness to his days was the children. Young Lady Almira and the happy Lady Hira. The girls would play games, which Ryker could hear from his secluded room. Their laughter and joy were the best part of his seclusion. Each time he watched them, he desperately desired to join their games and frolic in youth. But games were a thing of the past for Ryker Seaver.

A few years later, Lord Bach died. A solemn darkness overtook the fortress as sorrow seeped from the walls. He didn't expect the High Lord to enter his room after the burial of his son. But he did. Night had fallen and Ryker was hard at studying the nautical histories which Lord Beltran assigned that week.

"My lord!" He'd stood, toppling over his chair and making the single candle jumble.

The man said nothing. He was rigid, hard, a stone. He stared out the window like he often did whenever he would visit Ryker.

Ryker cleared his throat. "I'm so sorry for your loss, my lord."

Lord Beltran was silent for a long while. The only movement was his hair dancing in the evening breeze. Though Ryker knew much of tribulations, he didn't know what to say to the lord. It seemed words were inadequate for losing a child. As much as they were inadequate for losing his mother and family.

"My niece, Lady Hira, will be my heir," the lordship finally whispered.

Ryker recalled the girl with long red hair. She was about eight or nine by then. She loved to climb trees and run until she scraped her knees. But she never cried. She would hold in her tears, stubborn to let them go. She was fiercely bold and adventurous, and Ryker would often laugh at her anger towards the birds that would peck the fruit she wished to eat.

Lord Beltran turned to him suddenly. "She *must* live. No matter what, she *must*. You'll aid me in this, Ryker. She'll not know that you're her guardian when her time comes. You stay secret, you never tell her. You'll be her ghost, her shadow. You'll ensure she sits in the seat long after I'm gone. Swear it, boy. Swear it on your life. On your mother's memory. Swear it to me."

By then, Ryker was no longer a child. He was nineteen with a scruffy beard, but it didn't stop the high lord from calling him a boy. The foisting of a such a task on such a young man was terrifying, Ryker trembled but acquiesced. He wouldn't dare say no.

As the years passed, he scarcely saw the girl he'd promised to protect at all costs. She'd grown older, and thus, they expected her to act like a lady. He would only catch glimpses of her whenever she would escape the fortress on her horse, her wild red hair flying in the wind. He only ever saw her back. There was something incredibly defiant in her posture, and each time he saw her, he admired her more and more. She no longer sang and played games, but she would walk like her uncle and speak to others just as strongly.

Once, he'd accidentally been out past his curfew and he'd caught her sneaking back into the castle, sweaty, and looking very much like she'd been practicing swordplay. She'd flushed red and rushed past as she said "Apologies, Commander."

It was then that Ryker realized she thought he was Justan, who'd recently become the Commander of the armada. He'd opened his mouth to correct her but realized what a problem that would be, and instead watched her run with all haste to her rooms. He lingered on the spot she'd occupied and noticed she'd grown up, tall and strong, with fierce blue eyes and a freckled nose. A warmth crept over him, but he shook it off and made it back to his rooms. Ryker laid down at night thinking of the Lady Hira. He wished to speak to her and explain his role. He thought it would be good for her to know he would protect her at all costs. Perhaps they could be friends. He didn't have any friends. But the thought of Beltran finding out what he'd done soured his stomach.

Beltran always had his secrets, his plans, and he only provided Ryker but a portion of them. That's how he spent much of the next few years. Lingering in a tower, away from questioning eyes, away from the royal family. An ear for the High Lord to confess his fears that he wouldn't dare voice to others.

Until one day, a year after Lady Almira had married her first husband, and a few months after, he'd run into Hira in the hall. The High Lord woke him in the middle of the night. Lamp in hand, face hard as a pumice stone.

"Get dressed and come with me, boy," was all he'd said.

Ryker, in his mid-twenties by then, rushed after the man and descended with him into the dungeons. He'd expected to see many things down there, but never his brother, Justan. The brothers stared at one another, Justan in disbelief, Ryker in fear.

He'd numbly taken Justan's clothing and listened to Beltran's plan.

"No! Get me out! Ryker, get me out! Ryker! I'm your brother! Ryker, don't you hurt her! Don't you touch her! DAMN YOU BELTRAN! DAMN YOU AND YOUR ENTIRE FAMILY! I'LL MAKE YOU WISH YOU NEVER CAUGHT ME!"

Those were the words screamed as the door slammed shut.

In a few hours, Ryker had replaced his brother as commander. Out in the open, as if he were a normal man who'd not grown up in the shadows. The air felt too fresh. There was too much movement. He was uncertain of things, though he needed to appear aloof.

When Furia, thinking he was his brother, demanded sex, he performed as best he could. She shoved him off, annoyed at his floundering and hesitancy. He had tried to be sweet, like lovers should be. That's not what she wanted. His innocence quickly flittered away.

"Get off me," she'd snarled. "You've never fucked me this limp before!"

He'd bedded no one in his life. His lordship had covered much in his tutelage but never love making. Ryker knew little of what a man should do, and it was evident. He'd hid from Furia and trembled alone, cursing himself for such a reaction. He hated that he'd read the love poems of Jamsem, hated that he thought love was an innocent thing. That love was pure and magical, like the stars he'd long admired from his window.

It was a dark time for him. He became angry and bitter and lost all of his hope for the life he'd once imagined.

Then something happened that changed his outlook for the better. Little Quent, only ten years old, appeared at the port. He stared at his young brother, the one he never got to see, and the brothers embraced as if they'd known each other their whole lives. Ryker finally had someone that belonged purely to him. And he would protect him at all costs.

The desperation to truly become Justan took over his senses because he needed to live. He needed to be useful for Lord Beltran. If he couldn't pretend to be Justan, then what good was he? He was a ghost. So he took on a specialized behavioral tutelage. In each port, he bedded all the women he could. They taught him plenty, and he slowly began to resemble Justan. He personified Justan's charisma and debonair attitude, crude language, and cutting words. The only thing that mattered was being Justan and keeping Quent safe.

His little Quent, the only one who openly adored him and never questioned if his mannerism was Justan's or not. He didn't have to pretend around Quent. The boy was cheerful to take any attention from his older brother. Never judged him, never had ulterior motives. He wouldn't think it strange that Justan would hold him at night when he was sick or tell him tales of the ancient Garians and show him how to read the stars. And Ryker loved him with all that he was.

Then Beltran died, and it trapped Ryker. But he still had a mission because he'd made a promise. He'd promised to ensure Lady Hira rose to her High Seat. He'd make sure he succeeded in his promise.

He never expected the person who boarded his ship that morning. She was no longer a young girl. She was a woman. For the first time in his life, he was in the presence of a lady. He was unsure how to behave. Unsure if to be Justan or to show her who Ryker was. He wished he was *truly* Justan so that he would be worthy of someone like Hira Balik.

But he wasn't.

Ryker was a ghost. Ryker was a spy. Ryker was *dead*. A full grown man of thirty-one and he had no lands, no title, no money, he only had his pretense and his promise.

He'd lived so long as Justan, he'd forgotten to be himself.

When he made love to her, he pretended it was his first time. With someone he actually cared about and someone who cared about him. The true him. For he'd allowed his genuine personality to shine when alone with her. And she'd not minded it. She'd not scoffed at his knowledge of the histories. Or his desperate worry about Quent. On the contrary, she'd loved Quent as much as he did, and he couldn't ask for more.

But deceit was always thick on his tongue. It lingered acridly within his mind. When he thought she had died, he'd never descended into such darkness. Never had to pretend he was so unaffected by an occurrence. In those hours when she'd died, he'd failed. He was alone in the world with no hope of ever being himself. Of ever stopping the charade. Or ever telling someone what his real name was. But she'd come back, blessed by the gods. He'd almost confessed the entire thing to her, then and there, as they sat watching the sunset and speaking about dragons and myths. From that moment on, he saw her face in the stars.

But he'd sworn a promise to a dead man.

"You never tell her. You'll be her ghost, her shadow."

So, he was quiet. He held it all within himself. But tenderness had grown at the edges of his heart. He wished he had come down from his tower and played with her when they were children. Perhaps teach her how to properly climb trees.

And now he'd confessed the truth. In the process, he'd saved the queen and Hira. But who would believe such an unlikely tale? Did anyone believe ghosts when they whispered? Did anyone sympathize with reluctant spies? Did anyone accept men who lived in shadows?

No. They didn't. Men were judged by their deeds and his list of sins was great indeed.

But he *needed* to tell her. Ryker needed her to know because if she didn't… then what was the point of protecting her? What was the point of it all?

He finished his tale, swallowing thickly.

Ryker stared up at her—at her fierce face etched with a broken heart. He'd broken her in his attempts to keep to his task of protecting her. He'd broken her to save her from Furia. And he had a feeling she wouldn't understand. He didn't blame her. She was in the right, and he was in the wrong.

He had a feeling that much like her uncle, Hira Balik had taken whatever love she'd developed for him and turned it into a rock.

She'd methodically replaced her heart with it, so that any love she'd ever held for him was lost, encased in stone, surrounded by turbulent determination.

At that moment, he made a new promise. He would one day be worthy of her. One day, he would earn her forgiveness, even if it took years. He'd be patient. The stars were eternal, and they never stopped their light. And he was a Garian, a star-son of the night sky. He would be like the stars. A steady waiting light that remained constant until the moment it would shoot across the sky.

"And that is the truth of what happened and how I came to pass as the commander of the Istokian armada. For the past five years, I've carried the name of a man who hates everything I love and loves everything I hate. He may be in the cell, but I am in the prison," Ryker finished.

Chapter Fifty-Four

HIRA

In an instant, Hira unsheathed Ocean Fury. She pointed it with precision at his jugular. He didn't flinch. He didn't move. His eyes remained on hers.

"Do your lies have no end?" She pressed into his skin, the same skin she'd licked and kissed and nuzzled.

She hated that she wavered in her convictions, that her strength was conditional, that despite her tribulations, a part of her wished to believe him. To sink into his story. She very much recalled that night in the hall. It was when she first sneaked out to train, and she'd run into the commander. At the time, she *thought* he looked different. He'd always beheld her in contempt, but that one time he truly stared at her.

He swallowed and took a deep breath. "I was born a few minutes before Justan. I dare say it was the closest we ever were."

Hira yanked back her sword and scoffed. He couldn't stop his manipulations and his lies, drenching her once more with his deceit. How she hated him, how she hated that she still clung to the droplets of love. It would be easy to succumb to relief knowing he'd played a role with Furia and had been truthful with Hira.

"I'm leaving," she said as she turned from him.

He stood from the cot and took a step towards her, then he paused and held up his good hand. She didn't look at him, her fingers on the doorlatch. If she would meet his gaze, she knew she would find the warm brown of his eyes.

"He kept the scrolls in a secret place. Only Queen Almira knows where. His lordship was adamant that I should only reveal the truth once his daughter arrived, for only she could confirm my identity. Find them. Read them for yourself," he said in an earnest tone.

She clutched the handle tighter and glanced at him. Her face still etched with fury.

"My lady," his voice was soft. It made Hira flinch. "Each moment I had with you, when it was just the two of us, was real. If you knew the *real* Justan... you would've known."

She couldn't listen to his words anymore. They were *poison.* Everything about this was a cascade of falsity. She slammed the door behind her and grabbed a soldier.

"The moment we can, move him to the dungeons! I want him out of my sight!" she snarled, and the men quickly nodded as she stormed off.

Her mother's chambers were well-guarded but the king himself opened the door and beckoned her in. He smelled of seawater and the ointments used after the birth of a baby. The princess already had her blessings, and she'd missed it.

"How is my cousin?" Hira asked.

King Alton studied Hira with deep emotion. "You saved her, you saved them both. For that, I'm eternally grateful. Ask of me what you will, I'll grant it."

"I don't have the mind to answer such a question now," she said truthfully. What she wanted was not to feel anything—especially anything towards whoever the man was she'd fallen in love with.

"Of course, forgive me. You're tired," the king said.

Almira was in bed and the baby suckled quietly from her breast. The little girl made adorable noises of contentment. Her tiny hands fisted against Almira's brown flesh; her eyes closed. She was the loveliest thing Hira had ever beheld. Almira looked up at her cousin with a smile. She seemed serene and at peace despite the horrible day. Like a goddess against the white silk of the bedsheets.

"You look awful, cousin," Almira said.

The lady glanced down at herself. Her skin bruised and her hair still a mayhem.

"Yes. Captivity, near decapitation, war, a battle for the ages, and a birthing in the ocean will do that to someone." Hira sat in the chair next to her and pointed to the baby. "How is she?"

"Healthy and strong." Almira smiled as she ran her finger over the baby's head. Tiny light brown curls fuzzed up like a small poof.

"Have you named her?" Hira asked.

The baby stopped suckling and Almira unlatched her. In an unspoken conversation between the crowns, the king took the child and lifted her up. It was a lovely tender moment as he kissed her small, fisted hands and Almira covered her chest with the birthing cloth.

"She'll be known as the Princess Osaria, descendant of the first people," Almira said.

"One day she'll be the Queen of New Verden." The king settled the baby against his chest. She mewled, and he gently patted her bottom. "They have extensively instructed me on how to handle *my* child."

Almira ignored his jab and sighed. "M?"

Hira swallowed. "Dead. I was with her when she passed. She wasn't alone."

She didn't wish to linger in the memory of M. But the other option was thinking about Justan, or whoever he claimed he was. Neither was good.

The queen nodded, grief stricken.

"She'll have the funeral of a knight," the king said.

"Yes," Almira murmured. She grabbed Hira's hand, and they held each other tightly. "We have much to speak on, you and I."

Almira took her mangled arm and her mouth turned thin and hard.

"Did Furia do this?" Almira's voice was a burning blade. That sharpness that she exerted when needed flickered through.

Hira flexed her arm and allowed both the crowns to inspect the sight. "In a way, I suppose. Captain Strauss, a pirate, inflicted the wound."

Almira nodded. "We know of him. The man with the golden eye."

There was much shame that still lingered in her mind over her actions that day. How ignorant she'd been. "I challenged him to a duel when he commandeered the Sea Wife. I foolishly gloated in his defeat. He took my ruby blade and..."

She indicated to her arm with a shrug.

"That's a killing wound," the king said quietly, and Almira gasped, pulling her closer.

"It is." Hira nodded and met her cousin's eyes. "And I died after I agonized for days because I wouldn't let them take the arm. So, they took me to a witch. There's a lot more to it, Majesty."

And Hira continued her tale of horror.

"This dragon..." Almira said tentatively once Hira divulged that part of her journey. "Are you certain it was real and not..."

"She was real." Hira's voice was strong and sure. "And don't look at me like I'm mad. The girl you bid goodbye weeks ago died. I buried her and there she remains, on the stone floor of the prison below us."

She abstained from any mention of her connection with the commander. That burn was still red at the edges. Almira silently studied her, and Princess Osaria whimpered, but the king expertly turned the child and she settled, happy to remain in the thick of the adult conversation.

"You're so changed." Almira caressed Hira's face and her eyes saddened when she touched her butchered hair. "I hardly recognized you when I saw you. Did I damn you by sending you back?"

Hira certainly felt damned. Corroded and twisted. Bent at an unnatural angle, unable to straighten and be who she once was. Perhaps this is what people called 'growing up'. A most unpleasurable journey.

"I'm a little broken, but I still stand," Hira said. "I went through *Hell*. It was the worst time of my life, but I swear, had I not lived through what I did, I wouldn't be who you see today. My people need me and I'm ready to lead them proudly. Fear for those that try to oppose me or Istok."

The queen took a sharp breath, and she exchanged a look with the king. "I told father you would wake one day. I didn't know it would cost you so much."

Hira fisted her hand, studying her deformed fingers. "How did you know? About Furia?"

"A young girl stumbled into Easima. Beaten, starved, and nearly dead. Your mother and Ley Coster sent her. She brought me this letter." Almira handed her a well-worn letter, which Hira quickly read in confusion.

Hira shook her head. "*When?*"

Almira took the baby back from the king. The child was asleep, and the queen nuzzled her little face. "It took the girl months to reach me. She said she left the day father died, but how your mother knew father had died, I don't know."

Hira recalled the morning after the Battle of Mavros. "The Corsikan Torch. It was lit the morning after he died."

Almira's eyes lit up. "It connects to the -"

"The Dragon Torch," Hira finished, and the cousins smiled at one another.

Then Almira's face turned into a look of calculation. She was attempting to see the pieces of the puzzle. The princess whimpered, and she bounced her slightly. She seemed like such a natural mother, as if it didn't faze her.

"He kept so many secrets. In my heart I want to hold onto the love I had for my father, but... look what he's left us." Almira met Hira's eyes and they turned deathly dark. "Furia is still alive somewhere, licking her wounds. More dangerous than ever."

Hira nodded. "No body in the water means she escaped. She's joining forces with Arrigo. If she succeeds, every noble with an army that hates you or the king will rise with her."

Almira swallowed and watched the baby in her arms. "The Great Balikian War. Do you recall the witch's words?"

"War is inevitable at this point," the king said, and they both looked at him.

His face was dark, and he seemed angry, as if war took away from him something he'd wished for. Hira didn't understand. He'd always enjoyed war, at least it seemed like it. Perhaps he'd journeyed too, and while Hira became more brutal, he became more peaceful. Almira hung between the two of them like a balancing mother.

"Furia won't stop with harsh words from your strategic mouth," Hira said to Almira.

The queen sunk into the bed and closed her eyes. "There are two hidden sentences in the letter. Something about a secret key to a jail cell and a spy. Where's Sanaa? I need information on this Ryker. I assume he showed up. If not, I'll have to read through father's secret scrolls..."

Hira startled, "*What?*" Her tone was loud and harsh.

Almira blinked at her, and the baby screamed, angry at being disturbed. The king quickly took her and held her, to no avail. The queen pointed to the side room where a nurse came forth, and he followed the woman with the screaming baby in his arms.

She turned back to Hira. "Do you know Ryker? He's the one who allowed Sanaa entrance into the dungeons. He's been working for us all this time, a spy. Father said to trust him. That he was true. Did he aid you?"

For the first time in days, Hira felt as if she'd not eaten. She felt faint. Like she would collapse. Like her soul had stretched so thin it scarcely covered her body. She grasped the mutilated strands of her hair.

"Who is he?" Almira asked.

"I don't know!" Hira snapped. "I know nothing anymore!"

"*Cousin,*" Almira said in surprise at her tone.

Sanaa knocked at the door, then entered with Lord Thebo and Delara at her heels. Hira didn't want to have this conversation with everyone present. To make matters worse, the king returned, looking relieved now that the child was properly taken care of.

"We have set up food stalls, order is slowly returning, and I may have time for an ale." Thebo smiled and went to his niece, kissing her forehead. He peered at the king. "We can keep the platform up for the commander's execution if you like."

"No!"

Everyone turned to Hira, Sanaa, and Delara, who protested at the same time. The crowns and Thebo stared at them as if they'd all lost their minds. Almira's black eyes danced between Hira, her captain, and her usually silent guard.

"What exactly is happening?" Almira demanded.

"Yes, enlighten us all. When was this council for the commander enacted? It's got to be better than him saving himself by wounding Furia," the king said in a slightly miffed tone. He trained his glare on Sanaa. Perhaps he expected the outburst from many, but not from her.

The captain seemed embarrassed at coupling herself with Hira and Delara in the sudden entreaty.

"Commander Justan *is* Ryker," Sanaa said by way of explanation. She moved her hand about for emphasis. "Had it not been for him, we wouldn't have insight on Furia's plans, nor would we be able to enter Korkoran and rescue the lady before her public death."

Almira's head swiveled to Hira. She stared at her with wide eyes. "Is this *true*?"

Sanaa, annoyed at being questioned, said, "Am I not to be believed now? That I would lie for some *mediocre* man with a weak left turn?"

"He does *not* have a weak left turn," Hira bristled and turned to face her.

Sanaa raised a perceptive brow, and she almost saw a knowing smile on her lips as she leaned back and studied Hira. The lady, tired of being questioned and confused—amongst many happenings—grunted and glanced at the crowns who both openly regarded her.

"Commander Justan, or whatever he calls himself, is *my* prisoner. Not yours. His fate is in *my* hands. He's in Istokian land and thus he belongs to *me*," Hira said in a stronger tone than she'd intended.

The king, bright red by now, pointed at her. He'd never directed his anger at Hira, and she flinched. "Commander Justan aided Furia, almost killed my wife and your cousin. He sequestered you! Fed you lies! I don't care if he threw a last-minute harpoon to stop Furia, if he's a bloody spy or he opened a little gate, that hardly discards his actions. He must be punished. Treason is no trifling matter!"

"Begging your pardon, Majesty, but the lady is within her right," Thebo spoke, to the astonishment of all. "Or will you arrive in Zuri and demand the head of one of *my* prisoners?"

"Enough," Almira said in a harsh tone. "Fighting amongst ourselves will bring forth no resolution. Or have we forgotten that Furia and Arrigo are still out there? Likely building an army of malcontents to rival our own."

Anger seeped from Hira's pores as she refused to look at anyone, especially when they all pushed her to lead and now questioned her rule.

"Hira," Almira said in her most reasonable tone. "You must see that his actions on the ship were simply to save himself. He *took* me. I don't know what you've been through, what the commander made you believe, or what sentiments you think to have for him—"

"*Sentiments?*" Hira fisted her hands as she glared at the crowns. "Today, a friend has died in my arms. Do not confuse sentiment with weakness because it's not the same thing. I shouldn't have anyone question my decision at this moment simply because I *feel* things. I touched death's face multiple times these past few weeks, I found my mother dead, I watched my Ley be butchered, left naked and desecrated before the Istokian throne. I've been ousted out of my seat before all nobles! I'll explain no such thing to anyone, I've earned my words by blood and pain!" She pounded her chest, and it resonated in the room. "You wished me a High Lady, well here I am. And *this* High Lady will decide the fate of her prisoners. Where is the hidden key?"

Almira flinched, her face a myriad of words she wouldn't unleash before so many. "It's in your room. Father's old, gold-gilded desk. Second drawer, there's a hidden latch. His secret scrolls are also there."

Hira, flushed, stalked out of the room. She didn't expect Sanaa and Delara to be at her heels. She was halfway down the hall when she whirled on them, ready to argue if needed. What she found were two very sympathetic friends. She paused and attempted to gather her thoughts.

"I need to find these scrolls." She expected the women would leave her to her task.

To her surprise, the captain shrugged. "I enjoy reading."

Hira felt a strange sort of comfort. She'd been so alone these days that it seemed alien to allot them into her plans. "Then I'll need to question a prisoner or two."

"Will there be torture?" Sanaa raised a brow.

"Perhaps."

Sanaa and Delara peered at one another, and the taller one smiled.

"We've not had much adventure today. Might as well go," Delara said.

Isabelle Olmo

Chapter Fifty-Five

HIRA

It felt forbidden to enter her uncle's quarters. She took a deep breath and paused. These were *her* quarters now. Spotting the gilded desk, she went straight for it and emptied the contents, leaving the papers sprawled to the floor. Under the last parchment, Hira found a small latch and pulled it. There was a key in the compartment. Old, dusty, and forgotten. She stuffed it in her pocket.

Captain Sanaa bent and picked up some scrolls Hira had discarded. She turned them over in her hand. "This one has your name on it."

It looked inconspicuous, but sure enough, her name was there, written in her uncle's handwriting. She knelt and opened it. As she read the words of the dead man, she sat dejectedly on the floor, papers strewn about and her friends waiting for her direction. Tears, which she thought she'd lost, sprinkled against her lashes. Angrily, she wiped them.

Her uncle essentially stole a boy and kept him for his plans and schemes. This boy lived in the same castle as her, watching her from a window. Why had she never looked up? He'd forced this boy to become someone else, and somehow, in the ocean of lies, they'd met. Her uncle might've intended many things, but she doubted his niece loving that boy was one of them.

"What bothers you?" Delara asked, her voice neutral and kind, as she sat down on the bed and looked down at Hira.

She curled her fingers against the parchment and shook her head. "That he wasn't lying."

"The commander?" Sanaa asked, crossing her arms.

"He's not the commander." She looked at the women and laughed sardonically. "I know nothing of this man."

Sanaa scratched her chin. "I see. I suspected attachment, but not this."

"Suspected what?" Hira asked harshly. She sat there, holding tight to her tender chest. Her heart felt exposed, on display, where anyone could simply reach out and scar it.

"*Love*," Sanaa said it with distaste.

Hira slowly stood and faced her. "You think I'm weak because I allowed myself to love?"

Sanaa said nothing, her own face reserved. And though the captain seldom said much, Hira was keenly aware that love had broken the woman. Now they faced one another as mirror images of a polluted past.

Slowly, Hira nodded. "The funny thing about love is... that when you're in love, it doesn't feel like a weakness. When you're in love, you feel invisible. It's only when it betrays you that you realize what a liability it is."

"And you're afraid you'll have to forgive him," Delara said, standing to face them.

Seeing the reality, Hira almost gasped, "Yes."

"Bullshit," Sanaa snarled and grasped Hira's shoulder, pulling her in. Her face set and determined. "Listen to me, I know of this. I know the treachery of *love*. You don't have to forgive anyone if you're not ready. Forgiveness takes *everything* out of the wronged, our emotional strength, our fortitude, and leaves nothing for the assailant but to bask in *our* forgiveness."

Hira studied her face, her wide jaw, the muscles that ran over her cheekbones, and the curl of her lips. She saw herself in the captain and understood a harsh reality. If she didn't disentangle her hate, one day she would become embittered like the captain.

Slowly, she grasped Sanaa's arm and squeezed it. "I won't do anything until I'm ready. Until then... let's go question our prisoner."

When the three women entered the room, he woke up. Employing their intimidation tactic, they spread out and stared him down. He looked at each of them, but his eyes settled on Hira, who crossed her arms in a sign of indifference.

"State your name." Hira glazed him over with a look of disdain.

It was difficult to constantly hate him when she longed to believe him, to allot him forgiveness.

He swallowed, then quietly responded, "Justan Seaver."

Hira, enraged by his insipid statement, walked to him and smacked him. It was a resounding hit. He looked up at her, his eyes blazing, his cheeks pulled back tightly. If anything, he was more handsome than before. He'd not been this angry at her for a long time.

"Let's try again," Hira said between clenched teeth. "*What* is your name?"

His eyes flickered to Sanaa and Delara, who watched him without remorse. He turned back to Hira and shook his head.

"If you'd led the life I've lived, you wouldn't trust anyone, not even those cloaked in red," he said.

Delara shoved herself off the wall, and in a quick movement, she threw her ruby blade. It landed an inch from the man's head. He slowly looked at it, then back at her.

"Your name, *Garian*," Delara said in a curse-like manner. "I have plenty more knifes and you have plenty of body parts."

He looked at Hira, then fisted his hands into the linen of his bed.

"The king has asked for your head," Hira said as she lit her cigar, beholding him with cool eyes. She'd grown to ache for the smoke and the way it calmed her nerves. "He wants the head of Justan Seaver. On charges of kidnapping the royal heir to Istok, aiding a coup of Treveri, and most importantly conspiracy to commit regicide of the Queen of New Verden. The king said he would do it himself."

There was a small twinkle in his eyes as he watched her exhale. "Death doesn't scare me. I've died before. A thing we have in common."

Sanaa sat across from him and leaned forward. "You care for the boy? You know he'll be guilty by association. Not death, but jail. To rot in the dungeons of Mavros. It's not a pretty place. The scent of gangrenous skin permeates the walls."

He cast Hira an accusatory look. "You said you would protect him. You wouldn't do that to Quent."

Sanaa chuckled and Hira wordlessly passed her the cigar, which the captain took. "*She* won't. But the king will. Men in love…" the captain inspected him slowly, "do *silly* things."

He leaned forward and rubbed his hand over his face. Hira wished to believe his ruse, wished to believe he was a victim in all of this. "He's innocent. He knows *nothing*."

"And what is it he should know? I give you one last chance, Commander. Tell me your name and I can vouch for your life and Quent's freedom." Hira met his gaze.

He nodded and took a deep breath. "When your uncle died… I thought I would be trapped as Justan forever. But I knew it was more important than ever that I maintain the lie because I swore to him that I would protect you and help you as best I could."

"Protect her?" Sanaa pointed at Hira. "Excellent job."

"She would be dead if it weren't for me!" he yelled as he sat up and looked at Hira. "Furia wanted to kill you the moment we arrived at Korkoran. I convinced her to wait for the queen's arrival and set up a showy execution. She wished to have you raped, and I had to—" and he lost his words in a breath. "I had to tell her you enjoyed it rough, that it wouldn't be a punishment. So, they beat you up instead."

Hira's mouth dried, and she stood perfectly still as she studied him.

He looked down at his fingers. "A little over fifteen years ago, my brother and I boarded my father's ship for our maiden voyage."

"*Which* brother?" Delara asked.

"Let me finish!" he sighed and cursed. "Not Quent. My twin.

We were fifteen. It was the Sea Wife. Pirates attacked us not two days before arriving back home. That's how I got this." He pushed his bandages aside to show the ugly scar he'd once told her about. He'd lied about that, too. "I fell into the waters, but no one came to get me. Not my father, not my brother. Abandoned, I floated on debris for days. I had ocean sickness. I was delirious and at the edge of death, but a fishing expedition found me, and they brought me back to Treveri."

He sat up and winced.

"I went to find my father and brother at a pub we frequented, but the days at sea made me unrecognizable. That's when I heard my father tell my brother it was a good thing that I was dead. That way, he wouldn't have to plot my murder to inherit what was rightfully mine as firstborn. They laughed about it." His words dimmed to a whisper of pain.

Hira flinched and had to look away.

"I did the only thing I could think of. Like I told you, my lady, I went to the High Lord." He glanced between the women. "I was born Ryker Alsandar Seaver. First of my name, heir to Pinnacle Palace."

Warmth seeped into her as he pronounced his name in the proper Garian accent. As if he'd held those words within himself for so long, to allow them to live outside of his mind was a rare perfume, seldom enjoyed.

She had to take a breath. "And you swear this on Quent's life?"

He met her eyes. There was strength there. He was a man who knew when to show strength and when to hide it. A useful trait for a spy. "I do. And he's the most sacred thing to me, you know this. He's the only family I have. Only he doesn't know I'm really Ryker, the brother he believes is dead. So, I suppose I've fooled all those I love."

A burning ignited in Hira's belly, and she tightened herself against the softness of his tone. "Tell me about Justan."

Ryker grunted and shook his head. "Justan is my darling little brother, my twin. We are identical save for one minor detail. This," he pointed to his scar. "When I replaced him, I had to be stabbed again. The High Lord did the honors."

Hira's eyes flickered to his scar and back to him. "Where is Justan?"

Ryker laughed humorlessly. A soft, maddening tone entered his voice, "I think you know where he is."

Hira's hands trembled. As if they knew a ghost was nearby. "In this castle. In my dungeons."

He flinched. "You don't know my brother. He is devotion personified when it comes to Furia. And her to him, it is mutual. A complete obsession. It was always that way. Her desires are his desires, like she said to you. Everything is true. She is his religion. They think the same."

Hira stood suddenly. The key in her pocket itched, and she wished to meet the true Justan. "*Why* is he locked and hidden?"

Ryker scratched his beard. She noticed how long his fingers were. Callused from many years of handling ropes at the helm of a ship. "Because five years ago, the High Lord uncovered a plot for his assassination at the hand of his own daughter and Commander Justan. Lord Beltran captured him, and they hauled him to the dungeons. Unbeknownst to anyone, I took his place."

Sanaa pointed at his scar. "A wound to show that you bravely escaped with your life," she nodded. "Beltran was conniving."

"Yes. Even then, it was hard to convince Furia. I'm not Justan. I don't behave like him, and I don't speak like him. She was paranoid, she thought Beltran knew about the plot. The things I had to manage were pure insanity. Even as a child, she was always like that. She knew something was different, and two weeks later, Quent shows up on the docks. She's attributed my 'change' to Quent's presence." He looked away, his jaw tightening. "I've been thinking she purposely tortured him because she hated him. Felt Quent 'took me' from her."

Hira swallowed and gripped Ocean Fury. "Why would you do this? You've *fucked* this woman. You've pretended devotion."

The thought of them naked and tangled together made her ill despite her best efforts to remain unaffected. She couldn't. Not when she'd loved him, when she'd not even known his true name.

"I've *killed* for this woman," he spat. "Had to watch her torture people. You haven't seen a *glimpse*. She didn't show herself to you. She played the part of a lady for you, the lady she desperately wished to be."

"*Why*? Why have you kept up this charade?" Hira stepped closer.

"Furia regaled my father with stories of my sudden change. He demanded Quent be returned home. I refused. He froze all my assets. Or Justan's assets. The post gave me liberty when I didn't have Furia breathing down my neck. Also, Lord Beltran saved me. He kept me hidden. He fed me, clothed me, educated me. He only asked one thing. He only gave me this task. Beltran made me promise that I wouldn't reveal my identity until his heir was safely on the seat. He was... conniving yes, a terrible father, yes. But he was also my only friend. Maybe he confided things to me because I was a ghost. I didn't really exist. I had to show no emotion when I carried my High Lord's body out to sea. Since I was sixteen years old, he told me that for the good of Istok, I must keep his heir safe."

"You had plenty of time to confide in me on the ship!" Hira roared, refusing to digest his watery explanations. To absorb his truth would be to allow him leniency, and she was still too raw to contemplate that.

"Furia would've smelled the truth on you. She would've killed *all* of us. You had to remain innocent from the truth. I knew you had to arrive alive in Korkoran, and I had to wait for the queen." He laughed humorlessly, "Furia's paranoia brought Mr. Hyall on the ship, and he would follow my every move. She began withholding information from me, so I was blind to some of her plans."

"You should've told the queen when her father died," Sanaa said.

"So, we could be ignorant of Furia's plans?" Ryker snapped. "The High Lord kept this a secret for a reason, because he knew his firstborn was dangerous. He said I should not reveal my identity until Hira took the seat and that moment is now."

They were silent as they mulled over his words and the implications of the complex plan hidden from them. "Uncle coordinated a letter to Almira when he died. A girl delivered it a few weeks ago. He mentions you in it. He said to trust you, so I will."

"I don't trust spies," Sanaa said in an exhale of smoke.

"I was a *boy* when I was lost at sea. Raised in secret by a man who spent all his time calculating political moves. I contacted the queen to warn her about Antilay. Captain, I let you into the castle." He looked at Hira with wide eyes. "I shot Furia before she could kill you. I grabbed the queen because I had to provide *some* buffer of protection. If it weren't for me, you and the queen would be dead! I did *everything* his lordship asked of me. I always have. In the midst of this, I fell in love with you. I'm sorry about that." Ryker paused for a quick moment, then continued, "No. I'm not sorry. It was the *one* time I allowed myself a score of happiness."

Hira felt herself flush to her ears, unable to respond to his words. As if her very breath left her soul, and she didn't know where she stood.

Delara saved her from having to say anything. "Aye, he helped." She waved her hand about. "Enough with this. I believe him. I think it's high time we meet Commander Justan Seaver."

Chapter Fifty-Six

HIRA

The dungeons of Korkoran were a series of labyrinth-like structures. They built it before Lady Dominia's grandfather constructed the castle. It existed in pockets. A head jailor would be responsible for their section and only know the prisoners within their purview. This was to prevent communication between inmates.

But there were other sections, hidden along the coast, carved out of rock. They faced the Cliffs of Evike. Waves hit the stones at the base of Korkoran where the waters were unnavigable. It was said that from there, dragons were born. That once, the earth spurted them forth, casting them out of its belly and it had been in torment ever since.

There were a few cells for lifetime prisoners, which opened into the cliffs. They were beautiful, but treacherous. The prisoners suffered the splashing of the water and often soaking them with the torrential rains which pummeled Istok in the Fall. Lord Beltran didn't believe in lifetime imprisonment, so he rarely used them. He preferred a swift punishment or the option of being thrown out of Istok forever.

Ryker led the women past the cells that Hira recognized. Each syllable they said echoed into the darkness.

"He's been here for five years?" Delara asked. Her voice ricocheted off the walls, traveling for what seemed like miles.

Ryker carried a torch high above his head to illuminate their path. The plains of his back shifted when he walked. Hira's mind was in chaos over his actions and words. It took much determination to focus on the task at hand. She was about to meet the man whose name she'd whispered in bed.

"A little over. I visit him often," Ryker said over his shoulder. "Always attempting to make him see reason, but it's useless. The High Lord should've killed him. All that this incarceration has accomplished is making him angrier. He hardly sounds like a man who once commanded the armada."

His tone was bitter, and Hira could only imagine what it would be like to hate the person you were born with. To be so opposite that the mere fact Justan was alive angered him.

They followed a series of lit tunnels until it became more and more isolated. The ocean chill made the walls drafty. They walked until they saw no more guards stationed.

"We bring food and supplies on a monthly basis. I'm usually the one that brings the items, if I'm in port. If I'm not, it was Ley Wallace. Sufu takes care of him, but he won't live forever," Ryker explained.

"Monthly?" Sanaa asked, confused.

"Aye, he cooks for him. If food were to be brought daily, there would be too much contact," Ryker explained. "Guards would suspect."

"That means he didn't know of Furia's coup," Hira said.

Ryker glanced at her. "Nor Furia of him… if she had," he looked away. "We would all be dead."

They stopped before a wide door made of Duncan wood. The material was nearly impossible to break down.

"We reserve this place for the worst offenders," Ryker said.

"Or political prisoners," Sanaa pointed out.

"Or that." He slammed his palm on the door five times.

They didn't have to wait long for the center carving of the door to open. A man peered out that made Sanaa startle. He was of the old race, but he was an albino. Hira had never seen an albino before and was more interested in him than anything.

When Sufu saw Ryker, he smiled. "Master Seaver." He pressed his hand in a tulip-shape against his forehead.

Ryker returned the gesture with an equally pleasant smile. Sufu glanced at the women with slight apprehension.

"This is the Lady of Istok, Lady Hira, heir to the seat," Ryker explained. "She's come to meet her prisoner."

Sufu bowed his head, and the door opened. "How is the young Lord?"

Ryker smiled. "Young Master Quent is well. Hopefully, one day I can bring him."

Sufu's face shifted to worry. His pale lashes slightly trembled. "I don't know if that's a good idea. He's been angrier of late. A much different man than when I first arrived."

Ryker's jaw hardened, and he nodded. Sufu turned and led them into the passageway, paces ahead of them. Ryker's shoulder brushed against Hira's, and she tensed.

"You're very kind to him," Hira whispered.

He looked down at her. "I'm the only one who comes to see Justan. The least I can do is be kind. It's a lonely life Sufu leads, and he leads it with dignity."

"Surely, there's a better job for this man to do. Locked in here must be awful," Delara said.

But Sanaa shook her head. "They would shun him in Suid. Favia-cursed. Likely saved from death as a child."

"He enjoys his task and takes great care of his charge," Ryker said, his voice defensive.

They could hear the violent crashing sea as they entered a large room in the cave. There was a spectacular view of the turbulent ocean. The room contained a small cot and cooking implements. Some chairs, scrolls, and general household items.

Facing the waves was a great jail cell. The bars were thick and solid, made of white iron, the most salt-water resistant material in the world. It was difficult to see the actual cell because the ocean was bright against the room. But inside was furniture, books, chairs, a bed, and all the comforts never provided to a regular inmate.

"My *lord*, you have visitors," Sufu said, and the tone of respect was not lost on Hira.

The women paused as laughter began. Hira felt the hairs on the back of her neck rise and Sanaa unsheathed her ruby blade. Eyes watched them from the darkened cell, then a hand slowly emerged and grasped one bar.

"Well, well, well... if it isn't the *good* guys."

A man appeared from the shadows and Hira felt sick to her stomach. Like she'd ingested poison. It was *Justan*. It was Ryker. They were identical, but there was something so sinister about his smile and eyes that she shrank back against the vision.

Justan immediately focused on Hira and Ocean Fury. He threw his head back and laughed, cackling maliciously.

"The Lady of fucking Istok! What an honor, my lady!" his voice boomed.

It was like beholding an evil version of Ryker. Of the man who claimed to love her. The one who fretted over his brother's wellbeing. A twisted vision she would never forget. She pulled her wits about her and met his eyes, though it hurt to do so.

"What's your name, prisoner?" Hira stepped forward.

"Are we going to play *that*?" he asked with a mocked tone of sadness as he raked her over. "I know better games, girl. You might not like them, but I'll surely enjoy them. Sorry about your uncle. Can't say he didn't deserve it." He licked his lips as his eyes lingering on Hira. "What the hell happened to you?" He gnashed his teeth, delighting in her recoil. "It's been a while since any hand other than my own has wrapped itself around my cock. You're ugly and disfigured, but in this fucking place," he waved his hands in a wild gesture, "it matters little. After all, look what it does to a man like *me*."

Hira wasn't certain if he was putting on an act to insult her, or if this was how he usually was. Ryker, however, stepped forward and pointed at his brother. Watching them like this, facing one another, was disturbing enough.

"Do not speak to her like that," Ryker said, and Justan turned sharply to stare at him. His face shifted to disgust.

Ryker had been right. Had she known the real Justan, she would've never mistaken the two. It was as if the light of the sun met the storms of the night and in that meeting eclipsed the world.

"You seem worse for wear, big brother. I do hope it was Furia who stabbed you," Justan said with a delighted smile.

Ryker sneered at him, confirming the assumption.

Justan laughed once more, then hissed and pressed his hand against his cock, rubbing it back and forth. *"Fuck!"*

Sanaa made a noise of disgust. Justan studied her carefully.

"Oh, I'll be a gentleman like my big brother and hold that image until you leave. Don't want to disturb the delicate sensibilities of the *ladies.*"

Hira had enough of such vulgar displays. She stepped forward until she faced him, and he openly caressed her with his eyes. "I've things to say to you."

He licked his lips. "Of course, you do."

"Furia is *dead,*" Hira deadpanned.

His demeanor changed. His gaze darkened to an unearthly shade. "You *lie,*" his words came out in a hiss. Like the Favia when they lapped at her wound, delighting in her dance with death.

"You can thank your big brother for harpooning her," Hira walked slowly to him.

Justan's eyes narrowed on Ryker. "You *promised* me!" and his hands reached for him between the bars, his fingers curling into a claw. "You said you wouldn't hurt her!"

Ryker flinched. "She was out of control, Justan."

"If not him, someone else would've." Hira stepped in between the twins.

Justan's head swiveled to Hira, and he gnashed his teeth. "Show me her corpse or you're a liar."

The High Lady swallowed, aptly caught in tricky words. She lifted her chin. "The harpoon didn't kill her. She fell on an oil lamp and was consumed by fire before falling into the bay."

He slowly registered the news, closing his eyes and inhaling deeply. As if he was sensing Furia through his mind. "What a little liar you are, *Lady* Hira. Just like your uncle. Furia lives. I *feel* her. We are connected more powerfully than you know. She is a goddess. She will rise again, she will conquer. The blood in her veins is stronger than any of you."

She crossed her arms and didn't give into his words, even though they were already a fear in her mind. "She attempted a coup and failed. She was in this very castle."

Justan pressed his face between the bars. "She failed because she didn't have *me*," his stare flickered to Ryker. "*He's* a poor imitation. Like the Suidian wine sold in the ports of Norr. They call it *berry ale*. Did you know that *girl?*"

Hira scoffed and looked away.

"I told you there's no point," Ryker said. "He's always been obsessed with her."

Justan let out a snort of laughter. "I can imagine what Furia thinks of *Justan* now. Impotent, weak, salivating over our brother's wellbeing. Attempting to dissuade her plans instead of supporting her when you know very well, she has every right to take revenge! I delight in the fact that she killed Beltran—manipulating, corroded bastard that he was!"

"Have respect for the dead, man," Ryker snapped, his face flushed red.

"You're pathetic!" Justan continued his laughter. "A pitiable excuse for a brother! Limp dick. Always were! Even when mother was alive, you couldn't wait to get a little of her attention, bringing her flowers and writing her poems. Where were you when she gasped for her final frail breath? Did you tell the lady how you cried in the corners of the ship because you lost your *mommy?*"

"Shut up!" Ryker rushed at him, but Delara and Sanaa grabbed him before he could reach Justan. Hira had never seen him angrier. His neck veins bulged, and his face reddened.

"He's not worth it," Sanaa snarled.

Hira glared at Justan as she placed a firm hand over Ryker's chest. His heart beat erratically against his ribs. "For someone so caught in the charms of Furia, you're a funny one to label *him* pathetic."

Justan lost his smile. "Oh, girl… that lost puppy play is all *him*. That's never been me. I never begged for her attentions. She gave them *willingly*. When we fucked, it was…" he closed his eyes and pressed his face against the bars. "Pain so good it makes you cum at the thought. The moment you replaced me, she knew something was wrong. My girl is smart. What did she do? Attribute my personality change to the appearance of Quenty? What did Furia do to torture him?"

Ryker stared at his brother. "How did you know that?"

A wicked grin slowly emerged on Justan's face. She wouldn't confuse the two again after this moment. There was a chasm of difference.

"Because I know *my* girl. Did she poison the brat? Make him sick for years? Or took him to her favorite medics? Poor little brother," he sneered and turned to Hira. "Did you know that when we were young and they brought Furia to our home, my twin and I competed for her attentions?"

"I was a child, I didn't understand the evil in that woman," Ryker spat, he was so tense and angry that Hira had to stand next to him, afraid of what he would do.

"We would write her poems. My brother was better at it, but I dabbled." Justan shrugged. "One day, father said if you want her to notice you, you're going to have to set a higher standard," Justan said as he smiled at Ryker, who looked sick.

"Stop," Ryker said.

"Remember Kilsie? Our nanny's daughter? She was five," Justan breathed. "She had taken in a puppy that week and had been sleeping with the mongrel each night. It yelped and cried pitifully, driving Furia to madness. I hated to see her angry, so I did what any devoted suitor would do. I took my blade, sliced its throat, and left the body on Kilsie while she slept. When she woke, her screams filled the entire palace." He chuckled maliciously, studying his nails as if he were recounting a comforting tale over a winter ale. "I found Furia and whispered into her hair 'I did it for you.' My brother never wrote another poem again. That's when mother started hating me."

"Mother didn't hate you," Ryker insisted.

Justan's eyes brightened. "She was a *weak* woman. I abhor weak women."

"Have you no respect for the dead?" Sanaa hissed.

Ryker shook his head. "You don't realize the evilness in your words."

"But I *do*. You see, I've had a lot of time to think. And now I realize the world is full of people who believe they are good and just. Only, their actions are never good and just. *For the good of the people*, they burn the world down. And who suffers? Those peasants, too poor to know better, too poor to fight back. The only thing the royals have ever done for this world is fuck it up. So here comes Furia, with a legitimate reason for anger and you call her evil. You think she's worse than your queen? *Nay*."

"Almira would never!" Sanaa stepped forward.

Justan smiled widely. "Does it make you *uncomfortable*? Well, fuck your discomfort. Because guess what? The world is an uncomfortable, nasty place. Full of nasty people. You strut around believing you can make it paradise. It's not. It's Hell. You live here with the rest of us. Get used to it. Maybe one day you'll stop your little ideological parade and give into it. Like I have.

I spent too long being a respectable member of this society. I knew all the little chatter performed in little corners while holding little delicate glasses of wine. Five years in this hellhole puts things into perspective when you've got no one to speak to but this fucker," and he pointed to Sufu, who watched from a corner. "So now... if Furia wants the world, I'll give her the world. Rotten place that it is. Even if I have to kill every man, woman, and child. I'll do it *with pleasure*. I'll enjoy every second. Like all the royals before us, I won't watch the world burn. I'll light the damn match myself," he clutched at his bars. "Yes, I do evil deeds, but so do you!"

His words were so incredibly disturbing they reminded her of Ley Coster's death. She backed away. "There's a reason my uncle kept you here, hidden. A *secret*."

He delighted in the disturbance his rhetoric was causing. "Do you know what the beauty of a secret is? They tend to get out," he drawled. "And when I do, I'll find my Furia. Then I'll come after *you,* and all the kin in your line. Then you'll know what it's like to be hunted. And I *always* catch my prey."

Sanaa stepped forward and pulled out her sword. "This cell is too close to the secret stairway that leads to the Queen's quarters. We don't need him escaping and finding them. We kill him *now.* I'll do it."

Justan turned and studied her, his eyes sharpening. "I think I'd like that very much."

"He's baiting you," Ryker said. "We've never opened the door because we don't have the key. We lost it with the High Lord's death."

"I have it," Hira said and took pleasure in Justan's head, slowly turning to her.

"A little heirloom from our wise High Lord?" He cocked his head.

She pulled the key from her pocket and dangled it before him. "Your life is in *my* hands. And when this is over, when Furia's blood has painted my sword, I'll push you off this cliff and watch you drown."

"I look forward to that day, my lady. Send my regards to Quent. Hopefully, the little fucker didn't suffer too much." A smile glazed his face as he melted back into the shadows.

Hira grabbed Ryker before he could rush to the bars and hauled him to the exit.

"Seal this place!"

Isabelle Olmo

Chapter Fifty-Seven

HIRA

The next day, they lay Madhavi on an onyx stone, like all noble warriors. Sanaa kneeled first and paid her respects. She said the Suidian prayers and pressed her forehead against M's hand.

When she stood, she looked at Hira. "Suidians burn their dead immediately, an offering to the Great Eagle."

Hira nodded. "I'll have the knights provide you with what you need."

Delara bent forward with red, pained eyes. They had all been good friends. Perhaps this was what Hira missed most about being part of the Red Guard. The sense of unity and comradery between the women. They were a unit.

When it was Hira's turn, she stared at M's face; smooth and polished. No one would know that she died filled with arrows, using her body as a shield to protect the queen. Sanaa mentioned M was ill, *dying*. Hira was glad M's death led to an onyx stone, rather than a deathbed of agonizing pain. M would've hated that.

Hira touched M's face. All her warmth was gone. Her devilish humor and her laugher at stories that shouldn't be told in good company. She kneeled before M and her throat thickened. It took twelve arrows to bring her down. She was a true Suidian warrior of legend. Hira would write her name in the royal scrolls so that all that read them learned that Madhavi the Suidian Warrior died at the gates of Korkoran, protecting the queen during the Battle of the Usurper.

"Favia, take your warrior. Allow her into the land of the honored, for she died protecting her queen," Hira whispered.

When she stood, Sanaa held the red cloth in her hand and the three of them wrapped M's body. Then they stared at one another, as if realizing their dwindling numbers.

"Three gone, three left," Delara said rather somberly.

Hira took a sharp breath. "We have work to do. I don't believe that our coming to be Red Guards was a coincidence in this life. I think the sea gods brought us together because they heard the rumblings of the land."

It felt right to have this conversation while M was still around. Until the flames consumed her body, she was still one of them.

"Arrigo has gained a significant number of followers. The Norrian houses have split their support. They fight amongst themselves more than they fight Ouest. General Vine retreated most of the army out of the sector." Sanaa leaned against the wall.

Delara crossed her arms and signaled with her hand. "There are four grand houses of power in Norr. High Lord Dag still has a handle on House Ritter and House Benici. Lord Arrigo has taken back House Markey and House Cavallo. He controls half of Norr and he's set his eyes on Easima, as they always were."

"Who has the largest coffers?" Hira asked.

"Cavallo," Sanaa said. "They own the frozen gold mines off the Sea of Torkin. It means the east part of Norr has fallen. Dag remains in the West."

"And we still have his heir in the dungeons of Mavros?" Hira looked to Delara, who nodded. "Then Furia will soon control the north of Istok, where it meets with Arrigo's territory."

"What brings Ciraton to the economy?" Delara asked.

"Timber," Hira said grimly. "Before I ran away, I heard Uncle complain that Furia's mother sent less and less timber. If she cuts off our supply, which she will, we'll have to get our timber from Suid. It's a long journey."

"And expensive," Sanaa looked at Hira. "You still have your armada."

"I do." Hira rubbed her eyes. "But I have no commander."

"Ryker—"

"I don't know what to do about him yet," Hira stopped her, and Sanaa raised a brow.

"Don't let your feelings for him impede wise decisions. If he was an excellent commander, allow him to continue," Delara said, always wise and calm in her choice of words.

Feelings. She hated that she still had them.

"Plus, he's devoted to you," Sanaa said with a double-meaning smile. "Men are simple that way."

Hira sighed and rubbed her forehead, not wishing to abide on her relationship with Ryker Seaver. "Things were simpler when we only had to worry about the queen."

Afterwards, Hira went to see Almira. She should've come to her yesterday but exhaustion overwhelmed them all. They had to set things straight. Hira didn't wish to stay angry at her cousin. Perhaps they had to find a better way to communicate now that Hira no longer sat attentively at her feet.

The queen listened to the explanation of the Seaver twins while the baby suckled from her.

"I sense there is something you're withholding," Almira said, lightly patting the baby's bottom.

Hira looked down and studied her mangled hand. "You were right about what you said. During my journey here, I formed a romantic attachment with Commander Seaver."

"Ryker Seaver?" Almira clarified.

Hira nodded. She didn't see why she should be ashamed of the occurrences. He'd lured her in. The commander was handsome, charming, and kind. She couldn't pull apart which parts were true and which parts he'd pretended for the benefit of the crew loyal to Furia.

Almira took a deep breath and adjusted the baby on her breast with a wince. "It seems to me we should commend Lord Ryker."

"He *lied.*"

"Hira, if my father said to trust him, despite my anger at his actions, he wouldn't lie. We should consider Lord Ryker a friend and an ally."

Hira sat with her words, pondering them as one ponders a game. She hated to think that love could be a game. Perhaps she had idolized notions of love. That it should be pure and truthful. That once in love, everything would fall in place and no further worries would arise. Like the stories.

"Why romance me?" Hira hated the shakiness and desperation in her voice. But she needed to ask someone. She needed clarity.

Almira sighed. "Don't you think that perhaps he's earnest about his interest?"

Hira huffed and stood up. As she'd bathed last night, she finally inspected herself in the water mirror. She'd cried and that was her great shame. She'd never felt uglier and less desirable as a woman. Society ingrained in women's minds that they should be desired and lovely. Between the scar on her face, her twisted arm, her butchered hair, and her eyes a pit of ice, all her softness was pounded away and converted to pure rock.

"Don't be ridiculous. Look at me!"

Almira watched her pitifully. "I believe that Lord Ryker has an interest in you. Furia saw it and used it to her advantage to keep you distracted. You fell into her trap. You'll have to deal with that. Ryker is an excellent ally to have. He's a talented actor and could easily get back in her good graces as 'Justan' if we needed him to."

Hira could not believe her words. She stared at her cousin as if she'd lost her mind. She often forgot that while others lived their life one moment to the next, Almira never stopped calculating. Beltran had raised her as such.

"How can you say that? It's not fair to use him in that manner. He's paid his price for the past five years. His life should be his."

The Princess fussed, and Almira called the nurse and handed her the baby. She looked back at Hira with those piercing, unflinching black eyes. "You're my cousin and the Lady of Istok. You realize our lives are not our own and you cannot marry a man thought dead. A man without title, lands, or family."

Her words were the death knell long sounded. Hira knew them. Knew their patterns. But to know a bell will ring and to actually hear it ring are two different things.

"Will you do the same to your daughter?" Hira asked.

Almira flinched so hard Hira would've thought she'd hit her. She didn't meet Hira's eyes. "Osaria will have responsibilities she cannot ignore. She will have no choice if the king and I tell her to marry a man of our choosing. We are at *war*."

Hira whirled on her with a flushed face. All her feelings were on the verge of collapsing. Surely, it was too much for one person to feel it all at once.

"What are we fighting for? Land? Resources? Justice? Vengeance? We'll send peasants to die for a war *we* created! We twist it so that they believe winning is vital for them and their wellbeing. That our country will never be safe until they defeat the enemy in battle. But these wars are of our own making."

Almira's nostrils flared. "Just because the war was not of their making will not stop Furia and Arrigo from burning their crops, killing their children, raping their women, and making slaves out of the men. War affects all. It's our job, our *duty*, and responsibility to protect them as best we can. I don't want war!" She threw her hands up, "I'd like to be back at my castle, raise my child and fuck my husband all day long, but I don't have that liberty and neither do *you*."

She was silent, and Hira admitted she acted unfair. Almira never wished for war. She tried her best to avoid it, but it seemed the will of one would never conquer the will of the world.

"You should be veiled, cousin," Almira said softly after a moment.

"I'll not veil," Hira said forcefully. "Why is it women have to veil themselves and place their life on pause for a year while men trapeze around in glory? Who made *that* rule? Who created that custom?"

"You're angry—"

"*Yes*, I am. I'm frustrated! I've... been kidnapped and hurt, I've died, I've been deceived and used. People have died, my *mother* has

died! I'm tired!" Hira sobbed and pressed her hand to her mouth.
"I've a monster that looks like the man I love trapped in my own
castle. A woman is out there who wants to destroy us all. Still, I must
be the Lady of Istok, save our people, and lead them! It's too much
for one person. I need a rest."

Her entire body shook as she dwelled on her emotions, the
tender feelings she'd kept bottled up since she stepped foot in
Treveri. Like a dam long held at bay by mortar and rocks, Hira Balik
was crumbling, and she didn't know how to right herself.

"Do you truly love him?" Almira whispered after a while.

Hira shut her eyes. "I *do*. I'm ashamed that I do," she admitted
between clenched teeth.

Almira sighed and ran her fingers through her hair. "Don't be
ashamed of loving him. If father said he was to be trusted, then trust
him."

"What's the point? I can't marry him, even if I wanted to. Even
if I forgave him for the hurt and the *shame*, he's no one. You've said
it," Hira whimpered. "He's a ghost and I'm the Lady of Istok, whose
cunt you will sell to the highest bidder. Like your *daughter*."

Almira swallowed thickly and looked genuinely sorry. "Focus
on Istok, and all will fall into place."

Hira looked at her. "You know I'll do it. In the end, I'll do it.
I'll marry an ally for the sake of peace. I've always trusted your
judgement; you've always known best."

"I don't always know best," Almira said darkly. "There will be
times when I won't be around, and you'll have to make decisions
which will affect people. Then you too will carry the responsibility
for that."

Chapter Fifty-Eight

RYKER

When he was six, a fish bone wedged in his throat. He'd hacked and cried, believing his end was a moment away. His mother, with steady fingers, held him still. She expertly extracted it out of his mouth and held it up in triumph.

"Does that feel better?"

She'd smiled, and he'd thrown his arms around her, clutching her black hair, inhaling her scent and ensuring himself he wouldn't die, choking on a fish bone. It took a long while for him to eat seafood once more, always afraid of what small, ossified particle might kill him.

That's what these past few years felt like. A bone in his windpipe. Scraping bit by bit all the puzzle pieces which encompassed Ryker and replacing them with a Justan-shaped simulacrum. Like a skin-changer of legend, he'd mantled Justan and his idiosyncrasies over his body. The peculiarities of his brother etched in his veins until he was only a marionette that Justan, from his prison, controlled.

Somewhere along the line, he'd given up. He saw that now. He'd resigned himself to *being* Justan. And so, he'd taken the carcass that was Ryker Alsandar Seaver, swept all the mangled limbs into a bag and tossed it out to sea. Quent was dying—at least it's what Furia made him believe—and so too would Ryker. There was no point, no hope, no salvation. The embryonic process begun in the womb would reverse and so they would be one creature, one mind, one body once more.

But then Hira had come.

At the thought of her, he curled into himself. He was fifteen once more, looking down from the hidden servant's quarter, watching her climb a tree. In that moment, he understood why he always stared out the window. She was happy. A merry girl, always smiling and laughing and running. She was chaos, refusing to comb her hair, refusing to mind her gowns. She was free, and he was trapped. Like a princess in a story, who observed the world below, he watched and envied the way she carelessly lived, throwing caution to the wind. Each time he observed her, he'd wanted her to look up. Look up! Look at me. See me. Save me. Though she was just a child then, she was fire and fire was lionhearted.

When she stood being judged by Furia's court, she had entranced him. Shackled as she was, bloody as she was, he'd seen no one as powerful. As sure of themselves. He realized that the woman was afraid of nothing. Not of death. Not of pain. Not even Furia.

He'd loved her then. He might be her secret protector, but she was the hero he'd always longed for. She would release him from his torment.

When Hira came to him, she found him alone in his room. Yesterday she had removed the guards from his door so that he could walk the fortress as he wished. There was disappointment in her gaze at finding him waiting. As if she hoped he *would* leave, disappear. Confirm her hate. But he hadn't. He wouldn't. This fortress was his home. He had nowhere to go.

"My lady." He bowed his head. "You've just missed Quent. I'm afraid he's a little obsessed with the Red Guard. He follows Captain Sanaa everywhere."

Hira pretended aloofness. "I'm sure the captain must love that," she paused. "You look better."

He had a momentary thought. "If you've got the time, I'd like to show you something."

She raised a brow but said nothing. Tentatively, he stepped out of the room, and she followed a few steps behind, her hand still on the hilt of her sword. He took the path from the infirmary to the servant's quarter he'd inhabited for ten years. He noticed it was the same path he'd taken with Lord Beltran to begin his new life as a ghost.

When he reached the servant's stairs, she paused. "Where are you taking me?"

He glanced at her. "To my room. Where I lived for a decade."

Her eyes widened, and the red hairs of her lashes trembled slightly. There was a flash of anger on her face, though he wasn't certain *who* she was angry at. Perhaps her uncle. But he shouldn't recklessly attempt to determine her feelings. He'd rather wait until she was ready to share them.

Ryker followed the stairs he knew well, pausing when his shoulder smarted and he had to catch his breath. Hira said nothing, but she softened, and it seemed to him she wanted to ask if he was well, but she didn't speak.

When they arrived at his door, he unlatched it and opened it to allow her entrance. The room was the same. Piles and piles of scrolls, many of them containing his handwriting. The same window. The same dingy bed and wobbly chair.

She entered, her eyes lingering on the items within the small space. She took her time, thoughtful consideration, then finally walked to the window. He went and stood next to her.

"The gardens," she mumbled.

The temptation to study the soft curve of her neck, the pert nose, and the raised red brow was too great. She was so beautiful, so bright, like staring at the sun. Worth the burn to enjoy the warmth.

He pointed to the large oak tree which Hira loved to climb. "You always used your right foot to start your climb. You should've used the left. I... I always wanted to tell you."

Hira looked at him sharply and backed away, her breathing harsh as she said, "I don't know what to say to you."

Ryker flushed. He shouldn't have said that. What a fool he was.

But he'd not watched her with ill intentions. Trapped, he had nothing else to look at. She and Almira provided a daily distraction, a sort of almanac for the passing years.

"There was little to do for days on end. I apologize, my lady, I shouldn't have looked," he breathed.

But the lady, with her bruised face, cut lip, sharp eyes, and butchered hair, laughed sardonically. He didn't know where he stood with her. She was a cliff, and he was the ignorant traveler that would meet his demise for a chance to swim in the cobalt waves below.

"He trapped you. Just like he trapped Justan. He trapped you both," she said. "It's not right. None of this is right." She tossed some of his papers, pressing her hands against his handwriting. "I read his secret scrolls. I read his account. You were *fifteen*. Quent's age. He locked you here for *years*. In exchange for freedom, you had to become your brother."

Her words burned into him because he didn't like to linger on those thoughts. He recognized what Beltran did was wrong, but another part of him understood. There was nowhere else for Ryker to go. His mother was dead, and his father wished *him* dead. What was a fifteen-year-old boy to do? He had no money, no power, nothing but the rags he wore. He was an impoverished prince of a once great people.

"The queen wants to keep your identity a secret." Hira met his eyes and that strength he'd witnessed in Antilay was there. A fire that would save him. "I said *no*."

He couldn't breathe. His chest felt tight. Like he was at the end of a long hallway he'd been walking towards for years. He moved closer to her, as if she were that light of hope.

"*Why* did you say that?"

They locked eyes on one another, and he was a boy once more, alone with his thoughts. Lonely and cast aside. Petrified of being forgotten, of never being allowed out. Of being killed by his own brother and father.

"Because... you're entitled to happiness," she whispered.

Had it really only been a few days since she'd been his? Since she'd caressed his hair and nuzzled her nose to his temple? Once upon a time, she'd loved him. Once upon a time, he'd belonged to her. How he yearned to grasp the hands of time and turn back their path.

"And what about you? Are you entitled to it?" he asked, leaning in.

She broke the spell and looked away. "I'm the Lady of Istok. I've a country to run and a foe to defeat. War is brewing. Happiness is not my immediate concern."

And he keenly felt the loss of her innocence. Of the merry girl who sang songs while climbing a tree. The hardest part to admit was his own hand in the death of her innocence. He stepped closer and caressed her elbow. She inhaled sharply, tightening her jaw against the sensations his fingers caused her.

"Let me fight them with you, at your side. I ask for no return of sentiment, but I want to be on your team, back-to-back, swords at hand. I'll take that," he said fiercely. "Your weak left shoulder. My weak right."

She pulled her arm back. "I can't."

Pain drenched him. She was stubborn and hurt. He'd wounded her. She would not easily forget.

"You cannot forgive me, can you?"

More importantly, he realized that he'd not done anything to earn her forgiveness. A part of him foolishly expected that upon revealing the true nature of his identity, she would forget the past and the pain. But she wouldn't. Not Hira Balik. Not the fierce girl he loved. That wouldn't be her. He was unclothed, soft, and desperate. Ready to take what crumbs she would throw his way. He'd deceived her. He had to live with that.

"I don't know who you are," she finally said. The tears were pushing against her throat. "I fell in love with a fictional construction."

He shook his head. His fingers ghosted up to feel her cheek in a desperate plea. "I didn't pretend. I told you as much. When it was just you and me... *that* was real."

"You let me whisper *his* name in bed," her voice was a lacerated wound.

His hands dropped to his side. Each time she'd said 'Justan', he'd recoiled. A stark reminder that he was a marionette. A wooden boy, strings attached. Not real. A shadow at a window.

"I understand you, Hira Balik." The pain in his heart was unbearable. He was desperate to somehow stay near her, a useless shadow in her court. "Will I continue my post as commander?"

"I'm not sure," she said truthfully.

He nodded, pressing his tongue against his cheek as he breathed deeply.

"Then I have nothing. Same as I began. Would you... I know I've no right to ask, but... would you keep Quent under your wing? I'll have to make my own way and I won't have much to give him."

He was once more wounded, at the feet of House Balik, with nothing to his name.

She cleared her throat. "You rendered a great service to my uncle in your task. You'll be compensated. And yes, I'll take Quent as my ward. Unfortunately, he's a victim."

The minutes passed by in silence, inches from each other, neither meeting the other's eyes. He couldn't think straight. It was all ending. His mission. His time in Korkoran. He was finally free, and he'd never disliked it more.

Finally, he stepped back. "Thank you, my lady."

She nodded. "The king has ordered a feast to commemorate the birth of the princess. You're welcome to join us. You don't have to hide. I'll have... servants bring you clothing and..."

"Hira." He came closer to her. He brushed the tips of her hair, and she froze.

Then, to his horror, he broke through her defense and the tears erupted from her eyes.

"I wish you would've trusted me," and it came out like a sob. "I accepted death in that cell alone and without hope. A part of me *died* there. You *broke* me for a *task!*"

And he suddenly felt that he, too, was breaking. He too was pieces on the floor. Ryker didn't know what to do, what to say, how to fix it. He was alone at sea, watching the Sea Wife leaving him for dead.

She pressed her hand against her lips as she sobbed, hunched over.

"Had you said something sooner, would Ley Coster be alive? Would M? The entire world is on fire and how I wish I could get lost in your arms because gods help me, I still love you despite my anger."

She furiously wiped her tears against her shoulder, cleansing the evidence of her pain. A thickness coated his throat. A bone carving into the sinewy meat of his body.

"I am so sorry," he whispered.

And she met his eyes, a crystalline blue sharpened into daggers. "I know."

She turned and left. He stared at where she'd been, the imprint of her boots still on the dusty stone. A trace of her presence. He sat down on the seat he'd occupied for years. His legs were too long. Now he was grown. Outside, there were no joyous voices. No distractions.

He was a man with no name. A ghost.

Isabelle Olmo

Chapter Fifty-Nine

HIRA

Hira's heart was shattered in two. One part wished to forget the past and begin anew, the other was a withered stone of hate. She was most embarrassed to be found with red eyes by Ley Olan when he came to provide her with the requested reports. The Ley wisely said nothing, and Hira drove all notions of Ryker out of her mind as she listened to her Ley.

The celebration was the balm they all needed for the recent events. They arranged tables and chairs throughout the streets for the city to attend. Pounds upon pounds of scalla were roasted, and its peppered bouquet filled the hallways and put everyone in a jovial mood. Despite the burials of the morning, they looked forward to remembering the dead and basking in the new hope the princess brought.

Technically, Hira shouldn't be participating in the festivities. She should have veiled herself, but she shoved the black veil in the gown's pocket and carried the color like a knight would in battle. It's not that she didn't mourn her mother. She was too emotionally drained to dwell on much after she'd spent the afternoon crying.

Behind Almira, Hira would be the highest-ranking lady and would have to dance with the King, Lord Thebo, and many nobles.

It was not a night for armor and Almira had alluded to it in not so many words. Hira scowled at the cobalt blue gown Almira picked. The sleeves were long and intricate, and the neckline was so risqué, one could appreciate the swell of her tiny breasts. Most impractical for fighting.

In a fit of anger over the lack of control, she sat before her water mirror, naked, observing the many bruises marring her skin. There was still a sharp pain in her ribs from where she'd been kicked. She stared at her destroyed hair, the awful patches of baldness. Once upon a time, she'd cut her strands herself. It was one of her most empowering moments. A week ago, she lay prone, pinned to the ground as Furia butchered it and left her a sobbing mess on the floor.

Her eyes flashed to her ruby blade, and she grasped it. Without thinking, and ensuring she kept her eyes on her task, she shaved the remaining hair off her head. She used water and soap on the tricky bits, watching as the small scraps of hair scattered to the ground. She would start over, a fresh beginning.

When she was done, she was thoroughly bald. She oiled her scalp, soothing the redness the blade left in its wake.

For the first time in weeks, she could breathe. She'd *chosen* this. She controlled her body and her fate. Let them all gaze. She didn't care. She was the Lady of fucking Istok, and if Her Ladyship preferred to be bald, she would be bald.

The maids cried out at the sight of her when they came to dress her, but a sharp glare from Hira quieted them. They wordlessly dressed and adorned her with her ancestral jewels. When she next looked at herself in the water mirror, it amazed her to find she looked lovely and strong. With her hair gone, her eyes became the focus of her face. People would stare at her and *speculate*.

She idly considered hiding in the gardens or taking Quent on a ride to the coast to see the moon bathing the sea. But a knock sounded and the king himself came to escort her. *Oh, this was awful.* After their argument, she hardly knew what to say to him.

King Alton faltered for a moment at the sight of her appearance, then rapidly composed himself. He bowed and extended his hand. "My wise wife asked me to come and get you. She was afraid you wouldn't show." He smiled and brought her hands to his forehead. "You look wonderful, cousin."

"I look bald is what you mean," she quipped.

He continued to smile and shrugged. "I know many a bald man. Perhaps it's time to acquaint myself with bald women."

His majesty must've trained on how to appease women after his marriage with Almira.

"I should apologize for before," he said humbly. "I overstepped my boundaries."

She glanced at him. She'd never taken him for someone who issued apologies. There seemed to be many things she was ignorant about her cousin-in-law. Not wishing to continue her anger at him, she sighed and allotted room for friendship.

"Almira was right, quarreling amongst ourselves will solve little."

"Yes, she's always right, that one. Infuriating, really," he said with a wink as he led her to the hall.

Hira slightly relaxed. "*Most* of the time. We can't let her suspect."

"She's well aware of it," he said as he raised a brow, delighted in his own quips.

They nodded at a few passing nobles, both hating the pomposity. Both disliked the charade a false smile could conjure.

"Will the queen be joining us?" she asked.

"Later, she's making sure the princess is well-fed and asleep before she joins." He looked around the finely decorated room, the food laid out, the guests mingling and smiling. "I like the way you Istokians celebrate. The fiddled music, the dancing. I've even come to enjoy your peppered scalla."

Hira eyed the dance floor with apprehension. "I prefer fighting."

He grunted in agreement, "Give me a war over the finery of court. That's something we have in common. But the queen insists on these gatherings. Who are you and I to go against her will?"

She sensed a tone of teasing. "Well, you're the *king*."

He smiled widely. "Exactly."

She laughed, still not sure if it was appropriate, but he seemed in a jovial mood, which she attributed to the birth of his daughter.

The trumpets sounded when they entered the center of the room. The nobles raised their goblets and cheered. It became a sea of greeting faces she wasn't sure she trusted. They all pledged their allegiance to Istok and the *true* Lady of Istok. Her countenance startled a few, but nobles were experts at masking their true feelings, and so she knew she would also need to hide her emotions.

She was relieved when Lord Thebo rescued her, taking her by the arm and proclaiming her obvious hunger. Which was true, she could eat a bull by herself but knew that wasn't proper. The king welcomed all the nobles with false smiles.

Ryker and Quent were at the end of the table and Ryker's eyes were on her. She looked down at her goblet and desperately wished her complexion wouldn't flush so deeply. She could sense his attention lingering on her head, it was in the softening of his gaze.

The meal was served, and the chatter turned to choruses of delight. She hadn't enjoyed roasted pork in a long time and loved crunching on the crispy, salty skin.

It was at the end of the meal when Almira arrived. She stunned the nobles in her golden gown with a pattern of an eagle sewn into it. The skirt was wide to disguise her post birthing belly and Hira wondered if she would start a new trend amongst the ladies at court.

The King was instantly at his feet and helped her walk to the table in short, slow steps. No one could perceive if she was in discomfort because Almira was a grand actress. Before she sat, she welcomed everyone and assured them all the princess was in perfect health and was enjoying a long sleep after a good meal. When she spotted Hira, she faltered, her eyes widening at the sight of her, her nostrils flaring. Hira lifted her chin and coolly met her eyes.

Lord Barnabus stood with a wobble but held himself straight. "A toast. To the crowns, to the princess and her good health, and to our Lady of Istok. May her wisdom and bravery guide us!"

The entire hall drank to the health of all, and Hira smiled at Lord Barnabus, who glanced at her uncertainly. She nodded in encouragement. He'd done well.

The fiddles began, and servants moved the tables for the dancing to commence. Thebo shined within the social setting and rapidly became a sought-after dance partner. Suidians, after all, were quite the sociable bunch. He twirled the Istokian ladies with finesse worthy of envy.

King Alton extended his hand to Hira, and they twisted around and around in the manner of the quick jive. She stepped on his feet twice and he chuckled, which stopped her embarrassment. Then Lord Thebo took the next dance and a few other nobles, both Suidian and Istokians. When she was tired, Lord Barnabus came to her.

"I can't dance," he said rather desperately. "So, I shall escort the lady to her seat. If she permits."

She took his hand. "Of course."

"I also wanted to speak to you, my lady," he said in a hushed whisper. "I've thought about our discussion, and I very much would like to travel to the Free Isle."

For the first time this evening, her shoulders didn't tense. She smiled widely. "I'm glad to hear it."

He looked uncertain as he chewed on his lip. "But I can't do it alone. I'd never survive. I scarcely know how to use a blade!"

She tried not to laugh and tightened her hold on his hand. "I'll find you an escort, my lord. One that will keep you safe so that we can turn the tide in this war."

He meddled with his coiled coat. "Capital. Meanwhile, I shall prepare to depart! I've never been outside of Istok my whole life. I'm forty-six. It's rather pathetic. I imagine Zuri must be impressive, a white-stone city!"

She swallowed amusement at his excitement. He was so jovial and bright and such a contrast to the darkness she carried. She couldn't help but delight in his company. Perhaps this was what Ryker saw in her once upon a time.

Hira cleared her throat. "I'll send word, my lord. Thank you for the escort."

"Oh, yes!" he flustered. "At least I didn't have to dance!" He suppressed a mad laugh, "I'm terrible at it! Step on my own feet!"

After a while, Quent walked to Hira and grinned brightly. He was dressed in a fine suit of maroon velvet that fit him just right. He bowed before her.

"My lord, you look very handsome." Hira extended her hands, and he pressed them against his forehead.

He looked up at her with wide eyes. "And you are beautiful. Even with your hair gone. You're more beautiful than any other lady in this room." He realized Almira observed them. "After the Queen, of course!"

"Thank you." Hira bit her lip, clenching a smile between her teeth. "Would you care for a dance, Lord Seaver?"

He let out a huff of breath. "Yes. I mean… yes, my lady."

She allowed Quent to lead her to the dance and was glad there was a calm tune rather than a rushed one. It would save her feet instead of attempting to dodge his enthusiastic moves.

He leaned forward and whispered, "Did you learn that Justan is not Justan?"

"He told you?" Hira glanced at Ryker, who watched them. "Good. You must be aware of the truth."

He looked pensive. "Father seldom spoke about Ryker, but it's strange, isn't it? Thinking he's not *really* Justan. Ryker says the real Justan is not keen on me."

Hira squeezed his hand in reassurance. "I don't believe he cares for anyone other than himself and Furia."

They continued the dance, but Quent gave her a stare of determination. "I want to learn. I want to be strong like Captain Sanaa. That way, if the *real* Justan tries to hurt me, then I can battle and not retreat or wait to be saved.

She pulled him close, and it curled her stomach at the thought of Justan seizing Quent. What he would do just to please Furia. "Agreed, my lord."

"*Ryker* wants to keep me safe, but… I'm fifteen. I'm not a child anymore and I'm not ill. Plus, I want to wield a sword and one day become the greatest swordsman that ever lived," he said it with such passion that she had to admire his strategy.

"Considering you're my ward and under my protection, I'll make it happen," she said, and hugged him tighter.

He looked up at her with a slightly crestfallen face. "I'm your *ward*?"

She pushed back his hair and nodded. "Yes, darling. Ryker is technically dead, has no access to his inheritance, and Justan is in the bowels of this castle's prison. Until your father dies, you'll be my ward," she explained as the song ended.

"This means I can't marry you," he said with great sadness.

She floundered on what to say. Ryker had been right. "Quent…"

He bit his lip and shrugged. "I figured it was a longshot. You're very much in love with my brother and he's older and handsome. But I still hoped that maybe in a few years, when I'm stronger, you'd consider me."

She caressed his sweet face and pecked his cheek. "One day, a girl will come into your life and you'll forget all about me. You'll see me only as a loving older sister."

But he shook his head as his forehead wrinkled. "I'll *never* forget about you."

Ryker came and stood next to them and cleared his throat. Quent pulled back and glared at him. She stood awkwardly between the two without knowing what to say or what to do. Even less to consider what was proper.

"*Fine.*" Quent huffed and walked away dejectedly.

Hira stared after his slumped shoulders, and her heart twisted as if she negated his advances. She turned to Ryker, but before she could explain, he took her in his arms. She tensed for a moment, but the moment was a mere second.

"I think I broke his heart," she murmured.

His chuckle was deep, his rumbling chest made her shiver. "I told you he was smitten."

She wasn't sure if he spoke about Quent or of himself. He whirled her around on the dance floor with ease as she attempted not to blush under his gaze. The words spoken, and the acts played out in his rooms earlier were still vivid in her mind. It was enticing to have him hold her, his firm chest against her gown. No armor or leather to create a barrier.

And the fact was that despite everything, he brightened her senses and she yearned for him. She yearned to have him in her bed, naked and entangled in sheets. To her utter shock, he pressed his lips against the side of her head, lingering against her new baldness.

"Every man in this room stares at you and I wish to scream that I knew you first," he whispered.

Hira's heart would collapse within the confines of her chest. She kept her eyes on the encompassed revelry and said nothing. She couldn't. What her mouth would conjure and what her heart wished were two different things. Instead, she curled her fingers into his shoulder, and he pulled her closer.

"The queen watches us," he whispered in her ear.

She glanced at Almira and, sure enough, her face was tight. It was not that Almira didn't approve of dancing with such a man, it was that her calculating cousin understood Ryker Seaver was a landless gentry. A fine prospect for an ally against the fight with Furia, but not a candidate for Hira's attachments. Especially one that would kiss her in public.

"I'm thinking I should leave, try to find Furia myself. Finish her," Ryker said.

Having him gone forever caused an ache in her stomach. Damn her feelings and the internal tumultuous pain. The thought of Furia catching him, torturing him, ending his life almost had her gasping.

"She'll kill you if she has the chance," Hira breathed.

"I learned her tricks." He twirled Hira and brought her back into his embrace.

"And she learned yours," she hissed.

To dwell upon feelings as she danced before her entire court was a nightmare, but to wake one day and find him gone would be even worse.

"She doesn't know *me*, not the real me. Only *you* know that." His face was too close. This was most improper, but she couldn't pull away.

"Do I?" She studied his brows, the way they softly curved

downward.

His hand caressed her back through her gown. "You may not believe it, but you do."

She took a deep breath and let her body relax into him, mold to him. She remembered their entangled nights, his welcoming brown chest and how the rhythm of his heart lulled her to sleep. Closing her eyes, she chased away such a distracting memory.

Lord Barnabus laughed boisterously at something Lord Thebo said.

Ryker glanced at him. "Lord Barnabus is a fine man. I envied him greatly when he spoke on your behalf during your trial."

Throughout her demise, she thought she would never find humor again, and here he was, diverting her. She tried not to smile and pressed her lips together.

"You once called him a loaf of bread, if I remember correctly."

"*And* I said he could never handle you and I stand by that," Ryker said with unwarranted confidence.

She paused their dancing and fiercely met his gaze. She realized how much different this dance was from their previous one. Last time, she'd melted into his arms. Today, he was desperate to keep her because she'd floated far from him.

She raised a brow and leaned back. "A man doesn't have to *handle* me, my lord."

He flinched, but his hands didn't stray from her waist. On the contrary, he curled his fingers into her. "He shouldn't. You've learned to handle yourself just fine. But Her Ladyship must allow me to protect her. Even if she doesn't wish me to."

Hira swallowed and her lashes trembled. "Can you protect me from yourself?"

His mouth opened and his brown eyes dulled. She'd turned him down and there was nothing he could say. Her heart was still shriveled, curled in a corner where he'd left it.

Into her hand he stealthily slipped a small piece of paper, and for a mad moment she thought it was a love note. But he shook his head.

"Your mother left you this. I found it in her things when Furia took her rooms. I kept it so she wouldn't destroy it."

She glanced at the paper and nodded, her heart tightening as she pocketed the letter into her dress. His hands were back on her, and he drew her in.

Ryker's jaw tightened. "I've wronged you and I've not done anything to merit your forgiveness. I don't wish to be your awful secret that holds you on stolen nights. Or be in your bed conditionally. I don't want your pain to corrode who you are. Because I love who you are." His breathing increased as he shuddered, but his warm gaze didn't waver. "I want *all* of you. Your anger, your fury, your warmth, and your frigidity. I wish you to lead, so I may follow. I want to proudly walk with you in daylight. Before the Favia and the gods of old, I swear this to you tonight: I will be the man you *deserve*."

Warmth filled her from the crown of her head to the tip of her toes. In a moment of frailty, she considered forgiving him. Permit her emotions to lead and allow him into her life. As she opened her mouth, a dozen Korkoran Knights stormed into the hall.

"My lady! A breach in the dungeons!"

They both stared at one another.

"Justan," they said in unison.

Chapter Sixty

HIRA

Hira dashed through the hall, loathing that she had to lift her skirts to do so. She met Sanaa's eyes, and the captain was at her heels.

"You don't leave her side!" Sanaa snarled to the dozen young Red Guards surrounding the queen. Almira stood with a worried gaze as the king, Thebo, Ryker, and Delara rushed after them.

Someone released Furia's Korkoran Knights. Jails cells stood wide open with killed or wounded dungeon guards. Hira's instinct told her this was all Justan's doing. She didn't know how, but her mind kept going to the tone of respect in Sufu's voice.

Ryker led them to the hidden cell, and they lit the torches along the way, creating a path of light in the labyrinth's darkness.

"How evil can this man possibly be?" the king asked.

Hira could scarcely describe what an angry, freed Justan would bring to fruition. Her chest heaved as she attempted to control her panic.

"Evil, your Majesty," was all she could say.

Thebo was at her heels with a tight and outraged look. "Why didn't Beltran kill him?"

"I cannot ask questions of a dead man," Hira said in annoyance as the heavy door came into view.

Ryker rapped on it, and to their horror, it easily slid ajar. They looked at the darkened hall and weapons were quickly at hand. Sanaa handed Hira her extra blade. She'd never been angrier that she left Ocean Fury in her rooms.

Sanaa continued first, with a torch in her hand. "I should've killed him when I saw him."

"Indeed, you should've," the king snapped.

They prudently moved forward in the dark until they came to the opening of the cave. The cell was open, as Hira suspected. A dark-robed figure was on the floor. It was Sufu. Ryker rushed to him and flipped him over, and Hira screamed when she saw him.

He was alive, his mouth opened and moaning. Two bloodied empty sockets stared back as someone had gorged his eyes out. His ears bitten off. His face split open to the bone. The blood was stark against the pale skin. It was a wretched sight.

"Gods of the sea," Lord Thebo whispered in dismay.

Ryker found the key still clutched in his hand.

"He betrayed him, *used* him," Delara said. "Put him out of his misery!"

"That man stole a key and freed a prisoner," the king said.

But Ryker bent over Sufu. "What did he promise you?"

"He said he was my friend," Sufu whispered, the lacerations in his mouth causing him great agony. "He said... find the key from the lady's room... release me and Furia's men and I could stand once more under the sun."

The man moaned and choked on the blood spurting from his broken lips. But Ryker took his hands and clutched them tightly. His own face writhed in sorrow because he knew. He knew what it was to be trapped.

"Forgive me Master Ryker... I just wished for freedom," Sufu sobbed.

Hira felt sick, especially when Delara met her gaze with a knowing look. The man had been imprisoned all along. Her uncle captured him, making him fear the consequences of leaving the cell. Justan worked him over for years until the moment she'd dangled the key before his eyes.

The king and Thebo entered the cell and studied the items placed there. Luxuries that would never belong to a regular inmate.

"How long was he in here?" the king asked.

"Five years." Sanaa entered the cell and looked over Justan's scrolls. "He's no fool."

The king cursed and shook his head. "Which makes him even more dangerous. We're losing time. Let's hunt this scum down."

"Aye," Thebo agreed, and the men left.

Hira, not knowing what to do about Sufu, scrambled after them. She needed her sword and armor. They turned the corner and spotted the door closed. All three ran to it and their bodies slammed against it. It was locked.

The king yelled, pushed against it, and Thebo tried to no avail. Hira reached with her mangled arm and tried her strength, but nothing moved the Duncan wood door. The material mocked them, a sweet revenge from being hacked down from its comfortable home in the northern woods.

"Sanaa, Ryker! We're trapped! It's a trap!" Hira screamed, her heartbeat in her ears. Almira was up there. Almira and *Quent!*

Ryker instantly thought the same thing. He forced past them. "Quent! Quent!" He yanked at the door with a yell.

In the midst of his yells, the small window Sufu used to receive food slowly slid opened. The king moved Ryker aside and brandished his sword before him, pointing it at the hole. To Hira's horror, Justan peered in with a brilliant, satisfied smile. His lips were bloodied. It dribbled down his chin to his neck. His brown eyes were a carnivorous cloud of evil delight.

"Is that the *king?*" he said with a laugh. "Had I known that I'd get the rat along with the mice, I would've put on my embroidered jacket!"

The king slammed his palm on the door and raged. "How *dare* you trap me, vermin!"

Ryker pushed past Hira and stared at his brother. "Don't you dare touch Quent! Think about your actions!"

"Oh, do shut up, you pathetic embryo. I don't give a fuck about

Quent." Justan rolled his eyes and looked in on the cell, studying each of the angry people within. "Majesty, I'm sorry I can't stay and enjoy the festivities. I'm sure you put on a delightful party, but I've important work to do."

Hira, knowing there must be a way to convince him, something to offer him, clutched the window. "Justan, open this door. I swear on my house and on Istok that you'll see a *fair* trial. One you should've received from the beginning."

He watched her with that Cheshire grin, and she recoiled at the scent of blood that he exhaled in the chuckle. "You can't swear on something that's not yours, *girl.*"

Hira brightened, but before she could respond, the escaped Korkoran soldiers ran up to him. There was a commotion beyond the small window.

"Commander, we need to leave now! She was there, we got her. Let's go!" A Korkoran soldier said.

Justan grinned and peered back into the window.

"Got *who*?" The king said with rising panic. "Who do you have, you bastard? If you touched the queen—"

"Oh, I couldn't get to *her*. Unfortunately, she was heavily guarded by the brilliant Red Guard." His gaze flickered to Sanaa with a slow linger of malice and delight. "Thank you, Captain, I'm indebted. You were right. We *were* rather close to the secret stairway that led me to someone of *infinite* more value."

Silence descended upon them when he lifted his robe to show Princess Osaria sleeping peacefully on his arm. Her small brown curls a little halo around her, her tiny fist tucked under her chin, her long lashes brushing her chubby cheek. A minute cherub. The heir to the kingdom.

"Isn't she beautiful?" Justan asked in a mock whisper. "I can't wait until she calls me *father.*"

The king's knees seem to buckle. He strained his hand through the opening, a futile attempt to reach her. "No!" he cried in a desperate plea. "My kingdom, my entire kingdom, have it—give her to me!"

Justan pulled her away with a laugh. The baby woke and cried.

Her face reddening, her fists fought the air. She opened her small eyes, and it seemed as if she looked at her father, who gasped a moan of despair.

"Don't hurt her!" The king implored.

"Justan, please!" Hira clung to her cheeks, unable to fathom the horror of the situation. It was too ugly; it was too out of reason.

"I won't hurt her!" Justan rocked the baby, to no avail.

She cried, her small fists reaching out to the king, who howled with a wail.

"What sort of monster do you think I am? She's all mine now, mine and Furia's. We'll raise her as our own and teach her all about her bad mommy and daddy and how they didn't want her." He met the king's glare, and all playfulness fell from his face. It morphed into pure hate. "I've bid my days. Hour after hour. Making friends with pallid monstrosities and drenching myself in false promises. If you're under any delusions that I won't make you all pay for every second I spent in that hell, every second I falsified a friendship far below my station, then you're bigger fools than I thought. You'll understand pain. And *loss*. Like Furia did all her life. Like I have these past five years. *That's* vengeance," Justan finished with a hiss.

He gave the king one last spiteful glance, then left them.

The king shrieked obscenities at him. He pushed on the door, then collapsed into madness.

"OSARIA!"

Thebo tried to reason with him, but they had no words. What words could they say? What consolation and reassurance would suffice? Hira and Sanaa looked at one another as the implications coated them. The captain's demeanor was so stoic and dark that when she turned from the scene and stormed into the cave, Hira followed her.

Hira thought they would jump in the waters and attempt to capture them. But Sanaa strode to Sufu, still moaning on the ground. Without pausing, she rammed her sword into his chest. The man grasped at the sword and slashed his fingers against it. Hira had to look away. Sanaa pulled her sword and stabbed him again and again until he stopped twitching. She let out an angry yell and with one final blow; she decapitated the body, making the mutilated head roll on the floor.

Ryker entered the room and watched the captain in horror. "He was—"

Sanaa glared at him. "Speak to me again and you'll suffer his fate."

Hira moved between the two, though her thoughts were wild. She grasped Ryker's shirt. "How do we get out? We have to cut him off. We have to get her back!"

He shoved her hands away, his face a mask of bleakness. "There's no way out. He's been planning this escape for years. You showed him the key. He needed the key."

Hira pushed past him. The king was still roaring, his fists pounding on the door, splitting his knuckles. Then he made a horrible sound as he slumped to the floor. Thebo stood over him, at a loss for words. Delara studied the door, she wriggled the hinges and peered out the opening.

"I'm going to jump into the ocean," Hira said. Zeita didn't let her drown before, she wouldn't let her drown now.

The High Lord of Suid stared at her incredulously. "You'll die on those rocks before you can drown."

She yearned to yell, to bloody her knuckles battering the door, or to mutilate a dying man. "What will you have me do?"

"Everyone, shut up! Someone's coming!" Delara cried. "We're down here! We have the king!"

They all hollered, making as much noise as they could, hailing and begging for help. Soon, a dozen Black Knights arrived, and the king was on his feet. He pressed himself against the aperture.

"Get me out!" He resembled a madman as the knights scrambled to do his bidding.

One of them looked up. "Majesty, they've snapped the key! Fetch irons!"

"He took the Princess! Two of you, stay behind. The rest of you find the man called Justan Seaver." He grasped Ryker by the lapels of his jacket. "Looks just like him! Save my daughter, bring him to me dead or alive! He's with the false Korkoran knights. Go *now!*"

They did as they were told, thundering down the darkened caves after Justan. The other two carried irons and worked on the door.

"HURRY UP!" the king barked as the men grunted, manically attempting to succeed in their task.

They worked the inverted hinges from the iron and the king stormed out the moment they opened the door. They all followed behind him, through a gate, and were confronted with stairs that twirled into a pit of darkness.

Sanaa was already thundering down the steps with the king. "It's a long way down. Come on! We can catch them before they reach the boat!"

"Where does it lead?" Hira grasped the stone.

"The Cliffs of Lamya," Delara said, her voice tight but calm.

Hira screamed to her own guards. "Ships out to the Cliffs! Cut him off, send all the boats we can spare! Don't hurt the baby!"

At her call, the men nodded and moved towards the castle. Sanaa and Delara's torch guided them as the group descended into the pit. They ran most of the way, attempting not to fall into the spiral madness in the castle's belly. More than once, Hira tripped on her skirts, but Ryker turned to her and slashed a knife around the gown, allowing her more freedom in her steps. She noticed he limped, still smarting from his fresh wound. From that moment on, she took his hand as they plunged ahead.

"We're close!" Sanaa cried from below.

They hurtled down the stairs until they heard the ocean splashing, and they stumbled into a flooded cave. It was high tide and Sanaa quickly found the body of a drowned man. She shoved it aside with a growl and leapt into the sea.

"Gods, please -" The king jumped into the waters and swam.

He clutched the stone as he made it to the mouth of the cave. Hira dropped in after him, cutting through the water. They discovered more dead men with wounds.

"They didn't all fit into the small boat," Delara said darkly, diving under and gliding up to them.

"Where is the fucking boat?" King Alton screamed.

But Sanaa's face was still. She bobbed in the water, staring out the cave entrance into the vastness of the Istokian sea. Her hand slid up the stone and she discovered the remains of a rope which had once anchored a boat.

"It's gone," she despaired.

But Ryker yelled and smacked the wall with a curse. "He cannot get far in a dingy. I can hunt him down with the Sea Wife."

Hira followed, seeing his plan. "We'll cut him off!"

When she reached the steps, Thebo and Ryker hauled her up.

King Alton led the party as he jogged up the stairs, as if he needed no rest, pounding the steps up and up the spiral. Thebo hardly kept up. Their breathing was harsh, their lungs protesting against the exercise.

"He'll have to dock," Ryker said, gasping for air. "He's likely already in the city unless he's stolen one of our ships."

Hira nodded in agreement as he pulled her up to the next step. There were too many possibilities to consider, and they split their thoughts over an oceanic escape or a land one. When they emerged, the soldiers waited for them, and the king began yelling orders as Thebo instructed the captain of the Mesedi. Soldiers rushed out of Korkoran by the dozens and into the streets of Treveri. Chaos erupted as guests screamed when the knights marched through the hall, armed and ready.

That's when Almira came to them surrounded by the dozen young Red Guard who'd not left her side. She was calm and poised, looking impeccable and serene. She didn't know.

"I assume he escaped," Almira said with a raised brow.

The king paused his orders. His chest heaved. Almira studied him, his bloodied hands, all of them drenched and out of breath. She glanced at the group, then back at her husband.

"What happened?" she asked.

The king couldn't answer her. It filled him with shame. Hira, pitying him, addressed Almira.

"Justan Seaver took the baby," Hira said quickly.

Almira stared at her, her black eyes penetrating as she went eerily still. Her lips slacked, she grasped her belly.

"*What* baby?"

"Almira," the king whispered. "We'll find her. He couldn't have gotten far. We have ships out on the coast, men combing the city—"

"WHAT BABY?" She stumbled back.

He reached to her, but she moaned and pulled away from all who came near her.

"*Cuzo*, I'm sorry—" Sanaa tried, her voice unrecognizable.

But the Queen turned and shot down the hall towards her quarters. They all rushed behind her.

The Mesedi and Black Knights overwhelmed the hallways as they searched the castle, but Hira knew, deep in her gut, that it was too late. Justan was smart. He would've planned, he would be where they least expected. He'd out-thought them.

Hira didn't know how Almira ran up the stairs, but her determination was incomparable. When they reached the landing at the high quarters, all the soldiers and guards were still posted before the chamber, their weapons clean and their bodies relaxed.

"He couldn't have. She's safe!" Almira pushed the soldiers out as they made way for her, as she shoved open the doors to the chambers.

Inside the chambers was a silent, macabre display of bodies. Two young Red Guards were dead, one with a blade protruding from her back and another with a split throat. None of them with weapons at hand. Someone had calmly ambushed them. A maid laid out next to the antechamber door, killed in a swift, gory manner.

Almira let out a strangled moan and raced through the blood that slicked the floor. She left wet, bloodied footprints behind her as she ran. She entered the small nursery. Blood pooled on the ground, and there lay the nurse, dead with wide eyes, her mouth open in a scream that never materialized. The latch was wide open, the proof.

On the wall, painted in blood, was a grim message.

"For Furia."

The nurse had slumped and overturned the crib. The tiny golden cot was empty, nothing but soft sheets that once swaddled a princess.

Almira screamed. She grasped the sheets, threw them about as if she could find the child there. In the emptiness. King Alton sought to comfort her, but she pulled away from him. Her face a contortion of madness, grief, loss, and anger.

"Where is she, *Alton?*" her voice shrill, a penetrating hit.

"I'll find her! We have ships out there right now!" He struggled to grasp her shoulders, but she fisted her fingers into his shirt and howled. The despair cut into Hira and she gasped.

"He'll take her to Furia and Furia will *kill* her!" She manically looked around. "No Alton, bring her to me! I demand it!"

"I'm leaving to find her." He was clutching her as she gripped his neck, digging her nails into his skin.

And her mouth twisted. Almira, ever the realist, wailed deep in her chest. "*Why?* Why did you let him take her? Why?"

"I tried!" He drew her in as tears coursed down his cheeks.

Almira stumbled back, staring at him as if the king himself had allowed the abduction. "You're her *father!* My father would've destroyed himself to save me."

"*Almira,*" he whispered in a choke.

"You swore you would protect her! You swore with your cock *in* me you would—you are a *liar!*" she whimpered.

He stepped closer.

"DON'T TOUCH ME!" Her nails clawed her own skin.

Then she faltered and saw with horror that her breasts were wet. She became confused and pressed her palms to them. They were wet with milk that wouldn't be drank.

"*No!* This is for my baby!" She pressed her hands against her breast, attempting to keep the milk inside. "Alton, where is she? Where is she?"

And he had no words.

She slumped to the floor, falling like an empty sack, covering herself in the spilled blood. She sobbed uncontrollably. Horrible shaking screaming sobs, she yanked at her hair even when the king tried to stop her; she was beyond help.

She called for the princess over and over, huddled in one corner, snarling at anyone that came close. Then she pounded her

chest in agony.
    Pain. Pain. Pain.
    The queen had fallen.

Isabelle Olmo

Chapter Sixty-One

HIRA

It was as if the baby had died. The somberness of the situation descended upon them so quickly and heavily that Hira couldn't meet Sanaa's eyes. They fell for a well-placed trap and the queen was wounded.

No one was to enter the high quarters.

Sanaa placed ten guards at the door and twelve Black Knights. The rest ransacked the city to find the baby. Istokians themselves aided in the search, hunting through all homes and establishments. Even small children carrying candles searched corners for the stolen princess. They left no space unsearched. They plowed even the blades of grass to ensure they had not left her abandoned in a field.

Hira'd instructed her soldiers to search everywhere and expand to the countryside and the high seas. The entire kingdom searched for Osaria.

The Lady of Istok watched from a window as they enacted altars with the princess' name etched on stone. Elderly women lit candles and fervently prayed for the gods to protect the child and bring her home. They cried and begged, but they didn't understand that the Favia wished for such happenings. They wished the chaos, for they wanted war. A stolen princess was just what the people needed to support such a promise of bloodshed.

"She's gone," Delara said. "It's a useless pursuit."

Hira agreed but didn't voice it. It was too fresh in her throat. In desperation, she went to her rooms and yanked off her dress in angry tugs until it was a tattered mess on the floor. She donned her leather trousers, strapped Ocean Fury, and her ruby blade to her waist, ready to face the world.

As she moved to leave, she spotted the letter Ryker had brought. Her mother's letter. With trembling fingers, she opened it and read it in the dim light of her desk. As she read it, she sobbed. As if all the suffering and defeat of the past few weeks descended upon her, drenching and covering her. She missed her mother at that moment. She wished to shower Marai with all the tenderness she'd never shown her. Her mother had loved her in the way Almira loved her child and Hira had shunned her. She traced the patterns of her mother's words over and over, committing her words to memory.

"*You are strong, Hira,*" her mother wrote.

But how much strength did she need to survive such extreme pain and loss? Somewhere out there was a baby, crying for its mother, in the clutches of an evil person. She had no milk, no love, no comfort. The sense of failure was overwhelming, and Hira couldn't control her shaking. Her hands trembled so violently that she had to clutch them and bring them to her heart.

If Almira was broken, it fell to her. *She* would have to make choices far beyond what she thought she could do.

They were about to start a war for a child and a kingdom.

"*Wake up, Vishap!*"

The voice was sharp in her ears. She jumped to stand, toppling over her chair, and stared into the empty room. She swore shadows lingered there, lapping at her from the darkness.

"You think you won? You've not won." Her eyes locked on the black mass. "I'm still standing. I won't let you destroy this land."

The shadows hissed and curled, swirling and gnashing their teeth. They screeched, this time she could clearly discern their cries. Then, in an instant, the world exploded. The sound was so strong it reverberated throughout the castle. Hira fell on the floor, curling into herself and covering her head. More explosions and she scrambled up.

She ran into the hallway. Servants cried and clutched each other. Everyone seemed in a haze. Already guards rushed through the castle, mingled with the Suidian Mesedi, and Black Knights with buckets at hand.

"The armada is on fire!" they cried.

No! She joined them and dashed to the entrance when she stumbled into Sanaa.

"He's still in the city!" Hira roared at servants to bring them horses.

The Keepers scrambled to do her bidding and already Hira saw fire in the distance as more explosions shook Treveri. Istokians screamed as the chaos continued.

They rushed in the animals, and both she and Sanaa rode them with Korkoran guards down the streets. Hira's heart pounded and her hands fisted on the reins as she thundered to the port. When they reached Portales Street, which had the most picturesque view of the bay, she saw it was too late. Flames engulfed all the docked ships that were not out searching for the princess. It drenched the east side in blazes that reached the sky. The Istokian Armada was burning.

Hira gasped and moved to spur her horse, but Sanaa took her reins.

"It's too late," Sanaa said in a forceful tone. "Everything is too fucking late."

They tried to stop the fire, but the flames lapped at them. It forced her to order them all back. It ate the docks in ravenous hunger. They had to let the ships loose into the sea to save the other half of the armada and the city.

Then a figure emerged, and Sanaa pointed at it, pulling Hira's attention. From the smoke, developed a woman. A woman they both recognized. The witch that led them astray last year and had them rush to the king to allow Arrigo to take over Mavros.

She stared at Hira and Sanaa with malevolent intent. She raised her hand, a pyre of green flames on her palm. Then she thrust her hand out. Sanaa grabbed Hira, and she ducked them behind a crate of boxes. The witch attacked the boxes, and they burned.

The woman laughed over the roaring conflagrations. "Come out and face me, ladies!"

The two of them ran as fast as they could and hid behind the other crates. Another fireball exploded from the witch and incinerated their previous hiding place. More bolts would come.

"Weapons are no good!" Sanaa cried when Hira held up Ocean Fury.

"This is no mere weapon," Hira said. She knew she had seconds before their crate suffered the same fate.

She jumped up and faced the witch, sword at hand. The woman instantly spotted her, her eyes manic.

"Balikian," she hissed.

"*Witch*," Hira responded.

She held the bolt in her hand and flung it at Hira as she deflected it with Ocean Fury in her mangled arm.

Zeita, I carry your blood. Protect me, she thought.

It was a direct hit; the fire ensnarled the blade and swept up Hira's hand, but she didn't burn. It felt like an electric current. She was flung sideways, a rag doll, landing on the dock with a thump. The witch screamed with maniacal glee as Hira slowly sat up. She aimed at her again and once more Hira blocked with Ocean Fury; the sword took the hit but didn't burn. It flung her once more, a few feet away.

Hira was breathing deeply, her strength waning. She pushed herself up with a yell and once more hoisted her weapon as the fire shot came. This time, she felt the strain as Ocean Fury gave way. Burning pain coursed up her hand as it tossed her again.

"Hey!" Sanaa yelled. There stood the captain, having no magic weapon, wearing her armor, a warrior in red, facing the witch. "Come at *me*, you cunt!"

The witch turned her attention to Sanaa, even as Hira yelled for her to hide. Sanaa flicked her gaze to Hira.

"No!" Hira yelled as the fire bolt sped through the air straight at Sanaa. "No!"

A moment before she incinerated Sanaa, a tiny figure stepped before the captain. Their arms opened wide and floating a blue flame in them. She blocked the hit, encasing it between her two hands.

Hira recognized the person. It was the Suidian witch that saved her arm, the one who brought her to Zeita. The small woman, only three feet from the floor, her dark skin shining starlight, held the evil witch's fire within her hands.

"This is not your fight!" the attacker screamed.

The Suidian witch concentrated on the bolt, twisting it in her small hands, molding it into a ball. "You came to me once for help, Ignatia, and I helped you. I birthed your child Furia when she wanted to split you in half and now look at you. *Look* at you."

The other raged and pulled back her fire, but it didn't matter. The Suidian had the power source in her hands. She glared at Ignatia and released the ball of light. It flew straight at Ignatia and blasted her into the air, so far that Hira could no longer see her. She was lost and gone.

Hira gasped as she stared at the small witch that saved them. Then the woman collapsed, but Sanaa caught her before she fell on the ground and Hira ran to them. Sanaa looked up at Hira in confusion. Fearing magic but fighting gratitude towards the enchantress that saved them.

"She saved me once when she healed me. She saved us again." Hira touched the witch's face.

The woman opened her eyes and wheezed.

"Stay with us, small one," Sanaa hefted her up.

"Seek Leora on the Free Isle, Captain," she whispered. "Tell her I sent you. Tell her what's happened. Tell her you need her."

Hira clutched her small hands. Her skin felt like flattened paper after too much use. The witch smiled at her.

"You did well, *Vishap*. It was good to fight alongside you once again," she whispered, and her body collapsed in Sanaa's arms. Then it disintegrated to dust between the captain's fingers.

Around them, over a hundred ships floated out into the bay, lighting the black sky with smoke and red flames. The intense smoke would linger in her senses for months to come.

Dawn was but an hour away by the time Hira made it to the castle. In her sorrow, she dimly realized Ryker was missing. Panicked, she searched the castle. No one had seen him. Until she found a Keeper who admitted the commander asked for a sack of food and wore his sea coat.

He'd not been at the port, which meant he was at the beach.

Chapter Sixty-Two

RYKER

In the predawn hours, the world was at its most beautiful. The sky prepared itself for the masterpiece of a day. Ryker never tired of it. The stars were the clearest and the thousands of messages etched in their patterns were the most recognizable.

His mother's small boat floated at his feet, waiting with a downed sail, welcoming a Garian to take it to the end of the world. In the beginning, hundreds of these smaller boats coated the coastlines of Istok. Fishing and trading expeditions that made the Garians known for their navigating abilities.

Water was in his veins, and the sky beckoned him. He carried very little with him, things that reminded him of Quent, his mother, and Hira. Her handkerchief was tucked there, too.

Taking a deep breath for courage and wincing against the wound in his shoulder, he pushed the boat into the waters.

"RYKER!"

He stopped, holding the boat from the sea, snatching it, and looking behind him as Quent ran in the sand, tripping and crying out his name once more.

"Ryker!" he gasped, and Ryker's heart tightened.

He'd been a coward, not wishing to bid Quent a last goodbye.

To face the disappointment and hurt. But life seemed to swiftly begin its lessons. Quent stumbled and grasped the boat, yanking it back. He looked up at Ryker with such determination, he scarcely recognized his brother.

"I'm coming with you!" Quent said, already placing his foot on the gunwale.

But Ryker grabbed and pulled him out. "No. Not this time, Quent."

"Bull crap, Ryker! You're going to hunt Justan and I'm coming!" Quent's face was wild in the pre-dawn hour. "He's my brother too!"

With a sigh, Ryker hauled the ship back, mooring it on the beach and turned back to Quent, kneeling to speak to him eye-to-eye. And Quent cried, shaking his head.

"Don't leave me behind," Quent whispered with a trembling lower lip. "I'm a Garian too. I'm a star-son of the night sky."

His heart twisted into an unmanageable knot. He'd spent so long protecting Quent that he felt he was hurting him more than any other person before. Denying him the journey, making him stay behind, infantizing his capabilities. Ryker had done such wrong to Quent, in his desperation to save him he'd not prepared him for the world. Guilt was thick within Ryker; it was one of the many sins etched upon his soul.

"I don't know what lies ahead. I can't place you in that predicament." Ryker held his brother's small body one last time.

Quent pushed against him and grasped his brother's neck. His face was twisted and full of tears. "You lied! You told me you would never leave and now you leave!"

The emotions his small, innocent words caused within Ryker were impossible to rectify. He pushed Quent's hair back and kissed his forehead, committing to memory the smell of childish wonder that brought him peace on so many nights.

Quent sobbed even harder. "*Please,* don't leave. Please, don't leave me behind."

But Ryker grasped his face and pointed it at the stars, their cool light bathing them with their mercy. "Look up there, you see them?

When you settle in bed, I want you to look up. I'll be up there, watching over you. You're about to find out how harsh the world can be. I tried to protect you but I'm afraid all I've done is a disservice. You're going to grow up and be wiser than I ever could." And he kissed his cheek once more and pressed their foreheads together. "One day, we shall be together once more. One day, I'll have my own home and we'll be a family again."

"But we're a family *now*," Quent said between wails.

"And we'll never stop being one," Ryker whispered. "You are my treasured one, and I love you more than you'll ever know."

Ryker enveloped him in his arms as Quent's small body became wracked with sobs. He looked up when he heard a horse galloping on the sand. His gut twisted when he saw Hira. She jumped off the horse and ran to them. She paused as she watched them embrace. Her face was unreadable, shifting between concern and sadness.

"You mind Lady Hira and do as she tells you," Ryker said and finally extracted Quent's arms from him.

But Quent glanced at Hira, then back at his brother. "You stay alive. Don't make me have to avenge you."

Ryker smiled and held his face one final time before the boy, still crying, stumbled to Hira. She caressed his hair and handed over her horse's reins. With her eyes on Ryker, she slowly walked to him. Under the glow of the stars, which reflected on her newly shaved head, she resembled a warrior of old. He had a fleeting glimpse of something. Like a memory, not his. Like he'd been here before and history had doomed them to repeat it.

"Don't ask me to stay," Ryker told her.

"I'm not," she said and walked until they stood before one another.

Her eyes crystalline and wide as she studied his face.

"But... my uncle is dead. I'm in the High Seat. You fulfilled your promise. You're no longer a spy," she said in one breath as she scanned his face. "You've sacrificed too much for this. Let the armies hunt Justan down and bring her back."

But he knew in his heart they wouldn't find her. This was *his* task. Justan had done this, and the only one who could find his womb-mate was him, Ryker had to take down Justan. No one else. Justan was *his* responsibility and Ryker could never peacefully live while his brother was out there, committing such atrocities.

"I've the face of the man who stole the princess. What life do you think awaits me here? In any city? Peace? Happiness?" And he dared take a step toward her until he could feel the warmth of her body.

"You're not him," she said with a thinned mouth.

Softly, he touched her face and curled his fingers around her head, finding delight in the smoothness of her scalp.

"You looked beautiful tonight, my lady. It was a pleasure to dance with you," he whispered.

She pushed against him, grasping his coat. All the emotions she held within suddenly exploded and her face twisted. "Don't you dare let him kill you!"

His hand slid around her back, and he pulled her in, then nuzzled her face. She closed her eyes, and it seemed she finally allowed herself to drown in her emotions. To let go of the simmering anger she rightfully carried at his deceit. To allow him access to her heart and body. His lips found hers and they kissed each other desperately. She grasped Ryker so tightly he thought he would break.

The sun speared its first announcement of the day as he watched her.

"Remember that you saved *yourself*. You did all that for yourself. I simply had the pleasure of watching it happen. You're the strongest person I know. You are *formidable*. Lionhearted. A dragon. When this is over, I will take whatever you give me. Even if we must love one another in secret. I'll take that."

He kissed her, a passionate embrace, the saddest of all pleasures. She shook her head and pressed her face to his. From the folds of her trousers, she pulled a small bouquet. It was the strands of hair she'd cut tied in dried thistle. She pressed it into his hand.

"Until the day I can love you in daylight, marry you under Garian starlight, and call you my husband, I'll be for no other. For you have my heart." He could see the etches of heartbreak in her gaze, but she said it with conviction and strength. "Don't do anything foolish. Think of me and Quent."

He clutched the bouquet in his hand and held it to his chest, letting his eyes linger one last time on her beautiful eyes. She was a vivid painting, a masterpiece etched in honor and pain. He was the underserving bastard that held her love and he would never discard it again. From his soul, he unlatched the poem he'd composed, the words pulled from his sentiments and mixed with his yearning.

"I will think of you and Quent each second of every day. For years, you brought me happiness when I was alone in my room. You were the warmth beyond my window. Like all the ancestors before me who worshiped the sky, every night away from you, I shall paint your name into the stars."

Then, he parted from her and turned to his boat, pushing it out into the sea. As it glided into the Istokian waves, he jumped on it. He looked back at them both, holding onto one another and watching him leave. He may be on a quest to find his destiny, but his heart lay shattered on that beach.

"Zeita, that guides us all," he prayed. "Help me bring honor to my house once more. Allow me to return home. Allow me to return home to them both."

Isabelle Olmo

Chapter Sixty-Three

SANAA

Guilt was a strange emotion she'd seldom experienced. There was no escaping it now. She, who seldom spoke of things not her business, provided ample material for a travesty so large she couldn't quite grasp. The world was suddenly too wide to hold within her muscled arms.

Sitting at the base of the secret steps that led to their damnation, she drank heavily. Slowly, she inhaled the cigar in her mouth, blew out the blue smoke, and watched it twirl in the air. More drink, until she burped. She had removed her armor and leaned back in her plainclothes. She would never wear her armor again.

She'd failed. There was no point in anything else. Her cousin Edmee had won. Even in death she'd won. Her laugher danced in the air around her, a taunt. Almira defeated. The baby was lost. Witches battled in the open. Darkness covered the land.

She wanted nothing of it. Defeat felt rather liberating. No queen to guard, no tasks, nothing but her own problems to dwell upon. Perhaps she should return home to her country manor and bed every willing maid. Live the rest of her life heavy with whiskey and cunny juice. That sounded rather pleasant.

Soft steps sounded in the corridor, and she idly grasped her blade. Desperately wishing it was someone she could gut. As the person turned the corner, Delara revealed herself. Her long body illuminated by the torch she carried. She studied Sanaa with cool green eyes.

She snatched the bottle from the captain in two steps. Before Sanaa could protest, Delara had the liquor to her mouth, drinking deeply.

Then she wiped her lips. Her emotions were encased in shadows. "You've had your wallow. One doesn't give up simply because of one mistake. Come. Let's go."

Sanaa reluctantly followed Delara back to the castle, through the halls, the whimpering servants, and suspicious soldiers, all the way to the High Seat's war room. Within were people she didn't expect. They all sat and watched her, but no one said a word. A haphazard group of idiots with little in common.

The Lady of Istok entered the room, holding a plank of wood. She strode without preamble and tossed it in the middle of the room. The sun's rays bounced off the wood. It had an outline of a smoke ring, but it was undamaged.

"The fire was a farce. Magic fire," Hira snarled. "The ships we let loose are gone. Half of my armada has been stolen."

Sanaa could see how this would be a problem. However, she didn't understand how this was her problem. She raised her brow and met Hira's eyes, who studied her carefully.

"Where's your armor, Captain?" Hira asked.

Sanaa leaned against the wall and crossed her arms. She didn't owe anyone an explanation for her decisions. "I'm resigning my post as Captain of the Queen's Red Guard."

They all gawked at her, especially Delara.

"Captain..."

Sanaa flinched and looked at her feet, her jaw clenched. "I've failed at my duties. I've endangered the queen, and the princess has been stolen..." her voice faded, and she placed her fist against her chest. It was too much. Too much to feel when for so long she'd felt nothing.

"We've all *failed*," Thebo said from his sitting position. His elbows were on his knees and his head was in his hands.

But Her Ladyship stared at him with softened eyes. "You've not failed, my lord."

He raised his head to look at her, but his green eyes were ablaze with denial. His neck was taunt and corded and he seemed poised to kill and murder. Sanaa had never seen him as such, not in all her years knowing him.

"That bitch is still alive, isn't she? Now this witch fights with her? False fires that steal armadas? Who knows what they'll do to that baby? We might as well consider it *dead*," he spat.

Sanaa flinched, wishing to hit him. Wishing to make him eat his words. Osaria couldn't be dead.

"No, she's *not* dead. The captain and I will find her," Delara said, and stepped forward. This was news to Sanaa.

"No," Hira said.

Sanaa gave Hira a look that could kill. That Hira should stand and issue orders as Almira would was maddening. She wanted to wrap her hands around that pale neck and shake her. Though she realized it was not anger at the lady that consumed her.

"We answer to the queen, my lady, or must I remind you?" Sanaa snapped.

Hira squared off with her. She resembled the Great Dragon with her shaved head and armor. That girl who begged Sanaa for a post on the queen's guard was dead indeed.

"You're resigning your post; you answer to no queen."

Sanaa scoffed. She was formidable *now*. The dragon had certainly learned to swim.

"I don't answer to *you*," Sanaa said.

"No." Hira snapped to her. "But you do answer to the people of New Verden. We *all* do. It's time we stop thinking in such small ways. We must think of the *entire* world because the day is coming fast when it's no longer going to be Ouest against Suid. Suid against Istok. Istok against Norr. Soon all of New Verden must join against the foe who will try to destroy us all."

"The witch called it The Great Balikian War," Delara said. "I remember."

"More conjurers!" Thebo stood, his height towered over them all except for Delara, who didn't flinch at his outburst. He rounded on Sanaa and beheld her with disappointment. It was not the first time she'd disappointed a Suidian lord, and she boldly met his stare. "You should know better, Captain!"

"It's done!" Hira stepped in. "Some enchantress didn't cause this war. The deeds of the past brought it, and now we have to *deal* with it."

They said nothing. Sanaa fisted her hands, wishing to place them on Justan until his head bent at an unnatural angle.

"The queen has been compromised and we must make swift decisions. I'll take responsibility if she doesn't agree with our course of action." Hira moved her palm over her chest.

"And what is *your* course of action?" Thebo asked with a grunt. "Suidians will want revenge for the princess's kidnapping."

Her Ladyship straightened her shoulders and addressed him in an even tone. "From Suid, I need timber."

Lord Thebo, seldom surprised, reeled back. "*Ships.* Suidians don't build ships." He shook his head with a twist of his mouth.

But it did not dissuade Hira. "Istokians do. I'll send the Istokian builders to Suid to build up an armada. We need to defend the coastal lands. *Including* yours."

"You want *our* timber to craft Istok more ships?" He loomed over her.

Sanaa had no intention of stopping them if they wished to fight. She'd had enough of this.

"Not for Istok. For New Verden. We're going to make the kingdom an armada. Bigger and faster than the previous one. For that, we need your timber." Hira moved her hands in a scale motion. "You have the timber; I have the skilled workers."

He held her gaze without budging. "What of the princess? Who will rescue her?"

"Ryker will. No one knows Furia and Justan like he does." Hira's words caught in her throat. The poor girl was madly in love. A worthless love, if you asked Sanaa. All love was a waste of a perfectly good coupling.

Sanaa scoffed. "You think they're not prepared for that? They'll kill him on sight. I hope you bid farewell to your lover."

The boy named Quent, who had sat quietly next to Hira, jumped up. "My brother is one of the most skilled swordsmen. He's a star-son and difficult to kill. He'll bring her back. I'm certain he will!"

Sanaa watched him in surprise, and Hira held Quent's shoulder. The boy had followed the captain around in pure admiration, which made her uncomfortable. The last thing she expected was his ire.

"Which brings me to the second task..." Hira said. She looked at Lord Barnabus, who sat quietly in his chair, wondering how he ended up in this meeting. "Lord Barnabus will travel to the Free Isle in search of a weapon."

"What sort of weapon?" Delara glanced at the eccentric man.

"A *fire* weapon. One carried by hand," Hira explained, but Sanaa understood very little of her meaning. It enraged her that they would bother to speak of such idiocies at this time.

"It's a sort of apparatus that would compress pressure and redirect energy to a target. I haven't figured out the nuances, but once I get my hands on the prototype developed in the Free Isle, I can customize it for mass production! It'll be an invention that would change the scientific history and the world!" Lord Barnabus bustled with pride, but it only served for Sanaa to stare at him in disgust. What madness did he speak?

The Lady Hira didn't seem fazed, unlike the rest of them.

"Captain Sanaa, you're the most formidable and skilled warrior of my acquaintance. You've *also* been tasked with traveling to the Free Isle, haven't you? A dying wish is not to be ignored. Lord Barnabus needs an escort and protection," Hira said with insinuation.

Sanaa watched her in disbelief. That this petite girl, who once learned to fling a knife from Sanaa herself, would think to task *her* with *anything*.

"No." Sanaa remained unmoved.

But Hira was undeterred. "Just think, if we had this advanced weapon along with help from a witch that could battle Ignatia," Hira said. "*Please* escort Lord Barnabus. Aid him in his pursuit and bring the weapon to the queen. This is of utmost importance and discretion. Only those in this room know about this plan."

Sanaa remembered Almira's defeated form. The queen had not left her room, not even with the explosions. Meanwhile, Sanaa still recalled the witch's small body in her arms. She'd saved her. There was no denying that. She'd instructed her to find a witch. Sanaa cursed and sighed, pressing her fingers against her eyes. The fucking guilt. The godsdamn fucking guilt. She wouldn't hide in a country manor being eaten out for days while her friends fought a war.

She glared accusingly at Barnabus, who balked against his upholstered chair.

"That's not the only thing, Captain," Hira said, and touched Quent's shoulder. He looked at her curiously. "Lord Seaver is in danger in this city. He's my ward, and he has a great desire to learn and one day become a formidable warrior. I ask you, implore you, that you take him under your wing and make him your squire."

"I don't need a squire!" Sanaa stepped forward and Quent shrank back.

"You're going to send me away?" He stared at Hira with a broken face.

Sanaa wouldn't look. She didn't need more guilt. From the corner of her eye, she saw Hira place both hands on his shoulders.

"You don't want me anymore because Ryker is gone," the boy said in a soft voice.

Oh, gods of the sea!

"I want you very much. But your companion betrayed the crown, and you'll be associated with her evil deeds. Staying here in the city…. It's not safe, Quent. I stand by my statement that you need to learn to defend yourself and become strong," the lady craftily explained.

"I'm too little to travel as such." He glanced in fear at Sanaa.

The captain's nostrils flared.

Hira pushed his hair back. "You may come back when this is all behind us. You'll *always* be welcome in this castle."

The boy piteously sniffed as tears dribbled to his cheeks. Sanaa couldn't watch as she seethed.

"You're the only one who's ever been kind to me. No one else—aside from Ryker," the boy whimpered.

Sanaa let out another intricately crafted curse and glared down at Hira and Quent. She pointed an accusatory finger at the lady. "You're a manipulating bitch, my lady. You're *all* Balikian now!" Sanaa threw her hands up.

Hira raised her head without a word to deny it. Unbelievable.

Sanaa turned to Quent. "And you, *boy*, don't you want to be a warrior?"

He paled. "I—I do."

"Then how do you expect to do so by staying here and clutching the lady's skirts?" she snarled.

"She hardly wears skirts," he whimpered.

Sanaa loomed over him as he shrank back. "Pack. Your. Things."

"Y—yes, captain." he scrambled, then stopped, and pivoted. "I hardly have any things."

Sanaa thought she would hit them all. "Then it shouldn't take you long!"

He rushed out of the room and Sanaa glowered at the little bitch, desperately wishing to choke her. All her ire and frustration were bubbling within her.

"At your request, *my lady*, I'm escorting this pigeon," she pointed to the pale Barnabus. "And that runt," then motioned to the door, "across all Istok and Suid and into the Free Isle, which is a mess of harlots, thieves, and mercenaries. Then, back through Suid, the Pistian Sea and into Easima. All so you can learn how to kill people? With how I'm feeling, I could show you fifty ways to kill people."

Hira smiled that delighted smile of the one who'd won their wager. "I would never doubt your skill, Captain."

"If I may interrupt this state meeting."

None other than Kaia Kait lounged by the door, her small body still covered in weapons, as if she'd not been missing for the past few days. Sanaa thought she'd finally left, but that wasn't so.

"You seem to enjoy doing that," Thebo said with disdain.

Kaia ignored him. She trained her eyes on Hira, who watched her in slight confusion. "They say my sister died to save you. Is that true?"

Hira lost her frigidity as she gasped, and the women faced one another. "Do you regret saving me during the battle? For it was your arrows that protected me, weren't they?"

Kaia said nothing. Her cool eyes appraising her. "In my ear, amongst the chaos, I heard Tora. She said to me clearly, 'Let go of hate. Protect the redhead, for she is important.' And so I did."

Hira's lips trembled, and she looked as though she wanted to say something, but Kaia shook her head and held up her hand.

And she peered at Sanaa. "When do we leave?" A slow, self-satisfied smile formed on her lips.

"No." Sanaa sliced her blade through the air, though she wasn't certain when she'd grasped her weapon.

"You'll need an extra warrior," Hira said.

Sanaa would surely kill the lady in her own fortress. "A nice large party. Very inconspicuous. I assume you're sending Delara to escort the beast in the tower and make friends with the Norrians?"

Hira slowly nodded. Delara looked to protest.

"The queen had already made that decision, so you can blame her," Hira cut her off. "And please, get him there alive."

Hira walked to the center of her war room decorated with maps of her country and the seas. The emotionless murals of dragons beheld her in approval. The weight of what was to come pressed down on her, the worry, the tension. It was painted on her. She stood very much as Almira did.

"Three tasks. If we succeed, we have a chance," Hira said steadily.

"A chance for *what?*" Sanaa asked, her face still hard.

"A chance to win."

Chapter Sixty-Four

ARRIGO

Men might bathe themselves in idealism, but the world would forever be a slave to gold.

Morals can always be bent, twisted, and corroded with the right amount of coin. He had never met a pious person who didn't have a deep desire. He believed the gods made humans selfish and self-serving. And if the gods made humans covetous, who was Arrigo Markey to challenge the will of the gods?

In the far north of the world, snow blanketed the fields and there was little to do in winter but hunt, whore, and drink. The town was Spaltren. It was more of a sparse settlement, amid barley fields now barren. Small huts peppered the valley, their roofs sagging under layers of snow, their chimneys perpetually releasing small clouds of smoke that winnowed across the sky.

A cluster of buildings made up the town center, but the drinking hall at the far end of the village was the place he sought. There was a reason this establishment became so popular in the middle of the winter; berry ale.

Most berries die come the frost, but legend has it that witches loved the Mosaic berries so much they placed a spell over the bushes which surrounded the village. One frigid day, an industrious tavern owner discovered that if he fermented the berries, along with quality malted barley, he could produce near-sweet nectar. Perfect to warm your belly during the grayed months.

Arrigo had forgotten the cold of Norr, how it tore through silken threads and past artisanal leather boots right into the soft skin of his groin. The wind made his body dilatory and halted his thoughts to a grind. Still, he couldn't forget Almira, couldn't forget her scent or her undergarments. That scrap, once pressed against her soft cunt, which he kept buried in his breast pocket. He knew she yearned for him in the same manner he yearned for her.

He would destroy this kingdom for her. Clearly, she saw that and appreciated his arduous advances. Each dribble of blood from a kill was in her name, the memory of her coarse curls between his fingers teasing his sentiments.

Arrigo pushed the memories out of his head. His thick cock reacted to the flittering thought of his little queen and her mouth. Damn her, damn them all. He must focus and play his cards correctly. The perfectly played move would land her once more in his arms.

The men behind him paused and watched him. *Fools*, the lot of them. Not a shrewd mind amongst them. He had to do all the thinking himself. At the very least, the men behind him were warriors; it could be worse.

"What we do, m'lord?" a brutish one asked.

"*You* do nothing," Arrigo sneered. "Keep an eye out. If they draw blades, you stumble in and decapitate the man closest to *me*."

The ogre blinked, an adequate representation of his lacunae thoughts.

Arrigo fought not to roll his eyes. He attempted to calm his displeasure. He didn't need more enemies, and these men had been loyal to his father, and by extension, to Arrigo. It was best he continued to rely on his people. Arrigo's assiduous plans had been routinely thwarted by Hestian and his thirst for vengeance. Arrigo blamed him entirely. Had it not been for Hestian's irascible behavior, they wouldn't have jailed him. He could've killed the king while in battle and the Queen would've been trapped in the castle. Arrigo, naturally, would've been her violent protector.

Slowly, they rode their frozen horses between the darkened buildings. The few straggling villagers spotted them and wisely scurried back into their homes to speculate about the mysterious man with the silken threads.

They came upon the place he sought, the windows bright with glowing light. The noise within spoke of merry folk, toasting to whatever inconsequentiality was worth a drink and a laugh. Arrigo dismounted and nodded at the rest of his men to do the same. The men shivered, causing Arrigo's lip to curl into a snarl.

And they called themselves Norrians.

He yanked open the door, and the noise rose to cheers as the men inside laughed and told grand stories none of them had seen to fruition. As he stepped into the place, the joviality quieted when the bearded faces turned to him. Arrigo took stock of those within. There were about fifty men; a war party celebrating their latest victory.

There was Kastian Garr, a large man with wild black hair and a wooly beard that covered half his chest. He was a brutal assassin, but Arrigo felt hope that his plan would work. Amongst them was Earl Lavon, Hickon the Fourth, Lady Brocha who was Barrius' sister, and a few others not worth noting.

Arrigo delighted in their surprise. He strode, chest puffed, to the center of the room as his men spread out around him. He watched their faces, his sharp, eagle eyes steely cold as he slowly removed his gloves and tossed them to one of his men.

"My liege," Kastian Garr said in a near whisper.

Arrigo perused him critically. "Garr, is the ale as good as they say?"

The man held up his fisted hand, a stein of ale clutched in within his meaty grip. It sloshed nervously over the rim onto the wooden floor.

"Aye my lord." Garr set it down and stood to bow before Arrigo.

Thrilled, Arrigo turned to the rest, gauging their reactions to the act of Garr's allegiance. Most of the men shifted, uncertain as to

Arrigo's intentions, but most seemed confused about his identity. He'd been away from home for too long.

"Garr, be a champ and let your companions know who is in their midst," Arrigo said.

But it was Lady Brocha who stepped forward and considered him with unfettered eyes. "We have amongst us a most revered gentleman, lads. This here is Lord Markey."

The tonality of her voice flushed Arrigo with annoyance. She said it with a slight hint of sarcasm. The massive blonde woman stood swaddled in furs. Since she was a child, her gray eyes raged with battle-lust.

Murmurs rose amongst the men, but Arrigo kept his eye on her. *She* didn't fear him. She never had.

"Cousin, you must be chilled in those fine Easimian boots," Lady Brocha said and spat on the floor with a smirk. Arrigo flinched and fisted his hands.

"He's been in Ouest too long," Hickon said next to her. He smiled a toothless smile as he studied the heir. "Sharing meals with Istokians and Suidians."

Arrigo's chest tightened, shamed at having to rely on such fools and ingrates. In times past, a person such as Hickon wouldn't occupy the same room as House Markey. Now, Arrigo counted on his control of the Northern wild tribes to challenge his uncle. He sneered at Hickon.

"And how long have you been in Norr? Yet still, Dag controls the areas where the Northern tribes plant their seeds and hunt their snow elk," Arrigo spat. He knew such subjects were tender, inguinal wounds, easily torn open.

Hickon's face hardened, and his eyes narrowed. "Seven times I've made to kill the old man!"

"And yet he escapes you," Arrigo said frostily, a blissful aperture for an insult. "The old man must be cunning."

Any insult to battle-virility was of great offense to Norrians. He shamed them, and their faces turned red and haunted. Arrigo studied each warrior and delighted in the cowers of men far below his own station.

"For years I've provided each of you plenty of coin, *plenty* of silver," Arrigo said, pausing to scrutinize Brocha. She, at least, had the decency to raise her chin. "Not even you, *cousin*, could bring down an old man and his dogs. Barrius barely scraped the king's leg, and all it did was rally the people. *Fools*. Idiots! That *I*, the heir of Norr, should have to rely on such misfits!"

Brocha's exceedingly ordinary face flushed. "And how long did the heir of Norr maintain control of Mavros? You couldn't even locate Ivar, which was all I asked in payment."

"I took Mavros and asked for aid! Not one of you came! That you should call yourselves Norrians is laughable!" Arrigo yelled as he rounded them, slowly taking in their tattered attire and unpolished swords.

Arrigo's men tensed and the thickness of the room solidified as the two parties studied one another. Yes. His little conniving queen hid Ivar well. He knew her plans. She wished Ivar to be an ally, a puppet ruler to kiss the ring of the Ouest. But sharp words were a commonality in Norr. The Northern nobility were not so easily shocked as they preferred fists and ale to war council and wine.

"Laughable!" Hickon barked a laugh. "A pompous brat like you--"

Arrigo, done with such an exchange and eager to establish dominance, moved behind Hickon and quickly slashed his sword across Hickon's back. The man, more shocked than anything, screamed, then flailed and fell to his knees.

The room erupted into chaos, but Garr and Brocha bid them calm as Arrigo rounded on Hickon. They didn't share fights in Norr. A dispute was between the two parties, and the people of this unforgiving land forbid interference. The rest salivated at the violence, their mouths agape with delight. They placed secret wages; who would win, who would spill last blood. *Naturally*, Hickon was the favored party. Arrigo would teach them to not underestimate his own brutality.

He kicked Hickon in the stomach, then straddled the man and pressed his blade swiftly under his nose as Hickon blinked up at him. Shocked, his toothless mouth was wide with fear and the stench of neglected gums wafted up.

"My lord--"

But Arrigo sliced up with his sword and cut the man's nose clean off. The bloody gristle landed on the floor, leaving a concave opening in Hickon's face. The poor bastard screamed and clutched the gaping hole where his nose had been.

Arrigo calmly picked up the appendage and dangled it over the man's face. Hickon's eyes were wild and stunned as Arrigo smiled.

"Don't fret, dear Hickon. I won't kill you; I just think I like you better without a nose. You'll kill Dag, as I've asked you before, and perhaps you'll smell him better now."

Arrigo pushed himself from Hickon, who sobbed with indignation. The heir turned to Brocha, who looked down at the exchange with cautious apprehension. Arrigo tossed her the nose, and she caught it with disgust.

"Now… gather as many men as you can and march them to Ciraton. There we will meet with the formidable Lady Furia who has long been my most beneficial ally. She's gotten me an armada," he said with childish delight. "We're taking this kingdom down; I want Dag and the king *dead*."

Arrigo grasped an abandoned cup of ale and slurped it deeply as the surrounding men slowly pounded fists on the wooden tables, declaring him a winner over Hickon. Arrigo spat the ale on the floor and threw the cup across the room in disgust. He shuddered a breath as he beheld his little army.

"It tastes like *rot*." He rounded on them. "Too long has Norr slumbered. Too long we've been denied wine and had to scrape from wild bushes to quench our thirst. Our blades dulled. Our hunting scarce!" The men synchronized their support as Arrigo pounded his chest. "The West takes our land! And what do we do? We bend before whatever flaxen king decrees himself *our* lord. Norr crumbled the day Dag killed my father. That ends now! I have the blood of Northern kings in my veins! I'm the highest-ranking bastard in this kingdom, and we will rise! Today, the North stands!"

The men, delighting in the simplicity of his ideas, cheered and toasted. Spoke of new furs, and sweet wine, of war and power, of

Suidian beauties for their beds, and of Istokian armadas for trade.

"What of the Queen? Are we letting that Southern bitch live?" Brocha tossed the nose to Hickon. After all, it belonged to him.

Arrigo thought back on Almira, of her tits and the shape of her jaw—how wide such a mouth would open willingly for his cock. He licked his lips and stared down at his cousin.

"The Queen is *mine*. No one touches her. In the meantime, find me girls who are half Suidian. I want them bound and I want them scared. Not too many, just something for the road."

Isabelle Olmo

Epilogue

ALMIRA

The Queen of New Verden had not moved from her spot on the floor. Her legs twisted under her; her gown askew. These were her aunt's quarters. The latch that used to send her a letter of warning still flapped open. The proof of her salvation had been her damnation. They had stolen her daughter through that latch, taken in infancy before Almira could know how she preferred her food, how she preferred her cuddles. She'd had two days with her. That was her gift, and she'd not known it. She'd placed her in the nurses' arms, thinking she would have a lifetime to know the texture of her curls.

Like her mother before her, who never knew little Bach, who'd never heard his laughter when Almira chased him, and never saw his face scrunch up when fed carrots.

Sanaa had warned her the Favia didn't play fair. She'd fallen for the trap and lost her daughter. Her thoughts were in such a state of turbulent despair, she'd not noticed Alton had been gone. For hours. Or days? She didn't know. She didn't even notice when they removed the corpses left in the room.

It was not until he reentered their quarters, muddy, sweaty, and drenched in failure that she noticed. He set down his helmet and sword with a hard thump on the table. She watched his dejected posture, his head turned downwards, his hair falling over his face. His beard couldn't hide the sharpness of his jaw and how tightly he clenched it.

Any other day, she would've gone to him, draped her arms over him and comforted him. Waiting for him to confess his dark thoughts.

Not today. Not at this moment when her cunt still leaked. When their child was lost.

She startled when he screamed with a sudden ferocity and shoved his weapons off the table; the contents clanking on the stone and echoing in her mind. He slammed his fists four times, yelling louder each time.

"Fuck them!" he turned to her and exhaled. His body contorted in grief. "Talk to me, wife. Tell me it's my fault."

She wouldn't. She knew where the fault lay, the truth of it etched its thread in her heart.

"Did you find any trace?" It split her wide open. A chasm. All life drained from her and, on her lap, small droplets of milk dribbled from her nipples. Her belly still swollen. Sagged, emptied. A harsh reminder of what she'd lost.

He turned to her, his eyes wild, red-rimmed and raw. His handsome face was haggard, marred with defeat and anger. A storm of grief the likes she'd not seen since her father lost her mother.

His mouth soured. A twisted spine of pain. "I searched every valley, every hill, every home, every street. I rowed up the coast… nothing. Like the earth swallowed her."

His voice was a wasteland of despair and he cast his gaze away, as if he couldn't bear the looks she provided him. As if he covered himself in guilt for not being able to break through a door and save her. All the strength in his muscled body and he couldn't reach her. He clenched his fists in a futile gesture.

All Almira could recall was how she'd once offered her small baby on the alms' table over a bland meal.

Would she forget the softness of Osaria's hair? Would Osaria forget her? Never recall her mother and how Almira desperately birthed her in a bay?

Alton pressed his fingers against his forehead. "I'm marching the army north to Ciraton."

"You'll kill many Istokians," she whispered. The reality of what he would do dancing like moths in her brain.

He knelt before her, and she spread her legs for him as she studied his visage.

She realized he was at war. He was deep in the trenches. His sword was ready and hungry for blood. This was the man who killed Edgar, and she'd never beheld him before. She should've recoiled, she should've bid him for peace. But there was no peace in her. She'd tried with all of her skilled words to reach peace. Peace was not for the having. Peace was not for them. Not when the vital piece they created together was missing, and they both bled on the floor.

"Our baby is somewhere in the vastness of this world. She's crying, she's hungry, she's cold, and she doesn't know why she's been taken. You're the king of the world and not even you can find her," she said and as she did, something violent erupted inside of her.

So powerful was the hate she formed for Furia, for Justan, and Arrigo that it eclipsed the good in her. She set down the chain to the dragon she held within. Whatever love she had for Alton, she would attempt to bury it with her child. Perhaps it would fester in a grave. And if she didn't touch it, perhaps the gods would return her child. Love had no place within hate.

"I wish I were dead rather than her being taken," he confessed and leaned forward as if he sought reassurances.

"But you are with me." She spread her hands over his shoulders and pulled him in until his face was inches from hers. "I'm going to stand up from this floor, leaking tits and all, and I'm going to burn down the entire world to get her back."

He stared at her as if he'd never seen her before. His eyes tinged in slight fear. Let him fear her. They should've all feared her from the beginning. She had it in her. She'd always had it in her. But now the dragon was loose. Unchained.

"What about your dear peace, Almira? Don't you want that anymore?" Alton asked with slight apprehension.

"I want my daughter!" Almira screamed as she clutched him tighter. His jaw twitched. She couldn't control her emotions any longer, launching herself from grief, to anger, to disappointment. She was a storm.

She caressed his face and nuzzled his cheek, then pulled back. He beheld her carefully, and she smiled, caressing his lip. He fretted needlessly. She soothed his beard and smiled darkly, pecking his lips.

"Don't worry, my love. You always called me a dragon. Well... I think it's high time I lived up to my name. I will lay countries to ruin to get her back. Let the Favia *feast*."

TO BE CONTINUED

Lady of Istok

COMING 2024

CAPTAIN OF THE REBELS

A captain, an archer, an inventor, and a boy, travel to the Free Isle in search of a witch, a revolver, and a man named Kuimo.

The *Queen's Red Guard* is a five-part fantasy series.

JOIN ISABELLE OLMO'S MAILING LIST FOR RELEASE UPDATES!

https://mailchi.mp/441509191878/isabelle-olmo-books

ALSO BY ISABELLE OLMO

The Rose of Suid & The Last Balik
(A Queen's Red Guard Novella Collection)

https://www.amazon.com/Rose-Suid-Last-Balik-Collection-ebook/dp/B0B15KY4L6?ref_=ast_author_dp

ABOUT THE AUTHOR

Isabelle Olmo was born in San Juan, Puerto Rico and was raised on a steady diet of 80s fantasy films and Sweet Valley High. Her love for literature was developed at an early age when her grandmother gifted her a poetry collection.

She graduated with a degree in English Literature and a minor in Political Science from the University of Central Florida.

When she's not writing she loves to travel, cook, and drink wine. She dreams of one day living in Barcelona, her favorite city in the world.

Follow her social media:

Acknowledgements

Many people do not know this but I wrote *Lady of Istok* one month after I finished drafting *Queen and Conqueror* back in 2019. At the time, I felt like it would never be published. There was a sense of liberation that came from writing the chaotic storyline because I wrote it with no expectations. I wrote it for me. As drastic and dramatic as I dared. Fast forward to now, when it's published.

This story was read by only one person for nearly three whole years; my dear friend Armando. His response was "at first I wasn't crazy about Hira but by the end I was willing to give my left arm for her."

The editing process for this story was brutal and I owe a million thanks to my editors, Hina and Ashley who raked me through the coals, forcing me to do better. Be epic. My BETA readers for pointing out all the ways I could improve the story and dynamically engaging with me.

I need to thank all the amazing authors and readers I've met this year. Their encouragement and love for my story ebbed my uncertainty over sharing my writing.

Praise must the given to my family, my mom, brothers, nieces, cousins, and best friends who accepted not being able to see me or speak to me if I was in the editing cave. I value their understanding and their constant encouragement.

Last but not least, my cat Misha has left plenty of scars on my legs, voicing her displeasure at being ignored for some stupid fantasy story.

Ingram Content Group UK Ltd.
Milton Keynes UK
UKHW012334240723
425713UK00018B/289/J